PERSECUTED

Books by

Robin Parrish

Offworld

Nightmare

Vigilante

*Persecuted**

DOMINION TRILOGY

Relentless

Fearless

Merciless

*based on the film written and directed by
Daniel Lusko

PERSECUTED

I WILL NOT BE SILENT

ROBIN PARRISH

based on a Daniel Lusko film

BETHANYHOUSE
a division of Baker Publishing Group
Minneapolis, Minnesota

Published by Bethany House Publishers
11400 Hampshire Avenue South
Bloomington, Minnesota 55438
www.bethanyhouse.com

Bethany House Publishers is a division of
Baker Publishing Group, Grand Rapids, Michigan

Printed in the United States of America

Library of Congress Cataloging-in-Publication Data

Parrish, Robin.
Persecuted : I Will Not Be Silent / Robin Parrish.
pages cm
"Based on a Daniel Lusko film."
ISBN 978-0-7642-1267-3 (cloth : alk. paper)
ISBN 978-0-7642-1266-6 (pbk.)
1. Evangelists—Fiction. 2. Malicious accusation—Fiction. I. Title.
PS3616.A7684P47 2014
813′.6—dc23 2014003976

14 15 16 17 18 19 20 7 6 5 4 3 2 1

Foreword

Persecution is a subject that calls to mind the most incredible sufferings from all over the world, dating back to the days of Christ. Writing a movie called *Persecuted* comes with it a heavy task. Everyone can relate to the feeling of being persecuted for one's beliefs. The truth is many people feel persecuted, even within the Church, but few for the right reasons.

I want readers to know why I undertook this cause and why this particular story sits in front of them today. The stakes are high. I believe this project means life or death to those who are suffering from grave persecution all over the globe.

In America, we have become insulated in our lives to the point that few people, if any, seem to understand what it means to take up their cross and follow Christ. We're raised to think the Christian life consists of following a celebrity pastor and being involved in exciting events. This is not the case in much of the world today, as elsewhere persecution is something that is understood as part of the package in accepting salvation. Jesus said: "Blessed are those who are persecuted because of righteousness, for theirs is the kingdom of heaven." There is a power in suffering for the purpose of God, a power few have experienced in the West.

When persecution comes, few will be prepared for what comes with it. The story of this film is just the beginning of an awakening to prepare believers for a choice that will have to be made. I fear many will be wiped away, for the cares of the world will swallow them up. There is a cost to following Christ. Those who believe will know that cost, and they will have their reward in heaven. If you're asleep, I hope this wakes you up, because truth is stranger than fiction. If you're suffering worse conditions than those depicted here, don't lose heart, for God is with you. Bottom line: There's much more beyond the pages of this story; this is a symbol of the bridge I believe we must cross if we're to be joined with the remaining body of Christ around the world.

This is a wake-up call. Many of our freedoms granted to us by God will surely be ripped away unless we make a stand. This story is just the beginning.

Daniel Lusko,
writer and director of *Persecuted*

Congress shall make no law respecting an establishment of religion, or prohibiting the free exercise thereof.

—First Amendment to the
Constitution of the United States

The framers of our Constitution meant we were to have freedom of religion, not freedom from religion.

—Reverend Billy Graham

A man who won't die for something is not fit to live.

—Martin Luther King Jr.

Prologue

Boom.

Shot to the chest, instantaneous heart explosion. Emmett Olson. Brooklyn, eight years ago.

The next target came up. Mr. Gray took aim . . .

Boom.

Precision shot to the head, dead on impact. Gino Mendoza. Columbia, seven years ago.

He pressed the reset button on the panel in front of him. It triggered a belt in the ceiling of the shooting range that carried new paper targets into place. It was a huge place, larger than most, and Mr. Gray was setting each fifty yards away. But even so . . .

Boom.

Shot to the stomach, right where he'd aimed. Terrell Cobb. Tallahassee, five years ago.

He almost allowed a smile. That had been a more difficult, and therefore entertaining, job. The target wasn't supposed to just die but actually suffer for a bit first. So Mr. Gray had aimed for lower body mass. It had taken eight minutes for Terrell Cobb to bleed out over his kitchen floor.

You got what you paid for when you hired Mr. Gray. He was a professional.

His name, of course, wasn't really Mr. Gray. That was how he was known to those who employed his unique talents. Only a handful of people had had the misfortune of discovering the name he was born with, and he'd silenced them. Permanently.

Other men of his vocation would frown on assigning emotional values to past jobs. Mr. Gray found that it enhanced his skills.

He was about to take his next shot when his phone vibrated. No. Whoever it was could wait. The best marksmen could make any shot, even amid distraction.

Boom.

Head shot, double tap. Colton Lind. Tulsa, three years ago. The last hit he'd completed before taking on his new broader security assignment.

After taking a moment to ensure that his shots matched up with how he remembered the Tulsa job, he placed his gun down on the counter and pulled the phone from his pocket. It was the phone whose number he'd only given to his employer. It had already stopped ringing, but it logged the caller's number with a 202 area code. Someone here in Washington, D.C., but not his employer. The phone buzzed once. A message had been left.

Interesting.

Mr. Gray slipped the phone back in his pocket and returned his attention to the range. He had fifteen more shots to complete before he was ready for any distractions. Discipline and focus had gotten him this far. It was a core value—of his and of his clients.

The remaining shots went cleanly, with only the fourteenth slipping outside his intended area by more than an inch or two. Mr. Gray cleaned and packed away his gun, stowed his earplugs, and left the range, nodding once to the guard who'd been waiting for him to finish so the place could be closed for the night.

Only when he'd made it to his car—an intentionally unremarkable sedan with an intentionally remarkable engine under its hood—did Mr. Gray finally retrieve his phone and listen to the message left for him. The caller had followed protocol, sharing nothing about the desired job and providing only a phone number to an untraceable cell phone.

"Your employer," the message concluded, "suggested you as the best he'd ever met. He's been quite pleased with your assistance these last two years. I think you're exactly the right man for this opportunity."

Even without the caller's name, Mr. Gray could tell he was a politician. Elected officials were all the same, always trying to get people to like them.

Their pockets were deep, however.

Mr. Gray pulled an unused burner cell phone from his bag and placed the call to the number that had been left. When the call was answered, the unmistakable sound of a party—glasses clinking, forced laughter, even a band—could be heard immediately. "Go where no one can hear you or I will hang up."

"Got to take this," he heard the voice on the other line say and then the rustling of him walking away. Thirty seconds later, the caller said, "I'm alone."

"What's your need?"

"Oh. So, uh, what I need to know is how quickly you can go to work, once you've been given approval to proceed."

"Define *work*," said Mr. Gray, his patience being tested.

"Well, it's like this. For some time now I've been trying to convince my friend to join me in a vitally important initiative. I believe I still have a chance of winning him over, but if I can't, if he won't play ball . . . I may have need of your services."

Mr. Gray considered the man's words. Politicians usually dealt in vague terms, because clarity was too incriminating.

"Services?"

"Not that. Hopefully not that. But if he's not for us, then he can't be an obstacle. Your boss said you could handle this kind of complicated situation. You've helped him in the past."

"My fee is nonnegotiable," Mr. Gray said.

"Money is not a concern. Only success—and discretion, of course."

"I can guarantee both."

"That's why I called you."

"Send me the details electronically, along with payment in full. One hundred percent, in advance. Once that's done, I will present you with options for removing your obstacle. And anything else you may need."

"Excellent," said the politician. "You'll have both within the hour. I'll be in touch."

Mr. Gray clicked off, opened the phone, removed the SIM card, and snapped it in half. He'd finish destroying it at home, along with the phone. He glanced at his watch—1:30 a.m. Another productive day.

Starting the car, he began the drive back to the flat he'd secured as his base of operations here in Washington, D.C. It amazed him, after spending time on the ground in Iran, Afghanistan, Chechnya, and Somalia, how this city, in some ways, could be just as vicious. Just as dangerous. It suited him well.

Car pointed home, knifing through the quiet streets like a shark through water, Mr. Gray thought of the job that might wait ahead, that just might prove interesting. It was another chance to test his skills, another opportunity to put his training to work.

1

They were chanting. No, they were shouting. Screaming. This mob stationed outside the front gate, in the pouring rain, was screaming in shared outrage. But what were they saying? There was no audio on the news feed.

There were two sides to the mob, each as angry as the other. On one side were signs adorned with slogans like *Heaven is not a gated community!* and *I like your Christ, I do not like your Christians*. The other half of the mob held signs that said *Jesus is the way and the light!* and *Grace and truth come from Christ!*

Good grief, now they were singing.

John Luther turned his attention away from the TV monitor on the floor to his left, which had briefly cut away to the protestors outside Truth Ministries' headquarters. Now his own visage was back on the screen, where he was being broadcast live.

"Freedom has been under attack in every generation, and ours is no exception." John's sincere, steady gaze locked tight on the anchorwoman sitting across from him. He fought the urge to stare into the camera just over her right shoulder, as well as a vague desire to loosen his silk tie.

His surroundings were unusually sparse for a TV newsroom. CNW was as high-tech a network as any, and during his prior appearances he had always been seated in front of a green screen so that audiences would see an old Gothic church behind him. It was a different church every time, and John didn't recognize most of them. Just a visual cue to his vocation and traditionalist leanings, but it wasn't the image he would have chosen for himself. If he had to have a representative image projected behind him, he'd rather it be the stark beauty of an old wooden cross. Or maybe a picture of two hands with holes in the palms.

A tired-looking producer had explained to him an hour ago that they'd decided to go with a simple setup for this interview so that the focus would be on him, on this all-important occasion. It sounded nice, but John guessed they were in such a hurry to get him on the air that they didn't have time to assemble the usual background.

Seated across from him was Diana Lucas, CNW's most well-known and respected journalist. Blond and attractive, Diana had the kind of steely gaze that let her interviewees know this was *her* interview and she was in total control. She listened carefully to John's every word, though she didn't miss an opportunity to jump in when he paused.

"Who better to speak on the subject of freedom than you, John," she said. "You've been hailed as 'God's Ambassador' by some of the world's foremost dictatorships: Sudan, North Korea, and Iran. But there are those who claim that your ministry is intolerant, that it's condescending to people of other faiths. Some in Washington have said that your crusades may even threaten the freedoms of others."

John had sat across from her enough times to know that Diana Lucas approached every on-screen interview as a game of tactical chess, measuring the tiniest of facial tics and the most subtle vocal modulations with the skill of a criminal profiler. She knew exactly when to listen, and when to pounce.

Her pointed statement might have gotten under his skin a decade ago, yet this sort of exchange was old hat now. He shook his head and affected a sad expression.

"Diana, if I thought for one second that I could look down on anyone else for their beliefs, I wouldn't be sitting here. I'm not a Republican. I'm not a Democrat. I don't belong to any particular religious denomination. My personal history is no better than any of your viewers. Do you know what kind of person I used to be? Who I *really* was?"

Diana said nothing. Maybe she was waiting for him to bury himself with his own words. Or maybe she was genuinely speechless for once. John couldn't tell.

"An abusive, alcoholic, gambling drug addict," he explained. "And I deserved nothing less than death when God came into my life."

Diana's eyebrow twitched; it was barely visible, but John caught it. She'd allowed him considerable leeway, though her patience was running out now. He knew she was about to change the subject.

"So, John," she said smoothly, "what is your opinion of the primary tenets of the Faith and Fairness Act? And I quote, 'To *publicly* declare your religious beliefs in a way that permits equal time and respect to other systems of faith.'"

For the first time since the interview began, John bristled internally. But he swallowed it quickly, refusing to let her ruffle him on camera. "Freedom is fragile and costly," he said with conviction. "It must be constantly protected and defended by work and by faith."

Diana waited with her eyebrows pinched upward. John knew she was hoping for more, a stronger, more controversial sound bite.

It was awfully tempting to give it to her. But then why not? Why not say exactly what he was thinking? It was true, wasn't it? Come to think of it, people needed to hear it. If this bill passed Congress, there'd be many who wished that someone had come out and said it beforehand. John would never get a better opportunity.

He squared his shoulders. Yes, freedom had to be defended by work and faith. But also . . .

"Even by blood."

His voice resounded like a judge's gavel closing a heated court case. It was his final word on the subject, and he could see that even Diana sensed it. She jumped at the chance to end the interview there, transitioning effortlessly to a wrap-up of John's statements before handing things back over to the anchor desk.

John sat still in his seat, listening to her talk. Even after she was done, after she'd risen from her seat to shake his hand and thank him for his time, he remained frozen in place. Had he really just said that out loud? What was he thinking?

Well, now he'd really done it.

The board wouldn't approve of such strong words, as if suggesting their freedom to worship as they saw fit had to be defended with blood. But he would remind them that this bill was really happening, making this no time to soft-pedal or hold back. The easy thing would be to stay silent, but too much was at stake. They would be judged for how they acted right now—or refused to act.

No matter how many people would condemn him for it, or how many times it would be taken out of context in repeated news broadcasts, John knew it was the truth and had to be said. If not by him, then who? There probably wasn't anyone else influential enough to say it so that it mattered.

Maybe it had come across as too trite or too practiced. He hoped not. John found it hard to gauge his own on-screen performances. But he didn't just believe the words he'd said. He *knew* them to be true.

Not that long ago he'd been a wretched example of humanity who deserved the worst punishment eternity could offer. Not every man could understand the all-encompassing depths of God's amazing grace the way John Luther did. Not everyone knew what could be defended by blood.

2

39 YEARS AGO

The gunshot was so loud, it hurt John's ears.

As the cop knelt to the ground to check on the victim—his partner—the drug runner doubled back the way he came and made a run for it. Blood slowly pooled the ground underneath the fallen police detective, an elder member of the squad, while his partner frantically pulled a black radio from his belt.

"Officer down! Corner of West 5th and Buena Vista! Get the paramedics here *now*!" screamed the cop into the receiver.

John's heart raced with excitement as he watched the scene play out in front of him. He'd never seen anything so visceral, so realistic. He still couldn't quite believe he was here. It was like a dream.

Just ten years old, he'd lived a fairly sheltered life. The old man had seen to that. His father was a priest, a very respected and respectable one who clung to old-fashioned traditional values until they choked like that collar he wore around his neck. As such, he'd forbidden his son from engaging in most popular forms of entertainment and media—including movies. John had been invited to the cinema many times by friends from school, but his dad always said no.

A week ago John had presented his father with a crisp new report card bearing straight A's. It was the first time he'd ever scored top marks across the board, and it had required some seriously hard work in several disciplines that John found more challenging than most of the kids in his class. As a reward, the old man had offered him a free wish. Anything he wanted—within reason, not to mention budget—he could have.

John's wish was to see the big-budget buddy-cop movie that all the guys in school were raving about. Reluctantly his father had relented on his standard policy and agreed to take him.

The movie was only fifteen minutes in, and it was already the most exciting thing John had ever seen in his life. He already knew some of what was going to happen—that this older policeman who'd been shot was going to die, allowing the other cop to take on a rookie partner, kicking the story off for real—thanks to the kids at school. But he'd just learned that there was a big difference between hearing about something, and seeing and hearing it with his own senses.

Despite this, it wasn't a perfect experience. He could feel the disapproval emanating off his father in the seat to his right. Every time somebody on-screen uttered a word John only heard shouted by rough boys on the playground—words he never dared use himself—his father would let out a loud sigh or angrily mumble something indiscernible.

A minute later the older cop on the screen died from his gunshot wound, just as John knew he would. His younger partner stood to his feet, turned his anguished, outraged face to the sky, and screamed a single curse as loud as he could.

John knew his father would bristle at this, yet he wasn't at all prepared for what happened next.

Charles Luther, local priest and single father, cleared his throat loud enough for the entire theater to hear and stood. Everyone within a twenty-foot radius craned their heads in his direction. Charles squeezed past his son to exit the aisle.

"Come on, John," he said, seeming not to care about how loud he was talking.

What did he mean, "*come on*"? They weren't leaving, they couldn't. This was his wish, the reward he'd worked months for.

"I don't want to leave!" John whispered in reply, panic flooding his heart. He knew it wasn't wise to argue with his father, and under any other circumstances he'd already be on his feet, right in step behind the old man. But this was different. He'd waited so long for this!

Charles Luther froze and pointed his hard, expressionless gaze at his son. John swallowed but stood his ground. Or rather, sat.

"Get. Up." His father's words came out with his usual calm demeanor, but the undertone was painfully clear. John was now in serious danger of stepping over the line.

"But *why*?" John whispered. "You promised!"

"I won't have this kind of filth and violence filling your mind. We're going."

John had been angry before, many times. But never had he felt a rage so searing or urgent as what he felt at this moment. He turned his eyes back to the movie screen and replied, out loud, with a single word. "No."

The word had barely escaped his lips when he felt a painfully tight grip on his left forearm, jerking him out of his seat. No longer speaking, Charles pulled his son physically into the aisle.

"NO!" John screamed, pulling against his dad as hard as he could to try to get back to his seat.

Undeterred, Charles kept pulling. A big bear of a man, in another life he'd worked construction before entering Episcopalian priesthood, and still retained his strength of both muscles and will. His ten-year-old son was no match for him.

Still John refused to cooperate, pulling and screaming, "No! No! No!" as loud as he could. He was, as his father called it when they witnessed other children exhibiting this sort of behavior, causing *a scene*. And he didn't care.

His father was strict and relentless in his insistence on sheltering John from all things "worldly," and he also ruled the house with stern control that so stifled John he had trouble breathing. This was the first time John had ever dared to fight back against the old man, and he surged with the adrenaline rush, the feeling of exerting power. He wouldn't win, of course, and he knew he shouldn't be behaving this way. But he was proving right now that he *could* resist his father and make things difficult for him. It was strangely satisfying.

Charles dragged him, literally kicking and screaming, out of the theater and into the lobby, where a few dozen patrons turned in their direction. John was red in the face, screaming at the top of his lungs. He began to cry.

"But you promised!" he yelled. "You *promised*!"

"Yes, I did, John," Charles replied calmly. "And now I have to break that promise. Because I love you."

"Well, I *don't* love you!" John screamed. "I hate you!"

He didn't mean it, of course. But it felt good to hurt his father.

It was the first time he could ever remember seeing his father's stoic face show pain.

3

PRESENT DAY

They were still there. The protestors brandishing their big wooden signs like pitchforks and torches, right outside the studios of Truth Ministries. The rain was coming down harder now. Someone—probably Ryan—had left the small TV in his dressing room tuned to CNW, which was again showing a live view of the protests going on outside the building.

A CNW cameraman forced his way through the crowd like a shark drawn to blood, slicing to a point close to the studio entrance, where two voices were growing louder by the second. A man and a woman stood opposite each other. The microphone didn't pick up what the woman said, but when she shoved her large *Faith for Everyone!* sign into the man's face, it was pretty clear where she stood. The man swatted away the sign and replaced it with a well-worn Bible held high like a medieval sword.

The man's furious words were audible over the TV. "This is all I need!" he shouted. "God's Word! This is all anyone needs!"

The female protestor smacked the Bible away and onto the ground. The fundamentalist stood there for a moment, his mind unable to catch up to the sight of his treasured possession being cast to the wet ground like so much trash.

Then he snapped.

He threw himself at the woman full of red-faced rage and pain. The protestor gave back as good as she got, and as the TV camera captured the initial blows of their violence, the rest of the crowd made up of protestors and supporters—separated like football players on either side of the line of scrimmage—surged toward one another, launching punches and kicks in a thunder of fury.

The left edge of the camera's view caught a young woman leaning over to pick the Bible up off the ground. She clutched it to her chest protectively while closing her eyes. Around her the hatred swarmed, yet she seemed to be shutting out everything else, retreating deep inside herself for protection from the madness on all sides.

The CNW camera panned out slowly, poetically capturing the rain-soaked pandemonium erupting on Truth Ministries' doorstep. John was about to turn away from the TV when Diana Lucas's voice added a soundtrack to the on-screen action.

"'Faith must be defended *by blood*,'" she said in her most sincere intonation. "Those were the bold words of evangelist John Luther earlier this evening. And as you can see, they appear to have been taken literally by the crowd gathered outside the studios of Truth Ministries. Were his words incendiary? Our panel of experts is itching to answer that question. . . ."

Beneath the live footage of the fight, words scrolled across the bottom of the screen that included *Evangelist Calls on Christians to Fight Senate Bill* and *John Luther's War Cry*.

John sighed, slowly and deliberately sliding his watch over his wrist. How many children were starving to death right now? How many Africans were dying of AIDS at this very moment? How many believers in hostile nations were suffering for holding firmly to their faith? And yet a petty fistfight outside a television studio was what the national news was covering, using John's own words to fan the flames of hatred and prejudice.

He idly wondered if walking outside into the crowd might do anything to calm the swelling riot. But the thought passed quickly, as he knew that his presence would only have the opposite effect, and he didn't need to make things worse right now. Like it or not, he was a lightning rod in the public eye when it came to matters of faith. Everyone had strong feelings about the Faith and Fairness Act, and equally strong feelings about John Luther.

All John really wanted was to preach the Gospel. It was his reason for breathing. He wanted to share with any who would listen about the love and grace and forgiveness that had been given to him.

He turned off the television and sat down at his modest dressing table. Thankfully it had only been a short drive from CNW's studios across D.C. to his own ministry's headquarters on the outskirts of the capital. It gave him the time he needed to prepare. Hands clasped together and eyes closed tight, he prayed softly, "Lord, make me a channel of thy life, thy truth, thy way, thy words. Pure, honest, clean. Pure, honest, clean . . ."

John smoothed his hair back over his left ear, thinking of how he was the last person to judge those people outside in the rain. God knew he'd done worse things than starting fights in his day. Besides, human beings had been fighting over the Gospel of Jesus Christ for thousands of years and weren't scheduled to stop until time itself came to an end. And he had a feeling this particular confrontation might have been . . . helped along. He'd been behind the curtain of the media long enough to know how far they'd go to drive up ratings.

He just hoped the authorities could end the fight before serious injuries began racking up.

The clock on the wall told him it was almost time. John stood and buttoned the top button of his shirt. Tightened his red necktie. Then he began bouncing and shadowboxing around the room, punching at the air.

Left jab. *Breathe.* Right jab.

It seemed like the whole world wanted a fight. Maybe he'd give them one. His sermon tonight would be one for the books. All eyes were on him, and his only move was to come out swinging.

John stopped to button up his sleeve cuffs. On the inside of his left wrist he saw the small cross he'd had tattooed there years before he knew what it meant. It had been a joke—a jab at his father, Now . . . he leaned over the still-open Bible on the dressing table and read a few more words. Closing his eyes again, he prayed, "All I want is the truth. All I want is the truth."

A tiny knock came from the dressing room door. "Mr. Luther," a small voice said. It belonged to a young staff member. What was her name? She opened the door and stuck her head in. "Senator Harrison is here to see you."

Donald? What was he . . . ?

Oh. Of course. John should have seen this coming. Still, his old friend's timing was terrible. He had less than five minutes to show time.

"I can't talk to him right now," he told the staffer. Didn't he know that time was short, and John was supposed to be on in a matter of minutes?

"He *really* wants to see you," the girl replied, her voice rising. "I don't know what to say to him."

John held up his hands to calm her. "It's okay, it's fine. Just send him in."

He sighed.

Donald was here for one thing and one thing only. But maybe it wouldn't be so bad. He could dream, right?

Meh. If Jesus Christ could hold himself to a wooden cross in unimaginable pain for three hours, John could survive five minutes with Senator Donald Harrison.

4

The young woman at the door ducked out, barely getting out of the way of Senator Harrison, who slid into the room on shiny, spotless shoes like hot knives cutting butter. His eyes were heat-seeking missiles that locked immediately onto John.

Donald was in his late fifties, his perfectly coiffed hair prematurely white. A two-hundred-dollar haircut, John knew. The majority leader of the Senate was famous for his elocution skills and his ability to dominate any conversation. John had always appreciated his support and his friendship, but things had changed since they were young men. They had changed. At least in some ways. Donald was still a man who had little concept of another's personal boundaries, and an absolute ability to never take no for an answer.

"Hey, John!" Donald called out with a smile. "How we doing tonight?"

John took his old friend's hand and pulled him into a quick bear hug. He didn't want to be rude, but he needed to get to his pulpit.

"Oh yeah," Donald went on, "I just wanted to say I saw your

piece on *Primetime*. I thought it was very, *very* nice. Your transparency was very moving."

John smoothed back the hair over his ear again and glanced in the mirror. He knew the senator hadn't come all this way just to congratulate him on his latest press appearance. He'd come here for one thing, and they both knew what it was.

Donald sighed. "I know this isn't your cup of tea, John—"

"Then why do you keep pushing when you already know my answer?" John asked, trying not to sound impatient or exasperated, yet knowing he was failing at both.

"I really need your full support on the Faith and Fairness deal," Donald continued, as if John hadn't interrupted. "Your ministry reaches more people than the evening news! I know it's all just bureaucratic hoopla to you, but you're a fulcrum, John. A nexus. You stand in the middle of a crowd and turn one way, and the whole crowd turns with you. It's time to put them on the right path. Now, I need you to get up there on national television and announce that you fully support the bill. It could be the turning point for the whole thing!"

John closed his eyes and let out a breath.

Donald offered a tentative smile. "I'm counting on my friend to come through for me here."

The female staffer opened his door again. "Your wife and daughter are here."

John nodded in her direction, and she was gone. When he looked back at Donald, the senator was scowling. The stately gentleman was gone, and an imposing Beltway power broker stood in his place.

John doubted that Donald would ever get it. How could he? The man was a politician—and a very good one. What did he know about matters of the soul?

"What did God say about appeasing the masses, Donald?" John replied, standing toe-to-toe with the senator. "He said, 'I am the way. I am the truth. I am the life.' Not *one of* the ways, *the* way."

The senator was unmoved. "This isn't about that. This is about fairness and equality for all faiths, not just yours."

"Look." John felt his practiced cool beginning to crack, his pulse picking up. He grabbed his Bible and held it in front of his friend. "I'm not asking an imam to preach the Bible in a mosque, am I? All I'm focused on is preaching this book. It's not illegal to teach the Gospel in this country yet, is it?"

The temperature in the room shot up. Donald's cheeks flushed, and he rolled his eyes melodramatically. "I keep forgetting you're the sole proprietor of the Word of God."

John had to turn away and choke down the desire to shout the truth in Donald's face. Fighting wasn't the way. It wasn't what God wanted.

Donald let out a big breath. "This is a fine way to show gratitude to the people who have really helped you."

John turned back around. "I appreciate everything you've done. But you don't own me. And you've been thanked, plenty."

There was no mistaking the disappointment on the senator's face. "This bill is going to happen, and I'm offering you the opportunity to be on the right side of history."

Enough. John had no more time for this. He threw his suit coat on. "I *cannot* water down the Gospel to advance anybody's political agenda."

"Not everyone believes that heaven is a gated community, John," said Donald. Why did he sound so sad? He had to have known what John's answer would be before he came here. Did he come to the studio tonight to give John a warning? Or one last chance to jump on board?

The young girl opened his door again. "Sir, it's time."

Donald stood his ground and took on a much more formal tone. "I think I can speak for all of my colleagues in Congress when I say that we have reached the terminal end of our patience with you."

John wondered what that meant but chose to let the comment fall away. Neither Senator Donald Harrison nor all of Congress nor even the president himself held any power over John or the Christian citizens of this nation that did not first pass through the hands of God. His will would be done, no matter what.

John couldn't delay any longer. Yet he didn't want to end things this way with one of his oldest friends and supporters. Moving for the door, he stopped for a moment and gave Donald a friendly peck on the cheek.

"God bless you," he said, and hoped it meant something to the man.

Discussion over. It was time.

5

Ryan Morris bounced. Bobbing up and down in his jeans, expensive T-shirt, and sport coat, he stood in his customary spot just offstage, waiting for John to go on. Ryan was a handsome thirty-something with dirty-blond hair and chiseled features. He was as loyal and hardworking as they came, having dedicated his entire existence to furthering Truth Ministries. He had no family remaining, and no friends outside of the organization. It was his whole life.

John's calm always balanced out the buzz Ryan got at show time. They'd become a complementary pair over the years, and each knew the other's strengths and weaknesses as well as their own. Ryan was the unrelenting optimist, driven and enthusiastic at every turn. Quick with a joke or a hug, the man was like John's younger brother or son even. Someone who occasionally got a little too wild, and tonight he looked even more wide-eyed than usual. Like he'd had one too many cans of Red Bull before the show.

John marched through the dark backstage area toward the bright beacon that summoned him. The spotlight could be an intimidating place, but John had grown to love it. As always, he focused on that light, marching straight for it, because standing in that light was where he was able to speak the Gospel into the lives of those with ears to hear.

As he neared the stage, Ryan stepped forward to stop him for a moment. This was their ritual.

"You are gonna kill this thing like you always do," said Ryan, revving up his pep talk and gesturing in spastic arm movements. "You're *on fire*!"

He hadn't spoken to Ryan since returning from the CNW interview, but unsurprisingly his subordinate seemed to believe he'd nailed it. Ryan was always so quick to heap praise on him. John had asked him many times not to stroke his ego, as it made him horribly uncomfortable. But he'd come to realize that Ryan simply couldn't help himself. He believed so fervently in this ministry that any and every feat they accomplished—no matter how big or small—got him excited. They all knew what the stakes of John's interview would be.

"Right," John said with a deep breath. His apprehension at how he'd left things with Donald should have been buried, yet something small still nagged at him. And Ryan knew him too well. The man could tell something was bothering him.

"How are you feeling?" asked Ryan. "You good? You need anything?"

John shook his head while Ryan continued to gaze on him with concern. John felt a single bead of perspiration at his hairline. Ryan saw it too.

"You know what I'm thinking?" Ryan said, worried but growing excited again. "I'm gonna get you a driver to take you home after the show. You've got to take it easy, John."

No. Ridiculous. John didn't need a driver. He was fine.

"That's all right. I'll drive myself home."

John tried to slide past him, but Ryan wasn't done yet. He mirrored John's sidestep.

"Listen, listen," he said, gaining speed as he returned to pep-talk mode. "This media scrutiny comes and goes. You know that. All this talk of persecution is gonna die, and who's gonna be left standing? You are! Why? Because you're John Luther. So forget the politics. You get back in that ring and you bring those people out there what they came to hear. You bring the truth, brother! Go get 'em!"

John wasn't sure if he appreciated Ryan's over-the-top encouragement on this night or if he was growing tired of it. He was disheartened that he couldn't escape all the politics stuff even from his inner circle. He wearily nodded and walked past Ryan.

Ryan smiled and patted him on the back. He gave John a soft nudge in the direction of the stage. John turned his attention back to the spotlight. *For you,* he prayed silently. He took two deep breaths and then squared his shoulders. Finally he felt ready. It was time to put everything else aside, to leave the politics and the maneuvering in the rearview. It was time to step up to the podium and do the thing he was born to do, the thing that filled his heart with more purpose and fulfillment than anything else in this world.

It was time to share the Good News.

6

From Asia to South America, from Australia to Africa, John Luther has broken stadium records preaching the simple Gospel truth for many, many years!" boomed the gravelly voice of seventy-seven-year-old Dave Wilson. A senior member of John's board of directors, Dave was a zealot, a fiery devotee of both Christ and Truth Ministries. He also possessed a brilliant mind. Analytical and quiet, he was as passionate as Ryan and yet he approached life in a completely different way. They made a great team, offering their own unique perspectives on the world.

Dave's face was wrinkled and red at the moment, but he made no move to wipe away the sweat from his brow. He'd introduced John hundreds of times and yet still gave it every ounce of energy and fire he had, even after all the years. "Please do me a great favor and let's give a really warm welcome to John Luther!"

John's adrenaline surged as he parted the velvet curtain with a burst and strode confidently onto the stage. The bright TV lights enveloped him; somewhere across the years he'd come to enjoy their warm glow. There was something comforting about it. The two hundred-strong crowd—a filled-to-capacity number in the main studio—jumped to their feet and exploded in a roar of applause and whistles and cheers.

Bible in one hand, John patted Dave on the back with the other, then slid coolly into place behind the clear acrylic pulpit. Suspended behind him hung the circular logo for the show—*Truth Live* in white letters on a blue background. Stylized stalks of wheat representing the harvest ringed the outside edge of the circle, and the second *t* in *Truth* was a red cross. John held his Bible in the air, which he intended as a symbolic reminder that the audience's praise should be given to God, not to himself.

John projected his powerful voice into the microphone while gazing across the crowd.

"Tonight, I believe we are headed, as a nation, toward a great spiritual awakening. And yet many are telling you that if the government can unite all faiths under this new religious reform bill, that somehow world peace will come. But the Bible says that no government can ever bring peace to mankind!"

Senator Donald Harrison stood quiet, listening intently as he remained rooted to his spot in John's dressing room. He'd really thought John might come around, that he could be reasoned with.

His eyes swiveled toward the small television set, which blinked dark and then came to life again, now showing John Luther preaching on *Truth Live*. He loved the man, but what a stubborn fool John had become, how blind to the momentum of history's changing tide. Their conversations these days too often had turned into arguments, and Harrison couldn't understand why his friend couldn't see that he was standing in front of a tidal wave about to overwhelm him. The time for worry or pity was over. Donald had made his overture, many of them, but John had chosen his path. Now all Donald felt were frustration and disappointment. John's way of thinking was a relic of the past. How could he not see that? What would happen next, John was bringing on himself.

On the TV screen John was building momentum, his voice rising in volume and his gestures getting more animated. "Why? Because mankind has a disease. It's either the world and its religions and its politicians and its pleasures, or it's the Lord. Every human being who ever lived has had to make the same choice."

Donald pulled out his phone and redialed the last number he'd called.

"He's not on board," he said softly. Donald sighed. "Go ahead."

He put the phone away and cursed John's stubbornness under his breath.

John was breathing hard and sweating, working up to his crescendo.

"Many believe that religious reform will save us from war, from fear, and from terrorism. When has it?!"

"Never!" shouted the crowd.

John scanned the audience, looking as many of his parishioners in the eye as possible.

"Of course not," he said. "We know that only the Word of God can bring peace to the heart of man. You cannot legislate the power of God! You can't change your past, but Christ can with his blood! You don't have the power to do it yourself. But if you surrender to God, he'll give you the power to change your life and shape your future. Jesus said, 'I am the way.' Come to him now!"

7

A few miles away from Truth Ministries' studios, Mr. Gray, in his usual gray suit and dark tie, put his phone back into his jacket pocket. He drove a plain-looking black sedan the way one might pilot a tank, with a dour expression and unflinching solemnity. Driving slowly through downtown, he turned up the radio's volume. The preacher man Luther shouted through the vehicle's stereo speakers. He was well into his sermon now; he'd be done soon.

Not much time.

Finding the address at last, he brought the car to a stop in front of an old brick tenement and honked once, just as he'd said he would. A young girl soon emerged from an upstairs fire-escape door and wound her way down the wire-frame balcony and steps. Once her feet hit the pavement, he could see that she was quite pretty, and young, likely no more than sixteen or seventeen. She snapped and popped bubble gum, adding to her youthful appearance, but her eyes looked old. She'd seen life. As instructed, her clothes were nondescript—not overly conservative nor flamboyant but somewhere in between. She was old enough to suit his needs, yet young enough to retain her youthful vitality. He knew what went on in the apartment upstairs. Another year and the girl would probably look ten years older. But right now . . . she'd do.

Mr. Gray looked away as she approached, pretending not to have noticed her yet. She slipped lightly off the sidewalk and strolled over to the car. She was in no hurry. He turned off the radio as she knocked on the window. Rolling it down, he made eye contact.

"Want a ride, honey?" he asked.

She eyed him playfully, seductively. "Do you?"

He unlocked the passenger door. "Get in."

She rounded the vehicle and slid into the seat opposite Mr. Gray.

"What's your name?" he asked.

"Aaliyah," she answered, studying him with a smile.

"Get rid of the gum," said Mr. Gray.

She rolled her eyes but complied, sticking it onto a single finger.

Mr. Gray poured a pill into her hand from a prescription pill bottle, keeping his thumb over the word *Rohypnol* printed on it. He saw the greedy gleam in her eye. That was why she'd agreed to tonight, but the pill wasn't what she'd been promised. Rohypnol was a powerful sedative that relaxed the nervous system and made the user highly susceptible to suggestion. Fraternity brothers had abused its powers for years. Mr. Gray had no intention of taking advantage of this girl; that would be far beneath someone of his station. Yet he needed her drugged for what was to come.

"You've never had a ride like this before, Aaliyah," he said with a smirk. "I guarantee it."

She grinned back at him and tossed the pill into her mouth without even bothering to look at it. Mr. Gray handed her a can of soda, and she swallowed.

"Good girl," he said, starting the car.

Aaliyah eyed him sideways. She bit the gum off her finger and resumed chewing it as he drove into the night.

Roughly ten minutes later, Mr. Gray and Aaliyah slipped into the *Truth Live* studio to find it was mostly empty. Luther's sermon was long over, and most of the crowd had gone home—fewer potential witnesses. A few families remained, chatting among themselves. Just as Gray anticipated, Luther was still there, standing in the center aisle, not far from the stage. He looked tired even as he patiently greeted the attendees who'd lingered, shaking their hands and smiling for photos and saying prayers.

Mr. Gray grabbed Aaliyah by the hand and walked as quickly as he dared down the center aisle, approaching Luther from behind. The man was speaking to a family of four, thanking them for coming, when Mr. Gray tapped him on the shoulder. He decided he'd probably get further with the man if he acted apologetic and grateful. It had been a long night and he couldn't risk Luther deciding to pack it in.

"Mr. Luther, do you mind if we take a pic with my daughter real quick? She just loves this show," he said, smiling warmly.

Luther responded just as Gray had expected. He amicably put an arm around Aaliyah and smiled, waiting for Mr. Gray's camera phone to flash. Mr. Gray couldn't leave it at just one photo, though he knew he was pushing his luck.

"Oh, thank you, that's so great. Just one more, please?"

Luther had already relaxed, but he smiled again and resumed the pose. Gray noticed it was harder this time for the man to hide his weariness.

"Big smile!" coached Mr. Gray. "Excellent."

Okay, enough. No need to antagonize him.

"Thank you," said Luther, smiling again. He turned to Aaliyah and shook her hand. "Thank you for coming. Bye-bye." The preacher turned away, to another family waiting to meet him.

"Come on," said Mr. Gray to the girl, his voice barely audible.

He led her back out the same door they came in. One job done. But the night was just beginning.

8

It was late. All John Luther wanted was to be in bed, asleep.

He'd stayed far too long at the studio tonight, but so many had come to see him, to get a smidgen of one-on-one time with the famous evangelist. Some had driven hours to get to the D.C. studio, crossing entire states. One family had come all the way from Canada. How could he possibly disappoint them?

Except now he was paying for it. He wasn't as young as he used to be, after all. Still, what a great night it had been. God was so good. The sermon couldn't have gone better. He prayed that many, many souls would hear the message and give their lives to Christ. And if his viewers were inspired by his words to make their voices heard in opposition to the Faith and Fairness Act, all the better.

He loved getting one-on-one with people. It was way too easy to get bogged down in business matters and board meetings and talk shows, and forget the reason Truth Ministries existed in the first place. It was about winning souls to Christ. That was all that ever really mattered. Not the fancy studio, not his face on television, not his opinion being counted among the major issues of the day.

Sure, John was tired, but it was a *good* tired. He'd sowed the fields tonight, and it felt good. As much as he wanted his nightly swim, followed by deep, blissful sleep, he wouldn't have traded the chance to meet his parishioners for anything.

His eyes were glazing over as he drove out of town in his olive-green Toyota FJ Cruiser, off the highways and out of the bustle of the city, toward his home farther south in Virginia. A place with trees rather than monuments. He blinked suddenly, willing himself not to sleep yet. Home was just another twenty minutes or so.

Home.

He dreamed of climbing into bed beside Monica. What a woman she was; he loved her so much. Beautiful, kind, thoughtful, supportive, she was a great wife, and a truly amazing mother. He wondered if she would still be awake, waiting for him. She always said she never slept well when he wasn't home, but it was after one o'clock in the morning already. Besides, she wasn't terribly happy with him at the moment.

The same day that Donald Harrison had entered his dressing room and demanded his support for that idiotic bill, she'd shown up at the studios. He loved it when she made the trip in, though lately it seemed to mean that something was up. And usually something not good.

The dressing room door had flown open and in ran his daughter, Jodi, throwing her arms around his neck in that special way that little girls do only for their daddies. At seven years old, Jodi was as precocious as they came, and the everlasting sunshine in John's life. He'd almost given up on ever having kids—he was several years older than Monica, after all—but she wanted a child so badly. John was eternally grateful that she'd won that debate, because his little girl was more wonderful and beautiful and more filled with love and life than he could have ever imagined. He'd never loved anyone so selflessly in his life as he did Jodi, and it surprised him how easily she was able to pull that love out of him.

Monica walked in quietly behind her with an apologetic look on her face. The girl must have escaped her grasp and slipped down the hall. He smiled and shook his head gently, indicating that it was fine. He didn't mind.

He turned to Jodi. "What are you doing up?" he asked in mock disapproval.

"My recital is tomorrow and I needed to practice," she explained, wide-eyed. "Are you coming?" Her blond hair was in a ponytail, and she had on a polka-dot dress she adored.

John sighed, searching for words. How could he disappoint that beautiful face with its spray of freckles across her nose?

Monica walked up from behind and brushed a stray strand of hair out of the girl's face. "Sweetie, Daddy has a super important board meeting that's scheduled at the exact same time," she said. "He can't make it."

The tone in Monica's voice was unmistakable. John could hear the frustration and disappointment just below the surface. A quick sideways glance of her tired eyes confirmed it. When they fought, it was always about this. Balance. Time with the family. And guilt was always Monica's most effective weapon. But what could he do? Things were what they were and he couldn't change them. Truth Ministries was closing on some new properties tomorrow, the culmination of years of hard work. There was no way he could just skip it.

He and Monica had engaged in this argument year after year. Nowadays it was mostly fought with looks and inflections.

The ministry was important, there was no denying that. It was his mission, the purpose given to him by God. He was as sure of that as he was of drawing breath. But over the years, Monica had come to feel marginalized by it. It was a family affair at first, and then as the ministry grew ever bigger and the two of them finally had a child, things began to change. These days, Monica believed that as important as Truth Ministries was, it was always taking him away from his family—especially when they needed him most. Their little girl wouldn't be with them forever, she'd said once. And that he was just watching his board members get older. That had hurt. So did the pain in Monica's eyes when he missed another event. But what was there to say? John wished he could find a way to better balance the two sides of his life, but after twenty-plus years of ministry, he'd still not mastered that skill. There was always so much to do at Truth Ministries, and absolutely everything required his attention.

"Is there any way you can reschedule?" Jodi had asked in the dressing room, her eyes bright and hopeful.

Oh, how he hated disappointing his little girl. Nothing ripped his heart out more.

"I tell you what, baby," he said. "You go home with Mommy, straight to bed. And when you wake up, I'll be there. I promise."

"Breakfast in bed?" Jodi grinned.

John grinned back. "Breakfast in bed."

"Only I'm cooking!" proclaimed Jodi, full of glee.

John laughed. "Deal."

Even now, all alone in the Toyota in the dead of night, he couldn't help laughing again. There was truly no situation that could not be made better by Jodi simply being Jodi. He thought of waking her up in the morning and swinging her around her room in his arms. He thought of her adorable giggle, those mischievous eyes, and that smile that could light up the whole world.

John was still thinking of his daughter when he spotted the girl on the side of the road, trying desperately to get his attention by waving both arms over her head.

9

"What is she doing?" John mumbled. He leaned in toward the windshield to get a better look as he slowed the vehicle and pulled over.

Something in the back of his mind said *This isn't right*. Here he was, on a lonely old road in the middle of nowhere, and a young girl was flagging him down. There was nothing on this entire road except a Mini Mart gas station, lighting up a section of the road about a block ahead.

Before the SUV was fully stopped, she'd run frantically up to him and slammed her hands down on the hood. "Help me!" she screamed, staring wildly in all directions.

She looked drunk or high or something. But she was too young for that—probably fifteen or sixteen. And what was she wearing? Some kind of midriff-baring top and short shorts? It was cool out, and this girl was practically in her underwear.

This was very, very wrong.

But he couldn't just ignore her cries for help. She looked genuinely frightened out of her mind. What if something was really wrong?

He got out of his vehicle and rushed up to her. "Are you all right?"

"They're coming!" she screamed. She was completely crazed, just—

Wait.

He'd seen this girl before. Wasn't she at the broadcast tonight? Yeah, she and her dad had stayed late to meet him. . . .

"Who's coming?" he asked.

She spun around then and started to walk away.

John wasn't sure whether to chase her down or not. This was nuts. "Young lady, what are you doing out here by yourself?"

The girl paraded around the space in front of the Toyota, clearly not in her right mind. John was growing impatient; he wanted to be home and in bed. If this was just some stupid prank . . .

"Sweetheart, what are you doing?"

She faced him with a gleeful smile. A freezing chill ran down John's back.

"They're he-ere," she sang, grinning. "*They're he-ere.*"

A beefy arm suddenly had John in a headlock. His heart hammered hard against his ribs as he pulled frantically at the arm wrapped around his neck. It was hard like iron and immovable.

Something sharp stuck him in the neck, and darkness swallowed him.

John swam in and out of consciousness. He caught glimpses of moments that would be forever frozen in time as hazy memories. He was slumped in the passenger seat of his vehicle, with dark silhouettes of trees passing by the side window.

A hand ran across his body in places no one but Monica should be allowed. He wanted to squirm but couldn't get his body to move.

Who was driving his Toyota?

A flash of light made him stir again. He blinked just enough to see a camera phone being held out in front of him, taking photos of him with . . . with that girl. She was sitting on his lap, making vulgar poses and groping him. He wanted to tell her to stop, to force her off his lap, to take the phone out of her hand. But his mouth and body refused to work. He was so sleepy, he just couldn't stay awake.

The sound of a male voice roused him a third time. "Scratch his face."

John forced open his heavy eyelids for a moment to glance sideways. It was the girl's dad, the man from the studio who insisted on taking several pictures of John with his daughter. No, not his daughter. A father would never do this to his girl. Especially since he was watching her with calculating eyes, like a hawk watching its prey before striking.

The left side of John's forehead and face was suddenly on fire. He blinked and saw three of the girl's fingers withdrawing after scratching him. There were more flashes, forcing John to close his eyes again.

"You gonna teach me a lesson?" teased the girl between snapping pictures. "You're a bad boy, preacher man."

And then the darkness drowned John again.

10

33 YEARS AGO

I won't allow you to do this," said Charles Luther. He stood at their house's front door, his arms crossed over his chest. A tall, broad-shouldered slab of granite. Immovable.

"Doesn't matter. One way or another, I'm going," John said, glaring from behind the aviator-style sunglasses his father had given him for his last birthday. It helped—the old man not being able to look into his eyes. Made him feel bolder. A packed duffel bag lay at his feet.

He stared down his father from across the room, seething with anger. He was emboldened by three years of self-searching and teenage rebellion. And also three beers. He wondered if the old man could tell he'd been drinking. Probably could smell it on him, the bloodhound. It wasn't like it was the first time. But he'd always attempted to hide it before. Not this time. Not today. At sixteen it was entirely illegal for him to touch a can of beer, which was the main reason he'd done it.

But he liked the feeling of defiance. Doing something forbidden was thrilling, and his every rebellious action added to his father's grief. Something he rather enjoyed.

The old man had always been strict. But it went beyond that. Charles Luther was so convinced the world they lived in was full of corruption and suffering and evil, that he was determined to shield his son from it completely. John's friendships were judged, his every word and second scrutinized. There was little laughter in his home, and every time John tried to engage in something from the culture at large, his father would recite Philippians 4:8. "Finally, brothers and sisters, whatever is true, whatever is noble, whatever is right, whatever is pure, whatever is lovely, whatever is admirable—if anything is excellent or praiseworthy—think about such things." And he would recite it until it became nothing but a clanging gong that John had grown to despise. Now his days were mostly filled with silence. No conversation. No words. Just sixteen years at home that felt like solitary confinement.

"I'm done, Dad. I can't live in this house another minute. I'm so stifled here, I'm choking. *All the time*. I feel like I'm dying."

Charles sighed. "John, if I've been overprotective, I'm sorry. But I love you, and I don't want you to walk the same path I did. I want more for you. The road you're on leads only to destruction."

John went on glaring at his father. He'd heard all this before, so many times, and had no desire to hear it again. As a young adult his father had become an alcoholic, and his life fell apart because of it. He couldn't keep a job, he slept around, he was even homeless for about a year. As he'd told John countless times, God met him at his lowest point, and everything changed. He gave up all his destructive habits, got a solid job working in construction, and eventually entered seminary. The only evidence of that old life was the occasional cigar the old man indulged in.

John knew all of this to be true, but he didn't care. His father was so intent on keeping his son from becoming just like him that John felt nothing but rejected at every turn. Everything was so unfair here. He'd had enough.

But before he left, there was one question he had to ask. One unspeakable topic that had to be spoken. In sixteen years he'd never asked. He couldn't. It was unquestionably, unequivocally *off-limits*. But what if he never got another chance to ask?

"Where's Mom?"

Charles looked as if someone had punched him in the stomach. He took a tiny step backward.

"Where is she, Dad?" John repeated. "Is she dead? You've never told me a single thing about her, not one word. I don't even know her name!"

The old man studied his own feet.

"Debbie," said Charles. "Your mother's name is Deborah Letts. It was never my intention to keep her from you, son. I kept waiting for the right time to tell you, and well . . . I guess it never came."

Charles shifted his weight, unable to look John in the eyes. John had never seen his father look this uncomfortable. It was so painfully awkward, he almost felt bad for the old man.

"Were you married?" John asked.

His father shook his head. "I had just started my big construction job. I was changing, God was turning my life around. But I was—*we* were—young. And deeply in love. I think she's the only woman I ever loved. We were together for about five months when she became pregnant."

John's pulse began to rise. He couldn't figure out why this was making him angry, but his bitterness rose with his father's every word.

"So why isn't she here?" John spat. "How'd you drive her away?"

Charles looked down again. "The day after you were born,

I found a note on her hospital bed saying she was sorry but she couldn't stay. She'd discharged herself, and that was that. Your mother was . . . unique. Special. I suppose you could call her a 'free spirit.' She always dismissed anything I said about marriage or family."

"And now . . . ?"

"I never saw her or heard from her again," Charles said, his voice growing quieter. "I don't know if she's even alive. She made her choice and she never looked back. But I still think of her. Every single day. She destroyed me when she left, but a part of me still loves her."

When his father fell silent, John's anger evaporated. Of all the ways he'd imagined this conversation going, all the stories he'd concocted in his head over the years to explain his mother's absence, the reality was nothing like he'd expected.

"It wasn't because of you she left," John said, his voice barely audible and his eyes wandering far into the distance. "She ran from *me*, Dad. I'm the problem. I always have been. It's me. She knew it the first time she looked at me. There's nothing good in me."

Emotionless, he picked up his duffel bag and walked toward the door. He pushed past his father, but instead of a rigid wall of stone, the old man was more like a deflated balloon. He made no effort to stop John from walking out the door.

"John?" his father said when John was just outside.

John hesitated but didn't turn around.

"No matter where you go or what you do, I will always love you," said the old man softly. "There's nothing you could ever do to change that."

John's eyes stung, and a lump rose in his throat. But he swallowed it and kept walking.

11

PRESENT DAY

Tick, tick, tick. Mr. Gray studied his watch. Five more minutes ought to do it. He mashed down the gas pedal harder.

He glanced over to the passenger seat, where Aaliyah was having her fun. Doing her job.

The preacher was slumped in the passenger seat while Aaliyah sat in his lap, snapping suggestive selfies. She tossed her hair around, licked her lips, and stared melodramatically into the camera phone he'd given her.

She was better at this than he could have ever hoped. And only sixteen. What would come next would almost be a blessing for her.

One flash, then a second and third.

"That'll do," he said, then held out a hand in her direction.

She gave him the phone and popped her chewing gum back into her mouth.

Mr. Gray eased Luther's Toyota onto the side of the road, miles from where they'd tricked Luther into stopping. A red-and-white

Jeep was parked there, waiting for them. He stepped out of the vehicle, and Aaliyah followed suit, stretching her legs.

The phone still in his hand, Mr. Gray thumbed 911 and waited for the response. "Yeah, I'd like to report a car accident. One vehicle. Marker 134."

The operator repeated his words, "One vehicle. Marker 134."

"Looks like two people inside," Mr. Gray told her.

"Copy. Two persons with injuries?" she clarified.

"Yes. You're going to want to send an ambulance."

The call over, Mr. Gray threw his sports jacket over his shoulders and shoved his arms in. Aaliyah walked toward the trees that lined either side of the road. She lit a cigarette and took a long drag.

"Where do you think you're going?" he asked.

Aaliyah turned around and smiled. It was obvious she was enjoying herself, though how much of that was sincere and how much was thanks to the Rohypnol was anybody's guess.

"You just took his car," she said.

He smiled. "You like that, huh?"

She rolled her eyes but couldn't hide her sly grin. A light caught her eyes, and she turned serious. Mr. Gray knew she was staring at the red-and-blue lights of a police car. But no siren could be heard.

"The cops showed up?" asked Aaliyah, worried.

Mr. Gray shrugged. "Yeah. Are there any marks on you?"

She shook her head, then turned away from him again, so he could see there were no marks on her back.

"Come on," he prodded, smiling again. "Turn around for me."

Aaliyah spun to look into his approving face. She looked relieved that he was pleased with her work, and for just a moment he wondered what her story was. Was she an orphan? Had she never had a father and longed for that connection—even with a total stranger who'd hired her for a frame job? How did she end up here?

No one would ever get a chance to find out.

He backhanded her hard, and she was instantly unconscious. He lowered her to the ground and pulled out another syringe from his jacket and stabbed it into her neck.

The policeman, a big muscular man Gray called Mr. Broad, caught up to him just as Mr. Gray was pulling the syringe out of her neck. He stood to his feet.

"Get her in the car," said Mr. Gray and then headed back to Luther's vehicle, hearing Mr. Broad's grunt as he hefted the girl up. Gray approached the passenger side door and looked inside.

It was empty.

"He's gone," he said, no trace of worry in his voice. "Luther ran."

Mr. Broad, carrying Aaliyah, looked up in alarm. "But—"

Gray held up a hand, unconcerned. "Luther ran because that's what a guilty man does."

12

With great gasping lungfuls of air, John ran into the night. This was insane. He felt in his pockets, on his wrist. His watch was gone, as well as his car keys and wallet. They'd taken everything.

What was he doing, running through the woods in the middle of the night? He hadn't run this hard in years. How had it gotten to this? More pressingly, how long would it be before those two men noticed he was gone? There could even be gunshots fired in his direction any second now . . .

Wait. No, that didn't make sense. They wouldn't shoot at him. The man in the gray suit could have shot him in the car if he'd wanted John dead. So if they didn't want him dead, what *did* they want?

Just go, he told himself. He had to get as far away from them as he could. *Keep running*.

As he cleared a rise, he ran past something to his left between the trees, something just visible out of the corner of his eye.

His body was still sluggish from whatever they'd drugged him with, and it took longer than normal for his brain to catch up to his surroundings. Dazed, he stumbled to a stop and turned around. There stood two young people, probably twenty-somethings, both of them girls. One of them wore a hooded sweat shirt with the hood up around her head. She stood very still, holding a phone up at him. A camera, or video more likely. That was all he needed.

They shared a long, silent moment. The girls made no attempt to inquire about his safety or offer to help. But then neither did they rat him out to the two men down on the road below. John decided he should be grateful for small favors and let God worry about the rest.

Be ye thankful in all things . . .

The girl holding the camera phone looked pale, with heavily made-up eyes. Like a Goth, he thought. Is that what they were called? Goths? She had multiple piercings all over her exceptionally pallid face, and her clothes looked used and filthy, like they'd come out of a dumpster. Likely an addict, possibly even homeless. But why would she have a phone? Whatever she was, she certainly didn't seem to be interested in being his friend.

The camera girl's expression was blank, stern even. There was nothing on her face that he could discern—not even a fleeting curiosity. She was merely a bystander recording an interesting event.

Looking into her eyes and finding nothing there, no help, he turned and resumed his run.

A few minutes later, a small tree limb scraped across his forehead as he ran in the dark. He was so deep into the woods now, almost nothing was visible. He rubbed a sleeve against his head, found it stained with blood. He kept running.

Soon he had to stop to catch his breath. Without warning he doubled over and threw up on the ground, coughing and gagging. Was that the drug he'd been injected with? Working its way out of his system? Or just blind panic? John couldn't tell.

He placed a hand on his neck to feel his pulse. Predictably it was thumping harder than it had in years. He was so out of breath, he feared he'd never catch it. His lungs fought for air and his heart raced.

The darkness closed in once more, and John felt himself topple to the ground.

13

Monica Luther was afraid to turn over. She hadn't heard John come to bed last night, and she didn't want to find him *not there* now. But in her gut she had that horrible intuition. . . .

She rolled. His half of the bed was undisturbed.

Barring the occasional business trip, John always came home at the end of the day. Always. No matter what. Unless there was some big emergency to deal with, there was no way he would willingly not come home.

Okay, calm down, calm down. Maybe he was on the couch. Maybe he got in so late, he didn't want to wake her up. Or maybe he'd gotten up early this morning and was already downstairs, having breakfast with Jodi. Had she overslept? It wouldn't be like Jodi to stay quiet enough in the morning to let Mommy sleep in.

Monica rolled back over to glance at her nightstand. The alarm clock said it was 6:47 a.m. Well, that explained Jodi. She was a night owl like her dad; she rarely got up before seven. So what was going on with John? Monica told her heart to slow down, to stop trying to leave her chest. But it wouldn't listen.

Something was wrong. Terribly wrong. She could feel it.

Maybe she should call Ryan or Dave, find out if they'd seen John this morning. But she'd better do it quick; she'd have to get Jodi up for school in a few minutes.

Monica flinched and let out a clipped scream when the doorbell rang. Her heart jolted. Someone was at her door before seven in the morning. She wasn't even dressed yet. Who could possibly—?

Oh no.

She yelped again when a harsh banging reverberated throughout the house. Three knocks came from the front door, loud enough to be heard upstairs.

"Mommy?" called Jodi from down the hall.

Monica ran to her bedroom door, throwing her bathrobe on over her nightgown. "It's okay, sweetie. Just go back to sleep for a few more minutes."

Her heart thudded harder and harder as she descended the stairs as fast as she dared. She almost stumbled on one step, but caught herself just as the pounding on the door began again.

"Who is it?" she called out, rounding the bottom of the staircase.

"The police, ma'am" came the answer from a deep, gruff voice.

Monica hurried to the door, her fingers trembling as she unlocked the dead bolt and chain and flung the door open. Two uniformed police officers stood there, their expressions impossible to gauge.

"Is your husband home, Mrs. Luther?" asked the one on the left. The badge he held out to her said *Richards* on it.

Monica could barely process what was happening. The police were at her door, asking if John was here, and . . . *Was* he here? She'd never found out for sure. "Um . . . I don't think he is. I'm sorry, I'm a little disoriented. I just woke up."

The officer on the right, whose nametag said *Garcia*, spoke up. "May we come in?"

"Um . . . sure. I guess," Monica answered, still struggling to catch up. "What is this about?"

Officers Richards and Garcia ignored her question and stepped inside. They were followed by four more officers she hadn't noticed until now, each of whom slid into the house and moved off in a different direction. Just like that, the police were spreading out through her home.

"Wait," she said, her presence of mind finally returning. "Are you searching my house for something? Don't you have to have a warrant or something?"

Officer Garcia handed her a folded-up piece of paper. She didn't need to unfold it to know what it was.

She frowned at the two officers. "If you had this, why did you bother asking if you could come in?"

"Despite what you've seen on TV or read in crime novels, police officers do exercise common courtesy, Mrs. Luther," said Officer Richards.

There was a crash somewhere behind her, maybe the dining room? Monica frowned. Hopefully nothing was broken. More important, the noise had to have woken Jodi up. She'd be making her way to the stairs at any moment.

"In that case, I would appreciate knowing why you're here and what this has to do with my husband," said Monica.

Richards and Garcia exchanged a fleeting look. Were they under orders not to reveal too much to her?

"Do you know a teenage girl named Aaliyah Evans?" Garcia asked.

"No."

"You're certain?" asked Richards. "You've never heard that name before?"

"Never."

"Mommy?" said a small voice.

Monica spun in place. Jodi had moved very quietly down

the stairs and appeared right behind her mother. She sounded nervous.

"Why are the police here?" she asked.

Monica smiled at her daughter to lighten the mood. "They're explaining that to Mommy right now, sweetheart. Can you do me a favor and go get your school clothes on while I talk to these nice officers?"

Jodi obviously wasn't fooled. Monica knew her daughter could see her fear, and the girl glanced back and forth between the two officers and her mother, trying to find some answers. Greeted only with silence, she finally complied, shuffling across the hardwood floor and back upstairs.

The second she was gone, Monica faced the policemen again. "What is going on?"

"Aaliyah Evans is dead, Mrs. Luther," said Officer Garcia. "And I'm afraid your husband is our primary suspect. He hasn't been formally charged yet, but we have evidence that he was present at the scene of the crime when the girl died. And that he fled the scene immediately after her death."

Later, Monica would recall the sound of breaking glass at that exact moment. But she wouldn't be able to remember if something in the house had actually broken or if the sound had come from her world shattering into a million pieces.

14

Many hours later, John Luther slowly roused. He sensed a warm, dappled light on his face, and for a moment he forgot where he was. Why was the bed so hard? Why was that bird chirping so loudly outside his window? He was about to ask Monica to shut the window and put on a pot of coffee when he remembered.

His eyes opened tenderly, and he stared up into a maze of tree branches and bright sunlight beyond them. His lips felt swollen and cracked. Despite the sleep, he felt no more rested than he had before passing out. He was curled up in a burrow of leaves and fallen branches. With no small effort he pushed up onto his hands and knees, and then all the way to his feet. He steadied after a slight wobble and absent-mindedly put a hand over his abdomen. He was starving.

Worse, he was lost. He assumed he was still in Virginia, but he wasn't sure how long he'd been unconscious in the vehicle and how far they'd driven him. Turning in a circle he saw mostly trees, endless trunks of elms and oaks and firs. But there, finally, he saw the wreckage of his own flight. Bent branches and broken underbrush. Left without choices, he chose to backtrack down the path he'd carved last night.

The scent and sounds of the woods were instantly recognizable to John, though he couldn't quite place why they felt so familiar. It was only on stopping to rest and hearing a particular bird sing a quick six-note chirrup deep in the woods that he was transported back nearly forty years to his childhood—to the first time he'd run away.

He'd been eight or nine at the time, up in the woods with his father as the old man visited and thought about cabins. It was a pastime of sorts for Charles Luther, planning his future hideaway in the wilderness.

John couldn't remember why they'd begun to fight—maybe something about an X-Men comic book John had hidden away in his luggage—but he did remember the outcome. Charles ordered John out of the cabin they'd rented for the weekend and into the woods. He was to spend a half hour sitting in and thinking over God's creation before he could come back in for the night.

John had grabbed his backpack, pulled his hood up over his head to hide the anger burning on his face, and stormed out. He walked down the crushed-stone driveway, crossed the road, and plunged into the woods, not stopping to look back because he knew for certain Charles Luther was not following him.

The power in walking, in defying, fueled his legs. For the first half hour.

But then he stopped and sat down and suddenly the immensity of the woods weighed in on him, and he felt how alone he was. *"Pray,"* the old man used to tell him whenever he was scared, but John refused. He was scared, but he would not pray.

And he didn't—even when the sun fell low, and evening's cool hand started to grip him.

His backpack had a bit of food in it but nothing for warmth, and John realized—while he wasn't in great danger, as it wasn't that cold—it wouldn't do him any good to just stand out in the open. Scouting around the area, while the sun dipped lower and lower, he finally found a massive boulder with a snug depression at its base filled with fallen pine needles. The perfect size to tuck himself into.

Quickly, before darkness fell, he gathered a few pine boughs to pull up around himself and then lay down in his little den, eating what little food he had. He guessed he wouldn't sleep, but the next thing he knew, dawn had lifted night's grip and he crawled out.

He could see his breath, yet he felt *alive*. He'd made it through the night. On his own. Without his father. Without even a single prayer.

Hunger followed quickly, though, and he had no interest in spending yet another night tucked next to the boulder. Instead he climbed the rock and looked around deep into the woods, hoping to gather some sense of which direction to head. He soon began to panic—every direction looked exactly the same at first glimpse—but then he caught a sharp reflection of light and heard what had to have been a truck rumbling to life.

It took forty-five minutes to reach what he'd seen.

It was a camp. A scout camp perhaps, probably used mostly in summer, and so all the buildings stood abandoned. John didn't care; he was just thrilled to find some evidence of other humans. He spent the morning exploring—few of the buildings had been locked—and even found a box of saltine crackers that had been left behind and were miraculously untouched by rodents. John opened a sleeve and wandered his way past a strange dome-shaped greenhouse and down a path to the pool. He sat on the edge of the pool deck, took off his shoes and socks, and dipped his feet in the water.

"Those were going to be my lunch," a voice said from behind him, and John nearly choked on a cracker. He bolted to his feet.

A man stepped out from the pool house. He had on a green flannel shirt and denims supported by a carpenter's belt.

"I'm sorry," John said. "Didn't think there was anyone here." He couldn't tell if he was disappointed to have been found or thrilled to no longer be alone. "My name is John. I . . . I . . . got lost in the woods."

Half an hour later, the camp's caretaker had escorted John back to the rented cabin. The family car was still parked outside, but John's dad was not around.

"Probably looking for me," John said.

"I can wait around, if you like," the carpenter offered. But John said he was fine, and so the man drove off.

Hours later, Charles Luther returned. He had a stringer of rainbow trout in one hand and his rod in the other.

"Clean these for dinner," he had said to John, handing him the fish, and never said a single word asking about how the boy had spent his night.

John remembered how powerful he'd felt at the time—standing there, gutting and filleting the fish. Because, at least for one night, he'd won. He'd survived and found his way back home, and with no help.

The woods brought all that back to John as he, again, found himself lost and desperate. This time, though, he'd been humbled enough to pray. For direction and guidance. For a safe path home yet again. Then he set off once more into the woods.

Two hours later, he found the edge of the woods at last and stepped out onto a main road. He couldn't keep walking or he soon would collapse. Weary, dehydrated, and famished, he emerged from the woods to find himself behind a familiar-looking gas station. It was the Mini Mart, the one not far from where the girl had first flagged him down. Where this whole mess began.

At the rear of the store, attached to a streetlight pole, was something red, and it caught his eye. Walking closer, he saw it was an old pay phone. Hope flooded his heart; at last he could call Monica and get some help. But his hope evaporated when he stepped up and found nothing but a cord that was broken off where the receiver had once been.

John closed his eyes for a moment and let his head sag backward until it rested against one side of glass. He was so tired, so disappointed.

But he had to keep going. Just keep going.

John walked to the Mini Mart. At least there would be a sink where he could wash the blood off his face and get a drink of water. How long would it be before the effects of that drug wore off? He still felt horribly disoriented.

Inside the tiny store, a female clerk stood behind a counter reading a tabloid magazine. She eyed him so warily that he wondered what he must look like. She had long red hair and was maybe a little overweight. Did she have her finger on a panic button right now, waiting to see if he'd try to steal something or brandish a gun?

He was too tired to care.

"Key to the men's room?" he asked.

The clerk didn't respond. She merely stared at him.

So he turned right and walked through the store, looking, looking . . . *there*. The soda machine was perched on a long table affixed to one wall, alongside condiments, napkins, a coffee machine, and more. He pushed the soda machine's button for plain water and caught some in his hand. After pouring the handful into his mouth, he splashed a little on his face.

"That's for paying customers only."

He looked up. The clerk was still watching his every move.

His face wet, John quickly grabbed a few napkins from a dispenser and dried off.

"I'm sorry," she said. "Company policy."

Despite appearances, did she actually feel some sympathy for him? Particularly given how he must look? He glanced down to see ripped clothes, bloodstains, and dirt everywhere. But still, was he really *that* unrecognizable?

"Don't you know who I am?" he asked. He hoped it didn't sound pompous; he hadn't meant it that way. He was just so worn out that any hint of familiarity would be nice.

The clerk shook her head. "No idea."

John's head sagged again. "I'm . . ."

Ah, why bother? He wiped water drops from his tie and shirt with the napkins, then threw them in the trash. He walked toward the door.

"I apologize," he said, exiting the building. He knew he should be thinking about what would come next, how he was going to contact someone, but at that moment he felt only exhaustion, thirst, and a simple wish that he could fall once more into darkness.

Only this time it didn't come.

15

The halls of power at the J. Edgar Hoover Building were filled with clusters of agents engaged in hushed conversations. Whatever the big news was that everyone was whispering about, Agent Ashley Rivera had the feeling she'd missed it. She'd only arrived at work ten minutes ago, and had barely walked in the door when her partner summoned her to his office as quickly as possible.

Of course, referring to Agent Preston Clark as her "partner" was a slight misnomer. It was true that the two were a pair when working on cases, but his twenty-some years of experience at the FBI far outranked her two and a half. No one ever said it, but Clark was her mentor.

Agent Clark was tall and solid, a college linebacker in his day and something of a maverick at the agency. He was known for following protocol to the letter, but also for employing methods of investigation that were entirely his own. He relied on his instincts more than most federal agents were comfortable with, though he was also highly skilled in many disciplines.

"Seen this yet?" he asked as she walked through his office

door. He nodded at the flat-screen TV hanging from the wall to the right of his desk.

Rivera took her customary seat at the front of his desk and focused on the television. It was tuned to CNW, where one of their anchors was breathlessly relaying breaking news about an evangelist named John Luther. Rivera knew who Luther was; most everyone in America did. He was the most popular preacher in the country—possibly even the world. Luther was an outspoken, unapologetic evangelical, a virtue that made him plenty of enemies in Washington. And plenty of allies as well. Some loved him, some hated him. But everyone in D.C. respected him.

In the game of politics, John Luther was one of the few major players who held no public office.

A scroll at the bottom of the TV screen revealed the gist of the breaking news. A teenage girl had been found dead in Luther's car, Luther was the primary suspect and had fled the scene of the crime, and he was currently at large. A fugitive.

"So *this* is what all the chatter's about," Rivera said, running a hand through her long jet-black hair.

CNW splashed a photo of Luther that filled the entire screen. Luther was standing in it, his hands clasped in front, with a serene but serious look on his face. Behind him was an American flag, hung so that the stripes ran vertically. It almost looked like a presidential portrait.

Clark stabbed at the TV's remote and paused the live feed. "What do you see?"

It was a favorite exercise of Clark's. He had an uncanny knack for accurately determining guilt or innocence by "reading" the suspect's eyes. "The eyes are the window to the soul," he'd once told her. "Everything you need to know is there. You just have to look hard enough to see it." Shortly after being made partners, Clark had begun frequently engaging Rivera in this game. Most people believed that instincts couldn't be taught, but Clark was determined to instill them in his partner.

Rivera cleared her mind and stared into Luther's gray-blue eyes. She saw sincerity, though she knew that could be faked. Luther's eyes practically glowed with conviction and certainty of purpose. There was honesty, and lots of it. Some measure of ambition as well—probably more than he'd admit to. Was that a hint of patience? If so, was it the practiced kind that didn't come naturally? His eyes weren't unkind, but there was a distinct lack of humor. He was not a lighthearted man, and there was a great deal of pain in his past.

"Gut instinct . . ." she said, "he's a complicated man. But I don't see a killer."

Clark, who'd watched her closely as she made her determination, gave a slight nod. "Neither do I. But if drug use was involved, that changes all the rules."

"What makes you think drugs could be involved?" asked Rivera.

"Just a guess. But you're right. We need more to go on. The call came in twenty minutes ago. This is ours. You and I are going to bring this guy in before somebody else winds up dead—including him."

Rivera hesitated. That didn't quite add up. "Aren't fugitives under Marshal jurisdiction?" The purpose of the U.S. Marshals office was to hunt down fugitives and bring them to justice. This kind of thing wasn't unheard of for Feds, yet it was a bit unusual.

"Luther's unique status makes lots of folks up on the Hill very nervous. They want the FBI to take point."

Of course. When it came to politics, perceptions were all that mattered. And Congress would have an easier time molding the public's perceptions of John Luther if the FBI was running the investigation.

Clark unpaused the TV and caught it back up to the live

broadcast. CNW was showing an interview with John Luther, which was labeled PREVIOUSLY RECORDED in tiny letters in the top left corner.

"Do you know what kind of person I was?" asked Luther to whoever was interviewing him. "An abusive, alcoholic, gambling drug addict."

The face of popular journalist Diana Lucas replaced Luther's. She was speaking live. "That was John Luther, just days ago, admitting to a history of alcoholism, drug abuse, gambling addiction, and spousal abuse. It is not widely known among Luther's followers that he is currently married to his *second* wife, after his first marriage ended in a bitter divorce following allegations of abuse on Luther's part. He and his former wife eventually settled out of court, and today Luther is married to Monica Luther, with whom he has a daughter. He claims to be a changed man, having been 'delivered by God' from the destructive behaviors of his past. But only time and more information about the shocking events that took place last night will prove if that deliverance has stuck. . . ."

Rivera glanced at Clark. "I'll pull his criminal file."

Clark nodded. "Good. I've asked the police to let the agency conduct the girl's autopsy, so we should have those results in a few hours."

"What about the car?"

"It's being held for us," replied Clark. "The scene too. Let's get to work."

16

As the police searched the house, Monica sat at the dining room table for half an hour. Silent and alone.

She had no idea who this Aaliyah Evans was. But the whole thing had to be a mistake. It just had to be.

John had made his share of mistakes in the past, but he was different now. A good man. He was *more* than a good man—he was a man that countless others looked to, following his example and teachings. Monica hadn't known John before God came into his life. She'd heard stories of the wretched example of humanity he was back then. But the man in those stories was not the John she knew. He wasn't *her* John. She never wanted to meet that man.

Was it possible he could have slipped? Well, anything was possible. John was a flawed human being just like everyone else. No one was perfect. No one was immune to sin.

But he wouldn't do this. Monica's husband, the man she fell in love with and with whom she shared her life, would never, ever hurt anyone.

He wouldn't, right?

No. Of course not.

Unless . . .

Had something changed?

Had she missed the warning signs?

She stood and walked slowly to the kitchen. After digging in her purse, she retrieved her phone. What was his number? He was the last person she wanted to talk to right now, but few people spent more time with John and would have noticed any changes in John's behavior.

After two rings, Ryan Morris answered. "Yyyyellow?"

"Ryan, it's Monica."

"Well hey there, beautiful," he said. "Have you seen John this morning? He's not in his office, and we—"

"Ryan, something's wrong," said Monica.

As he so often did, he breezed right past her words. "Hey, is John feeling okay? I told him last night he was looking kinda pale. I hope he's not coming down—"

"*Ryan*," said Monica again. "John is missing. The police are here at the house, right now."

A brief silence was followed by, "What? What do you mean, 'missing'? Where is he?"

"I don't know, Ryan," she replied, rolling her eyes. "Something happened last night . . . something about a girl. I don't know any details yet."

Monica heard some kind of commotion in the background, people calling for Ryan.

"Hang on," he said. She heard shuffling and decided it was the sound of Ryan walking or jogging. Then there was louder hubbub, followed by the emotionless intonations of what sounded like a talking head on the TV news. She couldn't make out what the newscaster was saying.

Ryan was quiet for so long, she wondered if he was still holding the phone.

"Ryan?"

"You, uh . . . You'd better turn on the TV," he said.

For the second time today, Monica felt like she was going to throw up. If the media had already picked up on whatever happened last night, then it was over. Even if he was innocent, the media would make him *look* guilty. There was nothing television news networks loved more than a scandal. John was going to lose everything.

The world felt like it was moving in slow motion as she made her way to the living room and looked for the remote. The sense of dread was physical and overpowering.

Was any of this really happening? How could it be?

She found the remote on the couch, dropped it—when had her hands started shaking?—picked it back up, and pressed the power button. It was still tuned to CNW from the last time it was on.

Breaking News was plastered prominently at the bottom of the screen, with a smaller headline underneath that read, *Girl found dead in evangelist's vehicle.*

". . . highly respected evangelist John Luther, who has ministered to millions around the world, including sitting presidents and other global leaders, is the chief suspect in the alleged murder of Aaliyah Evans," said the news anchor. "We currently have no details on Ms. Evans, but police have confirmed to us that she was found dead shortly before dawn this morning, inside John Luther's vehicle, which Mr. Luther had apparently abandoned in an undisclosed location . . ."

Monica couldn't remember sitting down, but she was on the couch now. What had John been doing with a young woman in the middle of the night?

". . . manslaughter, possibly statutory rape, child endangerment, drug possession, and leaving the scene of an accident. Talk about a relapse—I don't know how a judge could overlook . . ."

God, please, no.

This couldn't be real.

17

The worst part was still being alive.

Standing outside the Mini Mart, John came to that slow realization. His head was finally clearing from whatever drug they'd used on him. Looking up and down the empty rural highway, John knew they had deliberately let him live, had likely wanted him to escape. It hadn't been mercy or kindness. Instead, there had to be some darker reason that he hadn't yet discovered. And now he was lost. Left here without a phone or money, hours from his home. He knew he had to find people to help him, but there were few options for next steps. Looking to his left, he began trudging in that direction.

What was that passage in the book of Matthew? The one about Jesus and the time he roamed the wilderness after Satan had tempted him? It said that angels had come to him and cared for him there.

"Lord," he whispered, "I sure could use an angel or two about now."

He was staggering, exhausted and thirsty. He hadn't felt like this in a very long time, not since the dark days before God came into his life. He'd forgotten how horrible it was, how he never wanted to feel like this again.

Minutes later, a white van appeared next to him, slowing to a stop. A woman popped her head out the side window. She had bright, fierce eyes, sharp cheekbones and chin, and long, curly brown hair. She wore a black T-shirt, not one but two cross necklaces, and one of her wrists was loaded with multiple bracelets that were a rainbow of colors. Thirty years ago she would've been a hippie. Today he'd see women like her in the audience, and the same kinds of faces in the crowds protesting him.

"Sir!" she called out.

John stopped short and walked over to her.

"You okay?" she asked.

"No," he replied wearily, out of breath. "I'm not okay."

John leaned forward to rest his head against the side-view mirror. The woman looked deeply concerned, studying him closely.

"Thanks for asking, though," he added.

"I'm Kathy from Helping Hands," she said. "I've got water and donuts if you want some breakfast." She produced an ice-cold bottle of water and handed it to him.

John accepted it gratefully, looking at the bottle as if it were the most precious gift he'd ever received.

Kathy smiled at him. "Not so long ago I looked just like you."

Oh. She thought he was homeless. Maybe even drunk.

John poured water into his mouth, swallowing the gloriously cold liquid greedily.

"The arms of God aren't as far away as you might think," Kathy continued, and John had to hold back a bitter smile.

He didn't have time to explain his situation to her. "Kathy, I need to borrow a phone."

She looked mildly surprised. "Okay," she said, reaching for the van's console, where she grabbed a cell phone. She offered it to him freely. Whoever this woman was, she was a godsend.

"Thanks," he said.

John turned and walked away, back around toward the rear of the van. He just wanted to get far enough out of earshot for a little privacy. Kathy opened the van's side door and peeked out, keeping an eye on him. She didn't seem to have much regard for her phone, so he had to assume she was worried about him.

Leaning against the back of the van for support, John made the call. The one person he needed to talk to first.

"Hello?"

"Monica!"

"John!" Monica whispered. Only she didn't sound relieved. "The police are here, and they're going through everything. They're talking about you like you're some kind of murderer! Where have you been?"

John stammered, "I . . . I don't know. I'm trying to figure it out. Something happened last night—"

"A girl is *dead*, John! They're saying you're involved. They're saying you killed her!"

Dead?

She wasn't dead when he ran from the car. She was fine. Drugged probably, but up walking around under her own power and seemingly feeling fine. How could she be dead?

It hit him.

It was *them*. Those two men—the one in the gray suit and the supposed cop.

That poor girl . . .

Dear God in heaven, they killed her.

18

I didn't kill anybody!" insisted John. "I woke up in the middle of nowhere. They took all my stuff—my car, my wallet, my ID."

Monica's silence was crushing. She believed him, didn't she?

"I'm coming home," said John. He knew it was madness, but he was just so tired.

"No! Don't!" Monica whispered. "*They're watching me.*"

John's muscles went weak, and he took a few steps backward until he fell against the van. Did Monica mean the police? Or . . . someone else?

He quickly ended the call, tried to compose himself, and edged around the van to hand the phone back to Kathy. He looked at the area around the van with new eyes. An oppressive, bright sun burned his skin as he spun around on the old hillside road. Dirt bordered both sides of the road, with higher hills on the right and dense woods on the left. The hills were clear and easily visible for as far as his eyes could see. But within the trees there could be anything.

Was he being watched right now? Or was he being paranoid?

Surely he wasn't important enough to warrant constant surveillance from . . . well, from whoever was doing this to him.

Who *was* doing this, anyway? Why was this happening to him?

"Can I give you a ride somewhere?"

John looked up. Kathy was still leaning out of the side of the van. Had she overheard his conversation with Monica? He'd spoken of killing, of someone being dead. Why wasn't she calling the police on the phone he'd just handed back to her?

She studied him intently as he did the same to her. He could discern nothing on her face except a sincere desire to help. No hint of deception.

John blinked, realizing he hadn't answered her question. His head was swimming with too many thoughts, and he felt dizzy. "What?" was all he could get out.

"Can I help you get somewhere? Someplace safe?"

Someplace safe. Where would that be?

He couldn't go home. The police were there and would have the entire neighborhood staked out by nightfall. The same went for the office; he couldn't possibly show his face there.

Was there anyplace safe for him anymore?

Well, I *could* . . .

There was one place John was always welcome, no matter what. And his connection to the place wasn't widely known, though it was a matter of public record and would surely come to light sooner than later. He didn't want to risk endangering anyone.

But maybe if he got there first, before the authorities . . .

Short of leaving the country, it was his only option.

"Downtown," he told Kathy. "I need to get to St. Peter's Church."

19

Senator Donald Harrison shook his head as he stared at the television screen in his office. The coverage had been playing for over an hour now. Nonstop reporting and analysis on four different networks about John Luther's shocking alleged drug relapse, possible murder of a teenage girl, and subsequent fleeing from authorities.

Donald located the TV remote on the corner of his desk and switched it off. Enough of this distraction. The Luther train had begun rolling away from the station, and there was no stopping it now.

"Well, here we go," he said to himself, rounding his desk and grabbing his coat before exiting the room.

He rode the elevator alone to the bottom floor, then strode out of it with confidence of purpose. Where were they . . . ?

There.

Coming in sight of the building's glass front door, he saw them, just as he'd expected. A moderately sized gathering of reporters, photographers, and camera crews stood a respectable distance away from the building's exterior, waiting for him to emerge.

Donald ran over in his mind a few ideas he'd had about what he would say when this moment came. Then he blew through the main doors and braced himself.

"Senator Harrison!"

"Senator!"

"Sir!"

The cacophony of voices came at him all at once as the crowd of journalists quickly converged around him.

"Senator!" cried a female reporter he recognized from one of the major networks. "You're a close friend of John Luther's. Do you care to comment on the charges he's currently facing?"

Donald cleared his throat, and everyone fell silent. More than a dozen microphones and recording devices were shoved up close to his face.

Affecting just the right note of concern and disappointment, he replied, "John Luther is a fine man. This is an absolute tragedy that's happened."

Another reporter spoke up. "If this ever goes to trial, will you be pushing for a lenient sentence?"

They might as well have been working off a prearranged script, ticking off Donald's anticipated questions one by one.

"Well, my heart goes out to his family," he said, managing to sound both stern and compassionate. "But regardless of who he may or may not have had relationships with, I want to see justice served."

Time to get moving again. He couldn't take the risk of appearing to *want* to speak to reporters about this. He pushed through the crowd and attempted to keep walking, knowing the reporters wouldn't let him go that easy.

The questions kept coming, fast and loud as he walked away, and he kept waiting to hear one he wanted to answer. Careful not to let his frustration show, he was nonetheless annoyed that their questions were turning inane. For several seconds there was nothing worth answering.

Finally he spun, walking backward, and offered a polished, flat politician's smile. Spreading his hands wide, he said, "I can't clean the world with soiled hands."

How was that for a sound bite, America?

Donald estimated that the line would be the lead-in for the John Luther news coverage for the rest of the day and much of tomorrow.

20

There it was. It took the better part of two hours to track down Luther's records, since most of them were police reports that came from disparate sources. Seemed Luther had spent a lot of his youth and early adulthood wandering from place to place. He'd been all over the country, from the looks of it.

Of greater interest to Agent Rivera was how difficult it had been culling his complete criminal history from the FBI database. The system was so sophisticated these days that a simple criminal report could usually be found in less than a minute. But Luther's records had proven difficult to track down. And even now, she'd only been able to compile a *criminal* history. She wasn't entirely sure that it was complete, even now, and his noncriminal records—marital status, deceased relatives, school records, and so on—were missing from his file.

It wasn't the first time she'd seen a file with conspicuously missing data. When the interests of one's benefactors in Washington were involved, those kinds of "public" records had a way of getting masked behind red tape.

Rivera knew that most agents hated chasing down records, but she'd always enjoyed it. There was something fascinating in learning about the things people did, the lengths they went to in order to get what they wanted, the capacity for evil that rested in the human heart, and the depths to which they descended and how they justified it. It was like reading forgotten pages from a volume of modern history, with a healthy dose of psychology thrown in.

She'd just begun skimming the report when Agent Clark walked into her office.

"Hear from the coroner yet?" she asked.

"Shouldn't be much longer. Autopsy's in progress now. O'Neill's doing it."

Rivera blinked. Franklin O'Neill was a senior agent, one of the "big office upstairs" guys who gave orders and supervised the work of underlings like Clark and Rivera. Many years ago he'd been a medical examiner, but he hadn't performed an autopsy in probably twenty years or more. Someone in Washington had to be applying some major pressure on the bureau if he had scrubbed up to perform Aaliyah Evans's autopsy himself.

"That his file?" asked Clark.

Rivera nodded. "He wasn't kidding on that TV interview. His criminal record is *not small.*"

Clark leaned in, reading the computer monitor from behind her shoulder. "Huh. Multiple arrests on drug possession, enforced rehab at twenty-six, license revoked for drunk driving at twenty-eight, three charges of domestic abuse . . ."

"All three of which were later dropped," Rivera added, pointing at a specific spot on the screen. "That was his first wife."

Clark nodded. "That date on the last reported incident—she filed for divorce just a few weeks later."

Rivera glanced at her mentor and partner. An unspoken question passed between them. How did he know the details of

Luther's divorce? And what else had he already found that she hadn't yet been able to?

He smirked at her sideways, then returned his eyes to the computer screen. That was probably all the answer she'd ever get. She knew Clark well enough to know that he had ways of finding things out that others couldn't or wouldn't. Sources, methods—sometimes it was just that uncanny intuition of his.

She returned her attention to the computer report. "What about the gambling? He mentioned gambling on TV, but I don't see anything here."

"He took over a dozen flights to Vegas over the years, but hasn't been since he turned his life around. It's a smart bet that he probably frequented Atlantic City at the time too, but by car."

Right. There would be no records of Luther flying to Atlantic City when he likely drove there.

Again, Rivera couldn't help wondering how Clark had gotten access to all of these personal details about John Luther. Was someone on the Hill feeding him intel? Someone who wanted to see Luther fall? Or maybe even someone who wanted to see Luther vindicated?

"So what we've got here is a dividing line," she said, summing up the report. "There's his old life, where he was toxic and self-destructive. And then there's his current life, where all of that stuff went away and he became a respected religious leader. The dividing line was probably a 'conversion experience' where he 'met God' or whatever. The question is, when did it happen?"

"Somewhere between fifteen and twenty years ago," Clark replied. Now he was studying her again. "And this is relevant how?"

He wasn't questioning her reasoning. He was testing it. Always he was testing her and how she functioned as an agent. "If we understand the circumstances of when and how he changed his life so drastically, it might help us better understand why he's flipped the switch back the other way, if he has indeed relapsed."

"Very good," said Clark.

If he was happy with her reasoning, then she was happy too.

21

Kathy's Helping Hands van came to a stop across the street from St. Peter's Church. John slid open the side door.

"God bless you," he said. "And thanks."

Kathy smiled warmly and placed a hand atop one of his. "No matter what, God is still with you. Never forget that."

"I'll try," John replied. He tried to smile back at her but couldn't quite manage it.

He stepped out of the van and glanced around. In so many ways it was just another small Virginia town. Far enough from D.C. and Richmond that commuters hadn't totally taken it over, it felt like a place out of time. Partly because every time John walked these streets he couldn't help but see how it looked twenty and thirty years ago when he'd prowled the area as a teen. The downtown block was remarkably empty for early evening. There were usually people out walking on errands, vehicles speeding about. Was it luck that no one was around to see him, or was it a little help from above? He was grateful either way.

Coming here may have been a terrible mistake. What if the old priest didn't believe him? What if the police showed up at the church while he was inside? What if that gray-suited man was hiding somewhere nearby, watching him right now?

He shuffled his feet, quickly crossing the street to the sprawling limestone church and entering through a set of double doors, painted red as the blood of a lamb.

The old priest stood at the altar at the front of the church, silently lighting dozens of votive candles in red glass holders. The red symbolized the blood of Christ, shed to redeem mankind. John recognized the votives as part of a traditional prayer vigil. Was he praying for John? Undoubtedly. But would he *believe* in John's innocence?

At least they were alone in the dark, cavernous sanctuary.

John struggled to move his aching feet down the center aisle, passing dozens of pews until he came within earshot of the priest.

"I didn't know where else to go," he said, an apology in his voice.

Charles Luther slowly raised his head, though his eyes stayed glued to the candles.

The relationship between the two men had improved over the years. They would never be best friends, but John had eventually let go of his self-hatred and the resentment he'd long carried against his father. And Charles had forgiven himself for his shortcomings as a father and tried his best to repair the relationship with his son.

"I don't know what you've heard," said John between weary breaths, "but, Dad, I didn't hurt anybody."

"I know you didn't, John." At last Charles turned to face his son. His black cassock was wrinkle free, his white clerical collar pristine. His expression was severe but not unkind. "Come with me."

John heaved a great sigh of relief as he followed his father through a side door into his personal chambers. Dingy brown walls were lined with shelves filled with hundreds of books. An old radio sent out a tinny news broadcast that was punctuated with occasional pops of static.

". . . victim has been identified as sixteen-year-old Aaliyah Evans, a runaway tragically found dead early this morning," said the newsreader. "The suspect in the alleged rape and murder of the young girl is John Luther, the renowned evangelist . . ."

Rape? It wasn't enough that they thought he'd *killed* her. Now they thought he'd raped her too?

Aaliyah Evans. So that was her name. Whatever her culpability in this crime against John, she didn't deserve to be murdered.

Charles crossed the room and turned the radio off.

"Monica and Jodi?" he asked.

John spotted a familiar painting hanging on one wall and scuffled slowly toward it. "They're at home, and they're safe. The police are there."

Something about the painting captivated him. It was a Caravaggio, a very well-known one, and a lifelong favorite of his father's. Entitled *David and Goliath*, it depicted David kneeling over the corpse of Goliath after his victorious battle against the giant. Goliath's head had been severed and lay in the foreground. It was simultaneously gruesome and beautiful.

Now John was facing his own giant, and he doubted it would go down as miraculously as the one in the painting. Or was he Goliath, having been toppled by a David he hadn't yet identified? Whoever had done all this to him was strong enough to have toppled his entire world with a single blow.

"Did I do this to myself?" he mused.

"It was only a matter of time, John," replied his father. "You're just a pawn in a much bigger game. It's about a powerful political movement based on deceit."

Political movement?

Political . . .

Donald.

Of course. John should have seen this coming. Donald had always been a dangerous kind of benefactor, but John never truly believed he would take the Faith and Fairness thing this far. Then again, maybe this went beyond Donald. The president himself was pushing the bill for all he was worth. But surely the leader of the free world had more important things to do than hanging John Luther out to dry.

How had he somehow become the linchpin in this big political power play? He was just a preacher of the Good News.

Charles crossed the room and handed John a small and very worn Bible. John looked at the leather-bound book in confusion.

"Why do these politicians hate me so much? Am I *that* much of a threat?"

Charles's features softened. "John, by the grace of God you were able to bring yourself up from the depths of degradation and form a wonderful ministry that has spoken the truth to millions of people. Now those who believe in nothing must bring you down. They have to destroy you to achieve their own goals."

John still couldn't believe all this. Why was it happening to him? How could it be that Donald and the rest of Washington's most powerful feared him so much that they had to eliminate him as an obstacle before they could get their bill to pass through Congress? It was impossible to get his head around. Sure, he'd spoken publicly in opposition to the Faith and Fairness Act a handful of times, but he couldn't possibly be so important as to single-handedly keep the bill from passing? Could he?

"Look," said Charles, "you're going to be charged with first degree murder. You have two choices now. You can turn yourself in, throw yourself on the mercy of the authorities, and hope for the best. I think you know how that'll turn out."

John's face was probably being printed on a bunch of those

Most Wanted posters right now. The evidence against him may have been circumstantial, but there was no way the police would ever believe him.

"So there's a second option," said Charles. "One you may not like very much."

"It doesn't matter what I like." John was tired but found his resolve growing with every passing second. He'd known Donald for almost a decade. How dare his friend do this to him? How dare he have an innocent girl killed to advance his agenda? "I'm going to prove the truth."

His father was resolute. "You do that, John," he said. "For that girl. And for yourself. You may be the only person who can."

22

32 YEARS AGO

How's the food?" asked Charles.

John smiled between mouthfuls of bread and tomato soup. "Better than I remember," he said, causing a line of soup to stream down his chin.

It was over five months since he'd walked out the front door of his father's home and never looked back. For a while at least. About a month into his self-imposed exile—or running away, depending on how you looked at it—he began second-guessing his decision to leave. His pride had prevented him from returning for quite a while, but soon he got so hungry and desperate for a warm, comfortable bed, he couldn't stand it anymore.

Not that he'd been exactly destitute or penniless, as they say. He'd managed to pick up odd jobs here and there, found some decent places to stay, though nothing fancy. There was the occasional homeless shelter, but he'd managed to avoid that sort of thing for the most part, sticking to motels and newfound friends willing to give him a place to sleep for the night.

He'd had to choke down a lot of ego to come back home. But it hadn't been as hard as he'd thought.

John knew the old man must be dying to ask him where he'd been and what he'd done while he was away, but to his credit he kept his questions to himself. While he welcomed John home with his typical stoicism after John knocked on the front door, John saw more going on inside the man than anyone else might have noticed.

Charles seemed to be fighting the urge to linger over his son as he ate his soup. He would disappear from the dining room and reappear every few minutes. He rarely said a word; it was like he was checking to see if John was still there. Or if maybe he'd imagined his son's homecoming.

"Your room is exactly how you left it," Charles remarked as John was finishing his last bite of soup.

John tried to offer a smile yet felt too awkward to pull it off. "Thanks," he said. "I could use a shower. Then I'll probably turn in."

Charles hesitated, searching his son's eyes with a trace of hope in his own. "So you're staying, then?"

John stood to his feet. "For now."

The next thirteen months were the most pleasant John could remember at home. Where his father had once been overprotective and domineering, he now swung to the opposite extreme. He refused to keep tabs on John's comings and goings, never remarked on John's attire, and pretended to be disinterested anytime he accidentally came across John engaging in any sort of personal activity, like listening to music or watching TV. Charles seemed determined to let his son live his life however he chose, but John knew the old man was terrified of pushing his son away again.

It was good to be home. But even though things were better, he still didn't belong there. Not really.

Late one night in the spring, John quietly packed his things and slipped out of the house before his father awoke. He knew his father would be awake by 5:00 a.m., and he didn't want to have to try to explain why he was leaving when he didn't really know himself. He knew only that he had to.

Unlike last time, he didn't want to leave the old man on bad terms. So he wrote a note and left it on his bed. It reassured his father that it wasn't about him—it was only about John. It answered what had to be Charles's biggest unspoken question, saying: I never found her. My mother. But I'm not done searching yet.

Atop the folded note he left the old pair of aviator sunglasses he'd been wearing the last time he left. The note explained why. *Hold on to these*, it said. *You need them more than I do. You spend all your time staring into the light. But I've never figured out how to.*

23

Present day

Steaming water washed away the muck of the last twenty-four hours, pooling blood and dirt under John's feet. It had very little pressure, and there wasn't much room to move in the tiny stall, but the heat felt wonderful to his tired muscles.

John felt old. Tired. He *was* tiny David staring down his own Goliath, and it seemed an impossible task. How was he supposed to uncover the truth about Aaliyah's death? How could he hope to expose a criminal conspiracy involving one of his oldest friends—activity of which he had zero proof? He wasn't an investigator, for heaven's sake.

But there was another thought nagging at John's senses. It had been there since this mess started late last night: How would Jesus react in John's place? What would Jesus do if someone framed him for murder?

The Bible said to turn the other cheek. Those were Jesus' own words, right out of the book of Matthew. John had read that passage many times. Christians loved to quote it, loved to hear it said aloud. It was a profound statement of mercy and grace and obedience. But John had always found it troubling, if not impossible to live out.

He'd never preached a sermon on this part of Scripture, because—though he would never say it aloud for fear of being judged—it struck him as another way of saying "lay down and die" or "encourage your enemies to crush you." Every time he read the fifth chapter of Matthew, he hoped that maybe the true meaning of the words had been lost to centuries and translations. Surely the Great Shepherd wouldn't expect his sheep to give themselves willingly to those who would gladly destroy them.

And yet the very next verse plainly stated exactly that. In it, Jesus compared being wronged to having your shirt stolen from you. His answer to this kind of injustice was not only *not* to fight back but to give the thief your coat too!

As hot steam entered his nose, throat, and lungs, John wondered how and if he was supposed to put this principle into action in the here and now. A girl was dead. Didn't the Bible also decry murder as a deplorable sin? Was John supposed to go to his enemies and ask them to kill him as well?

No. It couldn't be that. An innocent soul had been murdered, and under the perfect law of God's holiness, justice had to prevail. Evil could never be allowed to win. Always a price had to be paid for evil, a balancing of the scales. Jesus was a man of peace, but as God incarnate he couldn't abide injustice. Right had to triumph over wrong. If Jesus hadn't believed this, he would never have sacrificed himself to satisfy the wages of sin on the world's behalf.

In the end, vengeance would be the Lord's. Unquestionably. Only he was fit to judge and punish the guilty. But this wasn't about punishment. It was about stopping those who craved power at any cost from taking innocent lives to achieve their goals.

And yeah, John wanted his life back. Was that so wrong?

John ran a thick bar of soap across his arms and chest. The

last time anything had touched his chest, it was the girl, Aaliyah. She'd been just sixteen years old. The events of last night were starting to come back to him. She'd slipped her hand between the buttons on his shirt and massaged the skin underneath while snapping pictures. The thought made him shiver in revulsion.

More memories surfaced. The man in the gray suit . . . He'd watched with a kind of professional detachment as Aaliyah followed his instructions, running her hands over John's body . . .

He shuddered again.

Did that man answer directly to Donald? What was he, some kind of hired thug? Or was he an agent of the law gone bad? John squeezed his eyes tight, concentrating, trying hard to remember something he'd seen, some relevant detail about the man in the gray suit that was teasing at his mind. . . .

There it was. John opened his eyes and looked into his memories, where he stared down the barrel of a matte-black pistol that looked like molded plastic. Before becoming a preacher, he'd gotten to know a little bit about firearms, and he knew that this weapon was a Glock 22. The weapon of choice for most U.S. law-enforcement agencies.

Whatever he was, that man was a pro, and no stranger to taking a life.

How had he killed the girl? Did he shoot her in the head? Snap her neck? Did he choke the life out of her or did he poison her?

Did she have any idea when the two of them walked into the *Truth Live* studio that she would be dead by the end of the night?

John's eyes came into focus at the odd sight of a narrow spiral of blood amid the water at his feet. A red tendril slowly snaking through the shower water and into the drain.

The blood of the girl who died?

His own?

How much more blood would be shed in the days to come? And would he ever feel clean again?

24

Charles Luther was nothing if not prepared. As soon as he'd heard the news that morning, he'd known with absolute certainty that John would come to him for help. And that not long after John arrived, the police would follow.

He'd had most of the morning to consider this and make the necessary preparations. Soon he would find out if his plans were sound.

As John showered in the adjacent washroom, Charles stood at his office window keeping watch. The tall, narrow window offered a view of the downtown street that ran in front of the church. Today was Friday, which meant there were no services scheduled, just a few parishioners who would slip into the sanctuary to say their daily prayers. Any other visitors received would almost certainly be officers of the law. Whether they would be police, federal agents, or members of some other agency, he had no idea. But they would know that he was John's father, and they would almost certainly come carrying a warrant to search the premises on the chance that Charles was hiding and helping his son.

Which Charles had every intention of doing.

John had been at the church for over half an hour now, and every second he lingered he was in greater danger of being caught. But he had to get cleaned up and put on a fresh set of clothes. He was far too conspicuous, looking as he did before.

One of the first preparations Charles had made that morning was to find some street clothes John could change into. He'd considered running down to the local Goodwill store but worried he might be gone when John arrived at the church. Instead he'd raided the personal closet of one of his subordinates, a young priest named William. The two men's sizes weren't quite a perfect match, but it would have to do. William was a good man, and Charles promised himself he'd explain everything to the younger priest later.

The sun was drifting into the horizon when the unmarked sedan came to a stop in front of the steps leading to St. Peter's Church. At last. Charles was surprised it had taken them this long to come. Maybe it was divine intervention that slowed them.

He stepped quickly into the washroom, where John was getting dressed. His jeans were on, and he was just pulling a T-shirt over his head.

"It's time," Charles said. "Here's what I need you to do."

Less than two minutes later, Charles answered the ringing brass bell at the front door.

"Mr. Luther?" said one of the cops standing just outside the door. A woman, and a detective if Charles wasn't mistaken.

"Yes?"

"I'm Detective Millis, and this is Detective Chen," the woman said, gesturing to her partner. "May we come in?"

Charles smiled inwardly, knowing this was just a formality. These two could march straight into the church and do anything they wanted, and they good and well knew it. Still, he appreciated their manners.

"Of course," Charles replied. "The House of God is always open to those who seek him."

Detective Millis offered a friendly half smile as she stepped inside, while her partner appeared dour, unimpressed. "Why was the front door locked?" he asked.

Charles remained perfectly serene. "Purity of mind and body is one of God's commandments," he said. "Even priests must bathe."

Detective Chen examined him. "You don't look damp."

"The vestments of priesthood can take some time to gild oneself in, my son," Charles said. "Especially for those of us burdened with advanced years."

He led the two detectives down the church's main aisle, toward the altar, where the red votive candles were still burning. When Charles arrived, he turned to face the officers. "Now, how may I help you today?"

"You probably know why we're here," said Millis, her manner gentle.

"I know you're not looking for God."

Chen glowered. "Have you seen or heard from your son since last night?"

Charles was determined not to break his vows by lying to the officers. But he couldn't give John up to them either. Maintaining a perfect poker face, he replied, "John's no fool. He wouldn't reach out to anyone likely to lead you to him."

Chen and Millis exchanged a glance.

"If he isn't here, then you'll have no objections to us taking a look around," said Chen.

"If you find it reassuring, then by all means," Charles said. "I ask only that you not disturb our sacred vessels or other accouterments."

Millis said, "Of course," but Charles saw Chen roll his eyes as he looked away.

The two detectives first walked to the right side of the sanctuary, where the confessional was located. Charles took in a sharp breath as Detective Chen flung open the ornate wooden door on the right to look inside the priest's alcove. He found it empty. Chen next threw aside the curtain covering the opposite side of the confessional. Inside was a small bench for parishioners to sit on while confessing their sins. Like the priest's alcove, it too was empty.

Charles said nothing. He merely waited patiently and tried not to think about what his son was doing right now.

Once the door to his father's office had closed, John risked a peek around the corner. He was crouched at the end of the narrow hallway that led from the office to a storage closet where Eucharist supplies were kept. A tiny mechanical room was next door.

His father had the two cops inside his office, which meant John had to move. He was still clammy from the shower, and he wiped water from his forehead. John could hear the cops talking in muffled tones. He knew the office was a small room and that they wouldn't be in there long. He had to go, *now*.

As quietly as he could, he crept down the hall toward the office. His heart thudded heavily, his pulse racing. While hiding in the storage room, he'd put on some socks to help silence his footsteps. He prayed that the floors in the old church building wouldn't creak as he walked. The slightest sound and the cops would be on him. It would be over, all of it.

The voices were still speaking inside the office as he neared the door, yet it sounded like they were getting louder. Either the conversation had heated up or they were moving toward the door.

John slid past the office, gently opened the sanctuary door, and went inside. He heard through the door that the cops and his father had just emerged back into the hall. John knew his father would do his best to lead the detectives away from the sanctuary now, but he wasted no time in case they weren't compliant.

Still moving quick and noiseless, John shuffled down the altar steps and to the far side of the sanctuary. He entered the priest's confessional alcove and sat down. This was his father's plan; the old man had known the cops would check the confessional first. It was the oldest cliché in the book—hide the fugitive in the confessional booth. After checking it once, those searching would move on, and the tiny alcove would become the safest place in the building.

All he could do now was wait, sit still, and not make a sound.

25

Aaliyah Evans wasn't raped."

Agent Rivera looked up. Clark walked in, his eyes scanning the girl's autopsy report on the tablet computer in his hand.

Rivera was kneeling on the floor next to the passenger's side door, which stood open. She'd been inspecting the interior of John Luther's Toyota SUV in the FBI's forensics lab for the last hour. So far her findings confirmed everything the police had deduced.

Clark continued, "She was sexually active, but there's no evidence of rape."

"What's the cause of death?" she asked.

"Broken neck."

"That's consistent with what I'm seeing," she said. "I don't think she was wearing a seat belt. It looks like she was flung forward into the dashboard when the crash occurred." Rivera pointed to two spots on the vinyl dash that bore slight indentations.

Clark leaned over above her to get a closer look. "Hm," he said, and then went back to the tablet.

Rivera knew what he was doing. He was checking the autopsy report for bruises on the girl's body that lined up with the dents on the dashboard. He gave a brief nod, indicating he'd found what he was looking for.

"Okay," he said, regrouping. "I'm John Luther. I'm high or drunk, and I pick up a runaway junkie to join in on the fun. I have consensual sex with her—or maybe there's no sex at all. But then I wreck my car. Maybe I'm enjoying the afterglow. Maybe I'm just hammered. Either way, when I come to, the girl's crumpled on the floorboard, her neck snapped from an impact with the dash. So I . . . flee the scene on foot?"

Rivera hadn't been sure where her partner was going with this until he got to that last phrase. Now she got it. "Why didn't he leave the body and take the car?"

Clark looked her in the eye and nodded. "Not only did he leave *his car* at the scene of the crime, he left the girl's camera phone *on her person*, the very phone that held incriminating photos of the two of them."

Rivera pondered it. Was there a flaw in her partner's logic? Probably not, but he expected her to try to find one. It was part of their routine.

"It's conceivable that he could have been so high out of his mind that he wasn't thinking clearly," she suggested, even though she wasn't even buying it herself.

Clark frowned. Then something occurred to him, and he looked back down at the tablet. He swiped sideways several times, flipping through the report's pages. His brow furrowed, and his expression turned even more serious.

"What?" she asked.

Clark let out a slow breath, still reading. At last he looked up. "Evans's bloodstream showed toxic amounts of cocaine."

"Yeah," said Rivera. "We knew she was a drug addict already, didn't we?"

"But there was no powder residue found in her nostrils."

So she didn't snort the cocaine. Insufflation, as it was called, was the most common method of ingesting cocaine. Everyone knew this. But it was hardly the only available method of ingestion.

"I don't follow the significance," Rivera said, watching her partner.

"Alone, it's probably not significant," he replied. "But two other findings in the autopsy make it troubling."

Rivera extracted herself from the vehicle and stood, stretching her sore muscles. "I'm listening."

Agent Clark referred once more to the tablet. "Cocaine wasn't the only substance found in her bloodstream." He held out the device for her to see.

Rivera scanned the tablet's screen. "'. . . trace amounts of . . . Rohypnol.' That's the date-rape drug, isn't it?"

"It is," replied Clark, taking back the tablet.

Rivera took a breath, her mind spinning. "Okay. So he drugged her. Maybe she wouldn't get in the car with him otherwise."

"Maybe," Clark echoed.

Rivera pursed her lips. She knew Agent Clark was still holding back the most significant piece of evidence he'd read in the report. "What else?"

"Not every coroner would even think to check for this," he began. "But our guy did. God bless O'Neill . . . The cocaine in the girl's system saturated her bloodstream, but at the time of death, it hadn't been *digested*. At all."

Rivera blinked, then grabbed the tablet out of his hands. "You're kidding."

Clark said nothing, waiting for her to verify what the report stated.

And there it was. In the autopsy report, figures stating the amount of cocaine in the deceased girl's system, and a percentage showing how much was found in her digestive system. The first number was quite high. The second simply read *zero-point-zero milligrams*.

"The cocaine entered her system *after* she was already dead?"

Clark nodded. "Injected, most likely. Quite some time after she'd taken the Rohypnol."

Agent Rivera gave him back the tablet and crossed her arms. Her mind reeled, carefully piecing together everything she'd just learned. As usual, Agent Clark studied her.

"I don't like what this is adding up to," she said, looking Clark in the eye.

"Neither do I."

26

Obviously we're all in shock," said Ryan Morris. The man floundered in his seat, unable to conjure up words adequate for the situation. "I mean, the accusations . . . they're unbelievable."

Ryan was seated opposite Senator Donald Harrison, across his huge, ornate wood desk. Night had fallen, but that was of no concern—Donald considered himself always on duty. He watched this man he'd called to his office on *very* short notice. John always talked about Ryan's nearly hyperactive energy, and Donald could almost feel the man vibrating in the seat, barely able to stay still. His eyes shifted wildly around Donald's immaculate, intricately furnished office, visibly impressed. Each piece Donald had collected in his travels around the world. As a collection he knew they added up to prestige and power. But to be sure his visitor felt the full effect, Donald had asked his associate Mr. Gray to sit in on the meeting. His presence alone was enough to intimidate almost anyone.

Senator Harrison said nothing, allowing Ryan to squirm a little longer.

"But, uh . . . you tell me," said Ryan. "Where do we go from here?"

Donald smiled inwardly. People were so easily played. Like notes on a harp, he excelled at plucking them until they sang his tune. Not that he relished manipulating people, mind you. Or that he took pleasure from any of the actions he'd taken over the last twenty-four hours. They'd been difficult but necessary. It was all for the greater good.

Donald let out a measured sigh. "Well, what it is, is a tragedy. And the moment John comes in, I want to get him help and see him restored. Just as I'm sure you do."

Ryan nodded enthusiastically, but Harrison saw him shoot an anxious glance at Mr. Gray, who watched him with his usual focused intensity. As soon as he'd made eye contact with Mr. Gray, Ryan turned back to Donald fast, as if he'd done something wrong.

Harrison switched to his best fatherly tone. "Sometimes out of the ashes of tragedy comes opportunity."

If Ryan understood what Donald was hinting at, he didn't show it. He seemed to still be trying not to look directly at Mr. Gray.

All right then, Donald would just have to spell it out for him.

"How long have you worked with John?" asked Donald.

"Fourteen years," Ryan answered with a half smile.

"Fourteen?" Donald said, making himself sound impressed by the huge number.

Ryan smiled again and nodded.

Harrison knew exactly how long Ryan had worked with John Luther and Truth Ministries; he'd known long before tonight. He also knew that Ryan had entered full-time ministry after a bout with severe depression. His wife had left him, and subsequently they were divorced, plunging Ryan into the abyss of despair. He'd remained in a deep depression for almost a year, until he'd been dragged by a family member to a special church service—a service where the guest speaker was John Luther.

Donald would have felt sorry for Ryan if he hadn't found the man to be so grating. Fortunately his psychological profile made him the perfect candidate for the senator's needs.

"Well," he continued, solemn now, "to save this organization, it's going to take some bold leadership. We have a multitude in panic—millions of people who are going to feel unmoored, who are going to be looking for answers and direction. We need to show them all is not lost, and we have to speak into their lives a message of hope in these dark times."

Ryan leaned forward in his seat. He was a man desperate for hope, hanging on Donald's every word.

"How many people can you reach on your email database?" asked Donald.

"Oh, uh . . ." Ryan looked up at the ceiling, thinking. "We have a boatload. I'd have to check."

"But you *will* check, won't you, Ryan?" said Donald.

Ryan nodded again, eager to please.

Senator Harrison smiled a reassuring smile. He was coming to Truth Ministries' aid, and to Ryan's specifically. That was what he needed Ryan to take away from this meeting.

"I've been watching you for years now," Donald said. "You do fine, selfless work. Don't you?"

Ryan grasped for words again, but this time he blushed. "Well, I'd like to think God had a hand in it . . . but I appreciate that."

Still smiling with as much warmth as he was capable of, Donald went on, "This might be your time to shine. Great leadership knows when to seize opportunity."

Ryan looked overwhelmed, a dawning realization coming over him.

Finally. The simpleton was starting to get it.

"We need to bring this church together," said Donald, preparing for checkmate. "Now more than ever. We need to rise up and resurrect this ministry and take it in a brave new direction."

Ryan watched him with eyes wide. He was waiting to hear the senator's next words.

"Are you with me, Ryan?" asked Donald.

Ryan was clearly surprised to be offered the keys to the kingdom. But he was smiling. He let out a long breath. "I'm your man."

Donald grinned as Ryan rose from his seat and reached across the massive desk to shake his hand. "Glad to hear it."

He offered Ryan a fleeting, barely visible wink to seal the deal.

27

Just minutes after the police were finally gone, John was back in his father's office. The old man was offering John his best advice on how to proceed.

From one of the many books that filled the room's bookshelves, Charles surprised his son by pulling out a thick wad of rolled-up cash held together by a rubber band. John examined the book and found that a rectangular hole had been cut from the pages on the inside. A secret safe, made of paper. It looked like the old man had cut it out himself.

John knew his father cherished books, so he couldn't imagine any volume the old man would willingly carve up. He flipped over the hardback and couldn't help but smile. The spine read *The God Delusion* by Richard Dawkins.

He turned his attention back to the money. Charles Luther had never been rich. And the life of a priest was not exactly a lucrative one. Where had he gotten this much cash? Had he been saving up? For how long? There had to be five, maybe even ten thousand dollars in the roll.

He was about to pull off the rubber band when his eyes caught hold of something behind his hand. On Charles's desk was propped a small, square photo in a simple silver frame. John knew this picture. He'd given it to his dad a few months ago. It was a bright, sunny photo of John with Monica and Jodi. He had an arm around Monica, with Jodi situated in front of them both. John had his other hand on Jodi's shoulder. All three of them were grinning.

It had been a beautiful summer day—that day at the beach when they'd rented a three-seater bicycle. The photo was taken shortly after they'd returned the bike to that kooky rental guy who made Jodi giggle. Hearing her laugh always made her parents laugh, so they were all smiling extra big in this photo because of it. The rental guy took the picture for them.

That was such a great day. So much joy and laughter they'd shared.

How he missed them! He missed Jodi's laugh. Monica's touch. Her beautiful smile. Jodi's little hand in his. Her hugs. Monica's tender voice.

John suddenly couldn't remember why he always spent so much time working at the ministry. His wife and daughter brought out the best in him, and without them he was incomplete.

He picked up the photo and rubbed a finger across its glass surface.

Monica.

Jodi.

He needed them. And they needed him. No job—not even a ministry—was more important than that. They were his whole world, and he had to find a way back to them.

John wished he could hold both of them tight, right now. He didn't realize his father was watching until he wiped the moisture from his eyes.

"Don't do it, John," said Charles. John looked up at his father. "I know how much you want to be with them, son. When your mother left, I missed her more than I thought I was capable of. I would've done *anything* to be with her again. But you can't go to them. Not now."

John sighed. "I know. The police have probably staked out the neighborhood."

"Your head knows that," replied Charles. "What about your heart?"

"I won't, Dad. I can't."

"That's right, you can't. No matter how badly you want to. You'd only be endangering them."

John nodded and set the frame back down on the desk.

"I have something else for you," said Charles. He turned to a small, wooden keepsake box resting on one of the bookshelves. He pulled something out and returned to John. He handed it to his son.

John smiled when he saw the sunglasses in his father's hand. The aviator sunglasses. Was it . . . ? It was.

The same pair.

"You need these more than I do," said Charles with a half smile.

John accepted the glasses and turned them over in his hands. He couldn't believe his dad had kept them this long.

"Thanks," he said.

"Things are going to get worse before they get better," said Charles. "Don't you stop staring into the light, no matter what. You keep on looking into the light."

John looked down at the glasses again, and nodded.

"Now come on. We've got to get you out of here."

28

John followed his father down two flights of stairs into the church's basement. He'd never been down here before. The big, windowless room was partitioned off with makeshift walls, and there were old pews, tables, and chairs scattered about, along with other items like tarnished brass crosses, white cloths that were worn and dirty, and candles that had burned down almost to nothing.

Everything seemed damp, ancient, and gloomy. He imagined this as the kind of place slaves on the Underground Railroad might have been sheltered and hidden back in the nineteenth century. The kind of place no one in their right mind would expect any living creature to be found.

"Through here," Charles said. He led John through a narrow door made of rotting wood, into another partitioned room. They turned left and entered yet another tiny space in the basement.

This last room was somewhere in the middle of the basement, if John was estimating correctly. His father pulled on a chain hanging from the ceiling, and a single light bulb came to life.

The room was more or less square, and filthy. John imagined that his father's priests and other staff must've rarely had reason to venture down here.

"Grab the crowbar," said Charles.

Crowbar?

John glanced around, not seeing a crowbar until he looked back toward the door they had entered through. There, resting right beside the doorway, was the iron device in question. He picked it up, wondering what they needed it for.

"Here," said his dad, pointing at a rug on the floor in the center of the room, right under the hanging light bulb.

John moved forward as his father pulled up the rug. Underneath was a grimy old manhole cover.

He looked down at the metal cover, then glanced back up at his father. "And this is . . . ?"

"Your way out, John," replied Charles. "It goes right down into the sewer."

John's shoulders drooped as he thought of what it probably smelled like down there.

"The police are outside," Charles explained, "watching the building. If you have a better idea, I'm listening."

John frowned at the manhole, unable to think of another way to escape the police.

"Here," said his father, holding out a key chain with a single key dangling from it. "There's a ladder leading back up to street level a block and a half south of here. Use it and you'll find a burgundy sedan parked nearby."

John took a deep breath. This was it then. This was where it began. From here he'd either prove his innocence and get his life back or he'd be caught and probably lost forever behind endless reams of political red tape.

It wasn't like this was the first time he'd had to survive on his own. He'd left home many times as a teenager and then roamed the country alone as a young adult. He might be older now, but he was as mentally equipped for this as anyone could be.

"Thanks, Dad," he said, "for helping me."

"It's what I do," said Charles with a knowing smile.

"It's what you've always done," said John.

Ten minutes later it was starting to rain as Charles watched from his office window. He prayed John had the strength and faith to do this. His son was up against a lot more than one or two rogue federal agents. This was a political juggernaut that wouldn't go down without a fight. Could one man alone take down this Goliath?

Charles glanced at his Caravaggio painting.

No, that wasn't right. David was never alone, and neither was John.

Charles lit a cigar as he continued to look through the window. There he was. He watched as John's silhouette peeked around the brick corner of a building. A few seconds later, John emerged and walked with casual aplomb to the sedan that waited nearby. Soon he was gone, the old Volvo speeding off into the night.

The old man took a slow drag on the cigar as the car left his sight. Shaking his head, he mumbled to himself, "Dear God . . . This is really happening."

29

On the far end of town, John stopped the Volvo at the first motel he saw. It was a little after seven o'clock. The building looked on the gaudy side, all neon and chrome, as if the designers had tried too hard to make it hip and trendy. But it would do. Past the glass-brick front wall, John found a silver check-in desk with a clerk at the desk, who appeared far too young for the job. As he stepped closer to the counter, he noticed that she was pregnant—at least six months along—though her attire was far from modest.

Trying his best not to look conspicuous despite his sunglasses and crisp new leather jacket, he approached the attendant. "Hi."

"Hey," she replied.

"I'd like a room. Just for the night."

The attendant smiled. "I think we can manage that. Let me see what we have." She began typing on the desk's computer.

John glanced around the spacious foyer. A handful of people were coming and going, all of them a lot younger than himself. There was a flash of light beyond the glass entrance, and John sucked in a breath, jerking his head in the direction of the door. It was only headlights from a car outside.

He mentally kicked himself; the attendant had noticed his squirrelly reaction.

"Something wrong with your eyes?" she asked. Her voice was casual, unbothered. Just making friendly conversation.

But John was long out of practice at this sort of thing. How could he answer without making himself seem even more peculiar?

After way too many seconds had passed without his saying anything, he simply smiled, trying not to look sheepish. "No," he said with a shrug.

The girl waited, as if expecting John to remove the sunglasses. But he didn't.

She gestured at her temple, and it took John a few seconds to realize she was referring to the fingernail scars visible on his forehead and the side of his face. When he made no reply, she smiled a nervous smile and mumbled something John couldn't understand.

"How's the room?" John asked, trying to speed things along. She was trying to act normally, but he could tell that this pregnant girl couldn't have been more wary of his appearance and behavior. If he lingered much longer, she'd figure him out.

"Good," she replied. "I just need a credit card and a valid ID."

Before he could answer, a flat-screen TV affixed to the wall behind her caught his eye. It was CNW with breaking news. A young, clean-cut male reporter was speaking to the camera from a sidewalk in front of the U.S. Capitol. Under the young man was splashed the words *FBI Manhunt for Evangelist John Luther Under Way*. And in the top right corner of the screen was a sight that made John nearly double over.

It was one of the lurid photos Aaliyah had taken of herself with John when he was borderline unconscious. At least his eyes were closed in the photo, although now that he thought about it, he wasn't sure if that was a good thing or not.

At home, Monica was seeing this. What must she be thinking?

The board of directors at Truth Ministries were seeing it too. They had to be.

Not to mention his millions of supporters, the faithful viewers of his nightly broadcasts.

One thing he knew for certain was that Donald Harrison had just upped his game. Was he sending John a message? The senator *had* to know that John was out there somewhere, a fugitive in hiding yet hoping to exonerate himself. So he'd leaked this photo—and probably several others—to the media anonymously. Tightening the noose.

Donald knew John's agenda, and vice versa. And Donald knew that John had figured out his involvement. That he was likely the mastermind behind this whole mess.

So their friendship was over, and the game was on.

John blinked when he realized the attendant was staring at him as he was lost in thought, waiting to see the credit card and ID that he didn't have.

In the background, he heard the man on the TV saying something about "Mr. Luther's actions sending shock waves throughout the entire religious community . . ." He chose to ignore it.

John pulled out his roll of greenbacks and slid a hundred-dollar bill across the desk. "Will this work?" he asked in a hushed voice.

"It should be fine," said the girl. She didn't seem at all surprised to see the money, and John wondered how often people did this sort of thing. Or was she just really good at acting nonchalant?

John ran his fingers behind his ear, tucking back his hair, as she picked up the bill.

"I'll be right back," she said, flashing a winning smile. "I just need to go check on something really quick. Can you just wait here a moment?"

John's pulse jumped. This felt wrong. Was she pushing past

the usual paper work to give him a room anonymously, as he hoped? Or was she . . . ?

"... reported history of crime and addiction in Luther's apparently unstable early years," said the CNW reporter.

John frowned at the TV. Then he heard a voice whispering.

"I'd like to report a suspicious person, please," said the voice. It was the attendant, in an office adjacent to the front desk. She wasn't being nearly as stealthy as she seemed to think.

It had been a very long time since John had uttered a curse, but he was powerfully tempted to now.

He ran.

30

The police were gone, finally satisfied after hours of turning the house upside down. Or maybe it was Monica's life that was upside down, inside out, twisted and crumpled and gnarled beyond recognition. Again and again she kept coming back to the same question: How could this be happening?

John didn't do it. Of course he didn't. He wouldn't. He'd never in a million years.

But, quietly, in the back of her mind, she could hear the same awful whisper of doubt. He'd *been* this kind of man once in his life. Sure, it was long ago, but if he'd done it once, he could become that man again.

Monica's train of thought was interrupted by the sound of an acoustic guitar and a man's voice singing out the first line of "Amazing Grace."

Oh. Right. She'd almost forgotten Ryan was here. He'd arrived a little while ago, and he seemed . . . different. Monica had never been crazy about Ryan, but he was usually tolerable. Now something had changed. He held his chin a little higher, a smile played at the edges of his mouth, and he appeared rather pleased with himself. What was going on?

She didn't want to hear him sing. She was curled up on one end of the couch with one of her favorite handmade quilts—a gift from John for their tenth anniversary—deep inside her own world, watching nothing at all behind puffy eyes. She would have gone to sleep if her every muscle weren't so tensed up.

And Ryan wasn't helping.

"Ryan, please stop," she said.

He kept singing, ignoring her.

"*Please*," she repeated.

Ryan stopped. "I thought that was your favorite."

He was trying to comfort her, she realized. For some reason it made her uncomfortable. Unable to think of anything to say, she just looked away. The living room's big picture window was to her left; she kept staring out of it, wondering where John was, praying for his safe return, and hoping against hope to see him come walking down the sidewalk.

"All right," said Ryan.

She was vaguely aware of him standing and crossing the room to the kitchen. He soon returned and started talking again. Why couldn't he just leave her in peace? If she hadn't been so consumed with thoughts of John, she would have been able to think of a nice, not-terribly-rude way to get rid of him. As it was, she kept her mouth shut for fear of saying something she'd regret.

"Listen," he said, "I am *not* going to let you feel guilty for trying to take care of yourself."

Still she said nothing. She didn't care about herself at the moment. She cared about Jodi, and John, and about her family being whole again.

Something new occurred to her then. Had her father-in-law heard from John today? She'd be more surprised if he *hadn't*. If only there were a way to contact him, but the police had wired a tap to her phone before they left. Somewhere out there beyond the big window, police cars were on every corner throughout the neighborhood. She couldn't breathe without their knowing.

Ryan walked near and seated himself on the couch right next to her. This was quickly moving from uncomfortable to downright awkward. And now she saw what he had gone to the kitchen for. He'd poured himself a glass of white wine.

"I get it," he said. "Nobody saw this coming. Obviously. And now John is out there running around, doing . . . whatever he's doing. Personally I can't figure out what he must be thinking. If it were me, I'd put the needs of others before my own—you, Jodi, the ministry. I'd turn myself in."

Monica couldn't believe it. Ryan actually thought John was guilty. Which meant she had no use for this man. None whatsoever.

"I don't know if you remember," Ryan went on, trying his best to sound smooth, "but back before Jodi was born, I promised John that if anything ever happened to him, I'd watch over you like you were my own."

Monica had to fight hard to keep from rolling her eyes. Was he seriously hitting on her? *Now?* In the middle of all this?

"And as you know, I'm a man of my word." Ryan poked her playfully in the arm.

Monica wasn't feeling remotely playful just now. She glanced at Ryan with heavy eyes. Was he for real?

But then maybe she was being too sensitive. What if he was just trying to help her? Why should Ryan—John's right-hand man for over a dozen years—be the person whom she piled all her anger and frustration on? Did he deserve her ire?

Well, he certainly wasn't doing much to avoid it.

"In any case," he said, "have you heard from John?"

Monica looked away again. She didn't know what to say. Instead she simply closed her eyes while fiddling with her wedding ring.

"That's my point," said Ryan. "See? Me neither! I know how you feel. I feel the same way. And I can't stand what this is doing to you. I mean, he's left you alone here like you're a single mother or something."

She snapped, rounding on him. "No! He is *coming home* to this family."

Ryan looked at her with pity. "You have to accept this, Monica. Your husband is a fugitive."

Monica's eyes burned, but she refused to give him the satisfaction of seeing her cry. "No!" she said.

"He's a fugitive," he said again, this time with a harder edge that made him seem almost angry.

Monica *was* angry, and growing more so by the minute. "No!" She stood and walked to the window. Arms crossed, she stared out into the night.

Where is he?

There was a beep, and Monica watched in the window's reflection as Ryan pulled his phone out of his pocket and read a message.

"Sorry," he said. "We're having an emergency board meeting in an hour."

Wonderful. Now Truth Ministries was regrouping to decide how to go on without its founder.

"Anyway, I pray you're right about John," said Ryan. "I really do. All he has to do is show up, tell everybody what really happened, and we'll get to the bottom of this. But you know . . . God works in all things."

Monica watched the street out front as tears spilled from her eyes. She wanted to break down, to let it all out and cry on somebody's shoulder.

Yet it wasn't going to be a shoulder belonging to Ryan Morris.

31

John flicked off the headlights as he pulled the Volvo to a stop.

After fleeing the motel, he'd driven away as fast as the car would go. He had no idea where he was going; he just put as much distance as possible between himself and that place. For over half an hour he drove in a panic, not thinking about the direction he was going or where he might spend the night. He barely noticed stoplights, traffic signs, other cars on the road, or any other landmarks. He just drove.

So it was quite a shock for him to find himself coming up on his own neighborhood. Entirely without meaning to, he'd driven home. Ahead on the left was a little-used road that had recently been paved to make way for a whole new row of houses, most of which hadn't begun construction yet. From the outside looking in, most drivers had no idea that this dark, unlit, unmarked road connected with the neighborhood where John and his family lived. It was never used by locals, as parts of the street were still nothing but dirt.

He'd told his dad he wouldn't go see them. He knew he shouldn't. But he was so close to them now. They were less than half a mile away, and the itch to see them was so powerful . . .

Maybe if he just stayed in the car. It wasn't even eight o'clock yet. Monica would still be up, and the big living room window would probably be open.

John turned left onto the dark road. It was narrow, unmarked pavement for several hundred feet, and then a stretch of dirt at the end connected it to the street on which John lived. In no time at all he was less than a block from his house.

He saw no police cars or any marked vehicles anywhere near the house. In fact, the only car he didn't recognize as one of the neighbors was a red convertible, a 1957 Corvette. It was Ryan's car, and one of his prized possessions—a sporty little thing the man had bought after a nice bonus two years ago. A car as fast as the man himself. John hadn't expected Ryan's car here, but he guessed it made sense. Ryan was keeping the promise he'd made a long time ago.

Where were the police? Shouldn't they be watching the house?

With the headlights off, John pulled up the hood of the sweat shirt he wore under his leather jacket and circled the cul-de-sac a short way from his home. Driving past his house, he turned down a side street that gave him a perfect view through the picture window in front, if he craned his neck around to look out the back of the car. He turned the engine off and dropped lower in his seat, trying to hide as much as possible.

Monica rose from the couch and walked to the window. Behind her, Ryan sat on the couch and—was that a glass of wine?—talked. And talked. And talked some more. A pain struck John's heart when he realized Monica was crying. He could see a tiny reflection of light glistening on her cheek.

She wasn't crying because of anything Ryan said. John knew it was because of him. This big crazy mess was destroying her.

Did she believe in his innocence?

God, please give her strength. Ease her pain. Help her. Help me now.

The squawk of a walkie-talkie echoed down the street, and John's heart tried to escape from his chest. A patrol car was coming straight at him on the street ahead. The officer behind the wheel was sweeping a flashlight back and forth, examining every car, every trash can, every tree or bush he passed.

John quickly sank further into his seat, then pitched himself sideways so that he lay across the floor in front of both front seats. He heard the police car drawing closer and lay as still as he could, not moving an inch, not even breathing.

He heard the crackling sound of the patrol car's tires grinding slowly against the pavement, coming nearer, nearer, then stopping altogether. A light shone onto the seats just above him and lingered there for several seconds. John pressed himself into the floorboard as flat as he could.

His mind raced almost as fast as his heart. Why had he risked coming here? And why was the cop spending so much extra time on his car? Did they know what he was driving? They hadn't seen him exit the church. There were no cops at the motel, and he never saw the attendant come running out after him. There was no reason he could think of that anyone but his father would know what kind of car he was driving.

And yet here was this lone cop, scrutinizing his car more than any other on the block.

If the patrolman had been circling the neighborhood all night, then he would know that John's burgundy sedan was new. Maybe that was it. He was just making sure the car belonged here.

Except it didn't belong here.

At last the light receded and was gone, and he heard the car door open and slam closed before the cruiser rolled away again. John popped up and peeked over the edge of the passenger side window. He gasped.

All he got was a fleeting glimpse, but the driver of the police car looked terribly familiar. He'd seen this policeman before, and John didn't believe he was a cop at all. The last time John saw the broad-shouldered man, he was picking up the unconscious—or was she dead already?—body of Aaliyah Evans, next to the man in the gray suit who'd knocked her out.

He worked for Donald Harrison; he had to. And Donald had him here, watching to see if John attempted to go home. At least that meant they were leaving Monica and Jodi alone.

He needed to get out of here.

John glanced back at the house one last time, tears filling his eyes. Would he ever be with his wife and daughter again? He honestly didn't know. These people were dogging him at every turn. They seemed to have thought of everything.

Just as he was passing out of sight of the house, he saw Ryan emerge from the front door and walk toward his car.

32

Senator Donald Harrison glanced at his phone as it vibrated. He'd been expecting this call, having left the phone just to the side of his desk computer. He answered via speakerphone.

"They're starting, sir," said the voice of Mr. Gray.

Harrison said nothing, merely hung up. He turned to the computer and opened a program that played audio feeds and clicked the play button.

From the computer's speakers came the sound of several voices murmuring, as well as the screeches of sliding chairs. They were taking their seats. Good. The sound was coming through nice and clear. Donald would be able to hear the entire meeting.

Just a few hours ago, Donald called Ryan Morris to his office, pretending to back the man as the next and future leader of Truth Ministries. And that was important. Equally critical was when Mr. Gray opened the door for Ryan as he was leaving, and casually brushed against his sleeve, placing a tiny electric bug on his sleeve, just near the wrist. So long as Ryan didn't change clothes before tonight's board meeting at Truth Ministries—and why would he?—Donald would be able to listen in on the whole thing.

"I, uh, I think we all know why we're here tonight," Ryan

Morris began. Ryan had called the emergency meeting himself, at Donald's suggestion. "The accusations against John Luther have left us in a mighty awkward position, and now we have to decide where—"

"Let's not jump the gun here, Ryan," said another voice. Donald knew this one; it was Dave Wilson, the man best known for introducing John at the start of his telecasts. Donald had never had a formal conversation with the man, but he knew that Wilson was one of John's oldest friends. They'd known each other since before John became a minister. If anyone was going to be a problem on the board, it was likely to be Wilson.

"No," replied Ryan. "But we do need to look to the future. We're in a very precarious place here, and I think we need to establish governance for our unanimous cooperation with the Faith and Fairness Act, *prima facie*."

Wilson jumped in again. "According to our bylaws—"

"I think we're all very aware of the legal ramifications, but thank you, Dave."

A voice Donald didn't recognize spoke up. "Let him talk, Ryan." Some board member, Donald didn't know who, was reproaching Ryan. Wilson, several decades older than Ryan, was deserving of more respect than he was being given. Even Donald understood this.

It was one of the biggest risks in backing Ryan—the man was volatile, overly excitable, and a taste of power could make him seem too desperate. Donald needed the man to rein himself in.

There was a silent pause before Dave spoke again. "I just want to state for the record that I find the very origins of this meeting extremely distasteful. John Luther has more than earned our trust—many times over—and he deserves the benefit of the doubt. Before we do *anything*, we should hear the situation from John's perspective."

Dave Wilson was a hard-liner, always had been. A true believer, and absolutely loyal to John. But then, until a short while ago, Ryan Morris had been the same. Ryan was easily influenced, however. Donald doubted the rest of the board would be so easily swayed. Especially Dave.

"Look," said Ryan, "let's cut to the chase. We all hope John didn't do this. I for one believe the best of him. But we have to take into consideration not just our interests but the needs of the millions of people who've supported this ministry for years. We have a shared responsibility on their behalf."

Donald signed in relief. That was definitely a better path, and as speeches go, it wasn't bad. Certainly better than Donald had worried Ryan might be capable of.

"None of us would be on this board if not for John Luther," Ryan went on. "This ministry has changed all of our lives for the better. Unfortunately, John is *also* the reason we're having this meeting right now. We all believe he didn't kill that girl. But the fact that he hasn't taken into consideration our needs and the needs of the ministry . . . I don't know. Maybe that tells us something."

This was good, Donald thought. Ryan was hitting just the right note of fear. The room may have been filled with John's most faithful supporters, but they were also the people responsible for one of the biggest, most wide-reaching ministries in the world. Tapping into their fear of losing the organization, not to mention the human need for self-preservation, was a smart move.

"If our signing some piece of legislation sends a message to Washington that we're balanced, that we're in this for the long haul, then *I am for it*," said Ryan. "And written into this legislation for every single member of this board who complies—"

"Earmarks," interrupted Dave Wilson, his tone taking on a bitter quality. There was something else in his voice as well. A hint of resignation could be heard. Dave was losing this fight, and he knew it.

Donald smiled.

"There's a very generous tax package too," added Ryan, smoothing over Dave's animosity. "Dave, you're the one who's always told us to be prepared for the worst-case scenario. Well, brother, we're here! This is it."

A long silence followed, and Donald knew the dozen or so board members in that room were absorbing Ryan's words. The young man had been remarkably persuasive. Was it enough to get them all to agree? Or was the room filled with more nay-sayers like Wilson?

A new voice spoke up, another Donald didn't know. "I'm sorry, Dave, but I'm with Ryan on this. The individual tax benefit alone knocks this right out of the park."

Wilson said nothing in reply. Donald imagined him sitting stiffly in his seat, glaring at the rest of the board members, all of whom must've been in agreement with Ryan since no one was offering a counterargument. The old man was seriously outnumbered. At this point, he could either fall in line or abstain from the vote altogether. The latter option could even lead to his expulsion from the organization.

Donald very much doubted that Wilson's convictions would be strong enough to pit him against the majority. Or maybe he'd elect to side with everyone else in order to remain on the inside so that someone would still be there to represent John's interests.

Donald didn't care either way. It would be a unanimous vote, and that was all that mattered. Truth Ministries was officially on board with the Faith and Fairness Act.

At last.

33

25 YEARS AGO

John had to get out of there. He hated everything about this place: the stench, the scenery, and especially the company. The only good thing the abandoned duplex had going for it was that it had a roof to block out the rain.

He hadn't tripped in days and was longing for a good high. It wasn't that the goods were hard to come by here—dealers were in and out of this neighborhood all the time. He just didn't have any money to pay them.

John had spent the last decade moving, always moving. He'd chase work where he could, bum rides and food and shelter when he couldn't. He hadn't seen Virginia in years, and now he was as far west as he could get without drowning in the Pacific. Work wasn't that hard to get in Southern California, but there were precious few employers willing to hire a guy who spent his spare time chasing whatever high he could find. He spent one night a week at the local shelter to get a shower and a decent meal, but he didn't like how the people there were always down on him, trying to help him "turn his life around" or whatever.

At least he wasn't an addict. John refused to let himself be called that. Not like the two dozen or so other squatters who came and went from this old condemned house they shared. He didn't even know most of their names. Thankfully they left him alone most of the time.

John had claimed a small upstairs bedroom as his own a couple of weeks ago, but that didn't stop Crazy Karl from letting himself in and crashing in the corner every night. It wouldn't have been so bad if Karl hadn't snored so loudly. It hardly mattered. John rarely slept anyway.

It was somewhere in the middle of the night, and he was stretched out on the mattress on the floor he called his bed, listening to Karl snore, when he heard a familiar voice.

"Well, aren't you a sad sight."

John sat up and rubbed his eyes. Standing in the doorway was Charles Luther.

John blinked. He'd had a hallucination or two, but they'd always been wilder, fanciful. This one was as real as anything he'd experienced, and John just stared at his father in silence. Had the old man died and this was his ghost? He was dressed in his typical black attire and white collar. He hadn't seen the old man in more than six years, and yet he looked exactly the same.

"Can't say I'm surprised you ended up in a place like this," Charles went on. He stepped inside the room and closed the door.

John's brain was reacting slowly. This wasn't a poltergeist or a hallucination. This was real. His father was here. How in the world had he found him? "Dad?"

"Tell me, John," said Charles, walking closer. "In all this time, did you ever find whatever it is you're looking for?"

John opened his mouth to answer, then snapped it shut. It was the kind of question he expected from the old man, but why was he interrogating him now? Usually the first thing he did was try to help his son somehow. This was a new approach. Maybe it was his father's idea of tough love.

"No, Dad," John replied. "I haven't found it."

"That's because you're looking in all the wrong places," Charles said.

A moan coming from the corner gave way to Karl sitting halfway up and rubbing his eyes. "Who you talking to, man?"

"This is my father," said John.

Karl looked confused.

"Just go back to sleep," John added.

Karl did as he was told, collapsing back into his sleeping bag.

"You're such a disappointment, John," said Charles.

John shook his head, trying to clear away the fog inside it. "Why are you here?"

His father ignored him. He walked over to the nearest wall and leaned back against it, crossing his arms. "You've *always* been a disappointment."

Wait a minute. The old man had his flaws, but it wasn't in his nature to insult anyone—much less his own son. He'd never spoken to John like this before in his life.

And if John hadn't tripped in days, why was the room so bright? It had to be two or three o'clock in the morning, and there was no electricity in the building. Yet the entire room glimmered with a silver sheen.

Then he remembered. He'd scored some stuff a few hours ago, using the cash he'd lifted off a businessman down at the bus station. While the dealer promised that the stuff would bliss him out, what John was actually experiencing had a very different effect.

With a sudden panic he wondered what he'd taken. He glanced up at his dad, who merely stood there staring down at him with a frown, his arms still crossed. Only this wasn't his father at all. It was all in his head.

That train of thought was interrupted by a thunderous crash from downstairs, followed by a lot of yelling and screaming. This was no hallucination; John could tell that these sounds were the real deal. Even Karl heard them, because he'd bolted upright with a wild look in his eyes.

One voice overpowered all the rest. It took John a few moments to understand that it was being amplified somehow.

"Nobody move!" the voice called out. "This is a raid, and the entire place is surrounded!"

John swallowed and then jumped to his feet. He was extremely unsteady, and the room seemed to tilt back and forth like a boat on choppy waters.

The police were here. Someone must've tipped them off that this ancient place was being used as a safe house for people like him. What was he going to do?

He couldn't run; he was barely able to stand. John was used to the clarity and euphoria his drugs usually gave him. Tonight his brain was full of clouds, moving slow and filling his eyes with visions of things that weren't really there.

He was still pondering what to do when three policemen rushed into the small room and placed handcuffs on him and Crazy Karl.

"There were about five different ways you could have escaped from this," said his dad in a resigned voice. The old man shook his head sadly and looked at John with those heavy-lidded eyes of his. "If only you'd cared enough to get out."

Get out? Get out of what? This place? This lifestyle?

One of the cops grabbed John gently by the arm and escorted him from the room. He looked back one last time on his way out.

But his father was gone.

34

PRESENT DAY

Ahead and to the right was a trailer with a big banner attached to its front that read *American Woman*. It looked like some kind of tattoo parlor. There were a few leather-clad characters milling about just outside, even though the place was closed.

After driving for almost forty-five minutes, John brought the car to a stop in the dirt patch of land that served as the tattoo parlor's parking lot and switched off the engine. He was wheezing with labored breaths, taking in oxygen that was reluctant to fill his lungs. John had never experienced asthma, but he wondered if this was what it felt like. But no, it was more than that. His stomach churned, his pulse had shot up, and his head felt as if it might explode.

Was it a panic attack? Maybe.

He couldn't find a hotel where he could risk staying. He couldn't go home. He couldn't stay with his father. Was there any such thing as a safe place anymore?

John turned on the car's overhead light and reached into his inside jacket pocket, where he'd left the tiny Bible his father gave him back at the church. Shaking and unable to read, he pressed the small book against his forehead with his eyes closed, trying to draw enough strength from its worn cover to calm himself.

After a few minutes he was able to hold the Bible without shaking, so he opened it to a passage his father had left bookmarked using the book's frayed ribbon. A yellow highlighter made a few verses of Psalms, chapter seven, leap off the page. His eyes flitted back and forth over the words.

"'In you I put my trust,'" he whispered, nodding in agreement with the text. "'Save me from all those who persecute me. . . . If I have done this, if there is iniquity in my hands . . . let the enemy pursue me and overtake me, let him trample my life to the earth.'"

The psalmist's writing was so powerful, John felt as if it had been written with him in mind. The Word of God was speaking beautiful truth into his circumstances, into his life, and the thought of such providential writing that applied so perfectly to him today was too much. Combined with his loss and his longing for home, John was overcome.

He burst into tears, his shoulders shaking and his chest letting out heaving sobs. John couldn't remember the last time he'd cried like this, and it felt good.

He cried himself to sleep.

Consciousness returned to John slowly, his eyes squeezed together tight as he trembled. Harder and harder he shook, almost unnaturally fast. Was he really waking up? What was going on?

At last his eyes snapped open. He was lying on his side in

familiar surroundings. He was at home in bed. Morning light made the room incredibly bright, though his eyes adjusted quickly.

Even before he'd opened his eyes, he was aware that someone else was in the room. There was only one person it could be, but he was facing away from her.

"Monica?" he asked, turning over and sitting partway up.

She sat in a wooden rocking chair on the far side of the bed, rocking and staring out of the upstairs window. She was perfectly serene, her slow rocking oscillating in a steady rhythm. After a few moments, Monica turned to face him. Her mouth moved as she looked at him. She was saying something, yet no sound came out of her.

What was she saying? She was just a few feet away. Why couldn't he hear her?

When she finished with whatever she was saying, she turned back to the window, continuing her rocking as if he wasn't even there.

Confused, John lay back and found himself breathing much too fast. But he couldn't stop. He stared at the ceiling, wondering if he was going to hyperventilate, why he couldn't hear Monica's voice, why the room was so very bright . . .

He sat up straight with a jolt.

John was awake. His head had just jerked upright away from the car's headrest.

He looked around; it was morning. He was covered in sweat and breathing hard, and for a moment couldn't remember where he was. Then he noticed the tattoo-parlor trailer off to his right. He wiped sweat from his face and felt sandpapery stubble on his cheeks.

John opened the door and stepped out. He was a bit wobbly but managed to stay on his feet. Instantly his ears were filled with noise. It sounded like cars racing by. He looked around and saw the interstate about a hundred feet away and down a short ravine.

The morning air cleared out the cobwebs, allowing him to walk with purpose toward the American Woman tattoo parlor. He'd seen this place the night he'd been drugged. It was one of the only memories he had. Dashing away from the car, up and up and up, until he'd stopped and shared that strange moment with those girls. And the camera.

He'd remembered the camera only after Charles had asked him what his next step would be. How could he clear his name without proof? Only then did John remember there *was* proof. Those girls had everything, and after leaving them, he'd run past this shell of a building. He wasn't sure the two were connected, but it was his only shot of tracking them down.

He climbed the wooden ramp out front and marched through the front door.

35

It was a "blue jacket" day. Agent Clark was already wearing his when Rivera showed up at work, and she knew what that meant. Anytime they wore their navy rain jackets—the familiar ones with the big letters FBI emblazoned in yellow—it was a day for fieldwork. In this case, most likely interviews.

She hoped that didn't mean they were going to have to talk to the dead girl's family. Rivera hated interviewing victims' family members. It always left her feeling sick. Besides, the police should have already spoken to whatever parent or parents Aaliyah had.

"Manage any sleep?" she asked, trying to start the day in a bright place.

Clark looked up from his desk. "You know I don't sleep," he said. "Anymore."

Rivera closed her eyes and tilted her head toward the ceiling. Of course she knew that. "I'm sorry, Preston—Agent Clark. I wasn't thinking."

Clark waved it off with one hand and returned to whatever he'd been working on when she walked in.

A few years before Rivera joined the agency, Clark had lost his wife to a carjacking. Her body was found a few days after the crime, but the perpetrator was never caught. Agent Clark had almost cinched the noose around the guy ten months ago, but he managed to slip away yet again. Coming so near to finally closing the case had opened up all the old wounds once more, even though Clark worked his hardest to shove aside the anger and pain.

Still, he couldn't hide it from her. Rivera saw the subtleties in his facial tics that others didn't seem to notice. Clark himself had taught her how to read a person for the slightest of expressions. She guessed he never thought she'd be using the skill on him, the teacher.

Rivera never brought the subject up, having learned most of the details of the case from other agents. If Clark didn't want to talk about it, she would abide by his wishes. Rivera knew that the two of them had gained enough respect for each other that if he ever did decide to talk about it, she would most likely be the one he would go to.

"So what's on the agenda?" she asked him.

Agent Clark stood and rounded his desk. "Come on. I'll tell you on the way."

John Luther's home was surprisingly modest. Rivera had expected the world-renowned preacher to live in something more . . . palatial. But the house he shared with his wife and daughter was remarkably average. A simple two-story house in an ordinary residential development.

She actually respected Luther a little more for his living so modestly.

Clark reached over and rang the doorbell.

Soon a blond woman a good ten or fifteen years younger than John Luther answered the door. She was nicely dressed, but her mascara had turned to faint streaks running down the sides of her face, and her eyes were red and puffy.

"Monica Luther?" asked Rivera.

Her expression was vacant as she answered, "Yes?"

Clark spoke up. "We're with the FBI. I'm Agent Clark. This is my partner, Agent Rivera. May we come in?"

Monica looked them up and down. "Where's your warrant?" she asked. It wasn't said in a rude way. In fact, the woman sounded almost confused.

"We're not here to search your home, Mrs. Luther," said Rivera. "We're trying to find your husband before anyone else gets hurt, and we'd just like to talk to you for a few minutes."

"Oh," said Monica, still confused and distracted. "Um, okay. Sure."

Rivera and Clark exchanged a glance as they followed Monica into the house. She led them to the living room, where she sat in an armchair, the two agents on the couch.

"Can I get you coffee or anything?" asked Monica. The question sounded habitual, as if she was used to entertaining, but it wasn't warm or welcoming. It was sort of robotic.

"No, thank you, ma'am," replied Agent Clark. "You haven't seen or heard from your husband since all this began, have you?"

Monica looked him in the eye for the first time. "I wouldn't tell you if I had. John is innocent. There's no way he would ever kill anybody. He didn't do it."

The room fell silent for an uncomfortable few moments.

"Does your husband have any enemies?" Rivera finally asked. "Can you think of anyone who might want to frame him for something like this?"

Clark shot her a stern look.

"No, of course not," Monica said. "He's a preacher."

Rivera nodded slowly.

"Wait . . ." said Monica, her eyes growing wider and her voice louder as she added, "Why are you asking me about John being framed? Have you found something? Something that can vindicate him?"

Monica leaned forward, her eyes bouncing back and forth between the two agents. Rivera, meanwhile, wanted to shrink into her seat. She knew she'd said the wrong thing.

Clark stepped in with his smooth calm. "We're not prepared to rule out any possibilities at this time," he said. "What can you tell us about how and when Mr. Luther underwent his . . . conversion experience? The event that turned his life around?"

Monica sat back and collected her thoughts. "It happened before we met. John calls it his 'Damascus Road' moment. He was thirty-two or thirty-three at the time?—I forget now—and he was at the lowest low of his life. Drinking hard, addicted to drugs, recently divorced from Jackie, his first wife. He was angry at the world, at his father, even at God. Someone dragged him to this old-fashioned revival camp meeting thing, the kind they used to hold outdoors under a giant tent. His father's an Episcopal priest, you know, so he'd grown up knowing all about the Christian faith. But this was different from anything he'd experienced before. He says that the 'simple Gospel truth' he heard at that revival opened his eyes and his heart. That was the day everything changed."

"And he's never relapsed into any of his old habits—no drinking or gambling or anything?" asked Agent Clark.

Monica shook her head with conviction, but a tear escaped her eye. "No. Absolutely not."

Rivera found herself feeling for this woman. She didn't know why; she was well practiced at staying detached from individuals involved in a case. But Monica Luther obviously believed in her husband, even if some small part of her was terrified that her faith in John had been in vain.

"Please find him," Monica said with more tears. "His little girl needs him. I need him. Get him home safely to us."

Rivera was about to open her mouth to tell Monica that they would do their best when Clark, perhaps sensing her empathy with Mrs. Luther, cut her off. "We need to speak to your husband's friends. Can you tell us who he's closest to, outside of yourself and your daughter?"

Monica looked away, thinking. "Just members of his staff, I guess. There's Dave Wilson. He's known Dave for something like twenty years, I think. Some others on the board of directors. Oh, and Ryan. Ryan Morris."

Something about the way she'd said that last name caught Rivera's attention. It was a kind of vocal grimace. Was there an odd vibe between her and Ryan? Or was it between Ryan and John? Rivera filed that little tidbit away for later.

"Thank you for your time, Mrs. Luther," said Clark, standing to his feet.

Rivera followed suit, and Monica rose to see them to the door. Clark shook her hand and thanked her again.

"You've been very helpful," said Rivera, shaking Monica's hand. Before she could stop herself, she'd put her other hand on top of Monica's and gave it a reassuring squeeze. She immediately regretted the action and hoped Clark hadn't seen it.

But he had. He never missed anything.

When they were back in the car, Clark asked, "What was that about? You know better than to make a personal connection like that."

"I don't know," Rivera replied, and it was the truth. She didn't.

"Well," said Clark, "I suppose you were following your instincts, which is good. But personal feelings will always influence your objectivity as an investigator. What was it about her?"

Rivera wasn't sure she could explain it, but she decided to go with her gut. "She has so much conviction about her husband. It was something about the way she *believes* in him. She's one of the 'good guys.' I want her to win."

36

A blue haze hung near the ceiling, and the pungent, unmistakable smell of marijuana enveloped John as he walked into the tattoo parlor. It was an odor he hadn't been around for years, but one that was hard to forget. In the dim light, John could see that the place was even filthier on the inside than it was outside. Grime covered every window, and the heavy haze made the small space feel claustrophobic.

A man who appeared to be in his early twenties lazily looked up from a little welcome desk next to the door. The man was clearly stoned. "How can we help you?" he asked.

John didn't bother replying. He couldn't imagine anything he said would be taken seriously by this guy. Instead he stepped around the desk and headed toward the back of the trailer, where he saw another man, this one busy tattooing a woman's back.

He'd only made it a few feet when the stoner at the desk spoke again.

"Hang on a sec," he said. "I know you. You're that guy . . . that guy from the TV. Hey, man, what happened to your face?"

John instinctively put a hand up to hide the scratches on

the side of his face. In the back of the trailer, a short African-American decked out in a Capitals hockey jersey turned from his work and looked at John. The client, the woman with her back exposed, faced away from the man. Already the outline of a dragon snaked its way up her spine.

"You can't just let people walk back here like this," the tattoo artist scolded, pointing a tattoo needle at the one manning the front desk.

"Don't talk to him like that," replied the stoner. "Learn some respect, man. Nolan, this is that famous preacher from the television. You know?"

Nolan glanced at John. "Nope," he said, and turned back to his work.

A narrow door behind Nolan inched open, and a thin wisp of a girl emerged. She wore dark, baggy clothes that accentuated her skeleton-like appearance. Her eyes were as hollow as her expression. She stood there quietly, studying John.

He thought she looked familiar but he couldn't be sure.

"Sorry it's such a mess around here," she said, her voice lethargic. "I try, but he never cleans up after himself. Neither of them do."

"Scorpion woman," remarked Nolan, eying her with disgust.

The girl gave a half smile while keeping her eyes glued to John. "And you are?" she asked.

"I'm John Luther. I was assaulted near this shop the other night, and I was hoping one of you might have seen what happened."

The girl nodded as though understanding now what he was after. "He's here for the show," she said to Nolan.

Nolan looked at John again. "So you're a preacher?"

John nodded. "Yes, I am."

"He's a fugitive, Alex," the stoner said to the girl before turning to John. He looked giddy at the notion. "Aren't you? Man, that's hardcore."

"I know where you're coming from," said Alex. "That was some madness that went down. I even taped it."

John's breath stopped cold in his throat, and his mouth fell partly open. He'd been right! She was the one who'd been there making the video that night. John's heart began to swell; he just might be able to get himself out of this whole mess. But then he looked at the girl again—her cloaked expression and her wary eyes. No way was it going to be easy. Who was to say she wasn't lying to him?

"You really taped it?" he asked her.

Alex grinned and stepped closer until she was right up in John's face. And then he knew—she wasn't lying. But, just like that night, she wasn't going to help him either. At least not for free. She had him right where she wanted him, and they both knew it. "We got needs too," she said matter-of-factly. "You understand?"

He nodded. He didn't even want to think about what the girl meant by "needs," though he certainly could guess. Yet what other option did he have? He'd pay any price for her recording. If she wanted the clothes off his back, the watch on his wrist, even the car outside in the parking lot—she could have it all.

"So, my brother," she went on, "you better believe it's gonna cost you."

37

Senator Donald Harrison normally prided himself on being able to sleep through any turmoil or stress. He'd been in this game too long to let the worries of the day follow him into his dreams and knew that exhaustion was one of the worst things to pile on to a problem. Working in the Senate, running a campaign, dealing with angry lobbyists—such things took a focused mind, and that wasn't easy to maintain through the fog that came from an interrupted night. Even so, sleep had proven difficult as of late, and so he was wide awake, staring into the dim light of his bedroom when the phone rang. The phone he'd been instructed to keep for only one caller.

"Tell me you've found him," he couldn't help but grumble into the phone once the call was answered.

"The plan was to let him escape and resurface in his own time. He won't stay underground much longer," said Mr. Gray. There was an edge to his voice, and the slightest hint of surprise. Donald didn't like that at all.

"I need to know *what* he's doing, *who* he's talking to, and *where* he is!" insisted the senator. "Do you understand me?"

This part of the plan had never seemed like it would be a problem. How could John Luther manage to evade a man with as much training, resourcefulness, and cunning as Mr. Gray, a professional? It would almost be impressive if it weren't so maddening.

"I paid you in advance," he said, his blood pressure rising. "I hired you because you're supposed to be the best. But you've been outsmarted by a *preacher*!"

There was silence on the other end of the line. Beads of sweat popped onto Donald's forehead. He wondered if he'd gone too far.

But that would be ridiculous. *He* was the one calling the shots here, not his hired hand. A hired hand who was failing to deliver.

"Don't worry. I'll find him," said Mr. Gray, his voice like sandpaper rubbing against stone.

The line went dead.

Donald threw the phone down, took a deep breath and counted to ten.

He had to forget about John Luther. He had to forget about Mr. Gray and let the man do his job. Unfortunately they weren't the only challenges he was dealing with at the moment. The real reason he couldn't sleep right now—the thing that had been occupying the majority of his thoughts—was something far more positive thankfully. A light at the end of the tunnel for what had been some of the most difficult work he'd attempted to do in his entire career. Today, the final piece would fall into place. And not even John Luther, wherever he was holed up, could stop the march of progress any longer.

The world was ready for change. The world *would* change, and Senator Donald Harrison would be at the front of the line, leading the procession.

Glancing at the clock once more, he knew his night was over. There would be no more sleep for a while.

Donald rose, slipped on his robe, and stepped into the bathroom, where he splashed water on his face. He looked at himself in the mirror. Those that changed history were remembered forever. *That* was eternal life. He might just get there after all.

Donald practiced his smile. It looked flat and . . . *practiced*. He made a slow count to ten, clearing his mind, and then let the first positive thought he could find fill his mind.

Tonight's meeting. Tonight's meeting was the start of everything. His smile found its true shape but then just as quickly vanished. Senator Donald Harrison found himself looking at a tired man.

It had been such a long road to this evening. He still remembered the first discussion, years ago, about the greatest challenges facing the country in the next century and how he'd spent a long evening talking about religious polarization, both in the U.S. and around the world, with another senator from Oregon.

"The world doesn't need to be torn apart further. It needs to come together," the senator had said, and Donald had heartily agreed. He'd had his own reasons back then, but over the years he'd not only come to see the value of those words but embrace them as well.

The senator was addressing the very heart of spirit and body.

Donald had been raised a good Christian boy. His parents took him to Sunday school. He memorized verses from the Bible. He even went on a missions trip once.

But he knew now that Christians were too insular—too frightened by the ground they were losing, too focused on a message that was narrow and exclusive. Few of them really understood what matters of faith looked like to the rest of the world. They were too wrapped up inside their own self-serving little bubble. The real world was quite a different place than what was seen inside the small, white street-corner churches or the megachurches of America.

God, Donald Harrison knew now, was a story so much larger than any single religion could claim. And all acts of faith would lead to him. Donald had sat in a temple in Japan and saw God in the face of a young boy meditating. Good Minnesota Lutherans had shown him hospitality when he'd been snowed in for three days in Duluth. He'd heard the energy of the prayers of Muslim men faced toward Mecca in Abu Dhabi. For two hours he'd once sat in silence in a Quaker prayerhouse and left without anyone claiming to speak for God. He'd even taken in a sunrise with a group of atheists at Virginia Beach and heard them talk about nature's beauty in words common to every church and temple and mosque and synagogue across the world. God was everywhere.

But the people of the world could not find him by clamoring in different directions. They all needed to be heading in the same direction.

If it took a flute and a song, so be it, but the world needed a melody to follow. And for years now the Faith and Fairness bill had been developed to play that very melody.

It was fools like John Luther who were holding back progress. He was a relic of another time. A bully, in some respects—and the world had had enough of bullies.

John's face came to mind again.

He'd been a friend once, but the man was standing in the way now. Donald wondered if John had pieced together yet how this whole thing had come to him. He wondered if he would see the man in the future and whether he would see the recognition in his eyes that Donald had brought him low.

The thought did not give him pleasure. This was not about revenge. He didn't *want* this to go down the way it had, but John Luther and the Christians of this country had had their chance. Almost two hundred and fifty years of claiming to have all the answers, and yet those answers had solved nothing. Why did they have the same problems as everybody else? Shouldn't they have solved the world's issues by now?

Should human beings not, in these modern times, be more enlightened so as to rise above their petty differences? The fact that war was still so prevalent in the twenty-first century was proof enough that *unity* was the key to peace, the key to ending conflict around the globe. And the United States was poised to lead the way, to usher in that unity.

At long last it was time for the world to coexist.

Today's meeting would bring the final key player into the fold.

With that thought, Donald Harrison's smile formed wide and true again in the bathroom mirror. He stared into the face of a man who was ready to change the world.

Charles Luther had heard of the Sumac Alliance organization; he just never expected to receive a call from them. Ever since his son had risen to prominence, Charles had made it his duty to watch out for him—no matter whether John wanted him to or not. That often meant finding people who didn't necessarily want to be found. Early on, Charles focused on religious radicals from other nations, revolutionaries who might target his son to make an example of him as a "false prophet." It didn't take too long to realize that such threats might not come from outside America's borders but within. And that those who stood opposed to what John Luther valued might not threaten him with violence, but more quietly, with trying to silence him through the force of laws and politics.

The Sumac Alliance had come up as he'd made these inquiries. Each meeting of the Sumac Alliance went unadvertised, and attending was strictly invitation only. Just a dozen or so handpicked individuals, representatives from a spectrum of religious orders, a few of whom choosing not to publicize the fact that they were members. But each had been specifically chosen and was a believer in the cause.

Well, almost all of them.

Charles Luther was still trying to shake off his surprise at being asked to attend this meeting when his bishop called him to say an emergency would keep him from attending. Charles would normally have passed, but he couldn't deny the serendipity of this chance to see the people who, if not responsible themselves for framing his son, had certainly laid the groundwork.

"Besides," the bishop said, "I really believe you'll enjoy the sharing of ideas that takes place." He'd been pressuring Charles for years to "think in new ways" and to "ready the church for the new world." This was probably Charles's last chance before the man wrote him off forever.

Up a driveway ramp behind a wrought-iron fence, Charles walked until he reached the front door to the lavish manor. A security guard stood watch on the brick porch in front of double doors that led inside. The man eyed Charles as if he were a rodent.

"How can we help you?" the security guard asked in a decidedly *un*helpful tone.

When Charles reached the bottom of the porch steps, he looked up at the man. "I was asked to fill in for the bishop."

Without another word, the man escorted him to the door and opened it for him.

Charles had never been inside a place like this before. Ornate and extravagant, no detail had been overlooked. Every end table was handcrafted with an intricate design. Exquisite draperies framed the windows. Even the doorknobs appeared to be carved out of solid brass and polished to a high shine. He had no idea which room the meeting was in, but he didn't have to go searching. He just followed the sound.

That sound was the deep voice of Senator Donald Harrison, the man who was chairing the meeting.

"I think you all know that the Faith and Fairness Act is a dream I've had for quite some time. I want to thank Warner for hosting this—"

Harrison stopped abruptly when he saw Charles Luther enter the room.

"Father," he said, warm and inviting. "Thank you very much for joining us. Would you have a seat, please? I think it's time we got started." The senator gestured to an empty seat in the back row.

Charles dutifully complied, feeling dirty sharing a room with the man who'd turned John into a fugitive. Did Harrison even know that Charles was John's father? Surely someone as well informed as the senator would have access to those kinds of details. But then it wasn't exactly Harrison's idea that Charles be present at today's meeting; he'd been invited by the bishop, after all.

Had the bishop known of the pressure Senator Harrison had been putting on John? Did any of the members here know? Charles doubted it. But in their quietly uniting to back this bill, they'd made their stand. For most of them, someone like John Luther was simply behind the times, preaching a faith that didn't matter in today's world. Only someone like Senator Harrison understood how important John's voice behind the bill actually would be.

Harrison resumed his spiel. "As you all know, the Faith and Fairness Act is very close to my heart. It's been quite a struggle . . ."

Charles tried to focus on the senator's words, but from the moment he took his seat, his attention was drawn to a figure standing above Harrison on an overlooking balcony. The man leaned on the balcony railing, his hands clasped together, and watched the participants in the meeting. No, that wasn't right. He was watching only Charles.

So Charles stared right back. The man was half hidden in shadow, but he appeared to be dressed much like the security guard outside, wearing a crisp gray suit. There was something ominous about this person, whoever he was. His gaze, the blank stare of a predator sizing up his meal, triggered an instinct in Charles to shrivel, but he fought it. This man was bad news. Charles could *feel* it.

As Harrison droned on, expounding the infinite virtues of his multi-faith alliance, a battle was taking place in this very room. A war without weapons, without movement, without even words. Miles of animosity filled the short space between Charles and the man in the gray suit. Charles felt his mouth stretch into a scowl while his eyes grew harder and harder.

I'm watching you, the man on the balcony seemed to be conveying.

I'm watching you too, Charles sent back to him.

Donald Harrison was the kind of man who would stab you in the back while giving you a great big bear hug. He'd already proven that, and Charles disliked him for it. This man on the balcony was altogether different.

Hatred was beneath a person of his station, but Charles couldn't escape the feeling that as he looked at this shadow-cloaked man, he was staring into the face of the enemy.

38

A quick check at Truth Ministries revealed that Ryan Morris hadn't made it in to work yet today. So Agents Clark and Rivera positioned themselves right outside the adjacent parking garage in order to catch him on his way in. Clark parked the black SUV on the curb next to the garage's entrance.

"I'm sorry about before," said Rivera. "With Luther's wife."

"I know," replied Clark, his eyes on the parking structure. "It's not important."

If Clark decided it didn't matter, then Rivera knew to let the matter drop. Still, she wondered what it was about Monica Luther that had brought her own emotions to the surface like that. As an FBI agent, she'd been well trained to put personal feelings aside while doing her job. It was like an on/off switch. You went to work, and the emotions got switched off. You headed home and, *flip*, they're switched back on. History had proven time and again that sentiment was a liability—particularly in the field.

She thought again of Agent Clark and his personal tragedy. At least he'd had someone at one point in his life. Rivera occasionally wished she had a significant other at home waiting for her, but she was too busy with work to have time for pursuing a relationship. The simple fact was, her partner was the man in her life right now—even if there was no attraction or romantic interest between them. She didn't look at him that way, and she was certain he felt exactly the same.

"There he is," said Clark.

Rivera followed his gaze through the windshield to see a tall man with dirty-blond hair just emerging from the parking garage on the ground level.

She and Agent Clark exited the vehicle in unison and converged quickly on Ryan Morris. Rivera did a quick profile on the man as they approached. His clothes made a bold statement. He wore clean-cut jeans, a crisp black T-shirt, and a pastel-pink sports jacket without a wrinkle to be seen. His hair was styled with a healthy amount of gel, ensuring that even if it moved, it always fell right back into place.

But none of these things told her more about Morris than what she observed from his walk. There wasn't mere confidence in his gait. There was a *swagger* to it. Ryan Morris was a man awfully pleased with himself.

Morris was humming some indiscernible tune, and smiling at nothing in particular.

Already Rivera disliked this man. It wasn't hard to deduce that he had tasted power very recently—probably having taken over as interim president of Truth Ministries in Luther's absence—and found it quite to his liking.

Was it poisoning him? Too soon to tell.

"Excuse me, sir," said Agent Clark.

Morris faced them with surprise on his face, though Rivera thought it may have been an act. He should have easily seen them coming from his peripheral vision.

"Ryan Morris?" Clark asked.

Morris broke into a smug grin. "The one and only."

Rivera saw no reason to humor him. She cut to the chase. "We'd like to have a word. That okay with you?"

"For the FBI, I'd be honored," Morris said with a little too much sincerity. "Tell you what you do. If you'll go to my office, they'll set up an appointment, and *boom*, we're good to go."

So that's how he was going to play it. The *I'm so important that I'm much too busy to deal with you* routine.

Rivera was about to tell him what he could do with his precious schedule when Clark spoke up.

"This will just take a minute," he said.

Morris glanced back and forth between the two of them, still smiling but registering disbelief. Were they for real? Didn't they understand who he was?

Rivera understood him all too well.

"Well, I'm sorry but I've got a critical meeting I simply *cannot* be late for," replied Morris. He was trying hard to keep things light and jovial, but his true intentions were quite clear. "I will help you in any way you need, but as I'm sure you're aware, we're in crisis mode here."

"We really need to talk," said Clark in a tone that left no room for further argument, and for a brief moment, Rivera flipped her internal switch so she could enjoy watching Ryan Morris squirm.

39

John was ecstatic.

The girl at the tattoo place, Alex, had come through. It'd cost him a sizable chunk of the cash his father had given him, but it was worth every penny. He'd left that place with a digital thumb drive containing video of Aaliyah Evans's murder. John could plainly be seen as unconscious in the vehicle while the man in the gray suit struck her and then injected her with a syringe. The camera then followed John as he fled his attackers, and by the time it returned to John's Toyota, the two men there were positioning Aaliyah's body inside the vehicle. It looked as though they were *posing* her.

God was good. John would probably be cleared of all charges before lunchtime!

He pulled out the phone he'd found waiting for him in the burgundy car the other night and dialed his father's number.

"I have it, Dad," he said, his words pouring out in an excited rush. "I'm going to the police. Can you meet me there?"

"John," said Charles, his voice disappointingly less than enthusiastic. "I've been doing some digging and . . . there's something you need to know."

Whatever it was, it didn't matter. Hadn't the old man heard him? "Dad, *I have it*!"

"It's not that simple."

Not that simple? Of course it was. What was he saying?

Charles sighed. "You're in their way, son."

Forty-five minutes later, John was on a secluded bench at a park just outside of town. His father wore a grave expression as he walked the dirt path and seated himself to John's left. Whatever the old man had to tell him, it was bad enough that John's heart thudded louder at the sight of him.

For a moment they sat together in silence, listening to the birds chirping in the surrounding trees. Clouds had rolled in late in the morning, and the sense of dread building inside John seemed to feed them, turning them darker and darker. He almost hoped his dad wouldn't say anything at all.

John looked his father in the eye. An unspoken question passed between them. *Why are we here, Dad?*

Charles pulled out a photograph and passed it to his son. John's eyes fell on it and saw three people at what looked like some kind of inner-city charity event. On the far right was Aaliyah Evans, looking much as she did the night he first met her at the studios of Truth Ministries. On the far left was a black woman John didn't recognize. And standing between them with a broad smile on his face was Senator Donald Harrison.

John studied the picture for a minute, trying to get his mind around what he was seeing. It was hard to concentrate because he felt like he'd just been sucker-punched in the stomach.

He knew he'd been set up. But by *Donald*?

What was this?

"We were like brothers once," said John. "He supported Truth Ministries for years, when we were just starting out and he was a state senator. We had our differences these past years, but I just can't believe it's him."

Charles's expression turned bitter. "That girl was adopted by a woman named Shanice Evans just two days before she was found dead. This woman was able to bypass the waiting list and a lot of other formalities thanks to the assistance of your friend the senator—the majority leader of the United States Senate."

This was much, much worse than John initially thought. Did Donald really possess this kind of limitless power at his command?

"Now, aside from the president," Charles continued, "I don't know of many people who are better equipped to withstand a bullet like this. Nor better equipped to make sure your evidence never sees the light of day.

"Senator Harrison isn't in the video you have, and you won't be able to connect him to it. The media has already tried you and found you guilty. You need to be more careful than ever about who to trust and how to expose this darkness."

John had a feeling that was an understatement. Donald Harrison suddenly seemed positively untouchable.

"Look, son," said Charles. "For Senator Harrison, it's about power and money. But more important, it's about what he's a part of here. The people he's associated with. What the Sumac Alliance is trying to do. What this legislation is bound to do to Christians all over America.

"Look at China, Russia, Iran, North Korea—these nations where we don't bat an eye when the authorities drag people out of their beds in the middle of the night and imprison them under false charges. People are even relieved to see this happening, because they think their government is cracking down on crime."

Was the old man saying what John thought he was saying? Was he comparing the persecution and martyrdom of Christians around the world with what the Faith and Fairness Act would result in? Even with what John was experiencing right now?

"You ask most people in this country, right now," said Charles, "about the persecution of Christians, and most of the time they'll just smile at you and say, 'No such thing. Not here. Can't happen here.'"

John thought of a quote from the Bible, after Saul's Damascus Road conversion, when it was said that "something like scales fell from Saul's eyes." John's eyes had never been more open. When he'd argued with Donald these past years about the Faith and Fairness Act, they'd been religious arguments, about truth and grace and what set Christianity apart from Buddhism, Islam, and the other religions. Donald had made the argument again and again that no one religion could corner truth and that God was big enough to serve all religions, but he'd never talked about his pet bill as a threat. But the old man was right. There it was, plain as day. If it passed, the bill could be used to silence anyone they targeted.

It was overwhelming. Goliath had just grown about ten times bigger, and John felt smaller than he'd ever been.

"There's one thing you need to understand above all else," Charles went on. "The eyes of all Americans are on you now. People are looking for a symbol of truth and freedom. Someone who'll stand up against the cabal of thorny, powerful politicians. Who'll be unbending amidst all the lies and slanders that can be thrown at him. Who'll get back up when he's knocked down. And that's exactly what you're going to do, son. You're going to get back up."

John looked sidelong at his father, thinking only of his own insecurities and inadequacies, and of the many failures of his past. How was a man with so many flaws supposed to be a symbol before an entire nation? He was neither deserving nor capable of such a feat.

He sighed and closed his eyes, half in exhaustion and half in prayer. If this really was what God wanted of him, then God was going to have to take the wheel. John swallowed hard and then blinked back the tears suddenly filling his eyes.

"God will decide who's found wanting," said Charles. "They can't silence the truth."

John held out the USB drive he'd acquired at the tattoo place. "I want you to watch this, Dad."

Charles accepted it, turning the tiny piece of plastic over in his hand. He exchanged the flash drive for a keycard inside a paper sleeve. "Here," he said. "I got you a room. Go get yourself cleaned up. And get some rest. It'll do you good." He clapped John on the shoulder.

John stood, slow and unsteady. But before he left, he looked back. "I *am* going to expose the truth about Donald Harrison." John feared his words sounded as if he was trying to convince himself as much as his dad.

The old man smiled at him, and John knew that he was proud of his son, proud of the man he'd chosen to be.

John only hoped he would be found worthy of such approval.

40

Suck it up, Rivera told herself. She'd wanted this job so badly and had worked crazy hard to get here. She had the best partner of anyone in the agency. She couldn't just pick and choose the most palatable tasks. She took a deep breath and squared her shoulders. She needed to take the good with the bad.

Even so, there were two or three dozen things she would rather have been doing right now than climbing the steps to Shanice Evans's apartment. It had taken some time to find the right place. Evans lived on the third floor of a crowded inner-city apartment building. The place had to be at least forty years old.

Rivera watched as Clark knocked on the door.

"Who is it?" called out a female voice from inside.

"FBI, ma'am," answered Clark.

Rivera heard the hasty sliding of latches and turning of locks. When the door opened, a tall, slender black woman stood at the threshold. Modestly dressed in a simple T-shirt and jeans, she didn't look as tired or grief-stricken as Rivera had expected a mother who'd just lost her child to look. Instead she looked like someone frustrated that she'd been interrupted from watching her afternoon talk show.

Clark held up his badge and introduced himself and his partner.

"Come on in," said Shanice. She held the door open and stepped aside.

"Thank you," Rivera said as she walked by.

When they were seated on an old but clean-looking couch in the apartment's living room, Shanice patiently waited for the agents to speak. Rivera glanced around, noticed crosses hanging on the walls spread all around the room. They were made of various materials: wood, ceramic, glass, and chrome.

"Our condolences for your loss," said Clark.

Shanice nodded. "Thank you."

"May I ask, when was the last time you saw your daughter?"

Shanice sighed and said, "I'm sorry, I still haven't gotten used to Aaliyah being called my daughter. . . ."

"Why is that?" asked Clark.

Shanice looked back and forth between the two of them. She seemed unsure of how to respond. "Don't you know? I'd only adopted Aaliyah just two days before . . . well, before what happened to her."

Rivera and Clark exchanged a look, both thinking the same thing. Only *two days*? No way was that a coincidence.

Clark recovered quickly from the shock. "How long had you known Aaliyah before the adoption?"

Shanice looked at the ceiling, thinking. "About two months, I think."

Rivera raised her eyebrows. "That's a remarkably fast turn-around."

"And I never would have gotten custody of her so fast if not for the senator's help."

"What senator?" asked Clark.

"Senator Harrison," said Shanice.

Rivera knew that name. She shot another look at Clark.

"He accelerated the process?" said Clark.

"That's right."

"Why?" asked Rivera, unable to suppress her curiosity.

Shanice looked uncertain. "We were like a test case . . . or whatever you call it. There was this bill he was working on. I read some of it on the computer, but it was way beyond me. It was something to do with supporting different religions. I'm still not sure what it all had to do with me and Aaliyah."

Rivera looked to Clark, uncertain what question to ask next. This interview was not going anything like what she'd expected. She'd heard of the Faith and Fairness Act, as the bill had been in the news a lot lately. But what did that have to do with a teenage girl's adoption—and murder?

"Hang on a sec," said Shanice, jumping to her feet. She left the room and retreated to what was most likely a bedroom. About a minute later, she returned carrying a photograph. She handed it to Clark, who looked at it and then passed it to Rivera.

It was a photo of Shanice, Senator Harrison, and Aaliyah, all of them smiling into the camera. Harrison had his arms around both Aaliyah and her new mom.

"When was this taken?" asked Rivera.

"Um, about a week ago. There was this big dinner thing he invited us to."

Clark let out a breath. "Well, I think that's about all—"

"Just one more question, if that's all right," said Rivera, playing a hunch. "If it's not too personal . . . how would you describe Aaliyah?"

Shanice's lower lip quivered. "Beautiful. Troubled. She had a difficult childhood. But she was a good girl. Whatever she was doing that night . . . she didn't deserve this."

Five minutes later, as she and Clark were descending the stairs, Rivera began thinking out loud.

"The deeper we dig, the weirder this gets. Senator Harrison . . . isn't he the one who's a big supporter of Truth Ministries?"

Clark looked at her, nodded.

"So what's he doing clearing out the red tape for a teenage girl's adoption just two days before she's murdered?"

"That," replied Clark, "is all I can think about."

41

Hotel Blue turned out to be an almost entirely forgettable little spot just off the highway and about an hour outside of D.C. and a few towns over from Truth Ministries' headquarters. Each ground level room had a parking spot right outside, so John could slip in without his being seen. His father could not have chosen a more perfect hideout.

John showered, and as the scorching needles of water stung and burned, he closed his eyes and prepared for what was to come. He was done playing the victim. It was time to put a plan of his own into motion. But before he could play Donald Harrison's game, he needed to know that his family was okay. More important, Monica had to know he was innocent, and believe in him. Without her support and trust, all of this was meaningless. Of everything he'd lost in the last days, his wife and his little girl were the only things that kept coming back to mind. Everything else could vanish, but without them . . . he couldn't imagine how he'd go on.

Two hours later, John used side streets to make his way over toward Truth Ministries. He had no doubt, if they were looking for him, that his headquarters would be one of the places there'd be a set of eyes. But he knew the area better than most, and he had more experience than they realized with finding shadows and vanishing when needed. The years he spent wandering as a young man had taught him some hard lessons, yet they'd also made him adept at dodging others' notice. And cutting through alleys toward the parking garage of his headquarters, those lessons all came flooding back to him.

He found a dark corner to crouch in, right around lunchtime, and watched. Soon enough, Ryan's Corvette whipped into the garage and squealed into a space—John's designated spot at the parking garage. John winced. He'd assumed Ryan would have taken charge in his absence, but wasn't parking in John's spot taking it a little far?

He put it out of his mind. He had much bigger things to worry about.

John slipped out of his corner and stepped behind a pillar in the garage, watching Ryan with eyes shaded by the hood of his sweat shirt. When Ryan headed for the elevator, John grabbed a cart of janitorial supplies he'd grabbed earlier from a supply closet the staff always left open, and followed Ryan.

The sound of whistling reached John's ears. Ryan was in good spirits.

When Ryan reached the elevator, John was close enough to tap him on the shoulder. Ryan jumped and spun around.

"Hey," said John. "It's me."

Ryan's eyes nearly leaped out of his head, and his complexion blanched lily white. "John!"

John was so happy to see a friendly face, he threw his arms around Ryan and wrapped him in a tight bear hug.

Ryan pulled gently away and spoke in hushed tones. "What are you doing coming here? It's too dangerous!"

"I need your help," said John.

"You—you need money?"

"Whatever you've got on you."

Quickly, Ryan pulled some bills out of his wallet, folded and handed them to John. "John, the whole country is hunting you!"

John suddenly felt self-conscious and glanced around the garage's interior.

"It's unreal what they're saying," Ryan added.

John had no time to explain himself. He handed Ryan a piece of paper on which he'd scrawled *Hotel Blue, 717 Central Ave.*, and the name of the town.

"Can you get this to Monica?" he asked.

Ryan glanced down at the paper. "Sure," he said.

Behind his shoulder, John heard the familiar squawk of a walkie-talkie. He turned to see a patrol car idling in the garage entrance, the cop inside talking to the booth attendant. Instantly he began backing away from Ryan.

"I'll be in touch," said John before turning and striding away.

Across the street from the garage, Mr. Gray waited. He scanned the street back and forth, watching for Luther. The preacher had shown up half an hour ago in an ugly maroon sedan and disappeared into the garage, but he hadn't come out yet.

On the orders of the senator, Mr. Gray had been trying to track down the preacher. The man had turned out to be a much more entertaining and elusive prey than Mr. Gray expected. After following him to the church, Luther had somehow escaped unnoticed. There was a report of him showing up at a motel on the outskirts of town a little while later, but he was long gone by the time Mr. Gray got there. The clueless girl who'd called the police was no help at all. While Luther had kept a low profile since then, Mr. Gray knew that sooner or later he would show up at Truth Ministries. Men with power couldn't stay away from their thrones for very long.

His associate Mr. Broad was busy patrolling Luther's neighborhood in case he returned there. As far as Mr. Gray knew, there'd been no sign of him yet.

Wait. There he was. Mr. Gray saw Luther pushing a cart down the sidewalk just outside the garage. He looked spooked. He was wearing those ridiculous sunglasses again. Luther soon ditched the cart and sprinted across the street, back to his car.

Mr. Gray watched him back out, and when he was sure Luther wasn't looking, he did the same.

Harrison would be relieved. He'd grown worried that they had nothing tangible on the preacher, but now that he knew the preacher's vehicle, Mr. Gray had more than enough information. He memorized the license plate and if needed would be able to affix a GPS tracking unit on the car. The full resources of the CIA and NSA were at his disposal, thanks to the efforts of Senator Harrison.

There was nowhere the preacher could go now. Mr. Gray had him in his sights and imagined circling him—drawing ever closer until he finally got the call. And then the real fun would begin.

42

23 YEARS AGO

"Anyone sitting here?"

John glanced up at the source of the question, a middle-aged man standing next to him. He shook his head and returned to his meal.

It was a busy Thursday night at the shelter. At least a dozen other guests were eating at long tables in the small dining hall. This guy taking the seat next to him didn't look much like he belonged here.

"Enjoying your meal?" the guy asked.

Oh, wonderful. John had no desire to talk to anyone, but this guy wasn't picking up on his expression or body language. Or maybe he was, and he was ignoring it. Either way, John was annoyed.

He'd never been to this shelter before. He'd been in Chicago looking for work for less than a week, but he was coming up dry. John was thinking of moving on to Cincinnati or maybe somewhere to the south in the morning. But his tired body needed fuel first.

"Yeah," he replied, not making eye contact with the nosy guy.

"I made it," the man said with a smile.

John couldn't hide his surprise. "*You* cooked this?"

"Every bite," said the man, quite pleased with himself. "Do I make a mean corn-bread casserole or what? Come back next week and I'll make you some more."

John shook his head and rolled his eyes. This guy was wearing a white dress shirt without a single wrinkle to be found, pleated black dress pants, and well worn but stylish loafers. "You look more like a stockbroker than a cook," said John.

The man chuckled. "Not far off. I'm an accountant."

John sighed and took another bite of his food. "This is the part where I'm supposed to ask why an accountant is at a homeless shelter."

"Is it?" the man replied. "I thought that seemed pretty obvious. I volunteer once a week."

"That's *what* you're doing," said John. "Not *why*."

The corners of the man's lips playfully curled up. "Tell you what. I'll give you my 'why' if you give me yours. Why are you here?"

"Been traveling around, looking for work. Can't seem to convince anyone to hire me. Guess they don't like my hair." John's long locks extended past his shoulders and hadn't been cut in over a year.

"Or," said the man, "maybe it's the smell."

John felt his cheeks burn red. "What's that supposed to mean?"

"Sorry, my wife tells me I'm too blunt sometimes," the man said, looking sheepish. "You volunteer here long enough and you learn about various scents on people who come in off the street and what they are. And I know the burning-plastic-crossed-with-a-dollar-bill scent that's pouring off you is the distinct smell of cocaine."

John clenched his fists. How dare this total stranger—

"I've offended you! I apologize. Truly," said the man, and John had to concede that he seemed sincere about it. "You hang around here long enough and certain topics just become old hat. I shouldn't have opened my big mouth."

John relaxed but held on to his frown. "Forget it. You're not wrong, anyway. I'm not proud of it. I'm trying to kick the habit."

The man smiled. "You will. I'm sure of it."

John took another bite of food. "You are, are you?"

He nodded. "Absolutely."

"You don't even know me."

"True. But I see something in you that I don't see very often in the people who come here."

John stopped chewing. "Like what?"

"You're hungry."

John looked at him blankly. Was the guy making some kind of joke?

The man smiled. "I know, I know. That sounded ridiculous. But I'm not talking about food. You're hungry for *more*. You *crave* something more from this life. I can see it in your eyes. On your wrist."

John looked down and saw the small Celtic-style cross he'd had tattooed on the inside of his wrist. It had been a gag, just one more thing to annoy his dad. But *sometimes* he looked at it and felt uncomfortable. Not that he was going to give this man the satisfaction of being right. "Maybe," he replied. "Or maybe I just really like corn-bread casserole."

The man chuckled again. "Fair enough."

John took a big bite of the casserole and studied the man beside him. "Your turn. What's a successful accountant doing at a run-down, nasty old homeless shelter in the bad part of town?" John didn't know that the man was successful, of course, but he figured it was a safe bet.

The smile receded from the man's face. "I suppose . . . I'm soothing a guilty conscience."

John continued eating quietly, waiting for the man to explain.

"I make a lot more money than my family needs. And when I think of how many people in the world go hungry one, two, even three meals a day . . . I feel frustrated. And guilty. And a whole bunch of other things. We donate a lot of money to worthy causes, but it doesn't quite feel *real* if I'm not getting my hands dirty. So I come down here once a week and I cook."

John was surprised to find himself empathizing with this man he didn't know. He sat in silence and allowed the man's words to roll around in his head. Finally he finished his meal. It felt good to be full again. And he had to admit, the food was tasty. He stood. "Well. Thanks for the meal. And the rest."

"You're very welcome. Before you go, may I ask your name? I like to have names to go with the people I pray for on a regular basis."

John was surprised and really had no desire for this man or anybody else to spend time on their knees, lifting up his name to a God who probably wasn't even there. Yet for some reason his mouth formed the words anyway.

"John," he said. "John Luther."

The man put his hand on John's shoulder. "Thanks for the conversation, John. Stop by the next time you're in town. I'd be happy to cook for you again."

John nodded, then broke away from him. He was almost out the door when he stopped and turned back. "You didn't tell me your name," he called, not caring that everyone else in the room stopped talking and looked up.

"Wilson," the man replied. "My name is Dave Wilson."

43

PRESENT DAY

Senator Donald Harrison had turned in early and just drifted off to sleep when the phone rang. Tomorrow was a big day. The Sumac Alliance was holding its benefit luncheon tomorrow, and there was much to do beforehand.

Fighting the urge to grumble, Donald reminded himself that calls in the night came with the job. He was always on duty. Besides, it wasn't even that late yet.

Donald turned on the lamp on his nightstand, reached over, and grabbed the receiver. It was attached to an antique-style phone, a Christmas gift a few years ago from his wife.

"Hello."

"Senator," said an official-sounding voice, "I have the president on the line."

Donald quickly sat up, swinging his legs over the edge of the bed. "Put him through," he replied.

On the other side of the large four-poster bed, his wife rolled over toward him and groaned. He waved a hand, motioning for her to be quiet. "*The president*," he whispered.

"Donald," said the president in his trademark Southern drawl.

"Yes, Mr. President," said Donald. "How can I help you, sir?"

"I'd like to share a story with you, if that's all right." The president's drawl sounded even slower and more rounded than usual. In front of the press, the accent would almost disappear, but in more casual situations, and especially in the presence of bourbon, one could clearly hear the man's deep Georgia roots. Donald wondered if he'd had a drink or two tonight.

"Please," said Donald.

"You know that feeling you get in your gut when something just ain't right?" said the president.

Donald's breath slowed. He and the president had only been talking about one subject recently.

"Yes, I know the feeling, sir," he said.

The president was quick to continue his story. "When I was about eight or nine, I was walking barefoot on the back porch and I heard a rattling sound, like a kid's toy. There it was, all coiled up. An eight-foot-long eastern diamondback rattler. Its fangs were dripping, the whole bit. Do you know what I did?"

"Uh, no," Donald said, even though he had a good idea of where this was going. "No, sir."

"I wrapped my little nubs around it and I squeezed until that devil didn't have any fight left. Do you know why I did that?"

A cold shiver ran up and down Donald's spine. This story of the president's was detouring to a very dark place. "Why?" he said, his voice much quieter than he'd intended.

"Because if I hadn't done that," said the president, "the safety of my entire family would have been in jeopardy."

Something had spooked him, Donald realized. But what had changed? Had the president heard about Mr. Gray spotting John Luther at Truth Ministries this afternoon? Was he worried that Luther was going to go on the offensive, turning the tables on them? Did he know something Donald didn't? Or was he just losing his nerve, chickening out?

"Do I make myself clear?" asked the president.

He most definitely did. But Donald wanted to try to lighten the mood. The two politicians were still allies, after all, and friends. There was no need for this to turn ugly.

"By the way, sir," said Donald in a jovial tone, "did you happen to see the polls tonight? They looked superb."

"I don't think you're understanding what I'm saying," the president said. It wasn't a warning; it was a threat.

"I certainly do, sir," Donald assured him. "In a few months, this is all going to be forgotten and you'll be in your second term. Please, just let me handle this, Mr. President."

After a short pause, the president said in his most authoritative voice, "Donald, I wash my hands of this thing. John Luther is *entirely* your misfortune."

There was a sudden click, and the president's voice was replaced by a dial tone. Donald pulled the receiver away from his ear and looked at it. He had to fight the urge to pitch it and the entire phone across the room.

He silently cursed the president. And yet Donald knew he should have seen this coming. All politicians had in common one driving motivation, one overriding purpose above all else, and that was self-preservation. It was only a matter of time before the president withdrew his part in the plan connected with John, thus denying any culpability. It had always been their objective for John to remain on the run for a while as a fugitive; it was so much easier to discredit and marginalize him that way.

Now that the plan was under way, however, and John was out there, moving in the shadows—obviously trying to prove his innocence—the president had thrown it all back on Donald. It was his responsibility alone now. He'd get no credit if everything worked out and would take all the blame if it didn't. None of it could be traced back to the Oval Office.

Donald was angry at the president, but even angrier at John. Why did the man have to be so stubborn? Why couldn't he have just gone along with the Faith and Fairness bill to begin with? Then none of this mess would be happening now.

If this was how John wanted to play it, then Donald had no choice but to oblige him. Maybe it was time to take the game to the next level.

Thinking fast, Donald picked up the receiver again and dialed Mr. Gray's number.

He had to send John Luther a message.

44

Charles Luther fired up his old record player, moving the needle to a piano concerto by Mozart. One of his favorite pieces.

It was otherwise perfectly quiet in the old log cabin. Charles loved this place. He'd bought it ages ago and came here whenever he had some free time. It was situated deep in the woods surrounding Kings Mountain, just forty-five minutes from the North Carolina border, untouched by the lights and commotion and noise of even the smallest of towns, let alone the big cities. It was his sanctuary from the demands of a life of service.

Above his desk was a wall filled with newspaper clippings. It looked like the obsessive work of a criminal profiler or a private detective, but a great importance and purpose was behind Charles's collection. He'd been assembling evidence for months. Well over a year, in fact. Few others saw the mounting signs, but that hadn't stopped Charles.

He sat down at the desk and placed the tiny USB drive John had given him into a slot on the side of his laptop. Already open on the screen was a web browser window showing CNW's front page. The top headline read, *Truth Joins Sumac in Fight for*

Religious Reform. Sumac had made the announcement early this evening, yet astonishingly not a single journalist had made the connection between John's supposed sudden "relapse" and Truth Ministries' shocking policy change.

Charles frowned when a video window popped up as a red light on the little thumb drive flickered. Looking down through his reading glasses, he clicked the play button. The video showed John's Toyota, pulled over to the side of the road in an isolated area. John was slouched in the vehicle's front seat and looked to be unconscious. Just outside, the girl, Aaliyah, stood talking to a tall man in a gray suit. Was that the man from the balcony at the Sumac meeting? Aaliyah turned to face him, and he struck her, hard. He then stuck a syringe into her while holding her in a headlock.

Charles turned sharply in his seat. He'd heard something, a creaking maybe. His heart sped up, his nerves on edge. But the house was perfectly still.

He went back to the video and kept watching.

A moment later, he turned again. This time he looked in the other direction, but again there was nothing but silence—save for the record that was playing in the background. What was it he'd heard? Was he imagining it? Maybe it was some kind of feedback coming from the video.

He returned to his computer. John was right. If they could get the media behind it, this video could at least clear John. Nailing down the true guilty party would be another matter entirely. Tying the man in the gray suit to Senator Harrison, though, would be trickier, if not impossible. Still, there had to be a way.

Charles reached across the desk for his phone and dialed John. It rang for several seconds until an automated voice message finally answered. "Call me when you can," said Charles into the recording, rubbing his rosary beads. "I've found something."

The woods were deathly still, the only visible light coming from the moon. Well, that wasn't completely true. There was a soft orange glow in the distance ahead that must've been from the cabin.

Mr. Gray waved Mr. Broad on with one hand, a nickel-plated pistol in the other. By his own orders both men were wearing latex gloves and hairnets. They may have looked silly, but it was unavoidable. This operation required zero residual presence. Not a single strand of hair or the tiniest piece of flaked-off skin could be left behind.

It took some time to weave between the gnarled trees of this ancient forest, but they couldn't allow their approach to be heard by anyone.

At last they made it to the cabin and slowly climbed the outside stairs one at a time, making sure their footsteps made no noise whatsoever. The front door wasn't even locked.

Inside, Mr. Gray identified the music being played as Mozart's Piano Concerto in D minor. Second movement, if he was not mistaken. This man had exquisite taste.

He and Mr. Broad traced the music to its source, a side room off the main living area. A wooden door was shut tight between them and their target. Would it give them away when they opened it? Mr. Gray was considering searching for an alternative entrance to the room when he heard a voice speaking inside.

"Call me when you can . . ." Mr. Gray recognized it as Charles Luther.

As the man kept talking, Mr. Gray seized the opportunity to grab the doorknob and turn it, assuming the man's voice would mask any sound this made. He needn't have worried. The door slipped open soundlessly on well-oiled hinges.

Mr. Gray quickly took in the details of the room. Across the room, his back to them, Charles Luther sat at a small desk up against one wall. There was a laptop on the desk. The rest of the room had warm, inviting fixtures. A beautiful end table that held a record player. A lovely brass floor lamp with a stained-glass shade. Religious iconography and art adorned the walls.

Noiselessly, Mr. Gray padded across the floor toward the desk. When the old priest hung up the phone, he leveled a silver snub-nosed pistol just inches away from Charles Luther's right temple.

Without hesitation, he pulled the trigger.

The priest's head snapped sideways, then slumped forward.

Mr. Gray and Mr. Broad went immediately into cleanup mode. Mr. Broad lifted a black duffel bag and set it on the desk. He unplugged the laptop and placed it inside the bag, with the USB drive still attached to it. For good measure he took the telephone too.

Mr. Gray carefully placed the pistol in the dead man's hand. Might as well make it look like suicide. Even if John Luther would never buy it, the police might.

Five minutes tops. Whoever Charles Luther had called could return the call or be headed here any minute, and they needed to clear out fast.

Double-checking their work, Mr. Gray nodded to Mr. Broad, and the man slipped back out of the office. Mr. Gray followed, stopping only for one second to reach out a gloved hand and turn off the record player.

Music that beautiful needed an audience. For Charles Luther, there was now only silence.

45

It felt great to swim. John took lap after lap in the hotel's swimming pool, clearing his head and rejuvenating his sore muscles. He'd taken advantage of the fact that it was too late at night for anyone else to be in the pool, and now he had the whole thing to himself. In the water he was weightless, and in the water there was silence. Everything from the last days dissolved, at least for a few moments, and he actually allowed himself to feel normal for the first time in days.

He pushed himself, hard. Much harder than when he swam at the fitness center near his house. It felt as though he was trying to prove something, but he wasn't sure what. Several times he thought he'd be done, on his last lap, but then decided to do one more. Just stroke and kick and breathe, over and over and over.

When finally his legs and lungs burned equally and he could go no more, he retrieved his belongings from the side of the pool and stepped back into his room. He was inside drying off when he noticed a light flashing on the phone his father had given him, which had been poolside while he was swimming. He wasn't used to this thing yet, and so it took a moment or two to figure out what the light signified, finally realizing that someone had left him a voice mail.

John pressed for the message to play and heard his father's anxious baritone on the other end of the line. "Call me when you can," said his father on the message. "I've found something."

John's heart fluttered, but not because of his father's words. Something in his spirit was unsettled, though he couldn't say what. He recognized the feeling. He'd only had it a few times before in his life. Almost always he found out later that it was the Holy Spirit tugging at his senses, coaxing him to pray for Monica or Jodi, at a moment when they were in dire need.

He called his father back right away. It was on the sixth ring when John knew in his soul that something was terribly wrong.

John grabbed his leather jacket and raced out the door.

After a frantic drive up the road leading to Kings Mountain, John finally arrived at the cabin. The lights were on inside the place; he could just make them out from the road. His dad was home, yet he hadn't answered his phone. A short hike through the trees and soon John was standing on the front steps, breathing hard.

He burst through the door. "Dad?" he called.

No answer.

Any chance the old man could be asleep? It was pretty late, after all. Almost eleven o'clock now.

Maybe he was in his study . . .

He ran to his left and flung open the door. "Dad?" he cried.

Charles Luther was slumped over to one side in his desk chair, his eyes closed. John froze, terrified of moving closer, because that would make this real. One foot in front of the other, he slowly inched across the room, hoping his father would wake up and John would discover this had all been a bad dream.

When he reached his dad at last, John leaned around and confirmed his greatest, darkest fear. On the other side of the old man's head was a bullet wound, blood streaking out of it and trailing down his arm to his hand. Dangling from his hand was the string of rosary beads he was never without, blood dripping from the beads into a pool on the floor. A nickel-plated pistol was clutched in his father's hand, but John knew instantly it had been placed there by someone else. Staged. Just as Aaliyah's body had been arranged for the police to find in John's Toyota.

"*Noooo . . . !*"

All of John's strength rushed from his body, and he collapsed to his knees. He knelt next to his father's crumpled form and pressed his head against the old man's. He squeezed his eyes tightly shut and let all his pain and grief pour out in sobs.

When the initial gust of sorrow passed, it was replaced by a rage unlike anything John had ever felt. He clenched his fists and looked around for something to hit, but there was nothing in his father's home that he was willing to destroy.

With a dread-filled start, John glanced at the desk. It was empty. No computer . . . no USB flash drive. He yanked the drawers from the desk and rifled through them, but the drive was nowhere to be found. John ripped the gun out of his father's hand and then, just as quickly, collapsed into a ball on the floor, wracked once more with sobbing.

He'd fought this man. For years and years, they'd fought. And then for years he'd run. So much had passed between them, and only recently did John feel like all the wounds of the past might truly heal one day. But now there was no chance. Now . . .

This couldn't be happening.

Several minutes later, John managed to get to his feet. He staggered out onto the back porch. In one hand he held the pistol; in the other he carried his father's bloodstained rosary beads. His limbs were heavy and numb as he tottered over to the edge of the porch. He leaned out and looked back and forth, half wondering if he might spot his father's murderer. And he knew exactly who the killer would turn out to be—the man in the gray suit. But that man was acting on someone else's orders.

When John was satisfied that no one was around, he tilted his face skyward, trembling with anguish and fury. With all his might he screamed at the top of his lungs, "*Are you not true to your name?!*"

He heard no answer.

After John had exhausted himself screaming to the heavens, he shuffled back inside the cabin.

His father's body sat there in the desk chair where he'd left him. It was as if the old man had been frozen in time. What should John do with him?

Should he bury his father? No, he couldn't. A coroner would need to examine the body before it could be laid to rest. And even before that, there were procedures for this kind of thing. In any murder, police considered the body as evidence. In fact, he shouldn't disturb anything in this room; it was a crime scene. A crime scene he'd placed himself right in the middle of. He'd touched his father. He'd taken the gun from the man's one hand and the rosary from the other. It was too late to put them back. His fingerprints would be on them both.

But he couldn't just leave his father slumped over sideways like that. The very notion felt horribly disrespectful. In just a few short days the body would start to decay, to smell . . .

John felt a sudden nausea, thinking of his father in these kinds of terms. Could this really be happening? *No*. He swallowed hard. He wasn't going to desecrate the scene of the crime any further. There was enough of that already with the old man's blood.

Maybe he could call in an anonymous tip to the police. Yes, that would work!

John dialed 9 . . . then hesitated. He couldn't call it in. There was no way he could report what happened as a suicide. It was too late for that, with his fingerprints on the gun. More than that, it would be a lie—a lie so revolting he couldn't stomach the thought of it.

Besides, any murder connected to John himself would put an even bigger target on his back. John knew how the media worked. They knew he'd had a complicated and often strained relationship with his father. What reconciliation had come between them these last years had been out of the public eye. If there was any suspicion of foul play at all, he'd be guilty in the court of public opinion almost immediately. He was already a desperate fugitive wanted for killing a young woman. Would the murder of his father be that hard to add to the list?

John wanted justice to be served toward those who'd done this evil act, but he could hear his father's voice in his head, reminding him over and over that what was important now was for him to focus on the first task—proving his innocence. Doing that would certainly bring the men who'd executed his father right to him. They'd have no other choice.

John sighed. He had no choice either but to leave the old man exactly as he was. The first chance he could, once everything was settled, he'd make it right. But for now . . .

Looking once more into the study, his eyes caught sight of the wall behind his father's desk, where dozens of newspaper clippings had been cut out and taped to the wall. His father had attached a long string to the papers, making links and connections between various articles. For just a moment, John wondered if they were about him, cuttings and publicity from his past.

He took a step closer. No. The articles weren't about John at all. Not a single one showed any mention of him.

They were about Sumac. It was remarkable really, his father's charting a complete history of the Sumac Alliance. The timeline began with a piece on the formation of a Senate Judiciary Committee on International Religious Freedom, chaired by—surprise, surprise—Senator Donald Harrison. It was dated three years ago. From there, it was easy to see now, in hindsight, that Harrison had begun gathering like-minded supporters through contacts and associations he'd made on that committee. Donald had talked to him once, eighteen months or so ago, about Sumac and whether it was something John saw Truth Ministries being interested in, but John hadn't even given it a second thought. His organization's focus was on sharing the Gospel. That was all.

John wondered how long Donald had been planning the Faith and Fairness bill, putting the pieces into place to build support and momentum in order to get it passed someday.

Many other headlines charted the growth and shaping of the group, which called itself a "nonprofit organization devoted to protecting religious freedoms." John wanted to spit at the irony. There were ups and downs recorded here, triumphs and setbacks on Donald's mission to unite all the major religions and require them to play nice with one another. Plenty of pious quotes from the senator on the importance of religious entities respecting one another and being friends.

"Too long have the religions of this nation focused on what divides them, when there is so much we have to share in common," Donald had said in one article.

It all sounded so nice and friendly—on the surface. So much talk of "mutual respect" and "the inherent cultural and historic value of every system of belief." Nothing wrong with any of it, except that John knew all this rhetoric was merely the public face of Sumac. Donald's true motives went much deeper.

It had been bothering John since the very beginning. What was Donald really after with the Faith and Fairness Act? Was the goal of world religions standing side by side worth killing for? Something about it didn't ring true.

The last article was an analysis of the contents of the Faith and Fairness Act, which ended by pointing out that the bill was scheduled to go before the Senate in just a few weeks' time. The article was dated a little under a week ago.

John took a step back and examined the timeline as a whole. Why had his father been following Sumac's formation and progress all this time? This had to have taken him years to compile.

It came to John in a rush of understanding. The old man had known all along. He'd come to see Sumac as a powerful organization that would one day stand in direct opposition to his son's ministry. Truth Ministries had risen to become one of the most popular evangelistic ministries in the world. John himself had become something of a celebrity, his name well known around the globe.

Of course, Truth and Sumac would come into conflict. It was inevitable.

Charles couldn't have known that his son would one day be the target of a conspiracy to frame him for murder, thereby discrediting him. But he had been watching and waiting for a very long time.

John had always despised politics, but his father had demonstrated a keen eye for it and tried to convince his son of the importance of staying on top of international legislation. Although he'd been trying to interest John in politics for years, John never really understood his father's fascination with it.

Until now.

46

Have you had any further contact with John Luther?" asked Clark, as Rivera worked on attaching a wired microphone to Ryan Morris's chest.

Morris almost laughed at the very notion. "Not a peep."

Rivera was unimpressed by his ego. "You sure about that?"

Morris smiled that smarmy grin of his. "Hey, I'm on your side."

"The only way to be protected is to be completely honest," Rivera said, watching him. She glanced at Clark, who was studying him as well. His expression was blank, but Rivera noticed his jaw was clenched.

He didn't trust Ryan Morris. Rivera was glad.

It was awfully late for a clandestine meeting between John Luther and his wife, but Morris swore it was the time Luther had requested that he bring Monica to the Hotel Blue. There'd been no sign of the preacher yet.

"Hey, if he said he'll show, he'll show," said Morris, defensive. "What more do you want?"

Agent Clark kept his gaze leveled on Morris. "What I want,"

he said, "is for you to give us more information about the activities of Senator Harrison."

There it was at last. The proverbial elephant in the room. After their interview of Shanice Evans, it was Clark who'd posited that Ryan Morris owed his sudden promotion to the maneuvering of Senator Donald Harrison. And based on Morris's reaction to Clark's gambit just now, it looked like he was spot-on.

For the first time since they'd met him, Morris was taken aback and not quick to answer. "I . . . I can't speak to that," he said. "I don't really know him. Look, you've read John's file. He had it in him to do this."

Everyone does, Rivera thought. And it didn't escape her attention that Morris had just tried very hard to change the subject. "We're well aware of his history, thank you," she said with a sour note. She finished up with the wire and walked away. Rivera was worried that if she spent any more time in close quarters with this man, she might slug him.

And she was fairly certain that he'd flirted with her at least twice while she was applying the microphone.

Morris pulled his shirt down and stood. "Listen," he said, stepping closer to Clark and taking on a conspiratorial tone, "I don't mean to be disrespectful, but what do they pay you guys for?" He laughed and propped an arm on Agent Clark.

That was it. Now Rivera was certain she would have punched that stupid smile off his face if she were still standing close to him. For his part, Clark looked down at Morris's arm with a threatening gaze.

Morris removed his arm but kept his mouth running. "I mean, prostitution, addiction, gambling . . . it's written all over him. We thought he changed. And we're all about forgiveness and grace. But I gotta tell you . . . this has caused me to doubt my faith a little bit."

While he spoke, Morris opened the room's tiny fridge. Was

he seriously looking for a drink? As if they would let him consume alcohol while he was supposed to be roping Luther in for them! Disappointed to find the refrigerator empty, he turned to the floor-to-ceiling mirror affixed to the wall next to it and examined his appearance.

"But that's the lesson," he concluded.

Rivera watched Clark work. As always, she was impressed with his ability to get people to spill their guts. He switched gears.

"It must be really hard for you to have to take on all that responsibility," said Clark, "especially with no advance notice."

Ryan nodded enthusiastically, as if excited to extol his own virtues. "See, people forget this about Truth Ministries—the size of the thing. It has the same nuts and bolts as a Fortune 500 company. And I'm running it! This ain't no sleigh ride, trust me."

"Oh, I can imagine," said Clark, patronizing him.

Morris seemed to be oblivious. He strode to the hotel room's window and looked out, obviously hoping to spot John Luther approaching. He whirled back around to face the detectives. "All right," he said. "Let's do this."

Rivera glanced at Clark, and for just a second she was sure she saw him roll his eyes.

47

Monica.

John's father was dead, murdered as an obvious message, and now all John could think about was Monica. Was she next on the list? Would Donald go that far?

It was the thought that stopped the tears, at least for the moment. His eyes became laser beams, focused on a single target—Donald Harrison. Had Donald really done all this because of his precious bill? Had he murdered two innocent people to get the Faith and Fairness Act passed?

John prayed it wasn't so, but couldn't conjure any hope on the matter. Not anymore.

After driving back into the city, he went straight to the Hotel Blue, intending to rendezvous with Monica. She would be there. She had to be. How would she react when he told her his father had been killed?

The hotel was ahead on the left, and true to his word, Ryan had brought Monica. John knew because Ryan's Corvette was there in the parking lot. It was parked in a handicap space, but whatever. That was just Ryan being Ryan. At least he'd come.

John was about to turn into the hotel's driveway when he spotted an unmarked black SUV parked just outside the hotel, in front of a dumpster. Odd place to park. John lowered his window to get a better look. The white license plate on the back of the vehicle was government-issued.

Ryan . . . John grimaced as he pushed down on the gas pedal, speeding past the hotel.

Either Ryan had called the Feds or they had approached him. John hoped against hope it was the latter, because the former would mean that his most trusted lieutenant had betrayed him.

And that he could not fathom.

Mr. Gray had studied countless fighting techniques and styles, trained meticulously with firearms and weapons, and had been a voracious student in the lessons of pain to be able to become the kind of professional he was today. He'd never had the opportunity, though, to watch himself at work until this very night.

The USB drive's surprising footage had at first angered him. The world today with its ubiquitous cameras and constant unblinking eyes. He'd scouted that location days in advance and chosen it in particular for how deserted it often appeared. And still, there'd been someone watching. Filming.

Yet the anger he felt turned to fascination as the video played out. He watched himself move through the steps he'd coordinated in his head. Each and every movement planned and executed with precision. He hadn't lost a step in that respect.

On the screen he sent the girl reeling with a short blow to the head and then followed it up with the syringe. She never felt a thing. Behind her, he could see the passenger side door open and John Luther stumble to freedom, just as planned. After another minute or two of filming, the man emerged huffing and disoriented up the hill, the camera's lens watching him the entire way. Whoever shot the footage stayed silent. Then the man disappeared into the woods once more, and the camera rustled a bit before switching off.

But not until it had moved a few unsteady steps toward a worn-down trailer promising tattoos. Mr. Gray reversed the footage, then paused it when the building came up again. He stared at the screen, nodding slowly. His loose end had a home.

Pulling out both his phone and his Glock, Mr. Gray placed a single phone call. When it was answered, he said, "We have a complication, sir, but fixable."

The voice on the line replied simply, "Then fix it."

Mr. Gray clicked off, slipped on his suit coat, and hurried out to his sedan. He looked at the dashboard clock as he entered and made some mental calculations. Thirty-three minutes to drive there. Fifteen to do the job. Ten to clean the place. Thirty-three minutes back. Should everything fall into place, he'd be back by midnight at the latest. He gunned the engine and was on his way.

It turned out he'd been wrong about the timing. It took him thirty-one minutes to arrive. The stoplights had been in his favor.

Parking once more at the bottom of the hill, Mr. Gray pulled the gun from its holster, just in case of the unexpected, and took the same ragged path up that John Luther had the other night. Above him, the moon glowed silver, the only thing that had gone wrong so far. It would've helped to have had some cloud cover should someone happen to be watching again. These days, someone always seemed to be watching.

This time, though, no one was. He reached the American Woman tattoo parlor in silence, his approach muffled by the music rumbling from inside. Three rusted cars waited outside, a good sign that his target might be inside. The music rattled the frail bones of the building, and a few people let out shouts of excitement. A party. Mr. Gray had one guess what had funded the celebration.

He tucked his gun back in the holster and, making a last-minute correction in his plans, knocked on the door.

Nothing.

He knocked again, louder. This time someone inside turned down the music. Muffled questions were exchanged. He knocked one last time.

Finally the door squeaked open, and a red-eyed shirtless man looked out, an annoyed expression on his face. "Help you, man?"

"Sir, I'm with the task force searching for John Luther, the fugitive who disappeared around here a few nights ago. We're canvassing the area, talking to everyone we can."

"Sure, yeah. Umm . . ." Apparently lying didn't come easily when a person was stoned. "I don't think I saw any . . . uh, fugitives."

Mr. Gray motioned to the party still going on in the back of the building. "How about your friends there? Did any of them happen to see anything suspicious?"

"Kinda late, man," he whined, but when Mr. Gray didn't budge from where he stood at the door, he sighed and called, "Nolan!"

Soon a thin black guy slipped out from behind a curtain and approached warily.

Once Mr. Gray had finished asking the same few questions, the black guy replied, "Man, lots of strange white guys showing up here lately."

Mr. Gray smiled. "So you *have* seen John Luther—the preacher on TV."

"Yeah, we seen him. Was here yesterday. This soiree is in honor of him, in fact."

From the depths of the trailer, two new faces emerged, both of them women. One was blond and looked frail. The other had dark-rimmed eyes and a unicorn shirt on. Mr. Gray looked at both, and when the unicorn girl met his eyes, he saw her recognition. She'd had the camera. The one who'd done such a good job filming him.

"Did you tell anyone else?" he called to her.

"What?" Nolan said.

"Did. You. Tell. Anyone. Else," Mr. Gray repeated. This time the girl shook her head. He believed her.

"That's too bad," he said. In a flash, the Glock was out, and both men went down before they could even cry out. The girls took a minute longer, but the music was loud enough that he didn't worry if their cries had been heard. Just another wild party.

Mr. Gray looked at his watch. Fifteen minutes exactly.

It took ten minutes more, and American Woman burned as bright as the evening's moon.

On a phone call during the thirty-three minute drive home, Mr. Gray made assurances that all complications had been fixed. He made it back before midnight, just as planned.

The only task left for the evening was to destroy the flash drive. But maybe not right away. Maybe he would watch the video one more time.

48

Not knowing where else to go, John drove to St. Peter's, entering again through the secret sewer entrance he'd escaped from just a few nights ago. Though it felt to him more like *weeks* ago.

Had he been in a better frame of mind, it would have bothered him terribly that he was filthy and haggard, disheveled strands of hair hanging from his forehead. But this was a night like no other.

A young priest John didn't recognize was in the sanctuary, holding a small midnight mass. A line of about a dozen parishioners was lined up in the center aisle, with the priest standing at the altar and handing out the sacraments for Holy Communion.

John stepped forward and joined the line. He was the last one, and while the priest clearly didn't know him, he didn't deny him the bread and wine. John took them gratefully, ingested them, and then closed his eyes in an impassioned, sorrowful prayer. He knew for some it probably wouldn't be considered appropriate for him to partake in Communion, but he desperately needed a connection to his dad, and this place was all that was left of him.

Would God hear his prayers this night? Would he honor them?

Would he answer?

After the service ended, John remained in his seat. Once all the other parishioners had left, he made his way to the priest's office. His father's office, though he knew this younger priest would be using it tonight.

John opened the door without knocking and stepped inside. The priest stood in the far corner, hanging up his vestments in an armoire. He didn't turn as John entered, so he must not have heard him.

John was so distraught, and his standing in this room only made things worse. Dark, with little more than candlelight to provide illumination, it was like a funeral home late at night. Serene, but eerie and vacant.

"It feels cold in here without him," John said. Had he said it to the priest or to himself, he wasn't sure.

The priest turned with a look of surprise. "Sorry?" he said. As he got a better look at John, he grew visibly concerned. "Sir, are you all right? You don't look well."

John didn't *feel* well. He was pale and nauseous, cold sweat droplets covering his skin. He stepped farther into the room and took a seat in a violet wingback chair.

"He's dead," John said, sickened as the words touched his tongue. "He was executed."

The priest took a tentative step toward him. "Who?"

"Your priest," John said. He looked the young man in the eye. "My father."

The man's countenance changed dramatically. He seemed to have trouble digesting what John was saying. He knelt in front of John and placed a hand on his shoulder. Compassion poured from his features, accompanied by deep concern. Did he think John was a crazed homeless person or something?

"What do you mean?" asked the young priest gently.

John reached into his jacket pocket. "Exactly what I said," he replied. He produced his father's rosary, stained with his blood.

The priest's eyes grew bigger as they fell on the beads. He pulled back his hand from John's shoulder, and John saw the truth swallow him. He looked so grieved, John's heart was pierced all over again. Charles may have been John's biological father, but he was also this young man's spiritual father.

The priest blinked, his eyes filling with tears. "My name is William." He swallowed hard.

William. John remembered the name. "The last time I was here, my father spoke very highly of you."

William said nothing but held eye contact with John. He looked to be in shock, struggling to make sense of things, feeling the first onset of grief and disbelief.

"Can you help me, William?"

49

18 YEARS AGO

Sleep was always impossible to come by in jail. He'd tried the first few times he'd been arrested to at least get some shut-eye, but after the third time, John had given up on that hope. First, they never shut off all the lights. Second, there was the noise—the talking and cursing, the snoring, people going to the bathroom just a few feet away from him. Third was the terrible smell that seeped into his nose and mouth.

So here he was, wide awake after midnight, when a guard came to the cell door and shouted his name.

John was told someone had posted bail. The officer quickly led him out of the lockup area to the check-in desk, where his personal items were returned to him.

Who bailed him out? He looked around the waiting area, but there were no familiar faces. Had Jackie decided to forgive him? Again? No, she'd made her feelings very clear.

John exited the building and found it colder outside than he'd remembered. But then he remembered very little about when he'd been brought in several hours ago.

Parked right in front of the police department's front door was a familiar station wagon, its engine running and spewing visible exhaust out the back. And at the wheel sat Charles Luther, his dad. John tried to remember the last time he'd seen the old man. It had to have been more than a year ago. He certainly hadn't told his dad he was back in the area.

"Thanks," he said with sincerity as he got in the car. "How'd you know I was in there?"

"You're welcome," said Charles. He put the car in gear and pulled into traffic. "Alonso Marquez was on the desk when you were booked. He's part of my congregation and knew I would want to hear that my son was back in town."

John watched the dashboard clock tick by for six minutes while neither of them said another word. Finally he couldn't take it anymore.

"If you want to fuss at me or list all the ways I'm a disappointment, please have at it," said John. "I've got it coming."

"It's tempting," said Charles, a smile playing at the corners of his mouth, "but I'll pass. You're thirty-one years old, John. You're way beyond my disciplinary jurisdiction."

John looked down at his shoes and chuckled. Good ol' Dad. He hadn't changed. In some ways, John hoped he never would. Despite the lectures in the past, John couldn't deny that Charles had always been there when John needed him. Always. John's demeanor turned dark as he pondered that.

"Why do you still help me, Dad?" he asked. "We both know I don't deserve it. I've spit in your face a hundred times. I wouldn't blame you if you turned your back and never wanted to see me again."

"Well, maybe I know something you don't."

Charles turned and looked at him. "What?"

"I know what it means to be a father," he said, his eyes never leaving the road.

John wished he could be more like his old man. Mountains of patience, limitless grace, and never once, despite all John had done, had Charles hurled guilt in his direction.

"Since I paid for your freedom," said Charles without a hint of condemnation or even sarcasm, "would you mind telling me what I spent my money on?"

John's insides withered, and he was certain he'd just shrunk to about two feet tall. He tried hard to blink back the tears, but failed.

"Jackie called the cops," John said, his voice thick and heavy. "I hit her, Dad."

Charles absorbed this in silence as John wept softly.

"Has it happened before?" asked the old man.

John bit his lip and nodded.

"Are you always drunk when it happens?" asked Charles. Even though he was careful to keep the judgment out of his voice, John could still detect the disappointment his dad was unable to mask completely.

John knew his father could smell the alcohol on his breath right now. He nodded again.

"Why? Why did you do it, John? What happened tonight?"

John let out a long sigh. "We were arguing. About money."

Charles nodded. "Gambling again?"

"Yeah," said John. "Jackie kicked me out tonight. She said . . . She wants a divorce, Dad." He began to sob again, his eyes squeezed shut and his shoulders shaking.

After a few minutes, John collected himself and sat in silence again. If it was possible to feel worse about himself than he did at this moment, he couldn't imagine it. And to confess it all to the best man he knew, the priest who was his father . . .

He was drowning in shame.

Charles pulled the car over and stopped in a parallel parking spot.

"John," he said, turning his whole body toward the passenger seat, "I know you think you're the worst of sinners. But you're no worse than me. Or anyone else."

John looked at him but couldn't hold the old man's gaze. He stared forward and shook his head.

"You've been searching for something your whole life, son. And we both know it's not your mother."

No. It really wasn't. John couldn't explain what it was exactly. But it wasn't her. He'd given up trying to find her ages ago.

"If you want my opinion," said the old man, "that thing you've been looking for has been right in front of your nose the whole time."

John looked up as his dad pointed at something beyond the windshield. John leaned forward and peered through the glass. A block ahead and across the street was the silhouette of a small church. Backlit by streetlights, the black outline of a cross stood tall against the night sky.

John sighed. "Dad, you know how I feel about that stuff."

"I know," said Charles. "But just think about it, John. Please. For me."

John had no desire to give any thought at all to religion. He'd been bombarded by that sort of thing during his entire childhood and never wanted to think about it again.

But he couldn't say no to his dad. Not tonight.

"Okay," he promised. "I will."

Charles patted him on the leg. Turning back to the wheel, he asked, "So where can I take you?"

Only one answer came to mind. Before tonight, he would have been humiliated to admit it or say it out loud. But just now, he didn't care.

"Home?" he said. He was dead tired, his last resource of energy tapped out. He sniffed and wiped his eyes. "Can I just go home for a little while, Dad?"

The old man smiled.

50

PRESENT DAY

Monica couldn't help wondering why she was bothering to drop Jodi off at school each morning. As if everything were perfectly normal, as if her whole world weren't slipping from her a little more every minute John was away.

Yet life had to go on, and she had a responsibility to keep Jodi away from all this. It was what John would want, and what Monica wanted as well. Jodi was far too young to deal with the madness that was her parents' lives at the moment. As far as the girl knew, her dad was working away from home—called away on a trip somewhere. Jodi hadn't asked how long he'd be gone, and Monica hadn't offered an answer.

As she drove into the school parking lot, she wondered what kind of commentary it was on John's passion for Truth Ministries that his daughter found it perfectly normal not to see him for days and days. Monica turned off the ignition and sighed, thinking about where John could be right now. An ache filled her heart when she realized, for the hundredth time, that she had no idea where he was.

She took Jodi by the hand and walked with her through the steel double doors at the private school, where Jodi was in first grade. Jodi tugged at her hand when Monica led her past her classroom door.

"Sorry, sweetie," said Monica. She hadn't even noticed the classroom.

Was she even really here, in this building? Was any of this really happening? How could it be? Every teacher or parent that she passed in the hall gaped at her, though some of them had the good grace to look away and try to act like nothing was wrong. She hoped Jodi wouldn't notice the strange looks being sent their way.

Why was John staying so far away from her? Didn't he realize they were in this together, and that she could help him?

No. Monica was being too emotional. She told herself to think rationally, and she would know that John was keeping away from them in order to protect them. Plus, she was still under police surveillance twenty-four hours a day. If he came near, he would be caught.

She just felt so helpless, wanting to help him but not being able to—or allowed to. Even though she knew it was unreasonable, even though she was ashamed to admit it, in her weakest moments the worst thoughts and doubts still crept in. When she woke in the middle of the night, and the darkness pressed in on her, she couldn't help but worry that everything they were saying about John was true. He *had* done terrible things in his past. In the years they'd been married, they both knew several men in the ministry who'd fallen—who'd cheated on wives or taxes, who'd become overwhelmed by gambling or alcohol. One pastor they knew from Tacoma had even been arrested for domestic abuse. Good men fell all the time.

No, that wasn't fair. Monica knew her husband, and he was not a man who would murder. Even years ago, at his lowest of lows, when he was drugged out of his mind and drunk all the time, he would never have taken someone's life.

Monica looked around and found herself outside the school's front door. How had she gotten here? Did Jodi make it to her classroom? Had Mrs. Goodwin smiled and spoken to her as she always did when she dropped Jodi off in the morning?

She couldn't remember.

She sighed and walked to the car. On the driver's seat was a piece of paper she didn't recognize. It had probably fallen out of Jodi's backpack or something.

Monica grabbed the paper and slowly sat in the seat. She unfolded the paper and gasped when she recognized the handwriting—it was John's sloppy, oversized scribbling.

He was here! She glanced at the note and confirmed it. At the bottom of the page were written the words *Love, John.*

Monica spun in her seat, surveying the parking lot and the entire surrounding area. John had left the note in the car for her to find while she was inside with Jodi, so he had to be close by!

She looked and looked, praying for something, even just a glimpse of him. But wherever he was hiding, he was doing it well. She reminded herself that it wasn't like this the first time he'd gone off the grid. He spent so many years running from his father, from God, even from himself. He knew how to be invisible.

She gave up her searching and sank back into the seat to read his letter.

Monica,

I love you so, so much. I hope you still believe in me. I want to see you and Jodi, but I can't—they're watching you.

They shot Dad. He's dead, ~~and I don't know if I can keep~~ but I have to keep going.

I can't believe he's gone. (Don't tell Jodi yet.)

Please pray for me. I miss you both so much. But I have to finish this. One way or another, this will be over soon.

Love,
John

Monica's hand was over her mouth. She felt light-headed.

Charles . . . He was dead? But how? Why would anyone kill a priest? It made no sense.

And John . . . He would be devastated—no, *destroyed*—by losing his father. This couldn't be happening, it just couldn't.

How would she break it to Jodi? More and more over the years, Charles had become a part of their lives, and Jodi—who knew nothing of the hurts of the past—simply went nuts with joy over her granddad. But no, John said not to tell her yet. Good, that was good.

No, that was dumb. *Nothing* was good about any of this. Not one thing. Where was God now, when her family needed him more than ever?

She didn't care about the danger anymore. Why wouldn't John let her in?

John made it around to the rear of the school, where the playground was, just as Jodi's class came out to play. They always had a few minutes of playtime first thing in the morning, and there she was.

Monica would be reading his note right about now. He wished he could see her when she found it, hug her after she read it, cry with her when she found out about his dad. At least he could see Jodi for a few minutes, even if it was from a distance.

A locked iron gate stood between John and his little girl, but he could see her plainly. She was skipping through the playground, laughing and playing with the other kids. She was wearing that cute little pink dress, and Monica had braided her hair in pigtails.

John closed his eyes, trying to sear this image of Jodi into his mind. If this was the last time he would ever see his daughter, he wanted it to be this picture of her that he remembered. This one, perfect moment. She was free from the sorrows and dangers he now had to confront, and he was so grateful for that. Her innocence was intact.

He put a hand on the iron bars and leaned in. How he wished he could hold Jodi, feel her little arms squeeze him around the neck, receive her sweet kisses on that one spot she always gravitated to on his cheek. A single tear leaked out as he watched her play.

"Father, please protect my wife and child," he said under his breath.

With a deep breath, John stood up straight and put his sunglasses back on. His father was dead. For better or worse, John was the man he was today because of that man, and John would never see him again in this life. Then there was the evidence that could have exonerated him. It was perfect, iron-clad. He had to assume that Donald had destroyed it by now. Plus, his most loyal colleague, his most passionate supporter, may have betrayed him.

How could he have any chance of winning? Of *surviving* this madness? He still had something to live for. To *fight* for. Two somethings.

And they were enough.

51

It wasn't like Agent Carter to disappear, particularly so close to lunch. When he was in the office, Carter's lunchtime was one of the long-standing traditions the man had, and Rivera was worried that she hadn't seen her partner for over half an hour. She'd jumped up to grab a quick mug of coffee, and when she returned, his desk chair was empty and nobody had even seen him leave.

She sat down at her desk and pulled out her file notes. Despite every best intention, this case was getting under her skin. More than that, Washington, D.C. was getting under her skin. And she couldn't say she hadn't been warned.

Rivera had started her career as a local police officer in a small Wisconsin town just west of Madison. She graduated from the University of Wisconsin with dual honors degrees in criminal justice and psychology, and had the bureau on the top of her wish list. But then the hiring freezes came, and she knew her chances of being selected while completely green were almost nil. So she took the closest job she could find, crashed with her parents when off duty, and spent most of her hours chasing down drunk Sconnie high schoolers fishtailing from one side of town to the other. The local sheriff, Beth Gibson, had been perhaps the second best mentor she'd ever had—next to Clark. She'd been the one to warn Rivera that the grass she dreamed of might be greener, but that luxury came at a cost.

"Even in Madison," Gibson had said, "anywhere there's a building with a dome in this country, there's somebody who'll pull strings to get away with murder. Or if not murder, then something that'll seem just as bad. And the movies you see about honest cops who don't play along? They won't kill you—that's all fiction. No. If you don't dance for them, they'll bury you so deep in the organization, you barely have the authority to shut your own office door, let alone stand for what's right." The woman nodded. "Don't know what it is about domed buildings."

Rivera couldn't see the U.S. Capitol building from her desk, but somehow she felt its long shadow stretching ever closer. And then the shadow was there, black and solid and imposing. She looked up.

"Lunch," Clark said, motioning with a thumb.

"Where—?" she started to ask, but he held up a hand to silence her, and she knew better than to ask. Every desk had a set of ears behind it. While she trusted most of them, she knew some of that trust was misplaced. Clark trusted no one. It felt cynical, but it was probably safer in the long run.

They took the stairs rather than the elevator. Rivera guessed that was mostly so he could let off some steam.

"Not doing the usual?" she asked, chasing after him.

This was what worried her most at the moment. Agent Preston Clark, when at his desk during lunch at Quantico, never failed to follow the same routine. He would check his fantasy sports team online, eat a grilled-pork sandwich delivered from the Vietnamese restaurant down the street, and then he'd pull up every crime and automobile database to which he had access and spend the next twenty minutes looking for anything that'd help him hunt down the man who'd killed his wife. Every day he could, he made this search. It was his penance.

"We're going out for lunch" was his only reply.

They hit the ground floor, headed straight for the parking garage, and were soon driving out of headquarters. Rivera would let him explain when he was ready. For now, he kept silent. The drive only lasted four minutes before they pulled into a different Vietnamese restaurant, one Clark usually refused to eat at.

"We're not here under duress," he assured her. He looked around at the place and sighed. "Although I'd feel better about eating here if we were."

But to her, the restaurant looked like nearly every Asian joint she'd ever visited. In the back corner, she saw the reason for their visit. "Director Graves," she said.

"We are not here under duress," Clark whispered again, and this time she caught his tone. Graves wasn't here to pull strings. There was something else going on.

"Agent Rivera," he said, standing, "so glad you could join us. I know your partner here loves Vietnamese food, and I thought it'd be a good opportunity to break bread together. Or break *banh mi*," he laughed, then pointed to the omnipresent sandwich that could be found from here to Hanoi.

Rivera ordered a vermicelli salad with grilled shrimp and watched as her partner sighed his way through the menu, nearly in distress. He finally settled on a simple order of spring rolls and an iced coffee.

"Watching your figure, Clark?" Graves laughed at his own joke and then let his humor fade into an uncomfortable silence. He looked at Clark, who shrugged.

"Agent Rivera, your partner has just been in a meeting to which you were not invited. He was sworn *not* to mention anything said at that meeting, even to you. That order came from

Assistant Director Wesley Walters, and is one I insisted Agent Clark here not dismiss. But . . . since Assistant Director Wesley Walters reports to me—as much as I know he hates it—he's not in a position to give me such an order. And I happen to know what was said in that meeting."

The shadow had reached them for real this time.

"Your names are known," Graves began. "And for lowly agents, no offense, that's not a good thing. That means someone is watching you. That means someone is talking about you."

"Do you know where the pressure is coming from?" Rivera asked. She felt her blood rising. Clark sat calmly, and she could almost have punched him for it. Puppets, strings . . . she hated being yanked around by others.

"We do not, specifically. My protégé, Assistant Director Wesley Walters, has a certain talent for hearing things and knowing everyone. You may hear bitterness in my voice as I say it, but I must also give credit where credit is due. That skill is not one that can be learned. He's a natural, and I'm sure, when he's cashed in all his favors, he'll find a way to pay me back for whatever wrongs he thinks I'm paying him. I have no doubt that within a year he'll be my superior. In the meantime, he has control of the information, and we can only make suppositions."

The server arrived with their food, and for a few moments they all fell into silence as they ate. Clark looked miserable. Rivera thought her salad tasted fine. Fish sauce, noodles, shrimp, cilantro, bean sprouts. It wasn't rocket science.

"And so you want us to . . . ?" she finally encouraged. She wasn't sure yet why Director Graves had called them there, except maybe to be a monkey wrench in his subordinate's plans. And that felt just as manipulative.

"My preference in most of these situations is to let God sort out the guilty by who's left standing at the end. So often the sides that tangle against each other in this town are equally culpable, equally dangerous. Occasionally, though, something from the outside gets trapped in their way. And they've forgotten how to play against anything but their enemies."

He was being cryptic, but Rivera could read between the lines. She'd been feeling more and more like John Luther might have been set up. Clark would never let her make such a leap without solid evidence, yet just by agreeing to this meeting she knew he'd been having a similar hunch.

"So, we press on?" she asked. She still wasn't sure what was said in the meeting, but she could sure guess. Assistant Director Walters had likely asked, in a tone that was really a demand, that Clark focus his investigation more fully on Luther as their prime suspect. Anything else that came their way was to be ignored.

"Press on. Absolutely." Graves smiled, and having made himself clear, he pulled the morning's *Post* from his briefcase. Straining to read upside down, Rivera could see the front page article touted the upcoming vote on the Faith and Fairness Act. Senator Donald Harrison was getting himself a *lot* of press over it.

"Changing subjects, sir," she said. "What do you think of this bill that's up for consideration?"

"Faith and Fairness?" Graves said, glancing down at the article. "I would think *everyone* should be for fairness, don't you agree?"

Rivera stopped chewing. Something in the way he'd asked the question gave her pause.

"Fairness is a noble aim," she said, "although it seems like a strange demand to make of things that are often diametrically opposed. Forcing them to coexist, doesn't that render them meaningless? It's like saying 'I want to go up' and being forced to say 'I want to go down' at the same time. You get nowhere."

Graves squinted. "Nowhere indeed."

Clark, who'd mostly just been staring at his sad lunch, took one last small bite, chewed, then swallowed. "Sorry, but our time is up, Director. We should get back before anyone starts worrying about us."

Graves waved them off and settled back to his meal.

Rivera followed Clark across the restaurant on their way to the door. In her mind, she kept hearing the words of Sheriff Gibson, *"Domed buildings. What is it about those domed buildings."*

When they reached the door, Graves's voice stopped them before they could make their exit. "Truth wins, Agent Rivera," the man said. "Maybe not right away. But I pursued this career with that hope. Truth, someday, will win."

Stepping out into the growing shadows of the afternoon, Rivera wished she could believe him.

52

17 YEARS AGO

More than anything, John wanted a beer. In all his wanderings these last years, he wasn't sure he'd ever been quite so hot as now, working on this road crew, fixing sections of blacktop that had buckled under the merciless Georgia sun. To his left, a sun-dappled stream snaked its way alongside the road, glinting in the light. A beer and his feet in the water, that was what John Luther wanted more than anything.

"Luther!" the foreman shouted. John startled. He'd been staring off rather than working his pickaxe. He raised a hand to the man in apology but didn't lift his eyes. Eye contact just meant an opportunity for the man to lay into him again.

"Don't make Big Tony angry," said Miles Washington, a short man with the blackest skin John had ever seen. "His wife forgot to pack him coffee this morning, so he'll be worse than usual all day." In the weeks since John had secured this job, Miles was the only other worker to show up consistently and the only other person interested in sharing more than two words with him. What they'd learned over the last days was that they had a whole lot in common—including stints in prison, preachers for fathers, and everyday battles with some kind of addiction. For Miles it was gambling—dice, horses, college basketball, anything. John was just past one year without a drink or a pill. Anything. But the sun today might just be the ruin of him.

"Do you think, Miles," he said, "when you're a millionaire, you'd rather have a house in the mountains or a place on the ocean?" It was a game they'd invented a week ago to distract themselves and to pass the time. Each of them asking outlandish questions of what they'd do when their luck finally turned around.

"Mountains," Miles answered. "But next to a great big lake full of trout and perch for dinner. You?"

John nodded. "My father has a place in the mountains. He says he hears God there in a way he can't anywhere else." In years past, that kind of memory would just have made John bitter, but ever since his father had bailed him out a year ago, something had thawed between them. John still felt restless, still ended up leaving his dad's house after a while. But he sent postcards every few weeks now and even called the old man up last week just to talk. "But me, I'd buy a place in the south of Spain. Learn the flamenco and find myself a señorita."

"South of Spain?" Miles laughed. "What do you know about the south of Spain?"

John laughed along with him and then realized, just for those brief moments, he'd forgotten about his thirst for beer. The rest of the day went on like that. Hours spent dodging his craving, minutes spent enjoying the company of this man he called a friend.

When they finally packed it in, Miles approached John with a look of embarrassment on his face.

"What's the matter?" John asked.

Miles took a deep breath and kicked at the road. "I meant to mention it earlier, but . . . well, it's just strange." John waited, and the man finally continued, "It's my father, the bishop. Turns out he's in town."

John nodded.

"He got in contact with me. Told me he was setting his tent up for a few nights. There's a farmer who's letting him use his sweet-potato field, south of here down on Jackson. And tonight's the last night."

Miles still wouldn't make eye contact with John, who then realized this wasn't just information—it was an invitation. "Are you asking me to come with you?"

Miles shrugged. "I told the bishop . . . my father, that I'd try to swing by. And I *know* you ain't got nothing more important going on."

John couldn't argue that, and he surprised Miles by saying, "Okay, I'll go."

"You will?"

Any other night he probably would have made up some excuse, but the sun still looked like it was directly overhead, and John knew what would happen if he faced the heat alone tonight. It'd been a year and he didn't want to screw up. "A tent sounds cooler than that flophouse where I'm staying. Let's go."

Stopping only briefly to rinse off and change into something fresher, the two were soon headed out of town to the meeting. Down every street a handful of people made their way until there was a stream of folks chatting and laughing and kicking up dust. Half a mile from the tent, three enterprising young men had set up a spit and had barbecue roasting. Nearby a young woman was selling lemonade. Miles and John couldn't pass it up; they ate their dinner while walking the rest of the way to the tent.

Full and exhausted from the day, John took a seat near the back of the tent. Miles disappeared, apparently to go find his father and say hello. Just as he'd hoped, the tent's shadow cut the heat by at least fifteen degrees, and the lightest of breezes even managed to make its way to John's sweaty brow. This, he guessed, would be one of the greatest naps he would ever take in his life.

Only it didn't go that way.

Miles reappeared just as John was about to drift off, all nervous and chattering. Seeing his father had put him on edge the same way seeing Charles always got John's nerves to jangling.

"Said my sister might get engaged. And our old mutt lost an ear to a bobcat, of all things." Miles continued to natter on about places John had never been, people John didn't know, and family history to which John was not privy. John was just about to tell him to knock it off when a gospel choir burst into song from behind them and the show started.

And it was a show.

First the music. Then the testimonies. Then more music. Stories of changed lives. Healed joints. Twenty minutes of quiet prayer, where John *did* doze for a while, only to be woken by even more music—including a woman soloing on "I'll Fly Away," who may have been the best singer John had ever heard in his life. This wasn't a bad way to spend a night, after all. And it was for free. John thought he might have to give Miles some guff for not inviting him to the previous two nights.

Then everything whirled to a halt, and a man who looked a lot like Miles, only with less hair and more gut, sauntered up to the podium.

John waited, expectant. He'd seen revival preachers before, their energy and almost manic shouting about God. He'd enjoyed the show so far and wouldn't mind a bit more before calling it a night.

But Bishop Washington didn't shout or dance or anything like that. The man's voice was deep and low, so quiet when he first started that John actually had to lean forward to hear him.

He couldn't exactly say when in the next ninety minutes he began to cry, but at some point he became aware that tears were pouring down his face. At one point, Miles gave him a strange look and then passed over a wadded-up napkin left over from dinner. John didn't bother with the napkin. Instead he just kept listening.

How was it he'd never heard this before today? He knew his own father said these words most every week, yet he never really *heard* them. They just sounded like Charles.

Tonight, in Bishop Washington's hushed voice, they came in a whisper that sounded like the very thing he'd been trying to hear all his life.

"You've been looking," the bishop said. "Looking hard, looking everywhere. Searching for anything that'll last more than a few seconds, more than a few minutes, more than a night. And you might have found somebody, but I will tell you, even they will only last you for their life. But there *is* something, and when you find it, it'll never leave."

On and on the bishop preached. Simple and true. Jesus. And when the call finally came, when the invitation was made, John was the first to reach the stage.

"God has big things planned for you, friend," the bishop said, then nodded in blessing. Afterward, John was given a robe, dunked, prayed over, and sent back into the world with a Bible in his hand and a strange smile on his face, which he couldn't seem to stop.

Miles met him near the back of the tent, gnawing on a wing of barbecued chicken and sucking on a lemonade. "That," he said, "was not why I asked you here tonight." He shook his head and offered the drink. "You thirsty?"

"No," John said, still smiling dumbly. "No, I'm not thirsty at all."

53

Present day

The giant blue banner with the words *THE SUMAC ALLIANCE* glowed brightly, thanks to the spotlight pointed at it. Below the Sumac logo, in smaller letters, it read, *State & Church Unite for Community*. It was the perfect symbol, a summation of Donald Harrison's life's work, and he loved it.

This luncheon marked the culmination of years of hard labor, of pressing on in spite of the seemingly endless obstacles. Congress would pass the Faith and Fairness Act before the week was out. This was more than a banquet for Donald's supporters. This was nothing less than a celebration of Donald's vision and victory.

Pride swelled within him as he took the podium. It was centered on a long table at the far end of the room, right in front of that bold Sumac banner. Positioned emblematically at the table, on either side of the podium, were six of the most respected religious leaders in America. Representatives of every major faith, who had thrown their support behind the Faith and

Fairness Act. Among them, on Donald's far left, was perhaps his greatest victory: Truth Ministries' representative—and newly minted CEO—Ryan Morris.

Donald smoothed out his favorite necktie, a blue checkerboard pattern that always made him feel confident and powerful. "We never thought we'd see this day, did we?" he began. He bore a giddy smile as broad as the table flanking him and probably looked a little silly, but he didn't care. This was it. This moment. This was what his sacrifice and perseverance had been all about.

"But miracles can happen when we as a people unite with one voice!" he continued. "Our opponents boldly stated that we could never have Christians and Jews and Muslims standing together in solidarity. But they were wrong, weren't they? Dead wrong! This is the future of our evolution in this nation, ladies and gentlemen. This is no longer a 'Christian nation.' In fact, it never has been. The question now becomes: How can a government survive and prosper without the steadfast unity of its own diverse religious community?

"It can't," he concluded. "It simply can't."

John's heart and mind were on fire, flames fanned by utter disgust. The sheer gall of this man he'd once called a friend. It was unconscionable. Donald was actually *rejoicing* over his so-called hard work on this precious legislation of his. John wondered how many members of Congress Donald had pressured or bullied or blackmailed in order to get the bill passed.

William had turned out to be a godsend. In less than twelve hours, he'd already helped John in a number of ways. As part of the alliance, St. Peter's had received an invitation to today's event, and William was happy to let John fill the vacancy. The young priest had loaned John his black floor-length cassock and white collar, and he'd been able to enter the Washington,

D.C. Grand Hyatt, find the luncheon, and seat himself at the back of the room, out of the line of sight of anyone at the big table up front, where Donald was giving his speech. Sometimes hiding in plain sight was the last place people would think to look for you.

"Just as Martin Luther King Jr. faced violent opposition when he first birthed his dream of uniting people of all colors," Donald went on, "I have a dream too. A dream of a tradition of faith as diverse as our skins, walking hand in hand toward the light!"

Donald ended his speech with his arms lifted high. John had to admit, it was a strong performance. And full of conviction. Everyone in the room was in awe of the senator, leaping to their feet to give him thunderous applause.

And there was Ryan Morris. He was standing shoulder to shoulder with men and women of authority from various religions, with a broad smile on his face. Ryan was Judas—Judas at the Last Supper, kissing John on the cheek while stabbing him in the back. All while gleefully drinking Senator Donald Harrison's polluted Kool-Aid.

Unable to endure another minute in this room, John stood along with the cheering throng and used the commotion to bolt out of the hotel ballroom door. So many people, all tempted by the same message of equality and freedom. Yet as he descended in the elevator, John could think only of the death and ruin Donald Harrison had dealt in order to bring about his Faith and Fairness Act. With Ryan Morris a naïve but eager accessory to Donald's ambition.

John felt his face harden with outrage. He almost didn't notice the Secret Service agent standing guard at the front door, who spoke something into the radio hidden in his shirt sleeve as John passed by. Something about the man seemed familiar, and as John chanced a glimpse back, the man's flattened profile—as if he'd broken his nose far too often—snapped a memory into place. He'd seen the man on the video the night he'd been abducted. It was the same squash-faced man who'd carried Aaliyah Evans's body into John's vehicle after his escape. The same man who'd been patrolling John's neighborhood, posing as a police officer.

His pulse racing, John picked up his pace, almost running for the parking garage across the street. He skipped the elevator, instead ascending the stairs two steps at a time until finally bursting onto the top deck.

John's fist was clenched tight around his father's rosary beads as he jogged to the car, where William was at the wheel, waiting with the engine running. William pounded the gas pedal before John's door was even shut. They squealed their way out of the parking garage and into D.C. traffic, where William began taking side streets to lose any tails that might be following them.

John took deep breaths, trying to calm himself, but his anger at Donald could not be contained. To be betrayed by someone he once trusted, someone he thought he knew so well . . .

John nodded to himself. He *did* know Donald well. And maybe it was time to put some of that knowledge to work.

54

Two hours later, a smiling Donald Harrison treated himself to a well-deserved massage at his favorite Chinese day spa. "My one indulgence," he'd said through the years whenever he'd talk about the place. It always made him happy, and even now, wearing a spotless white terry-cloth bathrobe, he couldn't wipe the grin off his face as he glided into the private massage room.

So John decided he would have to do it for him.

Losing the gray sedan William had spotted after the Sumac luncheon hadn't been easy. They'd circled and weaved through the city streets for nearly twenty minutes before the car slipped too far behind and got trapped at a red light. Even then, John wasn't totally sure the tail was gone. He assumed it was the squash-faced man and the gray-suited man from the video. The two men could've been tracking them some other way, for all they knew. But they had to take the chance. John had this last move on the chessboard, and he had to take it now.

Donald's massages had been a bit of an inside joke between them when they were younger. Every big win or any hard political loss meant at least an hour of getting his muscles kneaded at this quiet little massage parlor. John had no doubt the man would show up here sometime shortly after his speech, and with some help from William in distracting the masseuse, John was able to slip into Donald's reserved room and wait.

The senator was still grinning when he shut the massage room door and turned around to greet his masseuse. He froze when instead he found John sitting in a chair near the door, mostly obscured by shadows. But John knew Donald could see enough of him to know who was sitting there.

He was quick to mask his initial shock, replacing it with the kind of expression reserved for being surprised by a visit from an old friend. "What are you doing here, John?" he said, smiling again.

John wanted to say so many things. He wanted to spit on this despicable man. Instead he just sat there, silent, looking at Donald with his most pointed glare.

He was pleased to see that Donald was visibly rattled. Immediately the man began backpedaling. "I'll make some calls. I'll . . . I'll see what I can do for you, John."

Slowly and deliberately, John shook his head. "No more lies," he said, leaning forward in his seat so that Donald could fully see him—as well as the pistol and rosary beads he held in his right hand.

"Why did you do this to me?" John asked. He was somehow feeling both angry and sorrowful at the same time.

Donald played innocent, trying to keep things friendly. "I don't know what you're talking about."

"I said *no more lies*," said John. "You knew that bill would never stand without my support."

Donald laughed, yet there was a note of bitterness to it. "John, you always had the moves, but you could never hear the music. This is the most crucial piece of legislation since the Bill of Rights! This is heaven on earth for somebody like you. Imagine it, would you? With the flick of a switch you could be preaching to every synagogue and temple and mosque known to man. No more terrorists, no more secrets, because we hold all the keys! Every faith on bended knee before the throne."

"Whose throne?" asked John.

"I'm not your enemy, John. The real enemy is some guy with a nuclear weapon in a suitcase, hiding in a mosque or a temple somewhere. And I can't get to him because I don't have the oversight."

John's ears burned red. Donald had to be kidding. *That* was what this was all about? Terrorism? Was he serious?

John stood and faced Donald, gesturing with the gun. His voice was so thick with emotion when he spoke that he barely got the words out. "You're telling me you killed an innocent girl, you *murdered my father*, and you destroyed my life . . . to protect the nation from *terrorism*?"

Donald regarded him as a slow child, struggling to understand a simple concept. "Sometimes in war there's collateral damage. It's for the greater good."

John's blood boiled over. Remarkably, in this moment of rage, God brought a line of Scripture to his mind. It flowed from his lips like rainwater. "'You, like a tree that bears no fruit, shall be swiftly cut down.'"

Donald frowned, and he shouted in a sudden outburst, "Stop with the Christian platitudes!"

John felt an odd calm settle over him. It had to be God, comforting him, giving him inner peace. But he also knew in an instant how this was going to end. "You called yourself a Christian at one time," he said.

"I warned you," replied Donald, "if you put your personal history out on the street, it would come back to bite you in—"

"Donald," John broke in, speaking slow and methodic, "I want to ask you a question."

But Donald was still having a different conversation. He was shouting again. "You thought you were bigger than the system, but you're not! You thought you could wash yourself in the blood of Jesus and your sins would be removed, but they weren't. You know, John . . . the public doesn't take kindly to a sexual predator on the loose."

John kept going as if Donald had said nothing. "Do you remember what the Lord said to David when Saul was delivered into his hands?"

Donald was irate. "Oh, *stop* with 'the Lord'!"

"The Lord said to David . . ." John turned and pointed with his eyes at an object sitting on a ledge just above the room's door.

Donald followed his gaze to see a digital camera. A camera that had recorded his every word. His eyes grew wide with horror just as John reared back and struck him on the head with the pistol.

"'Deal with him as you wish,'" John whispered as Donald fell to the floor.

John let out a breath and stood to his full height. For a long moment he stared down at Donald, who lay there unmoving on the bamboo floor.

He reached up for the camera, staring into it with righteous vindication. If America wanted a guilty party to blame two deaths on, John had one for them right here.

Live and on camera.

55

They didn't have long before the senator would come to and the man's true power would be revealed. How quickly could he and his men find John? He couldn't risk waiting around; he still had one more message to deliver. With William at the wheel, John pointed them southward, out of the city. He was headed home. What used to be home.

Hood up to obscure his features, John was a rolling storm as he burst through the front door of Truth Ministries' headquarters. What had they built here? For years, John assumed he was building the ministry on a foundation of solid rock, as a place devoted to God. But now those who were a part of it had been so quick to turn on him, to seize power and run with it. They'd twisted this beautiful, God-serving entity into a selfish, money-grabbing abomination.

How dare they?

This place was never about man's power. It was about the power of God changing people's lives! It wasn't a cult of personality around John. It was a group of men and women joined together in common purpose—sharing the Gospel with a world that needed it more than ever.

John stepped into the elevator, thinking how this place looked no different from any other time, and yet he saw it with new eyes now. It was different. *He* was different.

He steeled himself as the elevator silently rose.

On the top floor he exited and walked past a ponytailed janitor he couldn't remember, who was removing giant-sized framed photos of John from the walls lining the central hallway. One by one he took the photos down. John wondered what they were planning to replace them with. Photos of Ryan?

As he approached the double doors of the boardroom, he could hear someone's voice speaking authoritatively from inside. It was Ryan. He was praying.

"We are so thankful for your financial blessings, for your abundance of grace, for your showers of mercy, Lord—"

Repulsed, John charged through the doors. The lights were dimmer than usual. The board members were viewing computerized slides on a large white screen.

The room fell silent as he entered, and Ryan halted his praying.

John slammed the door behind him and pushed back his hood, revealing to them his weary but furious face.

"John!" cried Ryan.

With unnerving calm, John gave him a piercing look. "Take a seat, Ryan."

Although Ryan was clearly thrown by the interruption, he tried hard to hold on to control of the room. "John, I don't know what to say. We hate seeing you like this, me especially, but you can't just—"

John produced the gun from his jacket pocket and held it up in the air.

Ryan gaped when John pointed the gun at him.

"I'm only going to ask you one more time, Ryan," said John. "Sit. Now."

Ryan raised his hands and scurried to his seat. "Hey, it's your show."

John joined Ryan at the head of the table, where he looked down at the younger man's open laptop. On the display was the same collection of pie charts being projected up onto the big white screen at the far end of the table. John glanced up at the bigger screen and marveled at the slide labeled *Ministry Donations*, which had been broken down by demographic.

"Your portfolios must have skyrocketed," he remarked to everyone in the boardroom. "Anybody want to see the next slide?"

John scanned the members, who looked to be in shock. Ryan was glaring at him now.

"Hit the button," John said to Ryan.

No one in the room moved, including Ryan, who had control over the slides. The place was deathly silent.

John slammed his empty hand down on the table. It banged so loud that several of his former underlings jumped in their seats. "All right, I'll help!" he shouted.

"John, *stop*," said Ryan, and John heard anger rising in his protégé's voice.

John was about to strike the table again when Ryan finally pressed the button, advancing the slide. Now the big screen showed a bar graph with a snaking line pointing diagonally upward. John couldn't believe it. He knew he probably looked crazed to the board members, but he had no interest in their perceptions of him anymore.

"Now we're talking," he said. "Look at this! Look at those numbers. Not bad for *blood money*. Tell me, was it worth it?" He nodded at Ryan at the head of the table. "Again."

"John . . ."

"Hit the button!" John roared.

Shaking his head, Ryan complied.

John circled the table, working his way back to the projection screen. "Stop. There it is," he said, pointing to a graph on the screen with his pistol. "That's like, what . . . ?" He turned to Dave Wilson, who sat closest to the screen. "Help me out here, Dave—you're the numbers guy. That's like a two hundred percent increase in salary, isn't it?"

Arthur Lewis, another senior pastor on the board, spoke up. "John, please, be reasonable—"

John spun on him. "Reasonable? Is that how you got to where you're sitting today, by being reasonable?"

"John." Dave looked up at John over his glasses with hardened eyes. "Your uncompromising perspective is admirable. You know I've always admired it. But your approach is not always a practical one."

John stared Dave down, sadness rushing through him. Slowly, intentionally, he looked each board member in the eye, one at a time.

"With God's help I built this place," he said. "With my bare hands. Now you're all in bed with the government. You're taking their tax dollars, but do you seriously think they can't silence you anytime they want?!"

56

This was getting serious.

Rivera believed that John Luther was innocent, and she could tell that Clark did too, though he hadn't said it aloud. Their current working theory was that Luther had been set up by Senator Harrison, but they had no hard evidence to back it up. Clark was getting pressure from his deputy director for reports, Rivera knew that. And she knew Clark was stalling from giving anything up. She also knew that the deputy director himself was getting pressure. But from who? How far up the bureau's food chain did this go? Without knowing who had the most vested in the case, she and Clark had little recourse on moving forward. Certainly they couldn't request to place the senator under surveillance based purely on one of Clark's hunches.

First they had a bigger problem.

He's here.

Clark had received the text only minutes ago from Ryan Morris. Then came the apparently surreptitious phone call that allowed them to listen in on everything.

John Luther was up in Truth's boardroom this very minute,

agitated and dressing down his former lieutenants. Rivera figured those guys probably had it coming. When emotions ran this high, however, the situation was apt to become unstable, and fast. What if the events of the last week had pushed Luther over the edge? They couldn't take that chance.

While Clark drove, Rivera took the passenger's seat, clicked the phone to speaker, and listened to the situation unfold.

Before long they were parked in a secluded corner of the parking structure adjacent to Truth's headquarters. A tactical backup team had been alerted and was only three minutes out. Clark had shut off the van and sat listening in with Rivera. This might be the break they needed, if someone confessed. They needed to assess what was happening, yet Luther was still fuming at the Truth Ministries' board of directors.

"They've got a hook in your back!" said John Luther.

Another voice spoke up. "John, it wasn't always this way."

Rivera glanced at her partner. He mouthed *Wilson* at her. The current speaker was Dave Wilson, Truth's chief financial officer. She remembered reading in Luther's file that he'd met Wilson decades ago, and they'd been friends longer than anyone else on his staff.

"Obviously," Wilson continued, "what happened to you is unthinkable. But as far as this organization is concerned, we're here just picking up the pieces. We were asked to come here for damage control—"

"No! You're being manipulated. Just another pawn! And you don't even realize it because you're too blinded by ambition and greed."

Clark glanced over at Rivera. "He's losing it." He still seemed reticent. "We can't wait any longer," he said.

Rivera didn't want to agree, but she knew that she had to. The man was unstable, and they'd get nothing helpful from him today. She nodded.

Pulling a radio from the clip on her belt, she alerted the team. "This is Agent Rivera. Agent Clark is ordering an immediate breach. Remember, do *not* open fire unless you are fired upon."

John couldn't believe it. Even Dave had turned on him. He'd known that Ryan was a lost cause after seeing him at the Sumac luncheon. But Dave? Dave had believed in him from the very beginning—long before John believed in himself. John had been trying to convince himself that even if everyone else at the ministry had written him off, Dave would still be there fighting for him.

"What good can it possibly do," said Dave, "if we blow our entire credibility on one piece of legislation? The world wouldn't listen to us any longer. We were losing viewers. We'd be spending the rest of our lives wandering in the wilderness, shouting louder and louder. How many people can we reach that way?"

John was out of breath. Sadness fell on him like a waterfall. He appreciated that at least Dave had thought this through and wasn't just blindly following Ryan. But the conclusion he'd arrived at was so far off.

"Have all of you completely forgotten?" he said, quiet and disheartened. He looked around the room at these men and women who used to be his closest friends and confidants. He smiled at them. "There once was a Man who wandered in the wilderness. And he reached more people than you're *ever* going to reach now."

John glimpsed the slide on the screen again. *Money.* That was really what it all came down to.

If money was all they were after, then they could have it. John reached into a jacket pocket and took out the last of his father's cash. There was easily two or three thousand dollars left, and he held up the bills for everyone to see. Then he tossed the entire wad high into the air. He heard a couple of gasps as those in the room froze, watching the bills flutter gently down on them.

John turned to Ryan.

His own personal Judas. Sitting there, looking up at John with fear in his eyes. John felt a momentary surge of power seeing Ryan this way. Justice was so close; he had the gun after all. Yet he couldn't even bring himself to point it at the man.

Jesus forgave Judas.

John shuddered, all his anger suddenly spent.

He tossed the gun onto the boardroom table. It thumped against the table and spun to a stop right in front of Ryan.

John turned and, as he left the room without another word, he heard Ryan's voice behind him.

"That is the destiny of an intolerant man."

57

Damage control. It was usually Donald Harrison's second-best mode. He was best at being the proud champion, rousing people with his excitement and his words like he'd done this morning. But so much of politics was damage control, and he'd gotten excellent at it through the years too.

If only the bruise and knot on his forehead would let him focus. He was sure he had a concussion, but he hadn't even taken a moment to get himself checked out. That would come later. What needed to be handled first was the video. The video John Luther had filmed of him confessing to ordering the deaths of that whore girl and also John's father.

Somehow it hadn't made it on the news yet, yet he knew it would happen anytime now. Unless his associates could locate John and get that video out of his hands first. Damage control.

Massaging once more the throbbing bruise, Donald tried to think through all the eventualities. For a second he wondered if it had been a mistake to call the president so soon after his coming to at the massage parlor. Except he knew this was nothing he could hide. One way or another, someone in power would find out about the video. They always did. Demonstrating his loyalty to the president by keeping him in the loop was the smarter move.

Predictably the president was highly displeased. After dressing Donald down a bit, he directed him to "take care of the situation." Which Donald was already hard at work doing. His man had been alerted and knew what to do. Donald had no doubt he'd get a phone call soon, telling him the job was done and that Luther was no longer a problem.

But the phone call still hadn't come, and Donald decided not to take any chances. Someone in his position didn't take such chances during damage-control execution.

As soon as the media got wind of the situation, the press would descend on his home en masse. He had no intention of being here when that happened.

His master bedroom stood littered with clothes thrown everywhere, some in a pair of open suitcases, the rest draped across every available piece of furniture. Donald's wife was flitting about, sorting through armfuls of clothes. Across the room, their television was tuned to cable news, and Donald feared their going to "breaking news" any minute now. Once more his phone rang and once more Mr. Gray was calling to say they hadn't yet located Luther.

"Well then, where is he?!" Donald shouted into the phone. The man wasn't a ghost, after all.

As Mr. Gray replied, the doorbell rang downstairs. Donald gave a quick look outside, fearing a streetful of news vans. But there was nothing, other than a single jogger running alongside a golden retriever. With a sigh he went to answer the door.

"He can't be *that* hard to find!" Donald said, restating what he'd been shouting at Mr. Gray since he'd first called ninety minutes ago. Donald descended the winding, open staircase that led to the ground floor. "Listen to me. Clean this up. Whatever it takes. Are we clear?"

He reached the entrance and swung open the door. In the doorway stood Mr. Gray, holding his own phone to his ear.

"We're clear," said Mr. Gray.

Donald's breath caught in his throat, and he tried to slam the door shut, but Mr. Gray was too fast, positioning himself over the threshold. Donald was shoved back onto the floor as Mr. Gray flung the door open wide and stepped inside. Donald looked up to see Mr. Gray pulling out his Glock 22 and taking aim.

From above, Donald heard a scream. His wife stood at the top of the stairs.

Mr. Gray swiveled his gun upward and shot twice.

The screaming stopped.

Donald had no time to look up or even think of her, because in a flash Mr. Gray had the gun trained on him again. He opened his mouth to say something, anything, to beg for his life or offer Mr. Gray money, but he never got the chance.

The last thing that went through his mind before the gun fired was the single phrase *All for nothing*.

58

John saw the FBI men entering the stairwell from two flights above. He still couldn't allow them to catch him. He couldn't trust them. Senator Harrison's influence certainly reached down into the bureau, and he couldn't trust that they'd ever allow him to release the video. No, this needed to get to the media, and now.

He diverted quickly to the third floor, weaving through a roomful of cubicles. Several employees stood as he ran by, shocked and scared. He had no time to slow down. Using an external fire escape at the rear of the building, he was soon on the ground, dashing toward the car, where William waited with the engine running.

As they speeded down the road, his mind was racing along with the car. He'd put off this decision long enough. It was now time to decide where to go next. Should they take their chances and take the video to the police, or should they head straight for a TV news station?

John glanced at William. He was so grateful to the young priest for his assistance. No one could ever replace his father, but William had been there for him in his darkest hour. And it wasn't like the priest was obligated to help him. He was risking his life for John, and he barely knew him.

John turned and thanked him, patting William on the arm as the man drove. That was when the unmarked white sedan rammed into John's side of the car at high speed.

The burgundy car spun a full circle, with glass, metal, and rubber flying everywhere. The scents of burning rubber and hot metal filled John's nostrils as he fought to hold on to consciousness. A nasty gash on the side of his head was sending a stream of blood down through his sideburns, cheeks, and neck.

William seemed okay, since John's side had taken the brunt of the impact. Dazed, John looked up. The front right corner of the car was crushed in, but remarkably the engine continued to run. Yet all such concerns were erased when a very familiar man in a gray suit stepped out of the white car that had slammed into them, drew his side arm, and pointed it straight at John—all in one fluid motion.

"William!" John cried.

But there was no time. On the other side of the windshield, the man stood a mere ten feet away from John. There was nowhere to hide, nothing John could do as the gray-suited man pulled the trigger.

John was terrified. This couldn't be how it ended, not like this . . .

Miraculously, after piercing the windshield, the bullet missed its mark. John gasped when instead the bullet ripped through the left edge of his seat, barely an inch or two from hitting him.

William wasted no time but pushed down hard on the gas pedal. The rear tires spun in place for a few seconds, until the car gained traction and peeled away from the gray suit.

John leaned to his right to get a glimpse of the man through the side-view mirror. He'd barely caught sight of him when another bullet struck the car, from behind this time, and traveled through the rear window and into the back of John's seat.

Instantly John was thrown forward against the dashboard.

The car's momentum then yanked him back into his seat again . . . but something wasn't right. A sledgehammer had knocked into him from behind, and now there was a pain in his chest. John felt his upper abdomen and pulled back his hand to find it completely covered in red.

"John!" cried William. "You're bleeding!"

The young priest pushed the car even faster, tearing down the street at a dangerous speed.

"Hold on! The hospital's not far—"

"No!" cried John, wincing through the pain. "I'll be all right."

William looked at him, his eyes wide with panic. "But John—!"

"There's no time," said John, sucking in air. "The church . . . Please, we have to . . . get back to the church."

Ten agonizing minutes later, William stopped the car at the curb around back from the church. The car had barely come to a halt when John opened his door and staggered around to the other side. William got out as well and put out his hands to steady him.

"We have to get you help!" insisted William. "You're bleeding—"

John shoved the digital camera into William's hands. "I need you to do this."

William hesitated. John could see that he was concerned only with helping John.

"Please," said John, gritting his teeth. "They have to see it. Show them. Show everyone. For me. For my dad."

While the worry never vanished from William's face, finally he agreed and accepted the camera. "What about you?"

John gave him a weak smile. "I'm the target."

William understood. While he handled the video, John would make sure that Donald's minions pursued him instead of the priest. William placed a hand on John's shoulder, then ran into the church with the camera.

John slid into the driver's seat, trying to ignore the excruciating sensations all over his body. He pulled away from the curb and drove off.

These guys wanted him dead? Fine. John knew how to run. He'd done it for thirty-some years of his life. He'd run from his dad, from God, even from himself. He could run for years, if he had to.

If they wanted him, he was going to make them work for it.

59

Any reason to hang up the phone on her mother would have worked for Monica. She was looking around the house, trying to find Jodi, but she'd gone upstairs to do her homework. Monica had had the TV on all day, watching and waiting for any new information about John. At the moment, though, they were just showing a current weather map of the United States, and the weather was the last thing on her mind right now.

Monica had been on edge all day after finding John's note in her car. She looked down at the kitchen counter again where the note lay and read it again. *One way or another, this will be over soon*, it said. How soon? Monica had pondered that question all day.

She wanted so badly to call the police and report that Charles had been murdered, so they could try to catch the killer. But she didn't know how or where he'd been killed, and anything she reported now would probably get blamed on John. Monica couldn't take that chance.

The nagging doubts had lingered, despite her fervent efforts to keep them at bay. She believed John's letter. She believed he was innocent. But still . . . there was no evidence to prove it. Not yet anyway.

To her knowledge, he'd never lied to her. But there was a first time for everything. What if . . . ?

She shook her head, shooing the thought away.

Ten minutes ago, her mother had called for the sixth time today. Her mom was confused so easily nowadays, and she was still trying to get her head around the charges that had been filed against John. She'd always loved John like her own son—she even insisted on supporting John's ministry out of her retirement fund, despite their continual protests—but now that he was a fugitive, she was more baffled than ever.

"I can't understand why they don't just get that man on the television to find out who really killed that girl," she said into Monica's ear.

Monica sighed, cradling the phone in the crook of her neck. She knew that the "man on the television" her mom was referring to was in fact the main character from the TV show *Monk*.

"Mom, that—"

Monica's eyes connected with the TV in the living room, where Diana Lucas had just appeared with a huge *Breaking News* graphic underneath.

"Mom, I need to go. I'll call you back soon," she said, then hung up the phone. She rushed into the living room and turned up the volume.

". . . stress that the raw, unedited footage you're about to see has not been verified as evidence in the charges against John Luther," said Diana Lucas. "But our public submissions department has concluded that this video is authentic. Take a look."

Diana was replaced by a view from above of what looked like a massage table. A man in a bathrobe was standing near the bottom of the screen, close to the camera, while John faced him from a chair to his right.

Monica's heart ached at the sight of her husband, so gaunt, so hurt, so despondent. She prayed Jodi wouldn't come downstairs just now, to see her father like this.

"*Why* did you do this to me?" asked John, his voice so full of pain that Monica's eyes promptly filled with tears.

Those final tiny doubts that had plagued her vaporized the instant she heard those words escape his mouth. She didn't have to hear anything more.

She knew.

She also knew she might never see her husband alive again.

60

Luther was long gone. He'd escaped them again.

Rivera was almost glad. She trusted the other agents on her team, but tensions were running so high around this case, with so much pressure on everyone from the top down thanks to Capitol Hill, that itchy trigger fingers were inevitable.

She stepped out of the van as Clark approached. He'd just been up to Ryan Morris's office, debriefing various members of the Truth Ministries' board of directors who'd been present when John Luther interrupted their meeting.

Clark shook his head. "Nothing useful. Most of them were cagey. They're still in shock. Morris kept pushing Luther's 'instability,' but his stock with the others seems to be plummeting."

Rivera raised an eyebrow. "Shocking."

Clark held out a nickel-plated pistol. "Luther tossed it to Morris before he left."

Behind Clark, the six-member team of agents they'd sent into the building returned in a pair of black SUVs. One of them reported that the building was, as suspected, clear. There was no sign of Luther.

"So what's he thinking?" she mused. "Where does he go next? Home finally?"

Clark shook his head. "More likely he's gone to see the good senator."

Rivera's phone rang. She excused herself and stepped away.

A few minutes later, she returned to Agent Clark, who crossed his arms as he listened. "That was a friend at the local PD. Said he just heard a report that there was a two-car collision a mile west of here about twenty minutes ago. A witness claimed that a white sedan with tinted windows intentionally smashed into a burgundy car with two men inside—one of whom matched the description of John Luther."

"Could the other one be his father?" asked Clark.

"No," said Rivera. "Luther's driver was described as a *young* white male."

Clark nodded. "So . . . the preacher's found himself a friend."

Rivera sent him a meaningful look. "There's more."

Clark waited, listening. Three other members of the ground team wandered over to hear.

"My friend just got a second report from a local badge, who saw a damaged burgundy car turning onto Route 16, heading up Kings Mountain. Said there was a bullet hole in the windshield, and the driver was bleeding from the head."

"He's being chased, and he's unarmed now," Clark said, his voice tense. He paused, looked into the distance. "Kings Mountain . . . where did I just see that name?"

Rivera thought for a moment, then snapped her fingers. "Doesn't Luther's father have a cabin up there?"

She locked eyes with Agent Clark.

Clark whirled on the six other agents and gestured toward the SUVs. "We're rolling! Everybody load up right now!"

61

John had so little time left. He could feel his life draining away with the blood leaking from his body.

If he could just make it to the cabin, he might be able to prolong this enough to . . . to what? What was he hoping for here? That he might be able to hide long enough for someone to come to his rescue? He had *minutes* left, not hours. That he might evade his pursuer and get the drop on him? John had left his only weapon back in the boardroom.

If William had come through and sent the video to the media, then it was safe for him to go home, to the authorities, or to the hospital. But he had no way of knowing if that was done yet. Perhaps they'd sent someone after the man. So John had no choice but to run. His only other option was to lie down and die or let the man in the gray suit catch up with him and finish the job.

The pain had become so fierce, it would be awfully easy for him to give up the fight, to stop his running and let things play out however they would. But he couldn't do that so long as there was even the tiniest of chances that he might survive this ordeal and so be with Monica and Jodi again.

He forced himself to keep driving. Both hands on the wheel, one of them still clutching his father's rosary, and fighting the increasing pain all the way up Kings Mountain. He pushed the car as fast as it would go. In the distance, on the road behind him, John caught sight of a white car. But then the road curved, and the car vanished before he could get a good look.

Was it *him*? Probably.

"Come on, come on!" he muttered to the car, willing it to go faster.

William would come through. He had to.

The job was almost done; it would be over within the hour.

Mr. Gray had the preacher in his sights. Less than half a mile separated them on the rural road leading up to Kings Mountain. Mr. Broad was on his way, heading toward Luther from the opposite direction. The plan was to box him in, and then finish this thing once and for all.

Obviously the fool was headed for his father's cabin. He must've thought that his being there would give him some kind of advantage. Or maybe he just wanted to be in familiar surroundings when he died.

How bad was the wound he'd given Luther? It was impossible to tell until he got a closer look. But he was certain that his last bullet had made contact. Instincts built on more than two decades of service to his country told him that when the hollow-point bullet left his Glock, it hit Luther in the chest. And it was very likely a mortal wound.

Mr. Gray considered shooting out the tires of Luther's car, but decided against it. Truth be told, he was enjoying the pursuit. His job was usually so clinical, so surgical in its speed and precision. It was nice to leave standard procedure behind.

And he respected the man's fight. The senator had made a

mistake in underestimating Luther—a mistake Mr. Gray never made. Prey was prey until it was dead, and the senator paid the price for forgetting that lesson. Worse, his memory and legacy were going to be tarnished because the public would soon be learning about his role in the recent deaths.

Still, the man in the Oval Office wanted John Luther dead. It was probably a personal grudge at this point, but that information was well above Mr. Gray's pay grade. No matter, for it had no bearing on how he did his job.

The job was all that mattered. He'd taken care of the girl, the priest, and the senator. Only the preacher remained.

Soon that loose end would be neatly tied up too.

62

One look at the gas gauge told the tragic tale: John would never reach the cabin. Already the Volvo was starting to sputter, and in just a minute or two it would go no farther.

Thinking fast, John stopped the car on the side of the road and got out, stumbling into the cover of the woods. He pressed one hand to his chest, trying to stop or at least slow the bleeding—even though he'd already lost so much blood that it might not matter anymore.

The bullet had gone straight through him, since he was bleeding immediately from the front after being struck in the back. He didn't want to think about how much he was bleeding back there too, or about what the bullet might have damaged on its trip through his body. The pain was too intense to tell. It couldn't have been his heart—he would have died almost instantly. But there were other vital organs in the vicinity—lungs, liver, stomach—and wounds to any of those could certainly be fatal for him.

John's heart thumped harder when he heard the echo of a car door slamming not far behind him. As best he could, he broke into a run. In truth it was more of a sped-up hobble than a run.

He came across a dirt path, and something deep in his memory stirred. It was almost as if he'd been here before.

He stopped and spun in place. He'd heard a branch or a twig snap. Were those footsteps?

Taking a gamble, John turned onto the dirt path and pushed himself to run a little faster. Around a bend in the path he reached a clearing where the skeleton of an abandoned greenhouse stood atop a raised, round wood platform. The dome-shaped structure was empty, the glass panels gone. Only the geometric frame remained, outlining the structure that once stood there.

John jogged around the dome, not quite believing his eyes. He *had* seen this strange structure once before, years ago, the first time he'd run away from his father. And now he'd stumbled across it again. Only this time he wasn't sure he would escape.

He had to stop when a sharp pain deep beneath the bullet wound stole his breath away. He doubled over, using the raised wood platform for support. It was a relief not to have to hold up his own weight for a moment.

The moment ended when a gunshot rang out, and a piece of wood splintered just a few feet away from his head.

He looked up. At the far end of the clearing stood the gray suit, his gun raised. And the man wasn't alone—his police-car-driving accomplice was right there with him.

John breathed a quick prayer and took off running.

63

Agent Rivera loved driving. She'd proven to be quite adept at it too, even in highly charged situations. So good that Agent Clark let her take the wheel anytime they were in the field.

Through her dark sunglasses, Rivera spotted the three cars on the side of the road just ahead and slammed on her brakes. Almost as one, she, Clark, and the other six agents poured forth from their vehicles. She circled the car to join her partner while checking the ammunition on her side arm. The other agents did the same.

It was during their ten-minute drive there that the call had come in. CNW had broken the news that Senator Donald Harrison had framed John Luther for the murder of Aaliyah Evans. All to push a pet bill of his through Congress. Reportedly there was a video of Harrison confessing, which had been arranged by Luther so as to exonerate himself. That had taken some serious guts on the preacher's part, to confront the man who'd taken everything away from him and basically trick him into admitting what he'd done—on camera. It was smart, impressive, and the sort of tactic her partner would have employed in a similar situation.

In that moment, she and Clark knew their target was no longer John Luther. He was now free from blame. Their target was the muscle who'd been working for Harrison. His henchmen, be they hired thugs or government agents. It didn't matter. They'd betrayed their country as much as Harrison had, and they'd already proven themselves as extremely dangerous.

Orders had come in straight from the highest office at the Hoover Building. These men trying to kill John Luther had to be stopped, and at any cost.

On Clark's orders, the unit deployed some of its heaviest weaponry, including standard rifles, shotguns, and one sniper rifle. The agents under their command donned the black protective gear they reserved for the most dangerous of situations. A few of them even wore balaclava masks.

Rivera followed Agent Clark's lead, sticking to her navy-blue FBI track jacket, although this time they both wore ballistic vests underneath.

With speed and silence, the team entered the woods.

Another hundred yards along the dirt path, John came upon another clearing. There was a small storage shed full of debris and rusty steel barrels that looked as though it hadn't been seen by human eyes in quite a while. The camp had obviously been abandoned years ago. The path continued beyond the shack, and John kept moving.

The woods closed in around the path, and soon there were overlapping branches sticking out in John's way. He was forced to slow down, duck, and weave his way through the undergrowth.

Slowing down killed his momentum and forced his adrenaline to subside. The pain hit him again full force, and random moments from the last week flashed through his mind. Was this his proverbial "life flashing before his eyes" moment? Or were his emotional defenses simply being stripped away, allowing thoughts and feelings to surface after days of suppression?

He remembered shaking hands with Donald Harrison in his dressing room and embracing him in a friendly hug. This memory was then replaced with a mental image of Donald standing at the Sumac podium, smiling with his arms held aloft in victory before a standing ovation.

He thought of Ryan's pep talk the night of his last televised sermon. How ironic that Ryan had advised him to "forget the politics," when Ryan had been unable to focus on anything else when he took over the ministry.

And that night, the fateful moment after his sermon when he was approached by Aaliyah Evans and the man trying to kill him now, who posed as her father and asked him to have their photo taken with him. That strand of recollection led inevitably to mental flashes of Aaliyah with her hands all over him, taking pictures shortly before she was killed.

His most painful memory was seeing his father's dead hand—the hand which still held his rosary beads—with the old man's blood pooling on the hardwood floor below him.

That memory and the pain he'd endured lately were too much for John, and he stumbled on a low-hanging branch. He hit the ground hard, and his first attempt to stand back up failed as soon as it began with him right back down, flat on his stomach.

"People are looking for a symbol," his father had told him the last time they spoke together, in the park. *"Someone who'll get back up when he's knocked down."*

Squeezing his father's beads and drawing strength from his words, John pushed against the ground until finally he was back on two feet. The woods spun around him, but he shook away the sensation and pressed on.

Ahead he found the end of the dirt path and felt another sudden sense of *déjà vu*. He remembered this path and knew where it would lead. Soon enough he found a small, weather-beaten shack and a platform he knew led to the swimming pool. Only it no longer glistened like an oasis. It lay empty, cracked and vacant. This camp that had once been his salvation now looked like a graveyard. His graveyard.

John staggered onto the wood deck and began limping across it. He was thinking the empty pool might make a good hiding place, with its being partially belowground, when he reached the end of the deck and came face-to-face with the gray-suited man.

64

A split second after looking into the cold eyes of the man who'd been hunting him for almost a week, John was lifted into the air and thrown to the ground. He landed on his back, his head making a cracking sound against the old wood of the deck. The blue sky above and the surrounding trees swirled in and out of focus, darkness creeping into the edges of his vision like the tentacles of an octopus that was swallowing him whole.

The next thing he knew, the gray suit was yanking him up by his jacket collar until he was on his knees.

John closed his eyes and silently prayed, *If this is the end, my spirit's ready to enter the gates of heaven. But if it be your will, let me live to hold my precious ones again.*

When he opened his eyes again, he was staring into the black barrel of a revolver. Holding it was the second man, the gray suit's comrade, and John saw murder in his eyes.

This was it.

Agent Rivera caught up to her partner just as John Luther was tossed on the ground like a plaything. Luther was bleeding from the abdomen, had a sizable gash on his head, and was very likely delirious from the loss of blood. Did he even know what was happening to him?

Two men were there with Luther—the one attacking him, and a second man who stood behind Luther, holding a revolver. So this was them. The men working for Harrison. They didn't look like mercenaries or professional hit men. They looked like Secret Service.

Which meant that Senator Harrison had tasked his own personal Secret Service detail with eliminating the girl and framing John Luther.

Unless . . .

Unless their orders came from higher up.

That was a sobering thought, and not something for pondering right now. Rivera filed it away for another time.

Agent Clark took point, silently working his way forward, using the trees for cover to get as close to the tiny cabin as possible. Rivera followed his steps precisely, readying herself to back him up when he made his move.

The two men had Luther on his knees, execution style.

It was time.

Agent Clark moved out into the open, his weapon drawn, and stepped forward onto a twig. He'd done it on purpose, and it made a loud *snap*.

The two assailants turned in his direction. Luther lazily did the same. He was pale and barely conscious now.

"Put the gun down!" ordered Clark.

The men looked at each other with surprise, then scanned their surroundings. They were taking in the situation tactically, just as Rivera would have done. There were eight agents all together, moving in to surround the cabin. She doubted the two men could see their sniper, who'd taken up position a little farther away.

"On the ground! Now!" barked her partner.

The one holding Luther up produced a badge clipped to his belt.

"We're United States Secret Service," said the other one.

That was irrelevant as far as Rivera was concerned.

Clark too. "I said *put the gun down*!" he yelled.

The one who'd spoken put a hand in his pocket. "I'm just reaching for my ID," he said. "I'm putting my weapon down."

The other one let go of Luther and bent over to drop his gun on the ground.

"On the ground!" Clark repeated.

Rivera didn't like this. Something felt wrong about it. . . . Clark had to be feeling it too.

"We're all on the same team, pal," shouted the first man, the one wearing a gray suit.

As his friend bent over to drop his gun, Rivera saw the first man give him a hand signal.

She opened her mouth to warn Clark, but the second man was too fast. He had his revolver up and fired a perfect marksman's shot into Agent Clark's forehead.

No!

Rivera ran to her partner, found him crumpled on the ground. He was dead from the instant the bullet struck.

She glanced up to see the second man taking aim again with his revolver, but he had no chance of getting off a second shot. The sniper hit him three times, center mass. The bullets shredded through his chest, and he collapsed. Rage surged through Rivera as he landed on the ground with a hard thump.

When she looked up again, the first man was gripping a backup gun, pointed at her.

He fired.

65

John watched in horror as an FBI agent was shot and killed. His second attacker fell to the ground behind him. Then the gray-suited man was shooting again, and John heard a scream. He followed the sound to a female FBI agent, who was doubled over, lying on the ground and cradling her leg.

But she didn't stay down. With a cry of fury she propelled herself up to a sitting position, raised her gun, and shot back.

The sight gave John a fresh rush of adrenaline. As the gray suit made a run for it, John crawled on all fours to the end of the deck and launched himself over the edge, sliding down the sloped wall into the empty pool.

When he recovered from the hard landing, he propped himself up against the side of the pool. He heard several hurried footsteps not far away, in a rush to chase down their target.

Still holding his chest with one hand, John looked down at his wound. His shirt and pants were soaked through with blood. It hurt to breathe, and his breaths were coming too fast. He tried to slow them but couldn't. Lying next to him, also smeared with blood, was the cell phone his father had left him. It must have slipped out of his jacket pocket when he slid down into the pool. John picked it up, his fingers trembling.

It was over. He was dead already. He merely had to wait for death to finish its work.

But maybe he had just enough time left . . .

His limbs so heavy they were hard to move, he lifted the phone and hit speed dial. The number he'd programmed and had wanted to call a thousand times. The line was ringing as he placed the phone to his ear.

There was a click, followed by a small, beautiful voice. "Hello?"

"Sweetie," he whispered.

"Daddy!"

It was Jodi. As far as she was concerned, it was a normal day and her daddy was calling home just to talk.

"Hi," said John, anguished but smiling.

Thank you, Father, for letting me hear my little girl's voice one more time.

"I drew a picture at Sunday school," she told him excitedly. "Do you want to know what I drew for you?"

John was so overcome he could barely choke the words out. "Of course I do."

"Who is it?" said a voice in the background.

Monica!

"I'm talking to Daddy" was Jodi's casual reply.

John heard shuffling sounds, and then Monica grabbed the phone. "John!" She was already crying.

"Hey, beautiful," he said, still smiling.

"John, they're dropping the charges! It's all over the news!"

John's chest deflated in measureless relief. He closed his eyes. "You saw it . . . Good."

She knew. Monica was still talking, saying something about the president getting involved in absolving him, but all that mattered was that she knew he didn't do it. Now and forever, she knew he was innocent.

"Monica," he said, straining to speak, "I want to apologize for shutting you out. You are the love of my life, and you deserve so much better."

Tears spilled out on both ends of the phone line, Monica's coming with the short, gasping breaths that happened when she tried to stifle her crying.

"Listen," John said. "If I don't make it out of this, I want you to be free."

"No," she replied adamantly, though her voice was quivering. "You're coming home, John. It's over and it's time for you to come home to us."

John couldn't hold it in anymore. He was done. He had nothing left to do, no time left to live. He didn't know how to tell her that he was dying, that they would never see each other again in this life, that he wouldn't be there to watch Jodi grow, guide her into adulthood, walk her down the aisle at her wedding, station himself in the waiting room while she gave birth to their grandchildren.

He put down the phone and let the tears rain.

It was done. He was ready to let it all go. . . .

Until he heard footsteps shuffling across the deck planking above.

66

Agent Rivera was on her feet, pushing through the pain. There was only one thing she knew for certain, just one thought cycling through her mind over and over again.

The Secret Service man was going down, and she would be the one to take him out.

She was hobbling across the deck, scanning the area with her gun drawn, when a man's thick, muscular arm seized her in a choke hold from behind. The gun fell from her hands.

Rivera struggled violently against his iron grip and belted out a wrathful growl. But it was no use. The man was too strong.

A dozen feet away, the remaining members of her team scrambled into position, weapons raised at the Secret Service agent. But he wheeled her around to block their shots while aiming his own gun at her head.

"Stand down!" he ordered the FBI team. "I'll kill her!"

Rivera was livid. She bared her teeth, fighting this loathsome member of humanity and wishing she could end his life with nothing but her own hate.

With all his remaining strength, John used his final moments to climb up the edge of the pool, his hands and arms so shaky he could barely hold on.

In the late afternoon sun, something shiny caught his eye on an outcropping about a mile up the mountain. He squinted and tried to focus. It was a window in the side of a building. A log cabin. A familiar log cabin.

His father's home away from home.

Lying there on the deck right in front of him was the revolver that had been pointed at his head just minutes ago. Still holding the rosary beads, he picked up the gun with the same hand and aimed it.

The gray-suited man stood not far away with his back to John. It was the perfect opportunity to end this. And that man was threatening to kill the FBI woman.

He hated himself for thinking it, for needing to do it, for having his finger on the trigger. All of this had begun because everyone believed he was a killer. He'd sacrificed everything—even his own life—to prove that he wasn't. And now he had to be a killer in order to save a life. If these were the choices people had to face in this world, maybe it was best that he leave it.

His face twisted in anguish, John pulled the trigger with his last ounce of strength.

When the shot rang out, the Secret Service man let go of Rivera and fell. She knew right away that he was dead, without even checking his pulse, and a surge of satisfaction flowed through her. Along with tremendous relief that she'd survived.

Still . . . Clark was dead, her partner and mentor. She couldn't compute that fact. Not yet. That would take some time.

She glanced out at her FBI team, wondering which of them had circled around and taken out her captor from behind. Thankfully she counted six. They were all there, looking back at her, nodding. She let out a sigh.

Rivera turned then and saw John Luther. He was peeking over the edge of the empty pool with a revolver in his hand. His eyes were rolling back into his head, and his grip on the edge was slipping.

She rushed over and reached for him, but she was too late. He fell and collapsed at the bottom of the pool. And there was a long red trail of blood tracing from the spot where he'd clung to the pool's edge all the way down the wall to a puddle of blood beneath his broken body.

67

A full moon shone down on the emergency room parking lot as Monica haphazardly steered the family car into the lot and screeched to a halt.

Her mind raced, fearing the worst and knowing it had to be bad since he'd been rushed here. She sprinted from the car to the glass double doors, which opened far too slowly, and then up to the check-in desk.

Incredibly, no one was behind the desk. Then, on the other side of the room, she saw a familiar face. The woman was sitting in a wheelchair with her leg propped up.

"Um, it's Agent . . . Rivera, isn't it?" she asked.

Rivera looked terrible. Her hair was a tangled, matted mess, she looked impossibly tired, and she was grimacing in pain. But her expression softened when she locked eyes with Monica.

"Mrs. Luther," she said. "It's okay. He's alive."

Monica felt weakened by the news. "He is? Are you sure?"

Rivera nodded. "The doctors said that if it had been even ten minutes more . . . He should be out of surgery by now if you want to see him. I can get you into his recovery room."

Monica ran the backs of her hands across her eyes, wiping away tears. "Thank you. Thank you so much. For everything." Monica looked about. "I should thank your partner too. Where . . . ?"

Rivera looked down, and immediately Monica knew why.

"Oh," she said, struggling for words. "Oh no. I'm so sorry . . ."

Now it was Rivera's turn to wipe away tears. She nodded in gratitude for Monica's sympathy but said nothing.

Monica placed a hand on her shoulder and prayed aloud for her, right then and there.

Afterward, Rivera took her hand and gave it a gentle squeeze. "Come on," she said. "It's this way."

She led Monica in her wheelchair through a set of locked double doors—which she got opened by showing her FBI badge to a staff member—and into a large round area with twenty or so patient rooms fanning out from it.

"He's in 109, over there," said Rivera, pointing. "When he wakes up, tell him I said thank you."

Monica looked at her. "What for?"

Rivera's eyes met hers. "I went into those woods today to save his life. He saved mine instead."

With that, she spun in her chair and rolled away. Monica watched her go, amazed at her words.

Quickly she found the room, and a nurse led her inside. Monica's hands flew up to cover her mouth when she saw John. He was sleeping in a hospital gown, lying on his back, with a respirator and other equipment she didn't recognize hooked up to him.

A young man sat in a chair beside the bed. His head was bowed as if in prayer, but he looked up when Monica entered. He jumped to his feet and offered her the chair.

"It's an honor to meet you, Mrs. Luther," he said, offering to shake her hand. "Your husband's a remarkable man."

Monica reciprocated his handshake, trying to figure out if she'd met him before. He didn't look familiar at all.

"My name is William," he said. "I work—I *worked*—with John's father. At St. Peter's."

"It's nice to meet you, William," said Monica, putting the pieces together as she took a seat in the chair. "You . . . you helped him?" she asked, looking at John.

"Yes," said William. "After Father Charles . . . well, I've already made sure the authorities know about him. They've taken the body from the cabin."

Charles . . .

Monica teared up again. Without really thinking about it, she was on her feet again and throwing her arms around William's neck.

"Thank you," she said, sobbing against his shoulder. "Thank you for helping my husband."

68

TWO WEEKS LATER

The Truth Ministries' headquarters building loomed large in John's window as the car came to a stop near the front entrance.

Monica put the car in park and turned to her husband. "You sure you don't want me to come with you?"

John glanced at her, almost amused at the thought. "You'd have to smile and hug and pretend like you're not holding a grudge against these people."

Which she was. John was in the process of letting go of the hurt and betrayal he'd suffered from these men and women, but Monica hadn't progressed quite that far yet. She was still furious at the lot of them.

"I assure you," she said with a sly grin, "I wouldn't have to do *any* of those things."

John chuckled and opened his door. "In that case, you're definitely staying in the car. I won't be long."

On the top floor, John emerged from the elevator, cane in hand, to find the same ponytailed janitor he'd seen the last time he was here. Only this time he was hanging the framed posters of John back up on the walls.

He knew he looked better than when he'd been here two weeks ago. Monica had helped him to get into his favorite navy-blue business suit, a crisp white shirt, and a red silk necktie. She told him he looked "terribly handsome," yet he saw new wrinkles on his face alongside the healed-over scars.

John walked slowly down the hall, leaning on his cane, and his heart sank when he saw what was waiting for him. Outside his office was a gathering of a couple dozen staff members, all of them applauding his return. There were a few wrapped gifts and even a cake.

What was this? They were throwing him a party? They were acting like he was a cancer survivor or something.

Ryan wasn't among them. His contract had been terminated by the board the day after John was cleared of all charges. John had heard a rumor earlier in the week that Ryan had already started a new ministry of his own, somewhere in the South.

"We thought you were dead," said Arthur Lewis, who'd been named interim chairman of the board.

There were so many bright smiles, but John couldn't bring himself to conjure one. It felt beyond strange being back here. "So did I," he replied.

Walter Bailey, another board member, spoke up. "We're being flooded with donations!" he said. "It could be our best quarter ever!"

John had no reply to that. He couldn't shake the odd sensation he'd felt upon entering the building.

"It's so good to see you, John," said Walter. "You look great."

"No. I don't," John countered.

They were posturing for him, and he was already tired of it.

Walter seemed to notice his discomfort. "We prayed for you constantly," he offered. "We prayed over what to do."

Then John's oldest friend in the world, Dave Wilson, stepped forward from the crowd, smiling like everyone else. "Now that you've been cleared of the charges, we'll reconvene as soon as possible and get you reinstated."

Although John saw their mouths moving, all he could hear was their support of Ryan and the Faith and Fairness Act, their condemnation of him and their lust for government earmarks. Clearly the whole letting-go thing was still a work in progress.

Walter was talking again, and John had already missed some of what he'd said.

". . . normal, it'll be like nothing ever happened!" he said, beaming. "And we've got some ideas for the next quarter that we think you're going to be extremely excited about. Some incredible outreach opportunities!"

A part of John wanted to join in with their enthusiasm. But he just couldn't. Not even a little.

"We've gotten cards and letters from all over the globe, like never before," said Dave. "This level of support is unprecedented! The whole world is standing behind you, John. I firmly believe that God is going to take what happened to you and use it as a testimony to reach millions more for him."

A chorus of amens echoed across the gathering.

Everyone was watching him, waiting for him to say something, every eye expecting him to share in this joyous occasion. But John simply wasn't interested.

"Excuse me," he said as he weaved and pushed his way through the crowd. "Excuse me. Excuse me . . ."

He hobbled to his office, entering it for the first time in weeks. He glanced around the room. Where was it? He'd come for just one thing, and he was sure he'd left it in this room.

There it was, on his desk.

An old, tattered Bible. His father had given it to him years ago. Holding it gave him strength, determination, purpose. And, he realized, a strong sense of what would come next.

A moment from his interview with CNW just days ago flashed to mind. Diana just couldn't seem to believe that he was willing to take a stand.

"So if it comes to that, are you telling me you would be willing to fall on your own sword? For this?" she'd asked, incredulous. Sometimes people worked so hard to make a thing complicated, when really some things were actually very simple.

"Diana," he'd said, barely holding back a smile, "if you take away a man's right to speak his mind in a country founded on that very principle, you don't really have a country, now, do you? So there's really no sword left to fall on, is there?"

She hadn't had a follow-up question to that.

Simple, though, didn't mean easy. Nothing would be easy—the past days had shown him that much. A storm was coming, and it was simple to say one should stand firm in the face of its wrath. But when that wind began to howl . . . it would be far from easy to do so.

With one last look around his office, he carried the Bible back out into the hall. Walking faster than before, he brushed past the partygoers and didn't look back.

They were all sycophants, swaying to whichever way the wind blew. Would he ever be able to trust them again? Could they ever regain his respect?

Today that was inconceivable to him. But, he told himself, didn't everyone deserve a second chance?

After all, few men understood God's amazing grace and forgiveness better than John Luther.

The next day dawned, and John found himself staring into Monica's wide, alert eyes. He didn't want to guess at how long she'd been up. It was to be his first full day back to work and he could only guess at the whirlwind of thoughts racing through her mind. She said nothing, but instead just smiled at him and slipped from bed to begin their day. Coffee first. A shower. The ritual would begin once more.

John heaved himself up to a sitting position—it took so much effort to do such a small, simple thing—and let the joy wash all over him again. The last time he'd been in this position, he'd been leaning against the edge of a drained pool, watching the life flow from him, heartbeat by heartbeat. He didn't expect to see this room again. He didn't deserve to see this room again.

But if his life had taught him anything, it was that *deserve* had nothing to do with it. "If we all got what we deserve," his father would say on occasion, "there'd be no one left alive to complain about not getting what they want." At the time, he thought the old man was just ragging on him—and part of him was—but it was also at the heart of his world view. A world infused with grace, where only God's goodness meant anything. A sharp pang made him wince, but John realized it wasn't his wound that ached. It was his soul. He hadn't yet had the chance to even begin mourning the loss of his father and everything his death had cost them both. It would come in its own time—the pain and then the healing.

John had his eyes closed, thinking about his dad, when he heard giggling coming from his bedroom door, followed by the padding of footsteps.

Jodi . . .

One of her favorite games was to try to sneak into her parents' bed without waking them. She got the biggest kick out of them waking up and their delight at finding her there in bed with them. Only she rarely could stifle her giggles, and for a girl with small feet she often made a surprising amount of noise.

John played along, even giving a fake snore. A minute later when she climbed in next to him, her frigid feet grazed his legs, and he startled for real.

"Surprise, Daddy!" she shouted, then stuck out a tiny fist. John offered his fist too, and they bumped them together. It had been their solution when the doctor warned that hugging, even though meant with love, could aggravate his wound. For now, fist bumps would have to do.

Monica returned from the kitchen with two mugs of steaming coffee. "Two more minutes, sweetie, and then Daddy's got to get ready for work."

Jodi nodded and held out her first again.

He couldn't do it. Not so soon. Not when this was all he'd stayed alive for. He couldn't just jump back into the routine.

"Change of plans," he said and then asked for the phone.

Half an hour later, despite the worry expressed by the few people he'd talked with at Truth Ministries, he was out the door with his family. Monica wore a slightly dazed expression while Jodi gripped her daddy's hand as if she'd never let go.

He'd return to the ministry. Someday. And probably soon. But today he was with his family. Today he *was* living. Tomorrow the world could find him again.

"Where to?" Jodi asked, looking up at him.

"I think . . ." John said. "I think this is your day to drive."

And so she did. First was a stop downtown to pick up donuts for breakfast, then a visit to the zoo, where they all had to choose their favorite animal. Jodi had selected a lumbering black bear because she said it walked a little like Granddad. John and Monica shared a look. They'd told Jodi her grandfather had died—not mentioning how—but the news hadn't seemed to quite connect.

"It's okay," she said when they asked her how she was doing a few days later. "I'll see him in heaven."

Her granddad still found his way into her thoughts, and John wondered when the little girl would finally realize he was gone. Maybe at his funeral. Or maybe she already had. Maybe heaven was the right answer, after all.

The zoo was followed by a picnic, which was followed by a matinee of a movie Jodi had been "dying to see." Already his little girl was sounding like someone so much older. They ate popcorn and stayed all the way through the credits, not wanting to miss anything the filmmakers might be trying to hide from them.

Jodi yawned, and John could see their perfect day was reaching an end. He switched his cell phone back on, which he'd turned off when they'd left the house, to check the time and found himself staring at an unthinkable hundred-plus emails and seven voice mails. He thought the world would find him tomorrow, but it had managed to sneak in a grasp at him today.

"At least listen to the voice mails," Monica said, who'd been watching him. "You never know."

Three were from media outlets wanting to follow up on his story. Those he could pass on to the ministry's publicist to tackle. The fourth was from a literary agent telling him how he *must* get his story out there. That got deleted immediately. The fifth surprised him, a short message from Miles Washington, a voice he hadn't heard in years. The man had seen the stories, seen what had happened, and was just glad John was all right. And that if he wanted to call back, Miles might not get the call because he was staying at a cabin in the Tennessee Smoky Mountains, doing some fishing.

Monica asked him why he was smiling, and he waved her off as the sixth voice mail began. This one he also recognized, the Southern drawl like honey in a warm sun.

"Mr. Luther, this is the president, and I have a matter of some importance I'd like to discuss with you. . . ." The message went on, requesting that John get back to him as soon as he could. John felt his whole body tense and could feel his wound once more. This, more than anything, had brought him fully back to reality.

But it was the last message—a short follow-up from one of the president's staff who was calling to arrange a time to meet—that chilled John for another reason. "We're really hoping you get this scheduled shortly, Mr. Luther," the voice said. "So, please, call us at your earliest convenience. And we do hope you enjoyed the movie with that lovely wife and daughter of yours."

John looked around, eyes wild, though he knew there was nothing to see. They were all alone in the theater at this point. The credits had ended, and the two most important people in his life were staring at him with concerned expressions.

And John knew. It wasn't over yet. It might never be over.

Epilogue

Near the back of the White House press room, John leaned on his cane for support with one hand and held tight to Monica's hand with the other. The president was at the podium, under the bright lights, extolling the virtues of John Luther and Truth Ministries and decrying the deplorable actions of the late Senator Donald Harrison.

All told, seven people had lost their lives to Harrison's madness. A teenage girl. A priest. The senator himself, along with his wife. A highly respected FBI agent. And two officers of the Secret Service.

John was grateful not to be the eighth. And yet . . .

Something was still nagging him about the whole thing. A thought that had occurred to him while he lay in his hospital bed for days on end.

What if Donald hadn't been the true architect of all this?

Words from his father still rang in his ears: *"Aside from the president, I don't know of many people who are better equipped to withstand a bullet like this."*

John couldn't shake the feeling that that was exactly what

was happening. Even here, now, at this press conference the president had personally asked him to attend. It just felt like . . .

Damage control.

Watching the president speak now, with his good-old-Southern-boy charm and homespun smile, John was more sure of it than ever. Everything about the man felt counterfeit.

Then again he *was* a politician. And it was the business of politicians to manufacture personas that matched what the public wanted in their leaders. Maybe John was just being paranoid. But he didn't think so. Every ounce of his soul told him the president was guilty of murder.

"Decide what you're going to say yet?" whispered Monica.

John sighed, shook his head.

It had been a topic of great discussion at the Luther house over the last few days. Would John stand up in front of the world and do the song-and-dance routine that the president expected of him? Or would he go up on that stage and blow the whistle on the man who'd been at the heart of this entire sordid affair?

"Well, I do," said Monica, eying him with confidence. "I know exactly what you're going to say."

He looked at her. "Oh? What then?"

"I can't be the one to tell you," she said. "You have to figure it out for yourself. And you will. When you step up to that podium, you'll know exactly what to say."

Was she serious? Monica was enjoying herself. That much was certain. Or she could have been teasing him about his indecisiveness . . .

"What makes you so sure you know what I'm going to do before I do it?" he asked.

She leaned in. "Let's just say that in all the years I've known you, you've never once disappointed me."

He smiled at her. He'd spent every waking moment of the last two weeks with Monica, and he still couldn't get enough of her. What was he thinking, all those years that he'd excluded her from the ministry, from everything that was happening in his life?

Still holding her hand, he gazed into her eyes. "Thanks for coming with me."

Monica gave his hand a squeeze and looked back into his eyes. "Thanks for asking me to."

It was time. John gave Monica a peck on the lips and then pulled away to the spot just to the side of the stage, where he'd been instructed to stand.

"Ladies and gentlemen," said the president, "it is with great pleasure that I introduce a longtime friend of mine: Pastor John Luther."

Polite applause came from the reporters and journalists filling the room. But John's eyes were locked on the president, who with a wide smile walked across the stage and gave John a hug.

It was for the benefit of the cameras. Most of what this man did was.

John was taken off guard when the president leaned in close and whispered in his ear, still grinning, "Very few men defy their own government and survive. But you did, John. And now everybody in the world wants to hear what you have to say. So let's play nice, shall we? *Real* nice."

John felt shell-shocked as the president stepped aside, clearing the path for him to walk to the podium. Dozens of cameras flashed as he stepped forward and gripped both sides of the podium. He was a preacher preparing to deliver a sermon again. The only question was which sermon would it be?

Any lingering doubts he had about the president's culpability had just been erased. But outing the leader of the free world on national television could put him—and his family—right back in the crosshairs of the nation's powerful elite.

Did he dare go off script?

John Luther glanced at the president one last time before

letting out a slow, steadying breath. With grim determination he stared out at the press corps.

The cameras flashed once more in unison, and then the room turned deathly silent. Nearly all were leaning forward as they anticipated his address.

John Luther peered into the blinding spotlight until everything had dissolved into a greater light and he heard the whisper he'd hoped would come. He heard the whisper, and his heartbeat quickened.

He heard the whisper and he knew: *I will not be silent.*

Questions for Conversation

1. Do you feel your rights as a believer have been limited? Has this changed over the years? What do you think the future of religious freedom is in America?
2. Compare America's religious freedoms with what you know of other countries' values. In what ways do we stand tall for freedom, and in what ways do we fall short?
3. The Bill of Rights explicitly protects religious freedoms while also providing for a separation of church and state. Do you feel religion should be more represented in government? Where is the balance between being a nation under God and not forcing your faith on nonbelievers?
4. Romans 13:1–2 says, "Let everyone be subject to the governing authorities, for there is no authority except that which God has established. The authorities that exist have been established by God. Consequently, whoever rebels against the authority is rebelling against what God has instituted, and those who do so will bring judgment on themselves." How do you apply this verse when government stands in opposition to your faith?
5. What areas of American life today are particularly vulnerable to limitations of religious expression? How is faith

being challenged in the areas of same-sex marriage, workplace regulations, and public schools?

6. Have you ever been wrongfully accused of something? What emotions did you feel? How did you get through that situation?
7. How did John Luther's past help him in the novel? How did it hurt him? Are you more cautious when you know someone has a complicated and dark background?
8. What do you think Senator Harrison's true motives were? Are there some causes more important than an individual person's life?
9. What do you think it is that John Luther says in his address at the end of the novel?

Interested in Gathering More Information on Protecting Your Religious Freedoms? Check Out These Resources.

Alliance Defending Freedom: A unique legal ministry that has brought together thousands of Christian attorneys and like-minded organizations who work tirelessly to advocate for the right of people to freely live out their faith in America and around the world. http://www.alliancedefendingfreedom.org

American Center for Law and Justice: Focusing on U.S. constitutional law, European Union law, and human rights law, the ACLJ and its affiliated organizations are dedicated to the concept that freedom and liberty are universal, God-given and inalienable rights that must be protected. www.aclj.org

American Conservative Union: An umbrella organization harnessing the collective strength of conservative organizations fighting for Americans who are concerned with liberty, personal responsibility, traditional values, and strong national defense. www.conservative.org

If we ever forget that we're one nation under God, then we will be a nation gone under.

President Ronald Reagan

Robin Parrish has written for over a decade as a journalist on the cutting edge of Christian culture, from books and music to film. He is the author of the DOMINION TRILOGY and suspense novels *Offworld*, *Nightmare*, and *Vigilante*. Robin and his family live in North Carolina.

Daniel Lusko attended film school at the New York Film Academy and directed the multiple hit documentaries *Inside the Revolution* and *Epicenter*, based on Joel Rosenberg's *New York Times* bestsellers. Over the past two years, Daniel has directed his first action/adventure feature film *500 MPH Storm*, as well as the gritty crime drama *11 Seconds*. He is also writer and director of the thriller *Persecuted*, produced in collaboration with Gray Frederickson (*The Godfather*, *Apocalypse Now*). Daniel and his family live in New Mexico.

lonely planet

Discover Hawai'i, the Big Island

Experience the best of Hawai'i, the Big Island

This edition written and researched by

Sara Benson
Luci Yamamoto

Contents

Plan Your Trip

Discover Hawai'i, the Big Island

In Focus

Survival Guide

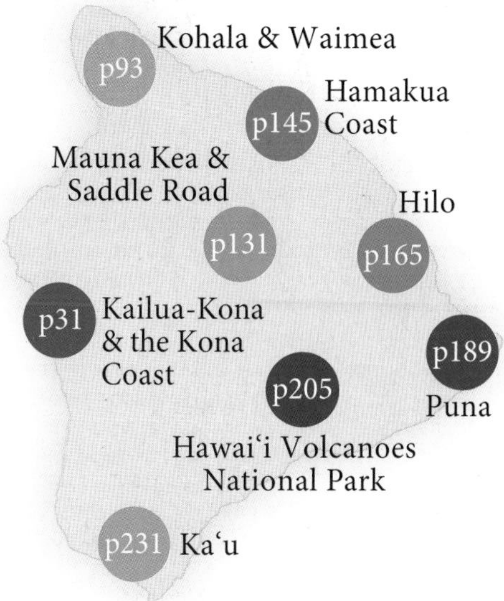

This is Hawai'i, the Big Island

We doubt it's possible to get 'island fever' on Hawai'i. The aptly named Big Island is fantastically diverse, with miles of highways and – better yet – byways to explore, from age-old fishing villages to modern megaresorts, from snowy peaks to sandy beaches. Hawai'i is twice as big as the other Hawaiian islands combined, and its dramatic terrain will surprise you and take you to extremes.

Less than half a million years old, Hawai'i is a baby in geologic terms. It's here you'll find the Hawaiian Islands' highest and largest volcanic mountains – and the world's most active volcano, spewing molten lava continually since 1983. Circumnavigate the Big Island and watch stark lava desert morph into rolling pastureland and misty valleys, weathered by rain, waves and time.

Ancient history looms large on Hawai'i, a place of powerful *mana* (spiritual essence). The first Polynesians landed at Ka Lae, where the windswept coast remains pristine and undeveloped, and Kamehameha the Great was born in Kohala. Hula and *oli* (chant) are powerful forms of living history on the Big Island, which has birthed legendary hula and Hawaiian music masters, as well as the celebrated Merrie Monarch Festival.

Plantation days are long past, but not their colorful legacy. Waves of immigrants who labored in the cane fields added their languages, foods and cultures to the mix. Today, there's no ethnic majority and common bonds are intangible: the pidgin vernacular, an easygoing manner and deep love of the *'aina* (land).

Hawai'i is untouristy. Thanks to its sheer size, there's lots of legroom. While Kona caters to travelers en masse, most island towns are rural and made for residents instead. Even the capital seat, Hilo, is a former plantation town that's still slow-paced and populated by *kama'aina* (people born and raised in the Hawaiian Islands). Wherever you go, there's a sense of freedom and frontier. The Big Island is a guaranteed *big* experience.

> *"Wherever you go, there's a sense of freedom and frontier"*

Pololu Valley (p121)

Hawai'i, the Big Island

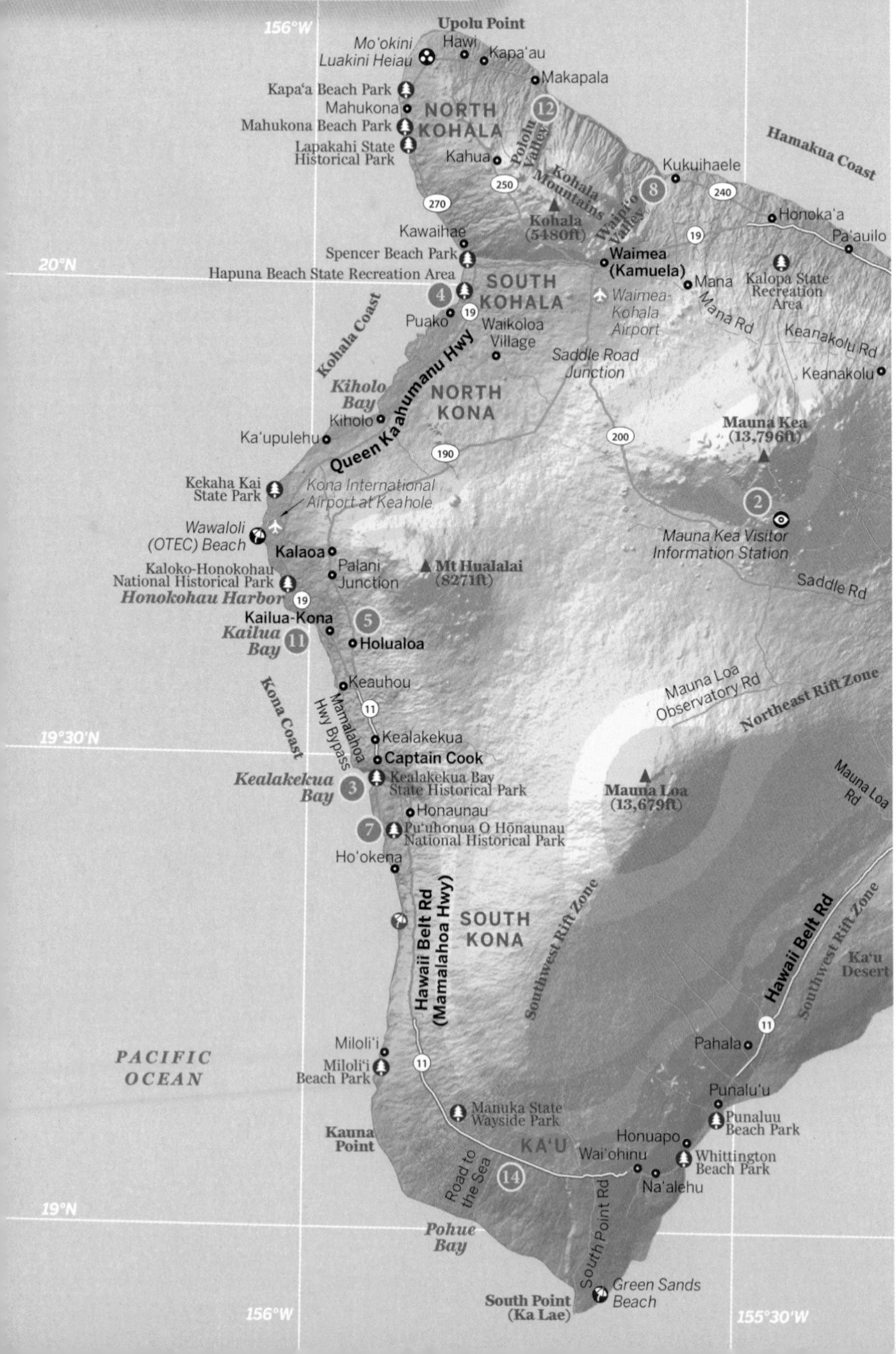

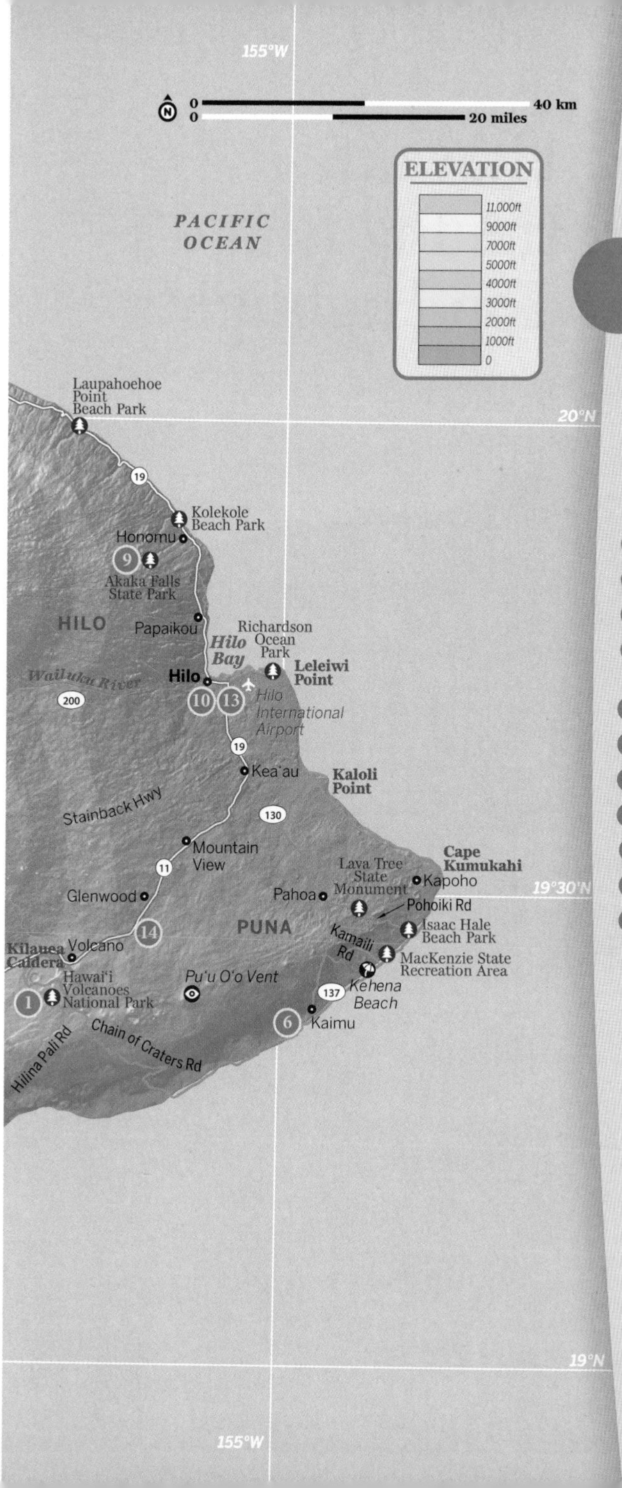

14 Top Highlights

1. Hawai'i Volcanoes National Park
2. Mauna Kea Stargazing
3. Snorkeling in Kealakekua Bay
4. Hapuna Beach
5. Kona Coffee Farms
6. Chasing Lava
7. Pu'uhonua O Hōnaunau National Historical Park
8. Waipi'o Valley
9. Akaka Falls State Park
10. Merrie Monarch Festival
11. Manta Ray Night Dive
12. Hiking into Pololu Valley
13. Hilo
14. Caving in Puna & Ka'u

14 Hawai'i, the Big Island's Top Highlights

Hawai'i Volcanoes National Park

The eerie glow of a lava lake, secluded palm-fringed beaches, ancient petroglyphs pecked into hardened lava, and miles of hiking trails through smoking craters, rainforest and desert – there's always so much more to explore at Hawai'i's number-one attraction (p205). The park is also one of the island's top spots to experience traditional Hawaiian culture at hula dance performances, annual festivals, concerts and talks. After dark, warm up by the fireplace inside the landmark Volcano House lodge, perched right on the rim of Kilauea Caldera. Kilauea Iki crater (p211)

1

TODD GIPSTEIN/GETTY IMAGES ©

PHILIP ROSENBERG/GETTY IMAGES ©

2

Mauna Kea Stargazing

It's breathless *and* breathtaking to be in the rarefied air of Mauna Kea (p138), Hawai'i's highest mountain and most sacred spot. Once the sun goes down, the stars come out – and so do the telescopes. Some of the world's clearest stargazing happens here. What you see through these telescopes, aided by enthusiastic amateur astronomers, you won't soon forget. For a trophy experience, show up here during a meteor shower. Above: Gemini Northern 8m Telescope, Mauna Kea

Snorkeling in Kealakekua Bay

It's all true – from teeming tropical fish to spinner dolphins lazily circling your kayak or catamaran. Tourist brochures hype this as the best snorkeling in the state, but in this case, you can believe it. New restrictions on kayaks can't tarnish the luster of this must-see spot (p71) – in fact, it's quite the opposite, as ecoconscious regulations are helping preserve the bay's underwater paradise. If kayaking doesn't float your boat, hike down instead to this historically significant spot, where Captain Cook perished.

3

The Best... Scenic Drives

CHAIN OF CRATERS ROAD
National park highway links volcanic craters downhill to the sea. (p212)

KOHALA MOUNTAIN ROAD (HIGHWAY 250)
Emerald pastures with black lava and white-sand beaches on the horizon below. (p113)

PEPE'EKEO 4-MILE SCENIC DRIVE
Jungle ramble across rivers and moss-covered bridges. (p163)

MAUNA KEA SUMMIT ROAD
Hawaii's highest-elevation mountain drive – oh, the sunsets. (p135)

MAMALAHOA HIGHWAY (HIGHWAY 180)
Coffee and mac-nut farms with skyline views of Kona's coast. (p61)

The Best... Hikes

KILAUEA IKI TRAIL
Hike across a moonscape in Hawai'i Volcanoes National Park. (p216)

POLOLU VALLEY TRAIL
Knees quake and spirits soar on this short, steep hike. (p121)

NAPAU CRATER TRAIL
Trek to the heart of an active volcanic eruption. (p217)

KIPUKA PUAULU
Native birdsong fills the sun-dappled forest on an easy nature walk. (p219)

MAUNA LOA OBSERVATORY TRAIL
Hard-core trek to a high-altitude summit – in just one day. (p142)

ROBERT HARDING PICTURE LIBRARY LTD/ALAMY

4 Hapuna Beach

Rock up to this half-mile-long powdery white-sand beach (p108), rent an umbrella and a bodyboard, and make one of Hawaii's most iconic beaches your personal playground. Surfboard, lounge chair or water wings – this beach has something for the whole family. While the basic A-frame camping cabins here are not for the finicky, the island's best beach is in your front yard – that's pretty hallucinatory. For more magic, detour just north to tranquil Mauna Kea Beach, sitting on crescent-shaped Kauna'oa Bay.

AGE FOTOSTOCK/ALAMY ©

5 Kona Coffee Farms

Christian missionaries planted Kona's first coffee trees. What began as an ornamental floral fad became a thriving agro-industry, as coffee farms worked by immigrants spread across South Kona's rain-kissed 'coffee belt.' Today rural byways wind past small, family-owned coffee plantations (p61), many of which let you drop by for a quick tour and free tastings of 100% Kona brews. Every November the whole community celebrates with the prestigious Kona Coffee Cultural Festival.

Chasing Lava

Pele, Hawaiian goddess of fire and volcanoes, is notoriously fickle. But if you're lucky, you may get the chance to see live lava crawling over and under newly birthed land (p202). Lava usually flows inside or around Hawai'i Volcanoes National Park, sometimes plunging into the sea, sending a steam plume skyward as hot lava mixes with roiling surf. Feel the heat on a walking or boat tour out of Puna.

Right: Lava from Kilauea Volcano (p208)

6

G. BRAD LEWIS/GETTY IMAGES ©

VAUGHN GREG/GETTY IMAGES ©

7

Pu'uhonua O Hōnaunau National Historical Park

Ki'i (deity images) watch over ancient temples at this historical site (p77) – known as the Place of Refuge – an unforgettable introduction to traditional Hawaiian culture. There's no better place to gain an understanding of the kapu (taboo) system that once governed life across the Hawaiian Islands. At nearby snorkeling spot Two-Step, look for *honu* (green sea turtles).

Waipi'o Valley

You can linger at the scenic viewpoint overlooking this lush green valley (p152), but the waterfalls, wild horses and wilder black-sand beach beckon. Hike down, ride horseback or even take an old-fashioned mule-drawn wagon to get you there. Experts can kayak in – when conditions are right. The most spectacular panoramas are from the grueling Muliwai Trail – head up, up and up some more for the money shot.

8

LONELY PLANET/GETTY IMAGES ©

The Best... Beaches

HAPUNA BEACH
Often voted the island's all-round top beach. (p108)

KIHOLO BAY
Soft black sands, sea turtles and a swimmable lava tube. (p90)

MANINI'OWALI BEACH
Easy access to a powdery white-sand beauty. (p86)

MAKALAWENA BEACH
Save a half-day to explore this hard-to-reach, idyllic strand. (p86)

BEACH 69
Swim, snorkel or laze at a gay- and family-friendly hangout. (p107)

Akaka Falls State Park

Crashing through the rainforest choked with fragrant ginger and giant philodendrons, this 420ft-high waterfall is no less spectacular for its easy access. Drive up, stroll a half-mile through what feels like Hollywood's version of Hawaii and there you are. Like all waterfalls on Hawai'i's windward coast, the park's two falls (p161) are most impressive during seasonal rains when they spill violently over the verdant cliffs. Poke around the tiny sugar-plantation town of Honomu once you're done ogling the towering falls.

9

RON DAHLQUIST/GETTY IMAGES ©

The Best...
Local Food

DA POKE SHACK
Fresh off the fishing boat *poke* (cubed, marinated raw fish) and plate lunches. (p46)

TEX DRIVE-IN
King of sugary, hot and filled *malasadas* (Portuguese doughnuts). (p151)

SUPER J'S
All homemade, *'ono* (delicious) Hawaiian recipes. (p70)

CAFE 100
Where the *loco moco* (dish of rice, fried egg and hamburger patty topped with gravy) madness all began. (p182)

VILLAGE BURGER
Big Island ranchers, farmers and fishers stock this cowboy country grill. (p127)

EMILY RIDDELL/GETTY IMAGES ©

10 Merrie Monarch Festival

What you saw at that resort luau? That's to hula what Velveeta is to cheese. If you really want to see how a hula *halau* (school) invokes the gods and legends through Hawaiian chants and dance, time your trip to attend this statewide hula competition (p177). Book early; people fly in from all over the globe for this one. Unless you're a serious hula aficionado, you're more likely to enjoy the pan-Pacific exhibition dances than the intense head-to-head competitions.

11 Manta Ray Night Dive

Diving at night is a thrill in itself, but once you turn on your light and attract a corps de ballet of Pacific manta rays, with wing spans of 10ft or more and tails like javelins, your life becomes segmented: before diving with mantas and after. Snorkeling with mantas can be even better because you're closer, but it's very popular, so don't be surprised if you get head-whacked by someone else's fins. Bring your own dive light and swim onto center stage with these graceful animals (p42).

CORNFORTH IMAGES/ALAMY ©

CULTURA RM/ADAM PASS PHOTOGRAPHY/GETTY IMAGES ©

12

Hiking into Pololu Valley

Waipi'o Valley or Pololu Valley? It's a tough call as to which of Hawai'i's emerald valleys threaded with waterfalls and blessed with a black-sand beach is more beautiful. But little Pololu (p121) retains a tranquility lost to Waipi'o since the invention of the monster truck. It takes a 10-minute downhill hike to get here, and it's the only way in. Combine your visit with lunch and a stroll around diminutive Hawi, Kohala's alternative arts hub. This northern thumb of land is old Hawai'i at its most evocative.

EMILY RIDDELL/GETTY IMAGES ©

13

Hilo

If one word describes Hilo (p168), that would be 'real.' This former sugar town had a life before tourism and remains refreshingly unpretentious, local and normal – if normalcy includes buoyant tropical greenery, drive-up beaches, unique museums, historic storefronts and sublime views of Mauna Kea and the Pacific. Here you'll rarely find tourist traps, but find yourself immersed in Hilo's diverse mix of residents, many whose ancestors arrived as plantation workers.

Left: Palace Theater (p185)

Caving in Puna & Ka'u

In Hawai'i, what you see on the surface is never the whole story. Beneath all the forest and volcanic flows lie elaborate systems of caves, caverns and lava tubes, multiplying by miles your exploration possibilities. The world's two longest lava tubes, Kazumura Cave (p192) and Kula Kai Caverns (p242), as well as a roadside lava tube that younger kids can walk through inside Hawai'i Volcanoes National Park, are among many options. Below: Kula Kai Caverns (p242)

14

LONELY PLANET/GETTY IMAGES ©

The Best... For Kids

CATAMARAN CRUISE
Snorkel with tropical fish, spy wild dolphins and humpback whales. (p38)

ZIPLINING
Hands on the cable, your heart will be in your throat. (p159)

KIKAUA BEACH
A protected cove perfect for little ones learning to swim or snorkel. (p87)

DAHANA RANCH ROUGHRIDERS
Giddyap like a *paniolo* (Hawaiian cowboy). (p124)

KULA KAI CAVERNS
Marvel at geological wonders on an educational tour. (p242)

Hawai'i, the Big Island's Top Itineraries

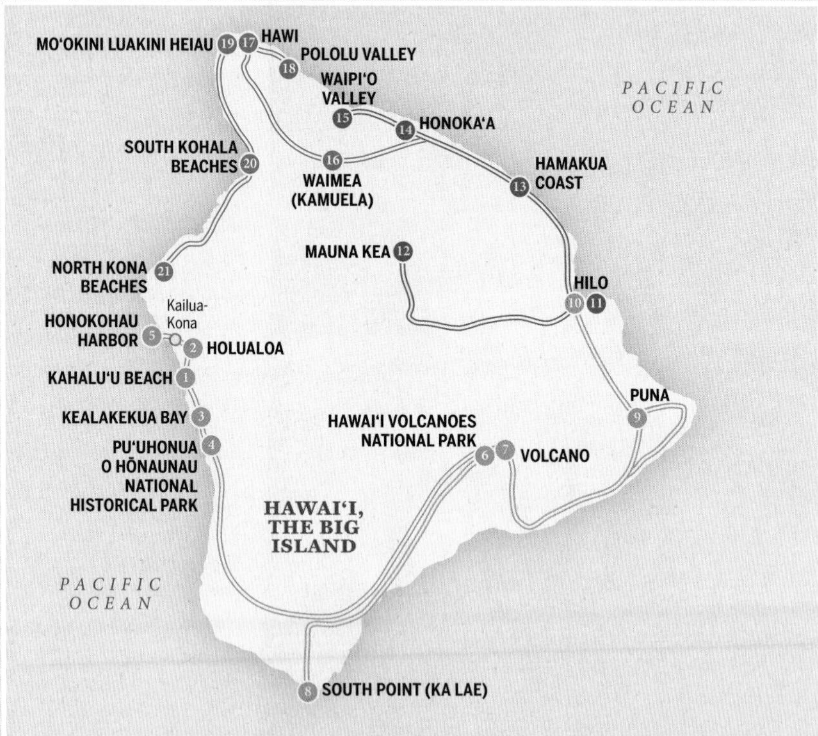

- **Kailua-Kona to Hawai'i Volcanoes National Park** four days
- **Volcano to Hilo** six days
- **Hilo to Waipi'o Valley** eight days
- **Waimea to North Kona** 10 days

Kailua-Kona to Hawai'i Volcanoes National Park

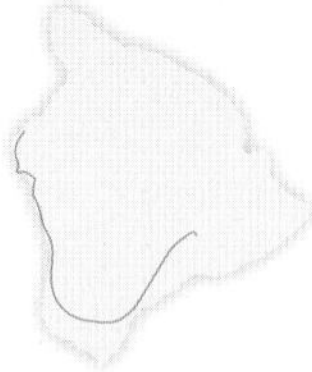

4 DAYS

GREG ELMS/GETTY IMAGES ©

Kayaking on Kealakekua Bay

1 Kahalu'u Beach (p54)

Teeming with tropical fish and sea turtles, this roadside beach is great for snorkeling or a surfing or stand up paddling lesson.

2 Holualoa (p59)

In the afternoon, drive upcountry to Holualoa. Browse high-quality island art galleries, sample Kona coffee from small family farms, and catch a spectacular sunset.

3 Kealakekua Bay (p71)

For day two, make reservations in advance for a morning snorkeling cruise or to paddle a kayak to the underwater wonders by the Captain Cook Monument.

4 Pu'uhonua O Hōnaunau National Historical Park (p77)

On day three, take an easy coastal walk around South Kona's 'Place of Refuge,' where ancient Hawaiian history and spectacular natural scenery converge. Afterward, duck next door to Two-Step for gorgeous shoreline snorkeling.

5 Honokohau Harbor (p80)

Don't miss night diving (or snorkeling) with giant manta rays – book ahead for boat tours. Show up early for a sunset walk around the ancient fishponds of Kaloko-Honokohau National Historical Park.

6 Hawai'i Volcanoes National Park (p208)

Set out early on your fourth day for the 100-mile drive over to East Hawai'i to visit the world's most active volcano. Diverse hiking trails and (if you're lucky) glowing after-dark views of a roiling lava lake await.

THIS LEG: 170 MILES

Volcano to Hilo

6 DAYS

JULIE THURSTON/GETTY IMAGES ©

Rugged coastline of South Point (Ka Lae)

7 Volcano (p223)

On the morning of your fifth day, browse or buy original works – photos, ceramics, blown glass – and meet the artists who created them at eclectic galleries hidden in the rainforest that embraces rainy, romantic Volcano village.

8 South Point (Ka Lae) (p239)

Backtrack past Ka'u's coffee farms and the sea turtles at Punalu'u Beach to stand at the southernmost point in the USA. It's also the place where ancient Polynesians first rowed ashore on Hawai'i. After standing at wind-blown Ka Lae, get ready for a long hike (or hop in a 4WD 'taxi') to unusually colored Green Sands Beach.

9 Puna (p192)

Get lost on day six in Puna, a district as nonconformist as it is beguiling. Little-traveled rural byways let you explore this region's wonders including tide pools, a black-sand beach and lava tree molds, plus there's a chance to perhaps see red-hot lava flowing into the ocean. Book ahead for dramatic lava boat tours.

10 Hilo (p168)

Drive north to Hilo to bed down tonight. With its scenic bay and lush greenery, Hawai'i's capital is a charmer. Stroll the retro-flavored downtown, with its local cafes, sushi bars and shops, to the EHCC Hawai'i Museum of Contemporary Art and Palace Theater.

THIS LEG: 200 MILES

Hilo to Waipi'o Valley

8 DAYS

'Imiloa Astronomy Center of Hawai'i (p172), Hilo

11 Hilo (p168)

On the morning of day seven, step inside one of Hilo's fascinating museums to learn about the Big Islands' volcanic origins, modern astronomy or destructive tsunami. Grab lunch fixings from Hilo's farmers and fish markets, then picnic in Liliuokalani Park, a bayside gem with Japanese gardens, pagodas and bamboo groves.

12 Mauna Kea (p134)

Drive up Hawaii's highest peak in time for sunset – the island's top spot for it – and then stick around for free stargazing programs outside the visitor information station. Taking a summit tour maximizes the literally breath-taking experience.

13 Hamakua Coast (p148)

Begin day eight by meandering through storybook rainforest along the short Pepe'ekeo 4-Mile Scenic Drive, passing the Hawaii Tropical Botanical Garden. Continuing north, stop at Akaka Falls State Park.

14 Honoka'a (p148)

On your way to Waipi'o Valley, pause in laid-back Honoka'a. Amble around downtown's antiques and art shops, or reserve ahead for a tour of nearby boutique farms that grow vanilla, honey, tea and more. Don't forget to fuel up with *malasadas* (Portuguese doughnuts) from Tex Drive-In.

15 Waipi'o Valley (p152)

No matter how you experience this waterfall-strewn, sacred 'Valley of Kings' – with a guide, on horseback or on foot – it will be memorable. Go solo to kick back on the black-sand beach at your leisure.

THIS LEG: 135 MILES

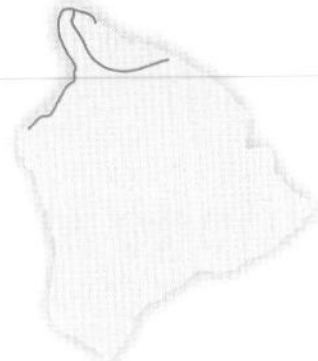

Waimea to North Kona

10 DAYS

Dahana Ranch, Waimea (Kamuela)

LONELY PLANET/GETTY IMAGES ©

16 Waimea (p122)

On day nine, giddyap on a morning trail ride (book ahead) across the heart of Hawai'i's *paniolo* (cowboy) country. Browse living-history exhibits at the town's heritage centers, then grab lunch.

17 Hawi (p113)

Follow scenic Kohala Mountain Rd (Hwy 250) through rolling green pasturelands to Hawi, a small, hang-loose town that's chock-full of art galleries and shops.

18 Pololu Valley (p121)

This valley offers eye candy from the road's-end lookout. A short, steep trail leads to the black-sand beach below.

19 Mo'okini Luakini Heiau (p115)

Unless you spent a lot of time swooning over Pololu Valley's rugged beauty, you'll also have time in the afternoon to visit this site, one of Hawaii's most sacred. It's nearby Kamehameha the Great's birthplace.

20 South Kohala Beaches (p97)

Don't miss sunset from one of South Kohala's drive-up beaches. Mauna Kea Beach is a favorite; Hapuna Beach is another all-around winner.

21 North Kona Beaches (p80)

Spend your last day adventuring to North Kona's wilder beaches – among the Big Island's very best. Dive into coconut-fringed Kiholo Bay, with its sea turtles and swimmable lava tube, or trek to Kekaha Kai (Kona Coast) State Park for powdery salt-and-pepper sands.

THIS LEG: 90 MILES

Get Inspired

Books

Saturday Night at the Pahala Theatre (1993) Lois-Ann Yamanaka's bracing stories written in Hawaiian pidgin reveal another side of 1970s Hilo.

Volcano: A Memoir of Hawai'i (1996) Poet Garrett Hongo traces his family's roots back to the evocative rainforests and lava flows of East Hawai'i.

Big Island Journey (2009) Sophia Schweitzer and Bennett Hymer share Hawai'i's rich history with 400-plus vintage photos.

Films

Keepers of the Flame (1988) Eddie and Myrna Kamae (www.hawaiianlegacy.com) profile revered Hawaiian cultural practicioners Mary Kawena Pukui, Iolani Luahine and Edith Kanaka'ole.

Li'a: The Legacy of a Hawaiian Man (1988) Another documentary by Eddie and Myrna Kamae celebrates prolific songwriter and musician Sam Li'a Kalainaina from remote Waipi'o Valley.

Music

Tell U What (2012) Ukulele prodigy Brittni Paiva's latest collection shows off her range.

Kona (2010) Master slack key guitarists Martin Pahinui, Daniel Akaka Jr and others highlight Hawaii's iconic instrument.

'Ohai 'Ula (2010) Kainani Kahaunaele is a gifted *haku mele* (composer of Hawaiian songs).

Websites

Mountain Apple Company on YouTube (www.youtube.com/user/mountainapplecompany) Watch Israel 'Iz' Kamakawiwo'ole to better understand what it means to be Hawaiian.

Toward Living Pono on YouTube (www.youtube.com/user/towardlivingpono) Snippets on poi, aloha and the Hawaiian language from iconic Big Islanders.

KonaWeb (www.konaweb.com) Despite the name, the whole island is covered, with handy links to cultural and performing-arts events, farmers markets, unique local products and more.

Hawaiian Lava Daily (http://hawaiianlavadaily.blogspot.com) Stunning photos and videos of Kilauea's red-hot lava action.

Short on time?

This list will give you instant insight into Hawai'i.

Read *Ancient Hawai'i* (1998) Artist and historian Herb Kawainui Kane depicts traditional Hawaiian ways in vivid detail.

Watch *The Punalu'u Experience* (2008) Danny Miller's documentary explains why Ka'u's pristine, black-sand beach is sacred.

Listen *Hawai'i Island...Is My Home* (2008) Slack key guitarist John Keawe's lilting instrumental and vocal tribute to the Big Island won a prestigious Na Hoku Hanohano award.

Log on GoHawaii.com (www.gohawaii.com/big-island) Official tourism website.

Hula performance with *ipu* (gourds)
WATERFALL WILLIAM/GETTY IMAGES ©

Hawai'i, the Big Island Month by Month

Top Events

Merrie Monarch Festival April

Hawai'i Island Festival September

Ironman Triathlon World Championship October

Kona Coffee Cultural Festival November

Waimea Ukulele & Slack Key Guitar Institute November

January

Waimea Ocean Film Festival

Watch eco documentaries, high-adrenaline sports footage and films about Hawaiian culture, with Q&A talks and outdoor activities over five days in Waimea and South Kohala in mid-January (www.waimea-oceanfilm.org).

March

Kona Brewers Festival

This beer fest (www.konabrewersfestival.com) on the second Saturday of March just keeps getting bigger. Sip dozens of handcrafted brews from across Hawaii, the western USA and elsewhere, all accompanied by live music and top island chef's food.

April

Merrie Monarch Festival

Hilo's premier event (p177) is a week-long celebration of Hawaiian arts and culture, starting on Easter Sunday. This Olympics of hula competitions draws top *halau* (schools) from all Hawaiian Islands, the US mainland and abroad. Plan ahead.

May

Lei Day

This statewide cultural festival kicks off on May 1 (Lei Day) at Kalakaua Park in downtown Hilo, with plenty of masterful lei on display, and continues with live music and hula at Hilo's beautiful Palace Theater.

(left) Dancers at the Merrie Monarch Festival
JOE CARINI/GETTY IMAGES ©

June

King Kamehameha Day

On June 11, a state holiday, join the crowds at King Kamehameha's birthplace in North Kohala for a flowery parade, arts-and-crafts fair, live music and food booths. More events take place on Mokuola (Coconut Island) in Hilo.

July

Fourth of July Rodeo

Held on the historic Parker Ranch, this annual event packs in *paniolo* (Hawaiian cowboys) and their fans for team roping, horse racing and other fun.

Kilauea Cultural Festival

This day-long festival in early July draws crowds to Hawai'i Volcanoes National Park to celebrate Hawaiian culture: there are lei- and basket-making demonstrations, hula dancing and even nose-flute jams.

Big Island Hawaiian Music Festival

A must for Hawaiian music fans, this two-day concert in Hilo features virtuoso performances by ukulele strummers, steel and slack key guitarists and falsetto singers in mid-July.

August

Hawaiian International Billfish Tournament

Kailua-Kona is the epicenter of big-game fishing, and this is Hawaii's grand tournament in late July or early August. Watch the weighing of the catch at Kailua Pier.

September

Hawai'i Island Festival

For '30 days of aloha' in September, this islandwide cultural celebration (www.hawaiiislandfestival.org) starts with a Hawaiian royal procession in South Kona and ends with a *paniolo* parade in Waimea. The Queen Lili'uokalani Canoe Races happen over Labor Day weekend.

October

Ironman Triathlon World Championship

This legendary triathlon is the ultimate endurance contest, combining a 2.4-mile ocean swim, 112-mile bike race and 26.2-mile marathon in Kailua-Kona on the second Saturday of October.

November

Kona Coffee Cultural Festival

Celebrate Kona's signature brew during the harvest season with 10 days of coffee tastings, farm tours, cultural events and a cupping competition in early November.

Moku O Keawe

In early November, this three-day dance festival brings together hula troupes from Hawaii, Japan and the US mainland for competitions, workshops and a crafts-and-clothing market, all in Waikoloa.

Waimea Ukulele & Slack Key Guitar Institute

In mid-November, aspiring musicians can study with Hawaii's foremost musicians at this three-day institute's workshops, whose legendary concerts and *kanikapila* (jam sessions) are open to the public.

Need to Know

Currency
US dollar ($)

Language
English, Hawaiian

Visas
Generally not required for Canadians or for citizens of Visa Waiver Program (VWP) countries for stays of 90 days or less with ESTA pre-approval.

Money
ATMs available in major towns. Credit cards widely accepted by most businesses (except some lodgings); often required for reservations. Traveler's checks (US dollars) occasionally used.

Cell Phones
Coverage spotty in remote areas. International travelers need GSM multiband phones; buy prepaid SIM cards locally.

Wi-Fi
Available at most accommodations; many hotels charge daily fees.

Internet Access
Cybercafes are scarce; access averages $6 to $12 per hour.

Tipping
Expected by bartenders, restaurant servers, taxi drivers etc. See p286.

When to Go

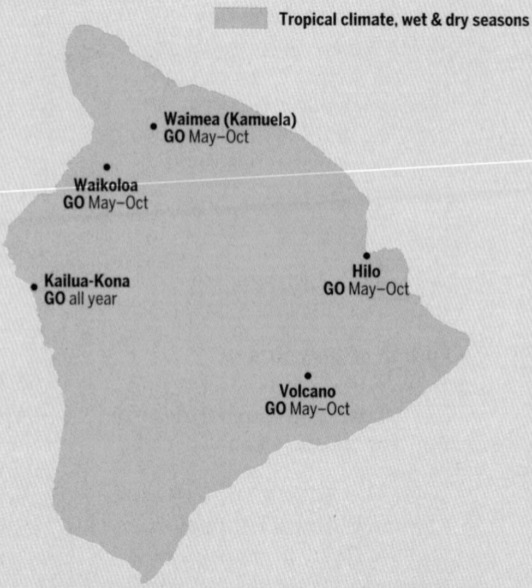

High Season (Dec–Apr & Jun–Aug)
- Accommodations prices up 50% to 100%
- Christmas to New Year and Easter most pricey, busiest
- Winter rainier (best for whale-watching and surfing)

Shoulder (May & Sep)
- Crowds and prices drop slightly between schools' spring break and summer vacation
- Temperatures mild, mostly sunny days
- Hawai'i Island Festival in September

Low Season (Oct–Nov)
- Airfares at lowest from US mainland and Canada
- More vacancies, accommodations rates lower
- Ironman World Championship (Oct), Kona Coffee Cultural Festival (Nov)

Advance Planning
- **Three months before** Decide which region's climate and attractions best match your interests. Search for internet deals on flights, cars and accommodations.
- **One month before** Reserve a spot on popular tours, such as nighttime snorkeling and diving with manta rays, lava-watching boats and Mauna Kea summit stargazing.
- **One week before** Confirm your travel bookings. Check weather forecasts to ensure you pack the right gear. Make spa and splurge-worthy restaurant reservations.

Daily Costs

Budget Less than $100

- Hostel dorm bed: $25–35
- Budget hotel or B&B room, shared bath: $55–80
- Local plate lunch: $5–10
- Bus fare (one way): $2

Midrange $100–250

- Room with private bath at midrange hotel or B&B: $100–200
- Rental car (excluding insurance and gas): per day/week from $35/150
- Dinner at casual sit-down restaurant: $20–40

Top End More than $250

- Luxury beach resort room: over $250
- Three-course meal and cocktail: $75–100
- Guided outdoor adventure tour: $80–200

Exchange Rates

Australia	A$1	$0.94
Canada	C$1	$0.92
Europe (euro)	€1	$1.38
Japan	¥100	$0.98
New Zealand	NZ$1	$0.87
UK	£1	$1.68

For current exchange rates see www.xe.com.

What to Bring

- **Driver's license** Needed to rent and drive a car.
- **Hands-free device** Talking or texting on a handheld cellphone while driving is illegal.
- **Hiking shoes** Broken in and sturdy enough for lava-rock terrain.
- **Long sleeves & pants** Breathable fabric to protect against sunburn and mosquito bites; lightweight waterproof jacket may be useful.
- **UV-protection sunglasses** For ocean glare and highway driving.
- **ID cards** Student, automobile association and AARP member cards for travel discounts.
- **Snorkeling gear** Bring your own if you'll snorkel often or are picky about fit and quality.

Arriving on Hawai'i, the Big Island

- **Kona International Airport at Keahole (KOA; p289)**

Car Rental-car companies at airport.

Taxi & airport shuttle Around $25 to Kailua-Kona, $35 to Keauhou, plus tip.

Bus One to three daily buses (none Sunday; $2).

- **Hilo International Airport (ITO; p289)**

Car Rental-car companies at airport.

Taxi Around $15 plus tip into town.

Getting Around

- **Car** Well-maintained highway circumnavigates island. Free parking widely available.
- **Bus** Hele-On Bus (fare $2) links major towns; limited runs, especially on weekends. Luggage, bicycle surcharge $1; no surfboards.
- **Bicycle** Decent roads for touring, but sun, wind and rain can be brutal.

Sleeping

- **Hotels & resorts** Prevalent on South Kohala and Kona coasts; top-end resorts offer the best beaches and splashy pools.
- **Condos** Mainly south of Kailua-Kona; ideal for independent travelers who prefer apartment-style amenities; discounted weekly rates.
- **B&Bs and inns** Generally reliable, with more space and amenities than comparably priced hotels; multinight stay often required.
- **Hostels** Simple private rooms and dormitory beds at rock-bottom prices.
- **Camping & cabins** Low-cost campsites and budget cabins at national, state and county parks; bring your own camping gear.

Be Forewarned

- **Vog** Volcanic smog can make sunny skies hazy. Short-term exposure not generally hazardous except for people with respiratory and heart conditions, pregnant women, young children and infants.
- **Coqui frogs** Nightly mating calls can disrupt sleep; inquire with accommodations if you're sensitive to noise.

Kailua-Kona & the Kona Coast

Since ancient Hawaiian times, the Kona Coast has been – and probably always will be – the Big Island's most popular playground. So alluring is this stretch of West Hawai'i's coast, it's not surprising that most travelers base themselves here. You can kayak and snorkel in aquamarine coves and lagoons one day, laze on a white- or black-sand strand the next, then cool off in the lush, green coffee belt on the slopes of Mt Hualalai. All the while, the natural beauty of Kailua Bay recalls its original role as an idyllic retreat for Hawaiian royalty. For visitors, the beach town of Kailua-Kona is a sunny delight and a hub for ocean sports. For locals who like to gripe, it's a sprawling suburb with nightmare rush-hour traffic, but others love the annual Ironman action and taking sunset cocktails by the surf. Stop by and see it all, then judge for yourself.

Kayaking, Kailua-Kona (p41)
ABRAHAM BOB/GETTY IMAGES ©

Kailua-Kona & the Kona Coast Itineraries

Two Days

❶ **Kailua-Kona** (p34) Dive right into the bay at Kailua Pier with whatever floats your boat – stand up paddling (SUP), surfing or outrigger canoeing. Take a guided tour of historical Hulihe'e Palace, once a royal retreat, as you amble down oceanfront Ali'i Dr. Grab sunset drinks at breezy Huggo's on the Rocks or the ocean-view lanai at Humpy's Big Island Alehouse.

❷ **Kahalu'u Beach Park** (p54) Roll out of bed early on day two, and check the weather first. Nice and calm? Head out for an early morning snorkel at this ever-popular beach, a quick drive or trolley ride south of Kailua-Kona. *Honu* (green sea turtles) and tropical fish abound in the bay's shallow waters.

❸ **White (Magic) Sands Beach** (p34) If it's looking choppy out there in the ocean, don't despair. Join the locals bodyboarding instead at this crescent-shaped strand closer to downtown Kailua-Kona.

❹ **Holualoa** (p59) In the afternoon, get out of town for a quick escape to this historic plantation community up in the hills. Do a slo-mo art-gallery crawl, followed by tastings and tours of Kona's famous coffee estates, only a short, scenic drive away.

❺ **Honokohau Harbor** (p80) Book ahead for inspiring nighttime snorkeling cruises and scuba-diving tours that visit the hidden haunts of manta rays along the Kona Coast. Most boats leave from this sportfishing harbor, just north of Kailua-Kona.

THIS LEG: 30 MILES

Four Days

1 Kealakekua Bay (p71) Begin your third day early, paddling a kayak across this crystalline bay and keeping an eye peeled for dolphins. The only way to enjoy some of Hawai'i's most phenomenal snorkeling at Ka'awaloa Cove is on a guided kayak tour or snorkel cruise, or by hiking.

2 Kona Coffee Living History Farm (p69) Travel back in time at this family-owned coffee farm that shows what life in South Kona was like for Japanese immigrant farmers in Hawai'i's prestatehood era.

3 Pu'uhonua O Hōnaunau National Historical Park (p77) Also known as the Place of Refuge, you can circumambulate ancient temples at this park deeply rooted in the Hawaiian religion and traditions. Have your snorkel gear handy for Two-Step.

4 Kaloko-Honokohau National Historical Park (p83) Start day four learning how ancient Hawaiians raised fish and crops on the inhospitable North Kona Coast. Fishponds and tide pools await at lava- and coral-strewn beaches.

5 Keahole Point (p85) Take in a lecture and tour of West Hawai'i's alternative-energy and sustainable-aquaculture projects; take the kids to Ocean Rider Seahorse Farm.

6 Kekaha Kai (Kona Coast) State Park (p86) These are the pristine, wild beaches you've been so eager to find – but you'll have to hike to reach the best of 'em. Then swim, snorkel and dream of sailing to Tahiti.

7 Kiholo Bay (p90) Hit this state-park reserve at the end of day four for wildlife spotting, a swimmable lava tube and one last brilliant sunset.

THIS LEG: 75 MILES

Kailua-Kona & the Kona Coast Highlights

1 Best Beaches: Kekaha Kai (Kona Coast) State Park (p86) Hard to get to, easy to love: snorkeling; sea turtles; soft, white sand.

2 Best Snorkeling: Ka'awaloa Cove (p73) Hike, kayak or cruise into Kealakekua Bay to this legendary spot teeming with underwater life.

3 Best Diving: Garden Eel Cove (p81) Aka Manta Heaven. Enough said! Thrilling after-dark boat trips depart from nearby Kailua-Kona.

4 Best Hawaiian Cultural Experience: Pu'uhonua O Hōnaunau National Historical Park (p77) Explore an ancient Hawaiian place of refuge.

5 Best Small Town: Holualoa (p59) Traditional Hawaiian craft and art galleries tucked among family-owned coffee farms.

Snorkeling, Kona Coast
JAMES R.D. SCOTT/GETTY IMAGES ©

Discover Kailua-Kona & the Kona Coast

KAILUA-KONA

Kailua-Kona, aka 'Kailua,' 'Kailua Town' or just 'Town,' makes a convenient base for exploring the entire Kona Coast, with its wild beaches; snorkeling with sea turtles and manta rays; upcountry coffee farms; and ancient Hawaiian sites by the ocean. In town, sunset by the seawall with a cold brew and a fish taco may be just what you're looking for at the end of another glorious day in the tropical sun.

Even so, Kailua can be a love-it-and-leave-it kind of place. Along Ali'i Dr, the main oceanside drag, traffic crawls bumper-to-bumper past tacky souvenir shops, waterfront bars and seafood restaurants. Sidewalk 'tourist information' booths sell every kind of tour and activity you might imagine.

Kahalu'u Beach Park (p54)
ANN CECIL/GETTY IMAGES ©

Beaches

Kailua-Kona might act like a beach town, but most of its in-town beaches don't rank among the Kona Coast's showstoppers.

White (Magic) Sands Beach Beach
(La'aloa Beach Park; Ali'i Dr; P) Over 3 miles south of Kailua-Kona toward Keauhou, this small but gorgeous roadside beach beckons with turquoise waters, tall palms and little shade. Its other nickname is 'Disappearing Sands,' because the sand can wash offshore literally overnight during high surf, exposing dangerous rocks and coral. As the surf settles, white sands magically return. It's a hot spot for body-boarding, or you can snorkel at the beach's southern end when waters are perfectly calm.

Facilities include restrooms, outdoor showers, drinking water, picnic tables, a volleyball court and lifeguard tower.

Old Kona Airport State Recreation Area Beach
(www.hawaiistateparks.org; Kuakini Hwy; 7am-8pm; P) The swimming is just so-so at this sandy but rock-strewn beach, just over a mile northwest of downtown Kailua-Kona. Come to picnic, explore tide pools and experience a laidback locals' beach. Just inside the south entrance gate is a pristine, sandy-bottomed pool for *na*

keiki (kids). At low tide, tiny sea urchins, crabs and bits of coral resemble lava-rock aquariums. When the surf's up, local surfers catch an offshore break here. Facilities include restrooms, outdoor showers, covered picnic tables and drinking water.

There's also a popular running track here. Just further south, the county-run **Kailua Park Complex** has an outdoor swimming pool, kiddie playground, tennis courts and ball-sports fields.

Kamakahonu Beach Beach

(👪) Kailua-Kona's only swimmable in-town beach is this teeny-tiny strand between Kailua Pier and Ahu'ena Heiau, where ocean waters are calm and usually safe for kids. Concession stands rent all kinds of beach gear here.

Sights

Ali'i Dr bombards you with surf shops and ABC Stores, but amid the tourist kitsch are a handful of historic buildings and landmarks worth seeking out.

Hulihe'e Palace Historic Building

(☎808-329-1877; www.huliheepalace.net; 75-5718 Ali'i Dr; adult/child $6/1; ⏰9am-4pm Mon-Sat) Imagine the life of Hawaiian royalty in this palace, a private oceanfront residence constructed in 1838 by Hawaii's second governor, John Adams Kuakini. It was originally built with lava rock, but in 1885 King Kalakaua plastered over it because he preferred a more polished style after his travels abroad. The two-story palace contains Western antiques collected on royal jaunts to Europe and ancient Hawaiian artifacts, most notably several of Kamehameha the Great's war spears.

Admission to the palace includes a 40-minute tour given by **Daughters of Hawai'i** (www.daughtersofhawaii.org) docents, who relate fascinating anecdotes about past royal occupants – including Princess Ruth Ke'elikolani, who typically slept outdoors in a *pili* (grass) hut.

Ahu'ena Heiau Temple

(www.ahuena.com; 75-5660 Palani Road) FREE After uniting the Hawaii's islands in 1810, Kamehameha the Great established the kingdom's royal court in Lahaina on Maui, but he continued to return to the Big Island. After a couple of years, he restored this sacred site as his personal retreat and temple. Notice the towering carved *ki'i* (deity) image with a golden plover atop its helmet: these long-distance flying birds may have helped guide the first Polynesians to Hawaii.

When Kamehameha I died at Ahu'ena Heiau on May 8, 1819, his body was prepared for burial here. In keeping with ancient Hawaiian tradition, the king's bones were secreted elsewhere, hidden so securely no one has ever found them (though some theorists point to a cave near Kaloko Fishpond).

Step inside **King Kamehameha's Kona Beach Hotel** nearby to view historical paintings and a mural by legendary artist and Hawaiian historian Herb Kawainui Kane. Also on display are a rare feathered helmet and cloak once worn by *ali'i* (royalty), ancient Hawaiian war weapons and musical instruments, and a whale's-tooth pendant strung on a braided cord made of human hair.

Moku'aikaua Church Church

(☎808-329-0655; www.mokuaikaua.org; 75-5713 Ali'i Dr; ⏰7:30am-5:30pm) FREE Completed in 1836, Moku'aikaua Church matches its island setting, with walls of lava rock hewn with stone adzes, smoothed with chunks of coral and held together by sand and coral-lime mortar. The interior posts and beams are constructed from ohia trees, while the pews and pulpit are made of koa, Hawaii's most prized native hardwood. The steeple tops out at 112ft, making this Kailua-Kona's tallest structure. The 11am Sunday worship service is usually followed by a short history lecture.

When the first Christian missionaries landed in Kailua Bay on April 4, 1820, their timing couldn't have been better. King Liholiho had abolished the traditional religion on that very spot just a few months before. He gave the missionaries this site, just a few minutes' walk from Ahu'ena Heiau, to establish Hawai'i's first Christian church.

Kailua-Kona

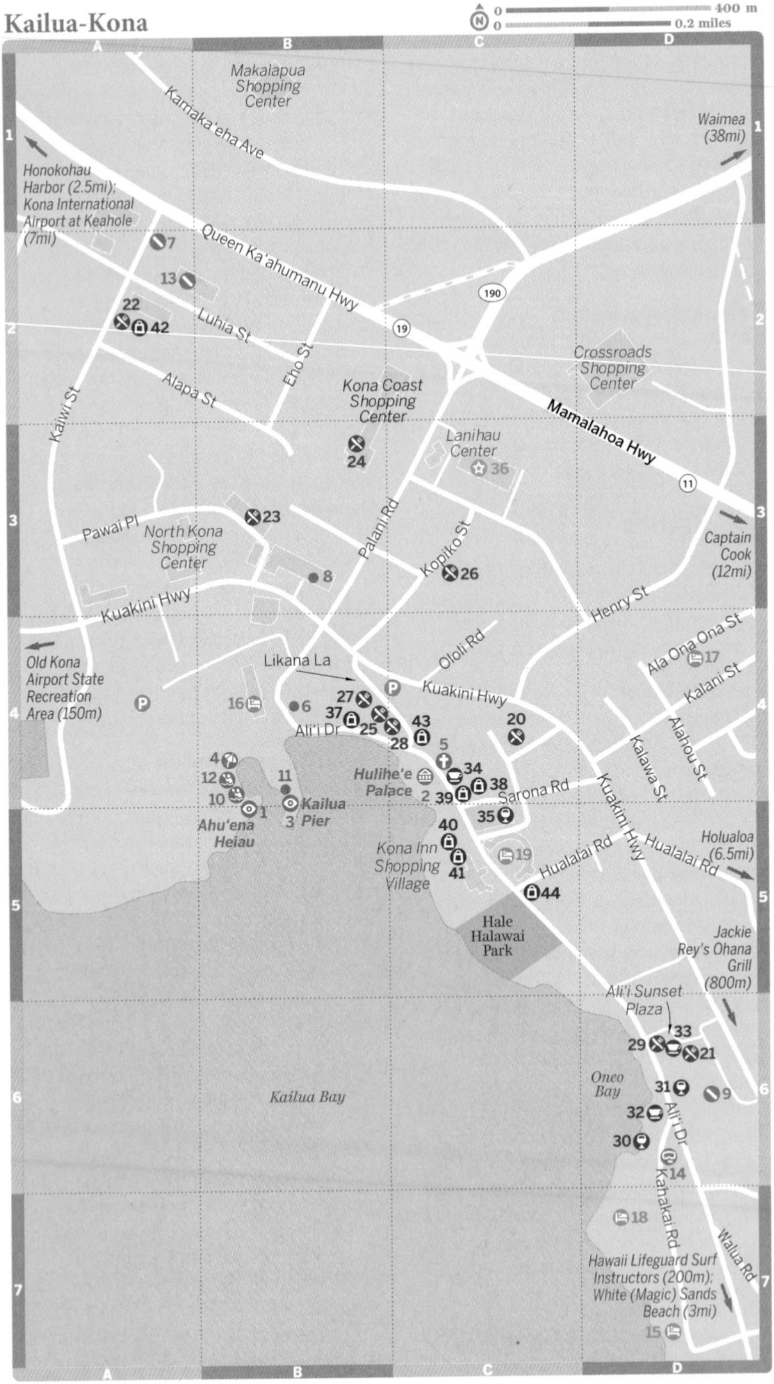
0 400 m
0 0.2 miles
Makalapua Shopping Center
Kamaka'eha Ave
Honokohau Harbor (2.5mi); Kona International Airport at Keahole (7mi)
Waimea (38mi)
Queen Ka'ahumanu Hwy
Luhia St
Alapa St
Eho St
Kaiwi St
190
19
Crossroads Shopping Center
Kona Coast Shopping Center
Mamalahoa Hwy
Lanihau Center
11
Pawai Pl
North Kona Shopping Center
Palani Rd
Kopiko St
Captain Cook (12mi)
Kuakini Hwy
Henry St
Ololi Rd
Old Kona Airport State Recreation Area (150m)
Likana La
Ala Ona Ona St
Kalani St
Ali'i Dr
Alahou St
Kalawa St
Hulihe'e Palace
Sarona Rd
Ahu'ena Heiau
Kailua Pier
Kona Inn Shopping Village
Hualalai Rd
Holualoa (6.5mi)
Hale Halawai Park
Jackie Rey's Ohana Grill (800m)
Ali'i Sunset Plaza
Oneo Bay
Kailua Bay
Kahakai Rd
Walua Rd
Hawaii Lifeguard Surf Instructors (200m); White (Magic) Sands Beach (3mi)

Kailua-Kona

Don't Miss Sights

1	Ahu'ena Heiau	B5
2	Hulihe'e Palace	C4
3	Kailua Pier	B4

Sights

4	Kamakahonu Beach	B4
5	Moku'aikaua Church	C4

Activities, Courses & Tours

6	Atlantis Submarines	B4
7	Big Island Divers	A2
8	Body Glove Hawaii	B3
9	Jack's Diving Locker	D6
10	Kai 'Opua Canoe Club	B4
11	Kailua Bay Charter Company	B4
12	Kona Boys Beach Shack	B4
	Kona Brewing Company	(see 23)
13	Kona Honu Divers	A2
	Lotus Center	(see 18)
14	Snorkel Bob's	D6

Sleeping

15	Hale Kona Kai	D7
16	King Kamehameha's Kona Beach Hotel	B4
17	Koa Wood Hale Inn/Patey's Place	D4
18	Royal Kona Resort	D7
19	Uncle Billy's Kona Bay Hotel	C5

Eating

	Basik Acai	(see 14)
20	Big Island Grill	C4
21	Island Lava Java	D6
22	Island Naturals Market & Deli	A2
23	Kona Brewing Company	B3
24	KTA Super Store	B3
25	Metal Mike's Twisted Pretzels	B4
26	Phuket Monkey	C3
27	Rapanui Island Cafe	B4
28	Scandinavian Shave Ice	C4
29	Sushi Shiono	D6

Drinking & Nightlife

	Don's Mai Tai Bar	(see 18)
30	Huggo's on the Rocks	D6
31	Humpy's Big Island Alehouse	D6
32	Java on the Rock	D6
33	Kanaka Kava	D6
34	Kope Lani	C4
35	Sam's Hideaway	C5

Entertainment

	Island Breeze Lu'au	(see 16)
36	KBXtreme	C3
	Lava Legends & Legacies - Journeys of the South Pacific	(see 18)

Shopping

37	Big Island Jewelers	B4
38	Conscious Riddims Records	C4
39	Crazy Shirts	C4
40	Honolua Surf Co	C5
41	J. Lambus Photography	C5
42	Kona Bay Books	A2
43	Na Makana	C4
44	Village Farmers Market	C5

Kailua Pier Landmark

Kailua Bay was once a major cattle-shipping area; animals were stampeded into the water and forced to swim to steamers waiting to transport them to Honolulu slaughterhouses. Now locals come to swim at lunchtime and canoe clubs launch their vessels here. The Hawaiian International Billfish Tournament (p43) kicks off here, continuing a sportfishing tradition begun in 1915 when the pier was built.

Activities

Other activity outfitters and tour companies are based at Keauhou, about 5 miles south of Kailua-Kona.

SWIMMING

With rocky shores and rough waters, Kailua-Kona isn't ideal for swimming – for that head to North Kona Coast beaches. Still, Kahalu'u Beach Park (p54), 5 miles south in Keauhou, is a good bet when conditions are calm, as is Old Kona Airport State Recreation Area (p34), especially with kids in tow.

BODYBOARDING, SURFING & SUP

White (Magic) Sands Beach (p34) is a favorite spot for bodyboarding. Local experts board surf at Banyans, north of White Sands, and Pine Trees (p85), south of the airport near Wawaloli (OTEC) Beach. Newbies can surf at Lymans, south of Banyans.

Ever popular, stand up paddling (SUP) delivers a core workout in the company of dolphins, turtles and tropical fish. The best part is anyone can do it – even the less fit can groove to this easy, fun

The Best... Kailua-Kona Sunset Views

1 Touching down at Kona International Airport (p52)
2 Kailua Pier (p37)
3 White (Magic) Sands Beach (p34)
4 Huggo's on the Rocks (p49)
5 Don's Mai Tai Bar (p50)

watersport. Give it a spin in Kailua Bay or Kahalu'u Bay, further south in Keauhou.

Hawaii Lifeguard Surf Instructors Surfing, SUP
(**HLSI; ☎808-324-0442; www.surflessonshawaii.com; 75-5909 Ali'i Dr; group/private lessons from $75/100**) Skilled, professional HLSI instructors have a minimum of 15 years' surfing experience and are all certified lifeguards. Join a group surfing or SUP lesson, or book a private one-on-one session (which is the only way that kids aged three to 10 years are taught at this school).

Kona Boys Beach Shack SUP
(**☎808-329-2345; www.konaboys.com; Kamakahonu Beach; surfboard/SUP set rental from $25, SUP lesson/tour $75/150; ⌚8am-5pm**) Organizes SUP lessons for beginners as well as more ambitious coastal paddling tours, and rents SUP sets and surfboards right on the beach. Call in advance to arrange group or private surfing or SUP lessons.

Kona Surf Adventures Surfing
(**☎808-334-0033; www.konasurfadventures.com; 75-6129 Ali'i Dr, Ali'i Gardens Marketplace; surfing lesson $99-150**) This surf school is run by California-born 'Kona Mike,' who comes with endorsements from novice students and veteran wave riders alike.

SNORKELING

For easy-access snorkeling, Kahalu'u Beach Park (p54), 5 miles south in Keauhou, is your closest and best option. To snorkel further afield, take a cruise from Honokohau Harbor or Keauhou Pier. Opt to depart in the morning, when conditions are calmer and clearer. Tour prices typically include snorkel gear, beverages and snacks; book ahead online for discounts.

Zodiac rafts are zippy and thrilling, capable of exploring sea caves, lava tubes and blowholes, but expect a bumpy ride and no shade or toilets. Catamarans are much larger, smoother and comfier but can't get as close into coves. Alternatively, many dive boats let snorkelers ride along at a cheaper rate.

Sea Paradise Snorkeling
(**☎800-322-5662, 808-322-2500; www.seaparadise.com; 78-6831 Ali'i Dr; snorkel cruise adult/child 5-12yr from $89/59**) Highly recommended outfitter offers morning snorkel cruises to Kealakekua Bay and nighttime manta ray trips (free rebooking if you don't spot any the first time out) on a smaller 46ft-long catamaran with a friendly, professional crew.

Fair Wind Snorkeling, Diving
(**☎800-677-9461, 808-322-2788; www.fairwind.com; 78-7130 Kaleiopapa St; snorkel cruise adult/child 4-12yr from $75/45**) The *Fair Wind II*, a two-story catamaran with two 15ft-long waterslides, sails to Kealakekua Bay every morning. Longer daytime cruises on the luxury hydrofoil catamaran *Hula Kai* explore less-trafficked waters ($149), while nighttime manta ray snorkel cruises are hugely popular ($99), so book ahead.

Captain Zodiac Snorkeling, Whale-Watching
(**☎808-329-3199; www.captainzodiac.com; Honokohau Harbor; snorkel cruise adult/child 4-12yr from $99/78**) In business with a jaunty pirate theme since 1974, Captain Zodiac makes daily trips to Kealakekua Bay in 24ft-long rigid-hull inflatable rafts that each carry up to 16 passengers.

Detour: Three Ring Ranch

Kona resident Dr Ann Goody communes with animals, fixes their broken bones and psyches, coaxes them back into their natural behavior and sets them free – or not: some rescued and exotic animals just can't cut it in the wild. That's when they become residents of her **Three Ring Ranch Exotic Animal Sanctuary** (**808-331-8778; www.threeringranch.org; 75-809 Keaolani Dr, Kailua-Kona; suggested donation $35; tours 11am-1pm, by reservation only**), a short drive from downtown Kailua-Kona.

An internationally accredited animal sanctuary, Three Ring Ranch currently hosts South African–crowned cranes, David and Goliath (a pair of gigantic African spur-thigh tortoises) and endangered endemic species such as the Hawaiian owl and nene (Hawaiian goose). Rescued from the failed Moloka'i Ranch safari park, the zebra Zoe has amelanosis, meaning her stripes are the color of sand and her eyes the color of the ocean.

Dr Ann Goody – who has been struck by lightning, tossed by a tiger shark and survived breast cancer – is as good with people as she is with animals. This, along with the unflagging support of her husband and business partner Dr Norm Goody, has led to an enormously successful educational initiative. Tours are by reservation only (children must be at least six years old). No drop-in visitors allowed.

Kamanu Charters Snorkeling
(**800-348-3091, 808-329-2021; www.kamanu.com; Honokohau Harbor; adult/child under 13yr $95/50**) Snorkel without crowds in the protected waters of Pawai Bay, just north of Old Kona Airport State Recreation Area. This 36ft catamaran maxes out at 24 people. Kamanu also offers a nighttime manta ray snorkel, but skip the dolphin swim – state law prohibits swimmers from getting closer then 150yd to these wild creatures to avoid disturbing them.

Snorkel Bob's Snorkeling
(**800-262-7725, 808-329-0770; www.snorkelbob.com; 75-5831 Kahakai Rd; 8am-5pm**) Rent snorkel masks (including corrective lenses for near-sighted folks), fins, reef walkers, wetsuits and flotation aids.

DIVING

The Kona Coast is known for calm, clear waters, unique lava formations and coral reefs. Near shore, divers can see steep drop-offs with lava tubes, caves and diverse marine life. Deeper waters contain dozens of popular boat-dive areas, including an airplane wreck off Keahole Point.

Most dive boats launch from Honokohau Harbor but have bricks-and-mortar offices in Kailua-Kona. Including all gear, the cost of a standard two-tank morning dive or one-tank night dive to see manta rays ranges from $110 to $150. Multiday PADI Open Water certification programs cost around $500 or more.

Jack's Diving Locker Diving, Snorkeling
(**800-345-4807, 808-329-7585; www.jacksdivinglocker.com; 75-5813 Ali'i Dr, Coconut Grove Marketplace, Bldg H;**) For top-notch introductory dives and courses, plus extensive programs for kids, this ecoconscious dive outfitter has a 5000-sq-ft facility with a store, classrooms, tank room and Hawaii's only 12ft-deep indoor dive pool. Sign up for a boat or shore dive, as well as a night manta ray dive. Snorkelers are welcome on many dive-boat trips.

Sandwich Isle Divers Diving
(**888-743-3483, 808-329-9188; www.sandwichisledivers.com**) This small charter dive-boat outfit run by a husband-and-wife team organizes personalized trips

(six-person maximum). These folks have decades of experience in Kona waters, and Captain Steve has a marine-biology degree.

Big Island Divers Diving, Snorkeling
(☎808-329-6068; www.bigislanddivers.com; 74-5467 Kaiwi St) Personable staff, an expansive shop and boat dives that are open to snorkelers all score big. This outfit specializes in night and manta ray dives. Black-water boat trips ($150 to $210) are for experienced – and, more importantly, fearless – divers only.

Kona Honu Divers Diving, Snorkeling
(☎888-333-4668, 808-324-4668; www.konahonudivers.com; 74-5583 Luhia St) Well-reviewed dive company schedules diverse boat trips, including manta ray night dives and Nitrox trips.

FISHING

Kailua-Kona is legendary for its big-game fishing, especially Pacific blue marlin (June to August are the best months), which can grow into 1-ton 'granders.' Sharing a charter boat starts at $95 per person for a four-hour trip or $250 all day. If you charter a whole boat, you can take up to six people for $450 to $600 for a half-day, or $750 or more for a full day. Ask whether the captain shares the catch.

Agencies book for so many boats that it's impossible to guarantee quality or consistency, but **Charter Desk** (☎888-566-2487, 808-326-1800; www.charterdesk.com; Honokohau Marina; ⌚6am-6pm) is reputable and can match you with 60 boats.

Captain Jeff's Charters Fishing
(☎808-895-1852; http://fishinkona.com) Captain Jeff is a straight shooter who offers tailored trips, insider advice and a share of the catch. Not for nothing, he has maintained the highest catch record in Kona for more than 15 years. Check his other website, **Kona Hawaii Fishing Report** (http://aloha-kona.com), for current sportfishing conditions.

Left: Surfing at Lymans Beach (p37) **Below:** Catamaran entering Keauhou Bay (p55)

(LEFT & BELOW) LONELY PLANET/GETTY IMAGES ©

Kayak Fishing Hawai'i Fishing, Kayaking

(☎808-936-4400; www.kayakfishinghawaii.com; guided tour $300) Imagine landing a 25lb ahi (yellowfin tuna) or *ono* (wahoo) fish from a kayak – not without a fight! This outfitter is based at Kawaihae Harbor, but travels island-wide.

OUTRIGGER CANOEING & KAYAKING

To see how outrigger canoeing pros do it, check out the January-to-May race schedule of the **Hawai'i Island Paddlesports Association** (www.hawaiipaddling.com). Over Labor Day weekend in late August and/or early September, don't miss the **Queen Lili'uokalani Canoe Race** (www.kaiopua.org) from Kailua Bay south to Honaunau.

Kona Boys Beach Shack Canoeing, Kayaking

(☎808-329-2345; www.konaboys.com; Kamakahonu Beach; tours $50-149; 8am-5pm) Experience what the original Polynesian settlers must have felt with the water rushing under their hull as they approached the volcanic shores of the Big Island. Paddle an outrigger canoe around Kamakahonu Bay or all the way from Keauhou to snorkel in Kealekekua Bay. Sea-kayaking tours often stop to snorkel too.

Kai 'Opua Canoe Club Canoeing

(www.kaiopua.org; Kamakahonu Beach) With this local club dedicated to traditional Hawaiian outrigger canoeing, visitors are welcome to join recreational paddling excursions leaving at 6am every morning except Sunday. There is no club office, so check the website for schedules and contact details. Trips launch next to Ahu'ena Heiau.

WHALE-WATCHING

Although snorkeling, diving and fishing tours often give you whale-watching opportunities during humpback season

Manta Ray Night Dives & Snorkeling

A night dive or snorkel cruise among Pacific manta rays is the aquatic thrill of a lifetime. Manta ray sightings are not guaranteed, no matter what boat operators promise, although some will let you repeat the cruise for free if none are sighted. If you're PADI-certified but rusty (or if it's your first night dive), a two-tank dive allows time to practice during the first afternoon dive.

Visit the **Manta Pacific Research Foundation** (www.mantapacific.org) website for responsible viewing guidelines for divers and snorkelers.

(December to April), you're more likely to see, and learn, more on specialized tours.

Dan McSweeney's Whale Watch Whale-Watching
(808-942-5376, 808-322-0028; www.ilovewhales.com; Honokohau Harbor; 2½hr cruise adult/under 12yr $110/99) Captain McSweeney's winter excursions focus on humpback whale sightings, marine conservation and education. Several other species of whales and dolphins can be seen in Kona waters year-round. Hydrophones allow passengers to listen in on whale songs.

Tours

Body Glove Hawaii Cruise
(808-326-7122, 800-551-8911; www.bodyglovehawaii.com; 75-5629 Kuakini Hwy; adult/child 6-17yr historical cruise incl dinner $115/83, incl lunch $88/68; 1pm Wed, 4pm Tue, Thu-Fri & Sat;) Popular historical cruises along the Kona Coast last three hours and feature a so-so buffet, live music and engaging historical narration. Staffed by a hospitable crew, the boat is wheelchair-accessible.

Kona Brewing Company Tour
(808-334-2739; http://konabrewingco.com; 75-5629 Kuakini Hwy; 30min tours 10:30am & 3pm) FREE Since 1994, this ecoconscious company has anchored Hawai'i's microbrewery scene. The once-small, family-run operation is now one of the nation's fastest-growing microbreweries – from Maine to California, you can sip 'liquid Aloha.' Complimentary tours include tasting samples. No reservations accepted; sign up in person at the pub.

Hawaiian Walkways Walking Tour
(800-457-7759; www.hawaiianwalkways.com; tour adult/child 8-12yr $119/99) Leads three-hour walking tours through the upland **Kona Cloud Forest Sanctuary**. Guides are knowledgeable about botany and geology, and the tour ends with a visit to Mountain Thunder Coffee Plantation (p61). Wear sturdy shoes.

Kailua Bay Charter Company Cruise
(808-324-1749; www.konaglassbottomboat.com; Kailua-Kona Pier; 50min tour adult/child under 12yr $40/20; usually 10:30am, 11:30am & 12:30pm daily;) Gain a new perspective on Kailua-Kona's coastline, its underwater reef and sea life from a 36ft glass-bottomed boat with a cheery crew and onboard naturalist. Easy boarding available for passengers with mobility issues.

Atlantis Submarines Boat Tour
(800-548-6262; www.atlantisadventures.com; 75-5669 Ali'i Dr; 45min tour adult/child under 13yr $109/45; 10am;) You read that right: a real-deal submarine descends up to 100ft into a coral-reef crevice and explores nearby shipwrecks. The battery-powered sub has 26 portholes and carries 48 passengers. Kids must be at least 36in tall.

Festivals & Events

Kokua Kailua Art, Food
(http://historickailuavillage.com) On the third Sunday of the month, local food vendors, artists and craftspeople set up booths along Ali'i Dr, which closes to vehicular traffic. The whole affair starts around 1pm and lasts until sunset, with free Hawaiian

music and hula dancing at Hulihe'e Palace starting around 4pm.

Kona Brewers Festival Beer, Food

(www.konabrewersfestival.com) On the second Saturday in March, Kona Brewing Company throws its annual beer bash, with proceeds benefiting local charities. Sample dozens of craft beers and island chefs' gourmet grinds. Buy tickets in advance online.

Hawaiian International Billfish Tournament Fishing

(www.hibtfishing.com) Hawaii's most prestigious sportfishing contest encompasses five days of fishing followed by weigh-ins and festivities at Kailua Pier. The tournament starts in late July or early August.

Ironman Triathlon World Championship Sports

(www.ironman.com) On the second Saturday in October, all traffic on Ali'i Dr halts for this human-powered endurance test that starts and finishes at Kailua Pier.

Kona Coffee Cultural Festival Coffee

(www.konacoffeefest.com) For 10 days in early November during the harvest season, the community celebrates Kona coffee pioneers and their renowned beans. Dozens of events include a cupping competition, art shows, live music and hula performances, farm tours, coffee tastings, a recipe cook-off and a coffee cherry-picking contest.

Sleeping

The quality of hotels and condos along Ali'i Dr in walkable downtown Kailua-Kona is only fair to middling. Many condos and vacation rentals are either along or near Ali'i Dr heading toward Keauhou, the beachy resort area just south of Kailua-Kona, or several miles upland on the cool slopes of Mt Hualalai.

Browse condo- and vacation-rental listings online at **Vacation Rentals by Owner** (VRBO; VRBO; www.vrbo.com), **Home Away** (http://www.homeaway.com/) and **Air B&B** (www.airbnb.com), or with local booking agencies **Affordable Paradise** (☎808-261-1693; www.affordable-paradise.com), **ATR Properties** (☎888-311-6020, 808-329-6020; www.konacondo.com), **Kona Hawaii Vacation Rentals** (☎800-244-4752, 808-329-3333 ; www.konahawaii.com), **Kona Rentals** (☎800-799-5662, 808-334-1199; www.konarentals.com), **Knutson & Associates** (☎800-800-6202, 808-329-6311; www.konahawaiirentals.com) and **SunQuest Vacations** (☎808-329-6438, from Canada 800-800-5662, from mainland USA 800-367-5168; www.sunquest-hawaii.com).

Wherever you stay, remember that oceanfront in Kona doesn't necessarily mean a sandy beach, as there's little sand along the rocky shoreline. Make reservations, especially during high season. Booking online in advance usually nets you the biggest savings.

Humpback whale, Kona Coast

STUART WESTMORLAND/GETTY IMAGES ©

The Best... Kailua-Kona & the Kona Coast for Kids

1 Kahalu'u Beach Park (p54)

2 Ocean Rider Seahorse Farm (p85)

3 Scandinavian Shave Ice (p47)

4 Fair Wind snorkel cruise (p38) to Kealakekua Bay

5 Hawaii Lifeguard Surf Instructors (p38)

6 Three Ring Ranch Exotic Animal Sanctuary (p39)

Koa Wood Hale Inn/ Patey's Place Hostel $
(808-329-9663; 75-184 Ala Ona Ona St; dm/r with shared bath from $25/55; reception 8am-noon & 5-10pm; @ wifi) Kailua-Kona's only hostel is a backpacker crashpad, with basic fan-cooled dorms and private rooms, a common kitchen and the usual crowd of 20-somethings, misfits and the globally road-weary. It's on a residential street within walking distance of Ali'i Dr. No drugs, alcohol or shoes indoors.

Royal Sea-Cliff Resort Condo $$
(info 866-733-0659, reservations 800-688-7444; www.outriggercondominiums.com; 75-6040 Ali'i Dr; studio/1br/2br apt from $145/175/230; P air-con @ wifi pool) This seven-floor timeshare complex feels almost like a hotel, giving you the best of both worlds. Immaculate units are generously sized and appointed with tropical furniture and lots of amenities – well-stocked kitchens, washer/dryers, two oceanfront pools, tennis courts and outdoor BBQ grills. Minimum two-night stay; mandatory cleaning fee ($40 to $60).

Kona Tiki Hotel Hotel $$
(808-329-1425; www.konatikihotel.com; 75-5968 Ali'i Dr; r $85-159; P wifi pool) You can afford oceanfront views at this retro three-story hotel, a quirky, well-kept 15-unit complex south of downtown Kailua-

Ironman Triathlon World Championship

Ironman Triathlon World Championship

When thousands of athletes and fans swoop into Kailua-Kona each October, locals gripe about traffic and crowds. But nobody can deny the thrilling spectacle of the Ironman Triathlon World Championship (p43). The granddaddy of triathlons is a brutal combination of a 2.4-mile ocean swim, 112-mile bike race and 26.2-mile run. And it has to be done in under 17 hours. Australian Craig Alexander set the current course record at eight hours, three minutes and 56 seconds in 2011.

Harsh conditions make the event the ultimate endurance test. Heat bouncing off the lava commonly exceeds 100°F (38°C), making dehydration and heat exhaustion major challenges. Many contenders arrive on the island weeks before to acclimatize. On race day, the world's toughest athletes are pushed to the max – in the past, they've included a 75-year-old nun, an Iraq war veteran amputee, and father–son Team Hoyt, with Rick pushing son Dick in a wheelchair (they're six-time finishers!).

Begun in 1978 by a US Navy man on a dare, the Ironman was labeled 'lunatic' by *Sports Illustrated.* Only 15 people competed the first year, and three didn't even cross the finish line. With that kind of crazy drama, the sports world was hooked. Today the event draws up to 2000 athletes from over 50 countries, everyone seeking the rights to 'Brag for the rest of your life!'.

Kona. Motel-style rooms are forgettably basic (no TVs, phones or air-con), but all have a fridge and enchanting lanai. Book well ahead, as the hotel regularly fills with nostalgic repeat guests. No credit cards.

Hale Kona Kai Condo $$

(808-421-3696, 808-329-6402; www.halekonakai-hkk.com; 75-5870 Kahakai Rd; 1br apt $150-215; P) All condos overlook crashing surf at this well-managed, oceanfront complex off the busy commercial stretch of Ali'i Dr. The 22 one-bedroom units vary in style, but each has a separate living room, full kitchen and ocean-view lanai. Poolside wi-fi only. Minimum-night stay varies.

Casa de Emdeko Condo $$

(808-329-2160; www.casadeemdeko.org; 75-6082 Ali'i Dr; 1br apt from $100; P) With Spanish-tile roofs, white stucco, immaculate gardens and two pools, this condo complex south of downtown Kailua-Kona is stylish and restful. Individually owned units are mostly up-to-date, peacefully quiet and reasonably priced.

Mango Sunset B&B B&B $$

(808-325-0909; www.mangosunset.com; 73-4261 Mamalahoa Hwy; r without/with private bath $100/120, all incl breakfast; P @) Hawaiiana-bedecked teak furnishings and bamboo accents spruce up the snug accomodations on this family-owned organic coffee farm. The best rooms offer sweeping ocean views from a shared lanai, and there's a common kitchenette. It's about a 15-minute drive from downtown Kailua-Kona, closer to the airport.

Kona Magic Sands Resort Condo $$

(800-244-4752, 808-329-3333; www.konahawaii.com/ms.htm; 77-6452 Ali'i Dr; studio apt $115-160; P) Large studios all have oceanfront lanai, but the 2nd- and 3rd-floor units are best. The location south of downtown Kailua-Kona is perfect for beach-goers. An all-concrete building keeps out some noise and heat, but not all units have air-con.

Nancy's Hideaway B&B $$

(866-325-3132, 808-325-3132; www.nancyshideaway.com; 73-1530 Uanani Pl; studio incl breakfast $120-140, cottage incl breakfast $130-150;) At this peaceful retreat, 6 miles upslope from town, pick between a free-standing studio or a one-bedroom cottage, each contemporary in design with its own kitchenette. No young children allowed.

Uncle Billy's Kona Bay Hotel Hotel $$
(808-329-1393, 800-367-5102; www.unclebilly.com; 75-5739 Ali'i Dr; r $99-135; P) In a pinch, head to this low-rent waterfront hotel. The good: it's right downtown with complimentary continental breakfast. The bad: street noise, frumpy interiors and kooky folks.

Kona Sugar Shack Vacation Rental $$$
(877-324-6444, 808-895-2203; www.konasugarshack.com; 77-6483 Ali'i Dr; ste $225-490; P) It hits the sweet spot for vacation rentals, right across the street from the beach. Friendly, artistic hosts have created a solar-powered oasis with funky, colorful and eclectic decor and relaxing, kid-friendly vibes. Extras include a shared outdoor kitchen, coin-op laundry, a miniscule pool and beach and baby gear to borrow. Rent the whole house for a family reunion. Expect a one-time cleaning fee ($125 to $275). Ouch.

King Kamehameha's Kona Beach Hotel Hotel $$$
(808-329-2911, 800-367-2111; www.konabeachhotel.com; 75-5660 Palani Rd; r $150-305; P@) A prime beachfront location and spiffy renovations are watchwords for the historic 'King Kam,' anchoring the north end of Ali'i Dr. Chic decor by the Courtyard Marriott chain, Herb Kawainui Kane's artwork and Hawaiian historical artifact exhibits in the lobby, a 24-hour fitness center and free wi-fi are all draws at this favorite with both vacationers and business types.

Royal Kona Resort Resort $$$
(800-222-5642, 808-329-3111; www.royalkona.com; 75-5852 Ali'i Dr; r $140-300; P@) Spread over three ship-shaped towers, this breezy, 1970s Polynesian fantasy has a tropical theme that lets you know you're in Hawaii. Although all rooms are remodeled, those in the pricier Ali'i and Lagoon Towers are worth an upgrade. A protected, saltwater lagoon is perfect for kids. Check out the long menu of spa services at the **Lotus Center** (www.konaspa.com).

Honu Kai B&B B&B $$$
(808-292-1775, 808-329-8676; www.honukaibnb.com; 74-1529 Hao Kuni St; d incl breakfast $220-255; P@) Amid tropical gardens, this plush, romantic four-room B&B is filled with rich fabrics, carved bedframes and Asian and Hawaiian decor. Guests share a hot tub, outdoor kitchen and rooftop lanai. Enclosed by rock walls, the private gated property is a 10-minute drive from downtown Kailua-Kona.

Eating

You don't have to spend a lot to devour *'ono kine grinds* (good food), but you'll usually have to venture further afield than Ali'i Dr, where most waterfront restaurants are disappointing and overpriced.

Da Poke Shack Seafood, Local $
(808-329-7653; http://dapokeshack.com; 76-6246 Ali'i Dr, Castle Kona Bali Kai; mains & meals $5-10; 10am-6pm) What's *poke*? Hawaii-style raw cubes of fish mixed with soy sauce, sesame oil, some chiles, seaweed and...well, the sky's the limit. This is the spot to get it, because these awesome *brah* (brothers) offer a huge variety of fresh-off-da-boat, homemade *poke,* side salads and plate lunches. Eat at picnic tables in the parking lot or take it to the beach.

Basik Acai Cafe $
(www.basikacai.com; 75-5831 Kahakai Rd; snacks & drinks $6-13; 7am-4pm Mon-Fri, from 8am Sat & Sun;) Healthy, wholesome acai bowls bursting with tropical fruity goodness, granola, nuts, shredded coconut and even cacao nibs, along with fresh juice smoothies, are made to order at this tiny upstairs kitchen that sources organic, local ingredients. It's expensive, but worth it.

Phuket Monkey Thai $
(808-333-5395; www.phuketmonkey.com; 75-5660 Kopiko St, Kopiko Plaza; mains $7-13;

10:30am-3:30pm & 5-9pm) Nearby Longs Drugs, this tiny strip-mall kitchen with a laughing monkey mascot dishes up real-deal authentic Thai food such as fiery lemongrass chicken, marinated beef salads and tangy pineapple curry. Order it 'super monkey' hot, if you dare.

Metal Mike's Twisted Pretzels Fast Food $

(Likana Ln; snacks $3-5; usually 11:30am-10pm Mon-Thu, to midnight Fri & Sat, noon-10pm Sun;) Metal Mike, who seriously looks like he spent time as a roadie, runs this rock-and-roll pretzel stand on a narrow alley by a parking lot just above Ali'i Dr. Go ga-ga over a dozen kinds of pretzels and dipping sauces, from cheesy jalapeño to white chocolate mac-nut.

Kope Lani Cafe

(www.kopelani.com; 75-5719 Ali'i Dr; snacks & drinks $3-7; 7am-9pm) Ali'i Dr is chock-a-block with coffee shops vending 100% Kona brews from upcountry coffee plantations. This sweet spot stands out, not just for its ocean views and ice-blended espresso drinks, but also its two-dozen flavors of Big Island–made ice cream.

Island Naturals Market & Deli Supermarket, Deli $

(www.islandnaturals.com; 74-5487 Kaiwi St; 7:30am-8pm Mon-Sat, 9am-7pm Sun;) This health-conscious grocery store has a fantastic deli making sandwiches, wraps and salads to go, plus a hot-and-cold takeout bar. Some organic and gluten-free options too.

Scandinavian Shave Ice Desserts $

(www.scandinavianshaveice.com; 75-5699 Ali'i Dr; snacks & drinks $3-8; 11am-8pm Sun-Thu, to 9pm Fri & Sat;) Shave ice is piled up here in huge, psychedelic mounds that are as big as your head. Dither over a rainbow variety of flavored syrups, then borrow a board game to while away an hour.

KTA Super Store Supermarket $

(www.ktasuperstores.com; 74-5594 Palani Rd, Kona Coast Shopping Center; 5am-11pm) The Big Island's best grocery chain, with many Hawaii-made products, anything from La-vosh crackers to *liliko'i* (passion fruit) jam.

Kona Brewing Company American $$

(808-334-2739; http://konabrewingco.com; 75-5629 Kuakini Hwy; mains $13-18; 11am-9pm

Luau (Hawaiian feast), King Kamehameha's Kona Beach Hotel

LONELY PLANET/GETTY IMAGES ©

Sun-Thu, to 10pm Fri & Sat;) Expect a madhouse crowd at this sprawling, ecosustainable brewpub, with torch-lit outdoor seating and laidback waitstaff. Everyone's here for the handcrafted 'liquid aloha' made on-site (Pipeline Porter and Castaway IPA are our faves). Pizza toppings verge on gourmet, but crusts can be soggy; BBQ sandwiches and fish tacos are better. Enter the parking lot off Kaiwi St.

Island Lava Java — Cafe $$

(**808-936-9766; www.islandlavajava.com; 75-5799 Ali'i Dr, Ali'i Sunset Plaza; breakfast & lunch mains $7-20; 6:30am-9:30pm;**) A convivial gathering spot for Sunday brunch or a sunny breakfast (served til 11:30am) with ocean-view dining on the sidewalk patio. The menu aims for upscale diner but hits closer to greasy spoon. Not everyone minds – especially with huge portions, Big Island–raised meats and farm-fresh produce and 100% Kona coffee.

Big Island Grill — Local $$

(**75-5702 Kuakini Hwy; mains $10-20; 7am-9pm Mon-Sat, to noon Sun;**) Big appetites are no match for the big portions served at this island-style diner. The island soul food is down-home country cooking, with *loco moco* (rice, fried egg and hamburger patty topped with gravy or other condiments), mahimahi fish-and-chips and slow-cooked *kalua* pork with cabbage always on the menu. Superfriendly service makes you feel like part of the *'ohana* (extended family and friends).

Rapanui Island Cafe — Asian $$

(**808-329-0511; 75-5695 Ali'i Dr, Kona Banyan Court; mains lunch $6-10, dinner $13-19; 11am-2pm Tue-Fri, 5-9pm Mon-Sat**) The New Zealand owners know Polynesian and Indonesian curries, which they prepare with tongue-tingling warmth. Various salads and satays, spiced pork and pawpaw chicken also make an appearance. Order the house coconut rice and wash it down with lemongrass-ginger tea.

Jackie Rey's Ohana Grill — Hawaii Regional Cuisine $$$

(**808-327-0209; www.jackiereys.com; 75-5995 Kuakini Hwy; mains lunch $10-16, dinner $15-33; 11am-9pm Mon-Fri, from 5pm Sat & Sun;**) Jackie Rey's is a casual, family-owned grill with a delightfully retro-kitsch Hawaii vibe. Haute versions of local *grinds* (food) include guava-glazed ribs, wasabi-seared ahi and *mochiko* (rice-flour-battered) fish with Moloka'i purple sweet potatoes. Locals, tourists, kids, aunties – pretty much everyone loves it. Pop by between 3pm and 5pm on weekdays for half-price *pupu* (snack or appetizers), tropical cocktails and island microbrews. Reservations recommended for dinner.

Sushi Shiono — Japanese $$$

(**808-326-1696; www.sushishiono.com; 75-5799 Ali'i Dr, Ali'i Sunset Plaza; a la carte dishes $4-17, lunch plates**

Kona Brewing Company beers (p42)
NIELS VAN KAMPENHOUT/ALAMY©

$10-19, dinner combos $20-37; ⏲11:30am-2pm Mon-Sat, 5:30-9pm Sun-Thu, to 10pm Fri & Sat) Inside a minimall, wickedly fresh sushi and sashimi are complemented by a tempting sake list. The joint is owned by a Japanese expat, who employs an all-star, all-Japanese (and all-male) cast of sushi chefs behind the bar. Skip the surf-and-turf combo plates. Dinner reservations recommended.

Drinking

Kailua-Kona's bar scene is pretty touristy, but there are a handful of places for a cocktail or a beer. Always a good fallback, Kona Brewing Company (p47) usually has live Hawaiian music from 5pm to 8pm on Sundays.

Huggo's on the Rocks — Bar

(☎808-329-1493; http://huggos.com; 75-5828 Kahakai Rd; ⏲4-10pm Mon-Thu, to midnight Fri, 5pm-midnight Sat & 5-10pm Sun) Right on the water, with a thatched-roof bar and live music nightly, Huggo's is an ideal sunset spot. Whether it's worth staying longer depends on who's playing and who else shows up. In the mornings, it reverts to **Java on the Rock** (**☎808-324-2411; www.javaontherock.com; 75-5828 Kahakai Rd; ⏲6-11am; Wi-Fi**) serving coffee and espresso drinks (give the bland breakfasts a miss).

Humpy's Big Island Alehouse — Bar

(☎808-324-2337; www.humpyshawaii.com; 75-5815 Ali'i Dr, Coconut Grove Marketplace; ⏲11am-2am Mon-Fri, from 8am Sat & Sun) With its enviable location on the strip overlooking Kailua Bay, Alaskan Humpy's would probably survive in touristy Kailua-Kona even without having dozens of craft beers on tap. Perch on the upstairs balcony, with its sea breezes and views, while live bands rock out. The kitchen stays open till 10pm daily, with a limited bar menu available until midnight. Happy hour runs from 3pm to 6pm on weekdays.

Kanaka Kava — Cafe

(75-5803 Ali'i Dr, Coconut Grove Marketplace; ⏲bar 10am-11pm, kitchen till 9:30pm) This tiny, locals' grass-shack hangout is the place to try Hawaiian-style kava (the mildly sedative juice of the *'awa* plant) or organic *noni* (Indian mulberry) juice, another herbal elixir. *Pupu* like squid luau and ahi *poke* are just an after-thought. Cash only.

Local Knowledge

NAME: PAUL STREITER

OCCUPATION: CO-OWNER, JACKIE REY'S OHANA GRILL

RESIDENCE: KAILUA-KONA

1 WHERE DO YOU GO ON YOUR DAY OFF?

I like Magic Sands (p34) right in town. It's a local favorite for people-watching and bodysurfing. In the winter, it gets a little rough and loses some of its sand; it's better in summer. My favorite all-round beach is Hapuna (p108) – phenomenal.

2 WHAT DO YOU RECOMMEND FOR TRAVELERS WITH KIDS?

The Fair Wind (p38) snorkel cruise to Kealakekua Bay is great. The crew is fun and kids love jumping off the upper deck or riding the waterslide into the bay. They always have fun sea toys that make you feel safe while snorkeling.

3 LET'S TALK FISH. TELL US SOMETHING WE DON'T KNOW.

The Big Island has amazing fishing grounds right off the coast – it's the best of all the Hawaiian Islands for fresh fish. The KTA Super Store (p47) on Palani Rd has the best fish counter. Top quality, nothing is ever frozen – this is the real deal. Try the *poke* (cubed raw fish mixed with soy sauce, sesame oil, salt, chili pepper or other condiments). For sushi, I like Sushi Shiono (p48), owned by a Japanese businessman who wants guaranteed good sushi when he's on the island.

4 YOUR RESTAURANT IS ON THE OFFICIAL IRONMAN ROUTE. WHAT TIPS DO YOU HAVE FOR FANS?

Watch the swim portion from Kailua Pier. The finish line is also a blast. Cyclists can feel like an Ironman for a day by renting a top-end road bike and pedalling the official Kailua-Kona-to-Hawi route.

Don's Mai Tai Bar Bar
(808-930-3286; www.royalkona.com; 75-5852 Ali'i Dr, Royal Kona Resort; 10am-10pm) For pure kitsch, nothing beats the lounge-lizard fantasy of Don's inside the Royal Kona Resort. Soak up the killer ocean views of the crashing surf – then lament the fact that the 10 different varieties of mai tai are all pretty lackluster (at least the little blue plastic monkey is yours to keep).

Real tiki fans roll in for **Don's Mai Tai Festival** (www.donsmaitaifest) in mid-August.

Sam's Hideaway Bar
(75-5725 Ali'i Dr; 9am-2am) Sam's is a dark, cozy (OK, some might say 'dank') nook of a dive bar. You'll rarely find tourists here, but there are always locals. On karaoke nights, don't act shocked when a 7ft Samoan guy tears up as he belts out 'The Snows of Mauna Kea.' The bar is hidden behind the shops fronting Ali'i Dr.

Entertainment

Kailua-Kona's two hokey, cruise-ship-friendly luau include a ceremony, a buffet dinner with Hawaiian specialties, an open bar and a Polynesian dinner show featuring a cast of flamboyant dancers and fire twirlers. Forego if any rain is forecast – an indoor luau ain't worth it.

KBXtreme Bowling, Karaoke
(808-326-2695; www.kbxtreme.com; 75-5591 Palani Rd; 9am-1am Sun-Thu, to 2am Fri & Sat;) Make a rainy day or dull night fun for families with a bowling alley, arcade games, a sports bar and a karaoke lounge. 'Xtreme' blacklight bowling parties take over Friday and Saturday nights; weekday afternoon bowling is discounted.

Regal Makalapua Stadium 10 Cinema
(808-327-0444; 74-5469 Kamaka'eha Ave, Makalapua Shopping Center; adult/child $10.50/7) Catch first-run Hollywood movies on 10 screens. Matinee showings before 6pm are discounted.

Island Breeze Lu'au Luau
(808-329-4969; www.islandbreezeluau.com; 75-5660 Palani Rd, Courtyard Marriott King Kamehameha's Kona Beach Hotel; adult/5-12yr $82/41; 5pm Tue, Thu & Sun;) Family-friendly luau benefits from a scenic oceanfront setting but crowds can reach up to 400.

Lava Legends & Legacies – Journeys of the South Pacific Luau
(808-329-3111; www.royalkona.com; 75-5852 Ali'i Dr, Royal Kona Resort; adult/child 6-11yr $67/33; 6pm Mon, Tue, Wed & Fri;) Assuage your disappointment in the buffet by taking a photo with the lithesome dancers.

Shopping

Ali'i Dr is swamped with run-of-the-mill, dubious-quality Hawaiiana and souvenir shops. Beware of 'Made in China' fakes.

J Lambus Photography Arts & Crafts
(808-989-9560; www.jlambus.com; 75-5744 Ali'i Dr, Kona Inn Shopping village; 11am-8pm Tue-Sat, to 4pm Mon) Josh Lambus's celebrated underwater photography has been exhibited by the Smithsonian, and he has taken some of the first recorded snaps of several deep-sea species. Pop into his gallery, then check his blog for Big Island adventure stories.

Big Island Jewelers Jewelry
(888-477-8571, 808-329-8571; http://bigislandjewelers.com; 75-5695A Ali'i Dr; 9am-5:30pm Mon-Sat) Family owned for nearly four decades, with master jeweler Flint Carpenter at the helm, this storefront sells high-quality Hawaiiana bracelets, pendants, earrings and rings, including pieces made with Tahitian pearls. Custom orders welcome.

Honolua Surf Co Clothing
(808-329-1001; www.honoluasurf.com; 75-5744 Ali'i Dr, Kona Inn Shopping Village; 9am-9pm) This island-grown surfwear shop is split right down the middle between styles for *kane* (men) and *wahine* (women). Board shorts, bikinis, hoodies, T-shirts and beach cover-ups will last you as long as an endless summer.

Hula dance performance, King Kamehameha's Kona Beach Hotel (p46)

LONELY PLANET/GETTY IMAGES ©

Na Makana Souvenirs
(808-938-8577; 75-5722 Likana Ln; 9am-5pm) Poke around this hole-in-the-wall shop for authentic made-in-Hawaii gifts, souvenirs and collectibles, with such unusual finds as Japanese glass fishing floats. Variable opening hours epitomize 'Hawaiian time.'

Crazy Shirts Clothing
(808-329-2176; www.crazyshirts.com; 75-5719 Ali'i Dr, Kona Marketplace; 9am-9pm) Once maverick, now mainstream, Crazy Shirts are worn mainly by tourists these days. The best designs feature natural dyes like Kona coffee, hibiscus, *ti* (a native plant) leaves and volcanic ash.

Kona Bay Books Books, Music
(808-326-7790; http://konabaybooks.com; 74-5487 Kaiwi St; 10am-6pm) Hawai'i's biggest selection of used books, CDs and DVDs, including Hawaiiana titles.

Conscious Riddims Records Music
(808-326-7685; www.consciousriddims.org; 75-5719 Ali'i Dr, Kona Marketplace; 10am-7pm Mon-Fri, to 5pm Sun) Drop by for reggae and Jawaiian (Hawaii-style reggae) music and dope clothing.

Village Farmers Market Souvenirs
(cnr Ali'i Dr & Hualalai Rd; 8am-5pm Thu-Sun) Sells a lotta phony shell jewelry and pseudo-Hawaiian knickknacks, but also fresh produce and flower lei.

Information

Media

Hawaii Tribune-Herald (www.hawaiitribune-herald.com) The Big Island's main daily newspaper.

West Hawaii Today (www.westhawaiitoday.com) Kona Coast's daily newspaper covers Kohala to Ka'u.

KAGB 99.1 FM (www.kaparadio.com) West Hawai'i home of Hawaiian and island music.

KKUA 90.7 FM (www.hawaiipublicradio.org) Hawaii Public Radio; classical music, talk and news.

KLUA 93.9 FM Native FM plays island tunes and reggae beats.

Medical Services

Kona Community Hospital (808-322-9311; www.kch.hhsc.org; 79-1019 Haukapila St; 24hr)

West Hawai'i's most advanced (level-III) trauma center, about 10 miles south of Kailua-Kona.

Longs Drugs (808-329-1632; www.cvs.com; 75-5595 Palani Rd; store 7am-10pm daily, pharmacy 7am-8pm Mon-Fri, 8am-7pm Sat & 8am-6pm Sun) Centrally located drugstore and pharmacy.

Money

The following banks have 24-hour ATMs and islandwide branches:

Bank of Hawaii (808-326-3900; www.boh.com; 74-5457 Makala Blvd; 8:30am-4pm Mon-Thu, to 6pm Fri, 9am-1pm Sat)

First Hawaiian Bank (808-329-2461; www.fhb.com; 74-5593 Palani Rd, Lanihau Center; 8:30am-4pm Mon-Thu, to 6pm Fri, 9am-1pm Sat)

Websites

Big Island Visitors Bureau (www.gohawaii.com/big-island) Travel planning info and comprehensive listings for festivals and special events.

KonaWeb (www.konaweb.com) Homegrown website for locals and visitors, with an islandwide calendar of events.

Getting There & Away

Air

Kona International Airport at Keahole (KOA; 808-327-9520; http://hawaii.gov/koa; 73-7200 Kupipi St) Mostly interisland and some US mainland and Canada flights arrive at Hawai'i's main airport, 7 miles northwest of Kailua-Kona.

Bus

Hele-On Bus (808-961-8744; www.heleonbus.org; 1-way fare $2, 10-ride ticket $15, monthly pass $60) Public buses run between Kailua-Kona and Captain Cook in South Kona (one to 1¾ hours) up to 10 times daily except Sunday; one or two also stop at the airport. Buses connect Kailua-Kona with Hilo (three hours) via Waimea (1¼ to 1¾ hours) three times daily except Sunday; one goes via South Kohala's resorts. Buses on the long-distance Pahala–South Kohala route (four hours) makes stops in Kailua-Kona, South Kona, Ka'u and sometimes at Kona's airport and in Keauhou; service is three times daily Monday through Saturday, once on Sunday.

All schedules and fares are subject to change; check the website. A $1 surcharge applies for luggage, backpacks or bicycles; no surfboards or bodyboards allowed on board. Children under 6 years old ride free.

Keauhou Trolley (808-329-1688; www.keauhouresort.com; 1 way $2; 9am-9pm) Also called the 'Honu Express,' this tourist trolley makes five daily round-trips between Keauhou and Kailua-Kona. Stops include White (Magic) Sands Beach, Kona Brewing Company, Kailua Pier and various shopping centers and resort hotels. Check current schedules and fares online.

Car

The drive from Kailua-Kona to Hilo is 75 miles and takes at least 1¾ hours via Saddle Rd, 95 miles (two hours) via Waimea and 125 miles (three hours) via Ka'u and Volcano.

To avoid snarly commuter traffic on Hwy 11 leading into and away from Kailua-Kona, try the Mamalahoa Hwy Bypass Rd. It connects Ali'i Dr in Keauhou with Haleki'i St in Kealakekua, between the Mile 111 and the Mile 112 markers on Hwy 11.

Getting Around

To/From the Airport

A car is almost necessary on Hawai'i, but if you're not renting one upon arrival at the airport, taxis are available curbside (book late-night pickups in advance). Taxi fares average $25 to Kailua-Kona or $35 to Keauhou, plus tip.

Speedi Shuttle (877-242-5777, 808-329-5433; www.speedishuttle.com; 9am-last flight) Charges about the same as airport taxis, but may be economical for large groups. Book in advance.

Bicycle

Home of the Ironman Triathlon World Championship (p43), Kailua-Kona is a bike-friendly town.

Bike Works (808-326-2453; www.bikeworkskona.com; 74-5583 Luhia St, Hale Hana Center; bicycle rental per day $40-80; 9am-6pm Mon-Sat, 10am-4pm Sun) Full-service bike shop rents high-quality mountain and road-touring bikes; rates include helmet, lock, pump and patch kit. Multiday and weekly discounts available. Second location in Waikoloa.

Hawaiian Pedals (808-329-2294; www.hawaiianpedals.com; 75-5744 Ali'i Dr, Kona Inn Shopping Village; bicycle rental per day $25-30;

9:30am-8pm) Rents well-used hybrid bikes for cruising around town; multiday and weekly discounts apply.

Bus

Both the public Hele-On Bus and privately operated Keauhou Trolley make stops within Kailua-Kona.

Car

Ali'i Dr in downtown Kailua-Kona is almost always congested. Free public parking is available in a lot between Likana Ln and Kuakini Hwy. Many shopping centers along Ali'i Dr have free parking lots for customers.

Moped & Motorcycle

Doesn't it look fun zipping down Ali'i Dr on a moped? And what a breeze to park!

Big Island Harley Davidson (**888-904-3155, 808-217-8560; www.bigislandharley.com; 75-5633 Palani Rd; motorcycle rental per day/week $179/763; 8:30am-6pm Mon-Fri, to 5pm Sat, 10am-4pm Sun**) Well-maintained Harley motorcycles come with helmets and rain gear to borrow. Book ahead online.

Scooter Brothers (**808-327-1080; www.scooterbrothers.com; 75-5829 Kahakai Rd; rental per 4hr/8hr/day moped $40/50/60, electric scooter $21/42/52; 10am-6pm Mon-Sat, from 9am Wed, by reservation Sun**) Get around town like a local, on a moped or electric scooter. The official riding area is from Hapuna Beach up north to Honaunau down south. Honda motorcycle rentals cost from $95 per 24 hours.

Taxi

Call ahead for pickups from the following taxi companies:

Aloha Taxi (**808-329-7779; www.alohataxihi.com**)

D&E Taxi (**808-329-4279**)

Laura's Taxi (**808-326-5466; www.luanalimo.com**)

AROUND KAILUA-KONA

Keauhou Resort Area

With its wide streets and manicured landscaping, Keauhou feels like a US mainland suburb: easy, pleasant and bland. Like most suburbs, there's no town center (unless you count the shopping mall).

View of Moku'aikaua Church and Hulihe'e Palace (p35), Kailua-Kona

PETER FRENCH/GETTY IMAGES ©

Rather, it's a collection of destinations: Keauhou Harbor for boat trips, beaches for snorkeling and surfing, condos and resort hotels for sleeping, and farmers markets for local flavor.

Beaches

Kahalu'u Beach Park Beach

(👪) Whether young or old, triathlete or couch potato, everyone appreciates the island's most thrilling, easy-to-access (and admittedly busy) snorkeling spot. Protected by an ancient breakwater (which, according to legend, was built by the *menehune*, or 'little people'), the bay is pleasantly calm and shallow. You'll spot tropical fish and *honu* (green sea turtles) without even trying. The lifeguard-staffed park has outdoor showers, restrooms, drinking water, snorkel and locker rentals and picnic tables.

Kahalu'u can be too popular for its own good, with snorkelers literally bumping into one another. The salt-and-pepper beach (composed of lava and coral sand) is often a mass of humanity, which you may find sociable or nauseating, depending. Come early; the parking lot may fill by 10am. Treading lightly is also important: follow coral-reef etiquette and stay back at least 50yd in the water (20ft on land) from all sea turtles.

When the surf's up (and it can rage here), expert surfers challenge the offshore waves and avoid strong rip currents on the bay's north side near the church. When conditions are mellow, beginners can learn to surf or stand up paddle here.

Sights

Kahulu'u Manowai Archaeological Site

(www.keauhouresort.com/learn.html; 78-6740 Ali'i Dr) FREE On the former grounds of the Outrigger Keauhou Beach Resort, just south of Kahalu'u Beach Park, three restored heiau (temples) and ancient Hawaiian petroglyphs are the centerpiece of a planned outdoor education and Hawaiian cultural center, sponsored by Kamehameha Schools and still under development in talks with the local community. For now, respectful visitors can explore the archaelogical sites during daylight hours. Check in at the security guardhouse and ask for a map.

At the north end of the complex is **Kapuanoni Heiau**, a restored fishing temple. Just south, **Hapaiali'i Heiau** was built 600 years ago and its construction aligns the temple with seasonal equinoxes and solstices. Both of these temples were painstakingly restored by Hawaiian cultural practioners, archaeologists and students in 2007.

Furthest south is **Ke'eku Heiau**, also recently restored. Legends say that Ke'eku was a *luakini* (temple of

Green sea turtle, Kahalu'u Beach Park
DR PETER M FORSTER/GETTY IMAGES ©

human sacrifice). Most famously, a Maui chief who tried to invade the Big Island was sacrificed here, and the spirits of his grieving dogs are said to still guard the site. Along the shoreline look for teeming tide pools and *ki'i pohaku* (petroglyphs) visible among the rocks at low tide.

Keauhou Kahalu'u Heritage Center Gallery

(www.keauhouresort.com; 78-6831 Ali'i Dr, Keauhou Shopping Center; ⌚10am-5pm) FREE To learn about the restoration of Keauhou's heiau (temples), visit this unstaffed cultural center, where small exhibits and videos also describe *holua,* the ancient Hawaiian sport of lava-rock sledding, at nearby He'eia Bay. The center is on the KTA Super Store side of the mall, hidden behind the post office near the public restrooms.

Keauhou Bay Harbor

Many tour cruises launch from the small pier at this protected bay. While not worth going very far out of your way for, the small beach, picnic tables and sand volleyball courts bring out locals. Facilities include restrooms and outdoor showers.

Against the hillside, a **plaque** marks the site where Kamehameha III was born in 1814. The prince is said to have been stillborn and brought back to life by a visiting kahuna (healer) who dunked him in a healing freshwater spring here.

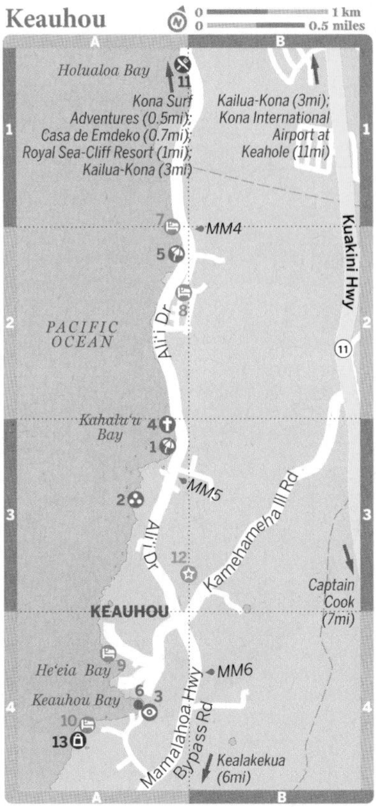

Keauhou

Sights
1 Kahalu'u Beach Park A3
2 Kahulu'u Manowai A3
3 Keauhou Bay A4
Keauhou Kahalu'u Heritage Center .... (see 12)
4 St Peter's Church A3
5 White (Magic) Sands Beach A2

Activities, Courses & Tours
6 Fair Wind A4
Kona Eco Adventures .... (see 12)
Sea Paradise .... (see 12)

Sleeping
7 Kona Magic Sands Resort A1
8 Kona Sugar Shack A2
9 Outrigger Kanaloa at Kona A4
10 Sheraton Kona Resort & Spa at Keauhou Bay A4

Eating
11 Da Poke Shack A1
Kenichi Pacific .... (see 12)
KTA Super Store .... (see 12)
Peaberry & Galette .... (see 12)
Sam Choy's Kai Lanai .... (see 12)

Entertainment
12 Keauhou Shopping Center A3
Regal Keauhou Stadium 7 .... (see 12)

Shopping
13 Ho'oulu Community Farmers Market A4
Keauhou Farmers Market .... (see 12)
Kona Stories .... (see 12)

Right: Sunset over Kahalu'u Bay **Below:** St Peter's Church
(RIGHT) ALVIS UPITIS/GETTY IMAGES ©; (BELOW) BOB POOL/GETTY IMAGES ©

To get here, turn *makai* (seaward) off Ali'i Dr onto Kaleiopapa St.

St Peter's Church Church
The much-photographed 'Little Blue Church' practically sits in Kahulu'u Bay. Made of clapboard and a corrugated-tin roof in the 1880s, it was moved here from White (Magic) Sands Beach in 1912. The church is on the *makai* side of Ali'i Dr, north of the Mile 5 marker.

Incidetally, an ancient Hawaiian temple, Ku'emanu Heiau, once stood here. Hawaiian *ali'i* (royalty), who surfed at the northern end of Kahalu'u Bay, prayed at the temple before hitting the waves.

Original Hawaiian Chocolate Factory Farm
(☎888-447-2626, 808-322-2626; www.ohcf.us; 78-6772 Makenawai St; tour adult/child under 12yr $15/free; ⏲usually 9am Wed & Fri, by reservation only; 👪) A must for chocolate fans, these one-hour farm tours detail how the *only* Hawaiian chocolate is grown, harvested, processed and packaged, followed by chocolate sampling and sales. Book tours by phone or email at least a week ahead. The factory is inland from Hwy 11 and King Kamehameha III Rd.

Activities

Some snorkel cruises and fishing trips booked out of Kailua-Kona depart from Keauhou Pier.

Kona Eco Adventures Ziplining
(☎808-324-4111; www.konazip.com; 78-8631 Ali'i Dr, Keahou Shopping Center, Suite 148; 3hr tour per person $149; ⏲hourly departures 8am-3pm, by reservation only) Hop aboard a shuttle to the upland slopes of Mt Hualalai, where two suspension bridges add to the thrill of eight short ziplines through ohia forest. Tours include snacks and drinks; participants must wear closed-toed shoes and weigh between 80lb and 250lb. The outfitter's storefront is not far from KTA Super Store.

Sleeping

Cheaper rates may be available by booking ahead online.

Outrigger Kanaloa at Kona Condo **$$$**

(800-688-7444, 808-322-9625; www.outriggerkanaloaatkonacondo.com; 78-261 Manukai St; 1br/2br apt from $229/275; P ❄ @ ≋) Tropical townhouse-style condos feel exclusive, sitting behind a private gate on an oceanfront lava ledge. Incredibly spacious, immaculate and fully equipped units gather in small clusters. One-bedroom condos easily fit a family of four. With three pools, night-lit tennis courts and an adjacent golf course, you can practically stay put. Multiple-night minimum stay (cleaning fee from $50).

Sheraton Kona Resort & Spa at Keauhou Bay Resort **$$$**

(866-716-8109, 808-930-4900; www.sheratonkona.com; 78-128 'Ehukai St; r/ste from $215/379; P ❄ @ ≋) Keauhou's only bona fide resort, the family-friendly Sheraton has a sleek modern design with hip boutique-hotel appeal. Despite having over 500 rooms, an oceanfront bar and restaurant with fire pits and live music (usually 6pm to 9pm nightly), and a massive pool with a spiral waterslide, unfortunately there's no beach. Manta rays gather off the rocky shoreline at night.

A mandatory resort fee (over $30 per night) covers self-parking, wi-fi, unlimited Keauhou Trolley rides, a morning yoga class and Hawaiian cultural activities.

Eating

Drop by Keahou's twice-weekly farmers markets for tasty, cheap *grinds*.

KTA Super Store Supermarket **$**

(78-6831 Ali'i Dr, Keauhou Shopping Center; 7am-10pm) Locally owned supermarket chain stocks groceries, beach snacks and drinks, with a full-service deli and bakery.

Peaberry & Galette Cafe **$$**
(808-322-6020; www.peaberryandgalette.com; 78-6831 Ali'i Dr, Keauhou Shopping Center; mains $7-14; 7am-7pm Mon-Thu, to 8pm Fri & Sat, 8am-6pm Sun) With 100% Kona estate-grown coffee, Illy espresso and Euro-bistro style, this cafe dishes up sweet and savory French crepes, plus satisfying salads, sandwiches, quiches and *liliko'i* (passion fruit)-lemon bars for dessert.

Kenichi Pacific Japanese, Fusion **$$$**
(808-322-6400; www.kenichihawaii.com; 78-6831 Ali'i Dr, Keauhou Shopping Center; a la carte dishes $3-18, mains $23-38; 5-9pm Sun-Thu, to 9:30pm Fri & Sat) Ignore the mall setting. Just savor the beautifully presented Pacific Rim fusion cuisine including tender miso black cod, Hawaiian *ono* (white-fleshed wahoo) topped with a cloud of *ponzu* (Japanese citrus sauce) and macadamia-nut-encrusted lamb. Sushi and sashimi cuts are fresh and generous. Happy hour (4:30pm to 6:30pm daily) brings half-price sushi rolls and drinks to the bar.

Sam Choy's Kai Lanai Hawaii Regional Cuisine **$$$**
(808-333-3434; www.samchoy.com; 78-6831 Ali'i Dr, Keauhou Shopping Center; mains lunch $10-14, dinner $17-36; 11am-9pm Mon-Thu, to 9:30pm Fri, 7am-9:30pm Sat, 7am-9pm Sun;) Sam Choy is one of the pioneers of Hawaii Regional Cuisine, an island-grown version of Pacific Rim fusion. At this casual eatery with dynamite sunset panoramas, the dinner menu is stuffed with haute fusion gastronomy like lamb chops broiled with soy, ginger and local bird-peppers, although execution falls short of the chef's sterling reputation. During happy hour (3pm to 5pm daily), nosh on *pupu* on the breezy ocean-view lanai.

Entertainment

Haleo Luau Luau
(866-482-9775; www.haleoluau.com; 78-128 'Ehukai St, Sheraton Keauhou Bay Resort; adult/child 6-12yr $82/52; usually 4:30pm Mon, also 4:30pm Fri late May-early Aug) The Sheraton's touristy luau weaves together Hawaiian themes and tales of ancient kings and battles, along with fiery dances from across Polynesia. The buffet is about as generic as you'd expect, but there's an open bar.

Regal Keauhou Stadium 7 Cinema
(808-324-0172; 78-6831 Ali'i Dr, Keauhou Shopping Center) Hollywood flicks fill seven screens. Matinee showings before 6pm are discounted.

Keauhou Shopping Center Music, Dance
(www.keauhouvillageshops.com; 78-6831 Ali'i Dr) FREE This shopping mall has hula shows from 6pm to 7pm most Friday nights. It also usually runs free Hawaiian craft workshops from 10am to noon every Thursday. Check the website for more cultural activities and special events.

Shopping

Ho'oulu Community Farmers Market Market
(www.hooulufarmersmkt.com; 78-128 Ehukai St, Sheraton Keauhou Bay Resort; usually 9am-2pm Wed & Sat) Unlike the touristy Kailua-Kona farmers market selling knickknacks from who-knows-where, this twice-weekly event focuses on small-scale farm and fishing bounty, including genuine Kona coffee and flower lei. Live music, island artists and takeout food vendors make this a must-do lunchtime stop.

Keauhou Farmers Market Market
(www.keauhoufarmersmarket.com; 78-6831 Ali'i Dr, Keauhou Shopping Center; 8am-noon Sat;) At this parking-lot farmers market with live Hawaiian music and a neighborly spirit, everything is Big Island–grown including seasonal fruits and veggies, organic coffee, homemade preserves and fresh flowers.

Kona Stories Books
(808-324-0350; www.konastories.com; 78-6831 Ali'i Dr, Keauhou Shopping Center; 10am-6pm Mon-Fri, to 5pm Sat, 11am-5pm Sun) Independent bookstore with a strong Hawaiiana section hosts community events for kids and adults. It's near KTA Super Store.

Information

Bank of Hawaii (www.boh.com; 78-6831 Ali'i Dr, Keauhou Shopping Center, Suite 131; 9am-6pm Mon-Fri, to 2pm Sat & Sun) ATM available inside KTA Super Store.

Keauhou Urgent Care Center (808-322-2544; www.konaurgentcare.com; 78-6831 Ali'i Dr, Suite 418, Keauhou Shopping Center; 9am-7pm) Walk-in clinic for nonemergency medical matters.

Longs Drugs (www.cvs.com; 78-6831 Ali'i Dr, Keauhou Shopping Center; store 7am-10pm, pharmacy 8am-8pm Mon-Fri, 9am-7pm Sat, to 6pm Sun) Convenient drugstore and pharmacy.

Getting There & Around

Nicknamed the 'Honu Express,' Keauhou Trolley (p52) makes five daily round trips between Keauhou and Kailua-Kona, stopping at White (Magic) Sands Beach, Kailua Pier, various shopping centers, resort hotels and elsewhere. Check current schedules and fares online.

Holualoa

POP 8540

It's well worth going out of your way to visit Holualoa, a bohemian coffee-farming village perched on the lush slopes of Mt Hualalai. Ramshackle retro buildings, a tight-knit community and a slower pace of life preserve old Hawaii right alongside contemporary art galleries. At 1400ft elevation, the climate is cooler and wetter, and the coastal views are magnificent.

Sights & Activities

Donkey Mill Art Center *Arts Center*

(808-322-3362; www.donkeymillartcenter.org; 78-6670 Mamalahoa Hwy; 10am-4pm Tue-Sat Aug-May, 9am-3pm Mon-Fri Jun & Jul;) FREE The Holualoa Foundation for Arts & Culture established this community art center in 2002. There are free exhibits, arts-and-crafts workshops, literary readings, performance art and film nights. If you're wondering about the name, the building was once a coffee mill with a donkey painted on its roof. It's 3 miles south of the village center.

Malama I'ka Ola Holistic Health Center *Health & Fitness*

(808-324-6644; www.malamatherapy.com; 76-5914 Mamalahoa Hwy) Inside a 19th-century doctor's office, this alternative-minded oasis offers yoga and Pilates classes, and massage, acupuncture, Chinese herbal medicine and organic skin treatments.

Festivals & Events

Coffee & Art Stroll *Art, Food*

(www.konacoffeefest.com) During early November's Kona Coffee Cultural Festival (p43), Holualoa hosts an incredibly popular, day-long block party.

Sushi platter, Kenichi Pacific

LONELY PLANET/GETTY IMAGES ©

Music & Light Festival Art, Music
(www.holualoahawaii.com) A small-town Christmas celebration with live music and a tree-lighting ceremony in mid-December.

Sleeping

Lilikoi Inn B&B $$
(808-333-5539; www.lilikoiinn.com; 75-5339 Mamalahoa Hwy; r incl breakfast $125-165;) All four rooms have an airy, modern art-gallery-in-the-tropics kind of vibe, blending cool monochromes with tasteful Hawaiiana. Each has a private entrance and access to a hot tub, guest laundry, kitchen and pick-your-own avocado and fruit trees. Enjoy the chef's restaurant-worthy breakfasts on a garden lanai. It's 3 miles north of Holualoa village.

Haleakala B&B B&B
(808-322-6053; www.haleakalabedbreakfast.com; 78-6612a Mamalahoa Hwy; d $130-150;) Setting this breezy, welcoming B&B apart are the breathtaking views – over coffee farms and mac-nut orchards all the way to the startling blue Pacific – from your private lanai or the shared hot tub. For *ipo* (sweethearts), the Kokua Nest is a private cottage suite with an outdoor garden shower. Rates include a local cafe breakfast voucher.

Holualoa Inn B&B $$$
(800-392-1812, 808-324-1121; www.holualoainn.com; 76-5932 Mamalahoa Hwy; r/ste/cottage incl breakfast from $345/385/550;) From gleaming eucalyptus floors to river-rock showers, serene beauty shines in every soul-soothing detail here. Common rooms are graced with Polynesian and Asian art and exquisite carved furniture that segue seamlessly into outdoor gardens and a pool, while the rooftop gazebo surveys the ocean. It's a peaceful, intimate retreat you'll long remember. No TVs, phones or children under 13 years old.

Eating

Holuakoa Gardens & Café Local, Organic $$
(808-322-2233; www.holuakoacafe.com; 76-5900 Mamalahoa Hwy; mains brunch $12-20, dinner $17-32; cafe 6:30am-3pm Mon-Fri, from 8am Sat & Sun, restaurant 10am-2:30pm Mon-Fri,

Decorated *ipu* (gourds), Ipu Hale Gallery

LONELY PLANET/GETTY IMAGES ©

Detour: Upcountry Kona Coffee Farms

Kona coffee has had gourmet cachet for decades, and today many coffee farms have opened roadside visitor centers and gift shops, where they give free samples and quickie tours. The best time to visit is during the harvest season, running from August through February, when 'Kona snow' (white blossoms) and 'cherries' (mature berry fruit) cluster on the coffee trees.

Mountain Thunder Coffee Plantation (☎888-414-5662, 808-325-2136; www.mountainthunder.com; 73-1944 Hao St, Kailua-Kona; 20min tour free, 3hr VIP tour adult/child under 6yr $135/free; ⏲tours hourly 10am-4pm, VIP tours 10am Mon-Fri by reservation only) is an award-winning farm lies upland in lush Kaloko Mauka, a 20-minute drive from downtown Kailua-Kona or Holualoa village. VIP tours (call 808-345-6600 at least one day in advance) give you a more in-depth look at Kona coffee, and let you roast a half-pound of beans to take home.

With jaw-dropping ocean views on a breezy lanai, an epicurean tasting room and eco-conscious farm, **Hula Daddy Kona Coffee** (☎808-327-9744; www.huladaddy.com; 74-4944 Mamalahoa Hwy, Holualoa; ⏲10am-4pm Mon–Sat) is the place to learn about cupping. Ask about unusual coffee-production techniques used to create its signature Kona Oli and Kona Sweet beans. It's less than 5 miles north of Holualoa.

Holualoa Kona Coffee Company (☎800-334-0348, 808-322-9937; www.konalea.com; 77-6261 Mamalahoa Hwy, Holualoa; ⏲8am-4pm Mon-Fri) at Kona Le'a Plantation does not use pesticides or herbicides on its small organic-certified farm, less than 2 miles south of Holualoa. As you drive up, watch out for the free-ranging geese who do double duty as lawn mowers and fertilizers!

Kona Blue Sky Coffee (☎877-322-1700; www.konablueskycoffee.com; 76-973 Hualalai Rd, Kailua-Kona; ⏲visitor center & gift shop 8:30am-4pm Mon-Sat, tours 9am-3:30pm Mon-Sat) is a convenient choice if your time is limited. This tiny coffee estate in Holualoa village offers a free walking tour that passes traditional open-air drying racks and includes an educational video.

from 9am Sat & Sun, also 5:30-8:30pm Mon-Sat;) The storefront cafe serves 100% Kona coffee, baked goods and sandwiches. Out back an organic, slow-food restaurant serves a sophisticated yet casual bistro-style menu that make the most of fresh, Big Island grown produce. Book ahead for dinner.

As one of Hawai'i's most dedicated establishments to supporting local farmers, it's no surprise there's a seasonal **Saturday farmers market** (⏲9am-noon Sat Apr-Oct) here.

Shopping

Holualoa is a tiny village but don't underestimate the quality of its artists. Along the Mamalahoa Hwy (Hwy 180) you'll find internationally known, highly commissioned artists creating art beyond the stereotypical tropical motifs. Most galleries and shops are closed on Sunday and Monday.

Ipu Hale Gallery Arts & Crafts

(☎808-322-9069; www.holualoahawaii.com/member_sites/ipu_hale.html; 76-5893 Mamalahoa Hwy; ⏲10am-4pm Tue-Sat) Magnificent *ipu* (gourds) are decoratively carved with Hawaiian imagery and dyed using an ancient method unique to Ni'ihau island, knowledge of which had been lost for over a century until a scholar rediscovered it in 1980.

Island Insights

Hawaiians wove the dried *lau* (leaves) of the hala (pandanus) tree into floor mats, hats, baskets, fans and other household items. Strong and flexible, *lauhala* is surprisingly hardy and long-lasting. Today, most *lauhala* is actually mass-produced in the Philippines and sold cheaply to unwitting tourists. But Holualoa's **Kimura Lauhala Shop** (**808-324-0053; www.holualoahawaii.com/member_sites/kimura.html; cnr Hualalai Rd & Hwy 180; 9am-5pm Mon-Fri, to 4pm Sat**), run by the Kimura family's fourth generation, sells high-quality, genuine Hawaiian *lauhala* handmade by local weavers, from traditional hats to signature lined tote bags.

Holualoa Ukulele Gallery Music
(**808-324-4100; www.konaweb.com/ukegallery/index.html; 76-5942 Mamalahoa Hwy; 11am-4:30pm Tue-Sat, other times by appt**) Inside a historic post office, owner Sam Rosen displays beautifully handcrafted ukulele made by himself and other island luthiers. He's happy to talk and show you his workshop. If you've got 10 days, he'll even teach you how to build your own uke.

Studio 7 Fine Arts Arts & Crafts
(**808-324-1335; http://studio7hawaii.com; 76-5920 Mamalahoa Hwy; 11am-5pm Tue-Sat**) A serene, museum-like gallery featuring prominent artist-owner Hiroki Morinoue's watercolor, oil, woodblock and sculpture pieces, and his accomplished wife Setsuko's pottery.

Dovetail Gallery & Design Arts & Crafts
(**808-322-4046; www.dovetailgallery.net; 76-5942 Mamalahoa Hwy; 10am-4pm Tue-Sat**) Showcases elegant contemporary work by Big Island sculptors, painters, photographers and furniture designers.

Getting There & Away

Holualoa village straggles along Hwy 180 (Mamalahoa Hwy), north of the Hualalai Rd intersection. Parking in the free village lot or along the highway's shoulder is easy most of the time, except during special events.

SOUTH KONA COAST

The dozen or so miles heading south from Kailua-Kona to Kealakekua Bay are among Hawai'i's most action-packed, historically speaking. It's here that ancient Hawaiian *ali'i* (royalty) secretly buried the bones of their ancestors, kapu (taboo) breakers braved shark-infested waters to reach the *pu'uhonua* (place of refuge), and British explorer Captain Cook and his rabble-rousing crew fatally first stepped ashore in Hawaii.

But you'd never know all that today, simply judging by the sleepy, small, yesteryear towns lined up along the Mamalahoa Hwy (Hwy 11). Upcountry lies Kona's coffee belt, where the slow pace of agricultural life continues on family-owned coffee farms and mac-nut plantations. Hidden down below, the coast may be short on sandy beaches, but it's long on snorkeling, diving and kayaking spots.

Most people drive to and around South Kona, but the public Hele-On Bus (p52) runs between Kailua-Kona and Captain Cook and buses on the long-distance Pahala–South Kohala route also make stops in Kailua-Kona and South Kona.

Honalo

At a bend in the road where Hwys 11 and 180 intersect, little time-warped Honalo is your first sign that more than miles separate you from touristy Kailua-Kona.

Sights & Activities

Daifukuji Soto Mission Temple
(**808-322-3524; www.daifukuji.org; 79-7241 Mamalahoa Hwy; usually 8am-4pm Mon-Sat**) On the *mauka* (inland) side of Mamalahoa Hwy, this Buddhist temple founded in

1914 inhabits a quirky red-and-white Hawaiian farmhouse. Inside are two altars, large drums and spiritual sculptures. Anyone is welcome to join the Zen meditation and tai chi sessions, Buddhist services and festival days.

Aloha Kayak Co Kayaking, SUP
(**☎877-322-1444, 808-322-2868; www.alohakayak.com; 79-7248 Mamalahoa Hwy; 24hr kayak rental s/d/tr $35/60/85, tours $75-99; ⏲usually 7:30am-5pm)** This Hawaiian-owned outfit knows local waters, offers half-day (noon to 5pm) kayak rentals and stand up paddling (SUP) gear rental. Kayak-snorkel tours go to Kealakekua Bay and other spots along the coast, seeking out sea caves and manta rays at night.

Eating

Teshima's Restaurant Japanese, Local **$$**
(**☎808-322-9140; www.teshimarestaurant.com; 79-7251 Mamalahoa Hwy; dinner mains $13-23; ⏲6:30am-1:45pm & 5-9pm; 👪)** For a real window into local life, grab a table at this family-run restaurant, which has been dishing up Japanese comfort food since the 1950s. It's more about the vintage atmosphere than the country-style cooking, which has as many misses as hits. That said, the sashimi is always superfresh and the tempura lightly crisp and golden.

Kona Coast

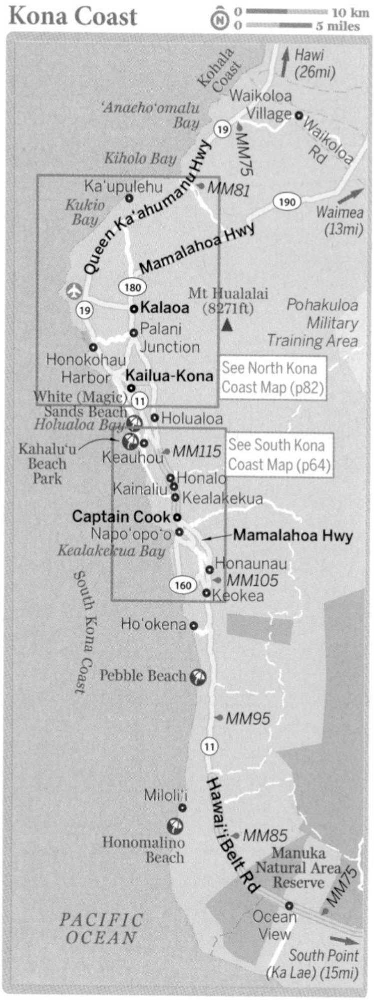

Kainaliu

Packed with antiques shops, art galleries and eclectic boutiques, Kainaliu is a lunch-and-linger town – handy if you get caught in the infamous 'Kainaliu crawl' traffic jam along the two-lane Mamalahoa Hwy.

Eating

Rebel Kitchen Sandwiches **$$**
(**☎808-322-0616; http://rebelkitchen.com; 79-7399 Mamalahoa Hwy; mains $9-16; ⏲11am-5:30pm Mon-Fri;** 🍸) Expect playful anarchy here, from the young counter staff to punk and reggae sounds streaming out of the kitchen. You know what else comes out of the kitchen? Amazing sandwiches. We'll fight you for the blackened *ono* with spicy Cajun mayo or Southern-style BBQ pulled pork.

Annie's Island Fresh Burgers Burgers **$$**
(**www.anniesislandfreshburgers; 79-7460 Mamalahoa Hwy, Mango Court; burgers $9-14; ⏲11am-8pm;** 🍸👪) 🌿 Annie's is where grass-fed Big Island beef and *panko* (Japanese-style breadcrumbs)–crusted fish with locally grown veggie sides (try

South Kona Coast

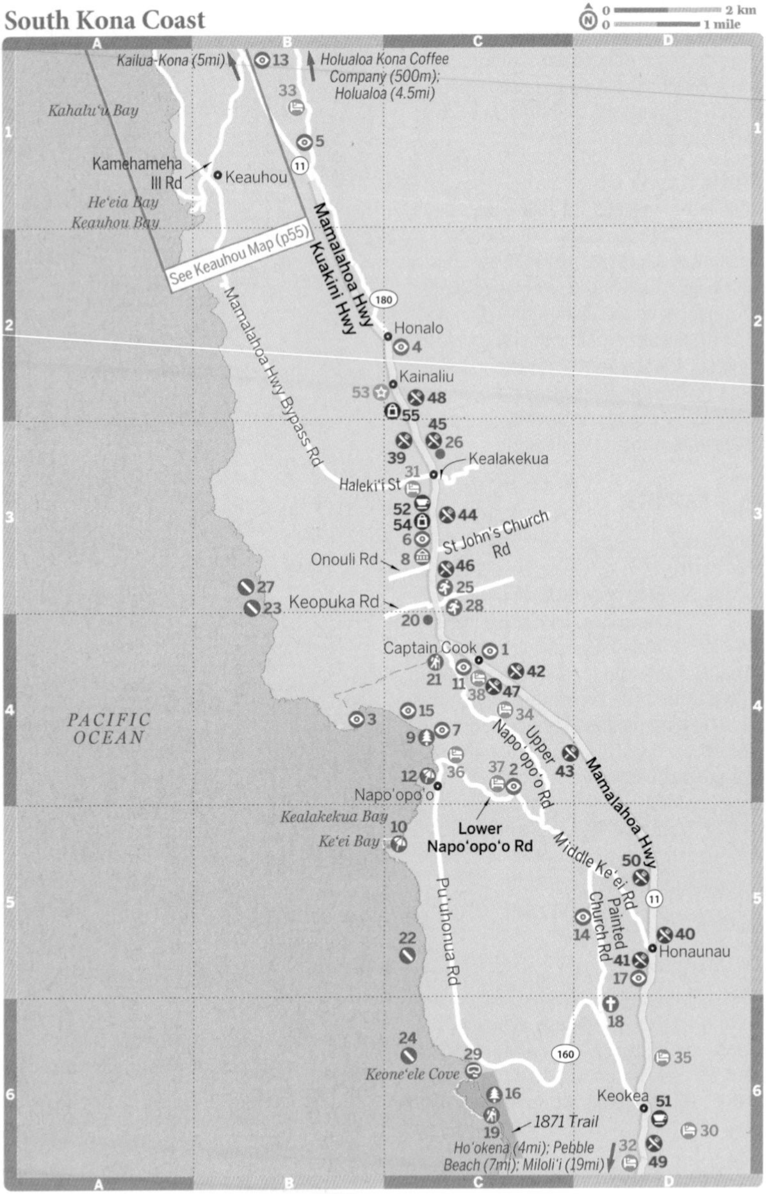

the purple potato salad) satisfy hungry road-trippers. Vegetarian? No worries – dig into a portobello mushroom 'burger' stuffed with Parmesan cheese and bulgur wheat.

☆ Entertainment

Aloha Theatre Theater, Cinema

(☎808-322-9924; www.apachawaii.org; 79-7384 Mamalahoa Hwy; tickets $10-25; ⏲box office

South Kona Coast

Sights

1 Amy BH Greenwell Ethnobotanical Garden ... C4
2 Big Island Bees ... C4
3 Captain Cook Monument ... B4
4 Daifukuji Soto Mission ... C2
5 Donkey Mill Art Center ... B1
6 Greenwell Farms ... C3
7 Hiki'au Heiau ... C4
8 HN Greenwell Store Museum ... C3
9 Kealakekua Bay State Historical Park ... C4
10 Ke'ei Beach ... C5
11 Kona Coffee Living History Farm ... C4
12 Manini Beach ... C4
13 Original Hawaiian Chocolate Factory ... B1
14 Paleaku Gardens Peace Sanctuary ... D5
15 Pali Kapu o Keoua ... C4
16 Pu'uhonua O Hōnaunau National Historical Park ... C6
17 Society for Kona's Education & Art ... D5
18 St Benedict's Painted Church ... D6

Activities, Courses & Tours

19 1871 Trail ... C6
20 Adventures in Paradise ... C4
Aloha Kayak Co ... (see 4)
21 Captain Cook Monument Trail ... C4
22 Coral Dome ... C5
23 Driftwood ... B3
24 Hammerhead ... C6
25 Kings' Trail Rides ... C3
26 Kona Boys ... C3
27 Long Lava Tube ... B3
28 Mamalahoa Hot Tubs & Massage ... C3
29 Two-Step ... C6

Sleeping

30 Aloha Guest House ... D6
Areca Palms Estate B&B ... (see 28)
31 Banana Patch ... C3
32 Hale Ho'ola B&B ... D6
33 Haleakala B&B ... B1
34 Ka'awaloa Plantation & Guesthouse ... C4
35 Kane Plantation ... D6
36 Kealakekua Bay Bed & Breakfast ... C4
37 Luana Inn ... C4
38 Manago Hotel ... C4
Pineapple Park ... (see 20)

Eating

39 Annie's Island Fresh Burgers ... C3
40 Big Jake's Island B-B-Q ... D5
41 Bong Brothers & Sistahs ... D5
42 ChoiceMart ... C4
43 Coffee Shack ... C4
44 Dave's Hawaiian Ice Cream ... C3
45 Ke'ei Café ... C3
Mahina Cafe ... (see 38)
Manago Restaurant ... (see 38)
46 Mi's Italian Bistro ... C3
47 Patz Pies ... C4
48 Rebel Kitchen ... C2
49 South Kona Fruit Stand ... D6
50 Super J's ... D5
Teshima's Restaurant ... (see 4)

Drinking & Nightlife

51 Kona Coffeehouse & Cafe ... D6
52 Orchid Isle Café ... C3

Entertainment

53 Aloha Theatre ... B2

Shopping

54 Discovery Antiques ... C3
Kiernan Music ... (see 48)
55 Kimura Store ... C2
Lavender Moon Gallery ... (see 55)
Reading Garden ... (see 47)
South Kona Green Market ... (see 1)

10am-4pm Mon-Fri) Repertory plays, indie films and live-music shows are on the program at this historic theater.

Shopping

Kiernan Music
Music

(**☎808-323-4939; www.kiernanmusic.com; 79-7401 Mamalahoa Hwy; ⏰10am-6pm Tue-Fri, to 5pm Sat)** Friendly owner Brian Kiernan has a talent for restoring vintage ukuleles and guitars, and he's a wonderful resource whether you're a curious beginner or a serious musician looking to buy a custom-made uke or archtop guitar.

Lavender Moon Gallery
Arts & Crafts

(**☎808-324-7708; www.lavendermoongallery.com; 79-7404 Mamalahoa Hwy; ⏰11am-6pm Tue-Fri, to 5pm Sat)** High-quality original paintings, prints, jewelry, pottery and handmade bags by Big Island artists fill the colorful storefront windows.

Kimura Store Arts & Crafts
(79-7408 Mamalahoa Hwy; 9am-5pm Mon-Sat) Long-standing family shop rolls out yards of colorfully patterned Hawaiian and Japanese fabrics.

Kealakekua

A sacred place whose name means 'pathway of the gods,' Hawaiian heiau (temples) and the secret burial caves of *ali'i* (chiefs) sat high upon these cliffs centuries ago. Today, this workaday town spread out along the busy Mamalahoa Hwy is South Kona's commercial center.

Sights

HN Greenwell Store Museum Museum
(808-323-3222; www.konahistorical.org; 81-6551 Mamalahoa Hwy; adult/child 5-12yr $7/3; 10am-2pm Mon & Thu) Housed in one of Kona's oldest buildings, this museum is a taste of old Hawai'i. Built in 1875 and meticulously restored, here educational docents in period dress bring Kona's multicultural and agricultural history to life as they wield dry goods and talk story. You'll usually smell sweet bread baking in the traditional Portuguese bread oven outside after 11am on Thursdays.

The museum is between the Mile 111 and the 112 markers on Hwy 11.

Greenwell Farms Farm
(808-323-2295, 888-592-5662; www.greenwellfarms.com; 81-6581 Mamalahoa Hwy; 8am-5pm, tours 8:30am-4:30pm) FREE Run by the Greenwell family and their descendants since 1850, this is one of Kona's oldest and best-known coffee plantations, roasting coffee cherries from over 300 local growers. Take a free tour (offered continuously throughout the day) and sample coffee and fruit at a shady picnic table. You can also purchase Kona Red, a juice made from coffee cherries.

The farm is between the Mile 111 and the Mile 112 markers on Hwy 11.

Activities

Adventures in Paradise Water Sports
(info 808-323-3005, reservations 800-979-3370; www.bigislandkayak.com; 81-6367 Mamalahoa Hwy, Kealakekua; surfboard/SUP rental per day $25/35, kayak-snorkel tour $80; usually 8am-5pm) At this professional water-sports outfitter, guides look after beginners well and lead kayak-snorkeling trips to Kealakekua Bay. Rental gear includes surfboards, bodyboards, wetsuits, stand up paddling (SUP) sets and prescription snorkel masks.

Kona Boys Water Sports
(808-328-1234; www.konaboys.com; 79-7539 Mamalahoa Hwy; s/d/tr kayak rental per day $47/67/87, tours $99-250; 7am-5pm) This laid-back pro water-sports outfitter is South Kona's largest. Kayaking, snorkeling and outrigger-canoe sailing trips visit Kealakekua Bay, or learn surfing and SUP from these brahs. Snorkel gear, SUP, surfboard and kayak rentals available. Call ahead for tour and gear-rental reservations.

Mamalahoa Hot Tubs & Massage Spa
(808-323-2288; www.mamalahoa-hottubs.com; 81-1016 St John's Church Rd; hot tub per hour for 2 people $40-50; noon-9pm Wed-Sat, by appointment only) Soak away your blisters or blues in a lush garden mini-oasis. The two teak-wood tubs, sheltered by thatched roofs that allow for stargazing, are open-sided yet private. Many types of massage, from Swedish to traditional Hawaiian *lomilomi* and hot stone, are available. Reservations required; ask about discount packages.

Kings' Trail Rides Horseback Riding
(808-345-0661, 808-323-2388; www.konacowboy.com; 81-6420 Mamalahoa Hwy; 2hr ride incl lunch $135; by reservation only) This family-run outfitter leads horseback trips across ranch lands on the slopes of Mauna Loa. Ask if trail rides along the coast near Kealakekua Bay have resumed.

Sleeping

Areca Palms Estate B&B B&B $$
(☎808-323-2276; www.konabedandbreakfast.com; 81-1031 Keopuka Mauka Rd; d incl breakfast $120-145; @ 📶) Country comfort and aloha spirit seamlessly combine in this spotless, wooden home. Airy rooms are meticulously outfitted, with lots of pillows and lush robes, and your hosts share their local knowledge freely. Kick back in the family room or watch a sunset from the hot tub. You'll eat like royalty with fresh breakfasts daily. Guests can borrow beach and snorkel gear.

Banana Patch Vacation Rental $$
(☎800-988-2246, 808-322-8888; www.bananabanana.com; Mamao St; studio $115, 1br/2br cottage $125/150; @) Let it all hang out in one of these comfortable, clothing-optional cottages secluded amid tropical foliage. Clean and tasteful, these rustic retreats are terrific for DIY naturists, who share the full kitchen and a hot tub.

Eating & Drinking

Dave's Hawaiian Ice Cream Ice Cream $
(www.daveshawaiianicecream.com; 81-6592 Mamalahoa Hwy; snacks $3-6; ⏰11:30am-9pm) Made on O'ahu, Dave's creamy concoctions are bursting with island flavors: *poha* (cape gooseberry), guava, *liliko'i*, coconut, *ube* (purple yam), chocolate-mac-nut, Kona coffee and more. Get a scoop inside a cup of rainbow shave ice.

Ke'ei Café Fusion $$$
(☎808-322-9992; www.keeicafe.net; 79-7511 Mamalahoa Hwy; mains $15-29; ⏰5-9pm Tue-Sat; 👪) At this long-standing outpost of haute island-fusion cooking, cracking peanut-miso papaya salad sets the stage for fresh catch of the day in fiery Thai curry sauce, tamed by sweet *liliko'i* cheesecake or mango cobbler for dessert. Some nights, the staff and kitchen are simply off their game, however. Reservations recommended; request a lanai table. No credit cards.

Kona coffee plant

Mi's Italian Bistro
Italian $$$

(808-323-3880; www.misitalianbistro.com; 81-6372 Mamalahoa Hwy; mains $14-35; 4:30-8:30pm;) This intimate eatery with class run by husband-and-wife team chef Morgan Starr and Ingrid Chan features homemade pasta, cioppino (seafood stew), meaty mains with organic Big Island–grown vegetables and housemade tiramisu soaked in Kona coffee for dessert. Reservations advised.

Orchid Isle Café
Cafe

(www.orchidislecoffee.com; 81-6637 Mamalahoa Hwy; 6:30am-2pm;) Hang out on the ocean-view lanai, surf the internet and refuel with Kona coffee and quiche at this cozy coffeehouse.

Shopping

Discovery Antiques
Antiques

(81-6593 Mamalahoa Hwy; 10am-5pm Mon-Sat, 11am-4pm Sun) Tin toys and aloha shirts, bric-a-brac and vintage Hawaiiana – who knows what you'll find at this secondhand antiques and curiosities shop. Bonus: it sells scoops of Tropical Dreams ice cream, made in Hilo.

South Kona Green Market
Market

(www.skgm.org; 9am-2pm Sun) Currently setting up at the Amy BH Greenwell Ethnobotanical Garden, this small farmers market with live music vends organic island-grown produce, artisanal foodstuffs and funky crafts.

Information

First Hawaiian Bank (808-322-3484; www.fhb.com; 81-6626 Mamalahoa Hwy; 8:30am-4pm Mon-Thu, to 6pm Fri)

Kona Community Hospital (808-322-9311; www.kch.hhsc.org; 79-1019 Haukapila St) Level-III trauma center with a 24-hour emergency room.

Getting There & Away

The long-awaited Mamalahoa Hwy Bypass Rd between Keauhou and Kealakekua allows drivers to avoid the worst of commuter traffic into and out of Kailua-Kona. The road connects Haleki'i St in Kealakekua (*makai* off Hwy 11 between the Mile 111 and the Mile 112 markers) to Ali'i Dr in Keauhou.

Captain Cook Monument (p72), Kealakekua Bay

Captain Cook

As the Mamalahoa Hwy winds south and the tropical greenery thickens, Captain Cook is a small town boasting big ocean views. Named after the ill-fated circumnavigator who died at Kealakekua Bay below, the town is peppered with B&Bs, roadside coffee-tasting rooms and kayaking outfitters.

Sights

Kona Coffee Living History Farm Historic Site

(808-323-2006; www.konahistorical.org; 82-6199 Mamalahoa Hwy; 1hr tour adult/child 5-12yr $15/5; 10am-2pm Mon-Thu, hourly tours until 1pm) Many coffee-farm tours are perfunctory 15-minute affairs. This tour run by the Kona Historical Society, an affiliate of the Smithsonian Institute, is different and deep. More than just an exploration of how coffee is grown and harvested, it's an evocative look at rural Japanese immigrant life in South Kona. Restored to Hawai'i's pre-statehood era, this 5.5-acre working coffee farm once belonged to the Uchida family, who lived here until 1994.

Several of the docents grew up on area coffee farms, so they speak from experience as they show you around the orchards, processing mill, drying roofs and main house. On easy walking tours, you'll learn how to pick coffee cherries and prepare a traditional *bentō* (Japanese boxed lunch) .

The farm is between the Mile 110 and the Mile 111 markers on Hwy 11.

Amy BH Greenwell Ethnobotanical Garden Gardens

(808-323-3318; www.bishopmuseum.org/greenwell; 82-6160 Mamalahoa Hwy; adult/child under 12yr $7/free; 9am-4pm Tue-Sun, guided tours 1pm Tue-Sat) Without pottery or metals, ancient Hawaiians fashioned most of what they needed from plants. This ethnobotanical garden preserves Hawai'i's endemic species dating from before Western contact and Polynesian-introduced plants in an *ahupua'a* (land division). Walk yourself along landscaped paths or take a guided tour to go more in-depth. Bring insect repellent.

The garden is between the Mile 110 and the Mile 111 markers on Hwy 11.

The Best... Kona Coast Outdoor Activities

1 Night dive or snorkel with manta rays near Kailua-Kona (p39)

2 Kayaking and snorkeling Kealakekua Bay (p66)

3 Hiking in Kaloko-Honokohau National Historical Park (p83)

4 Snorkeling at Two-Step (p77)

5 Off-roading or hiking to remote beaches in Kekaha Kai (Kona Coast) State Park (p86)

6 Lava-tube swimming at Kiholo State Park Reserve (p90)

Big Island Bees Farm

(808-328-7318; www.bigislandbees.com; 82-5780 Napo'opo'o Rd; 10am-4pm) At this roadside gift shop and tiny historical museum, genial staff will let you in on all the secrets of beekeeping, then give you a peek inside a living apiary and teach you how their award-winning, single-varietal and certified organic honey gets made. Taste a free sample of ohia lehua blossom honey spiced with cinnamon or the macnut blossom honey, and you'll be hooked.

Sleeping

Manago Hotel Hotel $

(808-323-2642; www.managohotel.com; 82-6151 Mamalahoa Hwy; s/d $56/59, with shared bath from $33/36;) This no-frills, historical hotel has been hosting travelers and islanders since 1917. Run by the family's third generation, the Manago has clean, spare, motel-style rooms without air-con; the best have private bathrooms and ocean-view lanai on the 3rd floor. Book far ahead, especially for the Japanese-style tatami room with futons and a *furo* (Japanese bathtub).

A koi pond and garden add to the breezy tropical atmosphere. This local landmark is between the Mile 110 and the Mile 111 markers on Hwy 11.

Pineapple Park Hostel **$**

(**877-800-3800, 808-323-2224; www.pineapple-park.com; 81-6363 Mamalahoa Hwy; dm $30, r shared/private bath $69/85; office 8am-8pm;**) South Kona's only hostel is your basic backpacker crashpad, run by a friendly if iron-willed proprietress. A sociable vibe makes up for cramped dorms (No 10 is best) and more comfortable (but still overpriced) private rooms. Look for colorful kayaks out front, between the Mile 110 and the Mile 111 markers on Hwy 11.

Ka'awaloa Plantation & Guesthouse B&B **$$**

(**808-323-2686; www.kaawaloaplantation.com; 82-5990 Upper Napo'opo'o Rd; r $125-150, cottage $159, ste $199, incl breakfast;**) Some places embody Hawaii's beauty effortlessly – like this guesthouse with wrap-around lanai, unparalleled coastal views and gracious hosts who show genuine aloha. Exquisitely decorated rooms (not all have private baths) with fine linens and cottages set amid organic coffee and macadamia-nut orchards are ideal for romance; so is soaking in the outdoor hot tub watching the sunset.

Luana Inn B&B **$$**

(**808-328-2612; www.luanainn.com; 82-5856 Lower Napo'opo'o Rd; d incl breakfast $170-210;**) Welcome to spotless Luana Inn, where each spacious, uncluttered and tastefully understated room has its own private entrance and kitchenette. Two rooms open right onto the pool and hot tub with jaw-dropping bay views, while two spacious suites share a sunny cottage. Over a lavish breakfast, pick your hosts' brains for Hawai'i travel tips – they've been around.

Eating

Super J's Hawaiian, Local **$**

(**808-328-9566; 83-5409 Mamalahoa Hwy; plates $8-12; 10am-6:30pm Mon-Sat**) The full title of this place is 'Ka'aloa's Super J's Hawaiian Food,' but everyone calls it Super J's. They also call it freakin' delicious. The *laulau* (pork, chicken or fish wrapped inside taro or *ti* leaves) is steamed until it's so tender it melts under your fork, the *lomilomi* salmon is perfectly salty – you'll even want second helpings of *poi* (mashed taro).

Site of Captain Cook's first landing in Hawai'i, Kealakekua Bay
SHELDON LEVIS/GETTY IMAGES ©

Best of all is the setting: you're basically eating in a welcoming Hawaiian family's kitchen. It's on the *makai* side of Hwy 11, between the Mile 106 and the Mile 107 markers.

Mahina Cafe Cafe **$**

(☎808-323-3200; 82-6123 Mamalahoa Hwy; breakfast & lunch mains $6-12; ⏰7am-3pm daily, 5-8:30pm Fri-Mon) Just south of the Manago Hotel, this simple diner run by two sisters serves made-from-scratch comfort food like pancakes slathered in *haupia* (coconut cream), *loco moco* bowls and mixed-plate lunches. Grab fresh, hot *malasadas* (Portuguese doughnuts) from the drive-through window.

Patz Pies Pizzeria **$**

(☎808-323-8100; 82-6127 Mamalahoa Hwy; slices/pies from $3/17; ⏰10am-9pm) Thin crust, zesty sauce: claims to dishing authentic NYC pizza are only slightly exaggerated at this native NYer's kitchen, just south of the Manago Hotel.

ChoiceMart Supermarket **$**

(82-6066 Mamalahoa Hwy; ⏰5am-10pm) South Kona's largest grocery store lets you stock up on beach picnic supplies.

Coffee Shack Cafe **$$**

(☎808-328-9555; www.coffeeshack.com; 83-5799 Mamalahoa Hwy; meals $10-15; ⏰7:30am-3pm) Perched precariously next to the highway, this longtime favorite banks on its vertigiounous views of Kealakekua Bay from the back deck – truly, you may never have another cup of 100% Kona coffee with a more inspiring vista. Sandwiches, salads and breakfasts can feed two easily, but taste so-so. Homemade desserts are killer: *liliko'i* cheesecake and Kona lime, coconut-cream or mac-nut pie.

Look for the historic building on the *makai* side of Hwy 11, between the Mile 108 and the Mile 109 markers.

Manago Restaurant Japanese, Local **$$**

(www.managohotel.com; 82-6155 Mamalahoa Hwy; mains breakfast $4-6, lunch & dinner $6-14; ⏰7-9am, 11am-2pm & 5-7:30pm Tue-Sun; 👪) Don't be put off by the bingo-hall ambience at this historic travelers' stopover, where locals devour the pork chops topped with gravy and onions, or try the fried whole '*opelu* (mackerel scad) or fresh catch in butter sauce. Each dinner plate is accompanied by Japanese pickles, miso soup and big bowls of rice. Simple diner-style breakfasts may be South Kona's cheapest.

Shopping

Reading Garden Books

(☎808-323-9540; http://thereadinggarden.blogspot.com; 82-6125 Mamalahoa Hwy; ⏰9am-6pm Mon-Sat, from 11am Sun) Teetering stacks of used volumes spread about in an ordered chaos, wrapping over walls and up staircases and even extending outdoors. Inside you may find proprietor Marcus Medler, whose hobby is restoring rare and vintage books.

Kealakekua Bay

Kealakekua Bay blends supreme natural beauty with ancient sacred sites possessing powerful mana (spiritual essence). Besides being of religious importance to Hawaiians, this also marks the spot where Captain Cook, and by extension the entire outside world, first set foot on Hawai'i, irrevocably altering the fate of the entire archipelago and the indigenous people.

This wide, calm bay, sheltered by a low lava point to the north, tall *pali* (cliffs) in the center and miles of green mountain slopes to the south, is both a **state historical park** (www.hawaiistateparks.org; ⏰sunrise-sunset) FREE and a marine-life conservation district. Off the Mamalahoa Hwy (Hwy 11), narrow Napo'opo'o Rd twists downhill for 4.5 miles to the bay, leaving behind rainy uplands and arriving at the often sunny coast. The road ends by the Napo'opo'o Wharf parking lot. Public restrooms are near the heiau (turn right).

Right: Kealakekua Bay **Below:** Snorkeling, Kealakekua Bay
(RIGHT) ALLAN BAXTER/GETTY IMAGES ©; (BELOW) JAMES WATT/GETTY IMAGES ©

Beaches

Manini Beach Beach

On its southern side, Kealakekua Bay is rocky and exposed to regular northwest swells, so swimming and snorkeling conditions are poor. That said, Manini Beach makes a scenic, shady picnic spot. If you do want to take a dip, despite the scattered, sharp coral and *a'a* (rough, jagged lava) along the shoreline, the best ocean access is to your right upon arriving at the beach.

From Napo'opo'o Rd, turn left onto Pu'uhonua Rd, then right onto Manini Rd. There's limited roadside parking.

Ke'ei Beach Beach

South of Kealakekua Bay, Ke'ei Beach is an attractive cove that's mostly too rough and rocky for swimming, except for a narrow sandy stretch at its northern end. When conditions are right, local surfers ride the long reef break here. Bayside, there's a small canoe and kayak launch and a few fishing shacks, but no public facilities. Be respectful of local residents – you're essentially walking in their front yards.

To get here, take the ragged 4WD road leading *makai* off Pu'uhonua Rd, about 0.3 miles south of Manini Beach Rd (if you hit Ke'ei Transfer Station, you've gone too far). Paved Pu'uhonua Rd continues another few miles south to Place of Refuge.

Sights

Captain Cook Monument Historic Site

From Napo'opo'o Wharf, this tall white obelisk is visible a mile away at Ka'awaloa Cove. It marks the spot where Captain Cook was killed in an armed confrontation with Hawaiians in 1779. In 1877, as an act of diplomacy, the Kingdom of Hawai'i deeded the land that the monument

stands on to Britain. Behind lie the ruins of the ancient village of Ka'awaloa.

Hiki'au Heiau Temple

Veer right at the base of Napo'opo'o Rd to reach this large platform temple. In front of the heiau, a stone beach makes a moody perch from which to observe the stunning scenery, but the surf is too rough to swim. Climbing on the ruins is kapu (forbidden).

Pali Kapu o Keoua Historic Site

Above Kealakekua Bay, the 'sacred cliffs of Keoua' were named for a chief and rival of Kamehameha I. Several high, inaccesible caves in these cliffs served as burial places for Hawaiian royalty, and it's speculated that some of Captain Cook's bones ended up here as well.

Activities

SNORKELING

At Kealakekua Bay's northern end, protected **Ka'awaloa Cove** ranks among Hawai'i's premier snorkeling spots. Protected from ocean swells, its aquamarine waters are especially clear. Tropical fish and coral are brilliantly abundant, and those with iron stomachs can swim out 100ft from shore to hang over the blue abyss of an underwater cliff.

If you're lucky, *honu* (green sea turtles) and spinner dolphins might join you, but remember not to approach these wild animals. By law, you must remain at least 50yd away from turtles, dolphins, whales and seals in the water. All Hawaiian sea turtles are endangered, so give 'em a break and never touch or try to ride them.

At the time of research, you could only visit Ka'awaloa Cove on a snorkel cruise leaving from Kailua-Kona or Keahou, on a guided kayaking tour by a South Kona outfitter or by hiking the Captain Cook Monument Trail.

KAYAKING

Controversy over overcrowding and environmental impact on the bay has resulted in new legal regulations for kayakers. Special recreational permits for transiting the bay, but not for landing at Ka'awaloa Cove or launching from Napo'opo'o Wharf, are currently available to individual kayakers in advance from the **Division of State Parks** (**808-951-9540; www.hawaiistateparks.org; 75 Aupuni St, Hilo; 8:30am-3:30pm Mon-Fri**).

Otherwise, your only other option (for now) is a guided kayaking tour by a state-permitted outfitter; check the website www.hawaiistateparks.org for a current list. Most tours launch from Napo'opo'o Wharf, paddling 30 to 45 minutes across the bay to Ka'awaloa Cove. Prevailing winds are from the northwest, so returning is usually faster and easier.

At the time of research, the only outfitters permitted to lead guided kayaking tours of Kealakekua Bay were Kona Boys (p66) in Captain Cook, Aloha Kayak Co (p63) in Honalo and Adventures in Paradise (p66) in Kealakekua.

DIVING

There are many good dive sites clustered around Kealakekua Bay, including **Ka'awaloa Cove**, with its exceptionally diverse coral and fish. Other sites further north include **Hammerhead**, a deep dive with pelagic action; **Coral Dome**, a big, teeming cave with a giant skylight; and **Driftwood**, featuring lava tubes and white-tip reef sharks.

In the aptly named **Long Lava Tube**, an intermediate site just north of Kealakekua Bay, lava 'skylights' shoot light through the ceiling of the 70ft-long tube, and you may see crustaceans, morays – even Spanish dancers. Outside are countless lava formations sheltering conger eels, triton's trumpet shells and squirrelfish.

HIKING

Captain Cook Monument Trail Hiking

While not a particularly interesting hike, the steep Captain Cook Monument Trail down to Ka'awaloa Cove gives a different perspective than paddling over in a kayak. Go early to avoid the heat, bring snorkel gear and pack plenty of water and insect repellent. The one-way hike down takes about an hour, losing 1300ft of elevation in less than 2 miles.

To get to the trailhead, turn *makai* off the Mamalahoa Hwy onto Napo'opo'o Rd; within the first 10th of a mile, park along the narrow road shoulder, wherever it's safe and legally signposted to do so. To find the trailhead, count five telephone poles from the start of the road – it's *makai* across from three tall palm trees.

The trail can be hot and buggy, with inspiring lookouts on the way down. The route is fairly easy to follow; when in doubt, stay to the left. Plan on twice as long for the uphill return, when you should stay alert for the trail's right-hand turn back up onto the lava ledge, or you'll end up on a 4WD road heading north along the coast – for miles.

Sleeping

Kealakekua Bay Bed & Breakfast B&B **$$**

(**808-328-8150, 800-328-8150; www.keala.com; 82-6002 Lower Napo'opo'o Rd; r/ste $165/240, 2br cottage $360;**) Gourmet breakfasts served in a Mediterranean-style villa are reason enough to stay here. Local goat cheese, macadamia-nut pancakes, fresh fruit plucked from the garden – you can't go wrong. That goes for the property itself too: three bright, sun-kissed rooms filled with tropical accents, and the six-person Ohana Kai Guest House, a hill-perched cottage with postcard views of Kealakekua Bay.

Honaunau

Growing by leaps and bounds amid thick coffee and macadamia-nut groves, Honaunau invites exploring without any must-do stops. Of course, nearby Place of Refuge (Pu'uhonua O Hōnaunau National Historical Park) is the star attraction, but meander down Painted Church Rd, stopping at fruit stands, honey farms and coffee shacks with sea views for less-trafficked diversions.

Sights & Activities

St Benedict's Painted Church
Church

(808-328-2227; www.thepaintedchurch.org; 84-5140 Painted Church Rd; services 7am Tue & Thu-Fri, 4pm Sat, 7:15am Sun) FREE A pulpit with a view, gravestones cradled by tropical blooms and a little chapel with floor-to-ceiling 'outsider art' make this church a picturesque side trip. A self-taught artist and Catholic priest, John Velghe, came to Hawai'i from Belgium in 1899 and he modeled the vaulted nave on a Gothic cathedral in Burgos, Spain. His trompe l'oeil artwork is delightful, in a naive art kind of way. Come early or late, when the light is softer and birds sing out.

Paleaku Gardens Peace Sanctuary
Gardens

(808-328-8084; www.paleaku.com; 83-5401 Painted Church Rd; adult/child 6-12yr $10/3; 9am-4pm Tue-Sat) Seven acres of shrines and meditation nooks await at this tranquil garden sanctuary tucked along Painted Church Rd. The innovative 'galaxy garden' is a mini Milky Way rendered in plants. A self-guided tour is a peaceful introduction to this unique, peaceful place. Check online for schedules of drop-in yoga classes and special events.

Society for Kona's Education & Art
Arts Center

(SKEA; 808-328-9392; www.skea.org; 84-5191 Mamalahoa Hwy) SKEA is a hotbed of activity, with pilates, Polynesian dance, tai chi and Japanese ink painting classes, art shows and poetry readings; check the online calendar. Around back at the **Kona Potter's Guild**, you can watch potters at work and buy their handmade creations.

The center is between the Mile 105 and the Mile 106 on Hwy 11.

Sleeping

Aloha Guest House
B&B $$

(800-897-3188, 808-328-8955; www.alohaguesthouse.com; 84-4780 Mamalahoa Hwy; r incl breakfast $125-230; @) If you're coming all the way to Hawai'i, you should have the finest digs. Heady views from the shared lanai, guest living room and, for the lucky ones, your own king-sized bed will make you swoon, guaranteed. Ocean vistas are complemented by luxurious amenities such as organic bath products and full breakfasts with local fruit and estate-grown coffee.

Access is via a unpaved one-lane farm road that's very steep and bumpy.

St Benedict's Painted Church
JOHN ELK/GETTY IMAGES ©

Hale Ho'ola B&B B&B $$

(☎877-628-9117, 808-328-9117; www.hale-hoola.com; 85-4577 Mamalahoa Hwy; r incl breakfast $125-165; @ 📶) This remarkably hospitable roadside B&B provides a homey, relaxed stay with three small but comfortable rooms downstairs in the main house. Despite comfy beds and private lanai with ocean views, the unfortunately thin-walled rooms are jammed together – they're not recommended for honeymooners or antisocial types. Robust breakfasts somewhat compensate.

Kane Plantation B&B $$$

(☎808-328-2416; http://kaneplantationhawaii.com; 84-1120 Telephone Exchange Rd; d incl breakfast $155-255; 📶) You'll be in excellent hands at this upscale historic home, where renowned Hawaiian artist Herb Kane once lived. Perched on a lush *mauka* hillside, the B&B shares the grounds with an avocado farm. Upstairs the most spacious Kanaloa Suite boasts a king-sized canopy bed and views of Kealakekua Bay from a private lanai. Breakfasts are gourmet, and the hosts are charming.

Eating & Drinking

South Kona Fruit Stand Market, Cafe $

(☎808-328-8547; www.southkonafruitstand.com; 84-4770 Mamalahoa Hwy; items $3-10; ⏰9am-6pm Mon-Sat, 10am-4pm Sun) Baskets overflow with everything from tart apple bananas to filling breadfruit, creamy *abiu* (sapote) and purple jaboticaba berries. Slurp a smoothie on the outdoor patio with gorgeous coastal views. Look for the pineapple flags on the *mauka* side of Hwy 11, between the Mile 103 and the Mile 104 markers.

Bong Brothers & Sistahs Health Food, Deli $

(www.bongbrothers.com; 84-5227 Mamalahoa Hwy; items $3-8; ⏰9am-6pm Mon-Fri, noon-6pm Sun; 🥡) 🌿 Food is politics at this small organic health-food store, vegetarian take-out deli and coffee shop inside a historic 1929 building.

Big Jake's Island B-B-Q BBQ $$

(☎808-328-1227; 83-5308 Mamalahoa Hwy; most mains $7-12; ⏰11am-6pm Sun-Thu, to 7pm Fri & Sat) Barbecued ribs, pork and chicken are slowly cooked up in the barrel smoker

Pu'uhonua O Hōnaunau National Historical Park

IMAGES ETC LTD/GETTY IMAGES ©

parked by the Mile 106 marker on Hwy 11. Chow down at picnic tables out back, or for DIY surf-and-turf, pick up some *poke* from the seafood shop next door.

Kona Coffeehouse & Cafe Cafe
(84-4830 Mamalahoa Hwy; ⌚7am-4pm Tue-Sat, 8:30am-2pm Sun) On the *mauka* side of Hwy 11, at the turnoff to Place of Refuge, this coffee shop is serious about 100% Kona brews, espresso and more. Gooey mac-nut caramel pies and *liliko'i* bars are homemade.

Pu'uhonua O Hōnaunau National Historical Park

Standing at the edge of thorny coastal plains and lava desert, this **national park (☎808-328-2326, 808-328-2288; www.nps.gov/puho; off Hwy 160, Honaunau; 7-day entry per car $5; ⌚park 7am-sunset, visitor center 8:30am-4:30pm)** fronting Honaunau Bay is one of the state's most evocative experiences of ancient Hawai'i. You'll almost always hear this park referred to as 'Place of Refuge,' because the name, meaning 'a place of refuge at Honaunau,' is such a tongue-twister.

Early morning or late afternoon is an optimal time to visit to avoid the midday heat and crowds. On the weekend closest to July 1, show up for the park's annual **cultural festival**, an extravaganza of traditional food, hula dancing, Hawaiian crafts and cultural demonstrations.

Sights

A half-mile walking tour easily encompasses the park's major sights. The sandy trail begins below the visitor center, where you can pick up self-guiding tour brochures and beach wheelchairs to borrow. Sights nearest the water require traversing rough lava, which makes them wheelchair-inaccessible.

The park comprises two sections: the royal grounds and the *pu'uhonua* (place of refuge). You enter via the royal grounds – a little village, really – where *ali'i* (chiefs) and their warriors lived. Leading up to the heiau is the **Great Wall** separating the royal grounds from the *pu'uhonua*. Built around 1550, this stone wall is more than 1000ft long and 10ft high.

The authentically reconstructed temple on the cove's point, **Hale o Keawe Heiau**, was first built around 1700. In ancient times, it contained the sacred bones of chiefs whose mana (spiritual essence) bestowed sanctity on those who entered the grounds. Surrounding the temple, ohia trees carved into *ki'i* (deity images) up to 15ft high stand guard.

Honu (green sea turtles) nibble and rest around small, sandy **Keone'ele Cove**, which was once the royal canoe landing. Also nearby are a royal fishpond, lava-tree molds, hand-carved koa canoes with coconut-fiber lashings and an open-sided, thatch-roofed *hale* (hut) where the park's cultural demonstrator talks story and carries on traditional crafts.

After wandering the self-guided trail, you might like to try some wildlife watching: humpback whales swim offshore in winter, along with sea turtles and dolphins year-round, and even hoary bats can be seen (after sunset is best).

Activities

Two-Step Snorkeling, Diving
Immediately north of Pu'uhonua O Hōnaunau National Historical Park, concealed within a (usually) placid bay, are ridiculously beautiful, vibrant coral gardens where reef and marine life seem locked in a permanent race to outstrip each other with the most eye-catching color palette. From above the water, your only indication of the action is the presence of boats leading snorkeling, diving, kayaking and SUP tours, plus the crowds gathering at the titular two steps.

There's no beach here – snorkelers use a stepped lava ledge beside the boat ramp to access about 10ft of water, which quickly drops to about 25ft. Look for, but by no means touch, the predatory, razor-sharp 'crown of thorns' starfish feasting on live coral polyps. Scuba divers can investigate a ledge a little way out that drops off about 100ft.

Island Insights

In ancient Hawai'i the kapu (taboo) system regulated every waking moment. A *maka'ainana* (commoner) could not look at *ali'i* (chiefs) or walk in their footsteps. Women couldn't cook for men, nor eat with them. Fishing, hunting and gathering timber was restricted to certain seasons. And on and on.

Violators of kapu were hunted down and killed. After all, according to the Hawaiian belief system, breaking kapu infuriated the gods. And gods wrought volcanic eruptions, tidal waves, famine and earthquakes, which could be devastating to the entire community.

There was one loophole, however. Commoners who broke kapu could stave off death if they reached the sacred ground of a *pu'uhonua* (place of refuge). A *pu'uhonua* also gave sanctuary to defeated warriors and wartime noncombatants (men who were too old, too young or unable to fight).

To reach the *pu'uhonua* was no small feat. Since royals and their warriors lived on the grounds surrounding the refuge, kapu breakers had to swim through violent, open ocean, braving currents and sharks, to safety. Once inside the sanctuary, priests performed ceremonies of absolution to placate the gods. Kapu breakers could then return home to start afresh.

The *pu'uhonua* at Honaunau was used for several centuries until 1819, when Hawai'i's old religious ways were abandoned after King Kamehameha II and regent Queen Ka'ahumanu ate together in public, overthrowing the ancient kapu system forever.

The best time to go is during a rising tide, when there are more fish. Year-round, freshwater springs can create blurry patches in the water, however. High winter surf means rough waters.

A privately operated parking lot here costs $3, or try to squeeze in along the road's shoulder.

1871 Trail Hiking

A 2-mile round-trip oceanfront hike leads to the abandoned village of Ki'ilae, where there's very little left to see. The visitor center stocks trail guides describing ancient Hawaiian archaeological sites along the way; among other things, you pass a collapsed lava tube and a tremendous, if overgrown, *holua* (lava-sledding course) that *ali'i* raced sleds down. Watch out for feral goats (but they're usually benign).

Ho'okena & Around

Most tourists zip right by the turnoff for Ho'okena, between the Mile 101 and the Mile 102 markers on Hwy 11. But meander just a couple of miles downhill to this fishing community and you'll be surprised by a gorgeous bayfront beach that locals love and, more importantly, are willing to share.

Ho'okena was once a bustling Hawaiian village. Novelist Robert Louis Stevenson wrote about his 1889 visit in *Travels in Hawaii*. In the 1890s, Chinese immigrants moved into Ho'okena, a tavern and a hotel opened, and the town got rougher and rowdier. In those days, Big Island cattle were shipped from the Ho'okena landing, but when the circle-island road was built, Honolulu-bound steamers stopped coming and most people moved away.

Beaches

Ho'okena Beach Park Beach

This modest, charcoal-colored beach is backed by a steep green hillside. When calm, the bay's waters are good for swimming, kayaking and snorkeling (although the bottom drops off quickly). Coral abounds, as do strong currents further out. When the winter surf is up, local kids hit the waves with bodyboards. You might spot dolphins and humpback whales offshore between December and April. Facilities include restrooms, outdoor showers, drinking water, campsites, a picnic pavilion and a concession stand.

Camping is right on the sand at the base of the cliffs. Ongoing security issues have been addressed by implementing a guard patrol and through the activism of the **Friends of Ho'okena Beach Park** (808-328-7321; http://hookena.org); you can obtain required camping permits and rent camping gear online or in person. Camping permits can also be obtained in advance from the county.

Pebble Beach Beach

Not quite pebbles, the smoky stones of this nonsandy beach at the bottom of the Kona Paradise subdivision range from gumdrop to palm-sized. It's a popular kayak put-in and offers a good dose of peace and quiet. Lounge for a bit, paddle a while or just watch the sun go down. If you enter the water, watch out for potentially fatal 'sneaker' waves.

The beach is a mile down very steep, winding Kaohe Rd, accessed between the Mile 96 and the Mile 97 markers on Hwy 11. Signs say 'private road' and 'keep out,' although the subdivision is ungated. Always ask permission from locals before entering.

Miloli'i

Miloli'i is a fishing village fighting to maintain its traditional ways while an upscale subdivision rises from the lava landscape around it. Miloli'i means 'fine twist,' and historically the village was known for skilled sennit twisters, who used coconut-husk fibers to make fine cord and highly valued fishnets. Villagers still live close

Hawaiian spinner dolphin, Ho'okena

to the sea, and many continue to make a living from it.

Privacy is paramount in these parts and curious tourists are tolerated – barely. The turn-off to Miloli'i is just south of the Mile 89 marker on Hwy 11; the village is 5 miles down a steep, winding, single-lane road that cuts across a 1926 lava flow.

Beaches

Miloli'i Beach Park Beach

This locals-only county beach park is pocked with tide pools. Visitors are generally unwelcome and facilities are limited to restrooms and picnic tables. Camping along the rocky shore is allowed (but not recommended due to security problems) with an advance county permit.

Honomalino Beach Beach

Instead of feeling like the unwanted guest you are at Miloli'i Beach Park, instead head to Honomalino Bay, less than a mile's walk south. With sand the color of all Big Island beaches crushed into one – green, gold, tawny and black – this beach has gentle swimming (for kids too) and reef snorkeling. Look for the marked public path beginning just beyond Miloli'i's public basketball courts by the yellow church and up the rocks.

When in doubt, keep to the right fork along the trail. Respect all private property and kapu (no trespassing) signs.

NORTH KONA COAST

If you imagine the Big Island is all jungle rainforest and white-sand beaches, the severity of the North Kona Coast will come as a shock. Infinite fields of black, broken lava-rock desert blanket this forbidding-looking shoreline. Yet always, at the edge of the horizon, the bright, sparkling blue waters of the Pacific beckon.

Turn off the Queen Ka'ahumanu Hwy (Hwy 19) and make your way across the eerie lava fields to snorkel with sea turtles, bask on almost deserted black-sand beaches and catch an iconic Kona sunset. On clear days, gaze *mauka* at panoramas of Mauna Kea and Mauna Loa volcanoes, both often snow-dusted in winter, and in the foreground between the two, Mt Hualalai.

Honokohau Harbor

Almost all of Kona's catch comes in at this harbor, about 2 miles north of downtown Kailua-Kona, including granders (fish weighing over 1000lb). Most fishing charters, dive boats and snorkeling and whale-watching cruises booked out of Kailua-Kona depart here.

Sunset, Honomalino Beach
ALVIS UPITIS/GETTY IMAGES ©

To reach the harbor, turn *makai* on Kealakehe Pkwy, just north of the Mile 98 marker on Hwy 19. The harbor provides public access to Honokohau Beach (p84) inside Kaloko-Honokohau National Historical Park.

Activities

DIVING & SURFING

From Honokohau Harbor south to Kailua Bay is a marine-life conservation district, accessible only by boat. This stretch of coast is littered with dive sites, including **Turtle Pinnacle**, a premier turtle-spotting site straight out from the harbor. Northbound toward the airport is **Garden Eel Cove**, aka 'Manta Heaven.'

Another good diving spot is off **Kaiwi Point**, south of Honokohau Harbor, where sea turtles, large fish and huge eagle rays swim around some respectable drop-offs. Nearby is **Suck 'Em Up**, a couple of lava tubes you can swim into, letting the swell pull you through.

Ocean Eco Tours Diving, Surfing

(808-324-7873; www.oceanecotours.com; 74-425 Kealakehe Pkwy, Honokohau Harbor; snorkel/dive boat trips from $99/119, group/private surfing lesson $95/150) For surfing lessons, this is the only operator permitted to surf within the boundaries of Kaloko-Honokohau National Historical Park. It also guides snorkeling and scuba trips along the coast, including night dives with manta rays. Stop by the small shop at the harbor to rent surfboards, bodyboards and snorkel or scuba gear.

FISHING

Scads of fishing charters leave from Honokohau Harbor. If you're just after the money shot, you can watch the boats as they pull up and weigh their haul at around 11:30am and 3:30pm. Entering the harbor area, take the first right, park near the gas station and walk toward the dock behind Bite Me Fish Market Bar & Grill.

KAYAKING

Plenty Pupule Kayaking

(808-880-1400; www.plentypupule.com; 73-4976 Kamanu St, Kaloko Industrial Park; kayak rental per day s/d $25/38, tours $80-250; 10am-5:30pm Tue-Sat) One of the island's top outfitters for adventure kayaking, these folks can recommend the best put-ins and snorkel spots, customize tours, teach you to kayak surf or take you kayak sailing, the latter particularly memorable during winter whale-watching season.

Tours

Hawaii Forest & Trail Van Tours

(800-464-1993, 808-331-8505; www.hawaii-forest.com; 74-5035B Queen Ka'ahumanu Hwy; tours adult/child from $159/139) This multiaward-winning outfitter caters to active travelers who want to delve into the Big Island's greenest depths. From the always popular Mauna Kea summit and stargazing van tours to exclusive guided bird-watching hikes in Hakalau Forest National Wildlife Refuge, you won't regret an adventure with these expert naturalists and ecosustainability stewards.

Eating & Drinking

Bite Me Fish Market Bar & Grill Seafood $$

(808-327-3474; www.bitemefishmarket.com; 74-425 Kealakehe Pkwy, Honokohau Harbor; mains $8-23; 6am-9pm;) Steps from the harbor boat ramp, stop into this bamboo-fenced place for a bottle of Longboard Lager and to spin yarns after a day of fishing. At dockside picnic tables, chow down on just alright fish sandwiches, tacos, ceviche, *poke* and seafood and *pupu* platters. Service from the tattted-out servers can be lackadaisical.

Kona Coffee & Tea Company Cafe

(www.konacoffeeandtea.com; 74-5035 Queen Ka'ahumanu Hwy; 7am-5:30pm Mon-Fri, 8am-5pm Sat, 10am-3pm Sun;) Life is too short for bad coffee: head here for award-winning 100% Kona grown on sustainable

North Kona Coast

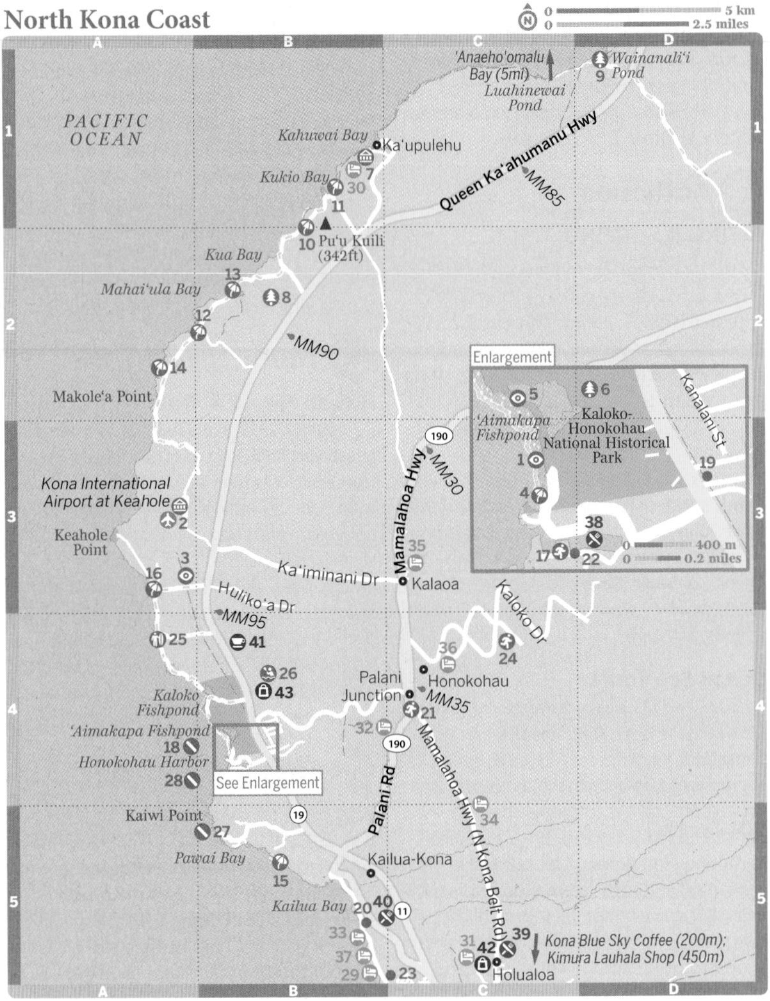

farms. Freshly roasted beans and toothsome mac-nut pies mitigate the location behind a gas station.

Kona Mountain Coffee Cafe

(☎808-329-5005; www.konamountaincoffee.com; 73-4038 Hukiloa Dr; ⏰8am-6pm Mon-Fri, to 5pm Sat & Sun) Just over 2 miles north of the harbor turnoff along Hwy 19, this farm-grown coffee roaster's retail shop and coffee bar also stocks baked goodies and snacks. It's a quick stop on the way to the airport.

Shopping

Kailua Candy Company Food

(☎808-329-2522, 800-622-2462; http://kailua-candy.com; 73-5612 Kauhola St, Kaloko Industrial Park; ⏰9am-5pm Mon-Sat) A detour to this chocolate factory shop is mandatory for every sweet tooth. Savor free samples of Mauna Kea 'snowballs' (white chocolate with shredded coconut), Kona coffee swirls, Hawaiian 'turtles' and tropically flavored truffles. To get here, turn *mauka*

North Kona Coast

Sights

1 'Aimakapa Fishpond ... C3
2 Astronaut Ellison S Onizuka Space Center ... A3
3 Hawaii Ocean Science & Technology Park ... A3
4 Honokohau Beach ... C3
5 Kaloko Fishpond ... C2
6 Kaloko-Honokohau National Historical Park ... D2
7 Ka'upulehu Cultural Center ... B1
8 Kekaha Kai (Kona Coast) State Park ... B2
9 Kiholo State Park Reserve ... D1
10 Kikaua Beach ... B2
11 Kukio Beach ... B1
12 Mahai'ula Beach ... B2
13 Makalawena Beach ... B2
14 Makole'a Beach ... A2
Manini'owali Beach (Kua Bay) ... (see 10)
Ocean Rider Seahorse Farm ... (see 3)
15 Old Kona Airport State Recreation Area ... B5
16 Wawaloli (OTEC) Beach ... A3

Activities, Courses & Tours

Captain Zodiac ... (see 38)
17 Charter Desk ... C3
Dan McSweeney's Whale Watch . (see 17)
18 Garden Eel Cove ... A4
19 Hawaii Forest & Trail ... D3
20 Hawaii Lifeguard Surf Instructors ... B5
21 Hula Daddy Kona Coffee ... C4
22 Kamanu Charters ... C3
23 Kona Surf Adventures ... C5
Malama I'ka Ola Holistic Health Center ... (see 39)
24 Mountain Thunder Coffee Plantation ... C4
Ocean Eco Tours ... (see 38)
25 Pine Trees ... A4
26 Plenty Pupule ... B4
27 Suck 'Em Up ... B5
28 Turtle Pinnacle ... A4

Sleeping

29 Casa de Emdeko ... B5
30 Four Seasons Resort Hualalai ... B1
31 Holualoa Inn ... C5
32 Honu Kai B&B ... B4
33 Kona Tiki Hotel ... B5
34 Lilikoi Inn ... C5
35 Mango Sunset B&B ... C3
36 Nancy's Hideaway ... C4
37 Royal Sea-Cliff Resort ... B5

Eating

Beach Tree ... (see 7)
38 Bite Me Fish Market Bar & Grill ... D3
39 Holuakoa Gardens & Café ... C5
40 Jackie Rey's Ohana Grill ... B5
'Ulu Ocean Grill + Sushi Lounge .... (see 7)

Drinking & Nightlife

Kona Coffee & Tea Company ... (see 19)
41 Kona Mountain Coffee ... B4

Shopping

42 Dovetail Gallery & Design ... C5
Holualoa Farmers Market ... (see 39)
Holualoa Ukulele Gallery ... (see 42)
Ipu Hale Gallery ... (see 39)
43 Kailua Candy Company ... B4
Studio 7 Fine Arts ... (see 42)

onto Hina Lani St off Hwy 19, then right on Kamanu St.

Kaloko-Honokohau National Historical Park

Just north of Honokohau Harbor, this 1160-acre **national park (808-326-9057; www.nps.gov/kaho; visitor center 8:30am-4pm, park 24hr) FREE** may be the Kona Coast's most underappreciated ancient Hawaiian site. Hidden among lava fields lies evidence of the innovations that allowed Hawaiians to thrive in this hostile landscape: fish traps, lava planters used to grow taro and other staples, plus the *ahupua'a* (land division) between Kaloko and Honokohau that gives the park its name. There are also heiau, burial caves and petroglyphs.

Despite the seemingly endless expanse of lava rock and unbearable midday heat, this is a good place to explore. Go in the early morning, late afternoon or when skies are overcast. *Kokua* (please) remember not to climb on, move, alter or deface any rock structures. Take special care not to disturb the endangered *honu* (green sea turtles), who haul out here to rest, feed and bask in the sun – it's illegal to approach them closer than 20ft away on land, or 50yd in the water.

The park's main entrance is off Hwy 19 between the Mile 96 and the Mile 97 markers, where there's a parking lot and a small, but informative ranger-staffed visitor center.

Sights

Honokohau Beach — Beach

At this beautiful hook-shaped beach with a mix of black lava, white coral and wave-tossed shells, the water is usually too cloudy for snorkeling, but just standing on shore you'll see *honu* (green sea turtles). You may spot more *honu* munching on *limu* (seaweed) around the ancient **'Ai'opio fishtrap**, bordered by a Hawaiian **heiau** at the beach's southern end. Inland are **anchialine ponds** – pools of brackish water that make unique habitats for marine and plant life.

To get here, turn right into the first parking lot at Honokohau Harbor (look for the small public coastal access sign). Near the end of the road is the signposted trailhead; a five-minute walk on a well-beaten path leads to the beach. You could also take the more scenic, if longer route by hiking to the beach along the 0.75-mile **Ala Hele Iki Trail** from the visitor center.

Kaloko Fishpond — Historic Site

At the park's northern end, Kaloko Fishpond is one of the most interesting sites because its massive rock retaining wall is being completely rebuilt, so it can once again be fished in the traditional way. Some speculate that the bones of Kamehameha the Great were secretly buried in a cave nearby.

From the park's visitor center, drive north on Hwy 19 until you reach a separate gated entrance at Ala Kaloko Rd. Alternatively, it's about a 1-mile hike north from the visitor center along the coastal **Ala Kahakai National Historic Trail**, a restored ancient Hawaiian footpath.

'Aimakapa Fishpond — Historic Site

In the park's southern section, 'Aimakapa is the largest fishpond on the Kona Coast. It's home to *ae'o* (Hawaiian black-necked stilt) and *'alae kea* (Hawaiian coot), both of which are endangered native waterbirds. Neaby look for the ancient remains of a *holua* (lava-sledding course).

Heiau, Kaloko-Honokohau National Historical Park

JOHN ELK/GETTY IMAGES ©

Keahole Point

Funny place, Keahole Point. Just offshore, the seafloor drops abruptly, providing a continuous supply of both cold water from 2000ft depths and warm surface water. These are ideal conditions for ocean thermal-energy conversion (OTEC), deep sea water extraction and aquaculture. All of this is happening here, plus there's a beach and one of the island's best surf breaks.

Beaches

Wawaloli (OTEC) Beach Beach

(Makiko Bay Dr; 6am-8pm) At the *makai* end of the access road to the Natural Energy Laboratory of Hawaii (Nelha), this quiet locals' beach is perfectly positioned for sunsets – never mind the jets flying overhead. Swimming isn't good here, except at high tide when the oodles of protected **tide pools** along the lava-rock coastline overflow. Bring a picnic and the kids. Facilities include restrooms and outdoor showers.

Sights

Hawaii Ocean Science & Technology Park Building

(HOST Park; 808-327-9585; http://nelha.hawaii.gov; 73-4660 Queen Ka'ahumanu Hwy; lecture & tour adult/student & senior/child under 9yr from $8/5/free) That funny-looking building with the gigantic solar panels is the **Natural Energy Laboratory of Hawaii (Nelha)**. This 'zero-net energy facility' was voted one of the USA's 10 greenest buildings in 2007. Learn about OTEC and research into alternative and renewable-energy technologies at Nelha's public presentations, which are followed by an abalone farm tour and tasting on Monday, Wednesday and Thursday or a solar-energy plant tour on Tuesday. Friday's 'Grand Tour' (reservations required) visits OTEC Tower and kampachi and abalone farms.

About 40 businesses call Nelha's HOST Park home, including **Kampachi Farms** (www.kampachifarm.com), the aquaculture gurus responsible for yellowfin tuna seen on haute island restaurant menus; **Kona Deep** (www.gotdeep.com), 100% Hawaii deep-sea water that's desalinated and bottled here, then sold as a tonic internationally; and **Ocean Rider Seahorse Farm** (**808-329-6840; www.seahorse.com; 73-4388 Ilikai Pl; tours adult/child 4-9yr $36/26; gift shop 9:30am-3:30pm, tours noon & 2pm Mon-Fri, also 10am Mon-Fri late Dec-Apr & Jun-late Aug;**), the only one of its kind in the country.

The turnoff is just over a mile south of Kona International Airport, between th Mile 94 and the Mile 95 markers on Hwy 19.

Astronaut Ellison S Onizuka Space Center Museum

(808-329-3441; http://hawaii.gov/koa/; Kona International Airport; adult/child under 12yr $3/1; 8:30am-4:30pm;) This little museum pays tribute to the Big Island native who perished in the 1986 *Challenger* space-shuttle disaster. Sitting between the aiport's departure and arrival buildings, you'll find kid-friendly exhibits and educational videos about space and astronauts. Items on display include a moon rock, a NASA space suit and scale models of spacecraft.

Activities

Pine Trees Surfing

Pine Trees is one of West Hawai'i's best surfing breaks. The break stretches along a pretty beach that is rocky enough to make swimming difficult. The final bay gets the most consistent yet more forgiving waves. An incoming midtide is favorable, but as the swell picks up in winter these breaks often close out.

Get friendly with local regulars if you want in on the action – this hot spot draws crowds, especially on weekends. Where the access road to Nelha veers to the right, look left for a rutted dirt road leading about 2 miles further south. You'll need a high-clearance 4WD to make it, or you can walk, but it's hot. The access road gates are locked between 8pm and 6am.

Kekaha Kai (Kona Coast) State Park

Most only accessible by 4WD or on foot, the gorgeous beaches of this **state park** (www.hawaiistateparks.org; 9am-7pm) FREE are all the more memorable for being tucked away on the far side of a vast desert of unforgiving black lava. Several beaches have remote coves where sea turtles gather and calm pools for swimming. The majority of the 1600-acre park is wonderfully undeveloped and brutally hot; bring water, food, sunscreen, a hat and sturdy hiking shoes or a 4WD vehicle.

Hard-core hikers can tackle a section of the coastal **Ala Kahakai National Historic Trail** from Kua Bay north via Kikaua Beach to Kukio Beach (2 miles each way), or south via Makalawena Beach to Mahai'ula Beach (4.5 miles each way). But beware that temperatures by midmorning can be broiling, and the trail has painful stretches of nothing but *a'a* lava.

Beaches

Manini'owali Beach (Kua Bay) — Beach

(www.hawaiistateparks.org; 9am-7pm) At this crescent-shaped beach with powdery white sand and little shade, sparkling turquoise waters are first-rate for swimming and bodyboarding (the latter especially in winter), and there's even decent snorkeling when waters are calm. Manini'owali draws major crowds, especially on weekends. To get here, turn onto the (unsigned) paved access road between the Mile 88 and the Mile 89 markers on Hwy 19, opposite West Hawaii Veterans Cemetery.

Mahai'ula Beach — Beach

Kekaha Kai (Kona Coast) State Park's largest beach has salt-and-pepper sand, rocky tide pools, shaded picnic tables and pit toilets. Swimming usually isn't good here, but during big winter swells, surfing happens. Walk a few minutes north along the coast to find a second, less rocky beach with soft tawny sands (nicknamed **Magoon's**), perfect for sunbathing and swimming. Access to Mahai'ula is via a chunky lava road between the Mile 90 and the Mile 91 markers on Hwy 19.

Although 4WD is recommended, many locals drive down the unpaved beach access road in a standard passenger car. Alternatively, you could traverse the 1.5 miles on foot from Hwy 19. Park at an improvised lot just inland from the highway and start walking or thumb it – drivers may take pity on your sun-beaten head and give you a lift.

Makalawena Beach — Beach

If what you're after is an almost deserted, postcard-perfect scoop of

Manini'owali Beach (Kua Bay)
TOM BENEDICT/GETTY IMAGES ©

soft, white-sand beach cupping brilliant blue-green waters (are you sold yet?), head to 'Maks.' Although popular, this string of idyllic coves absorbs crowds so well, you'll still feel like you've found paradise. The northernmost cove is sandier and gentler, while the southernmost cove is (illegally) a naked sunbathing spot. Swimming is splendid, but beware of rough surf and rocks in the water. Bodyboarding and snorkeling are more possibilities.

Practice aloha during your visit by packing out all trash and respecting the privacy of others. For locals, this is an unofficial camping and fishing getaway, and the growing popularity of these beaches among outsiders is contentious for some. Always give endangered sea turtles a wide berth – it's illegal to approach them closer than 20ft away on land, or 50yd in the water.

Getting to Makalawena requires extra effort. Take the unpaved Kekaha Kai (Kona Coast) State Park access road (4WD recommended, although many locals drive it in a standard passenger car), off Hwy 19 between the Mile 90 and the Mile 91 markers. Less than 1.5 miles later, at the road junction before the parking lot for Mahai'ula Beach, turn right. Park on the road shoulder near the cables restricting vehicle access to a service road, then walk north for 30 minutes across the lava flow and sand dunes to the beach, either following the service road or a rougher footpath over crunchy *a'a* lava.

Makole'a Beach Beach

Amazingly, this secluded black-sand beach belongs to Kekaha Kai (Kona Coast) State Park. Although there's no shade and it's too rocky for swimming, its natural beauty rewards those who make the effort to visit. To reach this small, dark treasure on foot, head south along Mahai'ula Beach and either follow the road or the coastline while making toward a lone tree.

With a 4WD, turn left at the road junction by Mahai'ula Beach, drive south for about 1000yd until you reach a path marked by white coral, then get out and hoof it as the lava becomes too rough.

The Best... Kona Coast Beaches

1 Kekaha Kai (Kona Coast) State Park (p86)

2 Kiholo Bay (p90)

3 Kukio Beach (p88)

4 Honomalino Beach (p80)

5 Ho'okena Beach Park (p79)

Ka'upulehu

Once a thriving fishing village among many dotting this length of coast, Ka'upulehu was wiped out by the 1946 tsunami and abandoned until the Kona Village Resort opened here in 1965. The resort closed indefinitely in 2011 after more tsunami damage caused by a massive earthquake in Japan. The luxurious Four Seasons Resort Hualalai remains open, however, as do some fine public beaches that you can visit for free.

Beaches

Kikaua Beach Beach

(family-friendly) Obviously artificial (a thin layer of sand laid over concrete is hard on the feet), Kikaua Beach has some things going for it. There's lots of shade, and a completely protected cove is perfect for teaching *keiki* (children) to swim and even snorkel. Around the kiawe-covered point are gaggles of sea turtles. Facilities include restrooms, outdoor showers and drinking water.

Public beach access is through a private country club and residential development. It's limited to 28 cars per day, so it never feels that crowded. To get here, turn *makai* onto Kuki'o Nui Rd

Right: Manini'owali Beach (Kua Bay) **Below:** Four Seasons Resort Hualalai golf course

(RIGHT) TOM BENEDICT/GETTY IMAGES ©; (BELOW) PETER FRENCH/GETTY IMAGES ©

near the Mile 87 marker on Hwy 19. Drive to the security guardhouse and request a parking pass and directions to the beach.

Kukio Beach Beach

From Kikaua Beach you could walk north to the scalloped, palm-fringed coves of Kukio Bay, officially part of the Four Seasons Resort Hualalai. There the sand is soft, the swimming is good (even for kids) and there's a paved trail leading north along the rocky coastline to another beach. Facilities include restrooms, outdoor showers and drinking water.

To drive here, turn onto Ka'upulehu Rd (unsigned) between the Mile 86 and the Mile 87 markers on Hwy 19. Drive straight ahead to the Four Seasons security guardhouse and request a beach parking pass. The 50-car beach parking lot almost never fills up.

Sights

Ka'upulehu Cultural Center Gallery

(**808-325-8520; 72-100 Ka'upulehu Dr, Four Seasons Resort Hualalai; 8:30am-4pm Mon-Fri**) FREE Inside the Four Season's Hawaiian cultural center, small but museum-quality displays are organized around a collection of 11 original paintings by Herb Kawainui Kane. Each painting is accompanied by a hands-on exhibit about traditional Hawaiian culture: shake an *'uli'uli* (feathered hula rattle), test the heft of a *kapa* (bark-cloth) beater or examine stone adze heads. On-site Hawaiian cultural practitioners actively link the present with the past by teaching classes (usually reserved for resort guests only) and giving impromptu Hawaiian arts-and-crafts demonstrations.

At the Four Seasons security guardhouse, tell them you're visiting the cultural center. Drive all the way downhill

to the resort's self-parking lot, from where it's a short walk to the center.

Sleeping

Four Seasons Resort Hualalai
Resort $$$

(800-819-5053, 808-325-8000; www.fourseasons.com/hualalai; 72-100 Ka'upulehu Dr; r/ste from $675/1475;) The island's only five-diamond resort earns its accolades with top-flight service and lavish attention to details like fresh orchids in every room, embracing lush gardens and an oceanview infinity pool. Some poolside rooms have rejuvenating lava-rock garden outdoor showers. The golf course and spa are both outstanding, or snorkel with 75 species of tropical fish in the King's Pond.

Eating & Drinking

'Ulu Ocean Grill + Sushi Lounge
Hawaii Regional $$$

(808-325-8000; www.uluoceangrill.com; 72-100 Ka'upulehu Dr, Four Seasons Resort Hualalai; mains $24-45, tasting menu from $65; restaurant 5:30-9pm, sushi lounge 5:30-10pm) *'Ulu* means 'breadfruit,' and this sustainably minded restaurant is all about locally sourced produce, seafood and meat – in fact, 75% of its dishes are made with Hawai'i-grown ingredients. The menu mixes tastes from *makai* to *mauka:* currried Kona mussels, kiawe-smoked potatoes and wild boar glazed with *liliko'i* (passion fruit). Too bad the food doesn't live up to the hype – or the sky-high prices.

The atmosphere is casually elegant, with glass-ball partitions and island artwork. Soak up sunset views from the 10-seat bar inside the sushi lounge. Dinner reservations are recommended for the restaurant.

Beach Tree
Californian $$$

(808-325-8000; www.fourseasons.com/hualalai; 72-100 Ka'upulehu Dr, Four Seasons Resort Hualalai; mains lunch $14-22, dinner $16-39; 11:30am-8:30pm;) You can't beat catching sunset from a cabana-style sofa while imbibing pricey tropical cocktails and noshing on *pupu*. A Cal-Italian menu of pastas, salads, sandwiches, burgers and pizzas is nothing to write home about, but the open-air oceanfront setting definitely has that barefoot romantic wow-factor. Live Hawaiian music plays until 8pm daily, and sometimes a solo hula dancer performs too.

Kiholo Bay

If you're looking for a beach with a little something for everyone, head to 2-mile-wide **Kiholo State Park Reserve (www.hawaiistateparks.org; 7am-7pm Apr-1st Mon in Sep, to 6pm 1st Tue in Sep-Mar)**. Incredibly, this oasis in the lava is not thronged by visitors, despite its gorgeous beaches, good chances for wildlife viewing and swimming through a lava tube.

At the south end of the main beach, take the lava-rock path toward the coconut grove in the distance, where there's a series of secluded, soft black-sand beaches. The lower the tide, the bigger the beaches, and when waters are calm, you can swim. Look for whales breaching offshore in winter. The coconut grove rings **Luahinewai**, a large, cold, spring-fed pond on private property (no trespassing).

Back at the main beach, you can explore on foot far to the north, especially when the tide's out. Seaweed-covered tide pools abound with *honu* (green sea turtles). Remember to keep back at least 20ft on land and 50yd in the water to avoid disturbing these endangered creatures – it's the law.

Once the gravel footpath heading north ends, look inland for **Keanalele (Queen's Bath)**, a lava tube filled with crystalline freshwater that beckons to strong, adventurous swimmers. Lots of folks stop here to wash off salt water, but because there's a living ecosystem inside the lava tube, don't enter it if you're wearing any sunscreen.

You can keep trekking north along the bay past an abandoned mansion and an authentic **Balinese house** (keep a respectful distance from both, as they're on private property). Past the remains of a gigantic ancient **fishpond** built during the reign of Kamehameha I, you'll come

Kiholo Bay

PHILIP ROSENBERG/GETTY IMAGES ©

Avoiding Car Break-ins at Beaches & Trailheads

For many, the Big Island's remote beaches and hikes are the main event – but they also make your rental car a prime target for thieves. Follow local advice: leave nothing of value in your car (yes, this includes the trunk). It's smart to get all your gear packed up before arriving at your destination.

Another local tip is to leave your doors unlocked so would-be ne'er-do-wells know there's nothing of value in the car. In this way, you can avoid a smashed window – which, as the confetti of broken glass in beach and trailhead parking areas proves, occurs fairly frequently.

Check your rental-car insurance policy before considering doing the same, however. This strategy can backfire, as it leaves your car wide open to stinky feral animals who may hop inside and make a huge mess that's impossible to clean up.

to **Wainanali'i Pond**, a lagoon where *honu* congregate.

To get to Kiholo Bay, turn *makai* onto the unmarked dirt road off Hwy 19 between the Mile 82 and the Mile 83 markers, just south of the scenic viewpoint. Drive downhill for less than a mile, taking the left-hand fork and parking by the abandoned roundhouse. You can also hike in about a mile from a small, rocky parking lot on the *makai* side of Hwy 19, just north of the Mile 81 marker.

Kiholo is a popular weekend **camping** spot for locals (get an advance state-park permit), but there's no potable water.

Kohala & Waimea

Kohala is a study in contrasts. South Kohala is the archetypal sun-and-sea resort mecca. Since the 1960s, swanky resorts and golf courses have transformed this stretch into the Gold Coast. From Waikoloa to Kawaihae, Hawaiian history is preserved in ancient trails, heiau (temples), fishponds and petroglyphs – although all you'll see from the highway is stark lava desert. In counterpoint to the south's desert climate and man-made attractions, North Kohala is lushly otherworldly, with magnificent pastureland, quaint plantation towns and Pololu Valley's cascading cliffs. It proudly remains rural with nary a high-rise in sight. Waimea, a ranch town in between, is a central stop for cross-island travelers.

Pololu Valley (p121)

Kohala & Waimea Itineraries

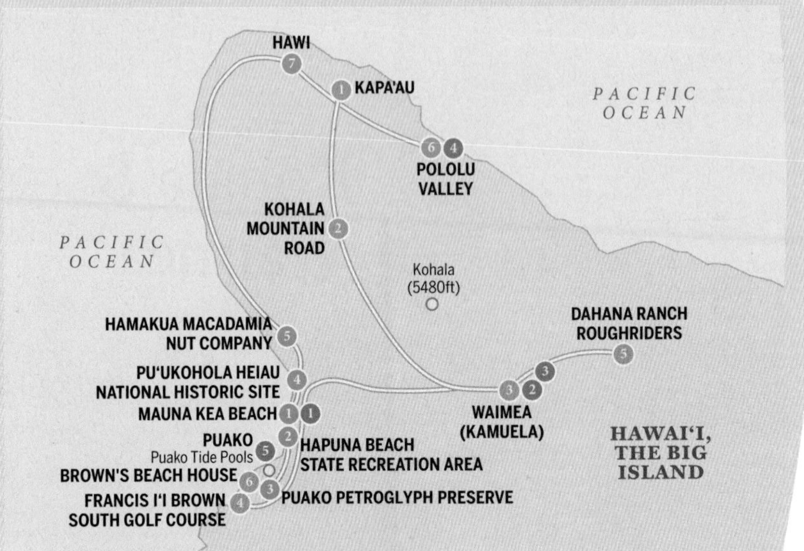

Two Days

1 **Mauna Kea Beach** (p108) Start your first day at this picture-perfect beach accessed through the Mauna Kea Beach Hotel, which reserves 40 parking spots for nonguests.

2 **Hapuna Beach State Recreation Area** (p108) As an alternative, try this awesome, easy-access public beach. Escape into shade for lunch at Monstera an *izakaya* spot (Japanese pub serving tapas-style food) at the Shops at Mauna Lani.

3 **Puako Petroglyph Preserve** (p104) A mini hike leads you to a fascinating tableau of petroglyphs. Explore sea life or watch the sunset from the Puako Tide Pools.

4 **Pu'ukohola Heiau National Historic Site** (p110) On day two, head to North Kohala, a world away with its lush forestland and village charm. Along the way, stop at this historic heiau, built by Kamehameha the Great during his fight for supremacy over the Hawaiian Kingdom.

5 **Hamakua Macadamia Nut Company** (p110) Who doesn't like macadamia nuts? Stop here for a free tour and ample samples.

6 **Pololu Valley** (p121) At the highway's end awaits Pololu Valley. The view from the lookout will only whet your appetite for deeper exploration into this mysterious valley. Hike down the short but steep and slippery trail to the beach.

7 **Hawi** (p113) End your day at this tiny town with outstanding art galleries.

THIS LEG: 32 MILES

Four Days

❶ **Kapaʻau** (p116) Follow the two-day plan, then join a morning zipline tour with Kohala Zipline or Big Island Eco Adventures. You'll be ferreted away into thick forest for aerial thrills and otherwise-inaccessible sightseeing.

❷ **Kohala Mountain Road** (p113) This bucolic, two-lane highway has such stunning views of the vast island, it's almost a traffic hazard.

❸ **Waimea (Kamuela)** Take a lunch break at Merriman's, one of the pioneering restaurants focusing on fresh local ingredients. Don't miss Isaacs Art Center, an impressive collection of fine art by late and living masters. Check the schedule for Kahilu Theatre, which hosts big-name performers.

❹ **Francis Iʻi Brown South Golf Course** (p104) The next day, head to this golf course at the Mauna Lani Bay Hotel & Bungalows. The juxtapositions of rugged lava rock and immaculate greens, massive mountains and the great Pacific, make Big Island courses distinctive.

❺ **Dahana Ranch Roughriders** (p124) Nongolfers can go horseback riding instead. At this ranch, even beginners learn to ride free on the range, not fixed 'nose to tail.'

❻ **Brown's Beach House** (p106) End your visit with a culinary extravaganza at this oceanfront icon, specializing in Hawaii Regional Cuisine (an island-grown version of Pacific Rim fusion) and stunning sunsets.

THIS LEG: 35 MILES

Kohala & Waimea Highlights

❶ **Best Beach: Mauna Kea Beach** (p108) Find powdery white sand and glassy water at this picture-perfect spot.

❷ **Best Art Venue: Isaacs Art Center** (p123) Size isn't everything, as this impressive fine-art collection proves.

❸ **Best Drink: Big Island Brewhaus & Taqueria** (p127) Prepare to be impressed by the lineup at this award-winning microbrewery.

❹ **Best Views: Pololu Valley** (p121) The lookout is the first of countless spectacular views along the valley trail.

❺ **Best Ocean Adventure: Kohala Kayak** (p108) Can't decide between paddling and snorkeling? Do both in the pristine waters of Puako.

Black-sand beach in Pololu Valley (p121)
TAN YILMAZ/GETTY IMAGES ©

Discover Kohala & Waimea

SOUTH KOHALA

The Queen Ka'ahumanu Hwy (Hwy 19) cuts through stark fields of lava. But a series of sumptuous resorts have created tropical oases along the water's edge, some containing the island's best beaches, some building their own. Meet the Gold Coast.

The waters off the Kohala Coast are pristine and teeming with marine life – and they're relatively uncrowded. The reef here drops off more gradually than along the Kona Coast, so you see sharks, dolphins, turtles and manta rays, but not large schools of tuna and other deepwater fish. Kohala is the oldest area of the Big Island: see lush coral growth and lots of lava tubes, arches and pinnacles.

A car is essential to get around South Kohala. While **Hele-On Bus** (**☎808-961-8744; www.heleonbus.org**) routes stop at the major hotels, they're geared for commuting hotel staff and run very early in the morning!

Golf course at the Waikoloa Beach Resort
GREG VAUGHN/GETTY IMAGES ©

Waikoloa Resort Area

POP 6362

Among South Kohala's resort areas, the **Waikoloa Beach Resort** (**www.waikolobeachresort.com**) is the most affordable and bustling. Its two mega hotels and golf courses aren't as prestigious as those further up the coast, but it does offer two shopping malls and the lion's share of events.

Note that the Waikoloa Beach Resort is not Waikoloa Village, a residential community further inland. To get to the resort area, turn *makai* (seaward) just south of the Mile 76 marker on Hwy 19. To get to the village for general services, such as a post office, turn *mauka* (mountainward) onto Waikoloa Rd north of the Mile 75 marker.

Beaches

'Anaeho'omalu Beach Park Beach
(**Waikoloa Beach Dr; 🕘6am-8pm**) 'A Bay' boasts easy access, salt-and-pepper sand and calm waters; it's the only place suited to windsurfing on Hawai'i. Classically beautiful, it's backed by hundreds of palm trees and makes for fantastic sunset viewing.

Drinking water, showers and restrooms are available.

The Waikoloa Beach Marriott fronts the beach's north end, but **ancient fishponds** add a buffer zone between the two. In that area, there's decent snorkeling directly in front of the sluice gate, where you'll find coral formations, a variety of fish and possibly sea turtles.

'Anaeho'omalu was once the site of royal fishponds, and archaeologists have found evidence of human habitation here dating back more than 1000 years. A short footpath with interpretive plaques starts near the showers.

To get here, turn left off Waikoloa Beach Dr opposite the Kings' Shops.

Sights

Waikoloa Petroglyph Preserve — Historic Site

(Waikoloa Beach Dr; dawn-dusk, 1hr tour 9:30am) FREE This collection of petroglyphs carved in lava rock is so easy-access that it merits a stop, although the Puako Petroglyph Preserve (p104) further north is more spectacular and not neighboring a shopping mall. Dating back to the 16th century, they're rather vague.

To get here, park at the Kings' Shops mall and walk for five minutes on the signposted path. Free guided tours of the petroglyphs are offered from 9:30am to 10:30am most Thursdays and Fridays, starting at the mall.

Activities

Ocean Sports — Water Sports

(888-724-5924, 886-6666; www.hawaiioceansports.com; 69-275 Waikoloa Beach Dr) Ocean Sports monopolizes the ocean-activity market in South Kohala. Fortunately the company is well run, if slightly steep in its pricing. Cruises include whale-watching ($119) and snorkeling tours ($147) aboard a 49-passenger catamaran. Departures from 'Anaeho'omalu Bay and Kawaihae Harbor.

At Anaeho'omalu Beach Park and the Hilton Waikoloa Village, this outfit also rents beach equipment.

The Best...

South Kohala Beaches

1 Mauna Kea Beach (p108)

2 Beach State Recreation Area (p108)

3 'Anaeho'omalu Beach Park (p96)

4 Beach 69 (p107)

Waikoloa Beach & Kings' Courses — Golf

(886-7888; www.waikoloabeachgolf.com; 69-275 Waikoloa Beach Dr, Waikoloa Beach Marriott; green fees guest/nonguest $135/165) The Waikoloa Beach Marriott boasts two top golf courses: the coastal **Beach course** is known for its par-five 12th hole; the **Kings' course** is more challenging and offers Scottish-style links. Tee off later and pay less (11:30am/1pm/2pm $115/105/85). Carts are mandatory.

Star Gaze Hawaii — Stargazing

(323-3481; http://stargazehawaii.biz; adult/child 5-11yr $30/15) Take advantage of Kohala's consistently clear night skies with professional astronomers and equipment. Locations include **Fairmont Orchid** (1 North Kaniku Dr; 7:30-8:30pm Fri), **Hapuna Beach Prince Hotel** (62-100 Kauna'oa Dr; 8-9pm Sun & Wed) FREE and **Hilton Waikoloa Village** (425 Waikoloa Beach Dr; 8-9pm Tue & Thu). Reservations are required.

Dolphin Quest — Wildlife

(800-248-3316, 886-2875; www.dolphinquest.com; 425 Waikoloa Beach Dr, Hilton Waikoloa Village; per person from $210, family encounter $1400; 9am-4pm) Minds differ on the ethics of captive dolphins. Judging by the popularity of this program, however, many have no qualms about paying big bucks for an encounter with this adored sea creature.

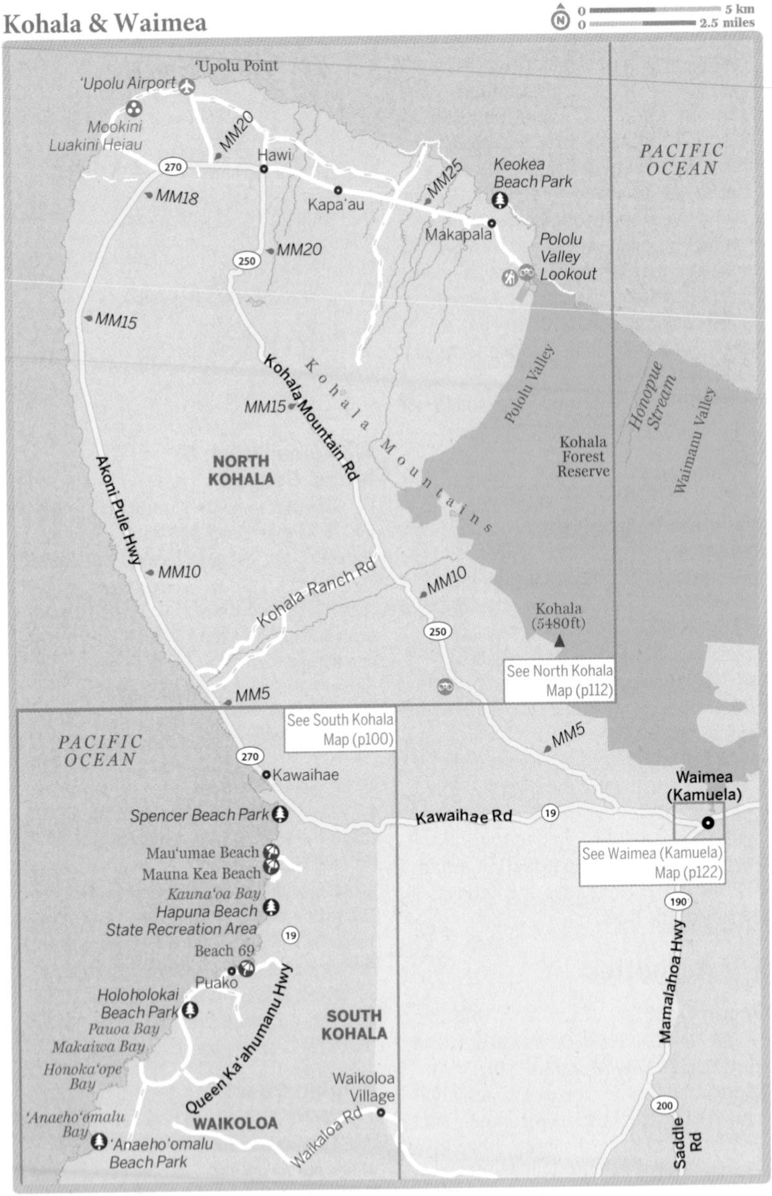

Hilton Waikoloa Village Pools Swimming

(☎800-221-2424, 886-1234; www.hiltonwaikoloavillage.com; 425 Waikoloa Beach Dr; nonguest pool pass up to 4 people $90; 🚸) Chances are, the pools at this over-the-top resort will thrill your kids. Besides two serpentine pools with multiple waterslides and waterfalls, there's a man-made beach. If your group numbers four, the fee *might* be worth a splash.

Ancient Hawaiian Art

Ancient Hawaiians carved *ki'i pohaku* (stone images), called **petroglyphs**, into *pahoehoe* (smooth lava). These mysterious carvings are most common on the Big Island, perhaps because it is the youngest island, with the most extensive fields of *pahoehoe*. The sketchy images include human figures, animals and canoes and other important objects. They're typically found along major trails or on the boundaries of *ahupua'a* (land divisions).

Touching the petroglyphs will damage them, so never step on or make rubbings of them. Photography is best done in the early morning or late afternoon.

Festivals & Events

A Taste of the Hawaiian Range Food

(www.tasteofthehawaiianrange.com; Hilton Waikoloa Village; admission advance/door $40/60) Celebrated Big Island chefs work magic with local range-fed meats and local produce in late September or early October.

Moku O Keawe Hula

(www.mokif.com; Waikoloa Resort Area; admission per night $15-25) This early November hula competition includes *kahiko* (ancient), *'auana* (modern) and *kupuna* (elder) categories. A decent alternate to the sell-out Merrie Monarch Festival in Hilo around Easter.

Sleeping

Waikoloa Beach Marriott Hotel $$$

(☎888-924-5656, 886-6789; www.waikoloabeachmarriott.com; 69-275 Waikoloa Beach Dr; r $200-450; P ❄ @ ≋) This airy, 555-room hotel fronts 'Anaeho'omalu Bay and thus boasts an awesome beach setting, plus three oceanfront pools. Renovated in late 2013, rooms feature quality beds (down comforters and high-count linens), tastefully muted decor and standard amenities, from cable TV to refrigerator.

Internet access is wi-fi in public areas and wired in rooms. Book ahead and online for deep discounts. There's a resort fee of $25 per day.

Hilton Waikoloa Village Resort $$$

(☎886-1234, 800-221-2424; www.hiltonwaikoloavillage.com; 425 Waikoloa Beach Dr; r from $225; P ❄ @ ≋) You'll either love or hate the showy, theme-park features of this 62-acre, 1240-room megahotel. There's no natural beach, so its highlights are manmade. Rooms are comfy enough but they're standard business class and neither luxury nor oceanfront. Due to sheer property size, getting around can be a hike and service somewhat impersonal.

The hotel is showing its age, but its larger-than-life decor could be a diversion for kids, with its monorail and boats navigating between three towers. Visitors must shell out $15/21 per day for self/valet parking. and $25 per day for resort fees.

Eating

Increase your dining options at Kings' Shops and Queens' MarketPlace, both located near the resort areas, and at Waikoloa Highlands Shopping Center, across the highway in Waikoloa Village. On Wednesdays, another option is the **Waikoloa Kings' Shops Farmers Market** (Kings' Shops; 8:30am-3pm Wed), which sells locally grown and produced edibles.

Island Gourmet Markets Market $

(Queens' MarketPlace; ☎886-3577) Spectacularly maintained and stocked, this is a one-stop shop for takeout food, freshly

South Kohala

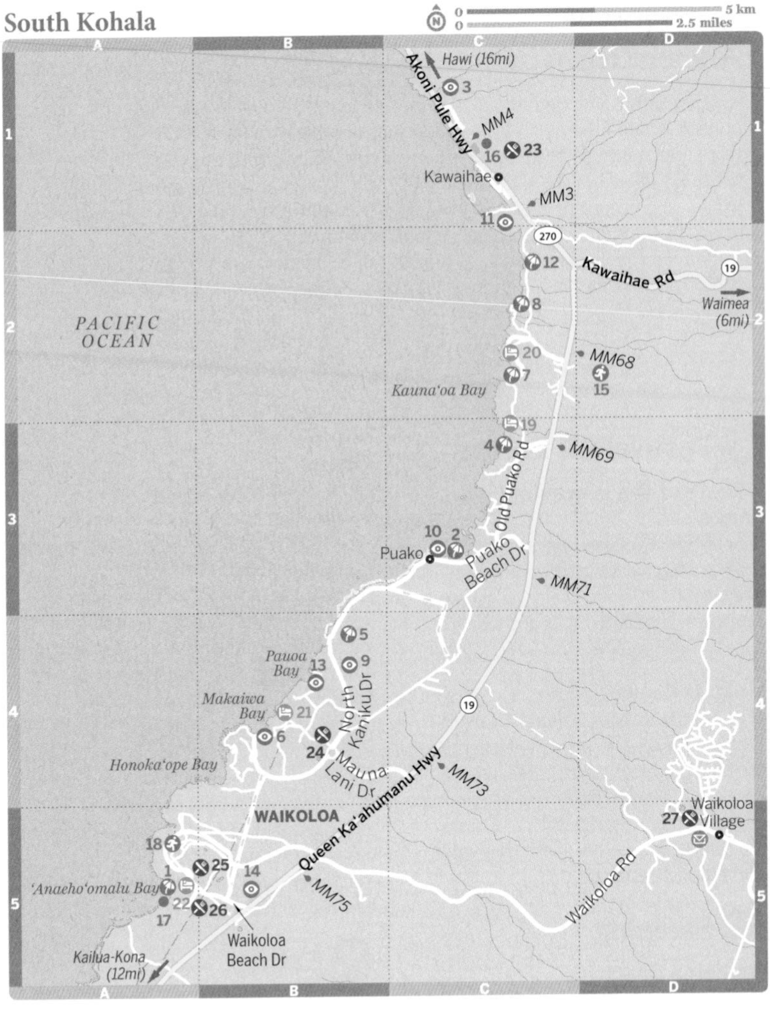

made sushi, basic and specialty groceries, magazines, gifts and more. There's a small patio for diners. A great option for healthy eats.

Inside the market, a little sushi bar called **Sushi Shiono** (☎886-3588; www.sushishiono.com; Queens' MarketPlace; ⏰7am-11pm) prepares rolls and *nigiri* (oblong-shaped sushi) by request, as well as packs to go.

Waikoloa Village Market Supermarket $

(☎883-1088; 68-3916 Paniolo Ave, Waikoloa Highlands Shopping Center; ⏰6am-9pm) Located *mauka* of the highway in Waikoloa Village, this branch of the excellent KTA Super Stores is a full-service grocery store with deli, bakery and ATM.

Pueo's Osteria Italian $$

(☎339-7566; http://pueososteria.com; 68-1845 Waikoloa Rd, Waikoloa Highlands Shopping Center; pizzas $14-18, mains $17-29; ⏰5pm-midnight

South Kohala

Sights

1 'Anaeho'omalu Beach Park A5
2 Beach 69 .... C3
3 Hamakua Macadamia Nut Company C1
4 Hapuna Beach State Recreation Area C3
5 Holoholokai Beach Park B4
Kalahuipua'a Fishponds .... (see 21)
6 Kalahuipua'a Historic Trail B4
7 Mauna Kea Beach C2
8 Mau'umae Beach C2
9 Puako Petroglyph Preserve B4
10 Puako Tide Pools C3
11 Pu'ukohola Heiau National Historic Site C1
12 Spencer Beach Park C2
13 Waikoloa Beach Resort B4
14 Waikoloa Petroglyph Preserve B5

Activities, Courses & Tours

Dolphin Quest .... (see 18)
Francis I'i Brown North & South Golf Courses .... (see 21)
15 Hapuna Golf Course D2
Hilton Waikoloa Village Pools .... (see 18)
16 Kohala Divers C1
Mauna Kea Golf Course .... (see 20)
Mauna Lani Sea Adventures .... (see 21)
Mauna Lani Spa .... (see 21)
17 Ocean Sports A5
Spa Without Walls .... (see 13)
Star Gaze Hawaii .... (see 19)
18 Star Gaze Hawaii A5
Star Gaze Hawaii .... (see 13)
Waikoloa Beach & Kings' Courses .... (see 22)

Sleeping

Fairmont Orchid .... (see 13)
19 Hapuna Beach Prince Hotel C3
Hilton Waikoloa Village .... (see 18)
20 Mauna Kea Beach Hotel C2
21 Mauna Lani Bay Hotel & Bungalows B4
22 Waikoloa Beach Marriott A5

Eating

Anuenue .... (see 16)
23 Blue Dragon Musiquarium C1
Brown's Beach House .... (see 13)
Cafe Pesto .... (see 16)
CanoeHouse .... (see 21)
24 Foodland Farms B4
Island Gourmet Markets .... (see 26)
25 Kings' Shops B5
Kohala Burger & Taco .... (see 16)
Merriman's Market Cafe .... (see 25)
Monstera .... (see 24)
Pueo's Osteria .... (see 27)
26 Queens' MarketPlace B5
Roy's Waikoloa Bar & Grill .... (see 25)
Sansei Seafood Restaurant & Sushi Bar .... (see 26)
Sushi Shiono .... (see 26)
Waikoloa Kings' Shops Farmers Market .... (see 25)
27 Waikoloa Village Market D5

Drinking & Nightlife

Luana Lounge .... (see 13)

Entertainment

Gathering of the Kings .... (see 13)
Kings' Shops .... (see 25)
Legends of the Pacific .... (see 18)
Mauna Kea Hawaiian Luau .... (see 20)
Queens' Marketplace .... (see 26)
Waikoloa Beach Marriott Sunset Luau .... (see 22)

Shopping

Waikoloa Highlands Shopping Center .... (see 27)

Mon-Sat, 8:30am-1:30pm & 5-9pm Sun) Run by a former top resort chef, this hidden gem will satisfy your cravings for gourmet-rustic Italian fare: pizzas, pastas and classics, including a yummy gorgonzola gnocchi. Everything is homemade and it's obvious. The Sunday brunch menu, from lemon-ricotta pancakes to a cherrywood bacon BLT, surpasses the standard buffet line.

Located in the Waikoloa Highlands Shopping Center, inland of the highway.

Sansei Seafood Restaurant & Sushi Bar — Japanese $$$

(☎886-6286; www.sanseihawaii.com; Queens' MarketPlace; mains $25-45, rolls $5-20; ⏰5:30-10pm, to 1am Fri & Sat) Local celebrity chef DK Kodama is known for innovative, fusion Japanese cuisine, such as his signature flash-fried ahi roll, and an extensive wine list. This newest branch might be a letdown to fans, with inconsistent service and less impressive execution. But it's worth a try, especially with the fantastic

50% early-bird discount. Free karaoke on Friday and Saturday after 10pm.

Roy's Waikoloa Bar & Grill Hawaii Regional Cuisine $$$

(886-4321; www.roysrestaurant.com; Kings' Shops; mains $30-35; 5:30-9:30pm) Always ridiculously bustling and noisy, Roy's will either delight or disappoint. We suggest that you focus on the food and not the atmosphere or sketchy service. The main courses, such as rack of lamb in a *liliko'i* (passion fruit) cabernet sauce or blackened ahi with pickled ginger, are less than cutting-edge today, but they generally don't disappoint.

Merriman's Market Cafe Mediterranean $$$

(886-1700; www.merrimanshawaii.com; Kings' Shops; mains $20-30; 11:30am-9:30pm) Foodies from sophisticated cities might find the Mediterranean-inspired fare unremarkable, but the kitchen does feature organic, island-grown produce and fresh local fish. Lunch is better value, with salads, sandwiches, pizzas and pastas under $20. Compared with the Waimea flagship, this alfresco cafe is more casual, affordable and touristy.

Entertainment

For nightlife, check **Waikoloa Nights** (www.waikoloanights.com) for special events, from rock concerts to hula shows. Free early-evening concerts featuring slack key guitar, ukulele and hula can be had at the Kings' Shops and Queens' MarketPlace shopping malls.

Waikoloa Beach Marriott Sunset Luau Luau

(886-6789; www.waikoloabeachmarriott.com; 69-275 Waikoloa Beach Dr; adult/child 6-12yr $97/43; 5pm Wed & Sat) This oceanfront luau features a Hawaiian-style dinner buffet, open bar and various Polynesian perfomances, including the Samoan fire dance.

Left: 'Anaeho'omalu Beach Park (p96); **Below:** Hilton Waikoloa Village (p99)

(LEFT) DANITA DELIMONT/GETTY IMAGES ©; (BELOW) WATERFALL WILLIAM/GETTY IMAGES ©

Legends of the Pacific Luau

(☎886-1234; www.hiltonwaikoloavillage.com/dining/luau.cfm; Hilton Waikoloa Village; adult/child 5-12yr/senior & teen 13-18yr $109/54/99; ⏲5:30pm Tue, Fri & Sun) The 'Legends of the Pacific' luau show features various South Pacific dances and includes a dinner buffet and one cocktail.

Mauna Lani Resort Area

Constructed in 1983 by a Japanese company, the Mauna Lani Resort Area resembles its neighbors, with high-end hotels, condos and golf courses. But it deserves special attention for its significant historical sites and for the Mauna Lani Bay Hotel & Bungalows' open attitude toward nonguests who come to explore its fishponds and trails.

Beaches

The best beaches for swimming or snorkeling are small and located around the two large hotels.

The beach fronting the Mauna Lani Bay Hotel & Bungalows is protected and relatively calm, but the water is shallow. Just 10 minutes south of the hotel by foot, In **Makaiwa Bay**, there's a small, calm lagoon fronting the Mauna Lani Beach Club condo. To get here, park at the hotel and walk south along the path past the fishponds.

One mile south of the hotel, there's a small salt-and-pepper beach at **Honoka'ope Bay**. When seas are calm, swimming and snorkeling are fine but not fantastic. The resort development fronting the beach reserves 20 daily parking spaces for nonresidents. To get here, drive toward the golf courses, turn left at Honoka'ope Pl and check in at the entry gate.

Located at the Fairmont Orchid, **Pauoa Bay** is an excellent, little-known snorkeling spot, which unfortunately is accessible only to hotel guests.

Holoholokai Beach Park Beach
(6:30am-6:30pm) Forget about sand and swimming here. Instead enjoy picnicking and strolling at this pleasantly uncrowded beach, blanketed by chunks of white coral and black lava. Facilities include restrooms, showers, drinking water, picnic tables and grills.

To get here, take Mauna Lani Dr and veer right at the circle; turn right on the marked road immediately before the Fairmont Orchid. The trail to the Puako petroglyphs starts here.

Sights

Puako Petroglyph Preserve Historic Site
With more than 3000 petroglyphs, this preserve is among the largest collections of ancient lava carvings in Hawaii. The simple pictures might not make sense to you, but viewed altogether, they are fascinating and worth a visit.

The three-quarter-mile walk from Holoholokai Beach Park to the preserve adds to the experience: take the well-marked trail at the parking lot. The walk is easy but rocky; wear sturdy footwear and expect blazing sun.

Kalahuipua'a Historic Trail Historic Site
(68-1400 Mauna Lani Dr, Mauna Lani Bay Hotel & Bungalows; P) FREE The first segment of this easy trail meanders through a 16th-century Hawaiian settlement, passing **lava tubes** once used as cave shelters and a few other archaeological and geological sites marked by interpretive plaques.

The trail then skirts ancient **fishponds** lined with coconut palms and continues out to the beach, where there's a thatched shelter with an outrigger canoe and a **historic cottage**. Continue southwest past the cottage to loop around the fishponds and back to the start (about 1.5 miles, round-trip).

Located on Mauna Lani Bay Hotel & Bungalows grounds, this trail starts at a marked parking lot opposite the hotel convenience store.

Kalahuipua'a Fishponds Historic Site
These ancient fishponds are among the island's few remaining working fishponds and, as in ancient times, they're stocked with *awa* (Hawaiian milk fish). Water circulates from the ocean through traditional *makaha* (sluice gates), which allow small fish to enter, but keep mature, fattened catch from escaping.

To access the fishponds directly (without taking the trail), exit the lobby of Mauna Lani Bay Hotel & Bungalows and go south toward the beach.

Activities

Mauna Lani Sea Adventures Water Sports
(885-7883; http://maunalaniseaadventures.com; 68-1400 Mauna Lani Dr, Mauna Lani Bay Hotel & Bungalows; snorkeling tour adult/child 3-12yr $99/45, whale-watching cruise $85/45) For snorkeling, whale-watching and diving tours, this outfit offers almost daily tours at decent prices. While Kailua-Kona is the Big Island's hub for snorkeling and scuba diving, the waters off Mauna Lani are excellent and much less crowded. You can also try stand up padding (SUP; rental and instruction $30/50 per 30/60 minutes).

Francis I'i Brown North & South Golf Courses Golf
(885-6655; 68-1400 Mauna Lani Dr, Mauna Lani Bay Hotel & Bungalows; green fees guest/nonguest $165/215) Mauna Lani boasts two world-class golf courses. The **South course** is more scenic and popular, with its signature 15th hole featuring a tee shot over crashing surf. The **North course** is more challenging and interesting, however, with a par-three 17th hole within an amphitheater of black lava rock.

Sleeping

Mauna Lani Bay Hotel & Bungalows Resort **$$$**
(808-885-6622, 800-367-2323; www.maunalani.com; 68-1400 Mauna Lani Dr; r from $400; P) The 342-room Mauna Lani has a loyal clientele for unfussy vibe and commitment to Hawaiian cultural stewardship. The grounds feature well-tended tropical gardens, hundreds of towering coconut palms and precious historic sites. Geared more for couples than kids, this is a solid upscale, if shy of luxurious, hotel.

Rates include basic services (eg parking, phone, internet access). Eco policies include use of solar power, drought-resistant grass and recycled water for irrigation. The **Mauna Lani Spa** (881-7922; www.maunalani.com; 68-1400 Mauna Lani Dr, Mauna Lani Bay Hotel & Bungalows; massages & facials from $159; treatments 10am-4pm) boasts lush landscaping and a lava-rock sauna; treatments are pricey, perhaps overpriced, but a memorable splurge.

Fairmont Orchid Hotel **$$$**
(866-54004474, 885-2000; www.fairmont.com/orchid-hawaii; 1 North Kaniku Dr; r $360-700; P@) Elegant and almost formal (for Hawai'i), the Orchid never lets you forget that you're at an exclusive, luxury hotel. The architecture feels rather continental, but the meticulously maintained grounds are buoyantly tropical. The 540 rooms are clean, modern and comfortable.

Amenities, such as in-room internet access ($14.50 per day), are rather pricey. Spa fans can experience outdoor treatments at **Spa Without Walls** (887-7540; www.fairmont.com/orchid; 1 North Kaniku Dr, Fairmont Orchid; massages & facials from $169; 7am-6pm), hidden amid orchids, palms and waterfalls.

Local Knowledge

NAME: DANNY AKAKA, JR

OCCUPATION: DIRECTOR OF CULTURAL AFFAIRS, MAUNA LANI RESORT

RESIDENCE: KAILUA-KONA

1 **WHAT ARE HAWAI'I'S MOST HISTORICALLY SIGNIFICANT SITES?**
Accessible heiau, such as Pu'ukohola Heiau (p110), Mo'okini Luakini Heiau (p115), and Pu'uhonua O Hōnaunau (p77), are foremost. I'd also recommend visiting Hulihe'e Palace (p35) in Kailua-Kona and Hawai'i Volcanoes National Park (p208). Waipi'o Valley (p152) is also impressive, not only for preservation of *kalo* (taro) culture but because it was once the seat of this island's government.

2 **WHAT'S A HAWAIIAN TRADITION THAT CONTINUES TODAY?**
Hawaiians always shared their bounty. No one went hungry. It was not quite barter, but more like mutual gift giving. If you grew taro in Waipi'o Valley and I had well-stocked fishponds, we would exchange and thus enjoy both. Likewise, today we never arrive for family visits empty-handed. I might go to Honolulu taking dried '*opelu* [pan-sized mackerel scad] and poi, and return with dim sum from Chinatown.

3 **WHAT DOES ALOHA REALLY MEAN?**
The word 'aloha' is a sacred Hawaiian word: '*Alo*' means being in the presence of another (or of the Supreme Creator, God). '*Ha*' refers to one's breath, life force or spirit. In the traditional greeting between Hawaiians, two people would come into each other's *alo*, touch nose to nose, which is known as *honi ihu*, breathing and sharing each other's *ha*. It was a spiritual exchange.

4 **HOW IS ALOHA USED TODAY?**
The word 'aloha' is used lightly today, to say hello and goodbye; but the profound meaning of aloha is to share spirit with one another.

Island Insights

In ancient Hawaii, the fish raised in fishponds were reserved for the *ali'i* (chiefs and royalty). Commoners who stole fish for their own consumption could be punished by death. When a chief wanted fish, the pond caretaker would simply net the biggest as they gathered for feeding. Sometimes, trained runners would transport fresh fish to distant royal tables. According to legend, they were wrapped in wet *limu* (seaweed) and arrived still wriggling, proof of freshness.

Eating

Foodland Farms Supermarket **$**
(**887-6101; 68-1330 Mauna Lani Dr, Shops at Mauna Lani; 6am-11pm**) Full-service gourmet supermarket with an impressive deli selection.

Monstera Japanese **$$**
(**887-2711; www.monsterasushi.com; 68-1330 Mauna Lani Dr; plates $16-30, sushi rolls $10-20; 5:30-10pm**) Chef Norio Yamamoto left his namesake restaurant at the Fairmont Orchid to launch his own *izakaya* (Japanese pub) venue. It's a looser, cooler place, where the menu ranges from classic *nigiri* sushi and tuna *tataki* (tuna seared and seasoned with ginger) to sizzling plates of kimchi stir-fried pork loin and teriyaki chicken.

Brown's Beach House Hawaii Regional Cuisine **$$$**
(**887-7368; 1 North Kaniku Dr, Fairmont Orchid; mains $40-60; 5:30-8:30pm Thu-Mon, til 9pm Tue & Wed**) Brown's remains a standout for those willing to pay. Expect gracious service and the finest local ingredients: the 'Sustainable Seafood Trio' features *shutome* (swordfish), mahimahi and *ono* (wahoo) from Kona waters, short ribs are braised with Kona coffee and the creamy risotto includes five types of Hamakua mushrooms.

Puako Petroglyph Preserve (p104)

Canoe-House Hawaii Regional **$$$**
(**☎881-7911; 68-1400 Mauna Lani Dr, Mauna Lani Bay Hotel & Bungalows; mains $35-44; ⏲6-9pm**) The Mauna Lani's flagship restaurant showcases local ingredients creatively, but simply. Those seeking a huge punch might find the dishes lackluster. A decadent option is the 'Captain's Table' (two to eight diners), a five-course meal specially designed in collaboration with the chef (per person $100). No complaints about the setting and service.

Drinking & Entertainment

Luana Lounge Bar
(**☎885-2000; 1 North Kaniku Dr, Fairmont Orchid; ⏲4-11pm**) A nice spot to unwind at sunset, with specialty drinks and tapas (small plates). The fish or burger sliders (three per order for under $20) make for a light, relatively affordable meal.

Gathering of the Kings Luau
(**☎326-4969; http://www.gatheringofthekings.com; Fairmont Orchid; adult/child 6-12yr $99/65; ⏲Sat from 4.30pm**) This luau spins a thread of storytelling to highlight slightly modernized versions of Polynesian and Hawaiian dance and music. It's notable for its above-average Polynesian dinner buffet and an open bar.

Puako

POP 772

Puako, a longtime beach community, is essentially a mile-long row of homes. The single road through 'town' is marked with numerous 'shoreline access' points. To get here, turn *makai* down Puako Beach Dr between Mile 70 and Mile 71 markers. You'll pass the **Hokuloa United Church** on your right. This cute little seaside church was originally built in 1860.

Vacation rentals abound here. Check www.2papayas.com and www.hawaiianbeachrentals.com for listings.

The Best... Kohala & Waimea for Kids

1 Horseback riding in Waimea or in North Kohala (p117)

2 Paddling with Kohala Kayak (p108)

3 Splashing around at Spencer Beach Park (p110)

4 Ziplining in Kapa'au (p116)

5 Exploring the Puako Tide Pools (p107)

6 Cooling off with shave ice at Anuenue (p111)

Beaches

Beach 69 Beach
(**⏲7am-8pm; 👪**) This lovely crescent of white sand is a local favorite but remains somewhat off the tourist radar. Both family-friendly and gay-friendly, the calm, protected waters are ideal for morning snorkeling. Around the boundary, shady trees provide welcome relief. Restrooms and showers are available; no lifeguards.

From Puako Beach Dr, take the first right turn onto Old Puako Rd. Find telephone pole No 71 (originally numbered No 69) to the left and park. Follow the 'road' to its end, and then tramp along the footpath that runs parallel to a wooden fence.

Puako Tide Pools Landmark
Puako is known for giant tide pools, some deep enough to shelter live coral and other marine life.There's no sandy beach, but a narrow strip of pulverized coral and lava covers the shore. It's ideal for beach walks and you might even see *honu* (sea turtles) sunning on the rocks.

To get to the pools, park along the road near one of six signposted 'beach access' paths.

Activities

For diving tours, book with Kawaihae-based Kohala Divers (p111).

Kohala Kayak Kayaking

(☎882-4678; www.kohalakayak.org; 3hr tour $70; ⏲depart 9am) Paddle and snorkel in Puako's pristine, less-traveled waters with knowledgeable, customer-service-oriented guides. Water depth is about 20ft; swim through underwater arches 10ft below. All levels are welcome; pedal kayaks are available for more stability.

Hapuna Beach State Recreation Area

Hapuna Beach is world famous for its magnificent half-mile sweep of white powder sand and fabulously clear waters. In summer, waves are calm and allow good swimming, snorkeling and diving, although the fish population has woefully declined since the 1980s. When the surf's up in winter, bodyboarding is awesome, thanks to reliable swells from the northwest. In general, Hapuna waters are too choppy for tots or nonswimmers. Waves over 3ft should be left for experts; drownings are not uncommon here.

The restrooms and picnic area at this **state recreation area** (www.hawaiistateparks.org/parks/hawaii; ⏲gate 7am-8pm; P) can be crowded and, at worst, grungy. Lifeguards are on duty. For nonresidents, parking costs $5 per vehicle.

To get here, take Hapuna Beach Rd just south of the Mile 69 marker. Arrive early to snag a parking space and a good spot. Bring industrial-strength sunscreen because there's virtually no shade.

Stay overnight in one of six state-owned **A-frame cabins** (per night residents/nonresidents $30/50) near the beach, an awesome location for sunset watching. While rather makeshift for the price, each sleeps four people on wooden platforms (bring your own bedding). Restrooms, showers and a cooking pavilion are available.

Mauna Kea Resort Area

The pioneering Mauna Kea development began in the early 1960s when the late Laurance Rockefeller obtained a 99-year lease on the land around Kauna'oa Bay from Richard Smart, owner of Parker Ranch. The Mauna Kea Beach Hotel was the first luxury hotel on the Neighbor Islands. 'Every great beach deserves a great hotel,' Rockefeller apparently said. Not everyone would agree, but he got his way here.

Beaches

Mauna Kea Beach Beach

Crescent-shaped Kauna'oa Bay (nicknamed 'Mauna Kea Beach' after Rockefeller built his landmark hotel on it) is blanketed in powdery white sand, while the clear waters are calm and shallow (generally less than 10ft). Snorkeling is best at the north end along the rocky ledge. This wonderfully uncrowded beach is open to the public through 40 parking spaces set aside daily for nonguests. Arrive by 9am and stop at the entry gate for a parking pass and directions.

Mau'umae Beach Beach

Lovely white sand, shady trees and glassy waters – this intimate beach can feel like your own. The downside: no restrooms. Plan accordingly and tread lightly on this locals' beach.

To get here, go toward Mauna Kea Beach Hotel, turn right on Kamahoi and cross two wooden bridges. Look for telephone pole No 22 on the left and park next to the other cars. Walk down the trail to the Ala Kahakai sign and turn left toward the beach. You can also walk here from Spencer Beach Park to the north.

Detour:
Ala Kahakai Trail from Kawaihae to Puako

For diehard sun worshippers, access South Kohala's signature beaches via a 6-mile stretch of the 175-mile **Ala Kahakai National Historic Trail** (www.nps.gov/alka/index.htm). You'll also cover pristine shoreline and natural anchialine ponds (pools of brackish water that provided drinking water to the ancients). You can start at any point along the way.

From the north, start at the southern end of Spencer Beach Park, where you'll pass thick kiawe groves until you reach Mau'umae Beach and eventually the Mauna Kea Resort Area, including the renowned golf course. After you navigate the Hapuna Beach, the trail continues down to Beach 69. The whole hike, especially the last leg, is scorching. Of course, you can turn back at any point.

Activities

Mauna Kea & Hapuna Golf Courses — Golf

(☎ Hapuna Beach Prince Hotel 880-3000, Mauna Kea Beach Hotel 882-5400; www.princeresortshawaii.com; Mauna Kea Beach Hotel, Hapuna Beach Prince Hotel; green fees Mauna Kea Golf Course guest/nonguest $230/255, Hapuna Golf Course $125) Designed by Robert Trent Jones, Sr, the **Mauna Kea course** is a 72-par championship course that consistently ranks among the top courses in the USA. The **Hapuna course** has a 700ft elevation gain and was designed by Arnold Palmer and Ed Seay.

Sleeping

Room rates vary significantly by season.

Hapuna Beach Prince Hotel — Hotel $$$

(☎ 880-1111, 888-977-4623; www.princeresortshawaii.com; 62-100 Kauna'oa Dr; r $200-500; ❄ 📶 🏊) The Mauna Kea Beach Hotel's 'sister' hotel offers good value and a primo beach setting. The architectural design is rather heavy-handed and rooms could use a facelift, but they're clean and come with large bathrooms. This hotel shares amenities with Mauna Kea Beach, and buses transport guests between the two.

Mauna Kea Beach Hotel — Hotel $$$

(☎ 866-977-4589, 882-7222; www.maunakeabeachhotel.com; 62-100 Mauna Kea Beach Dr; r $325-760; P ❄ 📶 🏊) This grand hotel on the Gold Coast is understated, quietly confident of its reputation. At first glance it might not wow you, but there is history here, among loyal returning guests and longtime staff. Rooms are regularly renovated and nicely maintained. The hotel's crowning jewel, however, is simply its location on Kauna'oa Bay, arguably the island's best beach.

Entertainment

Mauna Kea Hawaiian Luau — Luau

(☎ 882-5707; www.princeresortshawaii.com; 62-100 Mauna Kea Beach Dr; adult/child 5-12yr $96/48; ⏲ 6pm Tue & Fri) This outdoor luau show features standard entertainment (thrilling fire dance, group hula) and gorgeous beach setting. Buffet is generous and above average.

Kawaihae & Around

Kawaihae is a drab port town, where fuel tanks and cargo containers give off an industrial vibe. There's noteworthy dining, a family beach and historic heiau (temple) toward the south. For an insider's view of Kawaihae, see the **Pacific Worlds Kawaihae** (www.pacificworlds.com/kawaihae) site.

Beaches

Spencer Beach Park Beach

(👪) Shallow, sandy and gentle, this beach lacks the dramatic sweep of Mauna Kea or Hapuna, but it's ideal for kids and popular with local families. Come to swim rather than to snorkel; the waters are slightly silty due to Kawaihae Harbor to the north.

Located off the Akoni Pule Hwy just north of the Mile 2 marker, the park has a lifeguard, picnic tables, barbecue grills, restrooms, showers, drinking water and campsites (permit required). The campsites are exposed and crowded together, but it's the best camping beach north of Kona.

Sights

Pu'ukohola Heiau National Historic Site Historic Site

(**☎882-7218; www.nps.gov/puhe; 62-3601 Kawaihae Rd; ⏰7:45am-4:45pm) FREE**

By 1790 Kamehameha the Great had conquered Maui, Lana'i and Moloka'i. But power over his home island of Hawai'i was a challenge. When told by a prophet that he'd rule all of the Hawaiian Islands if he built a heiau dedicated to his war god Kuka'ilimoku atop Pu'ukohola (Whale Hill) in Kawaihae, Kamehameha built this massive structure.

He and his men formed a human chain 20 miles long, transporting rocks hand to hand from Pololu Valley in North Kohala. After finishing the heiau by summer 1791, Kamehameha held a dedication ceremony and invited his cousin and rival Keoua, chief of Ka'u. When Keoua came ashore, he was killed and taken to the *luakini* heiau (temple of human sacrifice) as the first offering to the gods. With Keoua's death, Kamehameha took sole control of the Big Island and by 1810 ruled all Hawaiian Islands.

Back then Pu'ukohola Heiau was adorned with wooden *ki'i* (statues) and thatched structures, including an oracle tower, an altar, a drum house and shelter for the high priest. After Kamehameha's death in 1819, his powerful widow Ka'ahumanu and son Liholiho, who abolished the kapu (taboo) system, destroyed the deity images and the heiau was abandoned.

Today, only the basic rock foundation remains, but it's still a massive 224ft by 100ft, with 16ft- to 20ft-walls. To get here, turn *makai* off the Akoni Pule Hwy halfway between the Mile 2 and 3 markers.

Hamakua Macadamia Nut Company Factory

(**☎888-643-6688, 882-1690; www.hawnnut.com; 61-3251 Maluokalani St; ⏰8am-5pm) FREE**

It's a tourist stop, but a darned good one, featuring a spanking-clean factory, gift shop and generous free samples.

Pu'ukohola Heiau National Historic Site

CASEY MAHANEY/GETTY IMAGES ©

Sacred Sites

Ancient Hawaiians built a variety of heiau (temples) for different gods and different purposes: healing the sick, sharing the harvest, changing the weather, offering human sacrifice and succeeding in warfare.

While some were modest thatched structures, others were enormous stone edifices, which today exist in eroded ruins that only hint at their original grandeur. After Kamehameha II (Liholiho) abolished the kapu (taboo) system in 1819, many were destroyed or abandoned. But on the Big Island, two of the largest and best-preserved heiau remain: Pu'ukohola Heiau (p110) and Mo'okini Luakini Heiau (p115).

Luakini heiau, for human sacrifice, were always dedicated to Ku, the war god. Only Ku deserved the greatest gift, a human life, and only the highest chiefs could order it. An enemy slain in battle was an acceptable sacrifice. But the victim had to be a healthy man, never a woman, a child or an aged or deformed man.

An eco-conscious company, it generates 75% of its energy needs from solar power and 10% from ground macnut shells. The Hamakua-grown nuts are excellent in quality and reasonably priced. To get here, turn *mauka* just north of the Mile 4 marker.

Activities

Kohala Divers Water Sports
(**882-7774; www.kohaladivers.com; 61-3665 Akoni Pule Hwy, Kawaihae Shopping Center; 1-/2-/3-tank dive $100/139/239; 8am-6pm**) This longtime outfit leads excellent diving trips throughout Kohala waters, plus snorkeling and seasonal whale-watching. One memorable trip visits a *honu* (sea turtle) 'cleaning' station where the turtles allow fish to pick parasites off their bodies.

Sleeping & Eating

In this rural residential area, the only lodging options are B&Bs and vacation rentals.

Hale Ho'onanea B&B $$
(**877-882-1653, 882-1653; www.houseofrelaxation.com; Ala Kahua Dr; ste $130;**) About 5 miles north of Kawaihae, find a terrific-value B&B suite atop peaceful grassy knolls 900ft above sea level. The Bamboo Suite includes kitchenette, private lanai, satellite TV, wi-fi, high ceiling, hardwood floor and stunning 180-degree horizon view.

Anuenue Ice Cream $
(**882-1109; Akoni Pule Hwy, Kawaihae Shopping Center; cones from $2.50, fast food $3.50**) Since 1998, Tim Termeer has delighted all comers with snowy shave ice and premium ice cream. Among his 35 flavors are ginger lemongrass, citrus mint and lavender lemonade. He also offers hot dogs, veg burgers and chili bowls.

Kohala Burger & Taco Burgers, Mexican $
(**880-1923; www.kohalaburgerandtaco.com; Akoni Pule Hwy, Kawaihae Shopping Center; mains under $10; 11am-7pm Mon-Fri, to 4pm Sat & Sun**) When only a real burger will do, come here for local grass-fed quarter-pounders with specialty toppings. But the real standouts are the fish tacos, quesadillas and dreamy shakes and malts.

Cafe Pesto International $$
(**882-1071; www.cafepesto.com; Akoni Pule Hwy, Kawaihae Shopping Center; lunch $11-14, pizza $9-20, dinner mains $17-33; 11am-9pm Sun-Thu, to 10pm Fri & Sat**) This well-loved favorite, serving eclectic, innovative cuisine you might

North Kohala

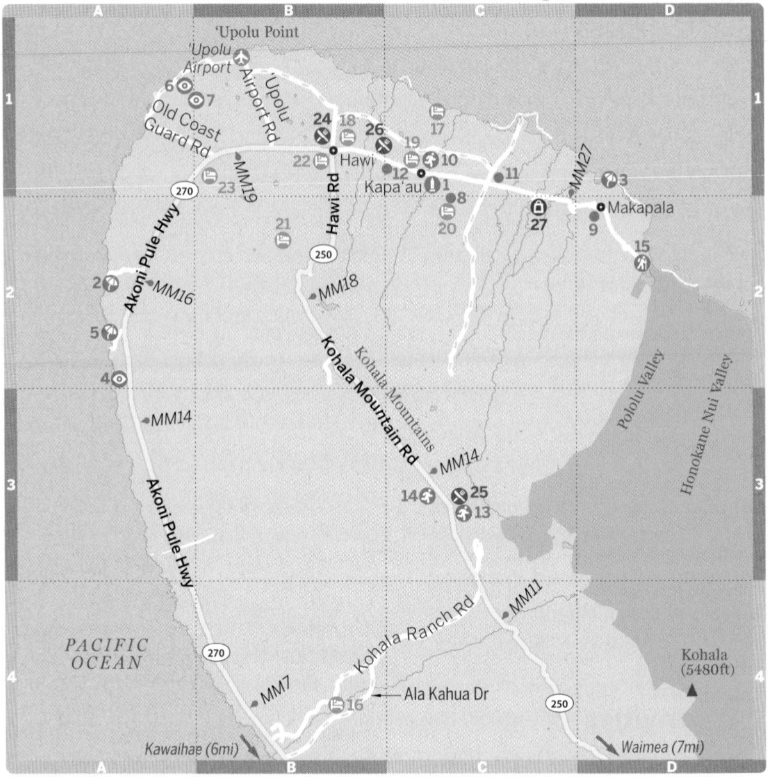

call Mediterranean with an Asian twang or Italian with an island twist. Choose from curries and Greek salads, seafood risotto and smoked salmon alfredo, piping-hot calzones and thin-crust gourmet pizzas.

Blue Dragon Musiquarium Hawaii Regional **$$$**
(**808-882-7771; www.bluedragonhawaii.com; 61-3616 Kawaihae Rd; mains $18-36; 5-10pm Wed-Thu & Sun, to 11pm Fri & Sat)** This roofless restaurant under towering palms features great live music five nights a week, starting at 6pm. The cuisine is hard to pin down, from stir-fries to curries to rib-eye steaks, but generally good. It's a convivial, family-oriented place for dinner; later, the potent specialty cocktails might tempt you to the dance floor.

NORTH KOHALA

Rural North Kohala is a charming mix of farmers and artists, of Native Hawaiians and haole (Caucasian) transplants, of rustic storefronts and dream homes. It makes for a fantastic day trip (or serene retreat), but because it's off the main highway, it remains a hidden gem.

Geologically the oldest part of the Big Island, North Kohala is the birthplace of King Kamehameha I and is rich in ancient history. In modern times, this region was sugar country until the Kohala Sugar Company closed in 1975. Today, Hawi and Kapa'au contain just enough art galleries, boutiques and distinctive eateries to succeed as tourist attractions.

North Kohala

Sights

1 Kamehameha the Great Statue C1
2 Kapa'a Beach Park A2
3 Keokea Beach Park D1
4 Lapakahi State Historical Park A2
5 Mahukona Beach Park A2
6 Mo'okini Luakini Heiau A1
7 Site of Kamehameha's Birth B1

Activities, Courses & Tours

8 Big Island Eco Adventures C2
9 Hawaii Paso Finos D2
10 Kamehameha Park & Golf Learning Center C1
11 Kohala Ditch Adventures C1
12 Kohala Zipline C1
13 Na'alapa Stables C3
14 Paniolo Riding Adventures C3
15 Pololu Valley Lookout & Trail D2

Sleeping

16 Hale Ho'onanea B4
17 Hawaii Island Retreat C1
18 Hawi Plantation House B&B B1
19 Kohala Club Hotel C1
20 Kohala Country Adventures Guest House C2
21 Kohala Lodge B2
22 Kohala Village Inn B1
23 Puakea Ranch B1

Eating

24 Bamboo B1
Gill's Lanai .... (see 1)
25 Kahua Ranch C3
Kohala Coffee Mill .... (see 22)
Minnie's .... (see 10)
Nambu Courtyard .... (see 10)
Sushi Rock .... (see 18)
Sushi To Go .... (see 10)
26 Takata Store B1

Shopping

Ackerman Galleries .... (see 10)
Dunn Gallery .... (see 1)
Elements .... (see 24)
Hawi Gallery .... (see 22)
L Zeidman Gallery .... (see 24)
Living Arts Gallery .... (see 18)
27 Rankin Gallery & Studio C2

At the road's end, time and the elements have carved the lush landscape into dramatic contours, culminating in Pololu Valley, the jewel of North Kohala.

This region has virtually no bus service, so driving is your only option.

Hawi & Around

POP 1081

Hawi (hah-*vee*) can fit all of its businesses within two blocks, but it looms large in picturesque charm, notable restaurants and shopping treasures. Mainland transplants are bringing big money to little Hawi and leading its transformation from boondocks to tourist destination. But it still offers only basic services, such as a post office, grocery store and gas station. Thank goodness, say the residents.

There are two ways to get here: the coastal **Akoni Pule Hwy** (Hwy 270) and the mountainous **Kohala Mountain Road** (Hwy 250). The latter is arguably the Big Island's best scenic drive, affording stupendous views of the coastline and three majestic volcanic mountains: Mauna Kea, Mauna Loa and Hualalai.

To experience both routes, go north to Hawi on the Akoni Pule Hwy, which navigates a region largely undeveloped and with spectacular views of the Pacific (and Maui in the distance). Just south of the Mile 14 marker, **Lapakahi State Historical Park** (**882-6207; 8am-4pm, closed state holidays**) FREE re-creates an ancient fishing village along an unshaded, 1-mile loop trail. Nothing is elaborately presented, so you need a wild imagination to appreciate the modest remains.

Further along, **Mahukona Beach Park** and **Kapa'a Beach Park** are fine for picnicking and sunset watching, but too rocky and rough for swimming.

On your return, go south on Kohala Mountain Rd, which gives more opportunity to witness the spectacular panorama. This road is called Hawi Rd close to town.

Sleeping

Kohala Village Inn Inn $

(**889-0404; www.kohalavillageinn.com; 55-514 Hawi Rd; r $75-85, ste $130;**) For budget travelers or those seeking digs in the heart of Hawi, this inn offers terrific value. In a plantation-era, motel-style building, no-frills rooms are clean and cozy, with wood-plank floors, pleasant lighting and cable TV.

Walls are rather thin and there's no view, but it's a fine place to rest your head.

Hawi Plantation House B&B — B&B $$

(☎(888) 465-8565; www.hawiplantationhousebandb.com; r $169-249; 📶) In a magnificently restored plantation house, choose from six lovely bedrooms of various sizes and sleeping configurations. All are smartly appointed and share a kitchen, a laundry room, a swimming pool, a gym and a tennis court.

Kohala Lodge — Vacation Rental $$$

(☎884-5105; www.vacationhi.com; 56-867 Kamalei St; $225-300; 📶) Tucked away in a treeline with sweeping views, this reproduction 19th-century *paniolo* (Hawaiian cowboy) ranchhouse (formerly known as Cabin in the Treeline) is unique in every way. The owner has showered attention to every architectural detail, from the lava rock fireplace to the period plumbing to retro-style appliances (that are actually high tech).

The house is located about 2 miles from Hawi, off Kohala Mountain Rd. Rates vary depending on season and number of guests. Book well in advance.

Puakea Ranch — Vacation Rental $$$

(☎315-0805; www.puakearanch.com; 56-2864 Akoni Pule Hwy; cottages $289-799; 📶 🏊) Dreaming of a secluded country estate? Live the dream in one of four meticulously restored cottages. Ranging from two to six bedrooms, each cottage enjoys its own bucolic grounds and includes kitchen, laundry facilities, and detached bathhouse with Japanese-style *furo* hot tub.

Striking just the right balance of luxury and authenticity, Puakea Ranch offers a unique alternative to the Gold Coast resorts. Located off a gated dirt road 3 miles from Hawi center.

Hawaii Island Retreat — Inn $$$

(☎889-6336; www.hawaiiislandretreat.com; At Ahu Pohaku Ho'omaluhia; r $425-500; 📶 🏊) 🍃 Modern-day seekers with money are the target audience for this high-end, off-the-grid, organic retreat center on 50 gorgeous acres. Here, leaving urban life behind doesn't mean giving up creature comforts, from spa services to an infinity pool. In addition to nine spacious rooms in the cliffside villa, there are seven yurts (per night $195).

Sushi Rock restaurant

LONELY PLANET/GETTY IMAGES ©

Detour: Mo'okini Luakini Heiau

Remote and strangely moving, **Mo'okini Luakini Heiau** (**373-8000; 9am-8pm, closed Wed**) FREE, near 'Upolu Point, is among the oldest (c AD 480) and most historically significant Hawaiian sites. Measuring about 250ft by 125ft, with walls 6ft high, the massive stone ruins sit solitary and brooding on a windswept grassy plain.

According to legend, the heiau was built from 'sunrise to first light' by up to 18,000 'little people' passing stones in complete silence from Pololu Valley – 14 miles away – under the supervision of Kuamo'o Mo'okini.

Five hundred years later Pa'ao, a priest from Samoa, raised the walls to 30ft and rebuilt the altar as his *ho'okupu* (offering) to the gods. He initiated human sacrifice, making this the first *luakini* heiau (human sacrifice temple).

In 1963 the National Park Service designated Mo'okini Heiau as Hawaii's first registered National Historic Landmark. Fifteen years later, it was deeded to the state. In 1978, the *kahuna nui* (high priestess) Leimomi Mo'okini Lum, the seventh high priestess of the Mo'okini bloodline, lifted the kapu (taboo) that restricted access to the temple.

To get here, take Old Coast Guard Rd, between the Mile 18 and 19 markers for just over a mile. Turn right onto a red-cinder road, blocked by a locked cattle gate. Call ahead for the gate to be unlocked (this is state land); otherwise park here (without blocking the gate) and walk 15 minutes to the heiau. There's an alternate route if you have 4WD: drive toward 'Upolu Airport, then turn south onto the gutted coastal road, which is impassable after rains.

Eating

Takata Store — Supermarket $

(**889-5413; Akoni Pule Hwy; 8am-7pm Mon-Sat, to 1pm Sun**) For groceries, try this well-stocked, family-run market between Hawi and Kapa'au.

Kohala Coffee Mill — Cafe $

(**889-5577; 55-3412 Akoni Pule Hwy; drinks $2-4, sandwiches $6-10; 6am-6pm Mon-Fri, 7am-6pm Sat & Sun**) A comfy place to hang out and treat yourself to muffins, fresh-brewed Kona coffee and heavenly Tropical Dreams ice cream. For breakfast, the souffléd eggs with cheese, onion, tomato, pesto and/or bacon is a winner.

Sushi Rock — Sushi $$$

(**889-5900; www.sushirockrestaurant.net; 55-3435 Akoni Pule Hwy; sushi rolls $7-19, mains $18-32; noon-3pm & 5:30-8pm Sun-Tue & Thu, to 9pm Fri & Sat**) This ever-popular sushi bar is famous for its fusion tropical sushi rolls, which might include papaya, mac nuts, Fuji apple or goat cheese. The menu also includes vegetarian/vegan rolls, creative salads and sandwiches, plus a wild selections of cocktails. Staff go out of their way to serve. Arrive early.

Bamboo — Hawaii Regional Cuisine $$$

(**889-5555; Akoni Pule Hwy, Kohala Trade Center; lunch $11-16, dinner $25-35; 11:30am-2:30pm Tue-Sun, 6-8pm Tue-Sat;**) Like a once-cool, now-retro aunt, this local icon is lovable and impossible to ignore. It's a winning combination, but don't expect innovation or mind-blowing dining. That said, the food is fine and the inviting interior – suspended Balinese umbrellas, twinkling Christmas lights and warm wood walls – is cheerful and pure Hawi.

Don't miss checking out the gallery upstairs.

Shopping

Living Arts Gallery Arts & Crafts
(www.livingartsgallery.net; 55-3435 Akoni Pule Hwy; 10:30am-5pm, to 8pm Fri) To appreciated the Big Island's extraordinary amount of artistic talent, come to this artists co-op. Members staff the gallery, giving you firsthand contact with some of the 65 artists represented here.

L Zeidman Gallery Arts & Crafts
(Hwy 270; 10am-5pm) The exquisitely crafted, museum-quality wood bowls made by the owner are mesmerizing en masse. Take one home for $150 to $2500.

Hawi Gallery Music
(206-235-1648; www.hawigallery.com; 55-3406 Akoni Pule Hwy; 10am-5pm Mon-Sat, 11am-3pm Sun) The ukulele as a work of art? Definitely, as this fascinating collection proves. In addition to gorgeous classics, check out the Cuban model made from a cigar box and the curvaceous Polk-a-lay-lee, a rare 1960s promotional item from a Chicago furniture store.

Elements Jewelry, Accessories
(www.elementsjewelryandcrafts.com; 55-3413 Akoni Pule Hwy; 10am-6pm) This jewelry and gift shop carries an eclectic collection of locally made finery.

Kapa'au

POP 1734

Kapa'au is another former sugar town refashioned into an attractive tourist destination. Although more scattered than Hawi, Kapa'au has a few good eateries and serves as a meeting point for several outdoor adventure tours.

Beaches

Keokea Beach Park Beach
(off Akoni Pule Hwy; gate 7am-11pm) While it has no beach to speak of, this park about 3.5 miles from Kapa'au has the best picnic spot around: an elevated pavilion with smashing views of a rocky bay and the motley crew of local surfers brave enough to test its dangerous shore breaks and strong currents.

Besides picnic tables, there are BBQ grills, showers, drinking water and portable toilets. The marked turnoff is about 1.5 miles before the Pololu Valley Lookout.

Sights

Kamehameha the Great Statue Monument

The statue on the front lawn of the North Kohala Civic Center has a famous twin in Honolulu, standing across from Iolani Palace. The Kapa'au one was the original, constructed

Kamehameha the Great statue

Ranch Life

Windswept pastureland. Grazing cattle. Cloud-dappled skies. North Kohala makes city slickers yearn to be a *paniolo* (cowboy), at least for a day. These working ranches give you that chance. Also see Hawaii Paso Finos (p118) in Kapa'au.

For horseback riding, **Paniolo Riding Adventures** (**889-5354; www.panioloadventures.com; Kohala Mountain Rd; rides $69-159**) offers a variety of rides (short, long, picnic and sunset) across 17-sq-mile Ponoholo Ranch and accommodates all levels. Horses are matched to a rider's level. This is the best choice for experienced riders. Boots, hats, chaps and jackets are provided.

Na'alapa Stables (**889-0022; www.naalapastables.com; Kahua Ranch Rd; rides $65-85**) offers rides across the pastures of 13-sq-mile Kahua Ranch, with nice views of the coast from its 3200ft elevation. Group rides are adjusted to the level of the least-experienced rider, so most rides are nose-to-tail.

If a down-home country barbecue is more your style, join the Richards family of **Kahua Ranch** (**882-7954; www.exploretheranch.com; Kahua Ranch Rd; with transportation $119, without $95, child 6-11yr half price, under 5yr free; 6-9pm Wed summer, 5:30-8:30pm Wed winter;**) for a hearty buffet dinner (including beer) followed by country music, line dancing, a campfire and Piggly Wiggly, the performing pig. The sprawling pastureland is perfect for sunset watching and stargazing by telescope.

in 1880 in Florence, Italy, by American sculptor Thomas Gould. When the ship delivering it sank off the Falkland Islands, a duplicate statue was cast from the original mold and erected in downtown Honolulu in 1883. Later the sunken statue was recovered and sent here, to Kamehameha's childhood home.

Kamehameha Rock Landmark

According to legend, Kamehameha carried this rock uphill from the beach to demonstrate his prodigious strength. Much later, when a road crew attempted to move it elsewhere, the rock stubbornly fell off the wagon – a sign that it wanted to stay put. Not wanting to upset Kamehameha's mana (spiritual essence), the workers left it alone. Don't blink or you'll miss it, on the inland roadside about 2 miles east of Kapa'au, on a curve just past a small bridge.

Activities

Kohala Zipline Ziplining

(**331-3620; www.kohalazipline.com; 54-3676 Akoni Pule Highway; adult/child 8-12 $159/$139**) Once you're up in the trees, you stay up for the whole canopy tour, which includes nine easy zips, five elevated suspension bridges between platforms, and two rappels. There are no superlong zips, but also no walking between elements. The course is built to blend with nature and cause no harm to trees.

Max eight per group; mandatory weight range 70lb to 270lb (kids must be at least eight years). A dozen three-hour tours go out daily.

Big Island Eco Adventures Ziplining

(**889-5111; www.thebigislandzipline.com; 53-496 'Iole Rd; $169**) The forest wilderness near Pololu Valley is a perfect setting for zipping, which you do eight times on this excellent tour, which also includes one

Below: Lei drape the Kamehameha the Great statue to commemorate the North Kohala Kamehameha Day Celebration; **Right:** Kahua Ranch (p117)

(BELOW) DANITA DELIMONT/GETTY IMAGES ©; (RIGHT) PETER FRENCH/GETTY IMAGES ©

suspension bridge beside a 60ft waterfall. The three-hour tour departs at least four times daily. Max 10 per group; mandatory weight range 90lb to 250lb.

Meet a half-mile up 'Iole Rd and then ride a 6WD military vehicle to the course.

Hawaii Paso Finos — Horseback Riding

(instructional tours $85-130) Paso Finos are the smoothest-riding horses in the world. Experience their bounceless gait and engaging demeanor in private or small-group activities. Learn horsemanship, riding, therapeutic communication and even yoga on horseback. A unique option for experienced equestrians.

Kohala Ditch Adventures — Kayaking

(☎888-288-7288, 889-6000; www.kohaladitchadventures.com; 53-324 Lighthouse Rd, btwn Mile 24 & 25; adult/child 5-11yr $139/75; ⏰7-11am & 12:15-4pm Mon-Sat) After an off-road excursion by Pingauer, a six-wheel Austrian military vehicle, you embark on a leisurely 2.5-mile kayaking trip through historic plantation irrigation ditches or flumes, including 10 tunnels. Guides are well-versed in island history. A unique culture journey, not a fast-paced action adventure.

Kamehameha Park & Golf Learning Center — Swimming, Golf

(☎golf center 345-4393, gym 889-6505, pool 889-6933; 54-540 Kapa'au Rd; ⏰pool 10-11:45am, 1-4:45pm, golf 8am-7pm, gym noon-8pm Mon-Thu, 7:45am-4:30pm Fri, 10am-4pm Sat) This county park includes a huge pool (call for schedule updates), tennis courts, gym with basketball courts and weight room, and playground. In back there's a privately run six-hole golf learning center where you can rent equipment and play all day for $10.

Festivals & Events

Kohala Country Fair Fair
(www.kohalacountryfair.com; Akoni Pule Hwy opposite 'Iole Rd) FREE This old-fashioned fair, held in the first week in October, brings together a smorgasbord of local artists and food, plus events including a Spam-carving contest, frog catching, equestrian demonstrations, tug of war and who knows what else.

North Kohala Kamehameha Day Celebration Historic Celebration
(www.kamehamehadaycelebration.org) FREE On June 11 join islanders in honoring Kamehameha the Great in his birthplace. The spectacular parade of floral-bedecked horseback riders and floats culminates in an all-day gathering with music, crafts, hula and food.

Sleeping

Kohala Club Hotel Inn $
(889-6793; www.kohalaclubhotel.com; 54-3793 Akoni Pule Hwy; r/cottage $56/90) Less than half a mile from Kapa'au, this laid-back inn offers clean rooms with private bathrooms for an unbelievable price. The main house contains four small, no-frills rooms with either a queen bed or two twins. The two-bedroom cottage is perfect for families.

Kohala Country Adventures Guest House Inn $$
(866-892-2484, 889-5663; www.kcadventures.com; off Akoni Pule Hwy; r $85-175;) For country livin', try this relaxed, lived-in house on 10 acres of ungroomed tropical gardens, with fruit trees, livestock and coastal views. The Sundeck Suite is comfy for families, with kitchenette, three beds and an open loft layout. Host Bobi Moreno puts everyone at ease.

Island Insights

South of Mo'okini Heiau is the apparent **site of Kamehameha's birth**, marked by stone-walled foundations. According to legend, when Kamehameha was born on a stormy winter night in 1758, his mother received a kahuna's prophecy that her son would be a powerful ruler and conquer all the islands. Upon hearing this, the high chief of Hawai'i ordered all male newborns killed. Thus, after Kamehameha was taken to the Mo'okini Heiau for his birth rituals, he was spirited away into hiding.

To get here, turn *makai* (seaward) on the dirt road about a quarter-mile south of Mo'okini Heiau.

Eating

Nambu Courtyard Cafe $

(889-5546; 54-3885 Akoni Pule Hwy; mains $9-12; 6:30am-2:30pm Mon-Fri, 7am-noon Sun) Pleasantly low-key, this owner-run cafe serves freshly made salads and sandwiches, espresso drinks and an unbelievable blueberry bread pudding. With lots of seating, indoor and outdoor, it manages to be both airy and cozy.

Gill's Lanai Cafe $

(315-1542; 54-3866 Akoni Pule Hwy; mains $6-9; 11am-5pm) With its umbrella-shaded patio and tiny kitchen, this avocado-colored roadside cafe offers a beach vibe and yummy fish tacos. Other favorites include bowls of ahi *poke* (cubed, marinated raw fish) and veg quesadillas. Service can be slow.

Minnie's Diner $

(889-5288; 54-3854 Akoni Pule Hwy; meals $7-9; 11am-8pm Mon-Thu, 11am-3pm & 6-8:30pm Fri, 11am-3pm Sat) This local-favorite family restaurant serves up generous burgers, sandwiches and plate lunches including mahimahi, Korean chicken and the house specialty, roast pork.

Sushi to Go Sushi $

(756-0132; 54-3877 Akoni Pule Hwy; rolls $6-10) Nothing fancy, just decent takeout sushi.

Shopping

Dunn Gallery Arts & Crafts

(884-5808; dunngallerywoodart.com; 54-3862 Akoni Pule Hwy; 10am-5pm Tue-Sat) Of the many wood art shops on the island, this one stands alone. The distinctive works here, gathered from 30 Big Island artists, represent a museum-quality collection. Contemporary, traditional, and functional pieces range from $20 to five figures.

Ackerman Galleries Arts & Crafts

(889-5138; www.ackermangalleries.com; 55-3897 Akani Pule Hwy; 10am-6pm) The Ackerman family has managed to combine art and commerce for 30 years. They have two galleries: the Gift Gallery has an excellent array of wooden bowls, glasswork and jewelry. Across the street, the Fine Art Gallery displays Gary Ackerman's impressionistic paintings of Hawaii and France (open from October to March and by request).

Rankin Gallery & Studio Arts & Crafts

(889-6849; www.patricklouisrankin.net; 53-4380 Akoni Pule Hwy; 11am-5pm Tue-Sat & noon-4pm Sun-Mon) Located midway between Pololu Valley and Kapa'au, this gallery is noted for its landscapes of Hawaii and the American West (and for the conviviality of Patrick Rankin, a local character happy to show you around his studio).

Also check out the adjacent Tong Wo Society building, a nicely restored temple that was once an opium den.

Pololu Valley

Marked by a row of mystical cliffs, this ancient valley is utterly memorable. It was once abundant with wetland taro, when Pololu Stream carried water from the deep, wet interior to the valley floor. When the Kohala Ditch was built in 1906, however, it diverted the water for sugar production. The valley's last residents left in the 1940s, and the area is now forest reserve.

The Akoni Pule Hwy ends at the Pololu Valley Lookout, the endpoint for those who do not hike down the trail.

Activities

Pololu Valley Lookout & Trail

Hiking

From the lookout, you can admire the spectacular coastline toward the east, but you must hike down to see Pololu Valley. The steep, rocky trail is doable for most, thanks to switchbacks and its 0.75-mile distance. Avoid trekking down after rainfall, since the mud-slicked rocks will be precarious. Makeshift walking sticks are often left at the trailhead. Parking is tight; there are no facilities.

At the mouth of the valley lies a rugged black-sand beach. The surf is rough, with rip currents year-round. Swimming is out of the question, even if you see local surfers testing the waves.

Hawaii Forest & Trail

Hiking, Swimming

(☎331-8505, 800-464-1993; www.hawaii-forest.com; adult/child under 12 $159/139) The Kohala Waterfalls Adventure includes a leisurely 1.5-mile loop trail to waterfalls (swimming included). Transportation from the Waikoloa Resort Area is included.

The Best...

Fine Art in Kohala & Waimea

1 Isaacs Art Center (p123)

2 Gallery of Great Things (p129)

3 Living Arts Gallery (p116)

4 Dunn Gallery (p120)

Parker Ranch (p127)

PETER FRENCH/GETTY IMAGES ©

Waimea (Kamuela)

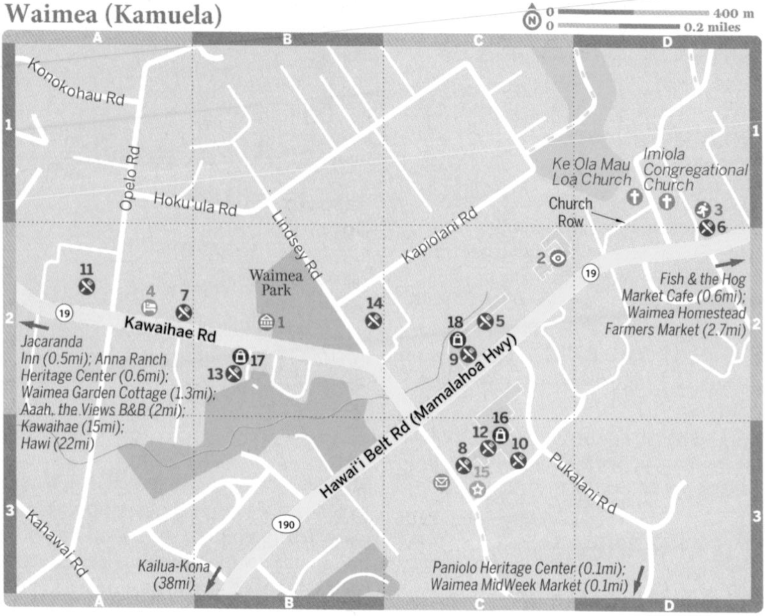

Waimea (Kamuela)

Sights
1 Isaacs Art Center B2
2 WM Keck Observatory Office C2

Activities, Courses & Tours
3 Mountain Road Cycles D1

Sleeping
4 Kamuela Inn A2

Eating
5 Aka Sushi Bar C2
6 Big Island Brewhaus & Taqueria D2
7 Hawaiian Style Cafe A2
8 Healthways II C3
9 KTA Super Store C2
10 Lilikoi Cafe C3
Merriman's .... (see 11)
11 Pau A2
12 Village Burger C3
13 Waimea Coffee & Co B2
14 Waimea Town Farmers Market B2

Entertainment
15 Kahilu Theatre C3

Shopping
Gallery of Great Things .... (see 13)
16 Parker Ranch Center C3
17 Parker Square B2
Reyn's .... (see 8)
18 Waimea Center C2
Waimea General Store .... (see 13)

WAIMEA (KAMUELA)

POP 9212

The misty rolling pastureland surrounding Waimea is perhaps Hawai'i's most unexpected face. This is *paniolo* (cowboy) country, and nearly all of it, including Waimea itself, is controlled by Parker Ranch, the fifth-largest cow-calf ranch in the USA.

From the highway, all you see are suburban strip malls, but closer inspection finds an extraordinary art scene, wide-ranging dining options, a shopper's paradise and rich cowboy heritage. Then there's the variety of transplants, including organic farmers, astronomers, artists and retirees.

Geographically, the town is split into a 'dry side' (west) and a 'wet side' (east), with the town center at the intersection of Kawaihae Rd (Hwy 19) and Mamalahoa Hwy (Hwy 190) roughly marking the transition.

For visitors, Waimea makes a good base to explore Kohala, Mauna Kea and the Hamakua Coast. The 2670ft elevation and evening fog can spell relief, but be prepared for chilly nights.

From Hilo, Hwy 19 is commonly called the Mamalahoa Hwy or Hawai'i Belt Rd, but west of Hwy 190 it becomes Kawaihae Rd, while Hwy 190 continues as the Mamalahoa Hwy.

Sights

Isaacs Art Center — Art Gallery

(**885-5884; www.isaacsartcenter.hpa.edu; 61-1268 Kawaihae Rd; 10am-5pm Tue-Sat**) FREE Set in a meticulously relocated 1915 schoolhouse, this series of bright, charming galleries displays a diverse collection of local and international fine art. The permanent collection features mostly renowned late masters, while the pieces for sale are by living artists. As you enter, take note of Herb Kawainui Kane's classic *The Arrival of Captain Cook at Kealakekua Bay in January 1779*. Works include paintings, pottery, furniture, jewelry and Hawaiian arts.

For deep pockets seeking the ultimate gift, this gallery is not to be missed. All proceeds go to the Hawai'i Preparatory Academy Scholarship Fund.

Rare Hawaiian Honey Company — Farm Store

(**775-1000, 888-663-6639; www.rarehawaiianhoney.com; 66-1250 Lalamilo Farm Rd; 9am-4pm Mon-Fri**) Sample unusual honey (imagine a pearlescent butter) at this welcoming sales/tasting room. The 'Rare Hawaiian Organic Kiawe Honey' (8oz jar $17 to 18) comes from a forest of kiawe trees in Puako. The thriving family-run business is the brainchild of former lawyer Richard Spiegel, who in the mid-1970s began collaborating with bees and the sweet nectar of kiawe flowers.

Anna Ranch Heritage Center — Historic Site

(**885-4426; www.annaranch.org; 65-1480 Kawaihae Rd; 10am-3pm Tue-Fri**) The life and times of Hawaii's 'first lady of ranching,' Anna Leialoha Lindsey Perry-Fiske, are celebrated at this 14-room historic ranch

Black-sand beach in Pololu Valley (p121)

ART WALASZEK/GETTY IMAGES ©

Island Insights

Waimea is also known as **Kamuela**, which is the Hawaiian spelling of Samuel, apparently for Samuel Parker of Parker Ranch. Maps generally list both names; the post office and phone book use Kamuela to distinguish this Waimea from those on O'ahu and on Kaua'i.

house, which contains impressive koa furniture, Anna's bountiful wardrobe and other memorabilia. Tours (10am and 1pm, $10) must be booked in advance. Located 1 mile west of town center.

Paniolo Heritage Center Museum

(854-1541; www.paniolopreservation.org; Pukalani Rd; 9am-4pm Wed) FREE The Paniolo Preservation Society is developing this museum at Pukalani Stables, where Parker Ranch once bred horses. It's a work in progress, currently housing a photo exhibit and a saddle-making operation. The real reward is the personal touch: staffers are happy to talk story about *paniolo* history.

Open on Wednesdays along with the Waimea Midweek Market (p127).

WM Keck Observatory Office Visitor Center

(885-7887; www.keckobservatory.org; 65-1120 Mamalahoa Hwy; 10am-2pm Tue-Fri) The lobby of this working office is open to the public. See models of the twin 33ft Keck telescopes, fascinating photos and a telescope trained on Mauna Kea. Informative volunteers prep you for a trip to the Mauna Kea summit.

Church Row Churches

FREE Home to Christians, Buddhists and Mormons, Church Row is a living history of religious life on the island. There are several noteworthy, if humble, structures along this curved street, including the much-photographed, all-Hawaiian **Ke Ola Mau Loa Church**. Look for the green steeple.

Next door is **Imiola Congregational Church**, Waimea's first Christian church, which originated as a grass hut in 1830 and was built entirely of koa in 1857. Here lies the grave of missionary Lorenzo Lyons, who arrived in 1832 and spent 54 years in Waimea. He wrote many hymns in Hawaiian, including the classic 'Hawai'i Aloha.'

Activities

Dahana Ranch Roughriders Horseback Riding

(888-399-0057, 885-0057; www.dahanaranch.com; 90min ride adult/child $80/70; rides 9am, 11am, 1pm & 3pm) Ride American quarter horses bred, raised and trained by third- and fourth-generation *paniolo*. On offer are open-range rides for kids as young as three, but also advanced rides for those who can canter. The ranch, owned and operated by a Native Hawaiian family, is 7.5 miles east of Waimea, off Mamalahoa Hwy. Reservations required.

Mountain Road Cycles Cycling

(885-7943; www.mountainroadcycles.com; 64-1066 Mamalahoa Hwy; bikes per day $30-45; 9:30am-5:30pm Mon-Fri, 10am-3pm Sat) In addition to renting bicycles, this full-service bike shop arranges mountain-biking and road tours starting at $50. It prefers small groups and serious riders.

Festivals & Events

Waimea Ocean Film Festival Film

(854-6095; www.waimeaoceanfilm.org) In early January, films, speakers, receptions and art exhibits showcase the beauty, power and mystery of the ocean. It's held in multiple venues in Waimea, Kohala and Kona.

Waimea Cherry Blossom Heritage Festival Japanese Culture

(961-8706; waimeacherryblossom@gmail.com; Parker Ranch Center & Church Row Park) FREE Dark pink blossoms are greeted with *taiko* drumming, *mochi* (sticky rice cake) pounding and other Japanese cultural events on the first Saturday in February.

Fourth of July Rodeo Rodeo
(☎885-2303; 67-1435 Mamalahoa Hwy, Parker Ranch Rodeo Arena; admission $6) Celebrating over 45 years of ranching, this event includes cattle roping, bull riding and other hoopla.

Waimea Paniolo Parade & Ho'olaule'a Parade
(☎885-3110; www.waimeatown.org) This mid-September parade of authentic *paniolo,* island princesses and beautiful steeds begins at historic Church Row Park and makes its way through town, followed by a lively fair in Waimea Park. In conjunction with statewide Aloha Festivals.

Round-Up Rodeo Rodeo
(☎885-5669; www.parkerranch.com; 67-1435 Mamalahoa Hwy, Parker Ranch Rodeo Arena; admission $5) This whip-cracking event is held on the first Monday in September after Labor Day weekend.

Waimea Ukulele & Slack Key Guitar Institute Concert Music
(☎885-6017; www.kahilutheatre.org; admission $20-64) This annual concert in mid-November is a dream opportunity to see Hawaii's musical greats. Past headliners include Ledward Ka'apana and Cyril Pahinui.

Christmas Twilight Parade Christmas
In early December, the town gets into the Kalikimaka (Christmas) spirit with a block party.

Sleeping

Kamuela Inn Inn $
(☎800-555-8968, 885-4243; www.thekamuelainn.com; 1600 Kawaihae Rd; r incl continental breakfast $69-94, ste $109-119; 📶) Resembling a typical motor inn, this local institution is an awesome value. Nothing's fancy, but rooms are clean and comfy, with a range of bed configurations and kitchen amenities. Rooms in the renovated Mauna Kea Wing are worth the extra cost, with open-beam ceilings and spiffier decor. The

Anna Ranch Heritage Center (p123)

JOHN ELK/GETTY IMAGES ©

spacious Executive Suite ($189) with full kitchen is ideal for families.

Waimea Garden Cottages Vacation Rental **$$**
(885-8550; www.waimeagardens.com; studio $155, cottages $170-185, incl breakfast;) On a well-tended property, find three spruce, well-equipped, country cottages around the owners' home. The largest, Kohala Cottage, has a full kitchen, enormous bath and adjacent walled garden. The cozy Waimea Cottage offers a fireplace, kitchenette and private patio. There's also a spacious studio near a seasonal stream.

Located a quick 2 miles west of town, near the intersection of Kawaihae Rd and Hwy 250. Three-day minimum stay.

Aaah, the Views B&B B&B **$$**
(885-3455; www.aaahtheviews.com; 66-1773 Alaneo St; r incl breakfast $189;) Run by a welcoming family, this B&B takes advantage of a uniquely designed house with lots of windows, peaceful mountain views and charming ladder-accessible lofts. The two-bedroom Treetop Suite is an especially sweet deal, with four beds and a private deck.

Enjoy generous breakfasts in your room or on a pleasant shared lanai. Located 3 miles west of town.

Jacaranda Inn Inn **$$**
(885-8813; www.jacarandainn.com; 65-1444 Kawaihae Rd; r/ste/cottage from $129/179/250;) Built in 1897, the Jacaranda has seen better days. While each of the eight rooms are indulgent, antique-filled visions (think four-poster beds, opulent tiled baths, carved furniture and oriental rugs), the property feels somewhat forlorn. Consider it a backup.

Eating

Waimea has a remarkable surplus of eateries to fit various tastes and budgets. The two malls, Waimea Center and Parker Ranch Center, offer numerous inexpensive restaurants, although some are only fast-food joints. You can also stock up on groceries at **KTA Super Store** (885-8866; 65-1158 Mamalahoa Hwy, Waimea Center; 6am-11pm), a large supermarket and deli with a pharmacy, and at **Healthways II** (885-6775; 67-1185 Mamalahoa Hwy, Parker Ranch Center; 9am-7pm Mon-Sat, to 5pm Sun), a natural food store and deli.

Waimea Town Farmers Market Market **$**
(8am-1pm Sat) With a circle of vendors around a grassy field, this farmers market has a friendly, cohesive vibe. Find artisan edibles, including handcrafted pasta and sausages, Thai plates and bread freshly baked in a mobile oven. While the specialty items such as tea, jam and honey are delightful, the selection of basic produce

Horseback riding, Dahana Ranch
LONELY PLANET/GETTY IMAGES ©

Of Cattle & Cowboys

Parker Ranch (www.parkerranch.com) was once the nation's largest privately owned ranch, peaking at 391 sq miles. Recently, however, the ranch has had to sell off parcels, including 37.5 sq miles to the US military in 2006. Today it's the fifth-largest cow-calf ranch in the USA, with at least 12,000 mother cows on 203 sq miles, and producing 12 million pounds of beef annually.

Big Island ranching goes back to 1793, when British Captain George Vancouver gifted King Kamehameha with a herd of long-horned cattle. Protected by the king's kapu (taboo), the herd proliferated and by 1815 was a menace.

Massachusetts mariner John Palmer Parker, who arrived here in 1809 at age 19, was deft with a rifle and hired to control the cattle problem. After successfully cutting the herd down to size, he received not only top-quality cows, but also the hand of one of Kamehameha's granddaughters and a prime piece of land. Parker Ranch was born in 1847.

is surprisingly limited. Located in front of Parker School in town.

Waimea Homestead Farmers Market Market $

(7am-noon Sat) This market, spread out on a grassy field, has a scruffy, local feel. It offers fruits and vegetables, eggs, preserves, flowers, meats, cheeses, tea, coffee, massages and scrumptious breakfasts. Located in front of the Hawaiian Home Lands office, near Mile 55 marker on Hwy 19.

Waimea MidWeek Market Market $

(Pukalani Stables; 9am-4pm Wed) This midweek market offers goodies including local organic produce, honey, handmade soaps, hot plate lunches and live *paniolo* music. Before browsing, visit the Paniolo Heritage Center, also at the stables.

Village Burger Burgers $

(885-7319; www.villageburgerwaimea.com; 67-1185 Mamalahoa Hwy, Parker Ranch Center; burgers $8-12; 10:30am-8pm Mon-Sat, to 6pm Sun) Burger connoisseurs, prepare to be impressed. Big Island beef, veal and lamb burgers are juicy and tender, while vegetarian options (Waipi'o Valley taro or Hamakua mushroom) are equally scrumptious. All major ingredients pass muster with locavores. Freshly cut fries and aptly named 'Epic Shakes' top it off. Seating is very limited, but there's ample space in the adjacent food court.

Big Island Brewhaus & Taqueria Mexican $

(887-1717; www.bigislandbrewhaus.com; 64-1066 Mamalahoa Hwy; mains $7.50-16; 11am-8:30pm Mon-Sat, noon-8:30pm Sun) The former Tako Taco has upped its game as a quality brewpub. Owner Thomas Kerns has created over a dozen memorable beers, including White Mountain Porter, rich with coffee and coconut, and Golden Sabbath Belgian Ale, which has a tremendous aroma. The setting is casual verging on sloppy. Go for the beer.

Lilikoi Cafe Cafe $

(887-1400; 67-1185 Mamalahoa Hwy, Parker Ranch Center; meals $9-12; 7:30am-4pm Mon-Sat) This cheery cafe serves healthy, innovative food such as a breakfast burrito with eggs, tofu and sweet red pepper, and hearty vegetable lasagne. Drink the fresh carrot, apple, beet and ginger 'House Cocktail' ($5.50) and conquer the world. Hidden in the back of the shopping center.

The Best... Live Performances in Kohala & Waimea

1 Blue Dragon Musiquarium (p112)
2 Kahilu Theatre (p129)
3 Kings' Shops (p99) and Queens' MarketPlace (p99)
4 Waimea Ukulele & Slack Key Guitar Institute Concert (p125)
5 Moku O Keawe (p99)

Waimea Coffee & Co Cafe $
(885-8915; www.waimeacoffeecompany.com; Kawaihe Rd, Parker Sq; sandwiches $8-10; 6:30am-5:30pm Mon-Sat, 8am-2pm Sun;) If you can snag a patio table, this is a lively hangout for espresso drinks and light fare. Service can be hit or miss, however.

Hawaiian Style Cafe Diner $
(885-4295; 64-1290 Kawaihae Rd, Hayashi Bldg; dishes $7.50-10; 7am-1:30pm Mon-Sat, to noon Sun) Big eaters will meet their match at this local favorite greasy spoon, especially popular for breakfast. Expect enormous Man v Food portions of *loco moco* (rice, fried egg and hamburger patty topped with gravy or other condiments), pancakes, fried rice, burgers and more. Not the place for health nuts and dieters.

Aka Sushi Bar Sushi $$
(887-2320; 65-1158 Mamalahoa Hwy, Waimea Shopping Center; sushi $5-10, bowls $12-16; 10:30am-2:15pm & 5-8:30pm Tue-Sat) Ignore the strip-mall setting: this is a gem for reasonably priced or takeout sushi. *Nigiri* (oblong-shaped sushi) and rolls have a high fish-to-rice ratio, and everything is fresh. Be sure to try the succulent *hamachi kama* (grilled yellowtail collar).

Pau Sandwiches, Pizzeria $$
(885-6325; www.paupizza.com; 65-1227 Opelo Rd, Opelo Plaza; pizza $17-28; 11am-8pm) This

Wok-charred ahi at Merriman's

LONELY PLANET/GETTY IMAGES ©

casual eatery serves reliably creative, tasty and healthful salads, sandwiches, pastas and over a dozen crisp, thin-crust pizzas.

Fish & the Hog Market Cafe BBQ **$$**
(**☎885-6268; www.hulisues.com; 64-957 Mamalahoa Hwy; sandwiches $10-13, barbecue $15-24; ⏰11:30am-8:30pm Mon-Sat**) Formerly known as Huli Sue's, this sit-down restaurant serves ribs, pulled pork, beef brisket and other kiawe-smoked meats with their signature BBQ sauces. Fish dishes, from gumbo to tacos, are well done. Save room for the famous banana cream pie.

Merriman's Hawaii Regional **$$$**
(**☎885-6822; www.merrimanshawaii.com; 65-1227 Opelo Rd, Opelo Plaza; lunch $11-15, dinner $30-50; ⏰11:30am-1:30pm Mon-Fri, 5:30-8pm daily**) Chef-owner Peter Merriman's Waimea namesake has long wowed diners with creative use of organic, island-grown ingredients. Today there are four sister restaurants and his original flagship might be slipping. But it's still the best fine-dining spot in town. The mahimahi marinated in *ponzu* (Japanese citrus sauce), wok-charred ahi and crispy molten chocolate 'purse' are classics. Lunch offers good value.

Entertainment

Kahilu Theatre Theater
(**☎885-6017, box office 885-6868; www.kahilutheatre.org; 67-1185 Mamalahoa Hwy, Parker Ranch Center; admission $20-54; ⏰box office 9am-3pm Mon-Fri, show times vary**) A hotspot for music and dance, this theater offers a variety of top performances – for example Hawaii icon The Brothers Cazimero, the latest Van Cliburn winner and the annual Waimea Ukulele & Slack Key Guitar Institute Concert. Check the website for upcoming shows.

Shopping

Three shopping malls line Hwy 19 through town: **Parker Ranch Center** (**67-1185 Mamalahoa Hwy**), where the stop signs say 'Whoa,' **Waimea Center** (**65-1158 Mamalahoa Hwy**) and **Parker Square** (**65-1279 Kawaihae Rd**). The first two have groceries and basics, plus restaurants and fast food; Parker Square aims for discriminating, upscale gift buyers.

Gallery of Great Things Arts & Crafts
(**☎885-7706; www.galleryofgreatthingshawaii.com; 65-1279 Kawaihae Rd, Parker Sq; ⏰9am-5.30pm Mon-Sat, 10am-4pm Sun**) This unpretentious gallery is crammed with antiques, high-quality art and collectibles from Hawaii, Polynesia and Asia. Among the Hawaiian crafts for sale is *kapa,* bark cloth painstakingly handmade by traditional methods. Best, there's something for every budget.

Waimea General Store Gifts, Homewares
(**www.waimeageneralstore.com; 65-1279 Kawaihae Rd, Parker Sq**) Shoppers, browsers and homemakers will enjoy the eclectic mix here, from Le Creuset and Japanese tableware to fancy toiletries and vintage hula-girl cards.

Reyn's Clothing
(**www.reyns.com; Parker Ranch Center; ⏰9:30am-5:30pm Mon-Sat, to 4pm Sun**) If you want to dress like a local, shop at Reyn's. Its classic, understated aloha shirts (which use Hawaiian fabrics in reverse) never go out of style.

Information

North Hawaii Community Hospital (☎885-4444; 67-1125 Mamalahoa Hwy) Emergency services available 24 hours.

Post Office (☎800-275-8777; 67-1197 Mamalahoa Hwy; ⏰8am-4:30pm Mon-Fri, 9am-noon Sat) Address all Waimea mail to Kamuela.

Getting There & Around

Kailua-Kona is 37 miles away along Hwy 190; Hilo is 51 miles away on Hwy 19.

On Monday to Saturday the Hele-On Bus (p96) goes from Waimea (Parker Ranch Center) to Kailua-Kona on its 16 Kailua-Kona route (65 minutes) and to Hilo on its 7 Downtown Hilo route (80 minutes).

Mauna Kea & Saddle Road

Caution: you're entering hallowed ground. According to the Hawaiian creation myth, this sacrosanct peak is home to the gods, the place between heaven and earth where *na kanaka maoli* (Native Hawaiians) were created. With its summit soaring 13,796ft above sea level, Mauna Kea – more precisely, its true summit, Pu'u Wekiu – is also Hawaii's highest peak, and the tallest volcano anywhere in the world's oceans.

Sacred status and chart-topping elevation aren't the only reasons to head up Mauna Kea. Travelers from the world over make their way to this literally breath-taking mountain for stellar stargazing and high-altitude hiking. Astronomers, too, covet the summit: with its unmatched collection of high-tech astronomical observatories, it's one of the best places on earth to observe the night sky.

Even just the trip getting here – along rolling Saddle Rd, then up Mauna Kea's skyscraping summit road – is adventure.

Mauna Kea summit at sunset

Mauna Kea & Saddle Road Itineraries

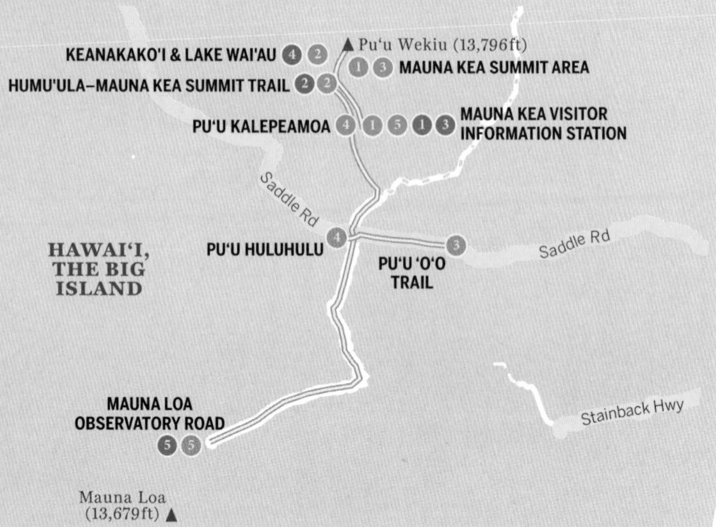

One Day

1 Mauna Kea Visitor Information Station (MKVIS) (p135) You'll probably be feeling the altitude by the time you reach this way station at 9200ft. Spend some time acclimatizing and picking the rangers' brains for fascinating facts about the mountain, modern astronomy and Hawaiian cultural traditions.

2 Keanakako'i & Lake Wai'au (p135) With a low-gear 4WD vehicle, if the weather is cooperating, keep driving up the mountain on its summit road. Stop partway up to hike to a shrinking prehistoric lake and an ancient Hawaiian adze quarry inside the Mauna Kea Ice Age Natural Area Reserve.

3 Mauna Kea's Summit Area (p135) You've made it! Drive the summit loop road around the 'golf ball' observatories perched high on the mountaintop. If it's a weekday, step inside the visitor gallery at the WM Keck Observatory.

4 Pu'u Kalepeamoa (p135) Drive slowly down from the summit back to the MKVIS. Across the road, take a 15-minute, mostly uphill hike to this top spot for sunset views. Have a flashlight handy for the after-dark return trip.

5 Stargazing (p138) Want your mind blown? Get some hot chocolate, bust out the warm jacket and mittens, and peer through powerful telescopes at distant corners of the universe during the MKVIS's free public stargazing programs held nightly, weather permitting.

THIS LEG: 16 MILES

Two Days

1 Sunrise on Mauna Kea (p135) Although light on traffic, dark and windy Saddle Rd makes a fairly challenging predawn drive – make sure the coffee is flowing as you catch the sun coming up over the clouds.

2 Humu'ula–Mauna Kea Summit Trail (p138) Fit and prepared hikers will want to hit this challenging trail by 6am, adding Hawaii's tallest mountain to their list of achievements. You'll be hiking at the knife's edge of the volcano and the sky. A short spur at the very top leads to Mauna Kea's true summit, Pu'u Wekiu.

3 Pu'u 'O'o Trail (p143) For a day hike that's not as heart-stoppingly strenuous, head east on Saddle Rd for this lovely loop. You'll cross forest, meadows and old lava flows in profound solitude, and you may spy colorful Hawaiian honeycreepers, such as the *'apapane* and *'i'iwi.*

4 Pu'u Huluhulu Trail (p143) Start this short leg-stretcher just before sunset. After a short walk up 'Shaggy Hill,' the entire Saddle Rd region will be laid out before you on clear evenings: Mauna Kea, Mauna Loa and Hualalai. The contrast between the lava flows and green shrubbery of the *kipuka* (oasis) is wild.

5 Mauna Loa Observatory Rd (p142) Here's yet another sunset option. Reaching the Mauna Loa Observatory (weather forecast: *cold*) at 11,150ft is a bit of a tricky drive, but you may be rewarded by seeing the mystical 'Mauna Kea shadow' over Hilo as you watch the sun go down. Inspired by the views? Come back tomorrow to tackle the hard-core Mauna Loa Observatory Trail.

THIS LEG: 42 MILES

Mauna Kea & Saddle Road Highlights

1 Best View: Mauna Kea stargazing (p138) Spy on our universe from Hawai'i's most sacred mountain.

2 Best Hike: Humu'ula–Mauna Kea Summit Trail (p138) Traipse among giant volcanic cinder cones above the clouds.

3 Best Place to Learn: Mauna Kea Visitor Information Station (MKVIS) (p135) Free stargazing programs, escorted summit tours and more fun for science geeks.

4 Best Ancient Hawaiian Site: Lake Wai'au (p135) Hawai'i's spiritual umbilical cord connects heaven and earth.

5 Best Adventure: Mauna Loa Observatory Trail (p142) Climb this massive mountain – in just one day.

WM Keck Observatory (p137)
MAGRATH PHOTOGRAPHY/NIELSEN/GETTY IMAGES ©

Discover Mauna Kea & Saddle Road

MAUNA KEA

Mauna Kea (White Mountain) is called Mauna O Wakea (Mountain of Wakea) by Hawaiian cultural practitioners. While all of the Big Island is considered the first-born child of Wakea (sky father) and Papahanaumoku (earth mother), the deity progenitors of the Hawaiian race, Mauna Kea is the sacred *piko* (navel) connecting the land to the heavens.

For the scientific world, it all began in 1968 when the University of Hawai'i (UH) began observing the universe from atop the mountain. Smart folks: the summit is so high, dry, dark and pollution-free that it allows investigation of the furthest reaches of the observable universe. Today, astronomers from 11 countries staff 13 observatories on Mauna Kea's summit – the largest conglomeration of high-powered telescopes anywhere in the world. They huddle in a small area of the Mauna Kea Science Reserve, a chunk of land leased by UH that encompasses almost everything above 12,000ft.

Many Hawaiians are opposed to the summit 'golf balls' – the white observatories. While not antiscience, they believe unchecked growth on the mountain threatens the *wahi pana* (sacred places) there, including heiau (temples) and burial sites. In a dramatic episode in 2006, an *ahu lele* (spiritual altar) built for ceremonies on the mountain was desecrated. Toxic mercury spills from some observatories have occurred, and damage to the mountain's fragile ecosystem is another arrow in the activists' antidevelopment quiver.

Nevertheless in 2011, plans were approved to build the Thirty Meter Telescope (TMT) here. While TMT will be the world's most advanced and powerful telescope, its structural footprint will be larger than all the observatories currently on the summit, with all the possible disruptions of natural and cultural resources that implies.

Saddle Road
LASZLO PODOR PHOTOGRAPHY/GETTY IMAGES ©

Sights

Mauna Kea Visitor Information Station — Visitor Center

(MKVIS; ☎808-961-2180; www.ifa.hawaii.edu/info/vis; ⏰9am-10pm) FREE Modestly sized, MKVIS packs a punch with astronomy and space-exploration videos, virtual observatory tours and exhibits on the mountain's history, ecology and geology. Budding astronomers of all ages geek out in the gift shop, where knowledgeable staff will help you pass the time acclimatizing to the 9200ft altitude.

Free public stargazing programs (p138) happen from 6pm until 10pm nightly, weather permitting. If you have a low-gear 4WD vehicle, escorted summit tours (p140) usually leave at 1pm on Saturdays and Sundays.

Inside the **gift shop** you can buy hot chocolate, coffee, packets of instant noodles and freeze-dried astronaut food to munch on; hoodies, hats and gloves to stay warm; and books about science and Hawaiian culture. Check the website for upcoming special events, such as lectures about science and Hawaiian culture, typically held on Saturday nights.

Across from MKVIS, a 15-minute uphill hike crests **Pu'u Kalepeamoa** (9394ft), a cinder cone offering glorious sunset views. Directly off the MKVIS parking lot is a small enclosed area where rare and endangered **silversword plants** grow.

As you drive 6 miles and 2500ft uphill from Saddle Rd to the MKVIS, you'll break through the cloud cover. The road is paved and normally accessible by 2WD vehicles as far as MKVIS.

Keanakako'i & Lake Wai'au — Archaeological Site, Lake

Just after the Mile 6 marker en route to Mauna Kea's summit area from MKVIS, pull into a paved parking area. Below is the trailhead to **Lake Wai'au**, the third-highest lake in the USA (it's disappearing fast), and **Keanakako'i**, a protected ancient Hawaiian adze quarry. It'll take an hour or so to hike to both the lake and the quarry, depending on your level of fitness and acclimatization.

A sacred place to Hawaiians, Lake Wai'au is the *piko* (navel, or umbilical cord) connecting heaven and earth. To ensure a baby has the strength of the mountain, real umbilical stumps were traditionally placed in the lake. Clay formed long ago by volcanic ash holds the water, fed by melting snow, permafrost and minimal annual rainfall. Since 2010, the lake has dramatically shrunk to 2% of its former size, and is now less than 1ft deep, but scientists don't know exactly why.

During Mauna Kea's ice age, molten lava erupted under its glacier, creating an extremely hard basalt, which ancient Hawaiians chipped into tools and weapons at Keanakako'i quarry. Some of these tools were used on Hawai'i to peck massive fields of symbolic drawings into hardened lava, including the Pu'u Loa petroglyphs in Hawai'i Volcanoes National Park. Entering the quarry is discouraged, as it's a fragile archaeological site of importance to Hawaiians, but the views from the trail are still worth seeing.

Mauna Kea's Summit Area — Landmark

At the top of Mauna Kea, massive round observatories rise up white and silver from stark terrain. It's a striking juxtaposition – you may feel like you've discovered a futuristic human colony on an alien planet. Staffed by scientists from around the world, these observatories compose the greatest collection of optical, infrared and millimeter/submillimeter telescopes on earth. At almost 14,000ft, the summit is above 40% of the earth's atmosphere and 90% of its water vapor, resulting in many cloudless nights.

It's a veritable UN on the mountaintop, with a bevy of countries administering different telescopes – Taiwan and the USA collaborate on the **Submillimeter Array**; the UK and Canada run the **James Clerk Maxwell Telescope (JCMT)**; and six nations share the **Gemini Northern 8m Telescope**. The **University of Hawai'i 0.9m Telescope** is now used mostly for training undergraduates. Most of these observatories are closed to the public,

Mauna Kea & Saddle Road

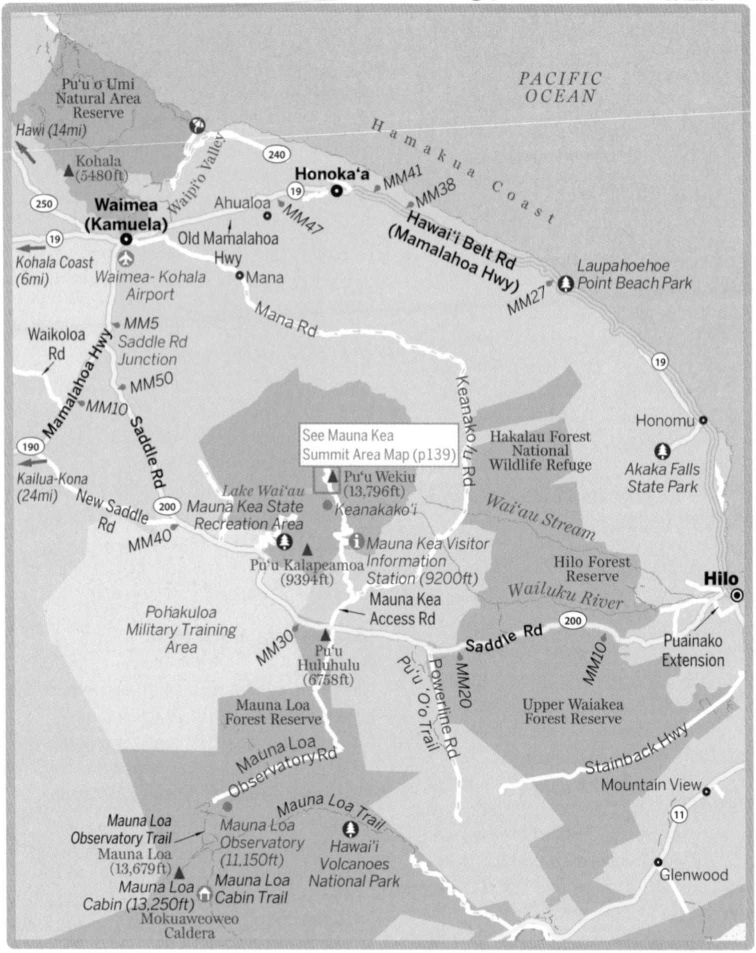

and none allow public viewing through their telescopes.

Sunsets are phenomenal from around the summit. All of Hawai'i lies below as the sun sinks into an ocean of clouds – while the telescopes silently unshutter and turn their unblinking eyes to the heavens. Look east to see 'the shadow' – the gigantic silhouette of Mauna Kea looming over Hilo. Moonrises can be equally as impressive: the high altitude may make the moon appear squashed and misshapen, or sometimes resemble a brushfire.

Be sure to bring long pants, a thick coat (or lots of layers), a warm hat and gloves. It gets cold up here. If you have a 4WD, you may drive to the summit in the daytime, but you must descend 30 minutes after sunset. It takes about half an hour to drive the 8-mile summit road, the first 4.5 miles of which are slippery gravel. Just before the pavement picks up again, the area on the east side of the road is dubbed **Moon Valley**, where Apollo astronauts rehearsed with their lunar rover before their journey to the real moonscape.

WM Keck Observatory Observatory (808-935-6268; www.keck .org; visitors gallery 10am-4pm Mon-Fri) FREE Near Mauna Kea's summit, the WM Keck Observatory has a visitors gallery with scientific displays, public restrooms and partial views inside the Keck I dome. Currently the world's largest and most powerful optical and infrared telescopes are housed here, a joint project of the California Institute of Technology (CalTech), the University of California and NASA. The two interchangeable telescopes can function as one – like a pair of binoculars searching the sky – allowing them to study incredibly distant galaxies.

In 1992, **Keck I** made a breakthrough in telescope design using a unique honeycomb feature made up of 36 hexagonal mirror segments that function as a single piece of glass. A replica of the first telescope, **Keck II**, went online in 1996. In 2013, scientists using Keck I discovered the most distant galaxy ever observed, a mere 13.1 billion light-years away.

Subaru Telescope Observatory (www.naoj.org; tours usually 10:30am, 11:30am & 1:30pm Tue-Thu) FREE Inaugurated in 1999 after almost a decade of construction, its $300 million price tag makes Japan's Subaru Telescope the most expensive observatory constructed to date. Its 22-ton mirror, reaching 27ft in diameter, is one of the largest optical mirrors in existence. Incidentally, Subaru is the Japanese word for the Pleiades constellation.

Observatory tours, which don't include looking through the telescope, are given in Japanese or English, but not both – so sign up early for your preferred language. Reserve tours online at least one week in advance. Children under 16 years old are not allowed on tours. No public restrooms.

Pu'u Wekiu Mountain

The short trail up this cinder cone to Mauna Kea's true summit (13,796ft) begins opposite the UH 2.2m Telescope. The hike is harder than it looks, and it's not necessary to go just to watch the sunset. Hawaiian cultural practitioners counsel against hiking due to the area's environmental fragility and cultural significance. At the true summit is a US Geological Survey (USGS) marker and an *ahu* (altar). Given the biting winds, high altitude and extreme cold, most people don't linger.

Island Insights

First snow is falling on Mauna Kea and, near the visitor information station, ranger James Keali'i Pihana – 'Kimo' as he's known – is blocking the frozen road in his pickup truck and explaining what Mauna Kea means to Hawaiians.

'To us, Mauna Kea is "the heavens." It is the place between heaven and earth... Mauna Kea is the center of our "Biblestory."

'Mauna Kea is the home of the snow goddess, Poliahu. Ceremonies are still conducted: equinox, solstices, first light. Lake Wai'au is sacred water. Umbilical cords were put in the lake for the protection of children.'

Kimo and others walked up the mountain in 1998 to voice their deep concern over the observatories. Sacred places and burial sites had been built on and disturbed, and new observatories were going up without consulting Hawaiians.

Consequently, a rally was held. Kimo says, 'Our people were ready to shut the road down.' It was a pivotal moment, and the politicians and astronomers responded. A Hawaiian advisory council was created, Kimo conducted cleansing rituals, and then he applied for a job. His most important task is communicating with Hawaiian leaders about what's happening on their sacred mountain.

The Best... Mauna Kea Webcams

1 CFH Telescope Timelapse Webcam

2 Joint Astronomy Centre Webcam

3 MKVIS Live Allsky Cam

4 NASA Infrared Telescope Facility Cameras

5 Subaru Telescope Webcams

Activities

STARGAZING

Although the high-tech telescopes inside Mauna Kea's summit observatories are closed to the public, the MKVIS (p135) hosts free nightly stargazing programs, weather permitting (no reservations necessary). Specialists focus high-powered scopes on the night skies, and travelers in wheelchairs have the use of adaptive scope attachments.

During big meteor showers like the Leonides in mid-November, MKVIS often hosts all-night star parties. Lunar eclipses and the monthly full moon are also popular with stargazers. Call ahead for special events and current viewing conditions.

HIKING

For sunset views without going to the summit, take the 15-minute, steep hike up **Pu'u Kalepeamoa**, starting across the road from MKVIS (p135). Heading toward Mauna Kea's summit area, you can hike to Keanakako'i & Lake Wai'au (p135).

Humu'ula–Mauna Kea Summit Trail Hiking

This daunting, all-day hike starts at 9200ft, then climbs almost 4600ft over the next 6 miles to Mauna Kea's summit. Expect thin air, steep grades and biting weather on this utterly exposed trail, where it often feels like you're going to step off the mountain into the sky. Plan on eight hours for the round-trip hike and bring a gallon of water per person – dehydration is a real danger at these altitudes. Don't hike in inclement weather.

Start by 6am to give yourself the maximum hours of daylight. Before hiking, register at the MKVIS (p135), where you can grab a hiking map and consult with rangers about current weather and trail conditions. (If it's closed, fill out a self-registration form and place it in the drop box.) Remember to take your time acclimatizing, with frequent rest and water breaks.

Park at MKVIS and walk up the summit road to where the pavement ends. Turn left onto a dirt side road and follow the brown-and-yellow Na Ala Hele signs for the Humu'ula Trail. The trail begins climbing doggedly upward, gradually getting slightly less steep after the first mile while it weaves among cinder cones. It's marked with poles and reflectors, as well as rock cairns. Avoid false spurs leading back to the summit road, which reappears after about an hour.

Most of the hike passes through the **Mauna Kea Ice Age Natural Area Reserve**. After about three hours you'll enter a broad valley, followed by a sharp, short ascent on crumbly soil over a rise to Keanakako'i (p135), an ancient adze quarry, with large piles of bluish-black basalt chips. Do not disturb anything in this protected area. Another mile-long ascent brings you to a four-way junction, where a 10-minute detour to the left reaches Lake Wai'au (p135). Back at the four-way junction, make your way north for the final upward push to the summit.

Suddenly the observatories pop into view and straight ahead is **Millimeter Valley**, nicknamed for the cluster of submillimeter observatories. The trail

Mauna Kea Summit Area

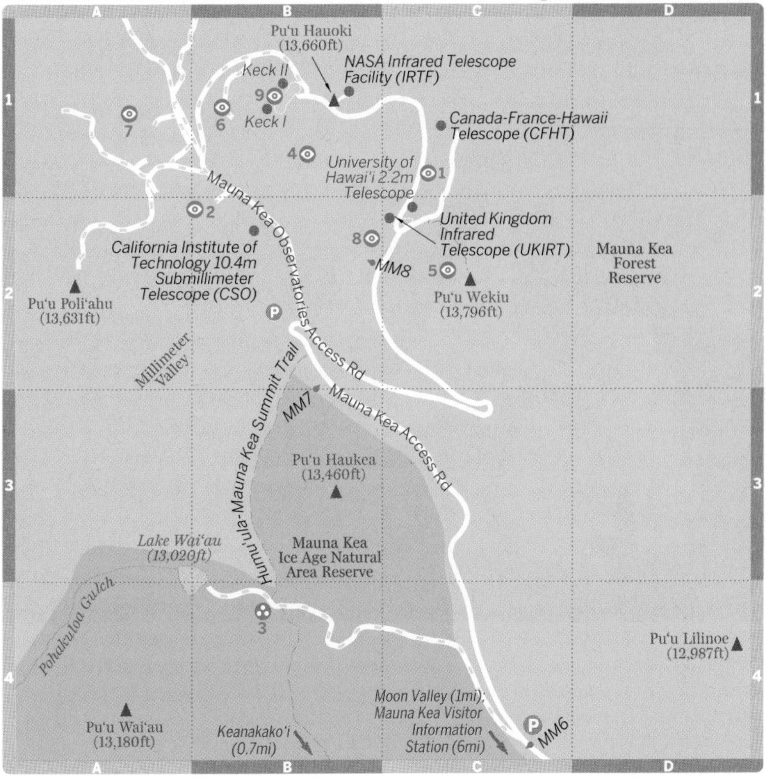

ends here at the road's Mile 7 marker, just below the hairpin turn; turn back here and you can descend the way you came on the trail or walk along the road instead. The latter is 2 miles longer, but faster and easier, and you're more likely (though not guaranteed) to get a lift down by hitchhiking.

If you really need to place a boot toe on Pu'u Wekiu (p137), Mauna Kea's true summit, follow the summit loop road up to the right (not the spur road into Millimeter Valley) for just over a mile. Past Mile 8 marker, where the road forks, veer right and look for a 'trail' opposite the **University of Hawai'i 2.2m Telescope**. This short spur trail-of-use descends steeply east, crosses a saddle and then scrambles up to the summit.

Mauna Kea Summit Area

Sights

1 Gemini Northern 8m Telescope C1
2 James Clerk Maxwell Telescope (JCMT) B2
3 Keanakako'i & Lake Wai'au B4
4 Mauna Kea's Summit Area B1
5 Pu'u Wekiu C2
6 Subaru Telescope B1
7 Submillimeter Array A1
8 University of Hawai'i 0.9m Telescope B2
9 WM Keck Observatory B1

SKIING & SNOWBOARDING

In January or February, enough snow may fall on Mauna Kea's heights to allow for winter sports. The so-called 'slopes' are crowded with locals using skis, snowboards, surfboards, bodyboards, inner tubes – whatever!

What concerns activists and conservationists is increased mountaintop usage during snowfall, combined with the degradation caused by monster trucks used to access the 'slopes,' thereby eroding natural habitat and culturally significant sites.

For those chasing this trophy experience, know that skiing Mauna Kea is entirely DIY. There are no groomed trails, no lifts, no patrols; exposed rocks and ice sheets are constant dangers.

Tours

MKVIS Escorted Summit Tour Guided Tour

(808-935-6268; www.ifa.hawaii.edu/info/vis; usually 1pm Sat & Sun) FREE You must provide your own low-gear 4WD vehicle to take advantage of these free guided summit tours (no reservations accepted). You'll spend the first hour acclimatizing and watching astronomy videos. After the orientation, you'll caravan up to the summit, where a docent talks about the telescopes, their history and what they're typically looking at. Tours visit at least one of the summit observatories, ending around 4:30pm. Most people stay for the sunset, then drive back down on their own.

Tours don't run when bad weather closes the road, so call ahead to check weather and road conditions. Children must be at least 16 years old.

Hawaii Forest & Trail Van Tour

(800-464-1993, 808-331-8505; www.hawaii-forest.com; tour $199; tours nightly, weather permitting) This top-notch, ecotour outfitter hosts a sunset and stargazing tour, with parkas, gloves and a picnic dinner at a private location. Knowledgeable guides take you to the summit, then conduct a tour of the heavens with an 11in Celestron telescope outside MKVIS. Pick-ups from near Kailua-Kona, Waiakoloa and the Hwys 190 and 200 junction. Participants must be at least 16 years old. Book early.

Left: Observatories on Mauna Kea's Summit Area (p135); **Below:** Hikers at the Mauna Kea summit

(LEFT) MICHELE FALZONE/GETTY IMAGES ©; (BELOW) GREG ELMS/GETTY IMAGES ©

Mauna Kea Summit Adventures Van Tour

(**☎888-322-2366, 808-322-2366; www.maunakea.com; tour $204**) The granddaddy of Mauna Kea tours has been taking folks to the summit for over 20 years. This outfit has vans with extra-tall windows and spacious seating. A hot dinner outside MKVIS, cold-weather parkas to borrow and stargazing through a 11in Celestron telescope are included. Pick-ups from Kailua-Kona, Waikoloa and the Hwys 190/200 junction. Children must be at least 13 years old.

Arnott's Mauna Kea Adventures Van Tour

(**☎808-339-0921; www.arnottslodge.com; 98 Apanane Rd, Hilo; tours $130-180; ⏲Mon, Wed & Fri-Sun**) Arnott's Lodge tours are for budget travelers, not serious stargazers. They're cheaper, leave from Hilo (or you can drive your own car and meet them on Saddle Rd) and the astronomy is bare-bones, with guides relying on laser pointers. BYO food and warm clothes.

Sleeping

The closest accommodations besides camping are in Waimea and Hilo.

Mauna Kea State Recreation Area Cabin $

(**www.hawaiistateparks.org; Saddle Rd; cabin $80**) At the Mile 35 marker is this public recreation area, with five bare-bones cabins (currently available on weekends only, but double-check this). Used mainly by local hunters, each cabin has six bunk beds, a basic kitchen and a toilet, but no water. Bring your own bedding and towels. Military maneuvers at nearby Pohakuloa Training Area can be very noisy.

Information

There are no restaurants, gas stations or emergency services anywhere on Mauna Kea or along Saddle Rd. Come prepared with a full tank of gas, warm clothing, sunglasses, sunscreen, snacks and plenty of water.

Dangers & Annoyances

Even at the MKVIS (9200ft), some visitors experience shortness of breath and mild 'altitude sickness' (acute mountain sickness, or AMS). At the 13,796ft summit, atmospheric pressure is less than 60% of sea level, and AMS is common. The risk increases with faster ascents and greater exertion; being physically fit offers no protection. All travelers to the summit should stop first at MKVIS for at least 30 minutes to acclimatize.

Symptoms of AMS include nausea, headaches, drowsiness, impaired reason, loss of balance, breathlessness and dehydration. AMS can lead to life-threatening pulmonary or cerebral edema. If you feel ill, descend immediately. Children under 16 years, pregnant women and those with high blood pressure or circulatory conditions should not go to the summit. Do not scuba dive for 24 hours before or after visiting Mauna Kea.

Be prepared for rapidly changing (and possibly severe) weather conditions, with daytime temperatures anywhere from 50°F (10°C) to below freezing and possible high winds. In winter, several feet of snow can fall, with road closures on the morning following a storm. Check weather and road conditions with the Mauna Kea Weather Center (**808-935-6268; http://mkwc.ifa.hawaii.edu/**) before heading up. Even when the fog's as thick as pea soup on Saddle Rd, it's crystal clear at the mountaintop 325 days a year.

Getting There & Around

Coming from Kona or Waimea, Saddle Rd (Hwy 200) starts just south of the Mile 6 marker on Hwy 190. From Hilo, drive *mauka* (inland) on Kaumana Dr (Hwy 200) or Puainako Extension (Hwy 2000), both of which become Saddle Rd. Start with a full tank of gas – Saddle Rd has no gas stations.

To get to MKVIS and the summit beyond, turn onto Mauna Kea Access Rd, near the Mile 28 marker on Saddle Rd. It takes about an hour to get to MKVIS from Hilo, Waimea or Waikoloa, or around 90 minutes from Kailua-Kona. MKVIS is 6 miles uphill from Saddle Rd; the summit is another 8 miles beyond the information station. Call (808) 935-6268 for current road conditions.

Driving to the summit requires a low-gear 4WD vehicle – there have been many accidents to underscore this point. Over half of the summit road is gravel, sometimes at a 15% grade. The upper road can be covered with ice, and loose cinders are always challenging. Drive in low gear and be particularly careful on the way down *not* to ride your vehicle's brakes, which can overheat and fail. Driving when the sun is low – in the hour after sunrise or before sunset – can create hazardous, blinding conditions. Plan to drive up to the summit during the daytime: the use of vehicle headlights is discouraged between sunset and sunrise, as they interfere with astronomical observations.

SADDLE ROAD

Off Saddle Rd you'll discover a few exceptional wilderness hikes, as well as one high-altitude scenic drive.

Sights & Activities

Mauna Loa Observatory Road Scenic Drive

Mauna Loa is somewhat of an enigma for visitors – it looms large all around, but how do you actually get on 'Long Mountain'? The answer is simple: drive up Mauna Loa Observatory Rd. This unsigned road starts near the Mile 28 marker on Saddle Rd, almost opposite Mauna Kea Access Rd and next to Pu'u Huluhulu. Delivering kicking views, the single-lane, 17.5-mile asphalt road ends at a parking area just below the **Mauna Loa Observatory** (11,150ft).

When weather conditions are just right, you can glimpse the 'Mauna Kea shadow' at sunset from here – a curious atmospheric phenomenon whereby Mauna Kea casts a blue-purple shadow behind itself over Hilo. The narrow road is passable in a standard car, but it's in varying condition and bedeviled by blind curves. Allow almost an hour. The road sometimes is closed in winter.

Mauna Loa Observatory Trail Hiking

The easiest way to summit Mauna Loa (Long Mountain) is via this trail. Drive up to Mauna Loa Observatory at 11,150ft, then pick up the 6.4-mile trail for the remaining 2500ft to the top. It's a steep, exhausting, all-day adventure, but an exceptional one that allows experienced hikers to conquer a 13,000ft mountain in one day.

Start before 8am. You want to be off the mountain, or at least descending, by the time afternoon clouds roll in. Starting from the road's end near the observatory, the trail is marked by *ahu* (cairns) that disappear in fog, rain and snow; if that happens, rangers advise seeking shelter and waiting until visibility improves. The faster and/or higher you hike the more likely your risk of altitude sickness.

The trail starts by crisscrossing a series of *'a'a* (rough) and *pahoehoe* (smooth) lava flows. After 3.8 miles and 2000ft in elevation gain, you'll arrive at majestic **Moku'aweoweo Caldera**. From the trail junction, it's just over 2.6 miles northwest to Mauna Loa's **summit** (13,679ft) or 2.1 miles southwest to Mauna Loa Cabin (13,250ft). It should take about half as long to descend. All told, plan on a 10-hour day. Bring plenty of extra water, food and a flashlight.

Day hikers do not need a permit, but if you want to overnight at Mauna Loa Cabin near the summit, register the day before at Hawai'i Volcanoes National Park's Backcountry Office (p216), where rangers can tell you about current trail conditions and water-catchment levels at the cabin. An alternative backpacking route to the summit, the multiday Mauna Loa Trail (p219), starts inside the national park.

Pu'u Huluhulu Trail — Hiking

The easy 0.6-mile trail up the cinder cone **Pu'u Huluhulu**, 'Shaggy Hill' (6758ft), makes a piquant appetizer before going up Mauna Kea. Inside a *kipuka* (volcanic oasis), the 20-minute hike climbs through native forest to the hilltop, from where there are panoramic views of Mauna Kea, Mauna Loa and Hualalai on clear days. The trailhead parking area is almost opposite the turnoff to Mauna Kea, near the Mile 28 marker on Saddle Rd. Don't confuse this hike with the Pu'u Huluhulu Trail (p217) in Hawai'i Volcanoes National Park.

Pu'u 'O'o Trail — Hiking

For a peaceful yet substantial ramble, take the Pu'u 'O'o Trail, a 7.5-mile loop traversing meadows, old lava flows and pretty *kipuka* forests filled koa and ohia trees and the songs of Hawaiian honeycreepers and other native birds. The signed trailhead parking area is almost exactly halfway between the Mile 22 and 23 markers on Saddle Rd. The trail is marked by *ahu*; it's easy to follow in good weather, less so in rain or fog. If in doubt, simply retrace your steps the way you came. Eventually, the trail connects with Powerline Rd (marked with a sign), a 4WD road that can be used as a return route, although this road dumps you out about a mile away from the trailhead parking area.

Local Knowledge

NAME: ROB PACHECO

OCCUPATION: OWNER, HAWAI'I FOREST & TRAIL

RESIDENCE: HOLUALOA

1 HOW MANY TIMES HAVE YOU SUMMITED MAUNA KEA?

I've been up there more times than I can count – hundreds of times. We all need beauty, awe and wonder in our lives. Mauna Kea does that for me.

2 WHAT'S THE BEST VIEW IN YOUR OPINION?

My favorite view is from outside the University of Hawai'i 2.2m Telescope, where you get unobstructed views to the western horizon; turn around and you have the same to the eastern horizon. Logistically, I like it because you can tuck yourself into the telescope when the wind is howling.

3 AS A NATURALIST, WHAT HIKE WOULD YOU RECOMMEND?

Off Saddle Rd, Pu'u Huluhulu is a great introduction to Hawai'i's native forests. You'll see rare endemic species, plus trees like sandalwood and koa. The views of the entire region are great, too.

4 SKIING ON MAUNA KEA: YOUR TAKE?

For me, Mauna Kea is not a recreational playground. On good snow days, of which there are only a handful each year, hundreds of people are up there skiing and sledding. Too many people. The Hawaiian-ness of the mountain is not on everyone's radar. My job is to help connect visitors to this land in deeper ways, to convert them from simple thrill seekers into stakeholders.

Hamakua Coast

Stretching from Waipi'o Valley to Hilo, the Hamakua Coast is wildly fertile and ruggedly beautiful. Here you'll find rocky shores and pounding surf, tropical rainforests and thunderous waterfalls. The color green takes on new meaning, especially in Waipi'o Valley, where farmers still grow taro, a native staple. Farther inland, farmers grow vanilla, tea, mushrooms and other innovative crops, modernizing and diversifying island agriculture. While drivers now speed along the highway, trains chugged along the coast during 'old plantation days,' when towering bridges spanned the gulches and sugarcane was king. Go slow here, taking back roads and stepping back in time.

Akaka Falls State Park (p161)
PETER FRENCH/GETTY IMAGES ©

Hamakua Coast Itineraries

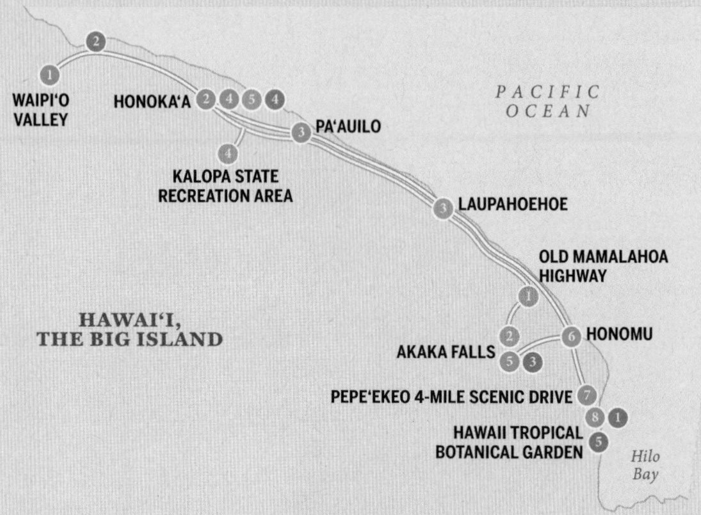

Two Days

1 Waipi'o Valley (p152) Start day one with the main event: hiking down into the valley. The view from the lookout is rewarding enough, but walk the 25% grade road to the bottom and write home about it!

2 Honoka'a (p148) Stop at this leisurely plantation/cowboy town and fuel up on *malasadas* (Portuguese doughnuts) at Tex Drive-In.

3 Hawaiian Vanilla Company (p148) Next is a trip to upcountry Pa'auilo, the island's bountiful breadbasket. Experience vanilla like you never have before at the Vanilla Experience Luncheon.

4 Café il Mondo (p151) End the day by returning to Honoka'a for freshly baked calzones and pizzas: you might even be serenaded by a guitar-strumming Brazilian.

5 Akaka Falls State Park (p161) The next day, head southeast to view the falls in flattering morning light; afternoon viewing guarantees gloomy backlit photos.

6 Hilo Sharks Coffee (p162) Stop in Honomu for locally grown coffee and chocolate, an unbeatable combination. Don't miss Mr Ed's Bakery for homemade preserves in 100 flavors.

7 Pepe'ekeo 4-Mile Scenic Drive (p163) Take this scenic drive and stop at What's Shakin' for a fresh fruit smoothie.

8 Hawaii Tropical Botanical Garden (p162) Leave lots of time to stroll amid wildly lush flora: gorgeous rain or shine.

THIS LEG: 40 MILES

Three Days

1 **Old Mamalahoa Hwy** (p151) If you have three days, start by following the two-day itinerary. On day three, detour to the old highway. Sometimes narrow and winding, it forces you to slow down, look around and truly appreciate the *'aina* (land).

2 **Ziplines** (p159) Get a bird's-eye view of the island's emerald expanse of forestland, plus waterfalls. Choose from two zip parks near Umauma Falls and one near Akaka Falls.

3 **Laupahoehoe** (p158) If zipping isn't your thing, take an agri-gourmet tour at Hamakua Mushrooms. Stop at the Laupahoehoe Train Museum and also the tsunami memorial at Laupahoehoe Point.

4 **Kalopa State Recreation Area** (p157) In the afternoon, luxuriate in your own private expanse of green. Hike the trails through native forest, play Frisbee on the lawn and breathe that fresh air.

5 **Honoka'a** (p148) Stay in town for the evening, catching a movie or show at the picturesque Honoka'a People's Theatre, built in 1930 and once the liveliest spot in town.

THIS LEG: 50 MILES

Hamakua Coast Highlights

1 **Best Garden: Hawaii Tropical Botanical Garden** (p162) Take a leisurely stroll through a rainforest jungle that meets the sea.

2 **Best Room with a View: Waipio Rim B&B** (p156) Behold Waipi'o Valley's green amphitheater from your bedroom!

3 **Best Waterfall: Akaka Falls** (p161) Walking to the lookout, past giant bamboo, ginger, ferns and orchids, is half the fun.

4 **Best Local Color: Honoka'a Trading Company** (p151) Browse through a mishmash of antiques and talk story with local characters.

5 **Best History Lesson: Hawaii Plantation Museum** (p163) See fascinating artifacts from plantation days, when Hawaii's multiethnic culture was born.

Laupahoehoe Train Museum (p159)

Discover Hamakua Coast

Honoka'a & Around

POP HONOKA'A TOWN 2258

Who would guess that Honoka'a was once the third-largest town across Hawaii, after Honolulu and Hilo? It was the hub for the powerful cattle and sugar industries, but was forced to reinvent itself when those industries crashed. By the time Honoka'a Sugar Company processed its last harvest in 1993, the town had dwindled in size and struggled to find new economic niches.

Taro farms in Waipi'o Valley (p152)

GREG VAUGHN/GETTY IMAGES ©

Eventually, entrepreneurial farmers diversified their crops and found success with niche edibles, such as mushrooms, tomatoes and lettuces, sold at farmers markets and prized by gourmet chefs.

You can catch Hele-On Bus (p96) to Honoka'a from Hilo or from Kailua-Kona, but service is infrequent. In and around town, you'll definitely need a car.

Sights

The following farms are located in pastoral **Pa'auilo** and **Ahualoa**, on the *mauka* (inland) side of the highway. All are small, family-run working farms, so you must book ahead for tours.

Hawaiian Vanilla Company Farm

(☎776-1771; www.hawaiianvanilla.com; Pa'auilo; tasting $25, afternoon tea $29, lunch per adult/child under 12yr $39/19; ⊙tasting 10:30am Mon-Fri, afternoon tea 3pm Sat, lunch 12:30pm Mon-Fri) The first commercial vanilla operation in the USA, this family-run farm is a model for successful agritourism. All of the edible tours are decently priced and worth your time. If time is short, stop by the **gift shop** (⊙10am-5pm) for vanilla-infused coffee, tea, bath and body products, and of course prime beans and extracts.

Mauna Kea Tea Farm

(☎775-1171; www.maunakeatea.com; 46-3870 Old Mamalahoa Hwy, Ahualoa; 60-90min tours per 2/3/4 or more people $30/25/20) If you're into tea, organic farming and philosophical inquiry, arrange a tour at this small-scale, family-run plantation. Its green and oolong teas are intended to represent the inherent 'flavor' of the land, not artificial fertilizers.

Hamakua Coast

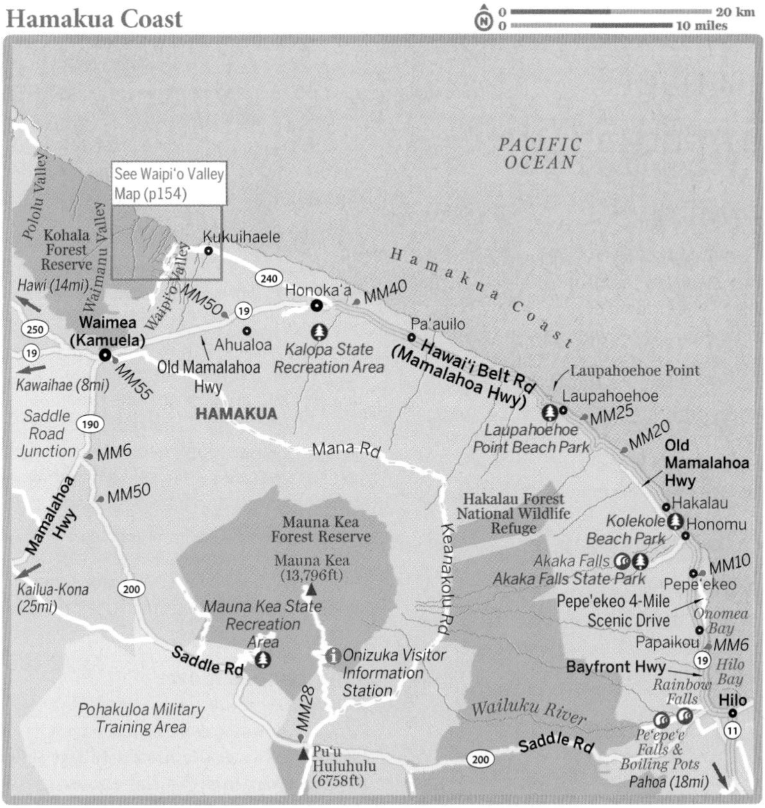

You can also meet the farmers at the Waimea Homestead Farmers Market (p127) on Saturday mornings.

Long Ears Coffee Farm

(☎775-0385; www.longearscoffee.com; tours $35) Try unique three-year 'aged' Hamakua coffee at this family farm. Wendell and Irmanetta Branco process their own and other Hamakua farms' beans, creating a sustainable agricultural economy for farmers here. On tour, you'll see the entire process: growing trees, harvesting cherry, pulping, drying, husking and roasting. Directions to the farm are given upon booking a tour.

Motta Ceramics Studio

(☎775-0856; http://gordonmotta.com; 46-4030 Pu'aono Rd) FREE After four decades as a potter, Gordon Motta knows a few things about throwing clay on the wheel. He also offers a free tour of his ceramics studio, stocked with high-quality porcelain stoneware at all stages of production, including finished gift items. Call for reservations.

NHERC Heritage Center Museum

(☎775-8890; http://hilo.hawaii.edu/academics/nherc/heritagecenter.php; 45-539 Plumeria St; ⏲9am-4pm Mon-Fri, to 1pm Sat) FREE Honoka'a will make a lot more sense if you visit here. Sponsored by the Northern Hawai'i Education and Research Center, it's mainly a large photo collection documenting the plantation era and its demise, but each picture speaks a thousand words.

From the main intersection downtown, follow Plumeria St uphill, turning right on Lehua St.

The Best... Hamakua Farm Agri-Tours

1 Hawaiian Vanilla Company (p148)
2 Hamakua Mushrooms (p159)
3 Mauna Kea Tea (p148)
4 Onomea Tea Company (p163)
5 Long Ears Coffee (p149)

Festivals & Events

Honoka'a Western Week Rodeo
(**Mamane St**) FREE In late May, sleepy Mamane St saddles up with a block party, parade, foot-stomping music and a rodeo.

Sleeping

Your best options lie just outside Honoka'a town, in misty upcountry Ahualoa and Pa'auilo pastureland. If money's not an issue, consider Kukuihaele and its incomparable views of Waipi'o Valley.

Keolamauloa Vacation Rental $$
(**776-1294; www.keolamauloa.com; 43-1962 Pa'auilo Mauka Rd, Pa'auilo; house per 2/3/4 people $100/125/150;**) This well-tended family homestead in Pa'auilo offers a modern homestay. The comfy two-bedroom house includes full kitchen, laundry facilities and access to the grounds: koa and fruit trees, vegetable gardens, pond and livestock. Guests are encouraged to participate in farm life. Discounts for long stays; surcharge for under four nights; plus there's a cleaning fee.

Waipi'o Wayside B&B B&B $$
(**800-833-8849, 775-0275; www.waipiowayside.com; Hwy 240; r incl breakfast $110-180;**) Loaded with character, this attractively furnished 1932 plantation house is a classic B&B, complete with welcoming host and sociable homemade breakfast. The five rooms differ markedly, but each enjoys designer touches, such as iron-bed frames, a wooden Chinese barber chair, shower skylight and hardwood floors.

Common areas include a living room with books and a large-screen TV (with DVDs), plus a spacious, secluded lanai. Located about 2 miles north of Honoka'a on Hwy 240.

Mountain Meadow Ranch Vacation Rental $$
(**775-9376; www.mountainmeadowranch.com; 46-3895 Kapuna Rd, Ahualoa; cottage $150, ste incl breakfast $115;**) This equestrian ranch on 7 acres offers a peaceful two-bedroom cottage that sleeps four and includes full kitchen, wood stove and washer/dryer. The B&B suite, attached to the main house, is ideal for two and, though lacking a kitchen, has a microwave, small fridge, and soothing dry sauna.

Waianuhea B&B B&B $$$
(**775-1118, 888-775-2577; www.waianuhea.com; 45-3503 Kahana Dr, Ahualoa; r $225-350, ste $400, incl breakfast;**) This striking inn combines eco thinking (solar power) with fine art and design (Tiffany lamps, Philippe Starck chairs, bright skylights and gleaming hardwood floors). Here, you get excellent hotel professionalism in rural solitude, but the vibe is strangely detached. Gourmet dinners (per person $58 to $68) are served on-site with 48 hours' notice.

Island Insights

The only Native Hawaiian governor in the history of the USA, John D Waihee III (served 1986–94), hails from Honoka'a.

Eating

Much of Honoka'a is closed on Sundays and possibly Mondays, too.

Tex Drive-In Bakery, Local $
(☎808-775-0598; www.texdriveinhawaii.com; Hwy 19; mains $5-10; ⏱6:30am-8pm) A *malasada* is just a doughnut, but Tex is famous for serving them hot and fresh. They come plain (96¢) or filled (add 35¢). Tex also serves decent plate lunches and *loco mocos* (rice, fried egg and hamburger patty topped with gravy or other condiments), with fish options and seasonal taro burgers.

Simply Natural Cafe $
(☎775-0119; 45-3625 Mamane St, Honoka'a; dishes $5-12; ⏱9am-3pm Mon-Sat, 11am-3pm Sun; 📶) A cozy go-to spot for wholesome eats, from taro pancakes to an open-faced spicy tuna melt. Kiddie menu and biodegradable takeout containers add to the appeal.

Honoka'a People's Theatre Cafe Cafe $
(☎775-9963; www.honokaapeople.com; 45-3574 Mamane St, Honoka'a; espresso drinks $2.50-4.50, sandwiches $5.50-8; ⏱7am-7:30pm Tue-Sun) In the theatre lobby, this friendly cafe serves espresso drinks, sandwiches and other light meals. A cozy hangout with counter or table seating.

Honoka'a Farmers Market Market $
(Mamane St, Honoka'a; ⏱7:30am-noon Sat) A small gathering, with fresh produce, directly from the farmers. Located in front of Honoka'a Trading Company.

Café il Mondo Italian $$
(☎775-7711; www.cafeilmondo.com; 45-3626a Mamane St, Honoka'a; pizzas $12-24; ⏱11am-8pm Mon-Sat) Honoka'a's gathering place specializes in pizzas, pastas and enormous calzones packed to bursting point. Sit at the convivial central table and mingle with locals. Bring your own wine and don't hesitate to share it.

Ahualoa Pastoral

For a peaceful meander, turn off Hwy 19 onto the Old Mamalahoa Hwy, just west of the Mile 52 marker. (Coming from Hilo, turn left at the Mile 43 marker opposite Tex Drive-In and then take the next immediate right.) This 10-mile detour winds through hill country, with small roadside ranches, old wooden fences and grazing horses. Take it slow, snap some pictures and get a taste of old-time Waimea. It's even more picturesque by bike.

Entertainment

Honoka'a People's Theatre Theater
(☎775-0000; www.honokaapeople.com; 45-3574 Mamane St, Honoka'a; movie tickets adult/child/senior $6/3/4; ⏱showings 5pm & 7pm Tue-Sun) In a historic building dating from 1930, this theater shows movies and hosts special events.

Shopping

Honoka'a Trading Company Antiques
(Mamane St, Honoka'a; ⏱10:30am-5pm) If a couple of Honoka'a aunties emptied their attics, basements and garages, it would look like this hangar-sized store. Weave through a worthy collection of vintage aloha wear, antiques, used books (great Hawaiiana selection), rattan and koa furniture, and real Hawaiian artifacts. Then talk story with the owner, quite a character herself.

Big Island Grown Gifts
(☎775-9777; bigislandgrown@hotmail.com; 45-3626 Mamane St, Honoka'a; ⏱9am-5pm Mon-Sat) Support local! This store carries an assortment of Big Island items, including bamboo T-shirts, koa jewelry, coffee and tea and natural soap (made by unforgettably named island brand Filthy Farmgirl).

Taro Patch Gifts
(Mamane St, Honoka'a; 9am-5pm) With a little of everything, this welcoming shop is a one-stop for souvenirs, from colorful ceramic dishes and breezy island apparel to Waipi'o Valley mouse pads and organic soaps. The shopkeeper's organic macadamia nuts, roasted in shell, are awesome.

Waipi'o Valley

At the end of the road on Hwy 240, you'll be blown away by the sight of Waipi'o Valley, the largest of seven spectacular amphitheater valleys descending from the Kohala Mountains. The valley goes back 6 miles, an emerald patchwork of forest and taro, where waterfalls plunge earthward from 2000ft vertical *pali* (cliffs). A river runs through it all, into a black-sand beach. Few sites rival sacred Waipi'o for dramatic beauty.

For 'stop and click' tourists, the scenic lookout is the final destination. To enter the valley, check out our two hiking options and talk to the ranger at the **information booth** (**8am-dusk**).

HISTORY

Known as the Valley of the Kings, Waipi'o was the island's ancient breadbasket and also the political and religious center, home to the highest *ali'i* (ruling chiefs). According to oral histories, several thousand people lived here before Westerners arrived, and the remains of heiau (temples) can be seen today. In 1823 William Ellis, the first missionary to descend into Waipi'o, estimated the population to be around 1300. In the 1880s Chinese immigrants began to settle in the valley's green folds, adding rice to the native taro cultivation.

In 1946 Hawai'i's most devastating tsunami struck the valley, traveling over a mile inland. Interestingly, no one perished despite the massive flooding. Once the waters receded, however, most people resettled 'topside' in Kukuihaele. The valley floor has been sparsely populated ever since, attracting only a few dozen nature lovers, recluses, pot farmers,

Waterford Public Library
860-444-5805
www.waterfordpubliclibrary.org

Title: Fodor's 2016 Hawaii
Author: Anderson, Karen,
Item ID: 31255005158509
Date due: 1/10/2019,23:59

Title: Discover Hawai'i, the big island : experience the
Author: Benson, Sara,
Item ID: 31255005113355
Date due: 1/10/2019,23:59

Our annual fund drive
is underway.
Please give if you can.

Left: Cliffs of Waipi'o Valley; **Below:** Waipi'o Wayside B&B (p150), Honoka'a
(LEFT) TAN YILMAZ/GETTY IMAGES ©; (BELOW) LONELY PLANET/GETTY IMAGES ©

hippies and *kama'aina* (people born and raised in Hawaii; literally, 'child of the land') seeking to reclaim their history.

Taro cultivation and poi production are building blocks of Hawaiian identity, and both valley residents and Native Hawaiians across the island fiercely guard Waipi'o Valley. It is strongly advised that you stick to established trails and avoid trespassing on private property if you enter the valley.

Sights & Activities

In addition to hiking, experienced sea kayakers can arrange custom tours with Plenty Pupule (p81) in Kona. Waipi'o Beach isn't swimmable, however, due to rip currents and treacherous undertow.

Hiking Etiquette in Waipi'o Valley

The first rule of backpacking etiquette is to leave no trace. This is critical in pristine, sacred places such as Waipi'o Valley. Inexcusably, some stick their garbage into crevices in the lava-rock walls surrounding the campsites. This attracts roaches and other pests. Some even abandon unneeded gear in the valley: tents, mattress pads, beach chairs, reef shoes, rope, canned goods, you name it. Carry out what you carry in.

Waipi'o Valley

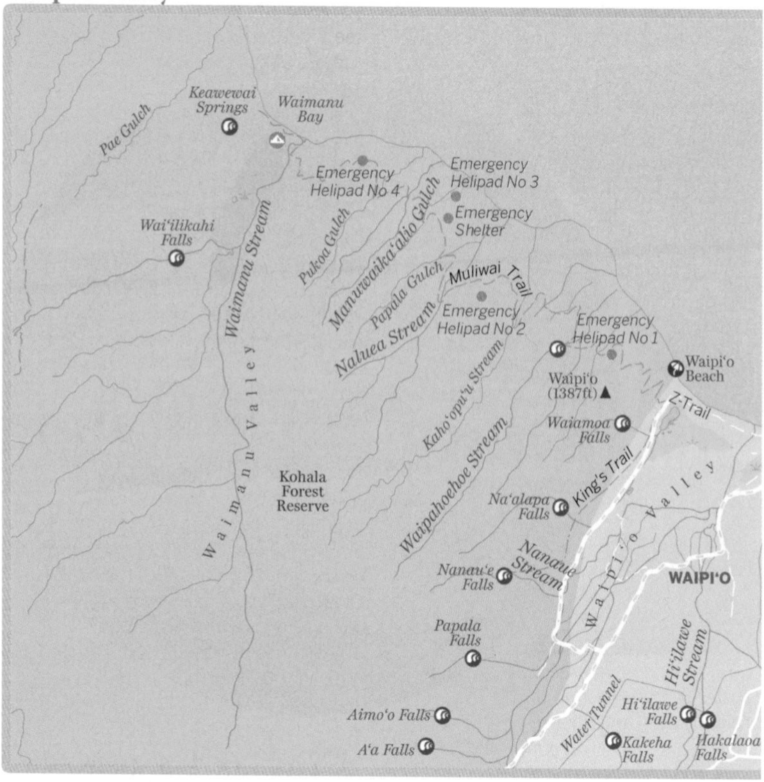

Waipi'o Valley Lookout Lookout
Located at the end of Hwy 240, this lookout provides a jaw-dropping view across the valley. One of Hawaii's iconic images.

Waipi'o Valley Hike Hiking
To reach the valley floor, you must walk or drive the incredibly steep road from the lookout. The road leads to Waipi'o Beach, and to explore further, the adventurous can follow the King's Trail to Nanau'e Falls.

Don't underestimate the steep road. If by car, you must have 4WD and use your gears for braking. Do not attempt it otherwise, as the road has a 25% grade and ends in a rutted mess that's even worse when wet. The trip takes about 15 minutes one way. If you hike down (allow for 30 minutes down, 45 minutes up), wear fitted shoes, as the decline will jam your toes. There's no shade or potable water.

Once on the valley floor, follow the road to **Waipi'o Beach**, passing the twisted remains of vehicles here to stay. There are bathrooms near the beginning of the black-sand beach. Don't even think of swimming here, even if you see local surfers paddling out. Midway down you'll have to cross **Waipi'o Stream**, which flows into the sea; best to do so by wading in the ocean, where there are no rocks. If there has been rain, you can see **Kaluahine Falls** cascading down the cliffs from whence you came. High surf makes getting to the falls more challenging than it looks. Ahead you'll see the Muliwai Trail zig-zagging up the cliffs on the other side of the valley, on its way to distant Waimanu.

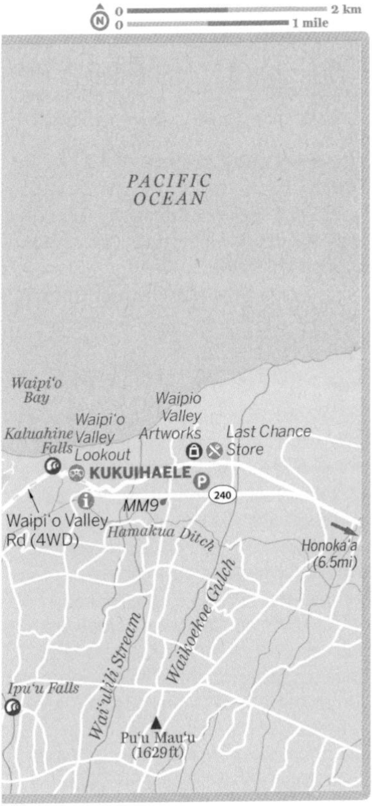

Once you cross to the base of the cliffs, you will see a trail that heads inland, next to a gate. The trail soon forks, with the Muliwai Trail heading upwards, and the **King's Trail** further inland, along a fence. As it parallels the valley walls the King's Trail passes through a natural botanical garden featuring coffee, *liliko'i* (passion fruit), monkeypods, papaya, elephant ear, avocado, and lots more. You might see friendly wild horses, descendents of domesticated animals left behind after the tsunami.

After a mile or so you'll reach a wire fence (passable on this public trail) and shortly thereafter **Nanau'e Falls**.

Muliwai Trail — Hiking

For expert trekkers only, this 8-mile back-country trail goes from Waipi'o Valley to Waimanu Valley, traversing steep, slippery and potentially treacherous ground. It takes 6½ to eight hours one way and requires crossing 13 gulches – brutal to ascend and descend, but lovely nonetheless, with little waterfalls and icy cold pools for swimming. Plan on camping in Waimanu Valley for at least one night. Don't attempt this hike during or after rains.

For detailed hiking information, contact **Na Ala Hele (☎974-4382; http://hawaiitrails.ehawaii.gov)** Trail and Access Specialist Clement Change in Hilo. Following is a general description of the hike.

To get to the Muliwai trailhead, you must first hike down into Waipi'o Valley. For overnight parking, your best bet is Waipi'o Valley Artworks (per day $15), a few miles from the Waipi'o Valley Lookout. Hike down into Waipi'o Valley and cross Waipi'o Stream, heading west.

The Muliwai Trail begins at the base of the cliffs on the west side of Waipi'o Valley. It starts by ascending over 1200ft in a mile of killer switchbacks. The hike out to Waimanu Valley is harder than the hike back, and the final 1200ft descent is extremely tricky. The trail is poorly

Island Insights

Kukuihaele means 'light that comes and goes' in Hawaiian, referring to the *huaka'ipo* (night marchers) – torch-bearing ghosts of Hawaiian warriors who pass through Kukuihaele to Waipi'o. As the legend goes, if you look at the night marchers or get in their way, you die. Survival is possible only if one of your ancestors is a marcher – or if you lie face down on the ground.

The Best... Hamakua Souvenirs

1 Big Island Grown (p151)

2 Hawaiian Vanilla Company (p148)

3 Waipi'o Valley Artworks (p157)

4 Woodshop Gallery & Cafe (p162)

maintained and extremely hazardous and partly washed out, with sheer drop-offs into the ocean and no handholds. If the descent is questionable, head back to a previous trail shelter for the night. Throughout, expect mud, mosquitoes, sun exposure and breathtaking views.

GUIDED HIKES & RIDES

Less-experienced hikers should consider exploring Waipi'o backcountry with guides.

Hawaiian Walkways Hiking
(808-457-7759; www.hawaiianwalkways.com; guided hikes adult/child $119/99; tours 9:30am) Go to waterfalls and swimming holes via a private trail.

Walking Waipi'o Hiking
(345-9505; www.walkingwaipio.com; adult/child 7-12yr $120/75; tours 8am Mon-Fri) An uncommon five-hour hiking trip on the valley floor, including swimming, led by a valley resident.

Waipi'o Ridge Stables Horseback Riding
(877-757-1414, 775-1007; www.waipioridgestables.com; rides $85-165; tours 8:45am) Tour the valley rim to the top of Hi'ilawe Falls (2½ hours) or combine with a forest trail ride (five hours), ending with a picnic and waterfall swim. Caters for all abilities.

Na'alapa Stables Horseback Riding
(775-0419; www.naalapastables.com; rides $85; tours 9am & 12:30pm Mon-Sat) Visit the valley on a 2½-hour horseback ride; children eight and over are welcome. Caters for all abilities.

Waipi'o Valley Wagon Tours Wagon Ride
(775-9518; www.waipiovalleywagontours.com; adult/child $60/30; tours 10:30am, 12:30pm & 2:30pm Mon-Sat) This 1½-hour jaunt in a mule-drawn wagon carts visitors around the valley floor.

Sleeping

Backcountry camping in Waimanu Valley requires a state permit from the **Division of Forestry & Wildlife** (974-4221; http://camping.ehawaii.gov; 19 E Kawili St, Hilo, HI 96720; fee per night nonresident/resident $18/12; 8am-4:30pm Mon-Fri) for a maximum of six nights. There are nine campsites (No 2, No 6 and No 9 are recommended) and facilities include fire pits and composting outhouses. For water, there's a spring about 10 minutes behind campsite No 9; all water must be treated.

Except for the yurt, there are no accommodations on the Waipi'o Valley floor. But there are excellent options in Kukuihaele, the residential community on the rim of the valley, including cliffside properties with spectacular views.

Waipi'o Valley Yurt Vacation Rental $
(345-9505; www.walkingwaipio.com; Waipi'o Valley; yurt per night/week $75/450) This off-the-grid, 14ft yurt by Waipi'o Stream is a unique opportunity to stay in the valley. It includes a kitchen with propane fridge and gas stove, plus a hot shower. The bed sleeps two but the kitchen/living area can accommodate more.

Waipio Rim B&B B&B $$$
(775-1727; www.waipiorim.com; studio $200) Get away from it all at this handsome studio, gloriously perched on a cliff near the lookout. From the private deck, all-around windows keep the fabulous view in sight. Microwave, refrigerator, fifth night free.

Cliff House Hawaii Vacation Rental **$$$**

(☎800-492-4746, 775-0005; www.cliffhousehawaii.com; Waipi'o Rd; 2br house $199, each additional person $35; @) Set on sprawling acres of pastureland, this house assures privacy and space. It's well equipped with two bedrooms, full kitchen, living and dining rooms, wrap-around lanai, satellite TV, washer/dryer and even a telescope for whale-watching. The same parcel contains the less dramatic but still beautifully situated **Hawaii Oceanview House** (☎775-9098; www.hawaiioceanviewhouse.com; 2-br house $165, each additional person $35). Minimum two-night stay.

Shopping

Waipi'o Valley Artworks Arts & Crafts

(☎800-492-4746, 775-7157, 775-0958; www.waipiovalleyartworks.com; ⏲8am-5pm) This inviting little shop wears many hats: stop for ice cream, sandwiches and snacks; browse the koa wood furniture, bowls and other crafts. It's also the best place to park your car overnight, if camping in Waimanu Valley (per day $15).

Kalopa State Recreation Area

Don't miss this idyllic 100-acre **state park** (www.hawaiistateparks.org/parks/hawaii/index.cfm?park_id=45; ⏲daylight hrs) FREE, with camping (first left as you enter), cabins (second left) and various gentle trails. Set in a quiet, native forest at 2000ft, it's fantastically lush and a great place for beginner or family camping. Group cabins (eight people max) have bunk beds, linens and blankets, plus hot showers and a fully equipped kitchen. **Permits** (residents/nonresident $60/90) are required.

The park comprises two overall trail systems (see the large map near the cabins). The first trail system starts where the road by the cabins ends. The easy 0.75mi **Nature Trail** passes through old ohia forest, where some trees measure over 3ft in diameter. The path can be overgrown so watch for the established trail. Skip the **Dryland Forest Trail**, which only goes 100 yards, and the **Arboretum Trail**, which is so overgrown that you might get lost. A small **Polynesian Garden** contains a dozen of the original 25 canoe plants, introduced to Hawaii by the original Polynesian voyagers for food, medicine and clothing.

The second, more-interesting, trail system leads into the adjoining forest reserve with old-growth forest and tremendous tree ferns. It starts along Robusta Lane, on the left between the caretaker's house and the campground, and goes about 600yd to the edge of Kalopa Gulch, through a thick eucalyptus

Muliwai Trail (p155)

JAMES OSMOND/ALAMY©

The Best...
Hamakua Coast for Kids

1 See Waipi'o Valley by horseback (p156)

2 Eat Tex Drive-In (p151) *malasadas* (doughnuts) with abandon

3 Stay on a family farm at Keolamauloa (p150)

4 Go ziplining

5 Go retro at the Back to the 50s Highway Fountain Diner (p160)

forest. The trail continues along the gulch rim for another mile, while several side trails branch off and loop back into the recreation area via the **Perimeter Trail**. Signage is confusing so you should sketch the map near the cabins for reference along the way. You can go over 4 miles on these scenic but spottily maintained trails.

To get here, turn *mauka* off the Hawai'i Belt Rd near the Mile 42 marker, at Kalopa Dr. Follow park signs for 3 miles.

Laupahoehoe

Laupahoehoe had its heyday when sugar was king, but it remains a solid village community with a pleasant beach park and a handful of attractions.

On April 1, 1946, tragedy hit the small plantation town when a tsunami 30ft-high wiped out the schoolhouse on the point, killing 20 children and four adults. After the tsunami the whole town moved uphill.

In February, the **Laupahoehoe Music Festival** (Laupahoehoe Point Beach Park; admission $10; 9am-5pm) comes to the beach park to raise scholarship money for local students. There's good eating, quality hula and tunes by favorite local musicians.

Laupahoehoe peninsula

PETER FRENCH/ALAMY©

Hamakua Ziplines

Ziplines are being strung all over Hamakua's rainforests and waterfalls. Which course is best for you?

Skyline EcoAdventures Akaka Falls (888-878-8400; www.zipline.com; 28-1710 Honomu Rd; $170; tours 10am-3pm) Skyline has the single best zip and it's a jaw dropper. The seven zips on this course get progressively longer and higher until you whoosh directly over a 250ft waterfall on a 3350ft ride! Weight 80lb to 260lb, ages 10 and up.

Umauma Falls & Zipline Experience (930-9477; http://umaumaexperience.com; 31-313 Old Mamalahoa Hwy; $189; tours 8am-3pm) The most consistently thrilling. None of its nine zips has the grandeur of Skyline's magnificent climax, but there are no bunny-slope lines and you'll see 18 waterfalls. Weight 35lb to 275lb, ages four and up.

Zip Isle Zipline Adventures (888-947-4753, 963-5427; www.zipisle.com; $147; tours between 9am-3:30pm) A good choice for kids and anxious first-timers. There are seven gentle zips, including a dual line, and a 150ft suspension bridge. Located at World Botanical Gardens, which you can enter for free. Weight 70lb to 270lb.

For other ziplines, see Kapa'au in North Kohala (p116).

Beaches

Laupahoehoe Point Beach Park — Beach

Only real crazy *buggahs* would swim at windy, rugged Laupahoehoe, where the fierce surf sometimes crashes over the rocks and onto the parking lot. But it's strikingly pretty, with a scenic breakwater and fingers of lava rock jutting out of the waves. It's popular with local families for picnics and camping (full facilities available).

Stop here to view the memorial for the 24 students and teachers who died in the 1946 tsunami. The school stood around the colossal banyan tree toward your right as you approach the park.

Sights

The 1.5-mile **scenic drive** to the point winds through a dense tropical jungle and longstanding plantation houses.

Hamakua Mushrooms — Farm

(962-0305; www.hamakuamushrooms.com; 36-221 Manowaiopae Homestead Rd; 70min tours per adult/child 3-11yr/senior $20/10/ 17.50; Tours 9:30am, 11am & 1:30pm Tue, Wed & Fri, 1:30pm Mon & Thu) A hugely successful boutique crop, Hamakua Mushrooms is favored by top chefs statewide. Its specialty mushrooms are cultivated in bottles and are immediately recognizable, especially the hefty Ali'i Oyster. The husband-and-wife owners give informative guided tours with a personal touch, including sauteéd samples. Their passion for mushrooms is contagious.

Laupahoehoe Train Museum — Museum

(962-6300; www.thetrainmuseum.com; 36-2377 Mamalahoa Hwy; adult/senior/student $6/5/3; 9am-4:30pm Tue-Fri, 10am-2pm Sat & Sun; P) This unassuming little museum is brimming with fascinating artifacts and photographs of the plantation railroad era, all contained in an old station agent's house. Don't miss the video of the long-gone coastal train, which showcases the amazing bridges that once curved along (and across) Hamakua gulches, until demolished by tsunami. Located between the Mile 25 and 26 markers.

The Best... Hamakua Green Oases

1 Waipi'o Valley (p152)

2 Hawaii Tropical Botanical Garden (p162)

3 Pepe'ekeo 4-Mile Scenic Drive (p163)

4 Akaka Falls State Park (p161)

5 Kalopa State Recreation Area (p157)

6 Scenic drive to Laupahoehoe Point Beach Park (p159)

Sleeping & Eating

Old Jodo Temple B&B **$$**

(**962-6967; www.vrbo.com/236574; r per night/week $150/950;**) This historic Buddhist temple (c 1899) is a gem hidden in the tropical valley near Laupahoehoe Point. Nicely restored by the owner-hosts, it's simple, retro and downright charming. Downstairs, the B&B area has two large bedrooms (sleeps up to seven), spacious living and dining rooms, airy porches and full kitchen.

For an additional charge, you could rent the entire house, which includes a large yoga space (formerly the temple), bedroom and bathroom upstairs. Washer and dryer available. Directions to the B&B are given upon booking.

Back to the 50s Highway Fountain Diner Diner **$**

(**962-0808; 35-2704 Mamalahoa Hwy; burgers $4-7, plates $8-10; 8am-7pm Wed & Thu, to 8pm Fri & Sat, to 3pm Sun**) Nostalgia reigns in this wonderful homage to Elvis, Marilyn and the boppin' '50s. Built in a historic plantation house, the old-fashioned counter and booths set the mood for burgers (made with local beef) and shakes. The menu has island favorites including fried *ono* (wahoo) filets with mashed potatoes, chili bowls, and pancake and egg breakfasts.

Hakalau & Around

It's a stretch to call Hakalau a 'town,' but it's home to an active residential community of old-timers and newcomers. There are no restaurants here, but stock up on homemade taro chips and other snacks at **Aaron's Blue Kalo** (**963-6929; 29-2110 Hwy 19; chips per bag $5-10; 9:30am-2pm Mon, Wed & Fri**).

Beaches

Kolekole Beach Park Park

Beneath a highway bridge, this park sits alongside Kolekole Stream. It's not a must-see, but there are pretty little waterfalls and full facilities. Daredevil locals surf and bodyboard at the river-mouth, but don't try it; it's rocky and currents are dangerous. Camping is allowed with a county permit, but the narrow area can get crowded and boisterous with picnicking local families.

To get here, turn inland off Hawai'i Belt Rd at the southern end of Kolekole Bridge, about 1300yd south of the Mile 15 marker.

Sights

World Botanical Gardens Gardens

(**963-5427; www.wbgi.com; MM16, Hwy 19; adult/child 5-12yr/teen 13-17yr $13/3/6; 9am-5:30pm**) Under development since 1995, this garden remains a work in progress. It is an admirable effort but plays second fiddle to the Hawaii Tropical Botanical Garden closer to Hilo. To get here from Hwy 19, turn *mauka* (inland) near mile marker 16, at the posted sign.

Sleeping

Akiko's Buddhist Bed & Breakfast B&B, Vacation Rental $

(☎963-6422; www.akikosbnb.com; s/d incl breakfast from $65/75, studio cottage $65-85, 3br house from $150; 📶) Immersed in tropical foliage, this peaceful retreat offers a variety of accommodations. The B&B rooms, with shared bath, are simple and clean, while two off-the-grid studio cottages allow a rare indoor-outdoor experience. For those seeking more space and privacy, the well-kept Hale Aloha house, with full kitchen, three bedrooms and two baths, is a fantastic value.

Most compelling might be owner Akiko Masuda, who invites guests to join morning meditation and coordinates a popular New Year's Eve *mochi* (Japanese rice cake) pounding festival. To get here, turn inland toward Wailea-Hakalau between the Mile 15 and 16 markers.

Honomu

Honomu is a quaint old sugar town that might be forgotten today if it weren't for its proximity to Akaka Falls. Life here remains rural and slow paced, now with retro wooden buildings sprouting shops and eateries.

Sights

Akaka Falls State Park Park

(www.hawaiistateparks.org; Akaka Falls Rd; entry per car/pedestrian $5/1) A worthwhile excursion, this park is visually outstanding and easily accessible. A half-mile paved path loops through enchanting rainforest, stopping at two lookouts. Your first stop, 100ft **Kahuna Falls**, is just a teaser for the truly grand **Akaka Falls**, which plunges 420ft into a deep green pool. Lush foliage includes banyan and monkeypod trees, seasonally blooming heliconia and giant bamboo groves.

To get here, turn onto Hwy 220 between the Mile 13 and 14 markers and then drive 4 miles inland. Cash or credit cards accepted.

Local Knowledge

NAME: AKIKO MASUDA

OCCUPATION: B&B OWNER SINCE 1991, COMMUNITY ORGANIZER, ARTIST, CHILDREN'S BOOK AUTHOR

RESIDENCE: HAKALAU

1 HOW CAN VISITORS HAVE A DEEPER CULTURAL EXPERIENCE HERE?

If you want to delve deeper on your trip, be willing to stay in one place, so staff or neighbors recognize you. Greet them every morning. The key is to develop trust with local people, and that takes time and lots of friendliness.

2 ANY ADVICE FOR VISITORS ON TRIP ITINERARIES?

Stay for a minimum of five days (or ideally two weeks). You can circle the island in a weekend and 'see a lot' but it's the people who make Hawai'i a very special place. Meeting people will change your life. Seeing the island... you might get a few nice pics.

3 ARE THERE RULES ON INTERACTING WITH LOCALS?

Locals are low-key, but appreciate a thoughtful gesture. One of my guests accepted free paddle boarding lessons from a local guy. I told [my guest], 'Don't take that at face value. Figure out a reasonable hourly rate. Then put cash in an envelope with a nice thank-you note.'

4 WHAT ARE SOME OTHER CULTURAL EVENTS WORTH SEEING?

The Merrie Monarch Festival (p177) showcases many cultures: hula is Hawaiian, but dancers have diverse ethnic backgrounds and *halau* (schools) come from Japan and the mainland. I'd also suggest the Waimea Cherry Blossom Heritage Festival (p124) and the King Kamehameha Day (p119) parade in North Kohala.

Sleeping

Palms Cliff House Inn B&B $$$
(**963-6076; www.palmscliffhouse.com; r incl breakfast $299-449;**) As elegant as a fine hotel, this well-run inn is also warm and welcoming. The eight ocean-view rooms are spacious, with upscale furnishings, and guests rave about the full hot breakfasts. Rates are steep, but discounts are often offered.

Eating

Hilo Sharks Coffee Cafe $
(**963-6706; www.hilosharkscoffee.com; sandwiches $6-7; 8am-6pm Mon-Sat, to 4pm Sun;**) This is *the* place to hang out in Honomu: great locally grown coffee, outdoor seating, wi-fi, creative sandwiches, refreshing smoothies, homemade chocolate and attractive prices.

Woodshop Gallery & Cafe Cafe $
(**963-6363; www.woodshopgallery.com; Hwy 220; lunch dishes $6-9; 11am-5:30pm**) From burgers and lemonade to homemade ice cream and espresso, it's all good and served with aloha. Following lunch, browse or splurge on the extraordinary collection of handcrafted bowls, photos and blown glass.

Mr Ed's Bakery Bakery $
(**963-5000; www.mredsbakery.com; Hwy 220; 6am-6pm Mon-Sat, 9am-4pm Sun**) Check out the staggering selection of homemade preserves featuring local fruit (jar $7.50). Pastries are hit or miss; some are cloyingly sweet, but the Portuguese sweet bread is a winner.

Onomea Bay & Around

Pepe'ekeo, Onomea and Papaikou are three plantation villages admired for their gorgeous landscapes and views.

Sights & Activities

Hawaii Tropical Botanical Garden Gardens
(**964-5233; www.hawaiigarden.com; 27-717 Old Mamalahoa Hwy, Papaikou; adult/child $15/5; 9am-4pm**) This is an absolutely fabulous botanical garden, beautifully situated by the ocean and superbly managed. A paved trail meanders through 2000 species of tropical plants set amid streams and waterfalls. Give yourself at least an hour for the walk, which ends at Onomea Bay.

The garden is located halfway along the Pepe'ekeo 4-Mile Scenic Drive. Park and buy your ticket at the yellow building on the *mauka* side of the road.

A guided tour ($5) is offered on Saturday at noon.

Hawaii Tropical Botanical Garden
TOM BENEDICT/GETTY IMAGES ©

Hawaii Plantation Museum Museum

(☎443-7679; http://memoriesofhawaiibigisland.com; 27-246 Old Mamalahoa Hwy; adult/child/senior $8/3/6; ⏲10am-3pm Tue-Sat) Don't miss this well-done museum highlighting Hawai'i's sugar industry, which spanned the mid-1880s to 1996. Museum curator Wayne Subica has single-handedly amassed this collection, which includes plantation tools, memorabilia from 'Mom & Pop' shops, vintage photos and retro signage.

To get here from Hilo, turn left just past the Mile 6 marker on the main highway; from Kona, turn right just past the Mile 8 marker.

Pepe'ekeo 4-Mile Scenic Drive Drive

The gorgeous rainforest jungle along this stretch of the Old Mamalahoa Hwy proves that those annoying showers are worth it. Cruising the narrow road, you cross a series of one-lane bridges spanning little streams and waterfalls, under a tangle of trees.

You can begin the drive from either end, but approaching from the south (Hilo side) involves an easy right turn between the Mile 7 and Mile 8 markers on the main highway.

Onomea Tea Company Farm

(☎964-3283; www.onomeatea.com; 27-604 Alakahi Pl; tasting $25) This 9-acre tea plantation offers tea tastings and tours. It's a small-scale operation, allowing for friendly chatting about tea and its cultivation. Website reservations are required.

Onomea Bay Hike Hiking

For a quick, scenic hike to the bay, take the Na Ala Hele trailhead on the *makai* (seaward) side of the road, along the Pepe'ekeo 4-Mile Scenic Drive. From Hilo, turn onto the scenic drive and go about 1.75 miles; look for a small sign marking the trailhead. Parking is tricky, but there's a small pullover spot just north of the sign.

After a 10-minute hike down a slippery jungle path, you'll come to a finger of lava jutting into the sea. A spur to the right leads to a couple of small waterfalls and a cove. Continuing straight brings you to the diminutive bluffs overlooking the batik blues of Onomea Bay. Hawaiian monk seals have been sighted here.

Eating

What's Shakin' Health Food $

(☎964-3080; smoothies $6; ⏲10am-5pm) Your fondest memory of the Pepe'ekeo 4-Mile Scenic Drive might be this fantastic roadside eatery. Just over a mile from the north end, look for the cheerful yellow cottage, which pumps out fantastic homemade food and killer smoothies (all fruit, no filler).

LYMAN HOUSE
MEMORIAL
The home of
DAVID BELDEN LYMAN
and
SARAH JOINER LYMAN
Missionaries of the
A·B·C·F·M· to the
Hawaiian People
Built in 1839

Hilo

Hilo should have an inferiority complex. It gets less than half of Kailua-Kona's tourists. But the townsfolk know better. Sure, it's rainy. But 130in of annual rainfall guarantees a leafy landscape, where waterfalls gush and every homeowner has a green thumb. Sure, it seems ordinary and familiar (despite its tropical splendor). But Hilo has enough critical mass to be a real community. This ain't no tourist town! Locals will outnumber you wherever you go. Since the 1990s, moneyed outsiders have been noticing this most livable place, boosting real-estate values and somewhat changing its boondocks reputation. But Hilo remains staunch to its plantation-era roots and unpretentious vibe.

Mission House (p169)
JOHN ELK/GETTY IMAGES ©

Hilo Itineraries

One Day

1 Hilo Farmers Market (p181) Time your trip for Wednesday or Saturday, when the market is in full swing. Go early to avoid traffic jams and bring cash for sweet bananas, juicy star fruit and fresh coconut.

2 Rainbow Falls (p173) If you're a waterfall aficionado, go in the morning for an optimal photo op.

3 Pacific Tsunami Museum (p172) It's impossible to understand Hilo's true grit without learning about its two catastrophic 20th-century tsunami. While downtown, stroll through old Hilo town, notable for its retro architecture, indie shops and scenic bay setting. Don't miss the stunning nature photography at Extreme Exposure Fine Art Gallery.

4 Suisan Fish Market (p181) Stop by for an assortment of takeout ahi *poke* (marinated raw fish) and succulent dried marlin.

5 Lili'uokalani Park (p169) Spend a leisurely afternoon picnicking or crossing the quaint bridges and stepping stones, all with a panoramic view of Hilo Bay. Walk across the paved footbridge to Mokuola (Coconut Island), another family favorite.

6 Hilo Bay Cafe (p183) To savor Hawaii Regional Cuisine, Hilo style, try this foodie favorite for dinner.

THIS LEG: 6 MILES

Three Days

❶ **Richardson Ocean Park** (p169) After following the one-day itinerary, next morning, wake early for a beach day. With sunning, swimming and snorkeling options here, there's something for everyone.

❷ **Itsu's Fishing Supplies** (p184) Cool off with a rainbow ice shave from one of Hilo's iconic mom-and-pop shops.

❸ **Kuhio Grille** (p183) Sate your appetite (and your curiosity about Hawaiian food) at this restaurant, known for its '1lb *laulau*' (pork or chicken and salted butterfish, wrapped in taro and *ti* leaves and steamed), *kalua* pork and poi.

❹ **Lyman Museum & Mission House** (p169) History buffs can see a variety of collections, from geology to ancient Hawaiian artifacts to plantation life. Don't miss the guided tour of the Mission House.

❺ **Takenoko Sushi** (p184) Reservations are imperative at this superlative eight-seat sushi bar.

❻ **Hilo Bay** (p168) On your third day, take the opportunity to revisit your favorite beach or park. If you've been itching to try stand up paddle (SUP) surfing – rent a board and launch into the calm waters of the bay.

❼ **Big Island Candies** (p184) Looking for gifts? The signature chocolate-dipped macadamia shortbread cookies are sure to delight.

❽ **'Imiloa Astronomy Center of Hawai'i** (p172) Spend a few hours here, especially if you're heading to the Mauna Kea summit. Catch an awesome planetarium show.

THIS LEG: 15 MILES

Hilo Highlights

❶ **Best Children's Beach: Onekahakaha Beach Park** (p168) Splash in kid-deep waters with lots of newfound playmates.

❷ **Best Picnic Spot: Lili'uokalani Park** (p169) Find a patch of lawn amid serene ponds, towering trees and Japanese bridges.

❸ **Best Local Food: Cafe 100** (p182) For local-style comfort food, join the lineup of locals at this iconic drive-in.

❹ **Best Block Party: Black & White Night** (p177) On the first Friday in November, downtown Hilo comes alive. Monthly 'First Friday' street fairs keep the party going year round.

❺ **Best Bargain Activity: Hilo Municipal Golf Course** (p174) Who cares if there are no seaside holes or resort glamour? This well-kept course is a fantastic value.

Lili'uokalani Park (p169)

Discover Hilo

HISTORY

Since its first Polynesian settlers farmed and fished along the Wailuku River, Hilo has been a lively port town. In the 20th century, it was the trading hub for sugarcane grown in Puna and Hamakua, connecting in both directions with a sprawling railroad, the Hawaii Consolidated Railway.

Back then, townsfolk set up homes and shops along the bay. But after being slammed by two disastrous tsunami in 1946 and 1960, no one wanted to live downtown anymore. Today, you'll find parks, beaches and open space along Kamehameha Ave.

When the sugar industry folded in the 1980s and '90s, Hilo focused its economy on diversified agriculture, the university, retail and, of course, tourism. While downtown Hilo is still the charming heart of town, the go-to retail destinations are the big chain stores (Walmart, Target, Home Depot, etc) south of the airport.

Richardson Ocean Park

LONELY PLANET/GETTY IMAGES ©

Beaches

Except for Honoli'i Beach Park, Hilo's beaches are located in the Keaukaha neighborhood. Here, they're listed as you'd reach them driving out of central Hilo. On weekends, expect jammed parking lots and steady traffic along Kalaniana'ole Ave.

All beach parks listed below have restrooms, showers and picnic areas.

Reeds Bay Beach Park Beach

At the end of Banyan Dr, this calm little cove is ideal for kids or stand up paddleboard (SUP) beginners. While centrally located, within sight of buildings and passing cars, it's a picturesque spot. Warning: a behemoth cruise ship might be docked in the distance.

Onekahakaha Beach Park Beach

Popular with local families, this beach has a broad, shallow, sandy-bottomed pool, protected by a boulder breakwater. The water is only 1ft to 2ft deep in spots, creating the perfect 'baby beach.' An unprotected cove north of the protected pool is deeper but can be hazardous due to pokey *wana* (sea urchins) and rough surf. Lifeguards on weekends and holidays.

James Kealoha Beach Park Beach

(Carlsmith Beach Park) Best for older kids and snorkelers, this county beach is nicknamed 'Four Miles' (the distance between the park and the downtown post office). For swimming and snorkeling, head to the eastern side, which has a deep, protected basin with generally calm, clear water and pockets of white sand. The park's western side is open ocean and much rougher. Locals surf here in winter or net fish. No lifeguards.

Wai'olena and Wai'uli Beach Parks Beach

(Leleiwi Beach) Rocky and ruggedly pretty, these side-by-side beaches (commonly known by their former name, **Leleiwi Beach**) are Hilo's best shore-dive site. You might see turtles, interesting coral growth and a variety of butterfly fish. The water is freezing until you go past the reef, and the entrance is tricky (ask for advice at Nautilus Dive Center). Lifeguards on weekends and holidays.

Richardson Ocean Park Beach

Near the end of Kalaniana'ole Ave, this pocket of black sand is Hilo's best all-round beach. During calm surf, the protected waters are popular for swimming and snorkeling, with frequent sightings of friendly sea turtles (keep your distance, at least 50yd in the water). High surf attracts local bodyboarders. Shaded by lots of coconut trees, the beach also makes a sweet picnic spot. Daily lifeguards.

Honoli'i Beach Park Beach

Less than 2 miles north of downtown Hilo, this protected cove is Hilo's best **surfing** and **bodyboarding** spot. When surf's up, it's jammed with locals and not a place for novices. Don't expect a sandy beach or ideal swimming conditions. It's all about the waves. Daily lifeguards.

From Hilo, take the Bayfront Hwy north; after the Mile 4 marker, turn right onto Nahala St and then left onto Kahoa St. Park on the roadside and walk down to the park.

Sights

Most sights are found in downtown Hilo, where historic early-20th-century buildings overlook the coast, which locals call 'bayfront.' Farther east sits Hilo's landmark dock, Suisan Fish Market, and the Keaukaha beaches.

Lili'uokalani Park Park

Savor Hilo's simple pleasures with a picnic lunch in **Japanese gardens** overlooking the bay. Named for Hawaii's last queen (r 1891–93), the 30-acre county park has manicured lawns, shallow ponds, bamboo groves, arched bridges, pagodas and a teahouse. At sunrise or sunset, join the locals and jog or stroll the perimeter, or simply admire the Mauna Kea view.

While here, cross the paved footbridge to **Mokuola (Coconut Island)**, a tiny island always lively with families, picnicking and swimming. Also adjacent to the park is **Banyan Drive**, Hilo's mini 'hotel row,' best known for the giant banyan trees lining the road. Royalty and celebrities planted the trees in the 1930s, and, if you look closely, you'll find plaques beneath the trees identifying Babe Ruth, Amelia Earhart and Cecil B DeMille.

Lyman Museum & Mission House Museum

(☎808-935-5021; www.lymanmuseum.org; 276 Haili St; adult/child $10/3; ⌚10am-4:30pm Mon-Sat) Compact yet comprehensive, this gem of a museum encompasses the tremendous variety of Hawaii's natural and cultural history. The adjacent Mission House, built by the Reverend David Lyman and his wife, Sarah, in 1839, adds a human element to the hinstorical facts. Well-trained docents give half-hour tours of the house at 11am and 2pm.

Downstairs in the museum, geologic exhibits include fascinating examples of lava rock, minerals and shells. Upstairs, learn about Native Hawaiians, with exhibits on ancient sports, religion and the kapu (taboo) system.

Hilo

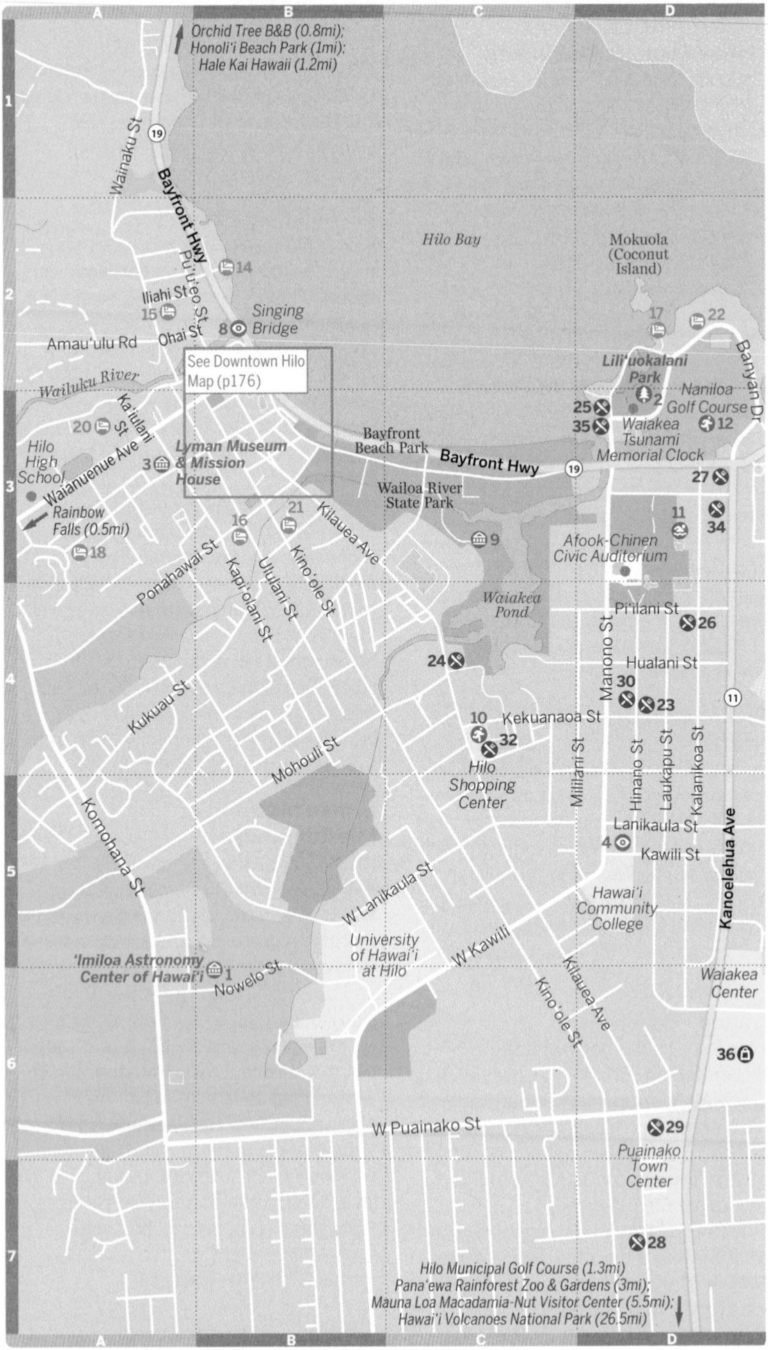
Orchid Tree B&B (0.8mi); Honoli'i Beach Park (1mi); Hale Kai Hawaii (1.2mi)
Hilo Bay
Mokuola (Coconut Island)
Bayfront Hwy
Wainaku St
Pu'u'eo St
Iliahi St
Ohai St
Amau'ulu Rd
Singing Bridge
Wailuku River
See Downtown Hilo Map (p176)
Lili'uokalani Park
Banyan Dr
Naniloa Golf Course
Waiakea Tsunami Memorial Clock
Ka'iulani St
Hilo High School
Waianuenue Ave
Lyman Museum & Mission House
Rainbow Falls (0.5mi)
Bayfront Beach Park
Wailoa River State Park
Kilauea Ave
Afook-Chinen Civic Auditorium
Ponahawai St
Kapi'olani St
Ululani St
Kino'ole St
Waiakea Pond
Pi'ilani St
Manono St
Hualani St
Kukuau St
Kekuanaoa St
Hilo Shopping Center
Mohouli St
Mililani St
Hinano St
Laukapu St
Kalanikoa St
Kanoelehua Ave
Lanikaula St
Kawili St
Komohana St
W Lanikaula St
Hawai'i Community College
University of Hawai'i at Hilo
W Kawili
'Imiloa Astronomy Center of Hawai'i
Nowelo St
Waiakea Center
W Puainako St
Puainako Town Center
Hilo Municipal Golf Course (1.3mi)
Pana'ewa Rainforest Zoo & Gardens (3mi);
Mauna Loa Macadamia-Nut Visitor Center (5.5mi);
Hawai'i Volcanoes National Park (26.5mi)

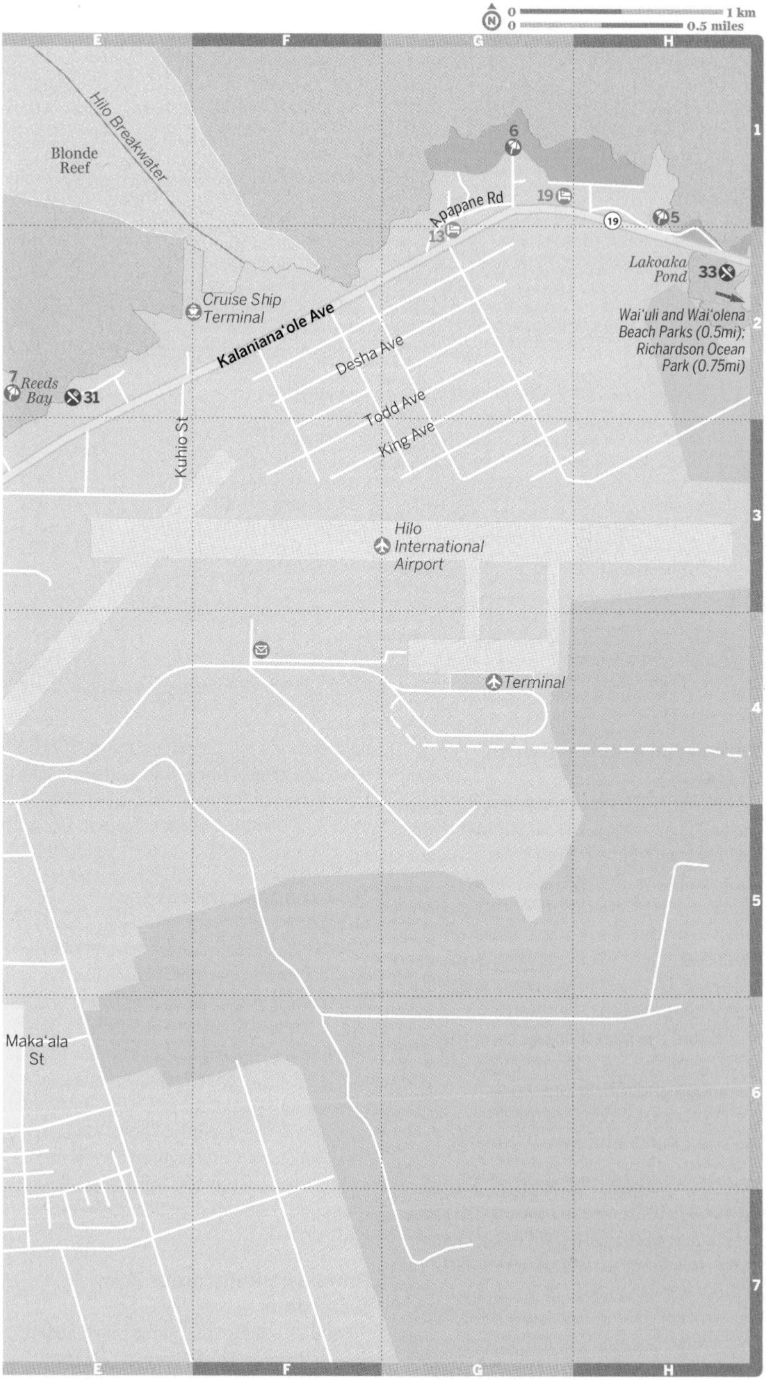

0 1 km
0 0.5 miles
Blonde Reef
Hilo Breakwater
Apapane Rd
6
19
13
5
19
Lakoaka Pond
33
Wai'uli and Wai'olena Beach Parks (0.5mi); Richardson Ocean Park (0.75mi)
Cruise Ship Terminal
Kalaniana'ole Ave
Desha Ave
Todd Ave
King Ave
7
Reeds Bay
31
Kuhio St
Hilo International Airport
Terminal
Maka'ala St

Hilo

'Imiloa Astronomy Center of Hawai'i — Museum

(808-969-9700; www.imiloahawaii.org; 600 'Imiloa Pl; adult/child 6-17yr $17.50/9.50; 9am-5pm Tue-Sun) 'Imiloa, which means 'exploring new knowledge,' is a $28 million museum and planetarium complex with a twist: it juxtaposes modern astronomy on Mauna Kea with ancient Polynesian ocean voyaging. Who would've thought that the mythical *kumulipo* (Hawaiian creation story) and the scientific big bang theory have parallels? It's a worthwhile family attraction and the natural complement to a summit tour. One planetarium show is included with admission.

Pacific Tsunami Museum — Museum

(808-935-0926; www.tsunami.org; 130 Kamehameha Ave; adult/child 6-17yr $8/4; 9am-4:15pm Mon-Sat) You cannot understand Hilo without knowing its history as a two-time tsunami survivor in 1946 and 1960. This seemingly modest museum is chock-full of riveting information, including a new section on the Japanese tsunami of 2011, which damaged Kona. Allow enough time to experience the multimedia exhibits, including chilling computer simulations and heart-wrenching first-person accounts.

Mokupapapa Discovery Center — Museum

(808-935-8358; www.papahanaumokuakea.gov/education/center.html; 76 Kamehameha Ave; check website for opening hours) FREE Did you know the Hawaiian archipelago extends far beyond the eight main islands to the Northwestern Hawaiian Islands, a long chain of uninhabited islets and atolls containing the healthiest coral reefs in the USA? Learn more about the islands' pristine ecosystems at this compelling museum, renovated and relocated in early 2014.

Pana'ewa Rainforest Zoo & Gardens — Zoo

(808-959-9233; www.hilozoo.com; 9am-4pm, petting zoo 1:30-2:30pm Sat) FREE

Four miles south of town, Hilo's sprawling 12-acre zoo is a fantastic freebie. Amid well-kept tropical gardens, see a global collection of monkeys, reptiles, sloths, parrots and more. The star is a white Bengal tiger named Namaste. Two play structures and a shaded picnic area make this a perfect family outing.

To get here, turn *mauka* (inland) off the Volcano Hwy onto W Mamaki St, just past the Mile 4 marker.

Rainbow Falls Landmark

A regular stop for tour buses, the lookout for this 'instant gratification' cascade is just steps from the parking lot. Depending on rainfall, the lovely 80ft waterfall can be a torrent or a trickle. Go in the morning and you'll see rainbows if the sun and mist cooperate. Waianuenue ('rainbow seen in water') is the Hawaiian name for these falls.

To get here, drive up Waianuenue Ave (veer right when it splits into Kaumana Dr) about 1.5 miles from downtown Hilo; follow the signage.

Pe'epe'e Falls & Boiling Pots Waterfall

Two miles past Rainbow Falls, and just as impressive, is another drive-up lookout, Pe'epe'e Falls & Boiling Pots. This unique series of falls cascading into swirling, bubbling pools (or 'boiling pots') might tempt you to hike in, but stay out of the water; currents are treacherous and many drownings have occurred. Restrooms available here.

EHCC Hawai'i Museum of Contemporary Art Art Gallery

(East Hawai'i Cultural Center; ☎808-961-5711; www.ehcc.org; 141 Kalakaua St; suggested donation $2; ⏲10am-4pm Mon-Sat) The best venue for local art is this downtown center, which displays the work of both professionals and amateurs. Exhibits change monthly, while workshops and classes (eg painting, drawing, ukulele and hula) are ongoing. Check the website for special evening concerts featuring top artists.

The Best... Hilo Freebies

1 Pana'ewa Rainforest Zoo & Gardens

2 Mokupapapa Discovery Center

3 Sweet samples at Big Island Candies (p184)

4 EHCC Hawai'i Museum of Contemporary Art

5 Ho'ike show at Merrie Monarch Festival (p177)

Wailoa Center & Wailoa River State Park Art Gallery

(☎808-933-0416; ⏲8:30am-4:30pm Mon, Tue, Thu & Fri, noon-4:30pm Wed) This eclectic, state-run gallery hosts a variety of monthly exhibits. You might find quilts, bonsai, Chinese watercolors or historical photos, all done by locals. Surrounding the center is a quiet state park on the Wailoa River.

The main park landmark is a 14ft, Italian-made bronze statue of Kamehameha the Great, erected in 1997 and restored with gold leaf in 2004. There is also a tsunami memorial and a Vietnam War memorial.

Mauna Loa Macadamia-Nut Visitor Center Factory

(☎808-966-8618, 888-628-6256; www.maunaloa.com; Macadamia Rd; ⏲8:30am-5pm) FREE Hershey-owned Mauna Loa provides a self-guided tour of its working factory, where you can watch the humble mac nut as it moves along the assembly line from cracking to roasting to chocolate dipping and packaging. The gift shop sells the finished product at decent prices.

To get here, follow signage about 5 miles south of Hilo; along the Mile 3 access road, see acres of macadamia trees.

Activities

While Hilo's coast is lined with reefs rather than sand, its gentle waters are ideal for stand up paddle (SUP) surfing; launch from Mokuola (Coconut Island), Reeds Bay or Wailoa River State Park. For surfing, head to Honoli'i Beach Park.

While diving is best on the Kona side, there are decent shore-diving spots in or near Hilo; inquire at dive shops.

Sun & Sea Hawaii Water Sports
(808-934-0902; sunandseahawaii@gmail.com; 244 Kamehameha Ave; SUP half/full day $45/65, 1-/2-tank shore dive $99/$129; 9:30am-5pm Mon-Fri, 9am-4pm Sat, 11am-3pm Sun) This friendly one-stop shop for ocean sports rents SUP packages and sells a variety of snorkeling, diving and swimming gear.

Nautilus Dive Center Diving
(808-935-6939; www.nautilusdivehilo.com; 382 Kamehameha Ave; intro charter dive $85; 9am-5pm Tue-Sat) Hilo's go-to dive shop offers guided dives, PADI certification courses and general advice on shore diving. If you're a certified diver, rent here and head to the best East Hawai'i dive site at Pohoiki Bay in Puna.

Orchidland Surfboards Surfing
(808-935-1533; www.orchidlandsurf.com; 262 Kamehameha Ave; 9am-5pm Mon-Sat, 10am-3pm Sun) Board rentals, surf gear, and advice from owner Stan Lawrence, who opened the Big Island's first surf shop in 1972.

Kawamoto Swim Stadium Swimming
(808-961-8698; 260 Kalanikoa St) FREE For lap swimming, this Olympic-sized, open-air pool is generally uncrowded during the day. Call for opening hours.

Hilo Municipal Golf Course Golf
(808-959-7711; 340 Haihai St; greens fee Mon-Fri $34, Sat & Sun $45) Hilo's main 18-hole course (locally known as 'Muni') offers a well-designed layout, friendly staff and good clubhouse restaurant. Morning tee times are favored by the local contingent;

Left: Onekahakaha Beach Park (p168); **Below:** EHCC Hawai'i Museum of Contemporary Art (p173)

(LEFT) GREG ELMS/GETTY IMAGES ©; (BELOW) LONELY PLANET/GETTY IMAGES ©

call ahead to avoid waiting. While reasonably maintained, expect some weeds and mud, thanks to Hilo rain.

Naniloa Golf Course Golf

(☎808-935-3000; 120 Banyan Dr; greens fee walk/cart $10/15) Despite its scenic location across from Lili'uokalani Park, this nine-hole course is good mainly for practice or for beginners. Grounds maintenance is so-so, but you might have the course to yourself.

Yoga Centered Yoga

(☎808-934-7233; www.yogacentered.com; 37 Waianuenue Ave; drop-in class $14; boutique 10am-5pm Mon-Thu, to 4pm Sun) In an attractive space downtown, this studio offers mostly flow classes and a boutique well stocked with quality mats and clothing.

Balancing Monkey Yoga Center Yoga

(☎633-8555; www.balancingmonkeyyoga.com; 1221 Kilauea Ave; drop-in class $10) Located at Hilo Shopping Center, this friendly studio offers a variety of daily classes.

Festivals & Events

Downtown Hilo hosts an art event on the **first Friday each month**, with live music, refreshments and extended hours at shops and galleries.

May Day Lei Day Festival Hula

(☎808-934-7010; www.leiday.net) Beautiful lei displays, demonstrations, live music and hula throughout the month of May.

King Kamehameha Day Celebration Historic Celebration

(☎808-935-9338; Mokuola/Coconut Island) Celebration of King Kamehameha, with hula, music, food and crafts, on June 11.

Fourth of July Independence Day

Entertainment and food all day at Lili'uokalani Park; fireworks display from Mokuola (Coconut Island).

Downtown Hilo

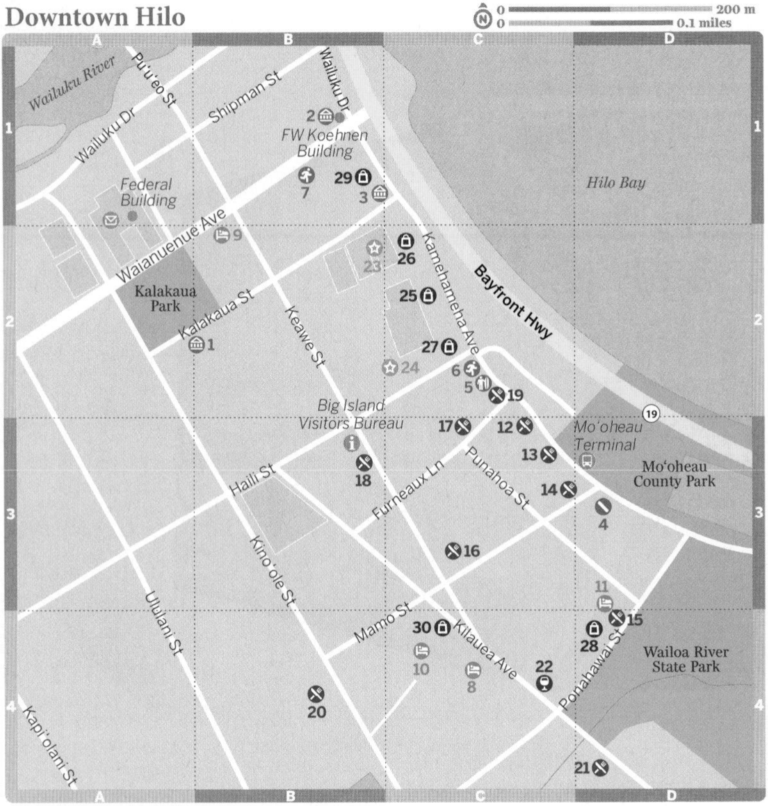

Downtown Hilo

Sights
1 EHCC Hawai'i Museum of Contemporary Art ... B2
2 Mokupapapa Discovery Center ... B1
3 Pacific Tsunami Museum ... B1

Activities, Courses & Tours
4 Nautilus Dive Center ... D3
5 Orchidland Surfboards ... C2
6 Sun & Sea Hawaii ... C2
7 Yoga Centered ... B1

Sleeping
8 D&S Bed & Breakfast ... C4
9 Hilo Bay Hostel ... B2
10 Lotus Garden of Hilo ... C4
11 Pakalana Inn ... D3

Eating
12 Abundant Life Natural Foods ... C3
13 Cafe Pesto ... C3
14 Hilo Farmers Market ... C3
15 Koji's Bento Korner ... D4
16 KTA Super Store – Downtown ... C3
17 Moonstruck Patisserie ... C3
18 Ocean Sushi Deli ... B3
Paul's Place ... (see 11)
19 Puka Puka Kitchen ... C2
20 Short N Sweet ... B4
21 Two Ladies Kitchen ... D4

Drinking & Nightlife
22 Grapes: A Wine Store ... C4

Entertainment
23 Kress Cinemas ... B2
24 Palace Theater ... C2

Shopping
25 Alan's Art & Collectibles ... C2
26 Basically Books ... C2
Dragon Mama ... (see 19)
27 Extreme Exposure Fine Art Gallery ... C2
28 Hilo Guitars & Ukuleles ... D4
29 Sig Zane Designs ... B1
30 Still Life Books ... C4

Championship Hula

The **Merrie Monarch Festival** (**935-9168; www.merriemonarchfestival.org; Afook-Chinen Civic Auditorium; 3-night admission $25-30**) swoops into town around Easter (late March or early April) and turns laid-back Hilo into *the* place to be. Forget about booking a last-minute room! This sellout three-day hula competition was established in 1964 to honor King David Kalakaua (1836–91), who almost single-handedly revived Hawaiian culture and arts, which had been forbidden by missionaries for 70 years.

Top hula troupes from all the Islands vie in *kahiko* (ancient) and *'auana* (modern) categories. *Kahiko* performances are strong and serious, accompanied only by chanting. *'Auana* is closer to the mainstream style, with sinuous arm movements, smiling dancers and melodious accompaniment that includes string instruments. The primal chanting, meticulous choreography and traditional costumes are profoundly moving.

The competitions are televised, but to see it live, order tickets by mail on December 26 (no earlier postmarks accepted); see the website for seating and payment info. The 2700 tickets sell out within a month. Book accommodations and car a year in advance.

Big Island Hawaiian Music Festival Music
(**808-961-5711; www.ehcc.org; 556 Waianuenue Ave, Hilo High School; adult/child $10/free**) A mid-July, two-day concert featuring virtuoso musicians in ukulele, steel guitar, slack key guitar and falsetto singing.

International Festival of the Pacific Japanese Culture
(**934-0177; Japanese Chamber of Commerce, 400 Hualani St**) FREE August celebration of the Japanese in Hawaii, featuring a lantern parade and Japanese tea ceremony at Lili'uokalani Park.

Hawai'i County Fair Fair
(**799 Pi'ilani St, Afook-Chinen Civic Auditorium; adult/student $3/2**) Pure nostalgia comes to town in September, with carnival rides, games and cotton candy.

Black & White Night Fair
(**www.downtownhilo.com; 5-9pm**) Downtown Hilo comes alive on the first Friday of November, with shops and galleries open late, artist and author appearances, and lots of live music.

Sleeping

In true Hilo style, there are few hotels, but the gamut of indie B&Bs, inns, and hostels. Note that many proprietors charge extra for one-night stays.

The Quirky Cottage Inn $
(**(770) 530-8788; www.thequirkycottage.net; 577 Kino'ole St; r $40-80**) Simple, clean, private and affordable. If these are your priorities, this no-frills inn is perfect. The two suites each include private bath and two separate sleeping areas ($80 for up to four guests); one even has a kitchen. The studio ($40), with fridge and microwave, is a budget traveler's dream. Owners Doug and Sue have run a successful B&B and their experience shows.

Lotus Garden of Hilo Vacation Rental $
(**808-936-5212; http://lotusgardenhilo.com; 140 Kilauea Ave; r $79-105, 2br cottage $120, per additional person $15;**) To immerse yourself in Hilo's charm, look no further than these brightly painted buildings. Of the two cottages, the Sugar Shack is available by room (shared kitchen and

bathroom), while the Lotus is rented as a whole. All accommodations are comfortable, reasonably priced and within walking distance of all you need. Friendly owners live on-site.

Hilo Bay Hostel Hostel $
(808-933-2771; www.hawaiihostel.net; 101 Waianuenue Ave; dm with shared bath $27, r with/without bath $77/67;) Perfectly situated downtown, this well-managed hostel occupies an airy, historic building with hardwood floors, remarkably clean restrooms and a kitchen in which you could cook Thanksgiving dinner. The crowd is older and diverse, creating a low-key, relaxed vibe.

Old Hawaiian B&B B&B $
(808-961-2816; www.thebigislandvacation.com; 1492 Wailuku Dr; r incl breakfast $85-125;) Perfect for discriminating budget travelers, these three pleasant rooms include private entrances and tidy furnishings. The Hawaiian Room (sleeps four) and Bamboo Room (sleeps three) offer great value. All open to a backyard lanai, with dining table, microwave and refrigerator. Located about a mile above Rainbow Falls.

Holmes' Sweet Home B&B $
(808-961-9089; www.holmesbandb.com; 107 Koula St; r incl breakfast $90-105;) Mr and Mrs Holmes's comfy B&B will immediately feel like home. The larger Blue Ginger room, with queen and twin beds, is worth the extra $15. Rooms are wheelchair-accessible and open into a common area with refrigerator and microwave. Located about 2.5 miles west of downtown, up Kaumana Dr, off Ainako Ave.

D&S Bed & Breakfast B&B $
(808-934-9585; www.dnsbnb.com; 150 Kilauea St; r $100, ste $125;) Located downtown, this B&B is convivial, casual and family friendly, run by a welcoming young couple. While simple, the rooms include minifridge and dining table and chairs, and they open to a shared patio where breakfast is served.

Uncle Billy's Hilo Bay Hotel Hotel $
(800-442-5841, 935-0861; www.unclebilly.com; 87 Banyan Dr; r $95-124;) Family-owned and operated by three generations, Uncle Billy's is a bargain. Expect a no-frills hotel in a terrific location. Rooms

Koi Room in the Orchid Tree B&B

PAULA BORCHARDT/GETTY IMAGES ©

overlook a courtyard of palms, red ginger and talkative mynah birds – or beautiful Hilo Bay (an ocean view for just over $100 is a steal!).

The hotel runs a convenience store (7am to 9:30pm daily) with a seating area, free wi-fi and powerful air- conditioning.

Arnott's Lodge — Hostel, Campground $

(☎808-969-7097, 808-339-0921; www.arnottslodge.com; 98 Apapane Rd; dm $28, r with/without bath $75/65; wi-fi) Hilo's longest-running hostel remains a solid value, with a variety of lodging options close to beaches. The $75 rooms are especially nice, with private garden views and bathrooms. Fringe benefits, such as free Sunday pizza and beer, add to the free-spirited camaraderie.

Hilo Tropical Gardens Guest House — Hostel, Campground $

(☎808-217-9650; www.hilogardens.com; 1477 Kalaniana'ole Ave; dm $25, d $55-65; wi-fi) Dorm and private rooms are tiny, but spick-and-span, amid a wildly lush setting. Pitch a tent (single/double $15/20) and suddenly you're camping in a jungle (warning: mosquitoes are voracious). Located behind Hilo Homemade Ice Cream store, just past Onekahakaha Beach.

Dolphin Bay Hotel — Hotel $$

(☎877-935-1466, 808-935-1466; www.dolphinbayhotel.com; 333 Iliahi St; studio/1br/2br apt from $119/169/189; wi-fi) This family-run hotel attracts countless loyal, repeat guests. No surprise. The 18 apartment units, each with full kitchen, are clean and conveniently located within a five-minute walk to downtown Hilo. Enjoy free coffee and locally grown fruit for breakfast amid tropical foliage. For longer stays, ask about the one-bedroom apartments in the **Annex** (per day/week/month $119/763/1600) across the street.

Around Hilo

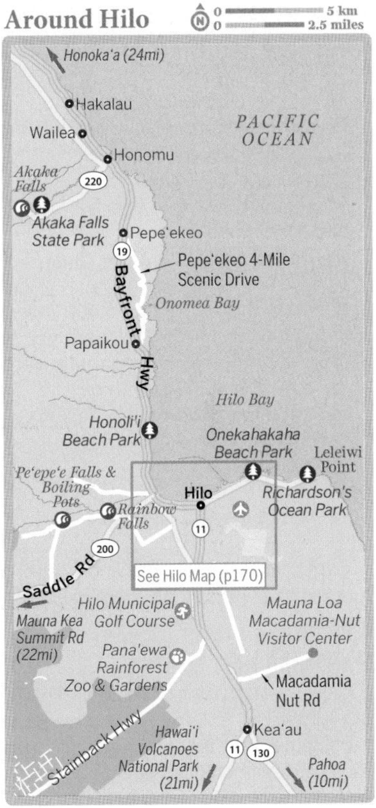

Hilo Bay Hale — B&B $$

(☎808-640-1113, 800-745-5049; www.hilobayhale.com; 301 Ponahawai St; r incl breakfast $139-159; air-con, wi-fi) In a gorgeously restored 1912 plantation home, two main-floor rooms feature private lanai overlooking charming koi ponds, while a ground-floor room boasts more privacy and space. Guests have access to the kitchen and laundry facilities. With two personable hosts, proximity to town and weekly discounts ($99 to $119 per night), you can't go wrong here.

Orchid Tree B&B — B&B $$

(☎808-961-9678; www.orchidtree.net; 6 Makakai Pl; r incl breakfast $150; air-con, wi-fi, pool) A few miles outside Hilo, this perennial favorite combines B&B friendliness with space and privacy. Couples will appreciate the stylish Koi Room with a gleaming hardwood floor and, yes, koi pond outside. The Hula Room is larger, containing two beds plus lounging area with plump, inviting sofas. Breakfast is served ouside in a communal 'surfer shack' patio.

Island Insights

According to Hawaiian legend, young prospective chiefs faced a ritual challenge: could they lift the 3.5-ton **Naha Stone**? The man with enough strength to budge the boulder was destined to reign all of the Hawaiian Islands. Along came teenage boy Kamehameha, who reputedly flipped over the stone (and proceeded to conquer and unite the Hawaiian kingdom). Today the Naha Stone, along with the upright **Pinao Stone**, are landmarks fronting the Hilo Public Library (p186).

To get here from Hilo, head north and turn right just past the Mile 4 marker on Nahala St.

Hilo Honu Inn B&B $$
(808-935-4325; www.hilohonu.com; 465 Haili St; r incl breakfast $140-250; wi-fi) In a lovely retro home, three custom-designed guest rooms accommodate different budgets. A worthy splurge, the Samurai Suite is utterly memorable, with genuine Japanese detailing, plus tatami floor, *furo* (soaking tub), tea room and sweeping (if distant) views of Hilo Bay.

Pakalana Inn Inn $$
(808-935-0709; www.pakalanainn.com; 123 Punahoa St; r $99-129, with kitchenette $149; air-con, wi-fi) With hardwood floors and clean-lined furnishings, this six-unit inn is an oasis just a block from the downtown farmers market. Rooms are average sized, but immaculate and airy, occupying the top floor of a building containing two recommended eateries. No on-site host, so you're on your own.

Hilo Hawaiian Hotel Hotel $$
(808-935-9361, 800-367-5004; www.castleresorts.com; 71 Banyan Dr; r $150-200, ste from $250; air-con, wi-fi, pool) Location, location. Hilo's biggest hotel has a prime oceanfront location, adjacent to Lili'uokalani Park. It's an apt choice for a largish hotel feel, air-conditioning, and round-the-clock staff. Rooms were renovated in 2013. If you can't afford an ocean-view room, head to the lobby cafe for morning coffee, free wi-fi and the spectacular view.

Bay House B&B B&B $$
(808-961-6311, 888-235-8195; www.bayhousehawaii.com; 42 Pukihae St; r incl breakfast $175; wi-fi) Just outside Hilo, across the Singing Bridge over the Wailuku River, find three immaculate guest rooms within sight and sound of the bay. Tastefully tropical themed, with classy hardwood and granite floors, each room includes a private lanai for in-room breakfasts. Rates have creeped up over the years, but this remains a solid choice.

Hale Kai Hawaii B&B $$
(808-935-6330; www.halekaihawaii.com; 111 Honoli'i Pl; r incl breakfast $165-179; wi-fi, pool) Four rooms below the main house enjoy panoramic ocean views and shared lanai. The Pele Suite is the best value, offering more space and kitchenette. Gourmet breakfasts are served on the upper lanai. Kids 13 and older only.

To get here from Hilo, head north and turn right on Pauka'a Dr, between the Mile 4 and Mile 5 markers.

The Inn at Kulaniapia Falls Inn $$
(808-935-6789, 866-935-6789; www.waterfall.net; 1 Kulaniapia Dr; r incl breakfast $189, guesthouse $279; wi-fi) Drive up, up, up 4 miles past acres of macadamia orchards to 850ft above sea level. Your reward? Ten rooms (in two buildings) and a pagoda guesthouse, exquisitely appointed with Asian antiques, in a fantastically verdant setting, complete with waterfall. The unlit road can be tricky at night. All power is hydroelectric.

Shipman House B&B B&B $$$
(808-934-8002; www.hilo-hawaii.com; 131 Ka'iulani St; r incl breakfast $219-249; wi-fi) Staying at the Shipman family's grand Victorian mansion is pricey, albeit peerless in historical significance. Queen Lili'uokalani played the grand piano, while

Jack London slept in the guest cottage. Surrounded by museum-quality antiques, three rooms in the main house are sedate and finely (although not luxuriously) furnished. In a separate cottage, two rooms are more casual and private.

Eating

Hilo Farmers Market Market $
(www.hilofarmersmarket.com; cnr Mamo St & Kamehameha Ave; 6am-4pm Wed & Sat) Hilo's gathering place is its downtown farmers market, which opened in 1988 with four farmers selling from trucks. Today, the market is bustling and attracts sizable crowds. A single pass through the food tent unearths luscious mangoes and papayas, massive avocados, whole coconuts, and bunches of anthuriums. Unfortunately, the produce sold here is not 100% locally grown. Craft tents entice tourists with 'Hawaiian' woodcarvings and shell jewelry, but most are cheap imports.

If you miss Wednesday or Saturday market days, you'll still find a row of daily vendors selling produce and flowers.

Kino'ole Farmers Market Market $
(cnr Kino'ole Ave & Kahaopea St; 7am-noon Sat) Hilo's 'other' farmers market is low-key and attracts mainly locals, with its 100% locally grown and made products sold by the farmers themselves. The 15 to 20 vendors supply all you need, including fresh produce, baked goods, taro chips, poi (steamed, mashed taro), plants and flowers. Parking is plentiful.

Suisan Fish Market Fish $
(808-935-9349; 93 Lihiwai St; poke per pound $13; 8am-5pm Mon-Fri, to 4pm Sat) For a fantastic variety of *poke* (sold by the pound), you can't beat Suisan, where you know the fish is freshly caught. The *shōyu* (soy sauce) ahi and *limu* (seaweed) ahi are tried and true. The takeout *poke* and rice bowl ($5 to $7) is an incredible deal.

Paul's Place Cafe $
(808-280-8646; 132 Punahoa St; mains $8-12; 7am-3pm Tue-Sat) In a three-table dining room, Paul serves absolutely scrumptious renditions of the classics, including

Local Knowledge

NAME: STAN LAWRENCE

OCCUPATION: BUSINESS OWNER AND SURFER, ORCHIDLAND SURFBOARDS

RESIDENCE: HILO

1 WHAT'S THE BEST SURF BREAK IN OR AROUND HILO?

There's only one: Honoli'i (p169). Thanks to the tradewinds, there's always something to ride here. Of course, it's hard to predict when waves will be extra big or small. It's also ideal because there are no *wana* (pokey sea urchins), unlike at Pohoiki (in Puna), which has sharp lava rock and lots of *wana*.

2 WHAT IS SURFING ETIQUETTE?

Give right of way to the next person in line and don't 'drop in.' Check the waves before entering. If you're in doubt, ask a lifeguard. And keep the beach clean. Don't litter.

3 WHAT MAKES THE BIG ISLAND DIFFERENT FOR SURFING AND OTHER WATER SPORTS?

Hawai'i is a young island, five million years younger than Kaua'i. There are fewer sandy beaches and developed reefs, and often the ocean hits against rocky cliffs. It's a more challenging place to surf.

4 WEREN'T THERE MORE SURF BREAKS BEFORE?

This island has changed a lot due to the lava flows: until 1990 there were 20 great surf breaks in Kalapana. That's why I moved to the Big Island in 1971. Suddenly the lava took Kalapana and [the surf breaks] were all gone. Some of the magic was lost. I still love the Big Island, but I miss the waves of Kalapana very much.

5 CAN DOWNTOWN HILO COMPETE WITH THE INFLUX OF CHAIN STORES?

If people, locals and tourists don't support small businesses, they'll someday be gone. At big chains, you don't get the same service.

Belgian waffles, robust salads and eggs Benedict featuring his special sauce. Everything's healthy, with lots of fresh fruit and veggies. If the place is full, wait or try again. You won't regret it.

Cafe 100 Local $

(808-935-8683; 969 Kilauea Ave; loco moco $2-5, plate lunches $5-7; 6:45am-8:30pm Mon-Sat) Locals love this drive-in for its generous plate lunches and 20 rib-sticking varieties of *loco moco* (dish of rice, fried egg and hamburger patty topped with gravy or other condiments), including fish and veggie-burger options. With a clean seating area and efficient service, it's local fast food at its finest.

KTA Super Store Supermarket $

Downtown (808-935-3751; 323 Keawe St, Downtown; 7am-9pm Mon-Sat, to 6pm Sun); **Puainako Town Center** (808-959-9111, pharmacy 808-959-8700; 50 E Puainako St, Puainako Town Center; grocery 5:30am-midnight, pharmacy 8am-7pm Mon-Fri, from 9am Sat) This popular, locally owned chain carries mainstream groceries plus a comprehensive deli with fresh *poke, bento* (Japanese-style box meals) and other ready-to-eat items.

Abundant Life Natural Foods Market $

(808-935-7411; 292 Kamehameha Ave; 8:30am-7pm Mon-Tue Thu-Fri, from 7am Wed & Sat, 10am-5pm Sun) Located downtown, this longtime health-food market has a takeout cafe (shuts down 1½ hours before closing time), serving smoothies and other standbys.

Island Naturals Market $

(808-935-5533; 1221 Kilauea Ave, Hilo Shopping Center; smoothies $3-3.75, deli dishes per lb $7; 8:30am-8pm Mon-Sat, 10am-7pm Sun) This well-stocked health-food store has a gourmet deli.

Grapes: A Wine Store Wine

(808-933-1471; www.grapeshawaii.com; 207 Kilauea Ave; noon-6pm Tue-Sat) This hidden treasure is owned by a true aficionado and packed to the rafters with global stock. Free wine tastings every other Thursday!

Koji's Bento Korner Local $

(808-935-1417; 52 Ponahawai St; loco moco $3.25-7.50; 7am-2pm Mon-Fri, from 9am Sat) The Koji *loco moco* – with two homemade hamburger patties, teriyaki sauce and gravy, one egg, two Portuguese sausages, macaroni salad and kimchee – is the stuff of local cravings.

Ken's House of Pancakes Diner $

(1730 Kamehameha Ave; meals $6-12; 24hr) There's something comforting about a 24-hour diner with a mile-long menu. Choose from macadamia-nut pancakes, Spam omelettes,

Fresh produce at the Hilo Farmers Market (p181)

LUCI YAMAMOTO

slow-cooked *kalua* pig plates and steaming bowls of saimin.

Miyo's Japanese **$$**
(808-935-2273; 681 Manono St; dinner $11-15; 11am-2pm & 5:30-8:30pm Mon-Sat) A longtime local favorite, Miyo's is known for homestyle Japanese meals and nightly crowds. Relocated in 2013, it's now larger, louder, and lacks it's former ambience, but the food is worth it. Try classics such as grilled ahi or *saba* (mackerel), tempura or *tonkatsu* (breaded and fried pork cutlets). Reservations are a must.

Restaurant Miwa Japanese **$$**
(808-961-4454; 1261 Kilauea Ave, Hilo Shopping Center; sushi $5-8, meals $14-25; 11am-2pm & 5-9pm Mon-Sat, 5-9pm Sun) Tucked away in a mall, Miwa is a low-key local favorite for traditional Japanese cuisine, includilng sushi. No surprises here, just satisfying dishes, such as grilled *saba*, teriyaki chicken and *tonkatsu*.

Puka Puka Kitchen Japanese, Mediterranean **$$**
(808-933-2121; 270 Kamehameha Ave; $10-12; 11am-2:30pm) This hole-in-the-wall serves Japanese-style plates, such as sautéed ahi and chicken katsu, but also various pita pockets, including a veg falafel option. Takeout bento boxes sell out well before lunch.

Sombat's Fresh Thai Cuisine Thai **$$**
(808-936-8849; 88 Kanoelehua Ave; dishes $8-16; 10:30am-2pm Mon-Fri & 5-9pm Mon-Sat;) Go here for healthy Thai classics made with local produce, fresh chef-grown herbs and lots of veg options. The restaurant interior is pleasant enough, but located in a deserted commercial building. Ideal for takeout.

Kuhio Grille Diner **$$**
(808-959-2336; www.kuhiogrille.com; 111 E Puainako St, Suite A106, Prince Kuhio Plaza; breakfast $5-10, lunch & dinner $9-20; 6am-10pm Sat-Thu, to midnight Fri) Large appetites will find satisfaction at this no-frills diner specializing in local favorites: taro corned-beef hash, oxtail soup, fried-rice *loco moco* and *laulau* (meat or chicken wrapped in taro leaves and steamed, Hawaiian style). Best suited for meat eaters.

Ocean Sushi Deli Sushi **$$**
(961-6625; 239 Keawe St; 6-piece rolls $3-6, meals $12-14; 10am-2pm & 5:30-9pm Mon-Sat) There's zero decor and hit-or-miss service. But rolls are cheap and creative – for example, combining fresh fish with macadamia nuts or tropical fruit. Not outstanding, but good value.

Hilo Bay Cafe American, Sushi **$$$**
(808-935-4939; www.hilobaycafe.com; 123 Lihiwai St; mains $15-30; 11am-9pm Mon-Thu, to 9:30pm Fri & Sat, 5-9pm Sun) Since 2003, this casually sophisticated eatery has wowed critics and put Hilo on the foodie map. The only drawback was its mall location. Now literally overlooking Hilo Bay, it's got the whole package, including full sushi bar. The eclectic menu features gourmet versions of comfort food, such as Hamakua mushroom pot pie and a local beef burger with garlic-salted fries.

The Best... Hilo for Kids

1 Picnic at Lili'uokalani Park (p169)

2 Cross a footbridge to Mokuola (Coconut Island; p169)

3 Splash around at Onekahakaha Beach Park (p168)

4 Stroll the Pana'ewa Rainforest Zoo & Gardens (p172)

5 Learn about voyaging at 'Imiloa Astronomy Center of Hawai'i (p172)

6 See a $2 movie at Kress Cinemas (p185)

Sweet Stuff

Hilo boasts a superlative lineup of sweets, which Neighbor Islands (and visitors in the know) crave until their next trip.

Big Island Candies (808-935-8890, 800-935-5510; www.bigislandcandies.com; 585 Hinano St; 8:30am-5pm) This immaculate candy factory welcomes visitors with generous samples, fantastic displays and beautifully packaged confections. It's a mecca for locals and Japanese tourists – and for anyone with a sweet tooth.

Moonstruck Patisserie (808-933-6868; www.moonstruckpatisserie.com; 16 Furneaux Ln; pastries & cake slices $4-5; 8:30am-4pm Wed-Sat) One discriminating foodie described Moonstruck's croissants as the best she's *ever* tasted. Judging from the accolades and local buzz, she might be right. Pastry chef Jackie Tan-DeWitt specializes in classic European pastries and unique cakes, cheesecakes and fruit tarts.

Hilo Homemade Ice Cream (808-217-9650; 1477 Kalaniana'ole Ave; scoops $3.50; 11am-6pm) To or from the beach, stop here for locally made flavors that ring true. Try rich macadamia-nut ice cream with zingy *liliko'i* (passion fruit) sorbet.

Itsu's Fishing Supplies (808-935-8082; 810 Pi'ilani St; ice shave $1.50; 8:30am-5pm Mon-Fri) For generations, this family-run shop has delighted kids of all ages with soft-as-snow ice shave (served between 2pm and 5pm). The red, yellow and blue 'rainbow' is a classic.

Two Ladies Kitchen (808-961-4766; 274 Kilauea Ave; 8-piece boxes $6; 10am-5pm Wed-Sat) Founded by two Hilo ladies, this hole-in-the-wall makes addictive island-style Japanese *mochi* (sticky rice dessert).

Short N Sweet (808-935-4446; www.shortnsweet.biz; 374 Kino'ole St; pastries $1.50-5, sandwiches $9; 7am-4:30pm Mon-Fri, 8am-3pm Sat & Sun) Whether you're seeking locally inspired pastries, gourmet focaccia panini, or a wedding cake made to order, this bakery-cafe is sure to please. We dare you to resist the 'homemade Oreo' or anything with tart-sweet *liliko'i*.

Takenoko Sushi Sushi $$$
(808-933-3939; 578 Hinano St; chef's choice $38, nigiri $2.50; 11:30am-11pm) Drop everything and make a reservation at this superb eight-seat sushi bar. Expect top-quality fish (mostly flown fresh from Japan), a spotlessly clean setting, expert sushi chef and gracious service. Each bite is a memorable experience. Three dinner seating times: 5pm, 7pm and 9pm.

Cafe Pesto International $$$
(808-969-6640; www.cafepesto.com; 308 Kamehameha Ave, S Hata Bldg; pizzas $10-20, dinner $18-30; 11am-9pm Sun-Thu, to 10pm Fri & Sat) Cafe Pesto is a safe choice, whether for business lunches or dinner with your mother-in-law. Set downtown in a lovely historic building, the versatile kitchen covers all bases with creative salads, risottos, stir-fries, pastas, seafood and chicken. Don't bother with the pizzas.

Ponds American $$$
(808-934-7663; www.pondshilohi.com; 135 Kalaniana'ole Ave; mains $20-25; 11am-9:30pm Sun-Thu, to midnight Fri & Sat) This steak/seafood/pasta restaurant will suit those hankering for familiar American food with an island twist. A big plus is the airy dining room overlooking 'Ice Pond.' Live music Thursday to Monday.

Queen's Court
American, Local $$$

(808-935-9361, 800-367-5004; www.castleresorts.com; 71 Banyan Dr, Hilo Hawaiian Hotel; breakfast adult/child $17/10, dinner buffet $40; 6:30am-9:30am & 5:30-8pm daily, to 9pm Fri-Sun) This longtime hotel restaurant is known for its all-you-can-eat weekend buffet dinners (seafood on Fridays and Sundays, Hawaiian on Saturdays). The airy dining room offers a spectacular view of Hilo Bay.

Seaside Restaurant
Seafood $$$

(808-935-8825; www.seasiderestaurant.com; 1790 Kalaniana'ole Ave; meals $25-30; 4:30-8:30pm Tue-Thu, to 9pm Fri & Sat) This old-school seafood restaurant specializes in fresh fish, from locally caught mahimahi to pan-sized *aholehole* (flagtail fish) raised in on-site Hawaiian-style fishponds. It's a sit-down restaurant, but the vibe is homey and retro. Portions are generous.

Entertainment

Palace Theater
Theater

(808-934-7010, box office 808-934-7777; www.hilopalace.com; 38 Haili St) This historic theater is Hilo's cultural crown jewel. Its eclectic programming includes art-house and silent films (accompanied by the house organ), music and dance concerts, Broadway musicals and cultural festivals. On Wednesday morning (from 11am to noon) it hosts 'Hawai'iana Live' (adult/child $5/free), a touching, small-town intro to Hawaiian culture through storytelling, film, music, *oli* (chant) and hula.

Kress Cinemas
Cinema

(808-935-6777; 174 Kamehameha Ave; tickets $2) When was the last time you saw a $2 movie? Enter on Kalakaua St.

Stadium Cinemas
Cinema

(808-959-4595; 111 E Puainako St, Prince Kuhio Plaza; tickets adult/child 3-11yr/matinee $9.50/6.25/7.50) Typical shopping mall cinema with the usual Hollywood showings.

The Best... Hilo Souvenirs

1 Aloha wear by Sig Zane (p186)

2 Antique-style map of Hawaii from Basically Books

3 Nature photography from Extreme Exposure Fine Art Gallery

4 Big Island chocolate at Hilo Farmers Market (p181)

5 Handmade ukulele from Hilo Guitars & Ukuleles

Shopping

While locals flock to the chain-heavy **Prince Kuhio Plaza** (808-959-3555; 111 E Puainako St; 10am-8pm Mon-Thu, 10am-9pm Fri & Sat, 10am-6pm Sun) south of the airport, downtown is far better for unique shops.

Basically Books
Books

(160 Kamehameha Ave; 9am-5pm Mon-Sat, 11am-3:30pm Sun) A browser's paradise, this shop specializes in maps, travel guides and books about Hawaii. Good selection for kids, too.

Still Life Books
Books

(808-756-2919; http://stillifebooks.blogspot.com; 134 Kilauea Ave; 11am-3pm Tue-Sat) Come for quality used books – primarily literary works – and to browse and talk ideas with the owner, a keen bibliophile.

Extreme Exposure Fine Art Gallery
Photography

(www.extremeexposure.com; 224 Kamehameha Ave; 10am-8pm Mon-Sat, 11am-5pm Sun) This informal gallery offers excellent nature photography, notably Kilauea's spectacular lava displays, and caters to all budgets, from framed prints to greeting cards.

Hilo Guitars & Ukuleles Music
(www.hiloguitars.com; 56 Ponahawai St; 10am-5pm Mon-Fri, to 4pm Sat) Find a wide selection of quality ukulele, from koa or mahogany collectibles to fine entry-level instruments.

Sig Zane Designs Clothing
(www.sigzane.com; 122 Kamehameha Ave; 9:30am-5pm Mon-Fri, 9am-4pm Sat) Legendary in the hula community, Sig Zane creates iconic custom fabrics, marked by rich colors and graphic prints of Hawaiian flora. You can spot a 'Sig' a mile away.

Alan's Art & Collectibles Antiques
(808-969-1554; 202 Kamehameha Ave; 10am-4pm Mon & Wed-Fri, 1-4pm Tue, 10am-3pm Sat) Glimpse old Hawai'i in this chock-full secondhand shop: vintage glassware, household doodads, aloha shirts, vinyl LPs and some collectible treasures.

Dragon Mama Homewares
(www.dragonmama.com; 266 Kamehameha Ave; 9am-5pm Mon-Fri, to 4pm Sat) Go home with exquisite beddings custom-made from imported Japanese fabric.

Information

Dangers & Annoyances

While relatively safe, be careful in downtown Hilo and avoid Kalakaua Park at night. Throughout Hilo, expect to hear coqui frogs, an invasive species, after dark. If you are bothered by noise at night, when they are most vocal, bring earplugs.

Internet Access

There's free wi-fi at Starbucks in **downtown Hilo** (933-3094; 438 Kilauea Ave; 4:30am-9pm, to 10pm Fri & Sat), **Prince Kuhio Plaza** (959-2492; 111 E Puainako St; 4:30am-10pm, to 11pm Fri & Sat), and their locations inside Target and Safeway, both near Prince Kuhio Plaza.

Bytes and Pieces of Hilo (808-935-3520; www.bytesandpiecesofhilo.com; 264 Keawe St; computer rental per 15/30/60min $3/5/8, wi-fi per day $5; 9am-6pm Mon-Fri, to 4pm Sat;) Four computers for rent, plus wi-fi, printing, faxing and scanning. The shop also sells vintage collectibles. Call to confirm hours.

Hilo Public Library (808-933-8888; www.librarieshawaii.org; 300 Waianuenue Ave; 11am-7pm Tue & Wed, 9am-5pm Thu & Sat, 10am-5pm Fri) If you buy a three-month nonresident library card ($10), you can use internet terminals for free and check out books.

Aloha wear

ANN CECIL/GETTY IMAGES ©

Medical Services

Hilo Medical Center (808-974-4700, ER 808-974-6800; 1190 Waianuenue Ave; 24hr emergency) Near Rainbow Falls.

Longs Drugs Kilauea Ave (808-935-3357, pharmacy 808-935-9075; 555 Kilauea Ave; pharmacy 7am-7pm Mon-Fri, to 6pm Sat, 8am-5pm Sun); Prince Kuhio Plaza (808-959-5881, pharmacy 808-959-4508; 111 E Puainako St, Prince Kuhio Plaza; pharmacy 8am-8pm Mon-Fri, to 7pm Sat, to 5pm Sun) General store and pharmacy; store hours run longer than pharmacy hours.

KTA Super Store (pharmacy 808-959-8700; 50 E Puainako St, Puainako Town Center; pharmacy 8am-7pm Mon-Fri, from 9am Sat) Supermarket with pharmacy. Store hours run longer than pharmacy hours.

Money

Bank of Hawaii Kawili St (808-961-0681; 417 E Kawili St); Pauahi St (808-935-9701; 120 Pauahi St)

First Hawaiian Bank (808-969-2222; 120 Waianuenue Ave)

Police

Police (808-935-3311; 349 Kapi'olani St) For nonemergencies.

Post

Downtown Post Office (808-933-3014; 154 Waianuenue Ave; 9am-4pm Mon-Fri, 12:30-2pm Sat) Located in the Federal Building.

Main Post Office (933-3019; 1299 Kekuanaoa St; 8am-4:30pm Mon-Fri, 9am-12:30pm Sat) Located near Hilo airport.

Tourist Information

Big Island Visitors Bureau (808-961-5797, 800-648-2441; www.gohawaii.com/big-island; 250 Keawe St) Basic info and brochures only.

Getting There & Away

Air

Hilo International Airport (ITO; 808-934-5838; http://hawaii.gov/ito; 2450 Kekuanaoa St, Hilo) Almost all flights to Hilo are interisland, mostly from Honolulu.

Bus

Hele-On Bus (808-961-8744; www.heleonbus.org; adult/senior or student $2/1) All buses originate at Mo'oheau terminal (329 Kamehameha Ave) in downtown Hilo. From here, buses go around the island, but service is infrequent, sometimes only very early in the morning (for work commuters) or only a few times daily. If you're going to a major destination (such as Kailua-Kona or a South Kohala resort) and staying within the area, the bus is a feasible option. Check the website for current routes and schedules.

Car

The drive from Hilo to Kailua-Kona (via Waimea) is 95 miles and averages 2½ hours. Driving on Saddle Rd can cut travel time by about 15 minutes. For rental information see p291.

For a retro adventure, see **Happy Campers Hawaii** (808-896-8777; www.happycampershawaii.com) which rents VW Westfalia pop-top campers/Vanagons that sleep up to four. From $120 per day, they're a steal – in great condition, with kitchenettes, sink with running water, cookware, bedding and more. Pick up and drop off in Hilo.

Getting Around

Bicycle

Cycling is more recreation than transportation in Hilo. **Mid-Pacific Wheels** (808-935-6211; www.midpacificwheelsllc.com; 1133c Manono St; 9am-6pm Mon-Sat, 11am-5pm Sun) rents mountain and road bikes for $25 to $45 per day.

Bus

The Hele-On Bus (p187) covers much of Hilo, although service can be infrequent. Check the website for current routes and schedules.

Car

Free parking is generally available. Downtown street parking is free for two hours; finding a spot is easy except during Saturday and Wednesday farmers markets.

Taxi

The approximate cab fare from the airport to downtown Hilo is $15.

AA Marshall's Taxi (808-936-2654)

Percy's Taxi (808-969-7060)

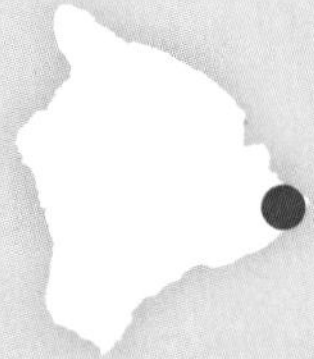

Puna

Even among locals, Puna is its own world, not far away but *far out*. The driving force is change. Here, the low-key plantation community has been inundated by an eclectic mix of mainland retirees, nouveau hippies, off-the-grid minimalists, funky artists, Hawaiian sovereignty activists, organic farmers, *pakalolo* (marijuana) growers and entry-level homeowners. While diverse, even divergent, all Punatics relish the laid-back, wristwatch-free lifestyle. They share a deep affinity for the volatile land, which Kilauea Volcano has repeatedly slathered with lava and blessed with black-sand beaches. If day-tripping here, avoid morning and evening rush hour: Puna, the fastest-growing district statewide, has become a sprawling suburb of Hilo.

Ukuleles at the Maku'u Craft & Farmers Market (p193)
LONELY PLANET/GETTY IMAGES ©

Puna Itineraries

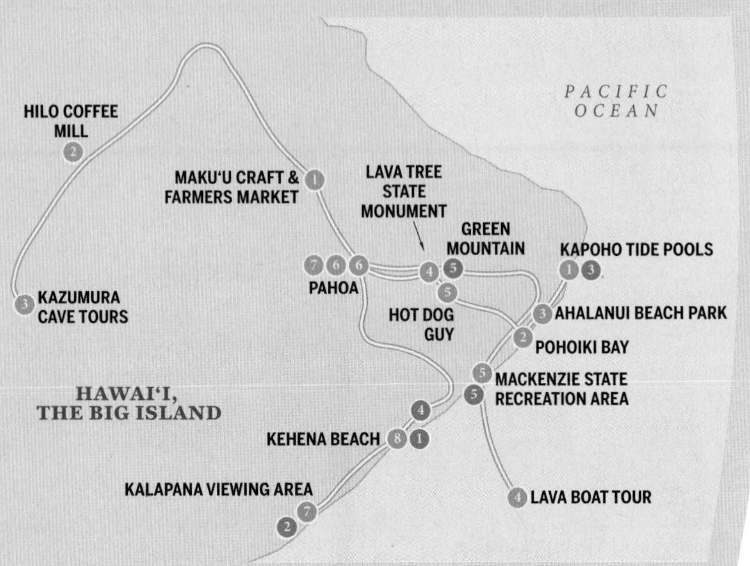

One Day

1 **Kapoho Tide Pools** (p197) Early morning is the best time to enjoy the serenity of these lava pools containing fish and an occasional sea turtle.

2 **Pohoiki Bay** (p198) Ace surfers and bodyboarders can opt to hit the formidable breaks here instead.

3 **Ahalanui Beach Park** (p198) Follow up at this easy-access hot pond; never empty, but soothing nevertheless.

4 **Lava Tree State Monument** (p196) Stroll through thick tropical forest, keeping your eyes peeled for hollow 'lava trees,' fascinating oddities of nature.

5 **Hot Dog Guy** (p197) If you're hungry, grab a bison, reindeer or beef hotdog grilled to order.

6 **Pahoa Fresh Fish** (p195) If a hotdog won't do, push on to Pahoa and fill up on fantastic fish and chips.

7 **Kalapana Viewing Area** (p201) If you're lucky and the flow is accessible, book a hiking tour to see red-hot lava. Hiking distances vary, but could be 3 or 4 miles one way over difficult terrain – expect a strenuous half-day to full-day adventure.

8 **Kehena Beach** (p199) If lava isn't viewable, take it easy at this freewheeling, clothing-optional black-sand beach.

THIS LEG: 25 MILES

Two Days

1 Maku'u Craft & Farmers Market (p193) If you're here on a Sunday, start day two by visiting this market – it distills the essence of funky, DIY Puna.

2 Hilo Coffee Mill (p193) On other days, wake up to fresh coffee and breakfast fixings at this friendly cafe. Coffee fans, the informative farm and mill tour is not to be missed.

3 Kazumura Cave Tours (p192) Head underground to explore the world's longest lava tube, mesmerizing in its size, darkness and silence.

4 Lava boat tour (p203) If lava is flowing into the ocean, it's a rare chance to get up close with Lava Ocean Adventures. Be prepared for choppy waters and unavoidable splashes.

5 MacKenzie State Recreation Area If the flow is inland or underground (or if you'd prefer peace and quiet), cobble together a picnic lunch and laze away the afternoon on a bed of ironwood pine needles.

6 Paradissimo Tropical Spa (p193) End your day with a pampering facial or massage – aah.

7 Kaleo's Bar & Grill (p195) Make a reservation at Pahoa's standby for well-made Hawaii Regional Cuisine. Another winner is Paolo's for Italian dishes in a cozy dining room.

THIS LEG: 70 MILES

Puna Highlights

1 Best Beach: Kehena Beach (p199) Let it all hang out at this bohemian black-sand beach, home to Punatics of all persuasions.

2 Best View: Molten lava close-up (p202) Hoof it over miles of rocky terrain and muddy jungle to get up close to red-hot lava.

3 Best Activity: Kapoho Tide Pools (p197) Snorkeling the shallow lava-rock tide pools awash in fish are fantastic for all ages and levels.

4 Best Day Pass: Kalani Oceanside Retreat (p200) Devote a day to your health, with yoga, massage, swimming and nourishing food at this longtime retreat.

5 Best Scenic Drive: Hwy 132 to Hwy 137 (p196) Puna's highways and byways are all scenic, but these two are especially mesmerizing and cover all of Puna's must-see sights.

Lava flowing from Kilauea Volcano near Kalapana (p201)
STUART WESTMORLAND/GETTY IMAGES ©

Discover Puna

Kea'au & Around

POP KEA'AU 2253

Between Hilo and Volcano, you'll whisk past former sugar plantations and mini villages. The main town, Kea'au, is just a cluster of gas stations and stores, including a supermarket, off Volcano Hwy (Hwy 11). Past Kea'au toward Pahoa, however, burgeoning residential subdivisions have transformed Puna into sprawling suburbs. If you want to explore Hawaii Volcanoes National Park from a balmier home base than Volcano, consider the lodgings tucked away here.

Hikers on Kilauea Volcano

SAMI SARKIS/GETTY IMAGES ©

Sights & Activities

Hi'iaka's Healing Hawaiian Herb Garden Gardens

(808-966-5956; www.hiiakas.com; 15-1667 2nd St, Hawaiian Paradise Park; adult/senior & child $5/3, with guided tour $15/10; by appointment)

Learn about medicinal plants at this lovingly tended acre of native, Polynesian-introduced and international herbs. The founding gardener and herbalist sells *noni* (Indian mulberry) and kava concoctions.

Fuku-Bonsai Cultural Center Gardens

(808-982-9880; www.fukubonsai.com; 17-856 Ola'a Rd; 8am-4pm Mon-Sat)

FREE Although well-intentioned, this bonsai nursery is mostly a salesroom for its commercial specialty: dwarf schefflera that can be grown indoors. Displays of mature bonsai are interesting, but grounds are poorly maintained.

To get here from Kea'au, drive south on Hwy 11 and turn left on Ola'a Rd between the Mile 9 and Mile 10 markers.

Kazumura Cave Tours Caving

(808-967-7208; http://kazumuracave.com; off Volcano Hwy, past Mile 22; tours from $30; by appointment Mon-Sat)

Since discovering that his property lies atop Kazumura Cave – the world's longest lava tube – Harry Schick has become an expert on lava caves and gives small tours (six people maximum) at reasonable cost. Be prepared to climb ladders and walk over rocky terrain, even on the shortest, easiest tour. Minimum age is 11; English proficiency is required. Make reservations at least a week ahead.

Kilauea Caverns of Fire Caving
(☎217-2363; www.kilaueacavernsoffire.com; off Volcano Hwy, before Mile 11; tours $29-79; ⏲by appointment) These tours through Kazumura Cave can run a bit large, up to 20 for the one-hour walk and up to eight for the three-hour adventure. But the shorter tour is a decent option for families, as the minimum age is five.

Sleeping & Eating

For groceries, stock up at **Foodland** (☎808-966-9316; 16-586 Old Volcano Rd; ⏲6am-10pm) or **Kea'au Natural Foods** (☎808-966-8877; 16-586 Old Volcano Rd; ⏲8:30am-8pm Mon-Fri, to 7pm Sat, 9:30am-5pm Sun), both at Kea'au Shopping Center, at the junction of Volcano Hwy and Kea'au–Pahoa Rd.

Butterfly Inn Inn $
(☎808-966-7936, 800-546-2442; www.thebutterflyinn.com; Kurtistown; s/d with shared bath $55/65) Geared for women travelers, this longstanding inn is a safe, supportive place in a comfortable home in Kurtistown. Two tidy rooms with private entrances share an ample kitchen, living room, dining deck, bathroom and outdoor hot tub.

Hilo Coffee Mill Cafe
(www.hilocoffeemill.com; 17-995 Hwy 11; ⏲8am-5pm Mon, Tue, Thu & Fri, 7am-4pm Sat; Wi-Fi) This tidy cafe makes for a pleasant stop, with ample seating, light meals, friendly staff, coffee (brewed and beans) and adjacent roasting room. Owners give personal, informative, 90-minute farm tours (with/without meal $20/15). Located roadside between the Mile 12 and Mile 13 markers.

Shopping

Dan De Luz's Woods Arts & Crafts
(☎808-968-6607; Hwy 11, past Mile 12; Wi-Fi) Master woodworker Dan passed away in 2012, but the grandson whom he trained is carrying on the family craft. The shop still carries numerous calabashes by this much-loved local talent.

Pahoa

POP 945

This former plantation town is the region's scruffy hub, attracting a variety of eccentrics and transplants. Rampant development hasn't toned down the fringe element here!

The main thoroughfare is signposted as Pahoa Village Rd. As you enter town, there are two shopping malls on either side of the highway: one with a supermarket and a hardware store, the other with Longs Drugs. In town, you'll find banks, gas stations, a post office and **Big Island BookBuyers** (15-2901 Pahoa Village Rd; ⏲10am-6pm Mon-Sat, 11am-5pm Sun), a well-run used bookstore.

Sights & Activities

Maku'u Craft & Farmers Market Market
(Hwy 130; ⏲8am-2pm Sun) Crowds converge here for wide-ranging offerings, including psychic readings, massage, surfboard repairs, orchids, jewelry and, yes, fruits and vegetables. Freshly cooked food includes Hawaiian, Mexican and Thai cuisine. Morning **cultural workshops** (⏲9am) give way to **live music** through the afternoon.

You can't miss it on the *makai* (seaward) side of Hwy 130 between the Mile 7 and Mile 8 markers.

Jeff Hunt Surfboards Surfing
(☎808-965-2322; http://jeffhuntsurfboards.com; 15-2883 Pahoa Village Rd; rental per day $25; ⏲10am-5pm Mon-Sat, 11am-3pm Sun) Jeff Hunt is one of the island's best board shapers, and at his little hut you can buy one, talk surfing and rent soft-top boards.

Paradissimo Tropical Spa Spa
(☎808-965-8883; www.spaparadissimo.com; 15-2958 Pahoa Village Rd; facials from $25; ⏲11am-5pm Tue & Thu-Sat) Owner Olivia is a tender soul with talented hands, and the organic spa products she uses feel like alchemy for the skin. Sauna and massage are also available.

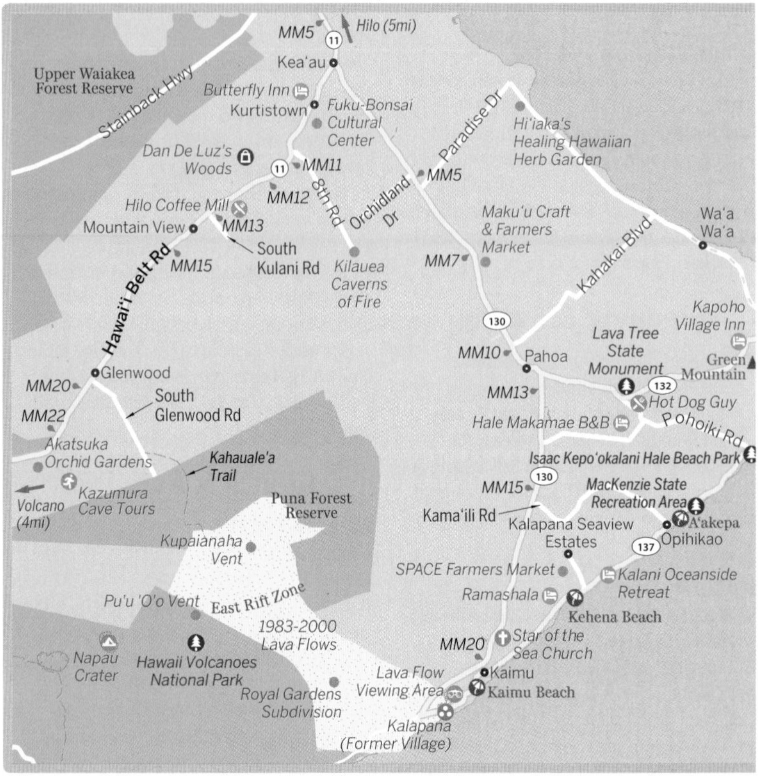

Pahoa Community Aquatic Center Swimming

(☎808-965-2700; 15-2910 Puna Rd; ⌚9am-5:30pm Mon-Fri, 9am-4:30pm Sat & Sun) For lap swimming, try this fantastic outdoor Olympic-sized pool behind the Pahoa Neighborhood Facility.

Sleeping

Hedonisia Hostel, Vacation Rental $

(☎808-430-2545, 808-430-9903; http://hedonisiahawaii.com; 13-657 Hinalo St; dm from $27, r with shared bath $55-70; 📶) A former junkyard converted into an organic farm/ramshackle hostel compound, with technicolor murals, Gilligan's Island huts, wild pigs and a school bus. Like-minded free spirits are invited to volunteer in the hostel for discounted stays. Located about 4 miles east of Pahoa.

Hawaiian Sanctuary Vacation Rental $

(☎800-309-8010; http://sustainable-hawaii.org; Mile 12, Hwy 130; r with shared bath $75-95) This permaculture farm offers internships for those interested in sustainable agriculture and going back to nature. Nightly stays are also offered, so visitors can eat vegan food and soak up the vibe. Located about 1.5 miles from central Pahoa.

Jungle Farmhouse Vacation Rental $$

(☎800-745-5049, 808-640-1113; http://pahoa.info; 15-3001 Mako Way; per night/week $139/700) Kick back at this beautifully maintained house, full of handpicked vintage furnishings, with three bedrooms, 1.5 baths, laundry facilities and an airy screened patio. Outside, enjoy fruit trees, chickens (fresh eggs!) and ducks. A

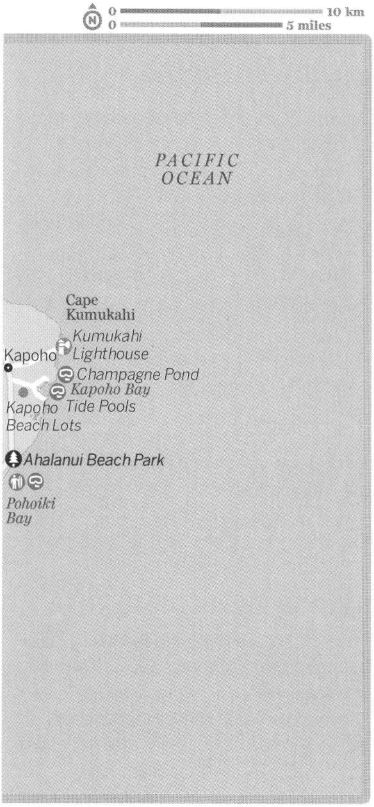

fantastic value, there's no extra charge for extra guests (maximum four total), and the weekly rate is a steal.

Hale Moana B&B B&B **$$**
(**808-965-7015; www.bnb-aloha.com; 13-3315 Makamae St; studio $110, 1-/2-br ste $145/165;**) In a clean-cut subdivision, this B&B (formerly known as Hale Makamae) is immaculate, family-friendly and a bargain. The suites are especially comfy, with well-equipped kitchenettes and enough space to spread out. The owner landscapes her 2-acre grounds superbly and is German fluent.

Eating

For such a small town, Pahoa has a decent bunch of eateries.

Pahoa Fresh Fish Fish & Chips **$**
(**808-965-8248; 15-2670 Pahoa Village Rd; mains $5-7; 8am-7pm**) Utterly unassuming in an ugly strip mall, this place makes fantastic fish and chips. Who knows what the friendly lady behind the counter is doing? Who cares? We'll come back for her perfectly battered and fried *ono* (wahoo) and mahimahi anytime.

Sirius Coffee Connection Cafe **$**
(**15-2874 Pahoa Village Rd; 7am-6pm Mon-Sat, to 3pm Sun;**) Yes, real espresso does exist in Pahoa! This simple space offers good coffee, internet and computer access, friendly service and baked goodies.

Island Naturals Market **$**
(**15-1403 Pahoa Village Rd; sandwiches $6-10; 7:30am-7:30pm Mon-Sat, 8am-7pm Sun;**) Here you'll find organic produce, healthy sandwiches, hot mains and the local nouveau hippie crowd.

Malama Market Supermarket **$**
(**Pahoa Village Rd, Pahoa Marketplace; 7am-9pm**) Pahoa's biggest grocer is best for basics.

Kaleo's Bar & Grill Hawaii Regional Cuisine **$$**
(**808-965-5600; 15-2969 Pahoa Village Rd; lunch mains $9-16, dinner mains $14-30; 11am-9pm;**) Pahoa's top sit-down restaurant serves island-fusion fare – such as a tempura ahi roll, orzo pasta salad, and coconut chicken curry – in a relaxed, family-friendly atmosphere. There's live music most nights. Definitely make a reservation on weekends.

Paolo's Bistro Italian **$$**
(**Pahoa Village Rd; mains $13-26; 5:30-9pm Tue-Sun**) This cozy, eight-table eatery executes Northern Italian dishes wonderfully. Bring your own *vino*.

Ning's Thai Cuisine Thai **$$**
(**15-2955 Pahoa Village Rd; mains $10-14; noon-9pm Mon-Sat, from 5pm Sun;**) Come for reliable Thai curries, lively salads and an emphasis on local, organic ingredients.

Luquin's Mexican Restaurant Mexican **$$**

(**☎808-965-9990; 15-2942 Pahoa Village Rd; mains $10-19; ⏰7am-9pm)** If you're craving Mexican fare, go to Luquin's for a fix, but it's nothing to write home about. The *liliko'i* (passion fruit) margaritas are memorable, however.

Entertainment

Akebono Theater Live Music

(**☎808-965-9990; Pahoa Village Rd; tickets $10-20)** This historical theater hosts all kinds of music, from Big Island Elvis to visiting jam bands. It's located behind Luquin's Mexican Restaurant.

Getting There & Away

Traffic between Hilo and Puna is a nightmare during commuting hours. By all means, avoid driving toward Hilo in the early morning and toward Kea'au and Pahoa in the late afternoon.

Hele-On Bus (**☎808-961-8745; www.heleonbus.org; adult/senior or student $2/1)** goes from Hilo to Kea'au and Pahoa several times daily.

Island Insights

Puna is home to the island's biggest concentration of nonconformists, New Agers, nouveau hippies and organic farmers – and it's also the island's gay capital. Here you'll find cruising and rainbow flags, gay-friendly places to stay, workshops and gatherings.

Highway 132

A good way to explore Puna is to navigate the triangle formed by three highways: Hwy 132, Red Road (Hwy 137) and the Kalapana Hwy (Hwy 130). It's even better on a bike!

LAVA TREE STATE MONUMENT

Entering this **park** (**⏰daylight hours**) **FREE** beneath a thick canopy of (invasive) albizia trees is an otherworldly experience. A short, paved loop trail passes through a tropical vision of Middle Earth, full of wild ferns, orchids, bamboo and strange 'lava trees.' These were formed in 1790 when Kilauea Volcano engulfed the rainforest with a flood of lava up to 10ft deep, enveloping moisture-laden ohia trees before receding. The lava hardened around the trees, which burned away, creating the hollow trunks left today.

To get here, follow Hwy 132 about 2.5 miles east of Hwy 130. Restrooms are remarkably tidy.

'Lava tree'

JOHN ELK/GETTY IMAGES ©

Red Road (Highway 137)

Nicknamed Red Road because its northern portion was originally paved with red cinder, Hwy 137 was repaved with black asphalt in 2013. It's still a mystical drive that meanders through tunnel-like canopies of milo and *hala* (pandanus) trees.

If exploring Puna on a day trip, drive east from Pahoa on Hwy 132; it's otherworldly as the jungly overgrowth thickens. Then head south on Red Road, which navigates from tropical jungle to vast ocean vistas. Return to Pahoa on Hwy 130, less scenic but avoiding backtracking.

Between this 'triangle' of highways, two back roads make intriguing detours or shortcuts: **Pohoiki Rd** connects Hwy 137 with Hwy 132, winding through storybook forest. Look for the roadside **Hot Dog Guy** (cnr Hwy 132 & Pohoiki Rd; hotdog $5-7; ⏲daily 'when it's not pouring'), selling bison, reindeer and beef hotdogs grilled to order.

Further south, **Kama'ili Rd** connects with Hwy 130 and, although less striking, is a pleasant country ramble.

KAPOHO TIDE POOLS

The best **snorkeling** in East Hawaii is this sprawling network of **tide pools** (suggested donation $3; ⏲7am-7pm), officially named Wai Opae Tide Pools Marine Life Conservation District. Here, Kapoho's lava-rock coast is a mosaic of protected, shallow, interconnected pools containing a rich variety of marine life, including saddle wrasses, Moorish idols, butterfly fish and sea cucumbers. Go deeper, heading straight out from the blue house, to see beautiful coral gardens (do not touch); sea turtles like the warm pocket a bit further south (keep 50yd distance).

Wear reef shoes to avoid cutting your soles on the lava rock. From Hwy 137, a mile south of the lighthouse, turn onto Kapoho Kai Dr, which ends at Wai Opae; turn left and park in the lot established by residents ($3 donation). This is not a public park, so there are no restrooms. If residents offer a portable toilet (for obvious reasons), they will request a

Local Knowledge

NAME: WAILANA SIMCOCK

OCCUPATION: FORMER HAWAI'I CULTURE AND PERFORMING ARTS DIRECTOR, KALANI OCEANSIDE RETREAT

RESIDENCE: FORMERLY KALANI OCEANSIDE RETREAT, PUNA; CURRENTLY HONOLULU, O'AHU

1 YOU TAUGHT HAWAIIAN STUDIES AT KALANI. WHAT ARE SOME GOOD HAWAIIAN PHRASES FOR TRAVELERS?

Everyone should learn the words used everyday like aloha and *mahalo* (thanks). In response, you might try 'no problem' *(A'ole pilikia)* or 'It's my pleasure' *(Na'u ka han'oli)*. It's a little more formal and a little more difficult!

2 PUNA IS CAPTIVATING. WHAT ARE SOME OF YOUR FAVORITE PLACES?

I surf, so the Pohoiki breaks are always calling. I like the first bay break called Elevators because it just rocks you up. Another place I really like is the lava tube at MacKenzie State Recreation Area. It's right behind the cliff 'where the spirits jump off.' Kehena Beach is a favorite of course – go before 10am for the best sun and water, and to see the dolphins.

3 DO YOU HAVE ANY TIPS FOR LAVA VIEWING?

The first place I always tell people to go is the new black-sand beach at Kaimu. The lava flow is changing all the time, which is important to remember. Also, there's no safe or right way to go to see the lava. It's a volcano – there's always an element of risk.

4 WHAT'S A GOOD KALANI ACTIVITY FOR PEOPLE WHO WANT A TASTE OF WHAT IT'S ABOUT?

Without a doubt, Ecstatic Sun-Dance. When we started this in 2000, six people and a dog showed up. Now we get about 300 people every Sunday and there's day care (but no dogs allowed). Everyone comes out – it's a highlight of this community.

Detour: Cape Kumukahi Lighthouse

Hwy 132 goes east until it meets Red Road at **Four Corners** near Kapoho. Once a small farming village, Kapoho became the victim of Pele (Hawaiian goddess of fire and volcanoes) in January 1960 when a volcanic fissure let loose a half-mile-long curtain of fiery lava in a nearby sugarcane field. The main flow of *pahoehoe* (smooth, flowing lava) ran toward the ocean, but an offshoot of *'a'a* (rough, crumbly lava) crept toward the town, burying orchid farms in its path. Two weeks later Kapoho's nearly 100 homes and businesses were buried.

When the lava approached **Cape Kumukahi**, however, it parted around the lighthouse, which survived. Old-timers say that the lighthouse keeper offered a meal to Pele, who appeared disguised as an old woman on the eve of the disaster, and so she spared the structure. Today, the lighthouse is just a tall piece of white-painted metal scaffolding, at the end of an unpaved 1.5-mile road from Four Corners. This is the easternmost point in the state, where you can breathe among the freshest air in the world.

From the lighthouse, trek 10 minutes over *'a'a* toward the sea to a rugged beach, too rough for swimming, but starkly memorable.

small donation to offset its maintenance; bring dollar bills.

KAPOHO BEACH LOTS

Slightly further north, there's top-notch snorkeling beyond the locked gates of this seaside community. Vacation rentals, such as **Pualani (☎805-225-1552; www.bigislandhawaiivacationhomes.com; Kapoho Beach Lots; 2-br house $150; @)**, an airy house with hot tub and wraparound lanai, are plentiful. Check vrbo.com and airbnb.com for listings.

If you stay here, you'll have access to **Champagne Pond**, a tranquil pool with sandy shores frequented by green turtles. It drew controversy when increased use by those driving here (on a rough 4WD-only road from Kumukahi Lighthouse) caused sanitation and other problems. Tread lightly.

AHALANUI BEACH PARK

The 'hot pond' is a spring-fed **thermal pool (⏲7am-7pm)** deep enough for swimming, easily accessible and often crowded. Water temperatures average 90°F (32°C) and the pool is very calm. During high tide, waves crash over the adjacent seawall, circulating the water, but there's still risk of bacterial infection. Early and late soaking is the best crowd-beating strategy. There are picnic tables, portable toilets and a daily lifeguard. Don't leave valuables unguarded.

ISAAC KEPO'OKALANI HALE BEACH PARK

This beach park, which goes by **Isaac Hale** (house; pronounced *ha*-lay) is a rocky locals' beach along **Pohoiki Bay.** Waters are too rough for swimming, but addictive to experienced bodyboarders and surfers who regard Pohoiki as the island's top break, despite the omnipresence of sharp *wana* (sea urchins). It's a scenic spot to witness pounding waves and local talent.

Some might find the local crowd and vibe intimidating; smile, ask questions and you'll be fine. There are picnic tables, outdoor showers and good **camping** facilities on a pristine lawn, with 22 sites and bathrooms with flush toilets and drinking water. A security guard checks permits (sketchy characters used to squat here).

MACKENZIE STATE RECREATION AREA

With a forest of ironwood trees edging sheer 40ft cliffs overlooking the ocean, this is a dramatic, gorgeous spot. During the day, it makes for quiet, uncrowded picnics. The trees provide plenty of shade, and their fallen needles blanket the ground like a carpet. **Camping** is allowed, but recommended only for large groups due to the park's isolation. Locals tend to go elsewhere because the park has a reputation for being haunted and was the scene of a few violent crimes decades ago.

The Best... Puna Views

1 Underground in Kazumura Cave (p192), the world's longest lava tube

2 Marine life in Kapoho Tide Pools (p197)

3 Molten lava by land or by sea (p203)

4 People-watching at Kehena Beach (p199)

5 Towering foliage in and around Lava Tree State Monument (p196)

KEHENA BEACH & AROUND

Beaches

Kehena Beach Beach

If any place captures the uninhibited vibe of Puna, it's this beautiful black-sand beach where all stripes – hippies, Hawaiians, gays, families, seniors, tourists – do their own thing. If nudity or *pakalolo* (marijuana) bother you, find another beach. On Sunday a drum circle invites dancing and even more communing. Think twice about swimming; the surf is treacherous.

To get here, turn into a small parking lot immediately south of the Mile 19 marker. A steep path leads down to the beach. Don't leave valuables in your car.

Sights

SPACE Farmers Market Market

(www.hawaiispace.com; 12-247 West Pohakupele Loop, Seaview Performing Arts Center for Education; ⌚8-11:30am Sat) Kalapana Seaview Estates, near the Mile 18, is home to the SPACE (Seaview Performing Arts Center for Education) Farmers Market, small but varied and lively. Keep an open mind as you browse tarot readers and tie-dyes, green smoothies and gluten-free breads. To get here, turn into

Kapoho Tide Pools (p197)
LONELY PLANET/GETTY IMAGES ©

the subdivision, turn right on Mapuana St and left on Kehauopuna St.

Festivals & Events

Puna Culinary Festival Food
(Kalani Oceanside Retreat & various farms; classes & tours $25, dinners $24) In early September, feast on Puna's farm-to-fork bounty at gourmet dinners, tours, markets and cooking classes.

Sleeping & Eating

Kalani Oceanside Retreat Resort $$
(808-965-7828, 800-800-6886; www.kalani.com; r shared bath $95, r $140-245; day passes 7:30am-8pm, Ecstatic Sun-Dance 10:30am-12:30pm Sun; @ ≋) Immerse yourself in the Puna mindset at this rustic 120-acre compound that hums with communal energy. Daily programs include yoga, meditation, dance and alternative healing. Note that workshops/retreats by visiting

Hidden Dangers in the Water

Frolicking in tide pools and hot ponds has a potential downside – bacteria, including staphylococcal. To minimize risk, go early in the morning when fewer people have entered the pools; go during high tide; and avoid Mondays and post-holidays. Most important, do not enter pools with open cuts and shower immediately after swimming.

Left: Kazumura Cave (p192); **Below:** Star of the Sea Church, Kalapana
(LEFT) ROBERT HARDING PICTURE LIBRARY LTD/ALAMY ©; (BELOW) GLOW IMAGES, INC/GETTY IMAGES ©

teachers are separate from ongoing programs. Nonguests can enjoy facilities on a **day pass** ($20). Weekly **Ecstatic Sun-Dance** (admission $15) gatherings attract the dreadlocked and tattooed.

An outdoor dining **lanai** (breakfast/lunch/dinner $13/15/24), open to nonguests, serves healthy buffet-style meals. Rooms are simple, with plywood floors covered in lauhala mats, and the **camping area** (tents s/d $40/55) is peaceful. To get here, turn inland from Hwy 137 between the Mile 17 and Mile 18 markers.

Ramashala Vacation Rental **$$**
(☎808-965-0068; www.ramashala.com; 12-7208 Hwy 137; r $50-200; 📶) Almost directly across from Kehena Beach, this architecturally delightful retreat offers six rooms in three sizes: the smallest come with a twin bed and shared bath, while the largest are mini apartments with full kitchens. High ceilings, hardwood floors, numerous windows, tropical grounds and two yoga studios make for an elegant private retreat.

Absolute Paradise B&B B&B **$$**
(☎888-285-1540, 965-1828; http://absoluteparadise.tv; Kipuka St; r $99-135, ste $164; 📶) Be treated as family at this gay-oriented, clothing-optional B&B a five-minute walk from Kehena Beach. The house and rooms, which vary in size and price, aren't extravagant, but are very comfy and clean.

KALAPANA (FORMER VILLAGE)

For generations, Kalapana was a close-knit fishing village near **Kaimu Beach**, the island's most famous black-sand beach. When Kilauea began erupting in 1983, the lava flowed downslope west of Kalapana. But in 1990 the flow inched toward Kalapana's 100 buildings. When **Star of the Sea Church** was threatened, the community moved it to safety in the nick of time.

Within the year, however, the village and beach were destroyed. Hawaiian residents were remarkably accepting of losing their homes to Pele, commenting that 'Pele's taking back the land' or 'She gave it to us and now she's reclaiming it.'

Today Hwy 137 ends abruptly at the eastern edge of the former village. At the dead-end, a makeshift **tourist stop** includes photos of the eruption and an outpost of the Hawaiian sovereignty movement. From here, you can take a short, but hot and rocky walk across lava desert to **New Kaimu Beach** (aka Coconut Beach), where hundreds of baby coconut palms surround a black arc of sand. The water is too rough for swimming, but it's a contemplative spot.

Eating & Drinking

Kalapana Village Cafe Local $

(12-5037 Pahoa Kalapana Rd, Hwy 137; mains $8-11; 8am-9pm) At the edge of civilization (or so it seems), this drive-in-style eatery serves decent burgers and plate lunches, plus ice-cold drinks. Restrooms open only to customers.

Uncle Robert's Awa Bar Bar

(3-10pm) In the afternoon, sidle up to Uncle's Awa Bar, where you can try kava (native intoxicant), listen to live music and rub elbows with local characters.

Highway 130

From Kalapana, Hwy 130 makes its way north to Pahoa and on to Kea'au.

Sights

Lava-Viewing Area Lookout

(hotline 808-961-8093; 3-9pm, car entry by 8pm) At the end of Hwy 130, there's a parking lot staffed by informative personnel, plus souvenir vendors and a few portable toilets. From the lot, you can walk over rocky terrain to a public lava-viewing area, but you might see only a plume of hot steam or absolutely nothing. Call the hotline for current info. The flow is unpredictable, so keep your expectations in check.

Star of the Sea Church Church

(9am-4pm) The historic Star of the Sea Church (also known as 'Painted Church') is noted for its trompe l'oeil murals that create an illusion of depth and expansiveness. Built in 1929, this tiny Catholic church's first priest was Father Damien, legendary for his work on Moloka'i with people suffering from leprosy. Originally in Kalapana, it's now off Hwy 130 at the Mile 20 marker.

Noisy Neighbors – Coqui Frogs

Hawaii's most wanted alien is the Puerto Rican coqui frog, only an inch long, but relentlessly loud. At sunset, coquis begin their nightly chirping (a two-tone 'ko-kee' call), which can register between 90 and 100 decibels from 2ft away. Even at a distance, their chorus maintains 70 decibels, equivalent to a vacuum cleaner.

Coquis accidentally reached the Hawaiian Islands around 1988, and they've proliferated wildly on the Big Island. Around Lava Tree State Monument, densities are the highest in the state and twice that of Puerto Rico. Besides causing a nightly racket, coquis are disrupting the ecosystem by eating the bugs that feed native birds. Light sleepers: bring ear plugs.

Activities

At the end of Hwy 130, there's nothing but vast fields of lava rock. Here, the main activity is lava viewing. Whether you see glowing, red lava depends on luck and timing. If lava is flowing into the ocean, a lava-watching boat tour is possible. If the flow is remote, the only option is a strenuous hike, covering miles of rugged terrain, in pitch darkness on the way back.

Bear in mind, the entire lava flow covers private land, and trespassing is illegal (although no one is cracking down on those crossing their property). If you walk across the flow – guided or unguided – you do so at your own risk. Dangers include unstable lava, sharp rocks, fires, gaseous explosion and simply getting lost in the dark. If you are injured, you could be stranded until other hikers discover you. Therefore, it's prudent to join a guided tour if you decide to hike to see the flow.

Lava Ocean Adventures Sailing
(**808-966-4200; www.sealava.com; tours adult/child from $150/125**) If (and this is a big 'if') lava is pouring into the Pacific, don't miss a once-in-a-lifetime boat ride it see it. Expect a turbulent ride; fit individuals only.

Ahiu Hawaii Hiking
(**769-9453; www.ahiuhawaii.com; tour per person $155; departures 8am & 4pm**) When the flow is too remote for most tours, these intrepid guides slog through muddy jungle and sharp lava rock to find it. For very strong hikers only.

Volcano Discovery Hawai'i Hiking
(**http://hawaii.volcanodiscovery.com; 4-14hr tours per person $150-400**) Run by a geologist, these customizable tours are informative, personalized and professionally run. Group size is limited for safety.

The Best...
Places with the Puna Vibe

1 Anything goes at Kehena Beach (p199)

2 Back-to-nature lodging at Hedonisia (p194) and Hawaiian Sanctuary (p194)

3 Ecstatic Sun-Dance at Kalani Oceanside Retreat (p200)

4 Far-out finds at Maku'u Craft & Farmers Market (p193) and SPACE Farmers Market (p199)

Native Guide Hawaii Hiking
(**808-982-7575; www.nativeguidehawaii.com; tour incl lunch per person $150; by appointment**) For the personal touch, Native Hawaiian and cultural practitioner Warren Costa offers customized all-day tours that reveal gems you wouldn't find on your own.

Poke a Stick Lava Tours Hiking
(**808-987-3456; http://lavarefuge.com; tour $100; 7:30am-4:30pm**) When the flow is accessible from their Kalapana property, this versatile couple takes groups out. They also offer vacation rentals.

Kalapana Cultural Tours Hiking
(**808-936-0456; www.kalapanaculturaltours.com; tour approximately $100**) Run by a local family, this is a solid choice for evening hikes when the flow cooperates.

Hawai'i Volcanoes National Park

It's safe to say there is no place on earth like Hawai'i Volcanoes National Park. Sulfurous smoke belches from the ground so voluminously it tastes like you're in hell. Ribbons of red lava flow from Kilauea – the most active volcano on the planet, ruled over by the Hawaiian goddess Pele – toward the sea, boiling it upon contact. Waving palm trees fringe white-sand beaches backed by jet-black lava fields, and above it all looms a snowy mountain, Mauna Loa. An entire day could easily be spent exploring sights along the park's scenic drives, but give yourself at least two – and don't miss seeing the lava lake glowing at night. After the sun goes down, soak in a hot tub secreted in the rainforest or put your feet up in front of the fireplace at cozy, romantic lodgings in artistic Volcano village.

Kilauea Volcano (p208)

Hawaiʻi Volcanoes National Park Itineraries

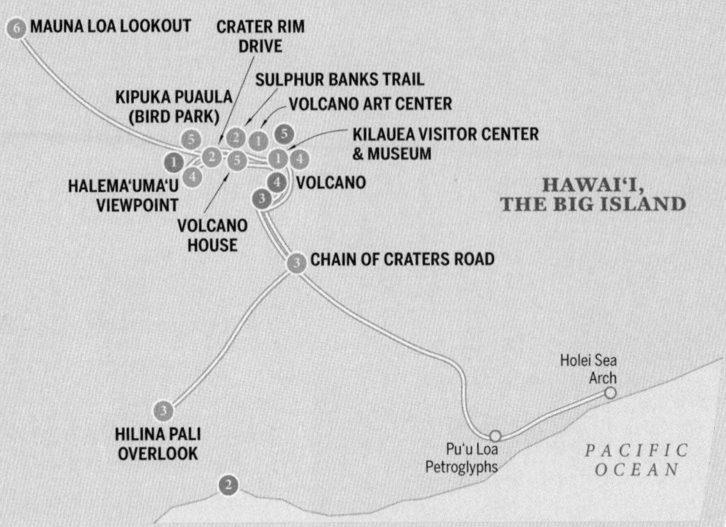

One Day

1 Kilauea Visitor Center & Museum (p208) Start day one early here, near the park entrance, to learn about the volcano and the park's natural history. Check daily schedules of ranger programs, eruption updates, sulfur-dioxide levels and road and trail closures.

2 Crater Rim Drive (p208) If Pele is up to her usual shenanigans, parts of this 11-mile paved loop road will be closed, but you should still be able to visit the Jaggar Museum, walk through Thurston Lava Tube and hike the Kilauea Iki Trail.

3 Chain of Craters Road (p212) Even if it's raining at the visitor center, drive down this scenic road to the coast, where you might still spot sunshine. Along the way, stop to hike to the Pu'u Loa Petroglyphs and snap photos of gravity-defying Holei Sea Arch.

4 Halema'umaʻu Viewpoint (p211) After sunset, backtrack along Crater Rim Dr to check out the ethereal glow of the lava lake deep within Halemaʻumaʻu Crater from the patio outside the Jaggar Museum.

5 Volcano House (p222) Even if you're not sleeping here, stop by this historic hotel perched on the rim of Kilauea Volcano. Its fireplace lobby, lounge and restaurant all enjoy panoramic crater-view windows.

THIS LEG: 55 MILES

Two Days

❶ **Volcano Art Center** (p209) By the Kilauea Visitor Center, immerse yourself in this high-quality gallery of traditional and contemporary island arts and Hawaiian crafts. If you're lucky, there'll be a hula dance performance or cultural arts demonstration happening.

❷ **Sulphur Banks Trail** (p209) Because this is day two, you may be ready for a more serious, all-day hike into the park's volcanic backcountry. If not, opt for this easy, but uniquely scenic trail just a short drive from the visitor center. It connects with the crater-rim walk past the hellish Steaming Bluff.

❸ **Hilina Pali Overlook** (p213) Bring a picnic along to this sea-view lookout, reached via a narrow, but paved scenic drive off Chain of Craters Road.

❹ **Volcano** (p223) Next it's time for lunch and art-gallery hopping in town, starting at the Volcano Art Center's Rainforest Gallery. Make reservations in advance to take a sustainable farm-and-forest walking tour with Tea Hawaii & Company.

❺ **Kipuka Puaulu (Bird Park)** (p219) A short drive west of Volcano lies this rainforest *kipuka* (oasis) spared by dramatic lava flows. An easy mile-long loop trail offers spectacular bird-watching for adults and kids alike – bring binoculars.

❻ **Mauna Loa Lookout** (p214) You've come this far already, so why not keep going? Narrow, pockmarked Mauna Loa Rd winds for over 11 miles up 'Long Mountain' to an unforgettable viewpoint over the volcanic caldera down to the coast.

THIS LEG: 50 MILES

Hawai'i Volcanoes National Park Highlights

❶ **Best View: Halema'uma'u Viewpoint** (p211) You may have to wait your turn to get a glimpse, but it's worth it.

❷ **Best Beach: Halape** (p218) A grueling hot hike with dizzying coastal views leads to this wild beach.

❸ **Best Hike: Kilauea Iki Trail** (p216) Trek across a lunar landscape of lava flows inside a living volcanic crater.

❹ **Best Activity for Kids: Thurston Lava Tube** (p212) Eerie walk through an underground tunnel carved by lava flows.

❺ **Best Entertainment: Volcano Art Center** (p209) Hula dancing, Hawaiian culture and craft workshops, concerts and more.

Volcano Art Center (p209)

Discover Hawai'i Volcanoes National Park

Nothing on the Big Island equals the elemental grandeur and raw power of the two active volcanoes encompassed by **Hawai'i Volcanoes National Park** (HAVO; ☎808-985-6000; www.nps.gov/havo; 7-day entry per car $10), established in 1916. With geological history dating back almost half a million years, this awe-inspiring park became Hawaii's first Unesco World Heritage Site in 1987.

The current eruption along Kilauea's East Rift Zone of Kilauea, the park's most active volcano, started on January 3, 1983, making it the longest in recorded history. Nearly 30 years of continuous volcanic action adds up to a lot of lava – some 2.5 billion cubic yards a day (that's 50,000 gallons a minute!), and 500 acres of new land. All of this boil, toil and trouble comes from the Pu'u 'O'o Vent, a smoldering cinder cone along the East Rift Zone.

Kilauea is a shield volcano, which means lava usually oozes and creeps along, with occasional earthquakes, lava fountains and lakes of fire. But it doesn't have the explosive gases of the more dramatic and deadly strato volcanoes found along the Pacific Ocean's Ring of Fire (eg Mt St Helens in Washington), which throw ash and flaming rocks into the air. Though languid, Big Island lava can still be deadly stuff, make no mistake: it consumes trees, houses, roads and anything else in its path.

Jaggar Museum
LONELY PLANET/GETTY IMAGES ©

Sights

CRATER RIM DRIVE

This incredible 11-mile paved loop road starts at Kilauea Visitor Center and skirts the rim of Kilauea Caldera, passing steam vents and rifts, hiking trailheads and amazing views of the smoking crater. At the time of research, the road beyond the Jaggar Museum and Halema'uma'u Overlook to the Chain of Craters Road intersection was closed indefinitely due to eruption activity.

Kilauea Visitor Center & Museum Museum

(☎808-985-6000; www.nps.gov/havo; Crater Rim Dr; ⏰7:45am-5pm, film screenings hourly 9am-4pm; 👪) Make your first stop the park's visitor center. On-duty rangers and volunteers can advise you about volcanic activity, air quality, road closures and hiking trail conditions.

Interactive museum exhibits are small but family-friendly, and will teach even science-savvy adults a lot about the park's delicate ecosystem and Hawaiian heritage. Pick up fun **junior ranger program** activity books for your kids before leaving.

Geology talks are given twice daily by the outdoor signboards, where ranger-led hikes and other activities are posted. A well-stocked nonprofit bookstore inside the visitor center sells souvenirs, rain ponchos, walking sticks and flashlights. Wheelchairs are free to borrow upon request. There are restrooms and a payphone outside.

Volcano Art Center Arts Center

(☎866-967-7565, 808-967-7565; www.volcanoartcenter.org; Crater Rim Dr; 9am-5pm) Near the visitor center, this innovative local art gallery spotlights museum-quality pottery, paintings, woodwork, sculpture, jewelry, Hawaiian quilts and more. The nonprofit shop, housed in the historic 1877 Volcano House hotel, is worth a visit just to admire its solid artisanship. Ask about upcoming art classes and cultural workshops here.

Sulphur Banks Landmark

(off Crater Rim Dr) Wooden boardwalks weave through to steaming Sulphur Banks, where rocky vents and holes are stained chartreuse, yellow, orange and other weird colors by tons of sulfur-infused steam rising from deep within the earth. That rotten-egg stench is from noxious hydrogen sulfide wafting out of the vents. The easy 0.7-mile one-way trail connects to Crater Rim Dr near the parking lot for Steaming Bluff. The latter half of the trail is wheelchair-accessible.

Steam Vents & Steaming Bluff Lookout

(Crater Rim Dr) Pumping impressive plumes of steam in the cool early morning, these vents make a convenient drive-up photo op. Steam is created when rainwater percolates into the earth, is heated by the hot rocks below and then released upward. For an even more evocative experience, take the short walk to the crater rim at Steaming Bluff, where the view looks like an inferno with steam pouring over the cliffs.

The Best... Hawai'i Volcanoes National Park at Night

1 Lava lake viewing from Jaggar Museum (p209)

2 'After Dark in the Park' evening programs (p221)

3 Na Leo Manu music concerts (p221)

4 Walking to Thurston Lava Tube (p212) by flashlight

5 Toasting your tootsies by the Volcano House (p222) fireplace

6 Live music and drinks at Uncle George's Lounge (p222)

Kilauea Overlook Lookout

(Crater Rim Dr) The Kilauea Overlook parking lot and picnic area provides a pause-worthy panorama, including views of Halema'uma'u Crater and the Southwest Rift. The latter's rocky fissure is bigger and longer than it looks: it slices from the caldera summit all the way to the coast.

Jaggar Museum Museum

(☎808-985-6051; Crater Rim Dr; 8:30am-7:30pm;) Big draws at this small one-room museum are the views and the real-time seismographs and tiltmeters recording earthquakes inside the park. Other exhibits introduce Hawaiian gods and goddesses and give a short history of the neighboring Hawai'i Volcano Observatory, founded by famed geologist Dr Thomas A Jaggar. Park rangers frequently give geology talks inside the museum. Wheelchairs are free to borrow.

Hawai'i Volcanoes National Park

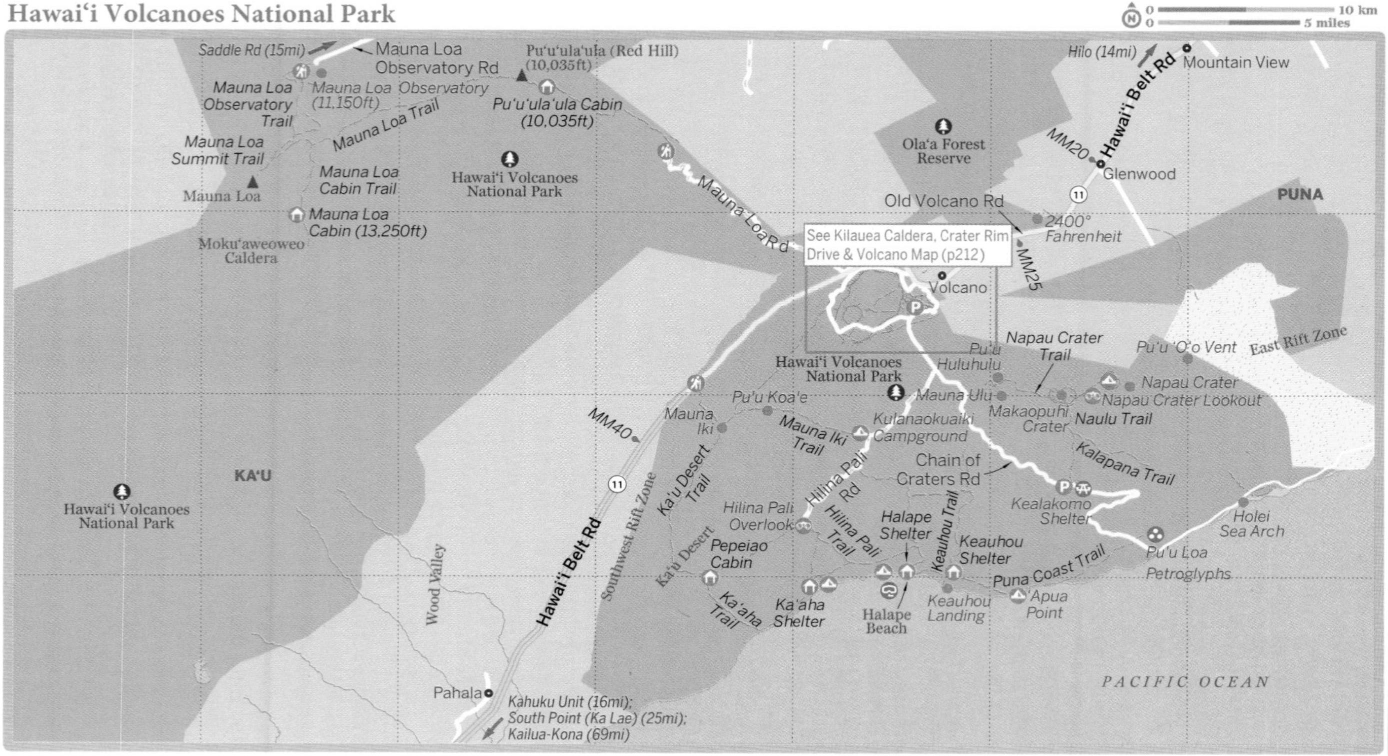

Halema'uma'u Viewpoint Lookout

(Crater Rim Dr) The original Halema'uma'u Overlook off Crater Rim Dr has been closed since 2008 due to ongoing volcanic activity. The next best vantage point is the patio outside the Jaggar Museum. Don't worry, the new viewpoint is still extraordinary: there's absolutely nothing like witnessing a huge smoking volcanic crater or roiling lava lake, especially after dark when the flickering hellfire glow is mesmerizing.

Halema'uma'u is really a crater within the crater of Kilauea Caldera. About 3000ft across and almost 300ft deep, it spews out a rising column of volcanic ash and gases, such as sulfor dioxide, that emerges from the great hole and billows into the sky, partly creating the vog (volcanic fog) that increasingly carpets the island (Kilauea's Pu'u 'O'o vent adds the rest).

How active Kilauea Volcano will be when you visit is subject to the whims of Pele, the Hawaiian goddess of fire and volcanoes who makes her home here, so don't count on a dramatic lake of fire. It's most advantageous to show up on clear nights after sunset. For more distant views of the crater, visit Volcano House near Kilauea Visitor Center.

Kilauea Iki Overlook Lookout

(Crater Rim Dr) When Kilauea Iki (Little Kilauea) burst open in a fiery inferno in November 1959, it turned the crater into a roiling lake of molten lava and sent 1900ft-high fountains of lava into the night sky. At its peak, the eruption gushed 2 million tons of lava an hour as the landscape glowed an eerie orange for miles.

From the overlook, you can view the steaming mile-wide crater below, which was used for filming the 2001 remake of *Planet of the Apes*.

Look for tiny hikers making their way across the crater floor to appreciate its massive proportions.

Halema'uma'u Crater: A Lake of Fire

On March 19, 2008, Halema'uma'u Crater shattered a quarter-century of silence with a huge steam-driven explosion that scattered rocks and Pele's hair (strands of volcanic glass) over 75 acres. A series of explosions followed, widening a 300ft vent in the crater floor, which as of early 2014 continued to spew a muscular column of gas and ash. The vent bubbles (but doesn't spurt) molten lava.

In 1823, missionary William Ellis first described the boiling goblet of Halema'uma'u, and this prodigious sight attracted travelers from all over the world. Looking in, some saw the fires of hell, others primeval creation, but none left the crater unmoved. Mark Twain wrote that he witnessed: '[C]ircles and serpents and streaks of lightning all twined and wreathed and tied together...I have seen Vesuvius since, but it was a mere toy, a child's volcano, a soup kettle, compared to this.'

Then, in 1924, the crater floor subsided rapidly, touching off a series of explosive eruptions. Boulders and mud rained down for days. When it was over, the crater had doubled in size – to about 300ft deep and 3000ft wide. Lava activity ceased and the crust cooled.

Since then, Halema'uma'u has erupted 18 times; it's the most active area on the volcano's summit. All of Hawai'i is the territory of Pele, goddess of fire and volcanoes, but Halema'uma'u is her home, making it a sacred site for Hawaiians.

Kilauea Caldera, Crater Rim Drive & Volcano

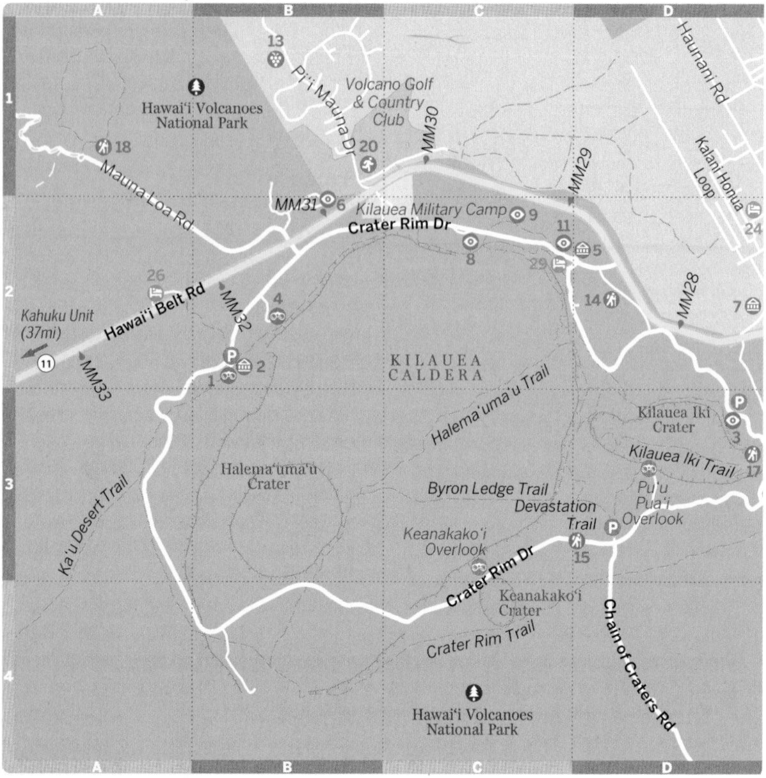

Thurston Lava Tube Cave

(off Crater Rim Dr; 👪) On Kilauea's eastern side, Crater Rim Dr passes through rainforest *kipuka* (oases) thick with tree ferns and ohia trees. An often overflowing parking lot is the access point for the ever-popular Thurston Lava Tube. All the tour buses stop here and it's a favorite with kids, so plan to come early or late in the day. A 0.3-mile loop walk starts in ohia forest filled with birdsong before diving underground through a gigantic lava tube that's artificially lit.

Lava tubes are formed when the outer crust of a lava river starts to harden but the liquid lava beneath the surface continues to flow through. After the flow drains out, the hard shell remains. Dating back perhaps 500 years, Thurston Lava Tube is a grand example – it's tunnel-like and almost big enough to run a train through.

CHAIN OF CRATERS ROAD

Turning south off Crater Rim Dr, paved Chain of Craters Road winds almost 20 miles and 3700ft down the southern slopes of Kilauea, ending abruptly at the volcano's East Rift Zone on the coast. Allow at least 90 minutes for the round-trip drive excluding stops. Drive slowly, especially in foggy or rainy conditions, and watch out for endangered nene (Hawaiian goose) along the way.

From the paved road you'll have striking vistas of the coastline far below, but for miles and miles the predominant view is of hardened lava. You can sometimes find thin filaments of volcanic glass, known as Pele's hair, in

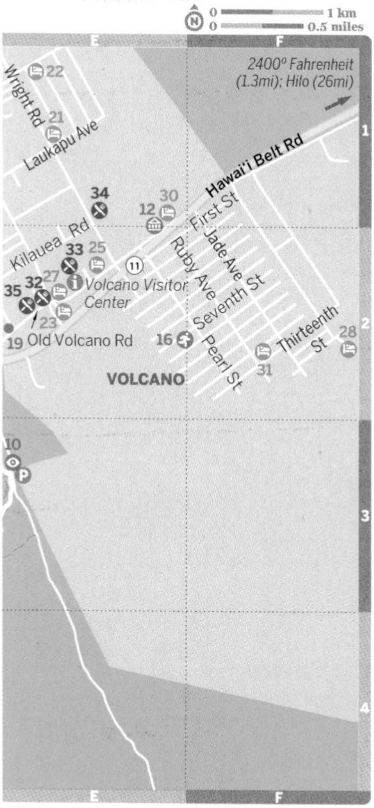

the cracks and crevices. The best time to photograph this unique landscape is in the early morning and late afternoon, when sunlight slants off the lava.

Hilina Pali Overlook Lookout

(Hilina Pali Rd) After a couple of miles of pit craters along Chain of Craters Road, you'll come to the turnoff for Hilina Pali Rd. Drive carefully on this narrow, one-lane paved road – especially because your eyes will be popping at the endless volcanic wastelands and spectacular northward views of Mauna Loa. After 5 miles, you'll pass Kulanaokuaiki Campground. The road ends roughly 4 miles later at the serenely beautiful Hila Pali Overlook.

From the road's end, you may be tempted to hit the **Hilina Pali Trail**, but the shoreline isn't as close as it looks. Hikers must be prepared for a rugged backcountry trek in extreme weather conditions.

Mauna Ulu Landmark

(off Chain of Craters Rd) In 1969, eruptions from Kilauea's East Rift Zone began building a new lava shield, Mauna Ulu (Growing Mountain). By the time the flow stopped in 1974, it had covered 10,000 acres of parkland and added 200 acres of new coastal land. It also buried a 6-mile section of the original Chain of Craters Road in lava up to 300ft deep. Today the signed turnoff for Mauna Ulu is 3.5 miles down Chain of Craters Road.

The Pu'u Huluhulu Trail (p217) and more demanding Napau Crater Trail (p217) begin here (backcountry permit required for the latter).

Kealakomo Lookout

(Chain of Craters Rd) About halfway along Chain of Craters Rd, this coastal lookout (elevation 2000ft) has picnic tables and commanding views. Below Kealakomo, the road descends long, sweeping switchbacks, some cut deeply through lava flows.

Pu'u Loa Petroglyphs Archaeological Site

(off Chain of Craters Rd) The gentle, 1.5-mile round-trip **Pu'u Loa Trail** leads to one of Hawai'i's largest concentration of ancient petroglyphs. Here Hawaiians chiseled more than 23,000 drawings into *pahoehoe* (smooth-flowing lava) with adze tools quarried from Keanakako'i. At the site, stay on the boardwalk at all times – not all petroglyphs are obvious, and you are likely to trample (and damage) some if you walk over the rocks. The trailhead parking area is signed between the Mile 16 and the Mile 17 markers.

There are abstract designs, animal and human figures, as well as thousands of dimpled depressions (or cupules) that were receptacles for *piko* (umbilical cords). Placing a baby's *piko* inside a cupule and covering it with stones was intended to bestow health and longevity on the child. Rangers occasionally lead hikes exploring petroglyphs beyond the boardwalk – inquire at Kilauea Visitor Center.

Kilauea Caldera, Crater Rim Drive & Volcano

Sights

1 Halema'uma'u Viewpoint B2
2 Jaggar Museum B2
3 Kilauea Iki Overlook D3
4 Kilauea Overlook B2
5 Kilauea Visitor Center & Museum D2
6 Lava Tree Molds B2
7 Rainforest Gallery D2
8 Steam Vents & Steaming Bluff C2
9 Sulphur Banks C2
10 Thurston Lava Tube E3
11 Volcano Art Center C2
12 Volcano Garden Arts E1
13 Volcano Winery B1

Activities, Courses & Tours

14 Backcountry Office D2
15 Devastation Trail D3
16 Hale Ho'ōla E2
17 Kilauea Iki Trail D3
18 Kipuka Puaulu (Bird Park) A1
19 Niaulani Rain Forest Tour E2
20 Volcano Golf & Country Club B1

Sleeping

Artist Cottage .... (see 12)
21 Chalet Kilauea Collection E1
22 Enchanted Rainforest Cottages E1
23 Hale Ohia Log Cabin E2
24 Holo Holo In D2
25 Kilauea Lodge E2
26 Namakanipaio Cabins & Campground A2
27 Volcano Country Cottages E2
28 Volcano Guest House F2
Volcano Hideaways .... (see 23)
29 Volcano House C2
30 Volcano Inn E1
31 Volcano Rainforest Retreat F2

Eating

32 Café Ohi'a E2
Café Ono .... (see 12)
Kilauea General Store .... (see 33)
Kilauea Lodge Restaurant .... (see 25)
Lava Rock Café .... (see 33)
Rim Restaurant .... (see 29)
33 Thai Thai Restaurant E2
34 Volcano Farmers Market E1
35 Volcano Store E2

Drinking & Nightlife

Uncle George's Lounge .... (see 29)

Holei Sea Arch
Landmark

Constantly brutalized by unrelenting surf, the coastal section of Chain of Craters Road has sharply eroded lava-rock *pali* (cliffs). Visible from near the road's end, this high rock arch is a dramatic landmark, carved out of a cliff by crashing waves.

End of the Road
Landmark

(Chain of Craters Rd) Quite. The road ends where the lava says it ends, having swamped this coastal section of Chain of Craters Road repeatedly between 1969 and 1996. The 'Road Closed' sign, almost entirely buried in lava, is a classic photo op. There's a simple info board and portable toilets here, plus a ranger outpost – but don't count on it being staffed unless lava starts flowing again nearby within hiking distance.

MAUNA LOA ROAD

If you really want to escape the crowds, drive 11.5-mile Mauna Loa Rd past hiking trailheads, majestic views and *kipuka* (oases) spared by massive lava flows. The road begins off Hwy 11 near the Mile 31 marker, just over 2 miles west of the park's main entrance. After a mile or so, before reaching Kipuka Puaulu, roadside picnic tables and pit toilets are the only facilities.

Lava Tree Molds
Landmark

(off Mauna Loa Rd) Near the start of Mauna Loa Rd, there's a turnoff to some neglected lava tree molds, deep tube-like apertures formed when lava flows engulfed the rainforest and hardened around the waterlogged trees instead of burning them upon contact. As the trees disintegrated, they left deep holes where the trunks once stood.

Mauna Loa Lookout
Lookout

(Mauna Loa Rd) It's a narrow, winding and potholed drive to the very top of lonely Mauna Loa Rd, passing heavily forested *kipuka* as you come ever closer to the world's most massive active volcano. Mauna Loa has erupted more than 18 times in the past century – the last eruption, in March 1984, lasted three weeks. At the end of the road lies epic Mauna Loa Lookout (6600ft) and the start of the exceptionally challenging, multiday

Mauna Loa Trail (p219; backcountry permit required).

For the best views, wander a short way down the trail for vistas that encompass smoking Kilauea far below.

KAHUKU UNIT

In 2003, NPS and the Nature Conservancy jointly purchased Kahuku Ranch, part of Hawai'i's largest traditional *ahupua'a* (land division). The biggest conservation land purchase in the state's history, this deal added a whopping 116,000 acres to the national park, increasing its size by over 50%.

Today, the park's **Kahuku Unit** remains largely wild and undeveloped. This is a real get-away-from-it-all destination, with no amenities besides outhouses. Four hiking trails – Pu'u o Lokuana (p220), Palm (p220), Glover (p220) and Kona (p220) – lead through green pastures and around volcanic cinder cones, lava tree molds, rainforest and lava flows. The 12-mile round-trip **scenic drive** is unpaved, but usually passable just over halfway in a standard car. Beyond the Palm Trail's upper trailhead, a high-clearance, 4WD vehicle is advised.

At the time of research, the Kahuku Unit (free entry) was open to the public from 9am to 3pm on Saturdays and Sundays, but double-check this at Kilauea Visitor Center before making the trip. The entrance is about 4 miles west of Wai'ohinu (p238), between the Mile 70 and the Mile 71 markers on Hwy 11. Ranger-guided hikes are offered some weekends (advance reservations not usually required.)

Activities

HIKING

Dust off your hiking boots: rainforest oases, lava deserts, secluded beaches, crater walks and the world's most active volcano all await on the park's 150-mile trail network, rising from sea level to the summit of Mauna Loa (13,679ft).

Be prepared for highly changeable weather: a hot sunny stroll can turn cold and wet in an instant. No drinking water is available, except possibly at primitive campgrounds (where it must be treated before drinking); plan to pack at least 3L of water per person per day. Campfires are prohibited. A compass and binoculars are handy, because misty or 'voggy'

Thurston Lava Tube (p212)

PHILIP ROSENBERG/GETTY IMAGES ©

Detour: Viewing the Lava Flow Up Close

Lucky travelers can view live lava making the 64-mile journey from the Pu'u O'o Vent to the ocean. Where the lava will be flowing when you visit and whether or not you can reach it are impossible to predict. Sometimes it's an arduous 13-mile round-trip hike from the end of Chain of Craters Road inside the park. Ask at the Kilauea Visitor Center, call the park or check the NPS website for updates.

It's usually a much easier hike to the flow from the free, county-run lava viewing area (p202) outside park boundaries at the end of Hwy 130 in Puna. If the show is really on, there will be surface flows, lava 'skylights' and flaming trees. When the flow mellows or changes course, you'll be able to see a steam plume during the day, and an unearthly red glow after dark. Bring a flashlight and water, and plan to stick around after sunset. You might be able to get even closer to the lava flow on a guided hiking tour or lava boat cruise leaving from Puna (p189).

Of course, all of this information is highly changeable – staying informed about the flow helps manage expectations (especially kids'). Lava entering the ocean is wondrous, but extremely dangerous. The explosive clash between seawater and 2100°F (1150°C) lava can spray scalding water hundreds of feet into the air and throw flaming lava chunks well inland. Unstable ledges of lava crust (called 'lava benches') sometimes collapse without warning. Several observers have been injured, some fatally, over the past decade. Always stay at least 500yd inland from the lava flow and heed all official warnings.

conditions and intense sunlight reflecting off lava can impede navigation.

All overnight hikes require a free permit, available in person up to one day ahead from the **Backcountry Office** (☎808-985-6178; Crater Rim Dr, Visitor Emergency Operations Center (VEOC); ⏲8am-4pm). Ask at Kilauea Visitor Center for directions, or check the park website, which has a downloadable backcountry trip planner covering potential hazards with safety tips and advice for protecting wildlife and archaeological sites.

If you prefer to join a group, the nonprofit **Friends of Hawai'i Volcanoes National Park** (☎808-985-7373; www.fhvnp.org; annual membership adult/student/family $30/15/45) leads weekend hikes and field trips, and organizes volunteer activities such as native forest restoration.

Kilauea Iki Trail — Hiking

If you can only do one day hike, make it this one. Beginning at the Kilauea Iki Overlook (p211) parking lot off Crater Rim Dr, this 4-mile, clockwise loop takes you through a jaw-dropping microcosm of the park. It quickly descends 400ft through fairytale ohia forest, then cuts across mile-wide Kilauea Iki crater. Scattered vents lace the crater's surface with ethereal steam plumes, while the wrinkly, often iridescent lava surface is peppered with *ohelo* shrubs, ohia trees and ferns.

Hitting the trail before 8am is a good way to beat the day-tripping crowds. The faint footpath across the crater floor is marked by *ahu* (stone cairns) to aid navigation. Don't wander off-trail to explore any steaming vents, lava tubes or caves without an experienced guide.

Geology-oriented trail brochures ($2) are sold at Kilauea Visitor Center.

Halema'uma'u Trail Hiking

Halema'uma'u Crater was indefinitely closed to hikers at the time of research due to ongoing volcanic activity, though short trail sections through ohia forest along the crater rim were open. When fully open, this 7-mile loop is one of the park's best day hikes, prized for its variety of ecosystems and colorful lava flows.

Devastation Trail Hiking

Although only 0.5 miles long, the paved, wheelchair-accessible Devastation Trail offers fantastic views of Mauna Loa looming over the sulfur-encrusted caldera. The 1959 eruption of Kilauea Iki toasted this rainforest, leaving dead trees, stripped bare and sun-bleached white, and tree molds. Now ohia trees, *'ohelo* shrubs and ferns are colonizing the area anew.

The prominent cinder cone you'll see along the way is **Pu'u Pua'i** (Gushing Hill), formed during the eruption. You can start the trail from either end at the Pu'u Puai Overlook parking lot or the Devastation Trail parking area further west, where Crater Rim Dr turns south.

Crater Rim Trail Hiking

Almost all of this trail was closed at the time of research, which is a pity since this 11.5-mile loop hike showcases just how dramatically the volcano has altered the landscape over time. Ask at Kilauea Visitor Center about which trail sections are currently open, usually short strolls of under a mile through ohia forest along the rim of **Keanakako'i Crater**, off Crater Rim Dr and Chain of Craters Road.

Pu'u Huluhulu Trail Hiking

This easy 2.5-mile round-trip hike begins at Mauna Ulu (p213) parking area off Chain of Craters Road. The trail ends atop a 150ft-high cinder cone, **Pu'u Huluhulu**, which is like a crow's nest on a clear day. Summit vistas net Mauna Ulu, Mauna Loa, Mauna Kea, Pu'u 'O'o Vent, Kilauea Volcano, the East Rift Zone and the ocean beyond.

A self-guiding trail brochure ($2), which includes perilous eyewitness accounts of the 1969–74 eruption, is sold at Kilauea Visitor Center.

Napau Crater Trail Hiking

An incredibly varied and satisfying all-day hike, the Napau Crater Trail passes lava fields, immense craters and thick native forest, ending with distant views of Pu'u O'o, the source of Kilauea's ongoing eruption. It's a 14-mile round-trip backcountry hike over rugged terrain, starting from the Mauna Ulu (p213) parking area off Crater Rim Dr. Backcountry permits are required for both day and overnight hikes.

Pu'u 'O'o Vent and its lava-flow path
STEPHAN HOEROLD/GETTY IMAGES ©

Self-registration is available at the trailhead, but it's smarter to pick up your free permit from the Backcountry Office (p216), where you can ask about trail conditions and closures in this geologically unstable area. The trail's first 5 miles follow what was formerly Chain of Craters Road, before lava swamped it; reticulite and Pele's hair (strands of volcanic glass) are strewn over the flows.

You'll pass lava trees and **Pu'u Huluhulu** cinder cone before veering left (east). On clear days the view is magnificent, with Mauna Loa to the northwest, Mauna Kea to the north and the volatile Pu'u 'O'o vent to the east. After descending across *pahoehoe* flows, you'll reach the south rim of jaw-dropping, mile-long **Makaopuhi Crater**.

Exiting a cool fern forest, you come to the rock walls of an old depository for *pulu,* the golden, silky 'hair' found at the base of *hapu'u* (tree fern) fiddlehead stems, with which ancient Hawaiians embalmed the dead. Tour helicopters whir overhead as fantastic views of the partially collapsed Pu'u 'O'o cone appear. Beyond the **Napau Crater lookout** junction is primitive Napau Campground (pit toilets, no water).

You can shave off about 4 miles round-trip if you start on the Naulu Trail from Kealakomo (p213) down Chain of Craters Road. However, you'll miss some of the grandest views and the huffing vents and cracks peppering the active rift.

Puna Coast Trails Hiking

You'll experience secluded snorkeling, white-sand beaches, soaring cliffs and savagely beautiful landscapes on these rugged backcountry trails. The main approaches – the Hilina Pali, Keauhou and Puna Coast Trails – are all hot, steep and strenuous, so bring lots of extra water. With an interconnecting trail network, you can design your own overnight trek.

Pick up your free overnight hiking permit (required) at the Backcountry Office (p216), where rangers have information on current trail closures and conditions, and just as importantly, water-catchment levels at primitive backcountry shelters and campgrounds.

With swimming and snorkeling, white sand and coconut trees, **Halape** is the most popular overnight destination,

Hiking, Devastation Trail (p217)

JOHN ELK/GETTY IMAGES ©

followed by **Keauhou**. Endangered hawksbill sea turtles nest all along the coast here, so travel responsibly.

The easiest route down to the coast is the gently sloping **Keauhou Trail** (6.8 miles one way); the trailhead is past the Mile 6 marker on Chain of Craters Road. The shortest route to Ka'aha is the **Hilina Pali Trail** (3.6 miles one way), which continues to Halape (8 miles), but it begins with a brutal cliff descent; the trail starts at Hilina Pali Overlook (p213).

Kipuka Puaulu (Bird Park) Hiking

(👪) If you're looking for a shady, 1.2-mile loop hike easy enough for young kids, this is it. This 100-acre sanctuary is a prime specimen of a rainforest *kipuka* (oasis), spared about 400 years ago by a major lava flow from Mauna Loa. Today native flora and fauna thrive here. The trailhead is just over a mile up Mauna Loa Rd, off Hwy 11.

This hike is best done in the early morning or at dusk, when you'll be enveloped by birdsong. You'll see honeycreepers – the *'amakihi, 'apapane* and *'i'iwi* – plus the inquisitive *'elepaio* (Hawaiian monarch flycatcher). The trees soar, so bring your binoculars and park yourself on a forest bench. You'll also pass a lava tube inhabited by a unique species of big-eyed hunting spider and lava-tree crickets.

Flora-and-fauna trail guides ($2) are sold at Kilauea Visitor Center.

Mauna Loa Trail Hiking

(off Mauna Loa Rd) The Mauna Loa Trail begins at the end of Mauna Loa Rd, off Hwy 11. All in, it's an extremely challenging (though nontechnical) 19.6-mile hike that ascends 7000ft and takes at least three days, although four is better for acclimatization and exploring the summit area. Rain, fog, snow and whiteouts can make the trail's *ahu* (cairns) hard to follow.

Two simple bunk-bed cabins are available on a first-come, first-served basis at Pu'u'ula'ula (Red Hill) and closer to the summit. Potable water might be available, but must be treated; inquire at the Backcountry Office (p216) when picking up your free permit (required). Be prepared for severe winter conditions year-round, as well as wildfires and volcanic eruptions (very unlikely).

The trail begins rising through an ohia forest and above the tree line. After 7.5 miles you'll reach **Pu'u'ula'ula (Red Hill)** at 10,035ft, offering views of Mauna Kea to the north and Maui's Haleakalā to the northwest. The next day, the 11.6-mile hike to the summit cabin (13,250ft) crosses a stark, stirring landscape of multicolored cinder fields, spatter cones and gaping lava fissures. Two miles before arriving at the cabin, turn left at the **Moku'aweoweo Caldera** trail junction for the summit cabin. The other fork leads to the 2.6-mile **Summit Trail**, for tackling the summit (13,679ft) on day three.

To summit the mountain in just one day, there's the Mauna Loa Observatory Trail (p142) off Saddle Rd.

Mauna Iki Trail Hiking

For solitude in a mesmerizing lava landscape, follow this trail into Ka'u Desert. Starting off Hwy 11 along what's commonly called the **Footprints Trail**, your initial commitment is low and variations allow for great route extensions. However, the entire trail section from the Jaggar Museum to Hwy 11 was closed at the

The Best... Hawai'i Volcanoes National Park Day Hikes

1 Kilauea Iki Trail (p216)

2 Kipuka Puaulu (Bird Park)

3 Pu'u Loa Petroglyphs (p213)

4 Glover & Kona Trails (p220)

5 Napau Crater Trail (p217)

Hiking & Backpacking Safety Tips

In Hawai'i Volcanoes National Park, both lava desert and coastal trails can be extremely hot and dehydrating. Heat exhaustion is a real danger. Sunscreen, sunglasses and a wide-brimmed hat are essential. When weather conditions turn windy and wet, hypothermia is possible even if temperatures stay above freezing. Always pack extra insulating, waterproof layers too.

Only fit and experienced high-altitude hikers should attempt Mauna Loa. It's critically important to acclimatize first. For 'altitude sickness' (acute mountain sickness, or AMS), descent is the only remedy. The mountain's high elevation causes extreme environmental conditions, making hypothermia a hazard. Winter-rated, waterproof clothing and gear are essential year-round.

time of research due to ongoing volcanic activity.

Look for the Ka'u Desert Trailhead parking area between the Mile 37 and the Mile 38 markers on Hwy 11. Start early, as midday can be brutally hot and dry. Initially, the trail is very clear, level and partly paved, threading through sand-covered *pahoehoe* flows to reach a structure protecting ancient Hawaiian footprints preserved in hardened ash.

Beyond here the trail is marked by easy-to-follow cairns. As you gradually ascend, views expand, with Mauna Loa behind and the immense Ka'u Desert in front. Less than 2 miles from the trailhead, you'll crest **Mauna Iki** and stand likely alone in the middle of a vast lava field.

Pu'u o Lokuana Trail — Hiking

Near the entrance to the park's remote Kahuku Unit, this easy 2-mile loop follows historic ranch roads through pasture lands. After passing lava tree molds, the route wanders around spatter ramparts from Mauna Loa's 1868 eruption. Follow an abandoned airstrip back to the road and climb the cinder cone that gives this trail its name for spectacular views.

Palm Trail — Hiking

A lonely semiloop inside the park's detached Kahuku Unit, this 2.6-mile ramble traverses pasture land with panoramic views. Highlights include ranching-era relics, remnants of native forest and striking volcanic features along a fissure from Mauna Loa's 1868 eruption. Start at the lower trailhead, an 0.8-mile walk downhill from the upper trailhead.

Glover & Kona Trails — Hiking

Deep inside the park's wilderness Kahuku Unit await the Glover and Kona Trails. The highlight of the 3-mile **Glover Trail** semiloop is standing at the edge of a huge forested pit crater, a deep bowl full of trees looking like the entrance to the underworld. Another semiloop hike nearby, the 3.8-mile **Kona Trail** passes through ranchlands and borders an 1887 lava flow.

The Lower Glover trailhead is on the right about 3 miles uphill beyond the Upper Palm trailhead (high-clearance 4WD recommended). The Glover Trail loops back to the upper trailhead near the end of Kahuku Rd, from where it's a 0.9-mile walk back downhill on the road to the lower trailhead. Alternatively, extend your hike by cutting west to the Upper Kona trailhead and ending at the Lower Kona trailhead, a short walk from the Lower Glover trailhead.

CYCLING

Volcano Bike Tours — Cycling

(**☎888-934-9199, 808-934-9199; http://bikevolcano.com; tours $105-129**) If you're into pedal power, Volcano Bike Tours offers guided cycling tours of the park on hybrid comfort bikes. Tours, which take off rain or shine and last three to five hours, follow Crater Rim Dr and Chain of Craters Road.

Festivals & Events

Check the park website or ask at Kilauea Visitor Center about free (or low-cost) special events, including **After Dark in the Park** natural history lectures, **'Ike Hana No'eau** cultural demonstrations and craft workshops, **Na Leo Manu** evening concerts and **Stewardship at the Summit** daytime volunteer activities.

Volcano Art Center Music, Dance
(808-967-7565; www.volcanoartcenter.org) Free Hawaiian craft demonstrations are given one Friday each month. The center also hosts arts, music and cultural events year-round, including popular concert, dance and theater performances here and at its Niaulani Campus in Volcano.

Hula Arts at Kilauea Arts, Culture
(www.volcanoartcenter.org;) A free series of outdoor *kahiko* (ancient) hula performances happens near the Volcano Art Center on one Saturday morning each month.

Kilauea Cultural Festival Culture, Arts
(www.nps.gov/havo/planyourvisit/events.htm;) For over 30 years, this annual cultural festival in July has celebrated traditional Hawaiian arts, crafts, music and hula. Free entrance to the park during the festival.

Sleeping & Eating

The park's two drive-up campgrounds are relatively uncrowded outside summer. Nights can be crisp and cool, however; you should bring rainproof gear. Campsites are first-come, first-served (seven-night limit).

Namakanipaio Cabins & Campground Cabin, Campground $
(info 808-756-9625, reservations 866-536-7972; www.hawaiivolcanohouse.com; tent site $15, cabin q $80) The park's busiest campground is off Hwy 11, about 3 miles west of the visitor center. Tent camping is in a small, unshaded meadow with little privacy. Facilities include restrooms, drinking water, picnic tables and BBQ grills. Book ahead for simple, A-frame wooden cabins with shared communal bathrooms and hot showers; check-in is at Volcano House.

Pu'u Loa Petroglyphs (p213)

SCOTT DARSNEY/GETTY IMAGES ©

Kulanaokuaiki Campground Campground $

(www.nps.gov/havo; Hilina Pali Rd) FREE About 5 miles down Hilina Pali Rd, this minimally developed campground has eight tent sites, pit toilets and picnic tables, but no water. Campfires are prohibited.

Volcano House Lodge $$$

(866-536-7972, 808-756-9625; www.hawaiivolcanohouse.com; Crater Rim Dr; r $185-385;) With an unforgettable location perched on the rim of Kilauea Caldera, the newly reborn Volcano House has long enjoyed its unique status as the park's only hotel. Ecoconscious renovations have brought long overdue upgrades to the restaurant, bar, fireplace lobby areas, gift shops and 33 spacious, if quite plain and thin-walled, guest rooms. Reserve well in advance.

Both the refurbished **Rim Restaurant** (www.hawaiivolcanohouse.com/dining/; Crater Rim Dr, Volcano House; breakfast buffet adult/child $18/9, lunch prix-fixe menu adult/child $19/11, dinner mains $19-39; 7am-10am, 11am-2pm & 5-9pm), serving better-than-average Hawaii Regional Cuisine (modern island fusion) crafted from local ingredients, and **Uncle George's Lounge** (Crater Rim Dr, Volcano House; 11am-9pm), a pint-sized bar with live music and food, have enormous windows that afford absolutely staggering volcano views (as do certain guest rooms). If you can't spring for the room, just sip a beer. Slowly.

Information

The park (808-985-6000; www.nps.gov/havo) is open 24 hours a day, except when eruption activity and volcanic gases necessitate temporary closures. For current lava flows and trail, road and campground status, check the website or call ahead.

The park's main entrance sits at almost 4000ft, with varying elevation and climates inside park boundaries. Chilly rain, wind, fog and vog (volcanic fog) typify the fickle weather here, which can go from hot and dry to a soaking downpour in a flash. Near Kilauea Caldera, temperatures average 15°F (8.3°C) cooler than in Kona, so bring a rain jacket and pants, just in case.

Dangers & Annoyances

Although few people have died due to violently explosive eruptions at Kilauea (the last was in 1924), other volcanic activity hasn't been so beneficent. You'll hear about tourists who ventured onto unstable 'benches' of new land that collapsed, for example.

Heed rangers' and park warnings. Stick to marked trails and don't venture off on your own – getting lost on lava is easier than you think. Watch your step, especially on glass-sharp *'a'a;* the bloody abrasions aren't pretty. Wear hiking shoes with good traction and ankle support, and carry at least 2L of water per person (more if you're hiking).

High concentrations of sulfur dioxide permeate the air, especially around Halema'uma'u Crater, sometimes closing Crater Rim Dr altogether. Anyone with respiratory or heart conditions, pregnant women and those with infants or

Bicycling, Hawai'i Volcanoes National Park

young children should be especially careful. When driving through especially voggy areas, keep the car windows rolled up and the air-conditioning running on recycled air. Drivers should also stay alert to avoid hitting an endangered nene (Hawaiian goose).

Websites

Hawaii Department of Health **(www.hiso2index.info)** Air-quality updates and current sulfur dioxide levels islandwide. For park-specific information, visit www.hawaiiso2network.com.

Hawaiian Lava Daily **(http://hawaiianlavadaily.blogspot.com)** Stunning photos and videos of Kilauea volcano's red-hot lava action.

USGS Hawaiian Volcano Observatory **(http://hvo.wr.usgs.gov)** Kilauea Volcano eruption updates, current earthquake and atmospheric conditions, and hypnotizing web cams.

Getting There & Around

The park is 30 miles (45 minutes) from Hilo and 95 miles (2¼ hours) from Kailua-Kona via Hwy 11. The turnoffs for Volcano village are a couple miles east of the main park entrance. Hwy 11 is prone to flooding, washouts and closures during rainstorms. Periods of drought may close Mauna Loa Rd and Hilina Pali Rd due to wildfire hazards.

The public **Hele-On Bus** **(☎808-961-8744; www.heleonbus.org; adult 1-way fare $2)** departs fives times daily (except Sunday) from Hilo, arriving at the park visitor center about 1¼ hours later, with one bus continuing to Ka'u.

In the park, cyclists are permitted only on paved Crater Rim Dr, Chain of Craters Road, Hilina Pali Rd and Mauna Loa Rd.

Volcano

Slow down: this is Volcano. Enveloped by cool mists and a mystical hush, this tiny town is hedged by ohia forest and emerald tree ferns. Many artists and writers find inspiration in this small, soulful place. Pull out your wet-weather gear, however: it can be cold and rainy.

Local Knowledge

NAME: EMILY PASTERCHICK

OCCUPATION: VOLUNTEER INTERPRETER

RESIDENCE: HAWAI'I VOLCANOES NATIONAL PARK

1 WHAT'S YOUR TOP SPOT IN THE PARK? THE ONE YOU KEEP COMING BACK TO?

The Kilauea Iki Trail. I can pick it up pretty much outside my door. I hike at least part of it every day. I've done it in a little over an hour – but that's with power walking across the crater. It usually takes two hours minimum.

2 IF YOU HAD ONLY THREE OR FOUR HOURS IN THE PARK, WHAT WOULD YOU DO?

There are shorter trails like Mauna Ulu where you'll see more of the park and fewer people. I'd also go to the Jaggar Museum and the overlook – this is the closest view of Halema'uma'u Crater since the road closures. The walk from the steam vents to the Sulphur Banks is cool too.

3 ASIDE FROM HIKING, WHAT DO YOU LIKE TO DO HERE?

My degree is in anthropology and so I often work at the Pu'u Loa petroglyphs, which are really interesting. Try and go in the early morning or late afternoon when the shadows are most dramatic. We're working to generate more interest in the ranger-led hikes there that take visitors beyond the boardwalk.

4 WOULD YOU RECOMMEND VOLUNTEERING IN THE PARK TO OTHERS?

Volunteering here has been one of the most exciting experiences of my life. Before I came here I knew nothing, but after two weeks of training I felt prepared – I knew about Hawaiian plants and animals, and traditional culture.

The Best... Hawaiian Cultural Experiences

1 Hula Arts at Kilauea (p221)

2 Kilauea Cultural Festival (p221)

3 Pu'u Loa Petroglyphs (p213)

4 Volcano Art Center (p209)

5 Hale Ho'ōla (p224)

Sights

Rainforest Gallery Gallery

(☎808-967-8211; www.volcanoartcenter.org; 19-4074 Old Volcano Rd; ⏰9am-4pm) A satellite of the Volcano Art Center (p209) in Hawai'i Volcanoes National Park, this gallery showcases local artists working in many different media; the adjacent shop offers remarkably handcrafted works for sale. Art workshops and performing arts events are sometimes held here too.

Volcano Garden Arts Gallery

(www.volcanogardenarts.com; 19-3834 Old Volcano Rd; ⏰10am-4pm Tue-Sun) Get inspired at charming artist-owner Ira Ono's working studio in the fern forest. You'll also discover an art gallery representing dozens of island craftspeople and fine artists, rotating art installations, gardens and Café Ono (p229). Check the online calendar for art workshops and special events.

2400° Fahrenheit Gallery

(☎808-985-8667; www.2400f.com; 11-3200 Old Volcano Rd; ⏰10am-4pm Thu-Mon) Drop by to watch Michael and Misato Mortara blow hot glass into mind-boggling bowls and vases. A tiny gallery displays their finished masterpieces – don't ask how much. It's off Hwy 11 at the village's eastern end.

Akatsuka Orchid Gardens Gardens

(☎808-967-8234; www.akatsukaorchid.com; 11-3051 Volcano Rd; ⏰9am-5pm) Famous for its unique hybrid orchids, this touristy showroom bursts with 200,000 blooming plants, shippable all over the world. Drop in for an olfactory awakening. It's off Hwy 11 between the Mile 22 and the Mile 23 markers.

Volcano Winery Winery

(☎808-967-7772; http://volcanowinery.com; 35 Pi'i Mauna Dr; tasting flight $5; ⏰10am-5:30pm) With grapes grown in Mauna Loa's volcanic soil, this winery inland from Hwy 11 pours bottles with some *very* unusual (read: supersweet) flavor infusions: tea, macadamia nuts, honey and guava.

Activities

Hale Ho'ōla Spa

(☎808-756-2421; www.halehoola.net; 11-3913 7th St; ⏰by appointment only) After a hard day hiking, relax at this day spa inside a private home with *lomilomi* (traditional Hawaiian massage) augmented by hula music, hot lava-rock stones or steaming bundles of medicinal herbs. Or maybe a volcanic mud facial or tropical body treatment – coconut-lemongrass sugar scrub, anyone? No walk-ins.

Volcano Golf & Country Club Golf

(☎808-967-7331; www.volcanogolfshop.com; 99-1621 Pi'i Mauna Dr; greens fees $56, club rental $20) With a lush setting beneath Mauna Loa and Mauna Kea, this straightforward 18-hole, par-72 course is a local favorite.

Tours

Niaulani Rain Forest Tour Walking Tour

(☎808-967-8211/8222; www.volcanoartcenter.org; 19-4074 Old Volcano Rd, Volcano Art Center's Niaulani Campus; ⏰9:30am Mon & 11am Sat; 👪) FREE Join an hour-long, half-mile guided nature walk through Volcano's rainforest. Guides cover the ecological importance and protection of old-growth koa and ohia forests, traditional Hawaiian uses of plants, and the role of birds in the forest. Call to ask about forest restoration volunteer workdays.

Tea Hawaii & Company Walking Tour
(☎808-967-7637; http://teahawaii.com; 1hr tour $25) Get an insider's look at Hawai'i's specialty tea cultivation on this sustainable farm and forest sanctuary, where you'll tour the tea gardens before tasting hand-picked black, white and oolong brews. Reservations required.

Hawaii Photo Retreat Walking Tour
(☎985-7487; www.hawaiiphotoretreat.com; 1-/2-/3-day tour $345/690/1035; by reservation only) Seriously aspiring photographers experience unbridled natural beauty on customized tours with professional shooters Ken and Mary Goodrich, who live in Volcano. Meals and transportation not included.

Festivals & Events

Volcano Rain Forest Runs Sports
(http://volcanorainforestruns.com) In August, this half-marathon, 10km run or 5km run/walk passes through Volcano village and nearby ranch lands.

Volcano Village Artists Hui Arts
(www.volcanovillageartistshui.com) FREE Tour pottery, fiber work, wood scupture, ceramics, woodblock prints, glass blowing and photography studios over a three-day weekend in late November.

Sleeping

Tranquil B&Bs and vacation-rental cottages grow around Volcano like mushrooms. Most require a two-night minimum stay, or else add a one-night surcharge or cleaning fee. For more listings, check **Vacation Rentals by Owner** (VRBO; www.vrbo.com), **HomeAway** (www.homeaway.com), **Air B&B** (www.airbnb.com) and local rental agent **Volcano Gallery** (☎808-987-0920; www.volcanogallery.com).

Holo Holo In Hostel $
(☎808-967-8025, 808-967-7950; www.volcanohostel.com; 19-4036 Kalani Honua Rd; dm $24, r with/without bath $75/60; @) Don't be put off by this hostel's exterior. Inside, the two six-bed dorms and four private rooms are sizable and cabinlike. The hostel, which has a well-equipped kitchen, is locked from 11am to 4:30pm daily, when guests

Wine tasting, Volcano Winery

ANN CECIL/GETTY IMAGES ©

must vacate. No credit cards or shoes indoors. Book ahead. The Hele-On Bus stops two blocks away.

Enchanted Rainforest Cottages Vacation Rental **$$**
(**808-443-4930; http://erc-volcano.com; 19-4176 Kekoa Nui Blvd; d $85-140;** wi-fi) Private, well-designed and impeccably kept, these cottages are harbored in a fern forest landscaped with footpaths and koi ponds. Both the light-filled Apapane Guesthouse – with a skylit bathroom, gas stove and full kitchen – and the smaller Hikers' Retreat studio attached to the main house have private lanai, immersing you in a leafy world of bird calls.

Volcano Country Cottages Vacation Rental **$$**
(**808-967-7960; www.volcanocottages.com; 19-3990 Old Volcano Rd; d incl breakfast $105-155;** wi-fi) Nestled in the rainforest, each of these cozy, centrally located cottages has a full kitchen with modern appliances (except for the studio, which has no kitchen). Privacy is assured, and there's outdoor space too, including a candel-lit hot tub hidden among ohia trees and ferns. Rates include self-catering breakfast fixin's.

Volcano Hideaways Vacation Rental **$$**
(**808-985-8959, 808-936-3382; www.volcanovillage.net; 6 Hale Ohia Rd; cottage $140-160;** wi-fi) On a quiet lane in Volcano town, all three of these historic cottages are spotless and expertly outfitted by energetic hosts, who provide everything from robes and a DVD library to freshly roasted coffee from the owner's farm. Depending upon which cottage you choose, perks include rain showers, whirlpool tubs, gas fireplaces, laundry rooms and kitchens.

Artist Cottage Vacation Rental **$$**
(**808-967-7261; www.volcanoartistcottage.com; 19-3834 Old Volcano Rd; cottage incl breakfast $129-149;** wi-fi) To all the artists and writers reading this: make your creative retreat here. On the grounds of Volcano Garden Arts (p224), this refurbished

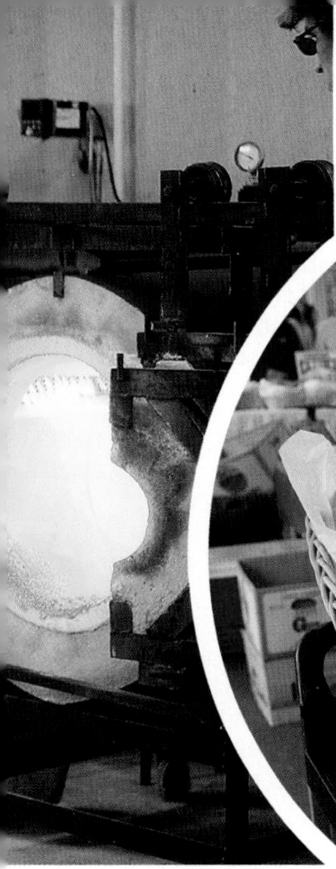

Left: Making glass art, 2400° Fahrenheit (p224) **Below:** Market in Volcano

redwood cottage full of original art has a sky-lit bedroom and bathroom with a giant walk-in shower. There's a full kitchen and a private outdoor hot tub. It's small – best for one or an intimate pair.

Chalet Kilauea Collection — Lodge $$

(800-937-7786, 808-967-7786; www.volcano-hawaii.com; 19-4178 Wright Rd; r $110-200, with shared bath $60-75; wi-fi) Three properties target three very different kinds of travelers. **Volcano Hale** is for hikers, with shared baths, a kitchen and a wood-burning fireplace lounge. A bit motel-ish, **Lokahi Lodge** is functional for families and has a garden hot tub. Romantic **Chalet Kilauea** evinces a cozy country-cottage atmosphere, with unique rooms and a treehouse suite. Breakfast buffet served (surcharge applies).

Volcano Inn — Inn $$

(800-628-3876, 808-967-7773; www.volcanoinnhawaii.com; 19-3820 Old Volcano Rd; r $99-149; wi-fi) Apart from aesthetic blunders (glaring signage, photos tacked to walls), this inn offers outstanding value. The main building contains immaculate rooms (corner rooms enjoy fern-forest views) and a positive community atmosphere. Family cottages come with kitchenettes and hot tubs. Rates drop for multiple-night stays. Takeout breakfasts and lunches available a la carte.

Hale Ohia Log Cabin — Cabin $$

(808-735-9191; www.homeaway.com/vacation-rental/p206956; Hale Ohia Rd; q $150; wi-fi) Step back in time to 'Old Hawaii' with a couple of nights at this sweet log cabin built in 1906. Century-old *sugi* pine trees grow in the yard, and notice the Hilo's Boy School carving on the cabin wall (the first headmaster built this cabin). There's a king and double bed in an upstairs loft, a modern kitchen and a wood-burning stove.

Volcano Guest House B&B $$
(☎866-886-5226, 808-967-7775; www.volcanoguesthouse.com; 11-3733 Ala Ohia St; r & ste $95-145, cottage $140-220, incl breakfast;) At this ecoconscious, family-run property, heart-warming rooms, suites and cottages with kitchettes sit among rainforest gardens, with a hot tub and laundry for guests' use. It's a value-conscious pick for families.

Kilauea Lodge B&B $$$
(☎808-967-7366; www.kilauealodge.com; 19-3948 Old Volcano Rd; r & cottage incl breakfast $190-205, house $220-295;) A tastefully renovated 1930s YMCA camp, this 12-room lodge is like a small hotel. Rooms embody upscale country chic with romantic accents like gas fireplaces, Hawaiian quilts and stained-glass windows. The honeymoon room has a wood-burning fireplace and private balcony, but even newlyweds have to share the garden hot tub. For more privacy, rent an off-property house.

Volcano Rainforest Retreat Vacation Rental $$$
(☎800-550-8696, 808-985-8696; www.volcanoretreat.com; 11-3832 12th St; cottage incl breakfast $145-295; @) Serenity abounds at these four individually designed cedar cottages, each artfully positioned with huge windows to take advantage of fern-forest views. Each has an outdoor hot tub or Japanese-style soaking tub. For added romance, in-room massage can be arranged in advance. Breakfast supplies provided.

Lotus Garden Cottages B&B $$$
(☎808-345-3062; www.volcanogetaway.com; r incl breakfast $185-210;) Choose among three sweet cottage rooms with rainforest views. The Aloha Moon and Hula Moon suites have cedar-plank walls, gas fireplaces, rattan furnishings and tall ceilings, while the unique Lotus Suite is outfitted with Asian antiques. Directions will be provided upon booking; no walk-in guests accepted.

Eating

Despite all the tourist traffic, Volcano has only limited eating options, and most are overpriced.

Café Ohi'a Cafe $
(19-4005 Haunani Rd; items $3-9; usually 7am-5pm;) This humble cafe's daily fresh soups in bread bowls, giant sandwiches and baked goods (try the chocolate-pecan tart) are all perfect for devouring on a hike or at picnic tables right outside. Breakfast croissants and cinnamon rolls kick off the day right.

Volcano Farmers Market Market $
(http://thecoopercenter.org; 1000 Wright Rd, Cooper Community Center; 7-10am Sun;

Volcano Rainforest Retreat

) The whole community comes out to this weekly market to buy farm-fresh produce, takeout meals, flowers, local crafts and more.

Volcano Store Self-Catering $

(19-4005 Haunani Rd, cnr Old Volcano Rd; 5:30am-6:45pm) Basic groceries, camping supplies and a few grab-and-go items. Friendly staff and two gas pumps.

Kilauea General Store Self Catering $

(19-3972 Old Volcano Rd; 7am-7pm) Slim pickings for groceries and premade snacks and meals. ATM and gas available.

Thai Thai Restaurant Thai $$

(808-967-7969; 19-4084 Old Volcano Rd; dinner mains $15-26; noon-9pm Thu-Tue, from 4pm Wed;) Locals claim it's the best Thai on the island. Classic *larb* (minced meat salads) and curries are all authentically flavored and well portioned, but don't let the servers intimidate you into ordering yours too mild. The dining-hall atmopshere can get crowded and stressed (dinner reservations recommended). Avoid tables in the kitschy gift shop or better yet, call ahead for takeout.

Lava Rock Café Diner $$

(808-967-8526; www.volcanoslavarockcafe.com; 19-3972 Old Volcano Rd; mains breakfast & lunch $7-11, dinner $11-24; 7:30am-9pm Tue-Sat, to 4pm Sun, to 5pm Mon;) This roadhouse joint is nearly always jumping, although the stick-to-your-ribs menu of huge burgers, seafood and pasta won't wow you, whenever it finally arrives at your table. For breakfast (served until 3pm), try the sweet French toast with house-made *liliko'i* (passion fruit) butter. Local musicians often play on Wednesday and Saturday nights.

Café Ono Cafe $$

(http://volcanogardenarts.com/cafeono.html; 19-3834 Old Volcano Rd, Volcano Garden Arts; mains $12-18; 11am-3pm Tue-Sun;) At an art gallery with a lovely garden for dining, you can lunch on organic vegetarian and vegan salads, sandwiches, soups, pastas and cakes. For what you get, it's slightly overpriced. Expect slowed-down service.

Kilauea Lodge Restaurant European, Local $$$

(808-967-7366; www.kilauealodge.com; 19-3948 Old Volcano Rd; mains breakfast & lunch $8-14, dinner $24-39; 7:30am-2pm & 5-9:30pm) Volcano's only high-end kitchen puts out a daily-changing dinner menu that oddly (and sometimes unsuccessfully) mixes European continental classics like duck *l'orange* and *hasenpfeffer* (braised rabbit) with fresh local seafood. Hardwood floors and a huge stone fireplace make the dinner atmosphere date-worthy. Service is outstanding; too bad the food is mostly mediocre. Make reservations.

Information

Most services are along Old Volcano Rd, including gas and a post office. Some businesses are cash only.

Volcano Visitor Center (19-4084 Old Volcano Rd; usually 7am-7pm) Unstaffed tourist information kiosk has brochures aplenty. Next door is a coin-op laundromat, ATM and hardware store selling some camping gear.

Ka'u

Ka'u is a wild and windy place where Big Island myths and ancient mysteries abound.

That makes sense, since Hawaiian history probably all began at Ka Lae (South Point), believed to be the site where wayfaring Polynesians first landed their canoes on Hawai'i. You could spend a day at Green Sands Beach or on the Road to the Sea and come away thinking there isn't much to this arid lava expanse other than a couple of hard-to-reach swaths of sand. But linger a while longer in the USA's southernmost region and you'll see why locals are so rabid to protect it. Ka'u residents have quashed coastal resorts, successfully lobbied for protected nature reserves and become pioneers of off-the-grid living. Even so, pristine areas like Pohue Bay have been slated for development. Are Ka'u's days as Hawai'i's outback numbered? Hedge your bets and head down here right now.

Ka Lae (South Point)
BRIGITTE MERZ/GETTY IMAGES ©

Ka'u Itineraries

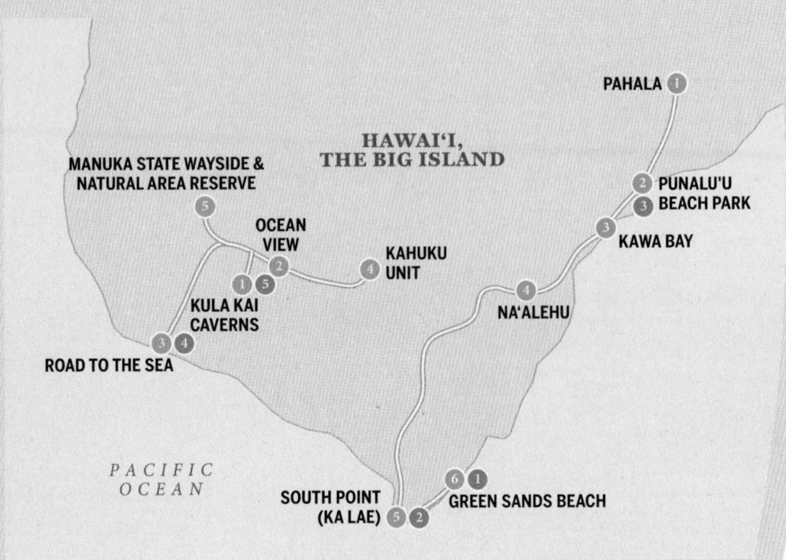

One Day

1 **Pahala** (p234) Start the day off right at Ka'u Coffee Mill, then drive through the sleepy old sugar-plantation town out to meditative Wood Valley Temple, a Tibetan Buddhist retreat center.

2 **Punalu'u Beach Park** (p235) When the wind and the waves are calm enough, wade into the ocean for a morning snorkel with *honu* (green sea turtles) at this phenomenal black-sand beach.

3 **Kawa Bay** (p236) Surfers with the guts and the gear will want to check out the sets at nearby Kawa Bay (aka Windmills), a hidden locals' beach accessed via an unmarked dirt road off Hwy 11.

4 **Na'alehu** (p236) Have you worked up an appetite yet? Keep heading south to sweet little Na'alehu for a hearty plate lunch at Hana Hou Restaurant, a folksy, neighborhood diner with toothsome take-out picnic fixings, or some soft Portuguese sweet bread from Punalu'u Bake Shop.

5 **South Point (Ka Lae)** (p239) Ramble down to the country's southernmost point, where locals go cliff jumping. Just wandering around you'll feel the mana (spiritual essence) of these ancient Hawaiian sites, including a fishing shrine.

6 **Green Sands Beach** (p239) This famous olive-green scoop of volcanic sand is about an hour's hike (or a faster 4WD 'taxi' ride) off South Point Rd. Don't count on swimming at this rough-and-tumble spot, known for high surf and howling winds.

THIS LEG: 40 MILES

Two Days

1 Kula Kai Caverns (p242) Plunge into one of the Big Island's best underground caving adventures. Soda-straw stalactites, moonmilk puffballs, pillars and columns: a lava tube's exoticism comes alive on guided tours. Children as young as six years old are allowed inside. Reservations are required.

2 Ocean View (p241) Fuel up your car's gas tank and stock up on snacks, drinks and to-go deli lunches from supermarkets in southern Ka'u's only commercial center.

3 Road to the Sea (p243) Ready for real adventure? You'll need a high-clearance 4WD vehicle to make it to the secluded beaches here, but it'll be worth it when you finally strip off your clothes in a mad dash toward the water. Set off early, say before noon.

4 Kahuku Unit (p238) high-clearance 4WD vehicle comes in handy, but isn't absolutely required for exploring this newest addition to Hawai'i Volcanoes National Park. Set on historic ranch lands in the shadow of Mauna Loa's massive lava flows, here hiking trails wind across green pastures, through lush rain forest and around colorful cinder cones and lava tree molds. Keep in mind this wilderness area may only be open on weekends.

5 Manuka State Wayside & Natural Area Reserve (p242) If you don't have a 4WD vehicle, or you're already itching to drive back around to the Kona Coast, make a quick pit stop at this little roadside oasis. A family-friendly nature hike strolls through shady native forest where unique endemic plants thrive.

THIS LEG: 52 MILES

Ka'u Highlights

1 Best Beach: Green Sands Beach (p239) Unusual olive sands put this on the Big Island bucket list.

2 Best View: Ka Lae (South Point) (p240) Watch crashing surf and dream of paddling to Tahiti.

3 Best Wildlife Watching: Punalu'u Beach Park (p235) Where *honu* (green sea turtles) bask in the sun.

4 Best Activity: Road to the Sea (p243) Get your kicks on a rugged 4WD adventure.

5 Best Rainy Day Activity: Kula Kai Caverns (p242) Take an underground tour of 'living museums.'

Green Sands Beach, South Point (p239)
ALVIS UPITIS/GETTY IMAGES ©

Discover Ka'u

Pahala

POP 1356

A former sugar plantation town now making a living growing coffee and macadamia nuts, Pahala dozes just inland from Hwy 11, south of the Mile 51 marker. Its quiet streets are lined with unrestored early-20th-century plantation houses – just squint to imagine the past. The unhurried town center, with a gas station, bank and post office, is at the corner of Kamani and Pikake Sts.

Sights

Ka'u Coffee Mill Farm

(**808-928-0550; www.kaucoffeemill.com; 96-2694 Wood Valley Rd; 8:30am-4:30pm**) This down-to-earth coffee farm roasts its own award-winning beans. Taste a variety of brews, which some connoisseurs rate as highly as Kona coffee, at the gift shop stocked with bags of beans to take home.

From Hwy 11, follow Kamani St inland, turn right onto Pikake St, then continue on Wood Valley Rd for about 1.5 miles.

Wood Valley Temple Temple

(**Nechung Dorje Drayang Ling; 808-928-8539; www.nechung.org; Wood Valley Rd; requested donation $5; usually 10am-5pm**) Just outside Pahala, this century-old, colorful Tibetan Buddhist temple is wonderfully juxtaposed against a lush 25-acre retreat center where peacocks roam free. The temple's official name, which translates to 'Immutable Island of Melodious Sound,' perfectly captures the valley's wind and birdsong.

Visitors are welcome to join daily chanting and meditation sessions (8am and 6pm), or to just visit the temple and gift shop. A meditative **guesthouse** (**s $65-75, d $85;**) lets you stay for a few nights.

Turn off Hwy 11 onto Kamani St, then turn right into Pikake St, which becomes Wood Valley Rd; the retreat is about 5 miles inland. It's a meandering drive up valley with farms, forest and one-lane bridges crossing babbling creeks.

Wood Valley Temple

PHOTO RESOURCE HAWAII/ALAMY ©

Ka'u

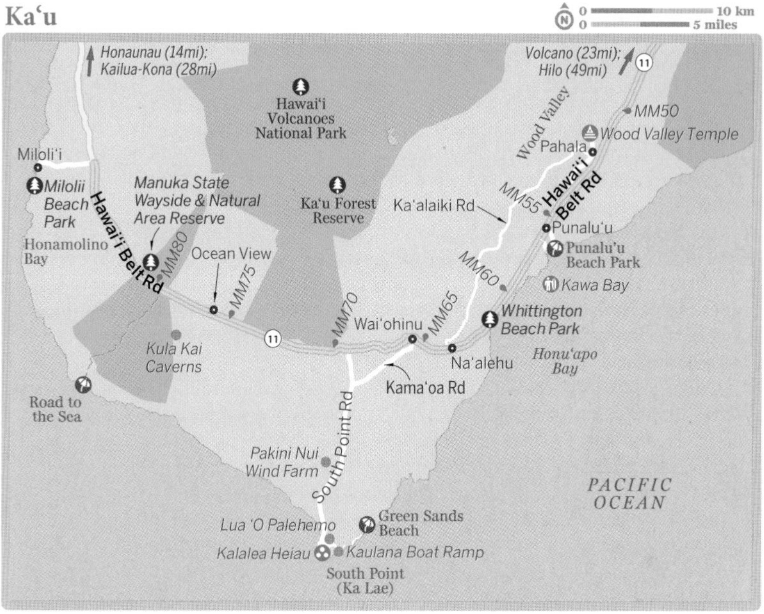

Festivals & Events

Ka'u Coffee Festival Coffee

(www.kaucoffeefest.com) In mid-May, Pahala wakes up with music, coffee, hula, coffee-farm and mill tours, farm-to-fork food, more coffee and even stargazing. No decaf allowed.

Getting There & Away

Hele-On Bus (**808-961-8744; www.heleonbus.org; adult 1-way fare $2**) One or two daily buses run between Pahala, Na'alehu and Ocean View, continuing up the Kona Coast to South Kohala's resorts. There's also one bus daily except Sunday between Hilo and Ka'u, stopping in Volcano.

Punalu'u

Once a major Hawaiian settlement during ancient times, today Punalu'u harbors a popular black-sand beach, known for sea-turtle spotting, and the Sea Mountain condo development, the only one of its kind on this coast – and perhaps the last.

Beaches

Punalu'u Beach Park Beach

On a pretty little bay is a black-sand beach where green sea turtles bask and feed. It's also one of the few beaches where rare hawksbill turtles lay their eggs, so be careful not to disturb their sandy nests. Most days the rough, cold waters are not good for swimming as there are forceful undertows – a lifeguard is posted – but when calm, snorkeling is a treat. The park has picnic pavilions, restrooms, outdoor showers, drinking water and a concession stand.

The northern part of the beach is backed by a duck pond and the remains of an old resort, rotting away in testimony to local economics and the anti-development movement. The ruins of the Pahala Sugar Company's old warehouse and pier lie slightly north. Follow a trail up the hill past the cement pier to find the ruins of **Kane'ele'ele Heiau**, an ancient temple where human sacrifices took place, in a vast field. The trail continues all the way to Kawa Bay via secluded coves, now protected as public land.

Protecting Hawaii's Honu

Hawai'i's gorgeous beaches and warm tropical waters attract more than tourists, they also attract *honu* (green sea turtles). Traditionally revered by Hawaiians, these magnificent creatures can be seen feeding, sunning and even nesting on Big Island beaches. Often considered an *'aumakua* (family deity or guardian spirit), *honu* appear in ancient petroglyphs too.

Sea turtles were once a prized source of food, but their capture and consumption was governed by ancient Hawai'i's strict religious laws. In modern times, governance has once again become necessary to prevent further damage to the beaches turtles depend on to reproduce. Development, tourism, hunting and harvesting of their shells have all contributed to a dangerously dwindling population.

Green sea turtles now abound in Hawai'i (look for them munching on seaweed in shallow, rocky areas). Less common are hawksbill sea turtles, called *honu 'ea*. The rarest turtles in the Pacific Ocean, they're easily recognized by their plated shells, beaked noses and clawed flippers. Spot them at Punalu'u or in remote coastal areas of Hawai'i Volcanoes National Park.

Before you get too close to the turtles, consider that only a very small percentage survive to return to reproduce. All Hawaiian sea turtles are endangered species protected by law and you must not approach them any closer than 50yd in the water and 20ft on land (this means kids, too!) – don't imitate tourists who crowd closely around, hassling these gentle reptiles.

To learn more about sea turtles and efforts to preserve critical habitat in Hawaii, visit **Save Punalu'u** (www.savepunaluu.org) and Maui-based **World Turtle Trust** (www.world-turtle-trust.org) online.

Come in the early morning, since the beach park quickly fills with picnickers and tour buses. Camping is allowed with an advance county permit. There are two signed turnoffs for Punalu'u between the Mile 56 and Mile 57 on Hwy 11.

Kawa Bay Beach

Surf's up at Kawa Bay, reached via a dirt road (stay straight, rather than taking any lefts) between the Mile 58 and Mile 59 markers off Hwy 11. Nicknamed Windmills, this is Ka'u's best surf break – paddle out from the beach's northernmost end. Locals also come here to picnic and fish; always respect their space.

Na'alehu

POP 866

Tiny Na'alehu is the southernmost town in the USA – a title it milks for all it's worth. Alongside giant banyan trees and pastel-colored plantation houses, Na'alehu has a lost-in-time rural feel that's underscored by the beautiful, but boarded-up Na'alehu Theatre, a 1940s movie house along the main road. Na'alehu is northern Ka'u's commercial center, with a supermarket, hardware store, laundromat, library, playground, post office, gas station and ATM. One or two daily Hele-On Bus (p235) services run between Pahala, Na'alehu and Ocean View.

Beaches

Whittington Beach Park Beach

North of Na'alehu, this small beach park has tidepools to explore, a fishpond frequented by birds, and the ruins of an old pier. Despite its name, there's no beach and the ocean is usually too rough for swimming, but hawksbill sea turtles can often be spotted. Facilities include restrooms, outdoor showers and picnic pavilions (no drinking water). Camping on the grass requires an advance county permit, but proximity to the highway means little privacy.

The turnoff to the park is between the Mile 60 and Mile 61 markers on Hwy 11.

Sleeping & Eating

Ka'u Coffee House & Guesthouse Hostel $

(808-747-4142, 808-896-9272; 95-5587 Hwy 11; s/d $35/50; cafe 11am-6pm Mon-Fri; @) On Hwy 11, this family-operated hostel does practically everything right. An upstairs hostel offers clean and tidy rooms and a relaxing community space, while the downstairs cafe serves a cooked breakfast (from $5 for guests), Ka'u coffee and veggie burgers and sandwiches at lunch. The Hele-On Bus stops out front.

Punalu'u Bake Shop Bakery $

(808-929-7343; www.bakeshophawaii.com; 95-5642 Hwy 11; items $3-8; 9am-5pm) Famous island-wide, this landmark bakery packs in locals and busloads of tourists, who come for sandwiches and a variety of flavored, doughy Portuguese sweet bread (purple taro!). Free samples aid in decision-making. Bonus: clean restrooms and a picnic area outside.

Ka'u Farmers Market Market $

(7am-noon Wed & Sat) A small but quality farmers market sets up in front of Ace Hardware.

Island Market Supermarket $

(95-5657 Hwy 11, Na'alehu Shopping Center; 8am-7pm Mon-Sat, 9am-6pm Sun) This well-stocked grocery store is the best between Hilo and Captain Cook.

Hana Hou Restaurant Diner $$

(808-929-9717; naalehurestaurant.com; 95-1148 Na'alehu Spur Rd; mains $8-16; 8am-7pm Sun-Thu, to 8pm Fri & Sat;) Here's your chance to eat 'the southernmost plate lunch in the USA' at a 1940s plantation-era family restaurant. Portions may not be as generous as the prices suggest, though. Stuffed sandwiches and wraps are great for picnicking, but the real draw is home-baked pies, like banana cream and macadamia nut. There's usually live music on Friday and Saturday nights.

Hana Hou Restaurant

ANN CECIL/GETTY IMAGES ©

Island Insights

For killer coastal views, pull off at the **scenic lookout** above Honu'apo Bay just northeast of Na'alehu. From the lookout you can see the cement pilings of the old Whittington Pier, which was used for shipping sugar and hemp until the 1930s. At the turn of the 21st century, the pier had a more scientific purpose for a few years, when a fiber-optic cable measuring the rising Lo'ihi Seamount, Hawai'i's active underwater volcano, was temporarily attached to the pier's pylons.

Shaka Restaurant American **$$**
(808-929-7404; 95-5673 Hwy 11; mains breakfast & lunch $8-14, dinner $12-22; 7am-9pm) This sports bar dishes up sloppy plates of grilled burgers, pizza and pub grub (the deep fryer works overtime). Cleanliness is questionable. Live music on most Fridays.

Wai'ohinu & Around

POP 230

Blink and you'll miss sleepy little Wai'ohinu ('sparkling water') between the Mile 65 and Mile 66 markers on Hwy 11. The village's claim to fame is its **Mark Twain monkeypod tree**, planted by the peripatetic author in 1866. The original tree fell during a hurricane in 1957, but hardy shoots sprang up and it's once again full-grown. There's a gas station and general store along the road through town.

Sights & Activities

Four miles west of Wai'ohinu, between the Mile 70 and Mile 71 markers on Hwy 11, lies the entrance to Hawai'i Volcanoes National Park's **Kahuku Unit** (admission free), which offers hikers the chance to explore historic ranch lands and lava flows (for more details, see p215). At the time of research, the Kahuku Unit was only open to the public between 9am and 3pm on Saturdays and Sundays. Check the park **website** (www.nps.gov/havo) for current opening hours and also schedules of ranger-guided hikes (reservations not usually required).

Sleeping

South Point Banyan Tree House Vacation Rental **$$**
(808-929-8515, 808-217-2504; www.southpointbth.com; cnr Pinao St & Hwy 11; d $100;) Fabulous studio apartment digs, equipped with a full kitchen and a hot-tub deck, seem to float in the branches of a giant banyan tree. Flooded with light, the octagonal two-story house is a private escape in a jungle of mango, lychee and *'ulu* (breadfruit) trees.

Hobbit House B&B **$$**
(808-929-9755; www.hi-hobbit.com; d incl breakfast & taxes $170-225) Powered by the sun and wind, this unique property is a fantastical hideaway. Perched atop a bluff with sweeping ocean views, the honeymoon suite with a full kitchen is a whimsically romantic escape. It's tucked half a mile up, up and up from Hwy 11.

Margo's Corner Campground, Cottage **$$**
(808-929-9614; www.margoscorner.com; Wakea St, off Kama'oa Rd; tent sites per person $30, cottages $90-130, all incl breakfast; @) Flying the rainbow flag high, this LGBT-friendly guesthouse is an artistic, alternative-minded stopover. Of the two cottages, the Adobe Suite is superior, with its wall of windows, double beds in Star Trek–like berths and private sauna. The garden setting is peaceful and even campers are offered breakfast and hot showers. No smoking on the property.

South Point (Ka Lae)

Ka Lae (literally 'the point') is the southernmost spot in the USA, but more importantly it's also a National Historic Landmark District where most historians believe that Polynesian voyagers first landed in Hawai'i. Turbulent and windy, this sacred place must have looked positively heavenly to ancient seafarers who traveled thousands of miles across open ocean using only waves, winds, sun, moon and stars to navigate.

Ka Lae was one of the earliest Hawaiian settlements, with rich fishing grounds offshore and freshwater available from nearby Punalu'u. These waters still sustain life and local families perch on the cliffs and fish the weekend away. The turnoff for narrow, mostly one-lane South Point Rd is between the Mile 69 and Mile 70 markers on Hwy 11. About 10 miles later, South Point Rd forks: veer right for Ka Lae or left for Green Sands Beach.

For a picturesque alternative, take Kama'oa Rd from Wai'ohinu to South Point Rd, a rolling country drive that deposits you just north of the **Pakini Nui Wind Farm**, where rows of high-tech windmills stand in cow pastures. Heading a few miles further downhill toward the sea, you'll pass the abandoned remains of a US government space-tracking facility that operated here during the mid-1960s.

The Best... Off-the-Beaten-Track Spots in Ka'u

1 Road to the Sea (p243)

2 Ka Lae (South Point; p240)

3 Kula Kai Caverns (p242)

4 Kahuku Unit, Hawai'i Volcanoes National Park

5 Wood Valley Temple (p234)

Beaches

Green Sands Beach — Beach

Also known as Papakolea Beach, this legendary green-sand beach on Mahana Bay isn't really *that* green, but it is a secluded, sandy strand. Its rare color comes from the semiprecious olivine crystals (a type of volcanic basalt) eroded from a cinder cone above, worn smooth by the relentless surf and then mixed with black sand until it sparkles in the sun. Swimming isn't advisable here (even

Ka Lae cape

on calm days) due to strong waves, with frequent high surf and howling winds.

To get here take South Point Rd, turning left after 10 miles. Follow this road until it dead ends at a grassy parking area (don't leave any valuables in your car). At this point you can hike – it's a dusty, hot and long 2.5-mile trek each way, so bring plenty of water – or pay around $10 to $15 for a ride in one of the local 4WD 'taxis' waiting to transport tourists.

If you choose to hike, start by walking toward the water, past the Kaulana boat ramp, and follow the rutted dirt road left through the metal gate. Then just keep going, enjoying the gorgeous undulating coastline and aiming for the uplifted, striated cliff-face in the distance.

Whether you arrive on foot or by 4WD, you'll have to scramble down the cliff to the beach, which has becoming a major tourist attraction despite the difficulty of reaching it. Go early, late or when it's overcast to beat the crowds.

Sights

Ka Lae Historic Site

(South Point Rd) Hawai'i's southernmost tip, Ka Lae feels like the utter end of the earth. Even with rushing wind filling your ears, an odd stillness steals over this sacred spot pulsing with potent mana (spiritual essence). But don't expect to be alone on the path, which is well-worn by visitors, heading south from the dirt parking area toward the light beacon. Standing near the actual point, you can imagine what it must have been like for ancient Polynesians to land here, fighting violent surf after months at sea.

The confluence of ocean currents just offshore makes this one of Hawai'i's most bountiful fishing grounds. Wooden platforms built onto the cliffs have hoists and ladders for the small boats anchored below, while local fishers brace themselves on lava-rock ledges partway down.

Daredevil locals like to cliff-jump into the surging waters here, but you might want to just peek over the edge, as you're many miles from help and hospitals. Behind the platforms, inside a large *puka* (hole), spy on the ocean raging upward and receding with the waves.

There are no facilities here except portable toilets.

Kalalea Heiau Temple

Near the dirt parking area for Ka Lae is this ancient temple and fishing shrine where Hawaiians left offerings in hopes of currying favor for a bountiful catch. A standing rock below the heiau is pocked with canoe mooring holes. Enterprising ancient Hawaiians would tether their canoes here with ropes, then let strong currents pull them out into deeper waters to fish.

Kalalea Heiau

Lua 'O Palehemo Historic Site

A short distance inland from the Kalalea Heiau is Lua 'O Palehemo, marked with a tree bent nearly horizontal by battering winds. From this brackish watering hole (*lua* means hole or pit in Hawaiian), views take in the massive flanks of Mauna Loa and the entire coast from South Kona to Puna.

Sleeping

Kalaekilohana B&B **$$$**

(**☎808-939-8052; www.kau-hawaii.com; 94-2152 South Point Rd; d incl breakfast $269;**) It's a rare place that's so welcoming you feel at once like a special guest and part of the family. But the *ho'okipa* (hospitality) here does just that. Upstairs, four airy rooms feature gleaming hardwood floors, luxurious beds, rainfall showers and private lanai. Downstairs, the gracious library and music room, a wide porch and complimentary drinks and snacks invite lingering. Directions will be given upon booking.

Ocean View & Around

Straggling alongside Hwy 11, Ocean View is divvied up between lusher Hawaiian Ocean View Estates (HOVE) *mauka* (inland) and arid Hawaiian Ranchos *makai* (seaward). Together they make up the largest subdivision in the USA. A persistent lack of jobs, blankets of vog and a reputation for illegal drugs keeps residential lots from being fully settled. This is Hawai'i's frontier, where people come to find themselves or get lost, scratching a pioneering existence out of desolate black lava.

Across Hwy 11 from each other near the Mile 76 marker, two shopping centers – Pohue Plaza and Ocean View Town Center – make up southern Ka'u's commercial center, with gas stations, supermarkets, fast food, ATMs and a laundromat. One or two daily Hele-On Bus (p235) services run between Pahala, Na'alehu and Ocean View.

Local Knowledge

NAME: JOHN REPLOGLE

OCCUPATION: CONSERVATION PRACTITIONER, NATURE CONSERVANCY

RESIDENCE: OCEAN VIEW

1 WHY IS KA'U SUCH A SPECIAL PLACE?

Geographically, it's the largest region in Hawai'i. It also has Ka'u Forest Reserve, the largest intact native forest in the state. Most importantly, it's home to Ka Lae (p240) and Kapalaoa – Hawaii's oldest archaeological site (currently closed to the public). Ka'u was once the seat of the Hawaiian Kingdom.

2 WHAT ARE SOME OF YOUR FAVORITE SPOTS IN KA'U?

I like to go to South Point to fish and hang out. The road down is an excellent cycling route. Lua 'O Palehemo (p241) is a place I like to share with people, especially in the early morning when you can see all the way down the coast. I take my grandchildren there a lot.

3 HOW ABOUT GREEN SANDS BEACH?

This is a beautiful, windblown piece of coastline (p239) worth visiting. But it's also fragile – do you see how many people drive there? It's eating away the land and accelerating erosion – it's better to hike anyway to get the full experience.

4 VISITING PUNALU'U AND SEEING THE TURTLES IS A PERENNIAL FAVORITE. DO YOU HAVE ANY TIPS FOR VISITORS?

There's the black-sand beach and the *honu* (green sea turtles), but the Kane'ele'ele Heiau is also there. Punalu'u (p235) was a prominent place in ancient Hawai'i. As for visitors, they should be very careful when swimming – there are major undertows at Punalu'u. While encountering *honu* is a unique experience, the turtles should never be hassled. Stand back and enjoy.

Sights & Activities

Kula Kai Caverns Caving
(808-929-9725; www.kulakaicaverns.com; 92-8864 Lauhala Dr; tours adult/child 6-12yr from $20/10) Top-notch underground tours are led by local experts who emphasize respectful stewardship of these 'living museums.' The geologically astounding caves belong to the world's longest lava tube system, reaching back into the bowels of Mauna Loa volcano. On the basic 30-minute tour, you'll enter a short, lighted cave section, where guides present Hawai'i's cultural and ecological history. Reservations are required.

There's also a longer 'crawling' tour ($60) and a two-hour extended twilight tour ($95). Group sizes are kept small, usually with a two- or four-person minimum. Children (minimum age six or eight years) are allowed on most tours.

Manuka State Wayside & Natural Area Reserve Park
(www.hawaiistateparks.org; Hwy 11) FREE This 13-acre reserve offers a very well-done nature trail. Proceeding through native forest on a lava rock path, and assisted by an interpretive trail guide, you'll identify 30 species of plants, and see a pit crater and lava flows. The entrance to the park and picnic area is off Hwy 11, just north of the Mile 81 marker.

Uninviting camping in an open shelter with concrete floors is allowed with an advance state park permit, but it's isolated, not always safe and there's no drinking water.

Sleeping

Lova Lava Land Vacation Rental $
(www.lovalavaland.com; Hawaiian Ranchos; yurt/VW bus $60/40;) This off-the-grid 'ecoresort' epitomizes Ocean View ingenuity. Guests sleep in VW buses in the middle of a lava flow and share a central compound with a fully equipped kitchen, herb garden, wi-fi and lava-rock shower. There's also a single yurt with a double bed, hardwood floors and moon roof. It's DIY living, with no on-site staff. A cleaning fee ($30 to $45) may be refundable. Directions will be given upon booking.

Leilani Bed & Breakfast B&B $$
(808-929-7101; www.leilanibedandbreakfast.com; 92-8822 Leilani Pkwy, Hawaiian Ocean View Estates; r incl breakfast $99-124;) On a tropical lot in the Hawaiian Ocean View Estates subdivision, the three plain-jane guest rooms here are a bit tight, but the well-tended grounds, complete with a covered BBQ area, and lanai (which doubles as an art gallery) compensate.

Eating

Ocean View Pizzaria Pizza $
(808-929-9677; Hwy 11, Ocean View Town Center; pizza slice/pie from $3/13, sandwiches $7-12; 11am-7pm, to

Lei of Lehua flowers
GREG ELMS/GETTY IMAGES ©

Detour: Road to the Sea

This high-clearance 4WD road crosses enough loose *'a'a* (rough, jagged lava) to shake your fillings loose. Once only for adventurers, these remote black-and green-sand beaches with looming cliffs are not the human-free pockets they used to be. You may find, after all the trouble of getting there, that the sea is too rough to swim and the beach too windy to enjoy. Even so, it's worth the trip for the scenery alone.

To find the **Road to the Sea**, turn *makai* (seaward) off Hwy 11 at the row of mailboxes between the Mile 79 and Mile 80 markers (look for the 'Taki Mana/Ka Ulu Malu Shady Grove Farm' sign). From there you'll drive 6 miles over rudimentary, seemingly never-ending lava. To reach the first and smaller of the two beaches at the road's end takes 45 minutes or so, depending on how rough you like your ride.

To reach the second beach, drive a half-mile back inland. Skip the first left fork (it's a dead end) and take the second left fork instead. Look for arrows painted on lava rock. The road jogs inland before heading toward the shore again, and the route isn't always readily apparent. There are many places you can lose traction or get lost. Almost a mile from the fork, you'll reach a red *pu'u* (hill). Park there and walk down to the ocean. If you decide to hike the whole distance to the second beach from the split in the road, it's about 1.5 miles each way. Bring as much water as you can carry, because it's a mercilessly hot and shadeless walk.

8pm Fri & Sat) The submarine sandwiches are filling, the pizza just OK. It's a place to eat, not linger. Better for takeout.

Malama Market Supermarket $
(92-8701 Hwy 11, Pohue Plaza; ⏲6:30am-8pm) Standard groceries, hot *hulihuli* (rotisserie-cooked) chicken, teriyaki-glazed Spam *musubi* (rice ball) and a lot more.

Ocean View Market Supermarket $
(Hwy 11, Ocean View Town Center) By the post office and an auto-parts store, this community grocery store sells hot food and sandwiches (get here early before they run out).

Hawai'i, the Big Island

In Focus

Hula at sunset

The Big Island Today

> *The trick now is to expand sustainable agriculture...and to convince everyone to 'eat local'.*

Drying coffee beans, Honaunau (p74), South Kona

ethnicity
(% of population)

if the Big Island were 100 people

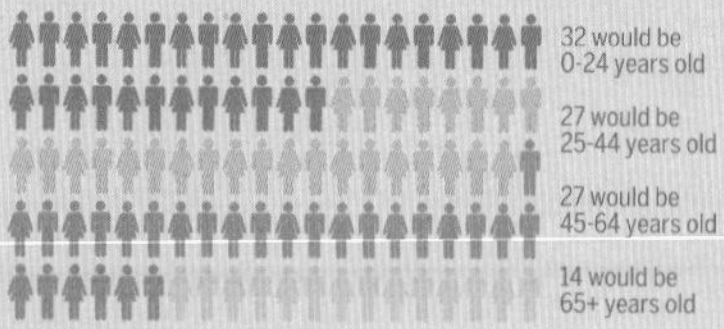

population per sq mile

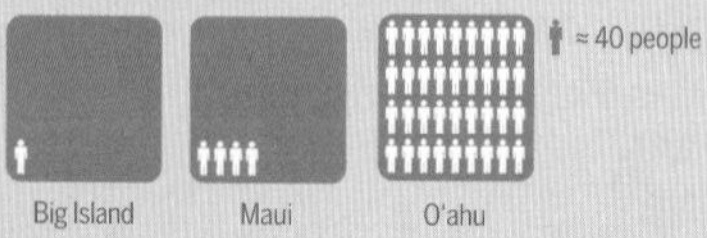

Economic Recovery

Since the 1960s, Hawai'i's economy has rested primarily on tourism, along with agriculture and real estate. But the 2008 national recession squeezed the influx of visitors (just over 1.3 million people in 2013, down 25% from its peak), and hotel occupancy has barely broken 60% since then, although room rates continue to rise. Japan Airlines inflicted another blow by ending its route to Kona International Airport (which Governor Neil Ambercrombie wants to expand) in 2010, and the loss of nonstop flights between San Francisco and Hilo also hurt.

During the recession, the island's overall unemployment rate hovered around 10% and home prices dropped, especially in Puna. The downturn affected the whole state, evidenced by furloughs for government workers (the island's biggest employment sector) and even public schoolchildren. But by early 2014, unemployment had shrunk below the national average of 7%, and real estate prices were rising. Visitors still face some economic fallout, as some state parks have started charging entry fees and have raised camping rates for nonresidents.

ANN CECIL/GETTY IMAGES ©

Sustainable Agriculture

Sugar plantations, which long dominated the state's agricultural landscape, are old news: the last commercial harvest on the Big Island was in 1995. Since then Hawai'i's agriculture has somewhat successfully diversified into signature coffee, papayas, macadamia nuts and orchids – as well as aquaculture and boutique crops from mushrooms, to vanilla to tea. The Big Island is still home to the state's largest cattle operation, Parker Ranch, and the state's last two remaining dairy cattle farms.

The trick now is to expand sustainable agriculture: to employ more island residents, to produce more food and to convince everyone to 'eat local.' The Hawaiian Islands import 85% to 90% of the food eaten here, and it will take many more farms to achieve food security (or, as some activists call it, 'food sovereignty') through greater self-sufficiency.

In 2013, after a long and bitter political fight, Hawai'i County Bill 113 was signed into law by Mayor Billy Kenoi. The law stops biotech companies from operating on the Big Island and prohibits farmers from growing any new GMO (genetically modified organism) crops, with an exemption granted for papayas. Farmers who opposed the bill argue GMOs are necessary to prevent crop-killing viruses that would decimate the industry.

The coffee berry borer (a small beetle native to Africa) was first discovered in Kona in 2010. With almost $30 million in annual revenue at stake, farmers feared economic disaster. Fortunately, a natural fungus that can be sprayed on coffee plants attacks the beetle, somewhat controlling the pest, which can never be eradicated. Quarantines will hopefully prevent the beetle from spreading to other coffee-growing islands.

Nature's Power

On the Big Island, nature is always in the news. Over the past few years, parts of the island have received the unwanted distinction of having the nation's worst drought, notably South Kohala and Ka'u. Meanwhile on the rainy windward side of the island, the longest lava flow in history continues, with spectacular displays inside Hawai'i Volcanoes National Park. New energy development projects are seeking to harness alternative energy sources – including wind, solar, sea and biomass – to sustainably power island homes, transportation and agriculture.

History

Ki'i, Pu'uhonua O Hōnaunau National Historical Park (p77)

LONELY PLANET/GETTY IMAGES ©

Hawaii's discovery is one of humanity's great epic tales, starting with ancient Polynesians who first found their way to these tiny islands. Almost a millennium passed before Western explorers, whalers and missionaries arrived. In the tumultuous 19th century, a global melting pot of immigrants came to work on Hawaii's plantations before the kingdom founded by Kamehameha the Great was overthrown, making way for US annexation.

Ancient Hawai'i

Although the discovery of Hawaii may have been accidental, subsequent migrations were not. Polynesians were highly skilled seafarers, navigating over thousands of miles of open ocean in doubled-hulled canoes without maps, and with only the sun, stars, wind and waves to guide them. Beginning around AD 300, they imported to these remote islands

AD 300–600

The first wave of Polynesians voyages thousands of miles by canoe to the Hawaiian Islands.

their religious beliefs, social structures and over two dozen food plants and domestic animals.

When, for unknown reasons, these trans-Pacific canoe voyages stopped around AD 1300, ancient Hawaiian culture evolved in isolation, but retained a family resemblance to cultures throughout Polynesia. Hawaiian society was highly stratified, ruled by a chiefly class called *ali'i* whose power derived from their ancestry: they were believed to be descended from the gods. Ranking just below *ali'i,* kahuna (experts or masters) included priests, healers and skilled craftspeople like canoe makers.

In ancient Hawai'i, clan loyalty trumped individuality, elaborate traditions of gifting and feasting conferred prestige, and a pantheon of shape-shifting gods animated the natural world. Strict religious laws, known as the kapu (taboo) system, governed what people ate, whom they married and dined with, and when they fished or harvested crops – essentially all human behavior. The penalty for breaking kapu was death.

The largest class was the *maka'ainana* (commoners), who could live wherever they pleased, but who were obligated to support the *ali'i* through taxes paid in kind with food, goods and physical labor. The lowest *kaua* (outcast or untouchable) class was shunned and did not mix with the other classes, except as slaves or human sacrificial victims (the latter were exclusively male).

The Best... Ancient Hawaiian Sites

1 Pu'uhonua O Hōnaunau National Historical Park (p77)

2 Puako Petroglyph Preserve (p104)

3 Pu'ukohola Heiau National Historic Site (p110)

4 Halema'uma'u Crater (p211)

5 South Point (Ka Lae; p239)

6 Keanakako'i & Lake Wai'au, Mauna Kea (p135)

First Western Contact: Captain Cook

In 1778, everything changed. On January 18, British naval explorer Captain James Cook, who was in search of the fabled Northwest Passage, accidentally sailed into the main Hawaiian Island chain. Ending 500 years of cultural isolation, his arrival irrevocably altered the course of Hawaiian history. Cook dropped anchor offshore to barter for fresh water and food, as he had elsewhere in the Pacific.

While Cook was already familiar with Polynesian culture from his previous voyages, Hawaiians knew nothing yet of Europeans, nor of the metal, guns and diseases

1778
Captain James Cook becomes the first Western explorer to 'discover' the Hawaiian Islands.

1810
Kamehameha I unites the major Hawaiian Islands into one sovereign kingdom.

1820
First American missionaries arrive at Kailua Bay, praying to convert Hawaiians to Christianity.

their ships carried. When Cook returned to Hawai'i in February 1779, he anchored at Kealakekua Bay to repair his ships and refresh supplies. When Cook tried to take a Hawaiian chief hostage in retaliation for a stolen boat, a battle ensued during which Cook, four of his sailors and uncounted Hawaiians died.

Once 'discovered,' the Hawaiian Islands became a prime Pacific waystation for traders, who would buy furs in the Pacific Northwest and stop here for supplies and fragrant *'iliahi* (sandalwood), then a valuable commodity in China. By the 1840s, the islands also became the whaling capital of the Pacific, with over 700 whaling ships stopping at Hawaiian ports annually. Some locals even jumped aboard to travel the world, since expert Hawaiian sailors were favored recruits by sea captains.

Kamehameha the Great

Kamehameha (meaning, 'Lonely One') was born in the Big Island's North Kohala district around 1753. Belonging to the *ali'i* class, he became a strong warrior under the guidance of his powerful uncle, Chief Kalaniopu'u. As a young man, Kamehameha was present with his uncle at Kealakekua Bay when Captain Cook was killed in 1779.

At the time, the major islands of Hawai'i, Kaua'i, Maui and O'ahu were independently ruled. Kamehameha fought for eight years to become the ruling chief of Hawai'i. Once he succeeded in 1791, he began a monumental campaign to conquer the other major islands. In 1810, after two decades of warfare, Kamehameha succeeded and became the first *mo'i* (king) of the Kingdom of Hawai'i, named after his birthplace.

During his nine-year reign, King Kamehameha I brought relative peace and stability to a society previously in flux with constant power struggles among *ali'i.* When he died in 1819 at his home in Kailua-Kona, two loyal chiefs buried him in a secret place to prevent rivals from stealing his bones, which were believed to hold great mana (supernatural power).

After Kamehameha I's death, his son Liholiho (Kamehameha II) became *mo'i* and his favorite wife, Queen Ka'ahumanu, became *kuhina nui* (regent). In a shocking snub to tradition, those two soon broke the kapu against men and women eating together and ordered many heiau (temples) and *ki'i* (deity images) destroyed. Hawaiian society plunged into chaos.

Christian Missionaries & Hawaiian Converts

Hawai'i's first Protestant missionaries chanced upon a fortuitous time and place to arrive. American Congregationalists from Boston landed at Kailua Bay on April 19, 1820, less than a year after Kamehameha I died. As Hawai'i's ancient religion had just been abolished, the missionaries found a receptive audience. However, new converts often quickly abandoned the church's teachings, reverting to traditional lifestyles.

1828

First coffee trees are planted in Kona by missionary Samuel Ruggles. Coffee beans

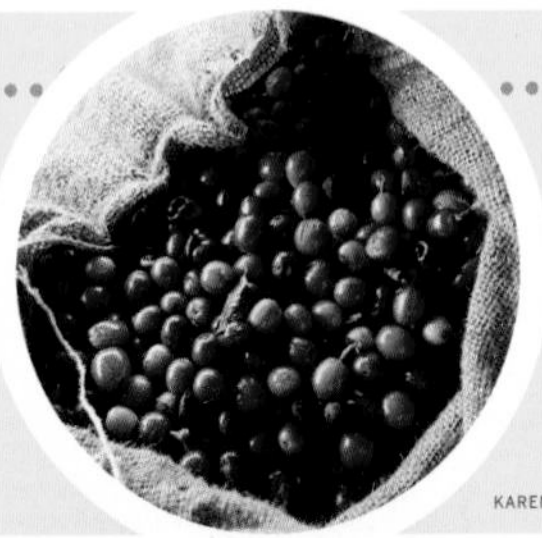

1863

Kohala Sugar Company, the island's first sugar plantation, is established.

The missionaries found one thing that attracted avid, widespread interest: literacy. Ancient Hawaiians had no written language; they preserved their mythology instead through lengthy oral epics, recited word for word by trained kahuna. The missionaries established a Hawaiian alphabet using Roman letters and zealously taught Hawaiians to read and write. This fostered a high literacy rate and the publication of several Hawaiian-language newspapers.

Eventually, however, missionaries banned the Hawaiian language in schools in order to distance Hawaiians from their 'hedonistic' cultural roots. They also prohibited hula dancing because of its lewd and suggestive movements, denounced traditional Hawaiian chants and songs that honored 'heathen' gods, taught women to sew Western-style clothing and abolished polygamy, which was accepted and necessary in this isolated island group.

The Best... History Museums

1 Lyman Museum & Mission House (p169)

2 Hulihe'e Palace (p35)

3 Pacific Tsunami Museum (p172)

4 'Imiloa Astronomy Center of Hawai'i (p172)

5 Laupahoehoe Train Museum (p159)

King Sugar in the Plantation Era

Ko (sugarcane) was a 'canoe plant,' introduced by the first Polynesians. When foreigners realized Hawai'i was ideal for growing sugarcane, they quickly established small plantations using Hawaiian labor. Many missionaries became influential advisors to the Hawaiian monarchy and received large tracts of arable land in return, prompting them to leave the church altogether.

By that time, the Native Hawaiian population had alarmingly declined, due to such introduced diseases as typhoid, influenza, smallpox and syphilis. To fill the labor shortage, plantation workers were imported from overseas. First, beginning in the 1850s, came Chinese laborers and soon after came Japanese and Portuguese immigrants. After the US annexed Hawaii in 1898, Puerto Ricans, Koreans and Filipinos arrived.

The rise of the sugar industry had a major impact on Hawai'i's social structure. Haole (Caucasian) plantation owners and sugar agents became the elite economic and political class, while Hawaiians and foreign laborers without land of their own filled lower-class ranks. Meanwhile, those diverse immigrant groups, along with the shared pidgin language they created, transformed Hawai'i into the multiethnic, multicultural society it is today.

During California's Gold Rush and later the US Civil War, Hawai'i's sugar exports to the mainland soared. As late as 1960, 'King Sugar' remained the state's largest industry. Due to cheaper labor and production costs abroad, however, Hawaii's sugar plantations began shuttering in the 1980s. Today there is only one working plantation left statewide, on Maui.

1882
Macadamia trees are planted on Hawai'i as an ornamental; the nuts aren't eaten till the 1920s.

1893
The Hawaiian monarchy, under Queen Lili'uokalani, is overthrown in Honolulu, ending 83 years of rule.

1912
Duke Kahanamoku wins Olympic swimming medals; he later becomes a global ambassador of aloha and surfing.

Hawaiian Kingdom Overthrown

Under the Hawaiian monarchy, foreigners had no way to own property because the king controlled the lands. With foreigners pushing to secure long-term property rights, in 1848 the kingdom's government enacted the Great Mahele, a revolutionary land reform act. Two years later the government further acquiesced by allowing foreign residents to buy land. Haole sugar growers and land speculators bought huge parcels for minimal sums from chiefs lured by quick money and from commoners ignorant of deeds, taxes and other legal requirements for ownership.

King David Kalakaua, who reigned from 1874 to 1891, fought to restore Hawaiian culture, arts and indigenous pride. He also had a fondness for drinking, gambling and partying, earning him the nickname 'Merrie Monarch.' In 1887 the Hawaiian League, a secret antimonarchy organization run by sugar interests, wrote a new constitution and forced Kalakaua to sign. This 'Bayonet Constitution' stripped the monarchy's powers, making the king a figurehead. It also limited voting rights, effectively allowing only wealthy businessmen and landowners to vote.

When Kalakaua died, his sister Lili'uokalani ascended the throne and tried to restore the monarchy. On January 17, 1893, a 'Committee of Safety,' composed mostly of haole

Koa bowls, Hulihe'e Palace (p35), Kailua-Kona

1946
Hawaii's most destructive tsunami, generated by an Alaskan earthquake, kills 122 people on the Big Island.

1959
Hawaii becomes the 50th US state; Daniel Inouye is elected first Japanese American in Congress.

1960
A tsunami generated off South America destroys over 100 buildings and kills 61 people in Hilo.

American residents and supported by US Minister John Stevens and a contingent of US marines and sailors, forcibly arrested her and took over Honolulu's 'Iolani Palace in a tense but bloodless coup d'état.

Becoming the 50th State

After the short-lived Republic of Hawai'i was annexed as a US territory in 1898, the road to statehood was long and bumpy. The islands presented some novel issues for the US federal government, including its distance from the mainland, strong labor unions and a huge nonwhite population. Likewise, statehood was a tough sell to the US Congress, but a series of significant historical events paved the way.

In 1936 Pan American Airways began regular commercial flights from the US mainland to Hawaii, launching the transpacific air age and the beginning of mass tourism. Wireless telegraph service, followed by telephone service, between Hawaii and the mainland alleviated doubts about long-distance communication. And, most importantly, WWII proved both the strategic military role of O'ahu's Pearl Harbor and the Hawaiian Islands generally.

While Southern conservatives, both Democrat and Republic, remained wary of the islands' multicultural melting pot, Hawaii became the 50th US state in 1959. After statehood, tourism exploded, thanks to the advent of jet airplanes and to the commercializing of Hawaii (think tiki craze, Blue Hawaii, aloha shirts and Waikiki). Hotel construction boomed and by 1970 tourism had added $1 billion to state coffers, surpassing both agriculture and US military spending.

Promised Land

In 1921 the US Congress passed the Hawaiian Homes Commission Act, setting aside almost 200,000 acres of government land for Native Hawaiians to lease for $1 per year. Unfortunately many of these lands are remote and lack basic infrastructure (eg roads, water, electricity) and applicants end up waiting for years, even decades. There are over 25,000 residential applicants on the wait list across the state, but fewer than 10,000 leases have ever been granted. Some applicants are elderly or even pass away by the time they receive a lease.

1971
Hilo's Merrie Monarch Festival holds its first hula competition, celebrating a cultural renaissance.

1978
The Office of Hawaiian Affairs (OHA) is established and holds Hawaiian Home Lands in trust for the benefit of Native Hawaiians.

1983
Kilauea begins the volcanic eruption that is currently the longest in recorded history.

Native Hawaiian Renaissance

In 1976, after the homegrown Polynesian Voyaging Society built and sailed the *Hokule'a* – a replica of a traditional Polynesian double-hulled canoe – succesfully round-trip to Tahiti, traditional Hawaiian knowledge was suddenly in demand again. The same year, a small grassroots group, Protect Kaho'olawe 'Ohana (PKO), began illegally occupying Kaho'olawe, an island taken by the US government during WWII and used as a practice bombing site.

After the state held its landmark Constitutional Convention in 1978, public schools started teaching Hawaiian language and Hawaiian-immersion charter schools proliferated. Small but vocal contingents of political activists began pushing for some measure of Hawaiian sovereignty, from complete secession from the USA to a nation-within-a-nation model. Today the US federal government still has not acknowledged Native Hawaiians as an indigenous people, however.

1993

Federal 'Apology Bill' acknowledges the USA's role in the kingdom's illegal takeover a century ago.

2002

Following Democratic Party corruption scandals, mainland-born Linda Lingle is elected Hawaii's first Republican governor in 40 years.

2008

O'ahu-born Barack Obama becomes the first African American US President; he is reelected in 2012.

People of the Big Island

Kahiko (ancient) hula performance with an *ipu* (gourd) drum

ALVIS UPITIS/GETTY IMAGES ©

Mention Hawai'i and you might start fantasizing about sandy beaches, swaying palms and blazing sunsets. But the heart of the Big Island is found elsewhere: in its diverse people. Whether residents are Native Hawaiian, kama'aina *(born and raised in Hawaii) or transplanted from afar, they're united by small-town values, respect for multicultural traditions, interrracial tolerance and their enthusiastic pursuit of 'the good life.'*

Big Island Identity

The Big Island is far from homogeneous, but overall the mellow vibe tends to smooth sharp differences between and among people. Most residents are easy-going and low-key, with a preference for unpretentious small-town life. Politically, the majority are moderate Democrats, often voting along party, racial, ethnic, seniority and local/nonlocal lines.

Locals embrace their longstanding connections, often maintaining friendships with high-school classmates and invariably bumping into familiar faces whenever they step out. As a rule, loud assertiveness is considered unseemly. It's better to avoid embarrassing confrontations and 'save face' by keeping quiet.

The most vocal, liberal and passionate speakers at community meetings are often brash mainland transplants pushing for environmental conservation, sustainability, slow growth and non-GMO food. 'Loudmouth haole,' locals might think. But other transplants quickly find their feet here: befriending *kama'aina* neighbors, growing backyard gardens, studying hula and simply slowing down and respecting local ways.

Locals generally support progressive trends, in keeping with the Hawaiian concept of *aloha 'aina* (love of the land). While Costco and Walmart might be anathema to politically left-leaning mainlanders, budget-minded locals just trying to get by welcome the discounts and variety. And despite guzzling expensive gas, a monster-sized pickup truck remains *the* status-symbol vehicle for many locals.

Hilo vs Kona

While Honolulu folk view Hilo, the capital town, as 'country' or even *da boonies* (the boondocks), everything's relative. On the Big Island, Hilo is 'town,' where people wear wrinkle-free aloha shirts and wristwatches to work in government offices. With the highest statewide percentage of Japanese Americans (33%), Hilo's plantation roots are clear.

In contrast, Kailua-Kona has become the island's economic powerhouse and a tourist hub. It's busy and 'haole-fied,' with a 48% white population due to an influx of new transplants. As a result, traffic along the Queen Ka'ahumanu Hwy is a nightmare and residents often gripe about the county's shortsightedness in improving Kona's jammed roads, compared with Hilo's well-planned system.

Lifestyle

The typical Hawai'i lifestyle is changing with the influence of newcomers and less-traditional younger generations, but Big Islanders generally center their lives around family. The workday starts and ends early; even workaholics tend to be backyard

Who's Who?

Haole White person, Caucasian (except local Portuguese). Often further defined as 'mainland haole' or 'local haole.' Can be insulting or playful, depending on context.

Hapa Person of mixed ancestry; most commonly referring to *hapa* haole who are part white and part Asian, Hawaiian etc.

Hawaiian Person of Native Hawaiian ancestry. It's a faux pas to call any Hawai'i resident 'Hawaiian,' thus ignoring the islands' indigenous people.

Kama'aina Person who is native to a particular place; literally 'child of the land.' In a retail context, '*kama'aina* discounts' apply to anyone with a Hawaii driver's license.

Local A person who grew up here. Locals who move away from Hawai'i somewhat retain their local 'cred.'

'Ohana Family. Extends beyond bloodlines to include close friends, co-workers, classmates and teammates.

Transplant Person who moves to the islands as an adult. Never becomes a 'local,' even after they've lived in Hawaii for many years.

gardeners, surfers or golfers. Not surprisingly, Hawaii residents have the longest life expectancy in the USA: 81.3 years.

The influx of mainlanders is obvious. Mainland transplants generally arrive with more money and different dreams – say, looking forward to a relaxed retirement, starting a B&B or a coffee estate, or just for youthful experimentation. On the Big Island, many mainlanders feel free to be more unconventional.

O'ahu and Maui expats constitute a newer wave of transplants. 'Hilo still feels like old Hawaii,' they say. Indeed, Big Island real estate remains the most affordable statewide, while urban problems from traffic to crime remain tolerable. 'High density' is still a foreign concept on the Big Island, where commutes can cover a lot of highway.

Regional differences can be stark. For example, Pahoa is teeming with off-the-grid types who grow their own food and live off bare essentials, eschewing creature comforts like hot showers. In Hilo and Kona, such a lifestyle is practically unheard of. There, locals tend toward more conventional 'American dream' lives, meaning marriage, kids, a comfortable home and stable employment.

Multiculturalism

Big Island immigrants are today overwhelmingly white, so the island's diversity stems from historical plantation-era ethnic groups: Native Hawaiians, Japanese, Filipino, Portuguese and Chinese. It's a unique mix that's remarkably different from mainland diversity, as it lacks significant African American and Latino populations.

During plantation days, haole were the wealthy plantation owners, and their legendary surnames remain household names (eg Parker Ranch, Lyman Museum). Their ingrained privilege is one reason why some resentment toward haole still lingers. However, prominent haole families were often close allies of high-ranking Native Hawaiians – or even related by marriage.

Hilo Farmers Market (p181)

Dos & Don'ts for Island Visitors

- Do be courteous and 'no make waves' (don't make a scene).
- Do try to use basic Hawaiian words, but don't speak pidgin.
- Do dress casually like locals do. Remove your shoes before entering homes and B&Bs.
- Do treat ancient Hawaiian sites and artifacts with respect. Don't collect or move stones.
- Do ask permission before picking flowers or fruit on private property.
- Do drive slowly and don't honk your horn except in an emergency.
- Do give a *shaka* (Hawaii's hand-greeting sign) if another driver lets you merge.
- Do tread lightly at 'locals only' beaches.

As time passes and the plantation era fades away, the traditional stereotypes, hierarchies and alliances are softening too. Besides, no ethnic group has ever kept exclusive for long anyway on Hawai'i. Instead different groups have freely adopted and shared cultural customs, from food to festivals. Today, folks of all ethnic backgrounds dance the hula, play the ukulele and study the Hawaiian language.

Today there is no ethnic majority in the Hawaiian Islands. Due to intermarriage, you cannot always assume a person's race or ethnicity by surname – many Native Hawaiians have Caucasian or Asian surnames. Generally, locals feel most bonded with other locals. While tourists and transplants are usually welcomed with aloha, they must earn locals' trust by being *pono* (respectful).

Religion

Although Hawaiians abandoned their ancient religion for Christianity soon after King Kamehameha I died, religious traditions survived underground. Today you'll glimpse them in public ceremonies, such as when a kahuna (priest) blesses the land during a groundbreaking. Many ancient historical sites – *pu'uhonua* (places of refuge), heiau (temples) and petroglyph fields – are also religious sites, chosen for the mana (spiritual essence) of the land. Certain natural features, such as Halema'uma'u Crater and Mauna Kea, are still considered sacred.

Many residents do not claim adherence to a particular faith, and the religious milieu is tolerant rather than dogmatic. The largest religious group is Roman Catholic, due to a significant Filipino population, followed by Mormonism, which has attracted many South Pacific converts. Mainstream Protestant Christianity is struggling with declining membership, while evangelical churches are burgeoning. Buddhism is prevalent among Japanese residents, and their temples are often important community centers.

Big Island Cuisine

Tempura ahi roll

BILL ADAMS/GETTY IMAGES ©

Forget pineapple-topped pizza; Hawaii's cuisine is no cliché. It's a multicultural flavor explosion, influenced by the Pacific Rim and rooted in the islands' natural bounty. The first Polynesians brought nourishing staples such as kalo *(taro),* niu *(coconut), chickens and pigs. Later plantation-era immigrants imported rice,* shōyu *(soy sauce), chilies and more. Over time, all these wildly different flavors became 'local.'*

Local Food

Cheap, tasty and filling, local 'grinds' (food) is the stuff of cravings and comfort. There's no better example than that of the classic plate lunch, a fixed-plate meal of 'two scoop' rice, macaroni or potato salad and a hot protein dish, such as fried mahimahi, teriyaki chicken or *kalbi* short ribs. Often eaten with disposable chopsticks on disposable plates, these meals pack a flavor (and caloric) punch: fried, salty and meaty. Nowadays healthier plates come with brown rice and salad greens.

Sticky white rice is more than a side dish in Hawaii. It's a culinary building block, an integral partner in everyday meals. Without rice, Spam *musubi* (rice ball) would just be a slice of canned meat. The *loco moco* would be nothing more than an egg-and-gravy-covered hamburger patty. Just so you know,

Spam-tastic!

Hawaii may be the only US state where you can eat Hormel's iconic canned meat with pride. Here in the nation's Spam capital, locals consume almost seven million cans per year.

Of course, Spam looks and tastes different in Hawaii. It's always eaten cooked, typically fried to a light crispiness in sugar-sweetened *shōyu* (soy sauce), not straight from the can. It's often served for breakfast with eggs and rice, or sliced and rolled into *musubi* (rice balls or blocks wrapped with nori), sold everywhere, even at mainstream chains like 7-Eleven.

During the plantation era, canned meat was cheap and easy to prepare for *bentō* (Japanese-style boxed lunches) taken to the fields. But Spam itself wasn't introduced to the islands until WWII, when fresh meat was replaced by standard US military rations. By the time the war ended, residents had developed an affinity for the fatty pork-based meat product.

If you acquire a taste for it too, pick up *Hawai'i Cooks with SPAM: Local Recipes Featuring Our Favorite Canned Meat* by Muriel Miura.

sticky white rice means exactly that. Not fluffy rice. Not wild rice. And definitely not instant.

One must-try local *pupu* (snack or appetizer) is *poke* (pronounced '*poh*-keh'), a savory dish of bite-sized raw fish (typically ahi), seasoned with *shōyu*, sesame oil, green onion, chili-pepper flakes, sea salt, *ogo* (crunchy seaweed) and *'inamona* (a condiment made of roasted, ground *kukui* – candlenut tree – nuts).

Another favorite local food is saimin, a soup of chewy Chinese egg noodles swimming in Japanese broth, garnished with green onion, dried nori (Japanese dried seaweed), *kamaboko* (steamed fish cake) and *char siu* (Chinese barbecued pork).

The traditional local sweet treat is Chinese crack seed. It's preserved fruit (typically plum, cherry, mango or lemon) that, like Coca-Cola or curry, is impossible to describe – it can be sweet, sour, salty or spicy. Sold prepackaged at supermarkets and Longs Drugs stores or scooped by the pound at specialty shops, crack seed is truly addictive.

Native Hawaiian Food

With its earthy flavors and Polynesian ingredients, Hawaiian cooking is like no other. But it's not necessarily easy for visitors to find – look for it at roadside markets, plate-lunch kitchens, old-school delis and island diners.

Kalua pig is traditionally roasted whole underground in an *imu*, a pit of red-hot stones layered with banana and *ti* (a native plant) leaves. Cooked this way, the pork is smoky, salty and succulent. Nowadays *kalua* pork is typically oven-roasted and seasoned with salt and liquid smoke. At a commercial luau, a pig placed in an *imu* is usually only for show (it couldn't feed 300-plus guests anyway).

Poi – a purplish paste made of pounded taro root, often steamed and fermented – was sacred to ancient Hawaiians. Taro is highly nutritious, low in calories, easily digestible and versatile to prepare. Tasting bland to mildly tart or even sour, poi is usually not eaten by itself, but as a starchy counterpoint to strongly flavored dishes such as *lomilomi* salmon (minced, salted salmon with diced tomato and green onion). Fried or baked taro chips are sold at grocery stores, gas stations etc.

A popular main dish is *laulau,* a bundle of pork or chicken and salted butterfish wrapped in taro or *ti* leaves and steamed until it has a soft spinachlike texture. Other traditional Hawaiian fare includes baked *'ulu* (breadfruit), with a mouthfeel similar to potato; *'opihi* (limpet), tiny mollusks picked off reefs at low tide; and *haupia,* a coconut-cream custard thickened with arrowroot or cornstarch.

The Best... Food & Drink Festivals

1 Kona Coffee Cultural Festival (p43)

2 Kona Brewers Festival (p43)

3 A Taste of the Hawaiian Range (p99)

4 Puna Culinary Festival (p200)

5 Ka'u Coffee Festival (p235)

Hawaii Regional Cuisine

Hawaii was considered a culinary backwater until the early 1990s, when a handful of island chefs – including Alan Wong, Roy Yamaguchi, Sam Choy and Peter Merriman, all of whom still have restaurants on the Big Island – created a new cuisine, borrowing liberally from Hawaii's multiethnic heritage.

These chefs partnered with island farmers, ranchers and fishers to highlight fresh, local ingredients and in doing so, transformed childhood favorites into gourmet Pacific Rim masterpieces. Suddenly macadamia-nut-crusted mahimahi, miso-glazed butterfish and *liliko'i* (passion fruit) anything were all the rage.

This culinary movement was dubbed 'Hawaii Regional Cuisine' and its 12 pioneering chefs became celebrities. At first, Hawaii Regional Cuisine was rather exclusive, found only at high-end dining rooms. Its hallmarks included Eurasian-fusion flavors and gastronomic techniques with elaborate plating.

Upscale restaurants are still the mainstay for Hawaii's star chefs, but now you'll find neighborhood bistros and even plate-lunch food trucks serving dishes inspired by Hawaii Regional Cuisine, with island farms lauded like designer brands on menus.

Who Invented Loco Moco?

Among Hilo's claims to fame is the *loco moco* (a hamburger patty, fried egg and gravy over rice). In 1949, the Lincoln Wreckers, a teen sports club, hung out at the now long-gone Lincoln Grill. Amid pinball machines and a jukebox, they'd fill up on cheap hot meals. One guy nicknamed Loco ('crazy' in Hawaiian pidgin) requested a new dish, so the owners offered him a big bowl of rice smothered with a hamburger steak and brown gravy for 25¢. This mishmash made the permanent menu and was named *loco moco* in honor of Crazy. Eventually eggs were added, and the rest is Big Island culinary history.

The Best... Sustainable Food Websites

1 Hawai'i Seafood (www.hawaii-seafood.org)

2 Hawai'i Agritourism Association (www.hiagtourism.org)

3 Edible Hawaiian Islands (www.ediblehawaiianislands.com)

4 Slow Food Hawai'i (www.slowfoodhawaii.org)

5 Hawaii Farm Bureau Federation (www.hfbf.org)

Hawaii's Locavore Movement

Many Big Islanders are backyard farmers, growing more apple bananas, star fruit and avocados than they can consume themselves. Still, a whopping 85% to 90% of Hawaii's food is imported, and food security (aka 'food sovereignty') is a hot topic. Small-scale family farmers are trying to shift the agriculture industry away from corporate-scale monocropping (eg sugar, pineapple) enabled by chemical fertilizers, pesticides, herbicides and genetically modified organisms (GMOs).

Diversified agriculture and agrotourism are booming on the Big Island. It's not just about Hawai'i's signature macadamia nuts and Kona coffee anymore, but a delicious range of locally grown edibles: Hamakua Coast mushrooms, vanilla, tomatoes and salad greens; Big Island abalone, lobsters and *kampachi* (yellowtail) from the Kona coast; grass-fed beef and lamb from Waimea; Kona chocolate; organic tea from Volcano and the Hamakua Coast; Ka'u oranges and coffee; yellow-flesh Kapho Solo papayas from Puna; and local honey. While the Big Island's egg and poultry farms are long gone, the state's two biggest cattle dairies still operate here.

Despite the popularity of Hawai'i's farmers markets, supermarkets still typically stock blemish-free Sunkist oranges and California grapes. An exception is the Big Island's KTA Superstores, a minichain that carries 200 products, including milk, beef, produce and coffee, from dozens of local vendors under its Mountain Apple Brand.

Coffee, Tea & Traditional Drinks

Hawaii was the first US state to grow coffee. World-famous Kona coffee wins raves for its mellow flavor with no bitter aftertaste. The upland slopes of Mauna Loa and Hualalai volcanoes in the Kona district offer an ideal climate (sunny mornings and afternoon clouds with light seasonal showers) for coffee cultivation.

While 100% Kona coffee has the most cachet, commanding upwards of $20 to $40 or more per pound, in recent years crops from the island's southernmost district of Ka'u have won accolades and impressed aficionados. Small coffee farms have also fruited in Puna and Honoka'a on the island's windward side.

Ancient Hawaiians never got buzzed on coffee beans, which were first imported in the early 19th century. Hawaii's original intoxicants were plant-based Polynesian elixirs: *'awa*, a mild, mouth-numbing sedative made from the kava plant's roots, and *noni* (Indian mulberry), which some consider a cure-all. Both of these drinks are pungent in smell and taste, so they're often mixed with other juices.

Tea-growing was introduced to Hawaii in the late 19th century, but never took hold as a commercial crop due to high labor and production costs. In 1999 University of Hawai'i researchers discovered that a particular cultivar of tea would thrive in volcanic soil and tropical climates, especially at higher elevations. Small, often organic, tea farms are now spreading around Volcano and along the Hamakua Coast.

Fruit trees also thrive here. Alas, most supermarket cartons contain imported purees or sugary 'juice drinks' like POG (passion fruit, orange and guava). Look for real, freshly squeezed and blended juices at health food stores, farmers markets and roadside fruit stands. Don't assume that the fruit is local, though.

Beer, Wine & Cocktails

Once a novelty, a handful of microbreweries are now firmly established on the Big Island. Brewmasters claim that the mineral content and purity of Hawai'i's water makes for excellent-tasting beer. Another hallmark of local craft beers is the addition of a hint of tropical flavors, such as Kona coffee, honey or *liliko'i*.

Lively brewpubs and tasting rooms where you can sample popular pours include ecoconscious Kona Brewing Company (p42) in Kailua-Kona, the Big Island Brewhaus (p127) in Waimea and **Hawai'i Nui Brewing** (Map p170; ☎808-934-8211; http://hawaiinuibrewing.com; 275 E Kawili; ⏰10am-6pm Mon-Fri) FREE (which also owns the Mehana Brewing Company label) in Hilo. The island's sole winery, Volcano Winery, is untraditional in its guava-grape and macadamia-honey concoctions – they're not to everyone's taste.

Every beachfront and hotel bar mixes tropical cocktails topped with fruit garnish and a toothpick umbrella. Hawaii's legendary mai tai is a mix of dark and light rum, orange curaçao, orgeat and simple syrup with orange, lemon, lime and/or pineapple juices.

Luau

In ancient Hawaii, a luau commemorated auspicious occasions, such as births, war victories or successful harvests. Modern luau to celebrate weddings or a baby's first birthday are often large banquet-hall or outdoor gatherings with the *'ohana* (extended family and friends). Although the menu might be daring – including Hawaiian delicacies such as raw *'a'ama* (black crab) and *'opihi* – the entertainment is low-key.

Hawaii's commercial luau started in the 1970s. Today these shows offer the elaborate pseudo-Hawaiian feast and Polynesian dancing and fire eaters that many visitors expect. But the all-you-can-eat buffet of luau standards is usually toned down for the mainland palate, with steamed mahimahi and teriyaki chicken. Most commercial luau are overpriced and overly touristy, although kids may enjoy them.

Coffee plantation, Kona
DENNIS MACDONALD/GETTY IMAGES ©

Hawaiian Arts & Crafts

Merrie Monarch Festival, Hilo (p177)

WILLIAM WATERFALL/GETTY IMAGES ©

Contemporary Hawai'i is a tropical garden of diverse cultural traditions, underneath which beats a Hawaiian heart. Since the 1970s, a revival of indigenous language, crafts, music and hula means visitors will find themselves surrounded by art, both ancient and new. E komo mai *(welcome) to this Polynesian island, where storytelling and slack key guitar are among the familiar sounds of everyday life.*

Hula

In ancient Hawai'i, hula sometimes was a solemn ritual, in which *mele* (songs, chants) were an offering to the gods or celebrated the accomplishments of *ali'i* (chiefs). At other times hula was lighthearted entertainment, in which chief and *maka'ainana* (commoner) danced together, including at annual festivals. Most importantly, hula embodied the community – telling stories of and celebrating itself.

Dancers trained rigorously in *halau* (schools) under a *kumu* (teacher), so their hand gestures, facial expressions and synchronized movements were exact. In a culture without written language, chants were important, giving meaning to the movements and preserving Hawai'i's oral history – anything from creation stories about gods and goddesses to royal genealogies. Songs often contained *kaona* (hidden meanings), which could be spiritual, but also amorous or sexual.

Today hula competitions take place across the islands, with hula troupes vying in *kahiko* (ancient) and *'auana* (modern) categories. *Kahiko* performances are raw and elemental, accompanied only by chanting and thunderous gourd drums. Costumes are traditional, with *ti*-leaf lei, *kapa* (pounded bark-cloth) skirts, primary colors and sometimes lots of skin showing. Western influences – English-language lyrics, stringed instruments, flowing dresses and pants, sinuous arm movements and smiling faces – may appear in *'auana* dances. Some *halau* even flirt with postmodern dance styles.

Hawaii's own Olympics of hula is Hilo's **Merrie Monarch Festival** (**☎935-9168; www.merriemonarchfestival.org; Afook-Chinen Civic Auditorium; 3-night admission $25-30**), held around Easter. A newer competition, **Moku O Keawe** (**www.mokif.com; Waikoloa Resort Area; admission per night $15-25**), takes place at Waikoloa in early November. Don't miss the year-round outdoor **hula performances** (**www.volcanoartcenter.org;** 👪) 🍃 at Hawai'i Volcanoes National Park.

Island Music

It would take a textbook to cover every genre of Hawaiian music, from traditional *mele* to contemporary vocalists, like the late Israel 'Iz' Kamakawiwo'ole, who marry Hawaiian and English lyrics. Away from the islands, however, most people aren't aware of the lasting contributions that Hawaiian musicians have made to modern music: the steel guitar, the ukulele and the slack key guitar.

Spanish and Mexican cowboys first introduced the guitar to Hawaiians in the 1830s. Fifty years later, teenager Joseph Kekuku started experimenting with playing a guitar flat on his lap while sliding a pocket knife or comb across the strings. He invented the Hawaiian steel guitar *(kika kila)*, which lifts the strings off the fretboard using a movable steel slide, creating a signature smooth sound.

Hawaiian Music Online

Hearing Hawaiian music is a great way to get pumped before, during and after your trip. The following websites let you dive right in:

- **Hawaiian Music Island** (**www.mele.com**) Online music and video retailer with links to award-winning Hawaiian artists and internet radio stations, with mainland and island concert listings.
- **Cord International** (**www.cordinternational.com**) Vintage music purveyor for everything from retro Japanese Hawaiian sounds to Les Paul's luau album.
- **Mountain Apple Company** (**www.mountainapplecompany.com**) Music label with the biggest library of contemporary and traditional Hawaiian music, plus free online clips and streaming radio.
- **Hawaiian Rainbow** (**www.hawaiianrainbow.com**) Live streaming of mostly traditional Hawaiian music; also available on a free mobile app.
- **Huapala** (**www.huapala.org**) Hawaiian music and hula archives include chants and songs searchable by island.
- **Dancing Cat Records** (**www.dancingcat.com**) Music label dedicated to Hawaiian slack key guitarists, offering free online album previews.

The Best... Big Island Albums

1 *'Ohai 'Ula* (2010), Kainani Kahaunaele

2 *Aloha Pumehana* (2009), Darlene Ahuna

3 *Hawai'i Island... Is My Home* (2008), John Keawe

4 *Songs from Hawai'i Island* (2007)

5 *Honey-Boy* (2002), Kekuhi Kanahele

6 *O Ke Aumoe* (1996), George Kuo

Heard all across the islands is the ukulele, derived from the *braguinha,* a Portuguese stringed instrument introduced to Hawaii in 1879. Ukulele means 'jumping flea' in Hawaiian, referring to the way players' deft fingers swiftly 'jump' around the strings. Both the ukulele and the Hawaiian steel guitar contributed to the lighthearted *hapa haole* (Hawaiian music with predominantly English lyrics) popularized in Hawaii and abroad after the 1930s. Today the ukulele is making a comeback as a young generation of virtuosos emerges, led by genre-bending, Billboard chart-topping rocker Jake Shimabukuro.

Since the mid-20th century, the Hawaiian steel guitar has usually been played with slack key guitar (*ki ho'alu,* literally 'loosen the key') tunings, in which the thumb plays the bass and rhythm chords, while the fingers play the melody and improvisations, in a picked style. Legendary musician Gabby Pahinui launched the modern slack key guitar era with his first recording of 'Hi'ilawe' in 1946. In the 1970s, Gabby and his band the Sons of Hawai'i embraced the traditional Hawaiian sound, spurring its rebirth. The list of contemporary slack key masters is long and ever growing, including Big Island–born Keola Beamer.

Hawaiian vocalists are known for a distinctive falsetto singing technique (called *leo ke'ike'i*) that stresses the break *(ha'i)* between lower and upper registers. The unquestioned leader of this style among women remains the late Genoa Keawe, whose impossibly long-held notes in the song 'Alika' set the standard (and set it high). Other notables include jazzy songbird Amy Hanaiali'i Gilliom and younger chanteuse Raiatea Helm, both Grammy nominees.

Traditional Crafts

The lei – a handcrafted garland worn around one's neck or head – is Hawaii's most sensuous and transitory art form. Traditional lei makers may use feathers, nuts, shells, seeds, seaweed, vines, leaves and fruit, as well as fragrant fresh flowers. In choosing their materials, lei makers tell a story – since flowers and plants may embody Hawaiian places and myths – and express emotions such as love, honor and respect.

In the islands' Polynesian past, lei were part of sacred hula dances and given as special gifts to loved ones, as healing medicine to the sick and as offerings to the gods. Today locals often don lei for special events, such as weddings, birthdays, anniversaries, graduations and other public ceremonies. A typical Hawaiian lei costs anywhere from $10 for a single strand of plumeria sold at the airport to thousands of dollars for a 100% genuine Ni'ihau shell lei necklace.

Other bewitchingly beautiful Hawaiian crafts include *lauhala* weaving, *kapa* (pounded-bark cloth) making and intricate featherwork seen in *kahili* (royal standards), capes and lei. When it comes to *lauhala,* weaving the *lau* (leaves) of the hala (pandanus) tree is the easier part, while preparing the leaves, which have razor-sharp spines, is messy work. Making *kapa* (called tapa elsewhere in Polynesia) is no less laborious: large sheets of hand-felted cloth are colorfully dyed with plant

materials and stamped or painted with bold geometric patterns, then scented with flowers or oils.

Ancient Hawaiians were also expert at woodworking, carving canoes out of logs and hand-turning lustrous bowls from a variety of beautifully grained tropical hardwoods, such as koa, kou and milo. *Ipu* (gourds) were dried and used as containers and as drums for hula performances and chanting. Contemporary woodworkers use native woods to craft traditional bowls, exquisite furniture, jewelry and free-form sculptures. Hawaiian bowls are not typically decorated or ornate, but are shaped to bring out the natural beauty of the wood.

All of these traditional Hawaiian crafts have become so popular with tourists that cheap imitation imports from factories across the Pacific and Asia have flooded island stores. Shop carefully, buy local and expect to pay more for high-quality handmade pieces, for example, at the **Volcano Art Center** (866-967-7565, 808-967-7565; www.volcanoartcenter.org; Crater Rim Dr; 9am-5pm), and Holualoa's **Kimura Lauhala Shop** (808-324-0053; www.holualoahawaii.com/member_sites/kimura.html; cnr Hualalai Rd & Hwy 180; 9am-5pm Mon-Fri, to 4pm Sat) and **Ipu Hale Gallery** (808-322-9069; www.holualoahawaii.com/member_sites/ipu_hale.html; 76-5893 Mamalahoa Hwy; 10am-4pm Tue-Sat).

Literature

Hawai'i's oldest storytelling was of ancient myths and legends, originally disseminated by oral tradition. In modern times, Hawaii's written literature was long dominated by Western writers who observed Hawaii's exotic-looking world from the outside, such as James Michener's best-selling historical saga *Hawaii*, Mark Twain's *Roughing It* and Isabella Bird's *Six Months in the Sandwich Islands*.

Since the 1970s birthed an ongoing renaissance of Hawaiian culture and language, locally born writers have created an authentic contemporary literature of Hawaii that evokes island life from an insider's perspective. Leading this movement has

Tobacco leaves, Pu'uhonua O Hōnaunau National Historical Park (p77)

Hawaiiana Classes

Explore Hawaiian language, art, music and dance at a variety of cultural classes, workshops and lessons held all over the island, including at beach resorts and hotels. Check calendar listings in the **Big Island Weekly** (www.bigislandweekly.com) and with the following places:

- **Volcano Art Center** (p267)
- **Society for Kona's Education and Art** (SKEA; 808-328-9392; www.skea.org; 84-5191 Mamalahoa Hwy)
- **Donkey Mill Art Center** (808-322-3362; www.donkeymillartcenter.org; 78-6670 Mamalahoa Hwy; 10am-4pm Tue-Sat Aug-May, 9am-3pm Mon-Fri Jun & Jul;) FREE
- **Keauhou Shopping Center** (www.keauhouvillageshops.com; 78-6831 Ali'i Dr) FREE
- **East Hawai'i Cultural Center** (East Hawai'i Cultural Center; 808-961-5711; www.ehcc.org; 141 Kalakaua St; suggested donation $2; 10am-4pm Mon-Sat)

Get a head start before your trip with online music lessons by slack key guitarist **Keola Beamer** (www.kbeamer.com).

been **Bamboo Ridge Press** (www.bambooridge.com), which for more than 35 years has published contemporary local fiction and poetry in an annual journal and has launched the careers of many well-known Hawaii writers.

In 1975, *All I Asking for Is My Body*, by Milton Murayama, vividly captured plantation life for Japanese *nisei* (second-generation immigrants) around WWII. Murayama's use of pidgin opened the door to an explosion of vernacular literature. Raised on the Big Island, Lois-Ann Yamanaka has won widespread acclaim for her poetry and stories (*Wild Meat and the Bully Burgers*, 1996), in which pidgin embodies her characters like a second skin.

Indeed, redeeming pidgin – long dismissed by academics and disparaged by the upper class – has been a cultural and political cause for some. The hilarious stories (*Da Word*, 2001) and essays (*Living Pidgin*, 2002) of Lee Tonouchi, a prolific writer and playwright, argue that pidgin is not only essential to understanding local culture, but also a legitimate language.

Family Travel

Stargazing, Mauna Kea (p135)

JOHN HOOK/GETTY IMAGES ©

With its phenomenal natural beauty, Hawai'i is perfect for a family vacation. Nā keiki *(kids) can play on sandy beaches galore, snorkel amid tropical fish, zipline in forest canopies and even watch lava flow. Then get them out of the sun (or rain) for a spell at family-friendly museums. Because long drive times can make kids antsy, you may not want to base yourself in just one place on the Big Island.*

Planning Your Trip

Mixing up natural and cultural sites and activities, as well as managing expectations, helps maximize children's fun. The latter is especially important when it comes to lava: kids may be sorely disappointed, expecting the fiery fountains dramatically seen on the Discovery Channel. Check current lava flows with the **Hawaiian Volcano Observatory** (http://hvo.wr.usgs.gov/activity/kilaueastatus.php) before booking an expensive helicopter or boat tour.

Choose accommodations based on your family's sightseeing and activity priorities. Resorts offer spectacular swimming pools, along with kids' activity day camps and on-call babysitting services. But some parents prefer the convenience and cost savings of having a full kitchen and washer/dryer, which many condominiums and vacation rentals offer.

Children often stay free when sharing a hotel or resort room with their parents, but only if they use existing bedding. Otherwise, rollaway beds may be available – sometimes free, but usually for a surcharge of up to $40 per night. At condos, kids above a certain age might count as extra guests and entail an additional nightly surcharge. Kids and even babies are welcome at some island B&Bs and inns, but not all.

Because Hawaii is a family-oriented and unfussy place, most restaurants welcome children, except for some high-end resort dining rooms. If restaurant dining is inconvenient, no problem. Eating outdoors at a beach park is among the simplest and best island pleasures. Pack finger foods for a picnic, pick up fruit from farmers markets, stop for smoothies at roadside stands and order plate lunches at drive-ins.

Commercial luau might seem like cheesy Vegas dinner shows to adults, but many kids love the flashy dances and fire tricks. Children typically get discounted tickets (and sometimes free admission when accompanied by a paying adult).

When deciding when and where to visit, know that most families choose the sunny leeward side of the island, staying around Kailua-Kona or on the South Kohala coast. The windward side of the Big Island gets more rain year-round and higher waves in winter, which can nix swimming. Year-round, vog (volcanic smog) can be a factor island-wide. Sometimes the air pollution is negligible, but at other times its health effects can be hazardous, especially for young children and pregnant women.

Resources

Travel with Children (published by Lonely Planet) Loaded with valuable tips and amusing tales, especially for first-time parents.

Lonely Planet (www.lonelyplanet.com) Ask questions and get advice from other travelers on the Thorn Tree's online 'Kids to Go' forum.

Go Hawaii (www.gohawaii.com) The state's official tourism site lists family-friendly activities, special events and more – just search the site using terms like 'kids' or 'family'.

Need to Know

- **Baby food and formula** Sold at supermarkets and pharmacies.
- **Babysitting** Ask your hotel concierge; some resorts offer day-care programs and kids' activity clubs.
- **Breastfeeding** Done discreetly (cover up) or in private.
- **Car seats** Reserve in advance through car-rental companies or Baby's Away.
- **Changing facilities** Ubiquitous in public restrooms except at beaches.
- **Cribs** Book ahead for rentals from Baby's Away.
- **Diapers (nappies)** Sold everywhere (eg supermarkets, pharmacies, convenience stores).
- **Health** Keep hydrated and wear sunscreen. Be careful when hiking over sharp *a'a* lava. Follow ocean safety rules and talk to lifeguards before getting in the water.
- **Highchairs & kids' menus** Available at most sit-down restaurants, except top-end dining rooms.
- **Strollers** Bring from home or reserve rentals with Baby's Away.

What to Pack

Hawai'i's small-town vibe means that almost no place – apart from star chef's restaurants and five-star resorts – is formal, whether in attitude or attire. You can let your kids wear T-shirts, shorts and rubbah slippah (flip-flops) just about anywhere. When visiting Hawai'i Volcanoes National Park and the island's windward side, rain gear and a sweater or fleece jacket will come in handy – those areas experience some wacky weather.

At tourist convenience shops, such as the ABC Store, you can buy inexpensive water-sports equipment (eg floaties, snorkel sets, bodyboards). In Kailua-Kona, Snorkel Bob's (p39) rents and sells all kinds of watersports gear for kids, from reef shoes to snorkel masks. If you do forget some critical item from home, **Baby's Away** (www.babysaway.com) rents cribs, strollers, car seats, backpacks, beach toys and more.

The Best... Children's Highlights

1 Three Ring Ranch Exotic Animal Sanctuary (p39)

2 Ocean Rider Seahorse Farm (p85)

3 'Imiloa Astronomy Center of Hawai'i (p172)

4 Pana'ewa Rainforest Zoo & Gardens (p172)

5 Hawai'i Volcanoes National Park Junior Ranger Program (p208)

6 Astronaut Ellison S Onizuka Space Center (p85)

Is My Child Old Enough?

Although parents will find plenty of outdoor family fun for all ages on Hawai'i, some activities require that children be of a certain age, height or weight to participate. Always ask about restrictions when making reservations to avoid disappointment – and tears.

- **To learn to surf** Kids who can swim comfortably in the ocean are candidates for lessons. Teens can usually join group lessons; younger kids may be required to take private lessons.
- **To take a boat tour** Depending on the outfit and type of watercraft, tours sometimes set minimum ages, usually from four to eight years. Larger boats might allow tots as young as two to ride along.
- **To summit Mauna Kea** Not advised for children under age 16 due to high-altitude health hazards.
- **To ride in a helicopter** Most tour companies set minimum ages (eg two to 12 years) and sometimes also minimum body weights (eg 35lb). Toddlers must be strapped into their own seat and pay full fare.
- **To go ziplining** Minimum age requirements range from five to 12 years, depending on the company. Participants must also meet weight minimums (usually 50lb to 80lb).
- **To ride a horse** For trail rides the minimum age ranges from seven to 10 years, depending on the outfitter and if your child has riding experience. Short pony rides may be offered for younger kids.

The Natural World

Scuba diving, Kaiwi Point (p81)

DOUG PERRINE/GETTY IMAGES ©

Calling this island big is no misnomer: Hawai'i claims twice as much land as the other Hawaiian Islands combined. Its landscape is so diverse that its alpine and lava deserts, wet tropical and dry forests, montane bogs and other ecosystems support the highest concentration of life-zone types on earth. Stewardship of these natural resources is a traditional Hawaiian value, reflected in aloha 'aina *– love and respect for the land.*

The Land

Myth and science dramatically mix on the Big Island, where plate tectonics and Pele, goddess of fire and volcanoes, conspire to create a powerfully majestic landscape.

Hawaiian volcanoes are created by a rising column of molten rock – a 'hot spot' – under the Pacific Plate. As the plate moves northwest a few inches each year, magma pierces upward through the plate's crust buried deep on the ocean floor, creating volcanoes. Straddling the hot spot today, the Big Island's Kilauea is the world's most active volcano.

Hawaiian volcanoes are shield volcanoes that erupt with effusive lava to create gently sloped, dome-shaped mountains. But they can also have a more explosive side, as Kilauea dramatically reminded onlookers and scientists in 2008. Since its current eruption began in 1983, Kilauea has added more than 500 acres of new land to the Big Island.

In Hawai'i Volcanoes National Park and elsewhere, you can observe hardened lava flows pierced by vents belching malodorous sulfur and walk through spectacular tubes, where past rivers of lava have cooled unevenly. If Pele is feeling frisky, you might witness lava flow, billowing clouds of steam during the day and glowing like hellfire at night.

The Best... Big Island Nature Escapes

1 Hawai'i Volcanoes National Park (p208)

2 Kealakekua Bay State Historical Park (p71)

3 South Point (Ka Lae; p239)

4 Waipi'o Valley (p152)

5 Kekaha Kai State Park (p86)

6 Mauna Kea (p134)

Wildlife

Born of barren lava flows, the Hawaiian Islands were originally populated only by plants and animals that could traverse the Pacific – for example, seeds clinging to a bird's feather or fern spores that drifted thousands of miles through the air. This evolutionary process accounts for the fact that over 90% of Hawaii's flora and fauna species are endemic (that is, unique to the islands), and also explains why they fare so poorly against invasive species and human-caused environmental changes. Unfortunately, Hawaii holds the ignominious title of being the 'endangered species capital of the world.'

Animals

Scientists estimate that successful species were established on the Hawaiian Islands maybe once every 70,000 years – and these included no amphibians, no mosquitoes and only two mammals, both now endangered: the Hawaiian hoary bat and the Hawaiian monk seal. The former are rarely seen, but the latter are increasingly hauling out onto Hawai'i's beaches (it's illegal to get closer than 50yd).

Up to 10,000 migrating North Pacific humpback whales come to Hawaiian waters for calving each winter. The world's fifth-largest whale, the endangered humpback can reach lengths of 45ft and weigh up to 50 tons. Other whales (such as blue and fin whales) also pass through. By federal law, you may not approach a whale in Hawaiian waters nearer than 100yd.

Show-stealing spinner dolphins are named for their acrobatic leaps from the water. These nocturnal feeders come into sheltered bays during the day to rest, especially along the Kona Coast. Because they are extremely sensitive to human disturbance, federal guidelines recommend that swimmers do not approach any wild dolphins closer than 50yd.

Hawai'i's coral reefs teem with over 500 tropical fish species, including bright yellow tangs; striped butterflyfish and Moorish Idols; silver needlefish and neon-colored wrasse, which change sex (and color) as they mature. Endangered *honu* (green sea turtles), hawksbill and leatherback turtles also swim in Hawai'i's waters and bask on sunny beaches (keep back at least 20ft on land, 50yd in the water).

Hawaii's endemic birds are often spectacular examples of adaptive radiation, but two-thirds are already extinct due to predatory feral animals (like mongooses and pigs) and diseases introduced by non-native birds. In Hawai'i Volcanoes National Park, you can catch sight of brightly colored Hawaiian honeycreepers, the royal *'io* (Hawaiian hawk) and the endangered nene (Hawaiian goose), Hawaii's official state bird.

Plants

Extravagantly diverse flora occupies every island niche. Of course, what you'll see today is not what the first Polynesians or ancient Hawaiians saw. Over half of native forests have already disappeared, mainly due to logging, agriculture and invasive plants. Most 'Hawaiian' agricultural products were originally exotic imports – including papayas, pineapples, mangoes, macadamia nuts and coffee.

In densely populated areas such as Kailua-Kona, you'll notice many of the non-native flowering plants grown in other tropical places around the world (bird of paradise, blood-red anthurium, orchids etc). But head inland to native forests and you'll see mighty koa and silver-tinged *kukui* (candlenut) trees forming a canopy over a mix of endemic flora. Out on lava flows, look for low-lying shrubs bursting with *ohelo* berries, emerald-green *hapu'u* (tree ferns) and blossoming ohia plants.

On the slopes of Mauna Kea, distinctive flora includes the yellow-flowered *mamane* tree and tiny-leafed *pukiawe* shrub with its red, pink and white berries. Back down by the beach, native coastal plants to look for include *'ilima,* its delicate orange-yellow flowers often strung into lei; pink-flowering *pohuehue* (beach morning-glory) with its dark green, glossy leaves; and *naupaka* shrubs, whose pinkish-white flowers look as if they've been torn in half (by a broken-hearted lover, according to Hawaiian legend).

Outdoor Adventures

Kayaking, Kealakekua Bay (p73)

DANITA DELIMONT/GETTY IMAGES ©

Everyone finds their own thrilling way to play outdoors on Hawai'i, whether it's exploring a lava tube or ziplining through the rainforest. How about nighttime scuba diving with manta rays or stargazing atop a volcano? Paddling a kayak, snorkeling with tropical fish and surfing are other diversions at sea, or visit sacred valleys on foot or horseback to get in touch with Hawai'i's true nature.

At Sea

With Hawai'i's long and strong tradition of communing with the ocean, you're sure to get wet on your Big Island vacation. Even if you've never snorkeled or surfed, this is a great place to start, with experienced outfitters on both sides of the island. Not much advance planning is required, save checking the weather – just get up and go.

Beaches & Swimming

On Hawai'i, coastal strands come in a rainbow of hues and infinite textures – with sand sparkling white, tawny, black, charcoal or green, and scattered with sea-glass, pebbles and boulders or cratered with lava-rock tide pools.

By law, all beaches in Hawaii are open to the public below the high-tide line. Private landowners can prevent access to their shoreline over land, but not by watercraft. Resort hotels often provide public beach access with limited parking spots, occasionally charging a small fee.

West Hawai'i is most inviting for swimming, including crescent-shaped Mauna Kea Beach and white-sand Manini'owali Beach with its brilliant turquoise waters, or try a short lap in Kiholo Bay's lava tube. East Hawai'i is generally rougher and mostly only for strong swimmers, although local families can be found at Hilo's beaches.

Bodyboarding

Bodyboarding (aka boogie boarding) rivals surfing and stand up paddling as the most popular way to ride Hawai'i's waves. Winter brings the best action to West Hawai'i at Hapuna Beach State Park, White (Magic) Sands Beach Park, Honoli'i Beach Park and Kekaha Kai (Kona Coast) State Park beaches, particularly Manini'owali (Kua Bay). If you really know what you're doing, venture to Puna's Isaac Hale Kepo'okalani Beach Park or Hilo's Honoli'i Beach Park, both in East Hawai'i.

Diving

Hawai'i's underwater scenery is every bit the equal of what's on land. Ocean temperatures are perfect for scuba diving, averaging 72°F to 80°F at the surface year-round. Even better is the visibility, especially in the calm waters along the Kona Coast, ideally during September and October.

About 700 fish species call these waters home, as do spinner dolphins, sea turtles and moray eels, so you won't want for variety – even during on-shore dives. If you've dreamed of diving, this is a perfect spot to learn, with a smorgasbord of dive operators offering open-water certification courses and beginners' dive experiences.

Among the most popular dive spots on the island is Ka'awaloa Cove in Kealakekua Bay. Other good West Hawai'i sites include Turtle Pinnacle, Harlequin, Aquarium and Suck 'Em Up along the Kona Coast, and Puako further north in Kohala. The manta ray night dive is a must, so book early. River runoff on the Hilo side usually means cloudy visibility, but Pohoiki in Puna – East Hawai'i's best site – teems with marine life.

For more tips, check out Lonely Planet's *Diving & Snorkeling Hawaii*.

Fishing

The Kona Coast is a deep-sea fishing fantasy: at least one 'grander' (1000lb or more) marlin is reeled in every year. With over 100 boat and kayak fishing charter companies leaving from Honokohau Harbor, the next one could be yours. These waters are also

Dive Safely & Responsibly

The popularity of diving puts immense pressure on many of Hawai'i's dive sites. Here's how you can help:

- Conserve Hawai'i's reef and marine ecosystems by using minimal-impact diving techniques.
- Respect Native Hawaiian sacred places, including fishing grounds.
- Do not feed any wildlife or disturb marine animals. It's illegal to come within 50yd of sea turtles, dolphins or Hawaiian monk seals, or within 100yd of whales. Don't ride on the backs of sea turtles, as this causes them great anxiety.

Warning! Don't go for a helicopter or plane ride or ascend to high altitudes (eg Mauna Kea, Mauna Loa) for at least 24 hours before or after scuba diving.

rich with ahi (yellowfin tuna) and *aku* (bonito or skipjack tuna), swordfish and mahimahi (dolphinfish). If you get to keep your catch, harborside Bite Me Fish Market Bar & Grill will cook it for you.

Kayaking

The warm, calm seas hugging the Kona Coast, combined with hidden coves and turquoise, fish-filled waters, make Hawai'i prime sea-kayaking turf. (Forget rivers – there are none.) Variants on the sport – fishing, surfing and sailing – are all possibilities, with guides and outfitters along the Kona and Kohala Coasts offering rentals and tours.

Kealakekua Bay, with its smooth waters and abundance of fish and spinner dolphins, is one of the state's most popular kayaking spots. Up north, the pristine coastline around Kiholo Bay offers solitude, while the reefs around Puako beckon paddlers to don their masks.

The Best... Big Island Adventure Tours

1 Lava boat tour in Puna (p203)

2 Ziplining in Kohala (p117)

3 Diving and snorkeling with manta rays along the Kona Coast (p42)

4 Mauna Kea stargazing (p138)

5 Sea kayaking during winter whale-watching season (p81)

Snorkeling

On the Big Island, you can step from the sand into crystal tropical waters teeming with vibrant coral and reef fish. Popular West Hawai'i snorkeling spots – like Kealakekua Bay and Kahalu'u Beach Park – are also teeming with tourists. To escape the crowds, go in the early morning (when conditions are best anyway), drive further up or down the coast (like to Beach 69 or Puako), or hike or kayak to more remote spots. In East Hawai'i, snorkelers can drive right up to Hilo's Richardson Ocean Park or detour down to Kapoho in Puna.

Always follow coral-reef etiquette: don't touch any coral, which are living organisms; watch your fins to avoid stirring up sand and breaking off pieces of coral; and finally, don't feed the fish. Snorkel gear rental costs around $10/25 per day/week, depending on quality. Most places rent prescription masks, which are essential for the myopic. Reef shoes are recommended for lava-lined shores.

Catamaran and Zodiac raft tours will transport you to prime spots and provide gear and food. On the Kona Coast, tours leaving from Keauhou Bay (instead of in-town Kailua Pier, or Honokohau Harbor north nearer the airprot) have shorter rides to Kealakekua Bay, meaning more snorkel time for you. Book in advance, especially during high season and for nighttime snorkeling with manta rays.

Surfing & Stand Up Paddling (SUP)

Ancient Hawaiians invented surfing (calling it *he'e nalu*, 'wave sliding'). On Hawai'i today, surfing is its own intense subculture as well as a part of everyday island life. Generally, winter northern swells are bigger and leeward breaks are cleaner. Check local tides, weather and swells online with *Hawaii Surf News* (www.hawaiisurfnews.com).

Along the Kona Coast, surf at Kahalu'u Beach Park, Banyans and Lymans, all south of Kailua-Kona, and Pine Trees near Wawaloli (OTEC) Beach. Down south in Ka'u, Kawa Bay has a left break that locals love. Consistent east-side spots are Honoli'i Cove in Hilo and Waipi'o Bay. Puna's Pohoiki Bay is much hairier, but experienced surfers will dig the reef breaks at Isaac Kepo'okalani Hale Beach Park.

Locals are usually willing to share surf spots that have become popular tourist destinations but they reserve the right to protect other 'secret' surf grounds. As a newbie in the lineup, don't expect to get every wave that comes your way. There's a definite pecking order and tourists are at the bottom.

The latest trend in surfing is stand up paddling (SUP) – which, as the name implies, means standing on the surfboard and using a paddle to propel yourself along flat water or waves. It takes coordination to learn, but it's easier than regular surfing.

Both surfboard and SUP rentals and lessons are widely available on the Kona and Kohala Coasts, and from a few outfitters in Hilo.

Whale-Watching

During their annual 6000-mile round-trip between Alaska and Hawaii – one of the longest migration journeys of any mammal – humpback whales breed, calve and nurse in the Big Island's nearshore waters between December and April.

Over 60% of the North Pacific humpback population winters in the Hawaiian Islands, so you'll have a good chance of seeing their acrobatics on a cruise, while kayaking or even from shore – don't forget binoculars. Tours run year-round from Kailua-Kona to view sperm, melon-headed, pilot and pygmy killer whales and, of course, dolphins.

On Land

Hawai'i has 11 of the world's 13 ecosystems, filled with exotic flora and fauna waiting to be seen. The island's unique geology offers all sorts of land-based adventures and it's a premier hiking destination. Travelers should pack a good LED flashlight for cave explorations, a rainproof jacket and binoculars for lava viewing and wildlife-watching.

Caving

Being the youngest Hawaiian Island and still volcanically active, Hawai'i is a caving hotspot, claiming six of the world's 10 longest lava tubes. No visit to the island is complete without exploring their dark, mysterious depths. In Puna you can tour parts of the Kazumura Cave, the world's longest and deepest lava tube. In Ka'u, the Kula Kai Caverns are geological wonders.

Cycling & Mountain Biking

Road cycling is tricky here, with narrow, winding roads light on shoulders. The Ironman route on Hwy 19 north of Kailua-Kona is an exception, and bike rentals are most readily available in Kailua-Kona. The **Hawai'i Cycling Club** (www.hawaiicyclingclub.com) offers information on island-wide cycling routes and events. Kona-based outfitter **Orchid Isle Bicyling** (☎808-327-0087; www.orchidislebicycling.com) organizes daily cycling tours and multiday vacations.

Golf

While playing on a championship course at a Kona or Kohala beach resort in the 'Golf Capital of Hawaii' can cost over $200 a round, Hawai'i's much more affordable municipal courses still boast scenery you probably can't get back home. Afternoon 'twilight' tee times are usually heavily discounted. Club rentals are sometimes available.

Visit www.teetimeshawaii.com for course descriptions and book-ahead tee times.

Helicopter & Air Tours

Flying over the world's most active volcano and gushing waterfalls provides unforgettable vantages you simply can't get any other way. That said, 'flightseeing' tours negatively impact Hawai'i's natural environment, both in noise generated and fuel burned.

Expensive helicopter tours are all the hype, but fixed-wing planes offer a smoother, quieter ride. Questions you should ask before booking either include: Do all passengers have a 360-degree view? Are noise-cancelling headsets provided? For the best views, sit up front.

Helicopter tours fly if it's cloudy, but not if it's raining – wait for a clear day, which is more likely during summer. Most tour companies offer online discounts (book in advance).

Recommended flightseeing outfitters include the following:

Blue Hawaiian Helicopters (☎800-745-2583; www.bluehawaiian.com) Reliable, dependable and high-volume company; departures from Waikoloa and Hilo.

Iolani Air (☎808-329-0018; www.iolaniair.com) Flightseeing tours in small prop planes take off from Kona and Hilo.

Paradise Helicopters (☎866-876-7422, 969-7392; http://paradisecopters.com) More personalized helicopter tours leave from Kona and Hilo.

Safari Helicopters (☎800-326-3356, 969-1259; www.safarihelicopters.com) Tours of East Hawai'i's volcanoes and coastline depart from Hilo.

Hiking

From an afternoon stroll through a lava tube to a multiday summit trek, the Big Island has wild walks. Hawai'i Volcanoes National Park boasts the most varied trails, but you can also hike to secluded Kona Coast beaches or easily explore petroglyph fields without leaving West Hawai'i.

Diving through an underwater cavern
BRANDON SAWAYA/GETTY IMAGES ©

Hike Safely & Responsibly

You don't have to worry about snakes, wild animals or poison ivy on Hawai'i. What you *do* have to worry about is lava – from ankle-twisting *'a'a* (slow-flowing rough and jagged lava) and toxic fumes to collapsing lava benches and hellishly hot conditions. Heed all posted warnings and hike with a buddy. Observe *kapu* (no trespassing) signs (residents of Waipi'o Valley are particularly territorial).

If you plan to hike anywhere here, sturdy, ankle-high footwear with good traction is a must. Flash floods are a real danger in many of the steep, narrow valleys that require stream crossings (yes, including Waipi'o Valley). You'll need to come prepared for winter mountaineering conditions if hiking to the summit of Mauna Loa or Mauna Kea is in your sights.

Camping permits are required for all overnight hikes, including in Hawai'i Volcanoes National Park and Waimanu Valley. It's best to bring your own backpacking gear from home. For anything else you need (or forgot to pack), try the Hawaii Forest & Trail (p81) headquarters in Kailua-Kona.

Both Hawaii Forest & Trail and Hawaiian Walkways (p156) offer recommendable guided hiking tours. Helpful resources for independent hikers include the following:

Na Ala Hele (www.hawaiitrails.org) Online maps and directions for public-access trails, including the long-distance Ala Kahakai National Historic Trail.

Sierra Club – Moku Loa Group (www.hi.sierraclub.org/Hawaii/outings.html; donation per hike for nonmembers $3) Island-wide group day hikes and volunteer opportunities doing trail maintenance and ecological restoration.

Horseback Riding

In Hawai'i's hilly green pastures, *paniolo* (cowboys) wrangle cattle and ride the range. Up in North Kohala and Waimea especially, as well as around Waipi'o Valley, you can arrange trail and pony rides and customized horseback tours. Book ahead.

Stargazing

From atop Mauna Kea, where international superpowered telescopes are trained on the heavens, scientists explore our universe. You can too – on Mauna Kea itself, with the eye-opening nightly stargazing program at the visitor information station. Kids under 16 can participate, but it's recommended they don't go to the summit.

Ziplining

If you're keen to zoom along suspended cables while the landscape whizzes by far below, several zipline outfitters now dot the island. Tours offer a totally different perspective on the island's forests, waterfalls and coastline. Plan on spending half a day on an adrenaline-pumping tour (minimum age and weight requirements apply).

Survival Guide

Beach in Kona
GLOWIMAGES/GETTY IMAGES ©

A-Z Directory

Accommodations

Rates

The following price ranges are for a double room with private bathroom in high season. Unless otherwise stated, taxes of 13.41% aren't included.

- **$** under $100
- **$$** $100 to $200
- **$$$** over $200

Reservations

Availability is scarcer during high season (mid-December through March or April, and June through August), around major holidays and special events. Book months in advance for peak periods, when room rates rise.

Amenities

- Accommodations offering online computer terminals for guests are designated with the internet icon (@). An hourly fee may apply (eg at hotel business centers).
- The wi-fi icon (wi-fi) indicates wireless internet access; a daily fee may apply. Look for free wi-fi in common areas (eg hotel lobby, poolside).
- A surprising number of hotels offer only wired in-room access; getting online may cost $12 or more per 24 hours.
- Air-conditioning (❄) is a standard amenity at most resorts. At some hotels, condos, hostels, B&Bs and vacation rentals, only fans may be provided.

Hotels & Resorts

- Ranging from no-frills motels to mega beach resorts, hotels typically offer full-time staff, daily housekeeping and amenities such as swimming pools (pool), bars and restaurants.
- 'Rack rates' refer to the the highest published rates. Hotels often hugely undercut rack rates to book as close to capacity as possible. Reserve ahead online for discounts.
- At some hotels, rates depend mainly on the view. Even partial ocean views cost 50% to 100% more than garden or mountain (or parking lot) views.
- Many hotel properties are entirely nonsmoking by law, with high penalty fees for noncompliance. If you need a smoking room, you must specifically request one (they're rarely available).

Condominiums

- Condos typically include separate bedroom(s), a full kitchen and a washer/dryer. Most condos are located around Kailua-Kona and bookable online. Units are privately owned and inconsistent in quality.
- Most condos require multiple-night minimum stays and offer weekly discounts. Condos are best for weekly or monthly stays; otherwise, the mandatory cleaning fee (averaging $75 to $150) negates any savings.

B&Bs, Inns & Guesthouses

- Hawai'i's B&Bs either serve breakfast or provide groceries for guests to prepare their own. Inns and guesthouses typically do not offer breakfast. Apartment-style amenities might include a kitchenette.
- Most B&Bs, inns and guesthouses require multiple-night stays. Always book ahead. Drop-in guests are discouraged and same-day reservations are hard to get.
- Rates typically cover two guests, with extra-person surcharges of $15 to $35. Children may not be allowed.
- Besides **Vacation Rentals by Owner** (www.vrbo.com), **HomeAway** (www.homeaway.

Book Your Stay Online

For more accommodations reviews by Lonely Planet authors, check out http://hotels.lonelyplanet.com. You'll find independent reviews, as well as recommendations on the best places to stay. Best of all, you can book online.

com) and **Air B&B** (www.airbnb.com), check online listings with the following:

Affordable Paradise (808-261-1693; www.affordable-paradise.com)

Hawaii's Best B&Bs (808-885-4550; www.bestbnb.com)

Hawaii Island B&B Association (www.stayhawaii.com)

Camping & Cabins

The island's best camping and cabins are inside Hawai'i Volcanoes National Park. State and county parks run the gamut; in general, easy-access roadside spots, especially at county beach parks, can be hangouts for drunkards and druggies.

Hawaii State Parks (808-961-9540; https://camping.ehawaii.gov/camping/welcome.html; 75 Aupuni St, Room 204, Hilo; 8am-3:30pm Mon-Fri) Advance state-park camping permits are required. Nonresident fees are $18 per campsite for up to six people ($3 for each additional person), $50 per A-frame shelter and $80 to $90 per cabin.

County of Hawai'i Department of Parks & Recreation (808-961-8311; https://hawaiicounty.ehawaii.gov/camping/welcome.html; 101 Pauahi St, Suite 6, Hilo; 7:45am-4:30pm Mon-Fri) Advance county-park camping permits are required. Nonresident campsite fee is $20 per person per night.

Happy Campers Hawaii (808-896-8777; www.happycampershawaii.com; rental per day from $120) Rents VW campervans with kitchenettes that can sleep up to four people, but you'll need separate campsite reservations. Pick-ups and drop-offs in Hilo (free airport shuttle service).

Climate

Location

The leeward (western) side of the island is usually hot and dry, while the windward (northeastern) side receives abundant rainfall year-round.

Elevation

The mountainous upcountry is noticeably cooler and wetter. This elevation difference is most marked on Mauna Kea and Mauna Loa, where overnight temperatures dip below freezing.

Seasons

When you're most likely to see major storms and flooding, the winter wet season (December to March) is rainier than the summer dry season.

Climate

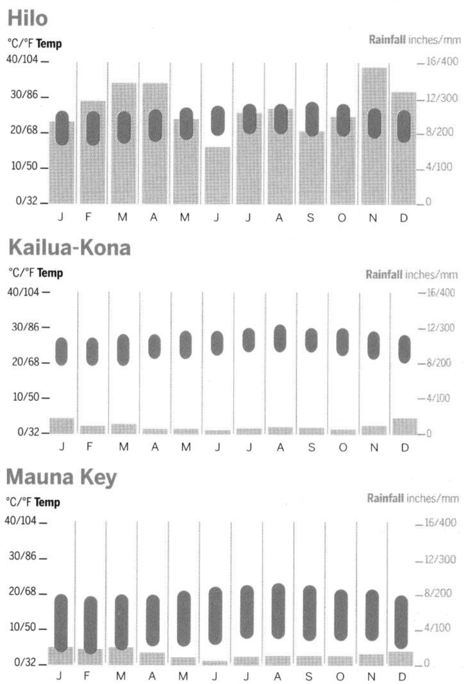

Customs Regulations

Non-US citizens and permanent residents may import the following duty-free:

- 1L of liquor (if you're over 21 years old)
- 200 cigarettes (1 carton) or 100 non-Cuban cigars (if you're over 18)
- $100 worth of gifts

Hawaii has stringent restrictions against importing any fresh fruits and plants. Because Hawaii is a rabies-free state, the pet quarantine laws are draconian.

Before leaving Hawaii, make sure that any fresh flowers or produce has been commercially packaged and approved for travel (or else you'll be forced to surrender those pineapples at the airport).

Discount Cards

Children, students, seniors, state residents and active and retired military personnel usually receive discounts at museums and attractions. All but children need to present valid ID proving their status.

Electricity

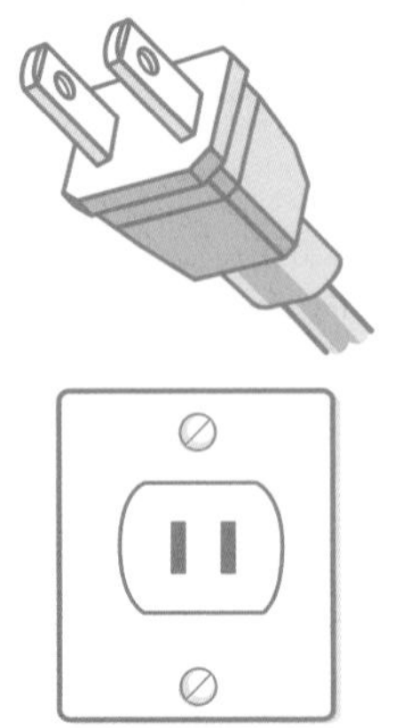

120V/60Hz

120V/60Hz

Food

Meals are early and start on the dot in Hawaii: typically 6am breakfast, noon lunch and 6pm dinner. Dress codes are relaxed (called 'island casual'), with no jackets or ties normally required. Men can get away with an aloha shirt and neat khaki or golf shorts at most resort restaurants.

The following price ranges refer to an average main course at dinner in a restaurant (lunch is usually much cheaper) or a set meal at a casual takeout eatery. Unless otherwise stated, taxes and tip are not included.

- **$** under $10
- **$$** $10 to $20
- **$$$** over $20

Gay & Lesbian Travelers

The state of Hawaii has strong minority protections and a constitutional guarantee of privacy that extends to sexual behavior between consenting adults. Locals tend to be private about their personal lives, so you will not see much public hand-holding or open displays of affection. Everyday LGBTQ life is low-key, and there's no 'scene' to speak of – it's more about picnics and potlucks, not nightclubs.

Connect with the following community resources:

Gay Hawaii (www.gayhawaii.com) Free website.

Odyssey Magazine Hawaii (www.odysseyhawaii.com) Free statewide monthly publication, archived free online.

Out in Hawaii (www.outinhawaii.com) Free website.

Out Traveler (www.out-traveler.com) Gay-oriented Hawaii travel articles free online.

Purple Roofs (http://purpleroofs.com) Directory of gay-owned and gay-friendly B&Bs, vacation rentals, guesthouses and hotels.

Pacific Ocean Holidays (☎ 808-923-2400; www.gayhawaiivacations.com) Personalized vacation packages for gay and lesbian travelers.

Internet Access

In this guide, the wi-fi icon (wi-fi icon) indicates that wi-fi is available. The internet icon (@) indicates that there's an online computer for guests or customers. Either could be free or fee-based.

- Wi-fi is now available at many accommodations; it's usually free at B&Bs, condos and vacation rentals.
- Bigger towns have at least one coffee shop offering free wi-fi or a pay-as-you-go internet cafe charging around $6 to $12 per hour.

Language

Hawaii has two official languages: English and Hawaiian. There's also an unofficial vernacular, called pidgin, a creole language whose colorful vocabulary permeates everyday local speech. While Hawaiian's multisyllabic, vowel-heavy words may look daunting, the pronunciation is actually quite straightforward.

Legal Matters

If you are arrested, you have the right to an attorney; if you can't afford one, a public defender will be provided free. The **Hawaii State Bar Association** (☎ 808-930-0872; www.hawaiilawyerreferral.com) makes attorney referrals.

In addition to Hawaii's road rules (see p292), be mindful of the following laws:

- Bars, clubs and liquor stores may require photo ID to prove you're of legal age (21 years) to buy alcohol. You must be 18 years old to buy tobacco.
- Drinking alcohol anywhere other than at a private residence, hotel room or licensed premises (eg bar, restaurant) is illegal, which puts beach parks off-limits.
- Possessing marijuana or nonprescription narcotics, hitchhiking and public nudity are all illegal in Hawaii.
- Smoking is generally prohibited in all public spaces, including airports, bars, restaurants and businesses.

Maps

Published by **University of Hawai'i Press** (www.uhpress.hawaii.edu), the fold-out, full-color topographic *Map of Hawai'i* ($4.95) details every bay, beach and gulch on the Big Island. **Franko Maps** (www.frankosmaps.com) makes full-color, waterproof and rip-proof laminated island maps showing beaches, snorkeling and diving spots, with a nifty guide to tropical fish. For exploring off the beaten path, Odyssey Publishing's Ready Mapbook series offers comprehensive road and street atlases for East Hawai'i and West Hawai'i ($16.50 each).

Money

ATMs

- ATMs are available 24/7 at most banks, convenience stores, shopping centers and airports.
- Expect a minimum surcharge of $2.25 per transaction, plus any fees charged by your home bank.
- Most ATMs are connected to international networks (eg Plus, Cirrus) and offer decent exchange rates.

Hawai'i vs Hawaii

The *'okina* punctuation mark (') is the Hawaiian language's glottal stop, which determines the pronunciation and meaning of words. In this guide, Hawai'i (with the *'okina*) refers to the island of Hawai'i (the Big Island), to ancient Hawai'i and to the Kingdom of Hawai'i pre-statehood. Hawaii (without the *'okina*) refers to the US state.

- Hawaii's two largest banks are **Bank of Hawaii** (www.boh.com) and **First Hawaiian Bank** (www.fhb.com).

Checks

Out-of-state personal checks are generally not accepted, except at some privately owned lodgings (eg B&Bs, condos, vacation rentals).

Credit Cards

Major credit cards are widely accepted. Typically they're required for car rentals, hotel reservations, buying tickets etc. B&Bs, condos and vacation rentals may refuse credit cards or else add a 3% surcharge.

Taxes

A 4.17% state sales tax is tacked onto virtually everything, including meals, groceries and car rentals (which also entail additional state and local taxes). Lodging taxes total 13.41%.

Tipping

Tipping is *not* optional; only withhold tips in cases of outrageously bad service.

Airport skycaps & hotel porters $2 to $3 per bag, minimum per cart $5

Bartenders 15% to 20% per round, minimum $1 per drink

Housekeeping staff $2 to $5 per night, left under card provided; more if you're messy

Parking valets At least $2 when handed your car keys

Restaurant servers & room service 15% to 20%, unless a gratuity is already charged

Taxi drivers 15% of metered fare, rounded up to next dollar

Traveler's Checks

Rather archaic nowadays, traveler's checks in US dollars are still accepted like cash at bigger tourist-oriented businesses in Hawaii, such as resort hotels. Smaller businesses such as grocery stores usually refuse them.

Opening Hours

Banks 8:30am to 4pm Monday to Friday, some to 6pm Friday; 9am to noon or 1pm Saturday

Bars & clubs noon to midnight daily, some to 2am Friday and Saturday

Businesses (general) & government offices 8:30am to 4:30pm Monday to Friday, some post offices also 9am to noon Saturday

Restaurants breakfast 6am to 10am, lunch 11:30am to 2pm, dinner 5pm to 9:30pm

Shops 9am to 5pm Monday to Saturday, some also noon to 5pm Sunday; major shopping areas and malls keep extended hours

Public Holidays

On the following national holidays, banks, schools and government offices (including post offices) close, and transportation, museums and other services operate on a Sunday schedule. Holidays falling on a weekend are usually observed the following Monday.

New Year's Day January 1

Martin Luther King Jr Day Third Monday in January

Presidents' Day Third Monday in February

Prince Kuhio Day March 26

Good Friday Friday before Easter Sunday (in March or April)

Memorial Day Last Monday in May

King Kamehameha Day June 11

Independence Day July 4

Statehood Day Third Friday in August

Labor Day First Monday in September

Columbus Day Second Monday in October

Veterans Day November 11

Thanksgiving Fourth Thursday in November

Christmas Day December 25

Safe Travel

For visitors who have an accident or become victims of crimes, the **Visitor Aloha Society of Hawaii** (VASH; ☎808-926-8274; www.visitoralohasocietyofhawaii.org) offers short-term nonmonetary assistance.

Hazards & Trespassing

Flash floods, rock falls, tsunami, earthquakes, volcanic eruptions, shark attacks, jellyfish stings and yes, even possibly getting brained by a falling coconut – the potential dangers in Hawaii might seem alarming at first. But like the old saying goes, statistically you're more likely to get hurt crossing the street at home.

Of course, that's not to say that you shouldn't be careful. First educate yourself about potential risks to your health and safety. This advice becomes even more important when you're engaged in outdoor activities in a new and unfamiliar natural environment, whether that's a snorkeling spot, a jungle waterfall, a high-altitude mountain or an active (and thus unpredictable) volcanic eruption zone.

Wherever you choose to explore, remember to mind your manners and watch your step. Hawaii has strict laws about trespassing on both private land and government land not intended for public use. Trespassing is always illegal, no matter how many other people you see doing it. Respect all 'Kapu' or 'No Trespassing' signs.

Always seek explicit permission from the land owner or local officials before venturing onto private or government land closed to the public, regardless of whether it is fenced or signposted as such. Doing so not only respects the *kuleana* (rights) of residents and the sacredness of the land, but also helps ensure your own safety.

Practicalities

- **Newspapers** Major dailies: *Hawaii Tribune-Herald* (p51); *West Hawaii Today* (p51); *Honolulu Star-Advertiser* (www.staradvertiser.com)
- **Radio** About 25 FM and five AM radio stations; National Public Radio (NPR) at lower end of FM dial
- **Time** Hawaii-Aleutian Standard Time (HST) is UTC-10. Hawaii doesn't observe Daylight Saving Time (DST). 'Island time' means taking things at a slower pace or being late.
- **TV & DVD** All major US TV networks and cable channels; DVDs coded region 1 (US and Canada only)
- **Weights & measures** Imperial system (except 1 US gallon = 3.79L)

Theft & Violence

The islands are notorious for thefts from parked cars, especially rentals (which are obviously tagged with bar-code stickers). Thieves can pop a trunk or pull out a door-lock assembly within seconds. They strike not only at remote trailheads when you've gone for a hike, but also at crowded beach and hotel parking lots where you'd expect safety in numbers.

As much as possible, do not leave anything valuable in your parked car. If you must, pack all valuables out of sight before arriving at your destination. Some locals leave their car doors unlocked with the windows rolled down to discourage break-ins and avoid costly damages (eg broken windows).

Stay attuned to the vibe on any beaches at night, and in places like roadside county parks, where drunks and drug users sometimes hang out. In rural areas of the island, there may be pockets of resentment against tourists, so be respectful as you explore off the beaten path.

Tsunami

Hawai'i is always at risk of tsunami, which have killed more people statewide than all other natural disasters combined. Hawai'i's tsunami warning sirens are tested on the first working day of each month at 11:45am, using the yellow speakers mounted on telephone poles. If you hear them at any other time, head for higher ground away from the coast. Telephone directories have tsunami evacuation zone maps. Turn on the radio or TV and listen for news.

Telephone

Cell Phones

International travelers need a multiband GSM phone to make calls in the USA. Popping in a US prepaid

Important Numbers

- Emergency (police, fire, ambulance): ☎ 911
- Local directory assistance: ☎ 411
- Long-distance directory assistance: ☎ 1-(area code)-555-1212
- Toll-free directory assistance: ☎ 1-800-555-1212
- Operator: ☎ 0

rechargeable SIM card is usually cheaper than using your home network. SIM cards are available at telecommunications and electronics stores, which also sell inexpensive prepaid phones, including some airtime.

Among US cell-phone service providers, Verizon has the most extensive network; AT&T and Sprint get decent reception. Coverage is good in bigger towns but spotty or nonexistent in rural areas.

Dialing Codes

- All Hawaii phone numbers consist of a three-digit area code (808) followed by a seven-digit local number.
- To call long-distance from one island to another, dial 1 + 808 + local number.
- Always dial 1 before toll-free numbers (800, 888 etc). Some toll-free numbers only work within Hawaii or from the US mainland and Canada.
- To call Canada from Hawaii, dial 1 + area code + local number (note international rates still apply).
- For all other international calls from Hawaii, dial 011 + country code + area code + local number.
- To call Hawaii from abroad, the international country code for the USA is 1.

Payphones & Phonecards

- Payphones are a dying breed, usually found at shopping centers, hotels, beaches, parks and other public places.
- Some payphones are coin-operated (local calls usually cost 50¢), while others only accept credit cards or phonecards.
- Private prepaid phonecards are available from convenience stores, supermarkets, pharmacies, etc.

Tourist Information

101 Things To Do (www.101thingstodo.com/big-island) Free publication describing major attractions.

Big Island Visitors Bureau (Map p176; ☎ 808-961-5797, 800-648-2441; www.gohawaii.com/big-island; 250 Keawe St, Hilo) Basic info and brochures only.

This Week (www.thisweek.com) Free tourist publication with handy maps.

Travelers with Disabilities

Accommodations

Major hotels are equipped with elevators, phones with TDD (telecommunications device for the deaf) and wheelchair-accessible rooms (which must be reserved in advance); most B&Bs and small hotels are probably not.

Guide & Service Dogs

Not subject to the general quarantine rules for pets if they meet the Department of Agriculture's minimum requirements (see http://hdoa.hawaii.gov/ai/aqs/guide-service-dogs for details). All animals must enter the state at Honolulu International Airport.

Tourist Information

For Hawaii-specific info on airports, all-terrain beach wheelchairs, transportation, medical and other support services, visit the **Disability & Communication Access Board** (☎ 808-586-8121; www.hawaii.gov/health/dcab/travel; Room 101, 919 Ala Moana Blvd, Honolulu) website. **Access Aloha Travel** (☎ 800-480-1143, 808-545-1143; www.accessalohatravel.com) is a full-service local travel agency.

Transportation

Rent wheelchair-accessible vans from **Wheelchair Getaways** (☎ 650-589-5554, 800-638-1912; www.wheelchairgetaways.com). Car-rental agencies may offer hand-controlled vehicles; reserve them well in advance. If you have a disability parking placard from home, bring it with you. Pu'uhonua O Hōnaunau National Historical Park and Hawai'i Volcanoes National Park lend wheelchairs free of charge.

Visas

Double-check current visa and passport requirements *before* coming to the USA via the Visas section of the US **Department of State** (http://travel.state.gov) website and the Travel section of the **US Customs & Border Protection** (www.cbp.gov) website.

Currently under the US Visa Waiver Program (VWP), visas are not required for citizens of 37 countries for stays up to 90 days (no extensions) if they register online at least 72 hours before arrival with the **Electronic System for Travel Authorization** (ESTA; https://esta.cbp.dhs.gov/esta/), which costs $14. Canadian visitors are generally admitted visa-free for stays up to 182 days.

Upon arrival, the Department of Homeland Security (www.dhs.gov) requires that almost all foreign visitors (currently excluding most Canadian citizens) have their digital photograph taken and electronic (inkless) fingerprints scanned; the process typically takes less than a minute.

Transport

Getting There & Away

Flights can be booked online at www.lonelyplanet.com/flights.

Air

Hawaii is a competitive market for airfares, which vary tremendously by season, day of the week and demand. In general, return fares from the US mainland to Hawai'i cost from $400 (in low season from the West Coast) to $800 or more in high season from the East Coast.

Airports

There are few direct flights to the Big Island from the US mainland or Canada. Most domestic US and international flights arrive at Honolulu International Airport on O'ahu. Travelers must then catch an interisland flight to one of the Big Island's two primary airports, Kona or Hilo.

Interisland airfares vary wildly; expect to pay from $80 to $180 one way. Round-trip fares are typically double that without any discounts. Usually, the earlier you book, the cheaper the fare.

Hilo International Airport (ITO; Map p170; ☎ 808-934-5838; http://hawaii.gov/ito; 2450 Kekuanaoa St, Hilo) Almost all flights to Hilo are interisland, mostly from Honolulu.

Kona International Airport at Keahole (KOA; Map p82; ☎ 808-327-9520; http://hawaii.gov/koa; 73-7200 Kupipi St) Mostly interisland and some US mainland and Canada flights arrive at Hawai'i's main airport, 7 miles northwest of Kailua-Kona.

Airlines

In addition to Hawaiian Airlines, the following carriers currently fly directly from the US mainland or Canada to the Big Island (usually to Kona): Air Canada, Alaska Airlines, American Airlines, Delta Air Lines, United Airlines, US Airways and WestJet.

The main interisland carrier – reliable Hawaiian Airlines – flies into Kona and Hilo. Commuter-oriented Mokulele Airlines flies into Kona and Kamuela (Waimea) airports with small turboprop planes. Another commuter carrier, Island Air, sometimes flies larger prop planes to Hilo.

Hawaiian Airlines (HA; ☎ 800-367-5320; www.hawaiianair.com)

Island Air (WP; ☎ 800-652-6541; www.islandair.com)

Mokulele Airlines (YV; ☎ 866-260-7070; www.mokuleleairlines.com)

Getting Around

Bus

It is possible to reach many places around the island with Hele-On Bus (p96), but services are infrequent, especially on Sundays and holidays. Always check the website or call for current schedules, routes and fares, which are all subject to change. Most routes originate from Mo'oheau Bus Terminal in downtown Hilo.

The one-way adult fare is $2 (including a free two-hour transfer), or buy a 10-ride ticket sheet ($15) or monthly pass ($60). You cannot board with a surfboard or bodyboard; luggage, backpacks, skateboards and bicycles are charged $1 each.

Bicycle

- Cycling around the Big Island is only for the adventurous and very fit who can cope with rain, sun, strong headwinds, narrow roads and oblivious drivers.
- In towns, cycling can be convenient for those comfortable riding in traffic. Dedicated bicycle lanes are scarce, however. The best places to rent, buy or repair bikes are in Kailua-Kona.
- Bicyclists are generally required to follow the same state laws and road rules as vehicle drivers. Cyclists under age 16 are legally required to wear helmets.

Road Distances & Times

To circumnavigate the island on the 225-mile Hawai'i Belt Rd (Hwys 19 and 11), you'll need at least five hours.

FROM HILO

DESTINATION	DISTANCE (MILES)	TIME (HOURS)
Hawai'i Volcanoes National Park	30	¾
Hawi	76	1¾
Honoka'a	41	1
Kailua-Kona	86	2
Na'alehu	66	1½
Pahoa	20	½
Waikoloa	72	1¾
Waimea	55	1¼
Waipi'o Lookout	50	1¼

FROM KAILUA-KONA

DESTINATION	DISTANCE (MILES)	TIME (HOURS)
Hawai'i Volcanoes National Park	98	2¼
Hawi	53	1¼
Hilo	86	2
Honoka'a	53	1¼
Na'alehu	59	1½
Pahoa	102	2¼
Waikoloa	26	¾
Waimea	40	1
Waipi'o Lookout	63	1½

Car

Automobile Associations

- For 24-hour emergency roadside assistance, free maps and discounts on car rentals and accommodations, join the **American Automobile Association** (AAA; ☎593-2221, from Neighbor Islands 800-736-2886; www.hawaii.aaa.com; 1130 N Nimitz Hwy, Honolulu; ⏰9am-5pm Mon-Fri, to 2pm Sat).
- AAA has reciprocal agreements with automobile associations in other countries (eg CAA); bring your membership card from home.

Driver's License

- US citizens with a driver's license from another state or international visitors with a valid driver's license issued by their home country can legally drive a car in Hawaii if they are at least 18 years old.
- Car-rental companies will generally accept foreign driver's licenses written in English with an accompanying

photo. Otherwise, be prepared to present an International Driving Permit (IDP), obtainable in your home country, along with your foreign driver's license.

Fuel & Towing

- Gasoline (petrol) is readily available in bigger towns. Fuel up before driving remote highways (eg Saddle Road).
- Gas prices in Hawaii currently average $4.30 per US gallon. Expect to pay 40¢ to $1.10 more per gallon than on the US mainland. Prices are lower in Hilo than Kailua-Kona.
- Towing is mighty expensive, costing about $65 to start, plus $6.50 per mile towed. Avoid trouble by not driving up Mauna Kea's summit road in anything but a 4WD vehicle, and never driving off-road, especially in sand or mud.

Insurance

- For damage to your rental car, an optional collision damage waiver (CDW) costs an extra $15 to $20 a day.
- If you decline CDW, you will be held liable for any damages up to the full value of the car.
- Even with CDW, you may be required to pay the first $100 to $500 for repairs; some agencies will also charge you for the car-rental cost during the time it takes to be repaired.
- If you already have vehicle insurance at home, it might cover rental cars; ask your insurance agent in advance.
- Some credit cards offer reimbursement coverage for collision damages if you rent the car with that card; check this before your trip.
- Most credit-card coverage isn't valid for rentals over 15 days or for 'exotic' models (eg convertibles, 4WD Jeeps).

Car Rental

The majority of visitors rent a car. Most agencies require drivers to be at least 25 years old; a few may rent to younger drivers for a hefty daily surcharge (check before booking). Having a credit card, not just a debit card, is usually necessary.

The daily rate for renting a small car usually ranges from $35 to $75, while typical weekly rates are $150 to $300; taxes, fees and surcharges can easily add $10 or more per day. 'Green' hybrid cars and 4WD vehicles are more expensive. Rates usually include unlimited mileage.

Book in advance online, then recheck periodically for lower rates. Reserve child-safety seats ($10 per day, or $50 per rental) when booking. Joining the rental agency's rewards program in advance (it's usually free) might entitle you to additional discounts and shorter queues at the airport.

Agencies serving both Kona and Hilo airports (except where otherwise noted) include the following:

Advantage (☎ 800-777-5500, 808-961-9193; www.advantage.com) Hilo airport only.

Alamo (☎ 877-222-9075; www.alamo.com)

Climate Change & Travel

Every form of transport that relies on carbon-based fuel generates CO_2, the main cause of human-induced climate change. Modern travel is dependent on airplanes, which might use less fuel per kilometer per person than most cars but travel much greater distances. The altitude at which aircraft emit gases (including CO_2) and particles also contributes to their climate change impact. Many websites offer 'carbon calculators' that allow people to estimate the carbon emissions generated by their journey and, for those who wish to do so, to offset the impact of the greenhouse gases emitted with contributions to portfolios of climate-friendly initiatives throughout the world. Lonely Planet offsets the carbon footprint of all staff and author travel.

Avis (☎ 800-331-1212; www.avis.com)

Budget (☎ 800-527-0700; www.budget.com)

Dollar (☎ 800-800-4000; www.dollar.com)

Enterprise (☎ 800-325-8007; www.enterprise.com)

Harper Car & Truck Rentals (☎ 800-852-9993, 808-969-1478; www.harpershawaii.com) The only agency with no restrictions on driving 4WD vehicles to Mauna Kea's summit. Damage to a vehicle entails a high deductible; rates are generally steeper than at other major agencies. Free Kona and Hilo airport shuttle service.

Hertz (☎ 800-654-3131; www.hertz.com)

National (☎ 877-222-9058; www.nationalcar.com)

Thrifty (☎ 800-847-4389; www.thrifty.com) Kona airport only.

Road Conditions & Hazards

- Roads and bridges can flood during rainstorms, especially in Hilo, Puna and Ka'u. Watch out for muddy, rocky landslides by gulches along the Hamakua Coast.

- Driving off-road or to Mauna Kea's summit is not for standard cars or novice 4WD drivers. In such remote areas, you'll be miles from any help.

- On narrow, unpaved and/or potholed roads, locals may hog both lanes and drive over the middle stripe until an oncoming car approaches.

- In hyphenated addresses, such as 75-2345 Kuakini Hwy, the first part of the number identifies the tax zone and section, while the second part identifies the street address. If numbers suddenly jump unsequentially, you've just entered a new zone, that's all.

Road Rules

Slow, courteous driving is the rule. Generally speaking, locals don't honk (except in an emergency), don't follow close (ie tailgate) and let other drivers pass and merge.

- Drive on the right-hand side of the road.

- Talking or texting on handheld devices (eg cell phones) while driving is illegal.

- Driving with a blood alcohol level of 0.08% or higher or when impaired by drugs (even if legally prescribed) is illegal.

- It's illegal to carry open containers of alcohol (even if they're empty) inside a vehicle; unless they're full and still sealed, store them in the trunk.

- Seat belts are required for drivers and front-seat passengers.

- Children aged three and under must be secured in a child safety seat. Those aged four to seven must use a booster or car seat (unless the child is 4ft 9in tall and can use a lap-only seat belt in the back seat).

- Speed limits are posted and enforced.

- Turning right at a red light is permitted unless a sign prohibits it.

- At four-way stop signs, cars proceed in order of arrival. If two cars arrive simultaneously, the one on the right has the right of way.

- When emergency vehicles approach from either direction, carefully pull over to the side of the road.

Motorcycle & Moped

- You can legally drive a moped in Hawaii with a valid driver's license issued by your home state or country. Motorcyclists need to have a valid US state motorcycle license or specially endorsed IDP.

- The minimum age for renting a moped is 16 years; for a motorcycle it's 21.

- Rental mopeds cost from $50/250 per day/week; motorcycle rentals start around $100 per day, depending on the make and model. A sizeable credit-card deposit is usually necessary. Most rental agencies are in Kailua-Kona.

- Helmets are not legally required for those 18 years or older, but rental agencies often lend them for free – use 'em.

- State law requires mopeds to be ridden by one person only and prohibits their use on sidewalks and freeways. Mopeds must always be driven single file at speeds not exceeding 30mph.

A-Z Glossary

a'a – type of lava that is rough and jagged

ae'o – Hawaiian black-necked stilt

ahu – stone cairns used to mark a trail; an altar or shrine

ahupua'a – traditional land division, usually in a wedge shape that extends from the mountains to the sea

'aina – land

ali'i – chief, royalty

aloha – the traditional greeting meaning love, welcome, good-bye

aloha 'aina – love and respect for the land

anchialine pool – contains a mixture of seawater and freshwater

'apapane – bright red Hawaiian honeycreeper

'aumakua – protective deity or guardian spirit, often an animal or ancestor

awa – see *kava*

broke da mout – delicious; literally, 'broke the mouth'

crack seed – Chinese preserved fruit; a salty, sweet and/or sour snack

e komo mai – welcome

grinds – food; to *grind* means to eat

ha – breath

hala – pandanus tree; the leaves *(lau)* are used in weaving mats and baskets

hale – house; hut

haole – Caucasian; literally, 'without breath'

hapa – portion or fragment; person of mixed blood

hapu'u – tree fern

he'e nalu – wave sliding, or surfing

heiau – ancient stone temple; a place of worship in Hawaii

holua – sled or sled course

honu – turtle

ho'okipa – hospitality

hula – Hawaiian dance form, either traditional or modern

hula 'auana – modern hula, developed after the introduction of Western music

hula halau – hula school or troupe

hula kahiko – traditional hula

'i'iwi – scarlet Hawaiian honeycreeper with a curved, salmon-colored beak

'iliahi – Hawaiian sandalwood

'io – Hawaiian hawk

ipu – spherical, narrow-necked gourd used as a hula instrument

kahuna – knowledgable person in any field; commonly a priest, healer or sorcerer

kalo – taro

kama'aina – person born and raised or a longtime resident in Hawaii; literally, 'child of the land'

kanaka – man, human being, person; also Native Hawaiian

kane/Kane – man; if capitalized, the name of one of four main Hawaiian gods

kapa – see *tapa*

kapu – taboo, part of strict ancient Hawaiian social and religious system

kava – a mildly narcotic drink (*'awa* in Hawaiian) made from the roots of *Piper methysticum,* a pepper shrub

keiki – child

ki – see *ti*

ki'i pokaku – stone carvings; petroglyphs

kiawe – a relative of the mesquite tree introduced to Hawaii in the 1820s, now very common; its branches are covered with sharp thorns

ki'i – see *tiki*

kipuka – an area of land spared when lava flows around it; a rainforest oasis

ko – sugarcane

ko'a – fishing shrine

kokua – help, cooperation; please

kona – leeward side; a leeward wind

Ku – Polynesian god of many manifestations, including god of war, farming and fishing

kukui – candlenut tree and the official state tree; its oily nuts were once burned in lamps

kuleana – rights

kumu – teacher

kupuna – grandparent, elder

lanai – veranda; balcony

lau – leaf

lauhala – leaves of the *hala* plant, used in weaving

lei – garland, usually of flowers, but also of leaves or shells

limu – seaweed

lomilomi – traditional Hawaiian massage; known as 'loving touch'

Lono – Polynesian god of harvest, agriculture, fertility and peace

luakini – a type of *heiau* dedicated to the war god Ku and used for human sacrifices

luau – traditional Hawaiian feast

mahalo – thank you

maka'ainana – commoners; literally, 'people who tend the land'

makai – toward the sea; seaward

mana – spiritual power

mauka – toward the mountains; inland

mele – song, chant

menehune – 'little people' who, according to legend, built many of Hawaii's fishponds, heiau and other stonework

milo – endemic hardwood tree

mo'i – king

nā keiki – children

naupaka – a native shrub with delicate white flowers

Neighbor Islands – the term used to refer to the main Hawaiian Islands outside of O'ahu

nene – a native goose; Hawaii's state bird

'ohana – family, extended family; close-knit group

oli – chant

'opihi – an edible limpet

pahoehoe – type of lava that is quick and smooth- flowing

pakalolo – marijuana; literally, 'crazy smoke'

pali – cliff

paniolo – cowboy

Pele – goddess of fire and volcanoes; her home is in Kilauea Caldera

pidgin – distinct local language and dialect, created by Hawaii's multiethnic immigrants

pikake – jasmine flowers

piko – navel, umbilical cord

pono – righteous, respectful and proper

poi – staple Hawaiian starch made of steamed, mashed taro

pupu – snack or appetizer; also a type of cowry shell

pu'u – hill, cinder cone

pu'uhonua – place of refuge

rubbah slippah – rubber flip-flops

shaka – hand gesture used in Hawaii as a greeting or sign of local pride

talk story – to strike up a conversation, make small talk

tapa – cloth made by pounding the bark of paper mulberry, used for early Hawaiian clothing (*kapa* in Hawaiian)

ti – common native plant; its long shiny leaves are used for wrapping food and making hula skirts (*ki* in Hawaiian)

tiki – wood- or stone-carved statue, usually depicting a deity (*ki'i* in Hawaiian)

ukulele – a stringed musical instrument derived from the *braguinha*, which was introduced to Hawaii in the 1800s by Portuguese immigrants

'ulu – breadfruit

Behind the Scenes

Our Readers

Many thanks to the travelers who wrote to us with helpful hints, useful advice and interesting anecdotes:
Lee Hundley, Amy MacNaughton

Author Thanks

Sara Benson

Mahalo nui loa to all of the locals who shared insider tips. Big thanks to my coauthor Luci Yamamoto, as well as to Cat Craddock-Carrillo, Kathleen Munnelly, Martine Power, Mark Griffiths and all of the other in-house LP staff who helped create this book. Thanks most of all to Jonathan Hayes for Fridays at the King Kam, Mondays at the Manago and Kona coffee almost every morning.

Luci Yamamoto

Mahalo to the locals who teach me more about Hawai'i every time I return. Thanks to those who helped me at LP, including Cat Craddock-Carrillo, Kathleen Munnelly, Martine Power, Mark Griffiths and Dianne Schallmeiner. Deepest appreciation to my coauthor Sara Benson, a real pro, and to my parents, who still make Hilo home to me.

Acknowledgments

Climate map data adapted from Peel MC, Finlayson BL & McMahon TA (2007) 'Updated World Map of the Köppen-Geiger Climate Classification', Hydrology and Earth System Sciences, 11, 1633–44.

Cover photographs: Front: Kukio Beach, North Kona Coast, Philip Rosenberg/Visual Photos/PacificStock; Back: Pololu Valley, North Kohala, James Flint/Alamy

This Book

This 2nd edition of Lonely Planet's *Discover Hawai'i, the Big Island* guidebook was researched and written by Sara Benson and Luci Yamamoto. The previous edition was written by Luci Yamamoto and Conner Gorry. This guidebook was commissioned in Lonely Planet's Oakland office, and produced by the following:

Commisioning Editor Kathleen Munnelly
Coordinating Editor Fionnuala Twomey
Product Editor Anne Mason
Senior Editors Claire Naylor, Karyn Noble
Book Designer Clara Monitto
Regional Senior Cartographer Mark Griffiths
Cartographer Julie Dodkins
Assisting Editors Penny Cordner, Kate Evans, Kate James
Cover Researcher Naomi Parker
Thanks to Anita Banh, Cat Craddock-Carrillo, Brendan Dempsey, Lauren Egan, Ryan Evans, Larissa Frost, Genesys India, Jouve India, Martine Power, Anna Richardson, Alison Ridgway, Wibowo Rusli, Dianne Schallmeiner, Juan Winata, Wendy Wright

SEND US YOUR FEEDBACK

We love to hear from travelers – your comments keep us on our toes and help make our books better. Our well-traveled team reads every word on what you loved or loathed about this book. Although we cannot reply individually to your submissions, we always guarantee that your feedback goes straight to the appropriate authors, in time for the next edition. Each person who sends us information is thanked in the next edition, the most useful submissions are rewarded with a selection of digital PDF chapters.

Visit **lonelyplanet.com/contact** to submit your updates and suggestions or to ask for help. Our award-winning website also features inspirational travel stories, news and discussions.

Note: We may edit, reproduce and incorporate your comments in Lonely Planet products such as guidebooks, websites and digital products, so let us know if you don't want your comments reproduced or your name acknowledged. For a copy of our privacy policy visit lonelyplanet.com/privacy.

Index

000 Map pages

H

000 Map pages

N

O

P

R

S

000 Map pages

NOTES

How to Use This Book

These symbols give you the vital information for each listing:

- Telephone Numbers
- Opening Hours
- Parking
- Nonsmoking
- Air-Conditioning
- Internet Access
- Wi-Fi Access
- Swimming Pool
- Vegetarian Selection
- English-Language Menu
- Family-Friendly
- Pet-Friendly
- Bus
- Ferry
- Metro
- Subway
- Tram

All reviews are ordered in our authors' preference, starting with their most preferred option. Additionally:

Sights are arranged in the geographic order that we suggest you visit them, and within this order, by author preference.

Eating and Sleeping reviews are ordered by price range (budget, mid-range, top end) and within these ranges, by author preference.

Look out for these icons:

★ Must-visit recommendation

FREE No payment required

A green or sustainable option

Our authors have nominated these places as demonstrating a strong commitment to sustainability – for example by supporting local communities and producers, operating in an environmentally friendly way, or supporting conservation projects.

Map Legend

Sights
Beach
Buddhist
Castle
Christian
Hindu
Islamic
Jewish
Monument
Museum/Gallery
Ruin
Winery/Vineyard
Zoo
Other Sight

Activities, Courses & Tours
Diving/Snorkelling
Canoeing/Kayaking
Skiing
Surfing
Swimming/Pool
Walking
Windsurfing
Other Activity/Course/Tour

Sleeping
Sleeping
Camping

Eating
Eating

Drinking
Drinking
Cafe

Entertainment
Entertainment

Shopping
Shopping

Information
Post Office
Tourist Information

Transport
Airport
Border Crossing
Bus
Cable Car/Funicular
Cycling
Ferry
Monorail
Parking
S-Bahn
Taxi
Train/Railway
Tram
Tube Station
U-Bahn
Underground Train Station
Other Transport

Routes
Tollway
Freeway
Primary
Secondary
Tertiary
Lane
Unsealed Road
Plaza/Mall
Steps
Tunnel
Pedestrian Overpass
Walking Tour
Walking Tour Detour
Path

Boundaries
International
State/Province
Disputed
Regional/Suburb
Marine Park
Cliff
Wall

Population
Capital (National)
Capital (State/Province)
City/Large Town
Town/Village

Geographic
Hut/Shelter
Lighthouse
Lookout
Mountain/Volcano
Oasis
Park
Pass
Picnic Area
Waterfall

Hydrography
River/Creek
Intermittent River
Swamp/Mangrove
Reef
Canal
Water
Dry/Salt/Intermittent Lake
Glacier

Areas
Beach/Desert
Cemetery (Christian)
Cemetery (Other)
Park/Forest
Sportsground
Sight (Building)
Top Sight (Building)

Our Story

A beat-up old car, a few dollars in the pocket and a sense of adventure. In 1972 that's all Tony and Maureen Wheeler needed for the trip of a lifetime – across Europe and Asia overland to Australia. It took several months, and at the end – broke but inspired – they sat at their kitchen table writing and stapling together their first travel guide, *Across Asia on the Cheap*. Within a week they'd sold 1500 copies. Lonely Planet was born.

Today, Lonely Planet has offices in Franklin, London, Melbourne, Oakland, Beijing and Delhi, with more than 600 staff and writers. We share Tony's belief that 'a great guidebook should do three things: inform, educate and amuse'.

Our Writers

SARA BENSON

Coordinating author, Kailua-Kona & the Kona Coast, Mauna Kea & Saddle Road, Hawai'i Volcanoes National Park, Ka'u After graduating from college, Sara jumped on a plane to California with just one suitcase and $100 in her pocket. Then she hopped across the Pacific to Japan, living for long stretches on Maui, Hawai'i, the Big Island and O'ahu and tramping all around Kaua'i, Moloka'i and Lana'i. Sara is an avid hiker, backpacker and outdoor enthusiast who has worked as a seasonal ranger for the National Park Service and as a volunteer at Hawai'i Volcanoes National Park. Already the author of more than 55 travel and nonfiction books, Sara also co-wrote Lonely Planet's *Hawaii* and *Discover Honolulu, Waikiki & O'ahu* guides. Follow her latest adventures online at www.indietraveler.blogspot.com, www.indietraveler.net, @indie_traveler on Twitter and indietraveler on Instagram.

Read more about at:
lonelyplanet.com/members/Sara_Benson

LUCI YAMAMOTO

Kohala & Waimea, Hamakua Coast, Hilo, Puna Luci Yamamoto is a fourth-generation native of Hawai'i. Growing up in Hilo, she viewed the cross-island drive from Hilo to Kailua-Kona as a rare, all-day adventure. Then she left for college in Los Angeles and law school in Berkeley – and even the Big Island seemed small indeed. Since covering Hawai'i for Lonely Planet, she's opened her eyes to the true greatness of her home island. Currently living in Vancouver, she feels privileged when *kama'aina* still consider her a 'local girl.' Follow Luci via her blog yogaspy.com and website luciyamamoto.com.

Published by Lonely Planet Publications Pty Ltd
ABN 36 005 607 983
2nd edition – Sep 2014
ISBN 978 1 74220 627 1

10 9 8 7 6 5 4 3 2 1
Printed in China